PATRIOT
ACTS

JIM LIES
&
GENE FRAZER

ISBN: 0984664416

ISBN 13: 9780984664412

This book is dedicated to James Lies, Sr., and all the other American men and women of "The Greatest Generation" who fought in World War II.

ACKNOWLEDGMENTS

We would like to thank our wives, Renee Lies and Jackie Thompson, for their patience, love, and support during the writing of *Patriot Acts*.

TABLE OF CONTENTS

TOM'S STORY: PART ONE

KURT AND ERIKA'S STORY: "THE BOOK"

TOM'S STORY: PART TWO

Beware the leader who bangs the drum of war in order to whip the citizenry into a patriotic fever. For patriotism is indeed a double-edged sword. It both emboldens the blood, just as it narrows the mind.

Julius Caesar

TOM'S STORY

PART ONE

CHAPTER 1

SATURDAY, JANUARY 10, 1998
Grand Forks, North Dakota

"I'm sorry to break our rule and call you, Tom, but I must see you as soon as possible. I need to know if you've kept your promise."

I hadn't heard the voice in almost twenty years, but I recognized it after the first few syllables. "Erika, I can't believe it's you! Where are you?"

"Can you meet me next Saturday in Fargo at one o'clock at the Holiday Inn? The one off of I-29?"

"Gee, why don't you get right to the point? And, yes, I've missed you, too, in case you're wondering. Of course, I'll see you. Have I ever refused you anything?"

I could feel the smile in her response. "Wonderful! I can't wait to see you again. So, did you keep your promise?"

"Yeah, a long time ago, but you and Kurt have left me thinking it was all just a wasted effort. Where've you been all this time?"

"Oh, Tom, we have so much to catch up on, but I can't stay on the phone too long. You can't be too careful, you know."

"Still the cloak and dagger stuff after all these years? I can hardly wait to hear the latest. You know this means I'll have to be a little creative with an excuse for my wife on Saturday."

"I'm sure you'll think of something interesting. After all, you talked her into marrying you, didn't you?"

"Glad to see you still have your sense of humor. It'll be great to see you and Kurt again. I can hardly wait!"

There was a long pause. "Kurt won't be with me. I'll explain when I see you."

"Seriously? He won't be there? Now I'm really curious. Is he okay? Can't you tell me something now? A week is a long time to wait."

"No, I can't. You know the phone rules."

"Yeah, unfortunately. Some things never change do they? Well, I've waited twenty years, so I guess another week won't kill me. In the meantime how about if I have your package waiting for you at the Holiday Inn?"

"That would be perfect. I knew I could count on you. I love you."

The phone went dead, and I stood in the hallway for a few minutes, contemplating the implications of her request. It was only ten o'clock in the morning, and I was alone in the house. Eventually—though part of me was resisting the impulse—I made my way down the stairs to the basement and started rummaging through the storeroom.

After a few minutes of shuffling boxes, I found the one I was looking for, the one I'd long ago marked "Tom: Hunting Gear" to ensure that my wife would never go near it. I picked it up and carried it to my office in the other corner of the basement. The years had weakened the packing tape to the point where it was barely holding the seams together, so the tape peeled off easily. The musty smell of damp paper rose up through my nostrils, reminding me of the box's history. It had survived floods, family moves, and the occasional weakness of my conscience when I had almost thrown it away. I pulled back the flaps and stared at the contents: lined notebooks scribbled full by hand, stacks of miscellaneous papers, random newspaper clippings, several plastic bags filled with audio tapes, and a thick manuscript held together by heavy rubber bands, simply titled, "Kurt and Erika."

I slowly unpacked the items, rediscovering each as I held it or read a key phrase. When I got to notebook numbered "1," I settled into my faded brown leather recliner under the window, opened the notebook and started reading. By the time I had finished the first few pages, thirty-two years had melted away, and I was back on the North Dakota prairie, reliving the day when I had first met Kurt and Erika.

CHAPTER 2

OCTOBER 8, 1966

The drake mallard crumpled and hit the water after the first shot. As I cautiously waded to retrieve it, the soft waves rocked it gently back and forth. Looking down, I was once again struck by the wonder of a scene I had witnessed hundreds of times. I marveled at the majestic drake as only a hunter can, inwardly wishing everyone could see the purple-tinted green head and purple-blue wing patches up close some time. As I reverently picked up nature's wonder, the water draining off its back sounded like water gushing from a faucet into a pail, shattering the morning stillness. I slowly waded back to the bank, found a dry patch of reeds and sat down to enjoy the silence. Gazing out over the slough in my camouflage hunting gear, I felt like a solitary sentry guarding a remote prairie oasis.

It was about ten-thirty on a brilliant Saturday morning, and that had been the last round of the day for my Remington 1100. The cloudless blue sky and bright sun exaggerated the golden reeds and grasses surrounding this small slough in the hilly country northwest of Bremen (population, about 75) in central North Dakota. After sitting for a few minutes, I picked up my decoys and the rest of my ducks and trudged to my dad's pickup parked about a quarter mile away.

"Old Ugly" was a sickly, pea-green relic that had served as the butt of my friends' jokes for many years. They insisted that General Motors had used that hideous color only once and then stopped immediately upon seeing the result. To dad and me the color did have an upside, though; it was so disgustingly distinctive that everyone knew who owned it. The locals considered us to be knowledgeable, respectful hunters, so once they recognized our truck, we hardly ever had to ask anyone for permission to hunt. But, today, for the first time in all my years of hunting, I had left the lights on and the battery was dead. "Old Ugly" wasn't going anywhere without a jump.

After cussing myself out for my stupidity, I walked up the trail to the top of a small hill to see if I could locate a farm. I'd gone exploring that morning, and the spot I'd selected for the day's hunt was outside of my normal boundaries, so I wasn't familiar with any farmers in this area. Earlier, following the ducks from their morning feeding back to the slough, I hadn't really paid attention to how isolated the area was. Now I was regretting my carelessness. Searching the horizon with my binoculars, I detected what looked like a man-made shelterbelt about two miles to the east and figured it must be protecting a farmhouse. It looked like my best hope, so I walked back to the pickup, put the decoys and ducks in the box, locked my gun in the cab, and started off across the prairie.

I love North Dakota, especially in the fall. On this day Mother Nature provided a feast of colors ranging from the deep reds and golden browns of the weeds and climbing brush to the yellows and oranges of the leaves drifting randomly along the ground. As a backdrop, the knee-high amber prairie grass danced gently in the light wind. Amidst this spectacular scenery my walk actually seemed enjoyable, except for the vague concern that I might not find a farm soon. The terrain was a little choppy, so I had to keep glancing down as I walked to make sure I didn't step into a hole and twist a knee or ankle. Still, I soon established a comfortable pace. Trudging along in my camouflage outfit and hunting boots, I couldn't help but return to the issue that had been nagging me for months: the probability that I would soon be drafted and sent to Vietnam.

I was scheduled to graduate in January from the University of North Dakota, which would end my student deferment. Single, 22, with no dependents and no job prospects, I was near the top of the list with my local draft board, so my fate was inevitable. I was finishing the last requirement for my education degree by student teaching at South Junior High in Grand Forks, a city in the northeast corner of the state where UND was located. Although I had been toying with the idea of extending my deferment by applying to law school, I just didn't think I had it in me to spend a few more years as an academic. Besides, part of me felt that law school would be taking the coward's way out.

As I ambled along, it didn't take much of a mental leap to replace the Dakota prairie with a rice paddy and my pseudo-military hunting garb with real GI fatigues. The harder part was substituting a human being for a mallard. I wasn't one of those gung ho "gonna' kill me some gooks" type of guys, but I believed I should serve my country just as my dad had done in World War II. I knew the war in Vietnam was escalating, and it wasn't the cakewalk many people had initially thought it would be, but it looked like we were finally committing enough resources to get the job done. Somebody had to stop the spread of communism in the Far East, and it looked like America was the only country up to the task.

I had been looking forward to talking things over with dad today, preferably while sipping thermos coffee and looking out over our decoys at our favorite duck slough. For the last four years my class load and the demands of playing college football had mostly eliminated my weekend hunting trips to New Rockford, our hometown of about 2,000 where dad owned the local hardware store. This fall, though, I was available to hunt with him every weekend until the ponds froze over and the last duck had migrated south. Unfortunately, a last minute emergency had kept him at the hardware store this morning, and I was disappointed that we had to postpone our conversation. Dad had joined up after Pearl Harbor and fought in the Battle of the Bulge, and, mostly because of my curiosity about his service in Europe, I had majored in history. By now I was quite well-versed about World War II through a series of research papers I had written about Hitler, the various German military organizations, and the morality of war. Dad and I hadn't really talked much about Vietnam yet, but with America at war and the draft now hanging over my head, things were coming full circle with him, and I welcomed his advice. It looked like tomorrow would have to be the day for our father-son discussion.

Eventually my walk brought me to a gravel road that angled toward the shelterbelt. Thankful for something else to think about, I followed the stony road for a short distance until I saw a dusty path veer sharply into the trees that partially concealed a small farm. The homestead consisted of only a few buildings: a barn, a garage, a machine shed, and a neat, white farmhouse with black trim and black shutters.

I walked up and knocked on the door.

—

A tall blonde swung the door open on the second knock. I guessed she was in her mid-forties, but it was hard to tell. She wore a simple housedress, typical of a farmer's wife on a Saturday morning, but her plain clothes could not hide her magnificence. She was the most striking woman I had ever met. Standing with one hand holding the storm door open, she asked serenely, "May I help you, young man?" When our eyes met, I felt a strange—almost spiritual—connection.

For a few seconds I could not speak, held captive by the purest, bluest eyes God had ever created. Feeling flushed, I finally managed to activate my vocal chords and utter a response. "My truck is dead, and I need some-one to give the battery a jump. Is your husband home?"

The doorway framed her slender, well-proportioned build perfectly. Long, natural blond hair accentuated the eyes, and a slight smile curled across her full, expressive lips. I had seen her for all of a few seconds, yet she radi-ated such warmth and confidence that I impulsively felt the urge to impress her, knowing all the while how ridiculous that seemed. I mean, this woman was old enough to be my mother! I was embarrassed at how good I felt in her presence, and inwardly I chastised myself for feeling like such an idiot.

"Well, I'm afraid I can't help you with your problem, but my husband will be home for lunch in about fifteen minutes, and I'm sure he can help. Would you like a cup of coffee?" A faint accent hinted at her identity.

"Yeah, thanks, but I'd better drink it outside. My clothes might be a little dirty." Actually, my pants had remained clean inside my waders, and I had left my soiled hunting coat in the truck because of the warm weather. I was only wearing a camo vest and a brown, long-sleeved shirt.

"Oh, don't worry. Just take your boots off and come on in. My name is Erika Heisler," she said as she extended her hand.

"I'm Tom Johnson," I said, shaking her hand. "This is very nice of you. I feel a little stupid about leaving my lights on. In all my years of hunting I've never done that before, and I'm sorry to be bothering you like this, and I promise I won't be here very . . ."

Erika gently stopped my rambling. "Excuse me, but are you from around here? I don't remember seeing you before."

"I grew up in New Rockford, and my parents still live there. My dad owns the Triple A Hardware store. I'm a senior at UND, but I always come home in the fall to hunt."

"I've only been through New Rockford once or twice," she said. "We usually shop in Maddock or Devils Lake. I have to finish doing some dishes, but I'll put some fresh coffee on. You're welcome to have lunch with us. Nothing special—just ham sandwiches, vegetables and coffee."

Then Erika gave me a coy little look that had probably reduced countless men to blubbering idiots. "Tom, I'm not in the habit of inviting strange men into my home, especially when my husband is gone, but you seem like such a nice young man. I'm a good judge of character, you know."

"Thanks for your hospitality," was the cleverest response I could muster.

"Why don't you go and wait in Kurt's office at the end of the hall while I get things ready in the kitchen? Today's paper is on the end table."

As I walked down the hall, Erika remarked, "You know, Tom, in all that hunting gear, you look just like a soldier."

Once in the office I paced nervously, absently surveying the stack of magazines on the end table: *Time,* the *Saturday Evening Post, Field and Stream* and a copy of a UND course catalog. "I can't escape UND," I thought, "even on a hunting weekend in the country." The bookshelves proved more interesting. The Heislers were either well read or they just liked to buy good books, because the shelves were lined with diverse works by many well-known authors. What intrigued me the most, though, was a six-inch pewter figurine standing on a small bookshelf. It was a Nordic warrior with one arm pointing a sword skyward and the other holding a lowered shield. I went over to get a closer look, and as I reached for it, my knee hit the upper row of books, jostling them and knocking a few over. Something fell out of one onto the floor. I leaned over and picked up two black-and-white photographs.

The first picture was of a handsome young soldier in a camouflage smock standing in front of a German half-track, vintage World War II. He wore no helmet or cap, and his dirty face was topped by unkempt blond hair. Pinned to his right collar tab were the runic flashes of the double S, signifying membership in the Waffen SS. Standing next to him was another young officer, dressed the same except for a field cap displaying the Death's Head symbol of the SS. I turned the picture over and read the handwritten notation: "Smolensk, 1941."

With trembling hands I picked up the second picture, a wedding photo. A radiant young woman in an evening gown stood alongside a dashing young man in a black SS dress uniform. The man was the hatless soldier in the first picture, and the woman was currently in the kitchen making me coffee.

I hurriedly put the pictures back in the book, shoved it into the shelf, grabbed the morning paper from the end table and sat down. I stared at the paper, unable to read a word. The pictures I had just seen were chilling. Most Americans had no idea what the Waffen SS was, but I was all too familiar with its sordid history. During World War II the Waffen SS had earned a reputation as brutal, fanatical fighters who asked no quarter in battle and gave none. They had burned entire villages to the ground and massacred civilian men, women and children in the process; they had also executed American prisoners at Malmedy, Belgium, during the Battle of the Bulge. As a group they had been condemned at the Nuremberg Trials for their horrific war crimes.

My imagination was racing with the excitement of my discovery, and I feverishly began creating possible explanations. Random bits of information rattled around in my brain like confetti in a windstorm as I struggled to organize my thoughts in a logical sequence. "My God," I thought, "the man who farms here belonged to the Waffen SS, the legendary 'Evil Elite' of Hitler's army. This guy is a war criminal hiding out on a farm here in North Dakota. Maybe my life is even in danger!"

"Tom, come into the kitchen. Your coffee's ready, and you can wash up." Erika's slight accent now sounded as if she were speaking pure German.

I walked into the kitchen and headed for the sink, struggling to maintain my composure. As I washed my hands, Erika left the house to greet her husband, who was coming up the driveway. She had taken her rings off, and they were lying near the edge of the sink. Normally I would take no interest in a woman's ring, but this ring—apparently Erika's wedding ring—made my heart pound even faster. The ring had a small diamond in the middle of three vertical lines that were connected from bottom left to top right by a fourth line. These lines formed a runic symbol called a Wolfsangle or Wolf's Hook, an image used by the Second Waffen SS Panzer Division Das Reich. There could no longer be any doubt about who these people were. It was as if God had not yet scared me enough and wanted to destroy my last ounce of composure. At that moment I wished I'd been an English major.

My mind was now in overdrive as I contemplated my next step. I was torn between two courses of action. Should I say anything to Erika and her husband? The historian inside me was captivated by the idea of furthering my knowledge firsthand through this couple. Maybe they could even tell me inside stories about Hitler, Das Reich and the fall of Germany that I could never uncover sitting in a library poring over dry historical tomes. And, if I didn't pursue this story, would I someday regret not following up on this once-in-a-lifetime opportunity? The practical side of me, however, was telling me to get my ass out of there as fast as I could and go alert the authorities. But who would I alert, and what would I tell them? "Hi, Mr. FBI agent. I'm a college student who wrote some research papers on World War II, and I just found a Nazi war criminal hiding out on a Bremen farm. Please go arrest him." Yeah, that plan had success written all over it.

Looking out the kitchen window, I saw a tall, slender man get out of a truck and walk toward Erika. They embraced, she told him something (probably about the idiot who had left his lights on), he laughed, and they came walking toward the house. By the time they reached the steps, I had formulated my plan. I would find out more about these two mysterious people because a chance like this would never come again. I needed to find a way to get invited back so I could make friends with them. Maybe then, over time, they would trust me enough that I would dare reveal that I knew their secret. If that moment never came and my suspicions seemed correct, I could always report them.

As they entered the kitchen Erika introduced me to her husband, Kurt, and explained my situation to him as we shook hands. He was a lean, handsome, well-built man in his forties, about 6'2", 175 pounds, with blond hair and blue eyes that defined a classic Nordic face. He carried himself with poise and confidence, but I sensed an aura of sadness about him. As Kurt examined me in my hunting gear, he said, "You remind me of some people I used to know a long time ago."

I thought I knew what he meant, but I played ignorant, hoping that someday soon I would get the chance to display my vast knowledge of the Waffen SS.

"Did you have any luck hunting?" asked Kurt.

"I only shoot greenheads, and I usually go home with my limit," I replied rather boastfully. "Do you want some?"

"No thanks. We get plenty of our own game here on the farm. Erika tells me you're going to have lunch with us, so why don't we sit down and eat? Then I'll drive you to your truck, and we'll get it started."

Over lunch we made the usual small talk about the weather, families and other safe subjects. I asked if they had kids, and Kurt said they were unable to have any. While I was struggling to come up with the appropriate condolence, Kurt said, "It really worked out okay. We don't have any kids to disappoint us, and now we have a lot more money to spend on ourselves."

Erika "shushed" him and said, "Please excuse my husband. He has a warped sense of humor sometimes. Actually, kids would've been nice." She then looked at Kurt with twinkling eyes and said. "When you're old and feeble and unable to take care of yourself, you'll wish we'd had a few kids to look after you, because I'll be out spending our retirement savings."

We all laughed, and Kurt reached across the table and tenderly held both her hands in his for a few seconds before Erika got up and asked, "Who's ready for apple pie and coffee?"

I've never refused pie in my life, and I wasn't about to start this day, especially when it meant that it would extend our time together. To me there's no such thing as bad pie, and Erika's was no exception. Over my second piece I mentioned that I'd seen the UND course brochure in the study earlier and asked if they were planning on taking some courses. Erika laughed and said, "No, we thought about enrolling in some extension classes a while back just for something to do in the winter, but decided we're too old for homework, so we just forgot about it. But once you're on the mailing list, it seems you just get that stuff forever. Say, you're from the University, why don't you go in and tell them they're wasting their money on us?"

As the conversation continued, I realized I was starting to like both of them, and vowed that I would be on my guard to remain objective if we continued the relationship. Who knew what atrocities Kurt might have committed with the SS?

After draining the last of his coffee, Kurt stood up. "Wow, look at the time. I've still got some chores to do, and I have to get into town before the stores close. We better start that truck of yours and get you on your way."

Erika came over to me, shook my hand and looked directly into my eyes. "Tom, it was a pleasure to meet you. If you come back and hunt around here again, please come and see us. We don't get much company, and sometimes it would be nice to hear a new voice and some different stories once in a while. Do you know any good stories, Tom?" She had that twinkle in her eye again, and Kurt just looked at her and rolled his eyes in mock disgust.

I was dying to say something clever about "old war stories," but caught myself in time. "I'll try to think of some, but I'm a pretty boring guy. Actually, I might forget about the ducks and come back just for the pie and coffee. Thanks for the lunch, Erika."

"You're welcome. Coffee's pretty much a sure thing around here any-time, but the pie is hit or miss. But come back and try your luck some time."

Kurt and I climbed into his truck and headed to the slough. I broke the silence first. "You ever get out and hunt, Kurt? I know a lot of places around here if you'd like to try a new spot some time."

"I'm pretty busy with the farm, so I don't do much real hunting. I just shoot a few birds around here when we feel like we want something dif-ferent for dinner. I guess I'm not much into shooting things these days."

As much as I wanted to follow up on the last comment, I didn't want to appear too eager, so I let it pass. "You know, I might come back here and hunt this slough before heading back to Grand Forks tomorrow. I got my limit pretty quickly this morning, and there are still plenty of ducks around."

"Why don't you try the sloughs on the other side of our property? We've posted them so they won't get over-hunted, but you're welcome to try them. Like Erika said, come and join us for a cup of coffee when you're finished. Sundays are pretty quiet around the place."

As we approached the truck to line up the batteries to attach the jump-er cables, Kurt couldn't contain himself. "Man, you sure don't sneak up on anybody with this beauty, do you? Can't say I've ever seen one quite this color, but I'll sure recognize it when you come back."

"Yeah, 'Old Ugly' is our special calling card. Even if people don't know who we are, they sure know the pickup. Don't worry, there isn't a joke we haven't heard, so we're way beyond being offended about it. But we've had it for so long, it's part of the family now."

We hooked up the jumper cables, I cranked the engine a couple times, and the truck roared to a start. I shook Kurt's hand and thanked him. He nodded, got back in his pickup and headed back to the farm.

As I drove back to New Rockford, I felt like I had made the greatest discovery since Stanley had found Livingston. As I relived the afternoon, the magnitude of the day's events sunk in, and I started getting excited all over again. Before I reached home I had to come up with a plan for the next day so I could meet with Kurt and Erika again without letting my folks know about my discovery. I knew my dad would want to go hunting on Sunday, so I decided to suggest to him that we go to church at seven o'clock that evening so we could hunt early in the morning. Then I could leave for Grand Forks by two o'clock, but instead of going straight there, I could go to the Heislers' slough to hunt and just drop in casually to say hello. This would allow me a good morning of hunting with dad and still leave some time to spend with Erika and Kurt in the afternoon.

Once I got home, it took all of my concentration to get through dinner with my parents without arousing their suspicions. In the end it was the banality of our daily routines that protected me from myself. They were used to having me come home and recount the day's hunting exploits over dinner, so I stuck with that approach until it was time to leave for church. When we returned, dad and I went right to bed so we could get up at four-thirty to get an early start.

As I lay in bed thinking back on the day's events, I couldn't help feeling proud about my detective skills in piecing together Kurt and Erika's backgrounds. I realized the circumstances that revealed the clues were totally random: Had I not knocked over a book in my clumsiness, I wouldn't have seen the pictures and suspected anything. Still, very few people— especially someone else my age—would have known enough about the military symbols to even question their significance. Without that knowledge, I would have left the Heislers and probably never seen them again. Instead, I was about to embark on an exciting historical adventure that could lead to great discoveries. I fell asleep very pleased with myself.

CHAPTER 3

On Sunday the weather again provided one of those autumn days that reminded me of why I had stayed in North Dakota to go to college: sixty degrees, bright sunshine and an endless clear blue sky. The hunt with dad was successful, but starting a conversation was a little difficult because of my preoccupation with the previous day's discovery. The events had certainly caused me to rethink my plan of discussing my draft situation with him. I didn't trust myself enough to think that I could have a discussion of any depth without somehow revealing what had happened the day before.

I did want to get his opinion of the Waffen SS, though, and I felt I could do that without making him too curious. I eased into a conversation about some of my research papers and told him how much I had been learning about World War II. Then I asked him a few general questions about his service in Germany. When I thought the timing was right, I asked him if he had ever come into contact with the Waffen SS.

"The SS?" he responded tersely. "They should all be in prison."

When I asked him to be more specific, he just looked past me, pointed his shotgun, and said, "Double at two o'clock." I was smart enough not to press the subject.

We finished our hunt and returned home by lunchtime. I told dad that I was going to make a leisurely trip back to Grand Forks and do some hunting on the way, so I stayed in my hunting clothes. I knew dad wouldn't be suspicious of this because I did it quite frequently; that's the curse of the hunting bug.

Around one-thirty or so I thanked my parents for the weekend and headed east on Highway 15 to Grand Forks, just in case someone was watching me drive away. I traveled east for a couple of miles before circling back west toward Bremen and the Heislers. Thinking about them, I wondered why former Nazis would pick remote North Dakota as a hiding place, until it hit me how brilliant their strategy was. The state has a large German population, especially around the Bremen area, and the Heislers could blend in there immediately without causing any suspicion. Most of the farmers kept to themselves and didn't meddle in other's business. Besides Germans, there were Swedes and Norwegians galore, and almost everybody had an accent of some kind, so there was nothing unusual about Kurt and Erika. (The distinctive accents are so prevalent I remember coming home from my first day of school and asking my mom why I talked so differently than the other kids.) All things considered, a farm near Bremen was the perfect hideout for foreigners who didn't want to be found.

I arrived at the farm about two-thirty, and Kurt and Erika were sitting around an old wooden table in the backyard. Hearing the car, they craned their necks trying to see who it was. Once they recognized me, they smiled and waved me up the driveway. They were more dressed up than they had been on Saturday, and as they walked over to greet me, I was struck by what a truly handsome couple they were. Kurt was trim and athletic, although he walked with a slight limp, and Erika was simply radiant. It was hard to tell whether it was her blond hair blowing in the gentle breeze, the sun dancing behind her as she walked, or her alluring smile that created such an effect. Whatever it was, it worked.

Kurt greeted me first. "Welcome back, Tom. I told Erika you might be coming back to hunt our slough today, but I thought you'd be here earlier."

"I hunted with dad this morning closer to home and decided to catch your sloughs on the way back to Grand Forks. I'm going over there in a bit, but I thought I'd come by and say hi first."

"Are you just hunting ducks today, or would you like to try to bag your limit on pie, too?" Erika couldn't hide her smile as she spoke.

"I don't think I've ever bagged my limit of pie, but if you're offering, I'll give it my best shot."

They led the way into the house, and we were soon gathered around the kitchen table sipping coffee and inflicting major damage on a freshly-baked cherry pie smothered with vanilla ice cream. We made small talk for a while, and then I shifted the conversation to move things forward. "I assume from your accents you're from Germany, but how long have you two been living in the States? Your English is excellent, so you must have been here for a while."

They exchanged a quick glance before Erika responded. "How long has it been now, Kurt? We've been here so long that the old country is just a fading memory."

"About twenty years now, I think. Yeah, that's right. We came over here a year after the war. Most of Germany was destroyed, so we thought as long as we were starting over, we'd like to be in a place that offered more opportunity, and America sure has plenty of that."

"Right after the war. Does that mean you fought for Germany? I'm sorry for asking, but I'm a curious history major, and I just can't help myself sometimes."

"Yes, like every eligible German, I was a soldier and fought for my country. I was luckier than most, though, and I survived. But that was a long time ago. America is our home now."

"It must have been tough leaving your homeland. How long have you been here in the Bremen area? And how did you wind up out here in God's country?"

Another quick glance passed between them, and the smiles were looking a little forced. "What, you don't think anyone would move here by choice?" Erika said, giggling. "Actually, we fell in love with the wide open spaces and the peace and quiet. We tried some bigger cities and decided the city life is not for us, too much traffic and not enough room to roam. We heard from other Germans that North Dakota was a good place, and there are a lot of them here, so we thought we'd give it a try. We moved out here in April and took this place on a rental basis with an option to buy. No one really told us how bad the winters could be, though, and now we're hearing all kinds of stories about blizzards and forty below zero temperatures. We might've had some second thoughts if we'd been warned. Are the winters really that bad?"

"Yeah, they can be, but if we warned everyone about the winters, we wouldn't get anybody to move here. We do welcome people of hardy stock, though. You've probably heard our unofficial state motto: 'Forty below keeps the riff raff out.'"

They laughed, thankful, I figured, that I wasn't pressing them for any more answers about their past. Before I could ask another question, Kurt had one of his own. "Tom, tell us about college. Erika tells me you're getting ready to graduate. What then?"

"Well, I'm not sure yet. I'm student teaching in a junior high school to finish my education degree, but I don't plan on teaching any time soon. I really don't have much control over my future right now."

Erika looked puzzled. "What do you mean?"

"My student deferment runs out when I graduate, so I'll be at the top of the draft list in Eddy County. That's one advantage—if you can call it that—of living in a small town. You always know where you stand in the draft. Anyway, I'm single with no dependents, so I'll probably get drafted as soon as I graduate."

"Drafted? Does that mean you'll have to go to Vietnam?" Erika was suddenly very serious.

"Probably. That's where most everybody is winding up these days, so my chances are pretty good. The army doesn't give you much choice about that. I'll just have to hope for the best."

"Don't you have any other options?" Kurt asked. "From the look of things, we could be in Vietnam a long time."

"My other options aren't very realistic. I'm thinking about asking for an extension to my deferment and applying to law school, but my heart really isn't in it. I don't think I could stand all the lawyer jokes I'd have to endure from my friends for the rest of my life." I paused for a moment while we all stared at our plates. "Well, there is one other thing, but it's kind of a long shot. You don't know of any drop-dead gorgeous women about my age who are dying to get married and start a family in the next month or so, do you?"

They both laughed, and Erika said, "I haven't seen many of those around here, but I could start asking around. You mean to tell me a handsome young man like you doesn't already have girls waiting in line?"

"Hardly. Truth is, I think I'm less afraid of the Viet Cong than the thought of getting married. Anyway, that's my sad story. Once I graduate in January, it looks like my future will be in Uncle Sam's hands."

I finished off the last bite of pie and stood up. "I better get going while there's still some daylight left to hunt. Thanks for the pie and the conversation. Can I use the bathroom before I head out?"

"Sure, just head down the hall and take a left," Erika said, pointing. "It's across from our bedroom."

When I got to the bathroom, the door to the bedroom was open, and I couldn't help but glance quickly inside. There was nothing out of the ordinary, but a grouping of black and white pictures on the nightstand close to the door caught my eye. There were several that looked like old family group shots from Germany and two larger individual photos. One was of an infant, a boy probably about a year old. The other one looked like Erika at about seventeen or eighteen, with shorter, darker hair. There were no other visible clues to their previous lives, and I didn't dare walk in and explore any further. I quickly used the bathroom and returned to the kitchen.

"Kurt, what's the shortest way to those sloughs you were telling me about yesterday?"

"Hold on a second. I'll walk you to your car and show you."

When we got outside he pointed to a rough path—just a couple of wheel ruts, actually—trailing off behind the barn. "Just take that about a quarter mile and turn right into the driveway with the locked gate. I forgot to tell you yesterday that the area's fenced. I keep the gate locked because we've had so many strangers around this fall. I keep a key hidden close by for the locals, though. About ten yards to the right of the gate, there's a 'No Trespassing' sign attached to a fence post. Just at the base of that post is a big rock, and under it there's a leather pouch with the key to the padlock on the gate."

"Thanks, Kurt. It's nice of you to let me hunt in your private pond. I hope I can do something for you sometime. I'll make sure there's nobody around when I come and go."

"Don't worry about it. It's not like I'm hiding gold bricks in there or anything. I'm just trying to keep it from getting hunted out. We hope we see you again sometime. Have a good hunt."

We shook hands and I was on my way. The key was right where he said it would be, and I had my limit of greenheads in less than an hour. By sundown I was well on my way to Grand Forks.

CHAPTER 4

My week of student teaching after meeting the Heislers was an absolute blur. I was so caught up in the excitement that I could barely function. I alternated between complete ecstasy about my discovery and total despair that I couldn't share it with anyone. It was difficult trying to live my normal life knowing what I now knew—a Waffen SS officer was hiding out close to my home!—and I had to constantly work at not blurting out everything to my friends, especially during nights out drinking with the boys. To combat this urge, I busied myself with re-reading my research papers so I would be ready to show off my extensive knowledge to Kurt and Erika when the chance presented itself.

I was dying to drive right back to Heislers the next weekend, but decided I had to be more subtle than just showing up at their door every Saturday or Sunday hoping for a piece of pie. I also hadn't had my talk with dad about the draft yet, and I needed to spend some time with him, so I formulated a plan for the weekend. I would go home and hunt around New Rockford as usual on Saturday, have a talk with dad on Sunday morning and then stop at Heislers Sunday afternoon to hunt. I wouldn't stop at their house, but they might see my car and invite me in. If they didn't, I'd just go back to Grand Forks and try it again the next weekend.

When I got to New Rockford on Friday night, Dad told me he would have to be at the store all day Saturday, so I wound up hunting alone. Our opportunity to talk came on Sunday morning after church. Mom was a hostess for a ladies brunch after the service, so Dad and I had a good chunk of time to ourselves. She had prepared some cold cuts and macaroni salad for us, so after a quick bite I cornered Dad in the kitchen before he could get to his favorite chair for a nap. "Dad, can we talk for a minute? I've got something I want to run by you."

"Sure we can, son, but before we get started, just tell me whether this is a 'pull up the chair' kind of chat or if we can finish it standing here in the kitchen."

"I think we need the chairs, Dad."

"Well, then, chairs it is. Let's go sit in the den. I'm gonna' be a bad boy and sneak a beer while your mom's away. You want one?"

"Sounds good to me."

Sitting face-to-face with my father, a can of Grain Belt in my hand, made me feel very much like an adult. I recalled the last time just the two of us had sat in the den talking. It was just before I had started college, when we were sitting there evaluating my scholarship offers. I had thought I was quite the adult then as I weighed all the options, projecting where I would eventually go in the NFL draft after a record-breaking college career. Counting back the years since that conversation made me feel even guiltier that I hadn't done this more often.

While I was lost in thought, Dad got a little impatient and jumped right in. "So what's on your mind, son? Could it have anything to do with Vietnam and the draft?"

I didn't even try to cover up my look of total surprise. "Yeah, matter of fact it does, but how the hell'd you know that?"

"Your mother and I have been talking about it for some time, wondering when you were going to bring it up, and we're not the only ones who are curious. This is a small town, after all, and it's a hot topic. Everybody around here knows you're close to the top of the list, and they keep asking us what you're going to do after you graduate. Besides, just because you've been away at college doesn't mean we don't know our own son. You've been acting pretty strange lately, and we just figured you've been worried about it. Your mother's having a hard time. I keep telling her you'll bring it up when you're ready, but I was starting to get concerned, too. You worried that you'll have to go to Vietnam?"

"Yeah, a little. I guess it's just seemed like a done deal for so long now that I haven't really given it much thought. My goal has been to graduate, and now that I'm almost there, I realize I haven't prepared much for the next step, except to sit back and wait to get drafted. I haven't looked for a job because I didn't think there was much point to it. It doesn't make sense to start a career somewhere knowing I'm going to be drafted soon. That doesn't seem fair to anybody."

"So what's there to talk about, then?"

"Well, there's one other option I wanted to run by you, but it's kind of a long shot. I'm thinking about applying for law school and extending my deferment for a couple of years, but I haven't been able to get comfortable with that. I mean ... I like school and all that, but ... well, I guess I don't know what I'd be doing there other than staying out of the draft. It's not like I'd be curing cancer or performing some noble service for humanity. Deep down I think I'd feel like I was taking the coward's way out and letting my country down."

I nursed my beer and looked at dad. He wasn't saying much, which wasn't unusual. He'd often let me talk through my problems when I was growing up, but I was looking for a little more than that here. True to form, he waited me out again. "One other thing's bothering me, too. I can't forget that you signed right up after Pearl and served your country, so I don't want to let you down, either. Can you help me out here, Dad? Whaddya' think I should do?"

Now it was his turn to take a sip of beer before speaking. "Well, that's a tough question, son. Do you want me to answer as a veteran or as a father whose son is about to be drafted?" He paused for a moment. "Who ever wants to go to war? No one, but someone has to go when our country calls. That's why we elect our leaders—to make these difficult decisions—and we have to support them. So, speaking as a veteran and a patriot, I guess I'd probably tell you to go."

I could tell he was just getting started, so I remained silent, closely examining the Grain Belt label.

"But as a father who recognizes that Vietnam is a different kind of war, I'm a little torn, and I'm not the only one with this problem. It's a subject of debate down at the Legion Hall because a lot of my vet buddies are going through this with their sons. Most of them don't want to hear anything about a different kind of war. They believe in 'My country, right or wrong' and think their sons ought to just quit whining and do their duty like they did. A few of us, though, are having a hard time totally buying this war and don't feel we should be sacrificing our children for a political mistake, but we're definitely in the minority. Clearly, your circumstances aren't the same as mine were. Back then we were attacked and had no choice about whether to go to war or not. It was either fight back or learn Japanese. This war is different. We didn't get attacked, and we're sending Americans halfway around the world to help solve another country's problems."

There is only so much to study on a beer bottle label, but I didn't make eye contact again because I knew the payoff was coming soon.

"It's really hard to be objective here, but speaking purely as a father, I don't think it would hurt for you to check out law school as an option. I know you don't want to run the store when I retire, and we've never had a lawyer in the family. That way you won't look back later and question yourself. Besides, law school may only postpone the inevitable. If we don't change how we're fighting this war, you'll probably be drafted in a couple years anyway."

"What do you mean change how … "

"Hold on, son. I want to respond to one other thing you said. That whole thing about not wanting to let me down is a load of crap. I don't ever want you doing something just because I did it. This is your life, and you have to make your decisions for your own reasons. Life's tough enough without being saddled with that kind of baggage." He drained the last of his beer and stood up. "Now, I've said my piece, and you're on your own. You know your mom and I will support you whatever you decide to do."

It was the longest speech I'd ever heard from dad, and he was clearly talked out. I had hoped that talking to him would reinforce my decision; instead, the discussion had only muddied the waters. I was unsettled, but I didn't know where else to take the conversation. Prior to dad's comments I was pretty much resigned to my fate, but his advice surprised me.

I couldn't have imagined that the gung-ho World War II veteran would encourage me to think things through more carefully before supporting my country. Between that advice and telling me not to worry about letting him down, I was wondering if he really did want me to go to law school.

Along with my confusion about the draft I also felt guilty about hiding things from dad. He'd shared more of his feelings in that short conversation than he'd shared in a long time, and I was aching to reciprocate by spilling my guts about Kurt and Erika. They were becoming a major force in my life, and it felt like a betrayal to keep them a secret. But as bad as I felt, I couldn't see a way to bring dad into that part of my life, at least not yet. One thing I was sure about, though, was that I didn't want to be around when mom got home. Knowing that dad and I had talked, she would want to rehash everything—complete with a mother's drama and the accompanying tears—and that was a scene I truly did not want to experience this day.

"Dad, I just realized that I need to get packed and get on the road if I'm going to make it back to Grand Forks before dark. Thanks for taking the time with me. You've given me a lot to think about, and I'll let you know what I decide about law school."

Forty-five minutes later I was unlocking the gate to the Heislers' sloughs. I walked in and positioned myself on the upwind side of the slough closest to the road and waited. It was a little too early in the afternoon for the birds to be returning from feeding, so I lay back among the reeds and dozed off for a while. I was awakened by the whistling wings of three blue-winged teal as they flew right over me. Their splash landings sounded especially loud and jarred me further awake. Peering through the reeds, I saw that the teal had joined a small flock of mallards about twenty yards off shore.

I edged closer to the shore to get a better shooting angle before I scared the ducks into flight. They had to be flying when I shot them; my hunter's pride wouldn't allow me to waterball a mallard, no matter what the circumstances. I carefully waded into the tall covering reeds. When the water was just above my waist, I slowly started to rise to a taller shooting position, but as I straightened up, my right foot came down on a jagged, slippery rock. I lurched forward, instinctively raising my right arm to keep my shotgun above water. As I did, the water started rushing into the front of my waders.

The shock of cold water jolted me upright, but the damage was already done. My waders were full up to my waist, and I had to get to shore quickly before they dragged me down. I struggled up the bank to dry ground, unbuckled the suspenders and peeled the waders down to my knees. The water came pouring out. I sat down and worked my soggy feet out of the boots, swearing all the while. I was soaked from my neck to my toes. I couldn't believe I'd been such a klutz.

"Can't say I've ever seen anyone sneak up on ducks like that before," a man's voice boomed from behind me. The sarcastic comment—which sounded like something my dad would say—startled me. I looked up to see Kurt standing about ten feet away with a big grin on his face. Erika was by his side. Kurt continued, "You leave your lights on, you fall into ponds. Tom, I'm not sure we dare let you hunt alone out here anymore. Are you all right?"

"Oh, man, this is all I need—someone to see this," I replied. "Yeah, I'm fine. Nothing injured but my pride. I can't believe it. For a second there as I was about to go under, I thought the last thing I'd see was a flock of ducks mocking me. They were cackling so hard it's a wonder they got airborne." By now I had my wool socks off, and I was wringing them out onto the ground. "I don't know what's worse, almost drowning or having you two here to see it. You've now witnessed my two most embarrassing hunting moments."

"Why don't you come up to the house and dry off? I can throw those clothes in the dryer, and they'll be done in no time." Erika was trying her best to sound sympathetic, but her voice inflections gave her away; she was working hard to stifle the giggles.

"It's okay. Laugh it up. I'd be laughing, too, if I were in your shoes. Your dry shoes, I might add. Right now I'm just glad you don't know any of my buddies. They'd pay anything for this story; it would keep them in insults for years."

"Don't worry. Your secrets are safe with us. Come on up. The coffee's on, and I'm sure I can find something to ease your pain," Erika offered.

"Instead of staying out here like a drowned rat? Hmmm ... I think I'll take the dry clothes and coffee."

"Smart choice. I'm sure your parents would be happy knowing all that college tuition wasn't wasted," Kurt said, picking up my shotgun and turning toward the house.

Inside the house I took my wallet out of my pants pocket and removed my driver's license and my emergency five-dollar bill and laid them on the kitchen counter to dry out. Kurt gave me a flannel shirt, sweat pants, and socks to wear, and Erika threw my wet clothes in the dryer.

Keeping with our newly established custom, we gathered around the table for apple pie and coffee. I tried to pry more information from them about their pasts, but this time they were having none of it. In between jabs at my hunting skills, they bombarded me with questions about my family, college and my future, and, try as I might, I couldn't change the subject.

After about a half hour I got up to check if my clothes were dry. When I returned, Erika and Kurt were standing at the kitchen counter, and Erika had my driver's license in her hand. She was shaking her head saying, "It can't be! It just can't be!"

"What? You can't believe the state would give me a license to drive?" I asked.

They both turned at the same time, clearly startled and looking guilty. Erika was the first to regain her composure. "Tom, I'm sorry we snooped at your license, but we were just seeing if it had dried out, and I noticed your birth date, July 18, 1944. That's the exact day one of our relatives—Kurt's nephew—was born in Germany. It just seems like such a coincidence that we would meet someone here who was born on the exact same day."

"Well, maybe fate left the lights on in my truck so we could meet. I'd much rather blame it on that then on my forgetfulness," I said, trying to keep it light. But I couldn't believe they would have that strong a reaction to a minor coincidence; it's not like I was the only person in the world born on that day. "Where's your nephew now, Kurt? Is he over here, too, or is he still back in Germany?"

Kurt looked at Erika and then at me. "He's dead, killed in an Allied bombing just before the end of the war. We haven't thought about him in quite a while, but the license gave us a bit of a jolt. Sorry, didn't mean to ruin the day."

"No, I'm sorry I made a joke about it. I was just trying to … "

"No need to apologize. You couldn't have known. Besides, that was a long time ago." Erika then turned on her light-up-the-room smile and said, "How are those clothes coming? Are they dry yet or are we going to have to put you up for the night?"

"They're dry, so I'll go change in the bathroom, and then I'll hit the road. I have some lesson plans to prepare for tomorrow, so I need to get back in time to finish them."

I changed clothes and we said our goodbyes in the kitchen. Erika gave me a hug, and Kurt and I shook hands. They told me to come back and see them soon, but Kurt couldn't resist the parting shot, "I'll keep a set of dry clothes ready for you just in case."

The parting felt warm, but different. Something about the relationship was changing, but I couldn't put my finger on what it was. That whole explanation about my having the same birthday as their nephew just didn't jibe with their actions. They were awfully distressed over a nephew who had died twenty-two years ago. I genuinely liked them both, but I was frustrated that I wasn't getting any further with my attempts to uncover their secrets.

There were only a few weekends of good hunting left, and after that I wouldn't have any reason to be at the Heislers—or home, for that matter— if I wasn't hunting. I never came back home during the winter except for holidays, and my parents would be way too suspicious if I suddenly started hanging around. And there was no story I could concoct that would allow me to be home and still disappear for long periods to see the Heislers. Mom would suspect—with a mother's attendant joy, I'm sure—that I had a secret girlfriend, but to make that work, I'd eventually have to produce one. I had to figure out a way to get more out of Kurt and Erika soon.

CHAPTER 5

As if I needed a reminder that my time was running out, the weather turned ugly the next week—rain and sleet with hard overnight frosts. The temperature bounced back up to the fifties by Friday, but I knew I couldn't press my luck for many more weekends. Somehow I had to find a way to broach the subject of Kurt's SS service with Kurt and Erika on my next visit.

My drive home was fine, but at dinner that night dad's announcement forced me to alter my weekend plans. He said that he had arranged for someone else to mind the store on Saturday so he and I could "make a day of it, just like the old days."

So we did. We left early in the morning and spent the day talking and drinking coffee and cursing our luck and chiding each other about missed shots; then we headed home and listened to mom make fun of our hunting antics, just like the old days. I thoroughly enjoyed every minute of it.

On Sunday, I hunted early at some of my favorite spots and then headed to the Heislers. When I drove up the gravel road to the farmhouse around ten-thirty, I still hadn't come up with a workable plan to get them to talk. As usual, they seemed happy to see me, and we were soon assuming our positions around the kitchen table, this time dipping fresh chocolate chip cookies into our coffee mugs. About a half hour into the conversation, while I was staring at Erika's wedding ring and wrestling with a subtle way to segue into a discussion about their lives in Germany—something like, "So, does anyone around here know you're a Waffen SS member, Kurt?"—Erika looked solemnly at him and said, "I think now's a good time to apologize to Tom, don't you?"

"Yeah, I guess so," he half mumbled.

Erika continued. "Tom, we have a confession to make. We weren't exactly truthful with you last week about the driver's license, and we've felt bad about it and want to clear things up." She paused to make eye contact with Kurt again, but he was suddenly captivated by the bottom of his coffee cup, so she continued. "We didn't have a nephew with the same birthday as yours. It was actually our only son, Jochen, who really was killed in an Allied bombing of Nuremberg in 1945. Very few people know about him, and it's still a painful memory for us, despite the years that have gone by. I hope you can understand why we're careful about discussing the war here in America. It's not a topic we bring up with folks we don't know well. We feel bad about deceiving you and hope you can forgive us."

This was the very opportunity I had been waiting for! Although I was saddened by their loss, I was excited about the opening that Erika's confession provided for me to reveal to them what I knew. Unfortunately, I didn't know what to say next. That usually didn't stop me from opening my mouth anyway, but this time I forced myself to think things through before saying something stupid. I couldn't blow things now that they were trusting me and sharing family secrets.

"I'm sorry about your loss. Thanks for confiding in me, but there's no need to apologize. It's really none of my business, and I do understand why you have to be careful talking about the war."

They both smiled, looking relieved. Erika spoke first. "It was a long time ago, and we thought we were well past the grieving stage, but when we saw your birth date on your license, we both had a rush of memories that caught us by surprise. We've talked about it a lot this last week, and we think it had something to do with our getting to know you and having a younger person around. Then to find out that you were born on the exact day as Jochen, well, that seemed spooky to us, like some kind of sign or something. You were making a joke when you said it must have been fate that brought you to us, but that's how it feels to us."

"Yeah, it was just a joke at the time, but now it seems more eerily correct than I could have imagined."

Kurt looked puzzled. "What do you mean?"

"Well, I don't know how to say this, but I haven't exactly been truthful with you, either. I know way more about you than you think, and I've been struggling to find a way to tell you what I know without alarming you. I guess now's a good time to come clean, even though I'm a little scared about what I'm going to say."

While they sat there looking totally bewildered, I decided it was now or never. I took a deep breath, and—with the arrogance and ignorance of my youth masquerading as confidence—I boldly blurted out, "Kurt, I know you were a member of the Waffen SS, and I suspect you're hiding out here."

They looked at me in stunned silence. I waited them out and watched the warmth drain out of Kurt's face before he finally spoke in cold, clipped tones, "What do you mean? I have no idea what you're talking about."

"You were a member of the Second Waffen SS Panzer Division Das Reich. Don't worry, I'm not going to turn you in or anything. I told you I was a history major, and I would just like to learn from you about Hitler and the Third Reich and the whole SS organization and your battles on the Eastern Front and ... " I stopped as I realized I was sounding like an excited third-grader.

They stared at me in disbelief. Erika was still speechless, white as snow. Kurt's eyes were icy slits. "Tom, how an earth did you make up such a story? I don't know how you could even imagine it."

"Well, Erika's ring, for one thing. I wrote research papers on the Waffen SS and Germany's role in the war for some of my classes. I know about your reputation and your various campaigns, especially in Russia. I know about your beginnings, how you grew, and how the Waffen SS made up the most powerful element of the German ground forces in the last years of the war. I also know the various symbols of the Waffen SS Divisions and that the Wolfsangle was the symbol for Das Reich. When I washed my hands in the kitchen sink, I recognized the Wolfsangle on the wedding ring Erika had left on the counter. That symbol is unmistakable."

I was amazed by the surge of confidence I felt relating my knowledge. Erika sat, visibly flustered. Kurt was also unnerved, struggling to come up with some kind of response.

Finally, after a long, tense pause Kurt said, "If you're as smart as you claim, then you'd know that many German war symbols were taken from historical artifacts. The design on the ring must be just a coincidence. Do you mean to tell us that you're creating this wild story just because Erika has an unusual ring?"

"No, there's something more telling than the ring. On my first visit I accidentally found your pictures in the books under the Nordic statue in the study. You know the pictures I'm talking about ... your wedding picture and 'Smolensk, 1941?'"

They looked at each other and slowly sank back into their chairs, but stayed silent.

I kept pushing. "How far do I have to go with this? Kurt, do I need to have you show me the inside of your left armpit? You know...the place where the SS tattooed your blood type? I bet I'll find either the tattoo or a scar where you had it erased, right? Look, if I was going to turn you two in, I'd have done it already."

They examined me for a minute, and finally Erika smiled and said meekly, "Maybe fate really did bring us together." She turned to Kurt. "Now what?"

Kurt sat ramrod straight, jaw clenched. "I don't think we have a choice. Now we're just going to have to shoot him and get it over with."

Before my adrenalin could kick in so I could make a dash for the door, Kurt lost his hard look and burst into laughter.

"Kurt, you are so bad sometimes! Don't even joke about something like that. Poor Tom's heart can't take much of that, even if he's a young man. Seriously, though, we knew this day would come eventually. I think it's time we trusted somebody. Why can't it be Tom?"

Kurt turned to me, serious again. "Congratulations, your college work paid off. You're right, I was a member of the Waffen SS, and Erika was ... well, I guess a little Nazi Princess. At least that's what I thought when I first met her. But before we say anything else, it's important that you level with us. Have you told anyone else about us, even your parents or some of your buddies? I don't want to sound too melodramatic, but our lives could be in danger if certain people knew where we were."

"No, I haven't said a word to anyone, honestly. Not that it wasn't hard. For me a couple beers are like truth serum. After the first weekend I was so excited about finding you I almost spilled the beans, but I've settled down, and I'm used to keeping the secret now."

"Good. Now that you've discovered our secret, we don't really know what to do. I'm sure you can appreciate how bizarre this is for us right now. We've been in the States for over twenty years, and we've come close to revealing ourselves a few times, but we could never overcome our fear of what might happen if people judged us too harshly. We hadn't anticipated anything like this happening, so our cover stories are a little rusty. Right now I think Erika and I need to discuss how much of our past we can share with you."

He took Erika's hand and said, "Excuse us while we go into our bedroom and talk for a few minutes." He glanced back at me as they headed down the hall. "Tom, this won't take too long. Just help yourself to whatever's in the fridge while we're gone."

While they were in the bedroom I poured myself another cup of coffee. I reveled in my triumph for a few minutes before reality suddenly kicked in, and the potential consequences of my actions hit me like a two-by-four between the eyes. Over the past couple weeks I had learned that there was a world of difference between suspecting something and knowing something, and I wasn't sure I could live with the consequences of my newfound knowledge. I had been so blinded in my selfish quest for war lore that I hadn't even considered that I might be endangering Kurt and Erika. On the other hand, what made me think I could trust them? Maybe they were planning on using me in some evil plot. Or what if they were in the other room discussing how to get rid of me? No one even knew I was here, and they could kill me and dispose of me without leaving a trace. My mind became numb considering the alternatives, but my gut was telling me that I wasn't in any danger. My gut was also telling me that there were still some cookies left that needed my immediate attention. I went with my gut on both counts and dipped another cookie as I waited patiently.

Ten minutes later Kurt and Erika were back in the kitchen sitting around the table with me. Kurt looked at me solemnly. "Tom, we're kind of at your mercy right now. You could leave here and turn us in, but we're hoping we've judged you correctly. We don't know exactly how to do this yet. We'll figure it out as we go, but we're willing to trust you further if you agree to some conditions. If you do, you'll be the first person to know our story, and we'll tell you things that we've never shared with anyone— probably way more than you can handle—including firsthand accounts of the Russian Front and other historical events. But we can't risk giving you our real names in case someone tries to get them from you sometime. What do you say? Can we trust you?"

I had to pause for a moment. "I want to say yes, but I need a little more information. Put yourselves in my shoes for a minute. I don't really know who you are or what you've done. Will I be getting in trouble by protecting a war criminal? And who are you hiding from that's so dangerous? I mean, the war's been over for more than twenty years."

"Those are legitimate questions, and I don't blame you for being cautious. I promise you, we're not wanted by the government, so you won't be committing any crime by keeping our information secret. As for the second question, we're not always sure who we're hiding from, but we can't explain that to you yet. I wish I could, but ... "

"Knowing all this is much harder on me that I thought it would be, and I'm not sure I'm up for all this. Can I hear your conditions before I decide?"

"I guess that's a reasonable request, isn't it, Erika?"

She nodded in agreement.

"First, as you've already promised, you can't tell anyone about us without our permission. Second, the only way you can communicate with us is to come here alone at prearranged times. Last—and this is non-negotiable—you must always park that god-awful truck in the garage. It'll draw way too much attention sitting outside." Kurt laughed heartily as he stated the last condition.

My mind was a jumble of conflicting thoughts. As eager as I was to hear their story, I felt like I was getting in way over my head. Could I handle something of this significance, or was it better to just walk away and continue on with my mundane life, forever wondering if I had passed up what might have been a life-defining moment? "Maybe all this is too much to expect of a college student like me. What if I just walk away and forget I ever met you two? You wouldn't be trusting me any more than you already are, and I could just get on with my life."

"Tom, we'll let you go if that's what you really want to do. But if you leave, you can never come back or try to find us again. And we can't take the chance that we'll be discovered, so we'll have to pack and leave here quickly."

Kurt paused for effect, which was totally unnecessary at this point. This was way more pressure than I had anticipated when I first saw the pictures and imagined the historical possibilities of getting to know them. I couldn't help but think about that old cliché: "Be careful what you ask for."

Erika spoke before I could respond. "Before you decide, though, you should know that—against our better judgment—we've grown quite fond of you and would like to see you again. It's obvious to us that you didn't know what you were getting into, and we understand your reluctance to get involved now that things are much more complicated than you'd planned. But we believe that because of these very circumstances, you're just the person to hear our story. So what do you say? Do you want to stay and learn some history firsthand? Or do you just want to go away and forget about us?"

As if I could do that! It was now or never for me. I was still torn, but by now my curiosity was outpacing my judgment, and the historian side of me was too strong to overcome. Besides, there was no way I could look into Erika's imploring blue eyes and say no, even if I wanted to. If I refused, I think I would be the first man to have ever refused Erika anything.

"Okay, I'm in, if you'll agree to one condition of mine."

"What's that?" Kurt asked cautiously.

"I want input on the pie selection, and I get a piece to go every now and then."

Laughing, Kurt stood up and shook my outstretched hand, and Erika followed with a warm hug. "Thank you for trusting us. I told you when we first met I was a good judge of character. But I must admit, I never imagined a college student would be the one to finally uncover us. Kurt, it looks like we've been worrying about the wrong people."

"Oh, I think we still have to worry about the same ones we've always worried about. In the meantime there's one question I've been dying to ask Tom. How did you ever 'accidentally' find those pictures of the Russian Front? I think we could've pulled it off if you hadn't seen the pictures."

"Through an innate talent that you're all too familiar with, my clumsiness. I bumped the bookshelf, a few books fell out and the pictures fell right to the floor. So it wasn't really fate that brought us together, just my lack of coordination."

The ensuing mirth helped release some nervous tension, especially for me. I felt like someone had taken the piano off my back, knowing that I could finally be honest with them. I didn't know what lay ahead, but at least I could relax around them on future visits. "You know, I hate to end this after we've gotten everything out in the open, but I have to get back to Grand Forks. I have some work waiting for me back in the real world."

"Sure, leave just when we were starting to get to know each other. Well, now you have something to look forward to besides pie on your next visit. Come on, we'll walk you to your car." Erika took my arm in hers and started for the door.

Outside, standing by my car, Kurt eyed all my hunting gear lying in the front seat. "You know, Tom, that day I took you to start your truck, your camouflage gear brought back some old memories. Camouflage clothing was unique to the Waffen SS—at least back at the start of the war—and driving across the wild, open prairie with you sitting across from me in your hunting clothes reminded me of Das Reich's mad dash across the steppes in Russia in 1941."

"Well, I suspected that's what you were referring to when you said I reminded you of someone you knew, but I didn't dare say anything at the time. And by the way, I know all about the SS's history with camouflage gear."

"Enough war talk, you two. Tom, now that there are no secrets, we'd love to have you stop by next weekend and really get into our life stories. But please be careful in the meantime. We're very dangerous people, you know." Erika's smile had me bordering on delirium thinking about what lay ahead.

Kurt feigned a scowl. "Don't be coy, Erika. You can still be such a flirt."

"Don't mind him, Tom. He's getting a little cranky in his old age. We'll see you next Saturday. What time would you like to come?"

"Well, how about if I show up early, about eight o'clock or so, so we can really get into it? I have a lot of questions, and we don't have many weekends left."

Erika looked at Kurt, and he nodded his okay.

"See you then. Drive home carefully, and remember ... We don't exist."

I left, giddy with excitement. As I relived the afternoon, the magnitude of the day's events sunk in, and I started trembling slightly. Now that my adrenalin had worn off, I was experiencing a combination of total elation and complete physical exhaustion. Excited as I was about the prospects of where this could lead, I couldn't help but scold myself for acting so brazenly and taking such risks. No one knew where I had been hunting today, and as far as I knew, Kurt and Erika were the only two people who'd even seen me and the car. Had they felt threatened, they could have killed me and hidden my body without a soul knowing about it. I tried to convince myself that with my size—6'1" and 200 pounds of solid German-Norwegian stock—I could have held my own in a fight, but given Kurt's military background and familiarity with killing, I doubt I would have stood much of a chance had it come to that. Still, even with that horrific outcome running through my mind, I couldn't help but rejoice over the result of my naïve brilliance. I didn't know exactly what to expect in the upcoming days, but I sensed that Kurt and Erika were gateways to a vast amount of historical information. I was counting on nothing less than a thrilling wartime saga.

CHAPTER 6

After that remarkable visit with the Heislers it became even harder to settle into my normal routine back in Grand Forks. I kept thinking about the possibilities before me while working hard to make sure I didn't accidentally reveal something to my friends. I didn't have a clue how the next visits with Kurt and Erika were going to go, but I had a lot of questions I wished I'd asked at our last meeting: Were we just going to sit around the table with me asking questions? Would I even get to ask questions? Was anything off limits? Could I take notes? And then there was the really big question that had been gnawing at me all week: Why were they so eager for me to hear their story if I could never tell anyone about them? This last question—coupled with their reluctance to reveal who they were hiding from—raised a red flag, because I couldn't come up with a plausible explanation for their behavior. So, my enthusiasm dampened, I came up with a plan to protect myself in case I was in some kind of danger. I would keep a written record of our meetings, or at least as much as I could remember, and make several copies. Then, if I ever felt threatened, I would have something to give to the authorities if I had to turn Kurt and Erika in.

On Thursday night before my next trip I bought a couple notebooks and wrote down questions by category, one question per page, leaving plenty of space for answers. I still wasn't sure how I was going to get Kurt and Erika to agree to let me take notes, but there was no way I could do it without them noticing. Actually, I was feeling more pressured by the circumstances of our situation. There were so many things I wanted to ask them about, but we were probably only going to get a couple more visits this year at best, and with the draft hanging over my head, I didn't know when I would ever see them again. This reality forced me to continually rethink my questions and my approach. There were some significant historical subjects—the campaigns Kurt had fought in, his knowledge of war crimes, whether they had met Hitler—that I was eager to ask about, but I didn't think I could be that forward right away. I also knew the alternative— never seeing them again and forever wondering about their story—would probably drive me crazy. By the end of the week, weary of rearranging lists and considering the myriad of possibilities, I just gave up and decided to wing it.

———

It was cold and raining when I arrived at the farm on Saturday morning. Despite my struggles during the week, I felt much more at ease than I had been on the previous weekend. Any fears I might have had about how the visit would go were dispelled as soon as I caught sight of them. They had heard me come up the driveway and were coming out of the house as I approached the garage. They seemed genuinely happy to see me. I drove my truck into the open garage stall as we'd agreed, grabbed the rope handle, pulled the overhead door down and walked over to greet them.

They led me into the kitchen, where Erika had a pot of coffee and a plate of fresh, homemade cinnamon rolls waiting for us on the table. "Tom," she said with a twinkle in her eyes as she poured me a cup of coffee, "it's a good thing you got here when you did. I had a harder time keeping these rolls from Kurt than I did protecting my virtue when we were first dating."

Kurt sighed loudly with what, by now, I realized was his stock reaction to Erika's barbs—an exaggerated eye roll accompanied by a back and forth head shake. "Not quite. If that were true, I'd have starved to death by now. But your cinnamon rolls are definitely worth a fight."

Erika snapped him with her kitchen towel, and he grabbed her in a warm embrace.

After a prolonged pause, I loudly cleared my throat and said, "On second thought, maybe I'm not old enough to hear your *whole* story."

They giggled as we pulled out chairs from the kitchen table and sat down. I brought my pen and notebook out of my knapsack and started reviewing my questions as I sipped my coffee and carefully assaulted the cinnamon roll, trying my best not to get sticky brown sugar all over my hands. I hesitated to break the jovial mood, knowing there really was no subtle way to ease into a serious war discussion.

Kurt beat me to the punch. "Tom, was your father in the war?"

"Yes, he was a major in the Forty-Second Rainbow Division in Europe and fought in the Battle of the Bulge."

"That's a bit of a coincidence. I was a major, too, and I was captured by the Americans during the Battle of the Bulge in December of 1944. I also fought against the Americans in Normandy, but I don't recall running into your father's division. Actually, I spent most of the war fighting Russians on the Eastern Front, which is where Germany really lost the war. "

Kurt placed both hands around his coffee mug. "Before we start getting into anything serious, have you had any second thoughts about this? You can still back out, but once we start, there's no turning back."

"Sure, I've had some second thoughts—even some third and fourth ones—but I'm ready to go if you are. How about you two? Are you nervous that I might blow your cover, whatever that is?"

"No, not at all. If anything, your discovery has forced us to finally talk about things we should have discussed long before this. We've always known this day would come, but once we got over the initial shock of being discovered, we felt liberated. It's only been a week since we told you the truth about ourselves, but everything has changed in that time. Now we feel we have to tell you our story, and we'd be disappointed if we didn't get the chance. So, by all means, let's get started with the story of Kurt and Erika."

"Any ground rules I should know about, or can I just fire away?"

"Just one thing," Erika cautioned. "We've been deceiving people for a long time, to the point where we have to stop and think sometimes about what's true and what isn't. We know it's going to take us a while to talk openly about some of these things again, so please be patient with us."

"Fair enough, and I'll make the same request of you. As you've probably noticed, sometimes my enthusiasm outruns my common sense, so please stop me if I seem rude or insensitive. Agreed?"

They nodded in agreement. Taking advantage of the good-natured tone we'd established, I took a gamble. "Before we start, there's one favor I'd like to ask of you. Since it's my curiosity about World War II and my questions about the morality of war that have really brought us to this point, I'm wondering if you'd let me take a few notes for the unit I'm doing in class right now. With Vietnam on the minds of so many young people, it seems like a good time to have a meaningful discussion about how and why countries get into war and how both sides—the occupiers and the occupied—are affected. I'm assuming you're going to talk about some of these things as we move forward, and some firsthand accounts of events—unattributed, of course—could really make history come alive for my classes. What do you say? Can you help a struggling student teacher out here?"

Neither seemed too surprised or disturbed by the request, but they took their time mulling it over before Kurt responded. "I guess we wouldn't mind, but it depends on the questions. Why don't you take a few notes and we'll look at them before you leave?"

"Sounds good, and I appreciate your letting me do this. I have a notebook here with a few questions written down that you can take a look at to see where I'm going," I said, handing the notebook to Kurt.

Kurt took the notebook, leafed through it and handed it back to me. "I don't see anything too dangerous. We'll probably be talking about a lot of this stuff anyway, so let's go ahead and see how it goes."

"Great. Now, there's only one more thing I need to know up front, and this isn't on the list you just saw." I hesitated for a moment, and then, remembering that my boldness had served me well up to this point, I continued. "Now that you've convinced me of the seriousness of your situation, and I know that I could also be in trouble if you're discovered,

I think it's only fair that I have some idea what I'm dealing with. I hate to start out so bluntly, Kurt, but since we've agreed to trust each other, I'm going to ask you a difficult question. Did you ever commit any war crimes?"

Kurt was taken aback by my abruptness. "Wow, you don't waste any time do you, son?"

There was a long pause before he spoke again. "I had hoped we could get to know each other better before we got into such things. You don't know much about me yet, and there's no way that your research could ever help you understand the horrors of the war on the Russian Front, so I hope you can avoid judging me until you hear my whole story, but you're right, you now have a stake in this, too. Perhaps it is best to get the difficult things out of the way first. Before I start, though, I'd advise you to put the pen down and just listen for a while. It's going to be hard for me to tell this and probably even harder for you to hear it, and none of this can ever show up in your notes."

Kurt took a deep breath and slowly exhaled before speaking. "Yes, I did commit war crimes, at least as I understand that term now. I had Russian prisoners shot, and I had some partisans—or people I suspected of helping the partisans—hanged. We'd just discovered a number of our missing comrades killed and horribly mutilated, and we needed to make an example. I suspect that some of those people were innocent, especially the women. This explanation probably sounds like a rationalization to justify such extreme acts, but at the time they seemed necessary to save more of my men. I concluded a long time ago that what I did was morally wrong. Now I don't ask for anyone's forgiveness except God's, and I ask for it every day."

I felt like I'd been kicked in the stomach. As I visualized peasant women dangling from ropes—gasping and struggling for their lives—how could I not judge him? From my studies I knew of such cruelty in the abstract, but it was much more sobering listening to someone sitting face-to-face with me actually confess to it. Yet, from what I had seen of Kurt over the past few weeks, I couldn't envision such a seemingly gentle, caring, intelligent man doing such things. Once again I was in an emotional no man's land, like a witness to a horrible car wreck, unable to look away while feeling guilty for not wanting to. I couldn't help but want to hear the rest of their story.

"You're right, this is hard to hear, and I'm having a hard time comprehending the magnitude of it, but I promised I'd hear you out, so I'll reserve judgment for a while. You say you felt it was the right thing to do at the time. How does a person ever get to that point?"

"Certainly not overnight. As you well know, Germany and Russia were led by fanatical dictators, and both saw the war as a battle for ideological and racial survival. As a result, the war in Russia was a different kind of war than the one the Allies fought on the Western Front. In Russia both sides totally abandoned proper conduct and the civilized rules of war. Our Waffen SS training conditioned us to neither ask for quarter nor give it. Combine that attitude with the ferocity of the Russians, who were defending their homeland and often shot by their own officers if they turned back, and you have a war that is beyond description. None of us—Germans or Russians—ever thought we'd survive if we were captured."

Kurt leaned forward and rested his elbows on the table. "But to really explain how I got to that point, I have to go farther back. You've studied our history, but I don't think outsiders can really understand what it was like to be in Germany during the 1930s. You can read about it, talk to people who witnessed it, and theorize about it, but unless you actually lived through it, it's hard to comprehend. I don't know how many more meetings we'll have to discuss these things, so for now I'll give you some background to start our conversation. I just hope that by telling you my story you'll at least start to understand how war can drive us to commit acts beyond our wildest imaginings."

I had overcome my initial shock, but to steady my shaking hands, I picked up my pen and shuffled through the pages of my notebook. "This is some of the historical stuff I was hoping you'd get into, so is it okay for me to take a few notes now?"

"Go ahead. I'll look at it all before you go anyway." He got up, went to the coffee pot, poured himself a refill and sat back down. He took a bite of his cinnamon roll, wiped off his fingers and began talking. "First of all, you have to understand that the remaking of Germany didn't happen overnight. We Germans didn't all wake up one day and vote to take over the world. Things were much more gradual than that. Pride, revenge, the desire to return to lost glories, finding someone to blame for our country's troubles … Hitler and his party leaders used these seductive tools brilliantly. The Nazis got us into organizations like the Hitler Youth before we really had a chance to grow up, and we endured an endless torrent of speeches, parades, and rallies until we were swept up into a mindless mob of devoted followers. As young, impressionable kids—I was only 15 when I left school to begin military training—we were naively brainwashed into believing Hitler was Germany's salvation before we even knew what we were saving Germany from. You Americans grow up dreaming of becoming doctors, lawyers, policemen, firemen. My friends and I dreamed only of being soldiers serving the Fatherland."

Erika broke in. "Tom, my background was quite different from Kurt's, and will, I hope, provide you with a different perspective. My father was a rich industrialist, and my mother was a very strong personality who championed the Nazi cause. Father helped rebuild the Reich, and the Reich, in turn, helped him. As powerful, highly respected members of the Nazi Party and the business community, my parents enjoyed privileged status in German society. I actually met Hitler a number of times growing up, and—I must confess—I enjoyed all the special attention that I was given due to my parents' status.

"Looking back, it's not hard to understand how they got that way. All during the Thirties Hitler kept making promises, and he delivered on them. People—especially people of the Aryan race like my parents—enjoyed being part of a resurgent country and their social standing within it. They tended to see only the good in the reform and ignored the bad, so there was no way a challenge to Hitler would come from within that group. You're the history major. Can you think of any government where the people in power ever suggested changing the system that got them there?"

"Not off the top of my head," I said, "but I'll give it some thought. Kurt, what about you? Were you a member of the Nazi Party?"

"No. I never actually joined the party, but by serving in the Waffen SS I accepted their teachings."

"Why? How could you accept such ridiculous nonsense?"

Kurt paused, glanced sideways at Erika and then back to me. "Is this where I'm supposed to be patient with your youthful rudeness?"

"Sorry, Kurt. You're right," I said, feeling foolish. "That was harsh. Please go on, and I promise not to be so rude."

Erika continued. "Regardless of the circumstances, we allowed ourselves to be seduced by the lure of power and prosperity. We were wrong and ... "

" ... and we should've known better than to follow Hitler," Kurt finished emphatically. "We Germans have been making excuses for Hitler for many years now, and that is what they are, excuses. But, to our eternal damnation, we failed to see what inhumanity his policies of Aryan supremacy and anti-Semitism would lead us to accept."

I put my pen down, thankful for a chance to clear my head. I looked at them and smiled weakly. "Sounds to me like you've been preparing these responses for a long time."

For some reason my comment had a relaxing effect. They shrugged sheepishly, agreeing that their answers sounded like textbook rationalizations. Nevertheless, they believed their summary accurately reflected what happened to most Germans: They were seduced by an evil genius who had succeeded in convincing them he was the only answer to Germany's problems.

Erika refilled our coffee cups. "You're right, Kurt," I said stabbing a second cinnamon roll. "These are worth fighting for."

We sat in silence as I finished the last bite of the roll and washed it down with coffee. "Let's continue. Kurt, why did you join the Waffen SS when you could have served Germany just as well in the regular army?"

"A couple reasons, I guess. The first was my older brother, Jurgen. He was five years older than me and had left home in 1930 when he was only fifteen. I'm not really sure how he got in, but he was one of the very early members of Hitler's personal bodyguard—the Leibstandarte Adolf Hitler—probably the most famous of the Waffen SS Divisions. My parents disagreed with his choice, and he became the black sheep of the family, but I idolized him, especially when he wore his magnificent black Leibstandarte uniform. I wanted to follow in his footsteps, even more so after hearing him talk about the special comradeship, or élan, of the

Leibstandarte. I just decided that if I was going to be in the army, I would serve with the very best."

He smiled mischievously at Erika. "But the thing that really pushed me over the edge was my burning desire to impress a certain blond beauty. I was convinced I had to be a member of Hitler's elite guard to ever win her heart."

"Sure, blame me," chided Erika. "I thought you were cute as soon as I saw that little boy lost look on your face that day outside your uncle's."

"I wasn't lost, and let's not go through that again."

"All I'm saying is that you didn't have to join the SS to impress me. I was already impressed."

"Sure, now you tell me. You could have saved me a lot of frustration by letting me know earlier."

Obviously, their humor had seen Kurt and Erika through some very difficult situations. Even now—recounting their roles during some of Germany's darkest times—they could still joke with each other. That friendly, affectionate sparring between them only reinforced my desire to know more about their lives together.

We continued our session until late in the afternoon, drinking coffee and talking, our relationship growing stronger with each passing hour. I completely lost track of time, and when I realized that it was nearly three-thirty, I knew I needed to end my visit quickly if I wanted to make it to New Rockford before dark. They seemed genuinely disappointed that I had to leave, and Erika asked if I could come by again the next day to continue our conversations. I had to be back in Grand Forks early on Sunday to prepare some new material for Monday's class, so I couldn't take her up on the offer, but we agreed to meet the next Saturday at the same time, weather permitting. Erika tried to get me to take some cinnamon rolls with me, but I told her I would have a hard time explaining to my parents where they came from.

Kurt said, "See, Erika, he's thinking ahead. I think he shows promise after all."

I gave Kurt my notebook to review. He studied if for a few minutes and turned to Erika. "I need to get some wood for the fireplace, so I'll walk Tom to his truck." He handed the notebook to me without a word, and I put it in my backpack. We walked to the garage in silence, but I could tell he had something on his mind. He opened the garage door and hesitated a minute before speaking. "Tom, you say your dad fought in the Battle of the Bulge. Have you ever talked to him about what he saw in combat?"

"Not really. He always steered me away from the specifics when I was younger, so we mostly talked about campaign strategy and stuff. Eventually I quit asking him about it. Why are you asking?"

"I know some of what you heard today was difficult to comprehend, and it'll probably weigh on you a while. If your dad was in some heavy combat, I'm sure he has some of his own experiences that he tries not to think about. Perhaps he has some stories that might help you better understand what it's really like on the front lines. Maybe it would be good to ask him again."

We stood in silence for a moment before Kurt continued. "There's one other thing I need to ask you about."

"What's that?"

"We know what a great hunter you are. Won't your folks get suspicious when you keep coming home without any ducks these days?"

"It's a good question, but, no, they don't. I often give away my birds to farmers or friends who don't hunt, so they never even bother to ask any more. Besides, even I get shut out once in a while."

CHAPTER 7

My next week in Grand Forks was an agonizing mental battle with myself. Reviewing my notes about the horrific deeds of the Waffen SS did little to reconcile my genuine fondness for Kurt and Erika with my knowledge of their pasts. He had killed innocent civilians, and she was from a Nazi family of staunch Hitler supporters. Finally, after days of intense soul searching, I decided that I shouldn't let my personal biases about morality prevent me from following through with this opportunity to explore history firsthand. If I wanted to be a serious student of history, I had to hear their whole story without passing judgment.

It also became clear to me—after spending hours trying to write down as much as I could remember about our conversation and then organizing my handwritten scribbles into some sort of order—that I had to come up with a faster, more efficient system. Just when I was feeling totally stumped about how to do this, a couple of real life events converged to help me out. While I was rummaging through boxes in my closet trying to find my research papers, I came across an old cassette recorder and a bunch of cassettes that my former roommate had left behind. He'd been struggling with a Spanish class and had bought the recorder and tapes to practice. A couple days later there was an article in the paper about Truman Capote, whose novel, *In Cold Blood,* was a runaway best seller.

Capote described how he had interviewed his subjects—two convicts who had murdered a Kansas family—without a tape recorder or notes present. He had trained himself to ask questions and then immediately after the interviews record everything he could remember, using his list of questions to trigger his memory of the answers.

I wasn't naïve enough to believe I could recall the Heisler conversations with Capote's level of accuracy, but I thought the tape recorder could help me out. If I wrote brief notes during the conversations—key phrases, dates, names and other pertinent information—and then recorded everything I could remember while I was driving home, perhaps I could be faster and more accurate. Then, between the notes and the tapes, maybe I could gather enough information to put together a cohesive narrative of our conversations. It certainly seemed worth a try, so I tested the format out a few times with my friends before leaving for the weekend. I made lists of some innocuous history questions, and, under the guise of doing research for my class, asked them on our nights out. Then I recorded everything I could remember as soon as I got back to my apartment. Surprisingly, the method worked quite well. The key, though, was to record everything immediately, because when I went back to review the tapes later, my memory about the specifics had already started to fade.

Loading the tape recorder and some notebooks into my travel bag Friday afternoon, I reflected on the amazing set of circumstances that had led me to the Heislers. Erika felt that my stumbling upon her and Kurt was more than a coincidence, and I had to agree. I was eager to see where the story would take me, and I promised myself that I wouldn't blow this chance.

C H A P T E R   8

Saturday's visit was less emotionally charged than that of the previous week. I didn't think I could handle any more descriptions of war crimes—at least for a while—so I asked about less sensitive topics. I started with "How did you two meet?" and they started talking and kept me writing for hours. They described their childhoods, their families, and their early lives in the context of the Germany that was emerging under Adolf Hitler. Their backgrounds were diverse, but equally fascinating, and I felt I had a front row seat to history as I absorbed their personal histories for most of the day. Kurt even started talking about some of his combat experiences in Russia.

As the afternoon wore on the conversation flowed much more naturally. They tried to get me to talk more about myself, but I kept the dialogue centered on their life in Germany. It was obvious from their interaction with each other that they had worked so hard over the years at keeping their pasts hidden that they had not even spoken with each other about many of these events. It also became clear to me how much it meant to them to finally talk with someone about their past. Around three o'clock I put my pen down and told them I was done for the day so I could get home by dark.

While I was packing up my things, Erika asked if I could come again the next weekend.

"This time of year the weather's pretty unpredictable, but I'll be back if the ponds and sloughs don't freeze over. If they do, I won't be able to make it, because my folks would get too suspicious if I came home when I couldn't hunt. I've never done that while I've been in college, except for holidays. And I can't try to sneak here to see you without going home. Too many people around here know me, and if anyone saw me and mentioned it to my folks, I could never come up with a believable explanation about why I was here and didn't come to see them."

"If the ponds freeze, when will we see you again? Now that you've got us talking, we can't seem to shut up," Erika said.

"I'll be home for Thanksgiving and Christmas for sure, and we'll just have to see what happens. The rest of my family will be there, and it'll be much harder for me to get away for any length of time with so many people around. It's just not like me to disappear for long periods of time when I'm not hunting. So if we don't connect over the holidays, I don't know when the next time will be. Then there's always that little overseas war that might rearrange my schedule a bit."

"Tom, please don't make jokes about the war around us." There was concern in Erika's voice. "After all, you're starting to feel like a son to us, and we're concerned about your future, too. We just have to find a way to get together sometime. We'd hate to have you go off to war without even getting to say goodbye."

"Well, I appreciate that, and I'd hate to leave without seeing you, but the rules are that our meetings have to be prearranged, and I don't know how to do that on the spur of the moment. Any suggestions? Would it be okay if I just called you?"

Given the time we had spent together and how close we'd become, I expected a quick, positive response. All I got was awkward silence.

They looked at each other for a while before Kurt finally spoke. "Tom, there are some reasons why phone conversations between us wouldn't be a good idea. I think the safest way for you to contact us is to write a letter. From Grand Forks it will only take a day or two to reach us, and you should know your plans that far in advance. Just don't put a return address on the letter. Will that work?"

"Only when I have some lead time," I answered. "It won't work when I'm here for the holidays and find some time at the last minute, so I guess that's out. But even when I know a couple days in advance, how will we arrange a time?"

"Why don't you give us your phone number, and we'll call you after we receive your letter?" Kurt said. "Just let us know when you'll be home. That'll work much better for us."

"I guess that'll work," I mumbled as I wrote out my phone number on a piece of notebook paper, "but I'm confused by your need for such secrecy. Why is a phone call or a return address on a letter such a threat?"

"Tom, I'm sorry we can't tell you everything right now, but please trust us a little longer," Kurt said. "We've come a long way together in just a few weeks, and we've trusted you completely with some very sensitive information. Believe me, we want our friendship to grow, and we wouldn't do this unless we thought it was absolutely necessary."

He handed me a folded piece of paper. "Just use this address to reach us."

I looked at his writing. It was a post office box in Bremen. "Okay, if that's the way it has to be, here's my number. I don't have a roommate or anything, so there shouldn't be any problem when you call me. I just hope this plan works. As for next weekend, just watch the weather forecast. If we get a hard freeze, I won't be here, but if the weather holds, let's make it around noon next Saturday."

"That sounds good, Tom, and thanks for your understanding. Let's hope for a nice weekend so we can see each other again soon." Kurt patted me on the back as he spoke.

"But since we're being so careful about the rules, I insist on enforcing one that you seem to have forgotten about," I said sternly.

"What's that? I can't think of anything that we've missed." Erika was frowning with concern.

"Next Saturday I want fresh apple pie with real whipped cream topping."

Amid the laughter, Erika said it wouldn't be a problem.

The goodbyes were getting harder with each visit, and this one was made more difficult by our knowledge that this might be the last time we would see each other for a long time, or ever again. When I finally steered the truck out of the driveway, I looked back for a last glimpse and saw them—each with an arm around the other—waving at me as I drove out of sight.

On the drive home I pulled out the tape recorder and set it on the seat and held the microphone in one hand. I was eager to try out my new technique, and I started recording everything I could remember about the day's conversations. I was amazed at how much I could remember and got so involved in the process that I missed the turn to New Rockford by several miles and had to turn around and go back. When I was within a few blocks of home I still had some things left to record, so I pulled into the empty St. James High School parking lot and sat there for fifteen minutes to finish up recording my notes and reflect on the day.

By now I was getting used to my weekends of contradictory emotions, and this one was no different. Just when I thought we had turned the corner on the relationship, they threw a curve at me with their reluctance to let me call them. If they were willing to call me, it meant that they just didn't want calls coming into their house. Could they be worried about their phone being tapped? If so, who would be doing that, and why? And obviously they didn't want a return address on the envelope so nothing could be traced back to me. Was I being used for some devious purpose? That didn't seem to make sense, because Kurt was right when he said they had revealed a lot to me. If it were all true, I could certainly do more harm to them than they could to me. So far I had done nothing incriminating, nor had they asked me to do anything other than to hear their story. If they ever asked me to do something questionable, I could simply decline. I didn't think I was being duped, at least not yet. But I had to admit, if this was some kind of con, Erika and Kurt were really good at it, and I was very pleased with myself for having the foresight to protect myself with my notes and tapes.

As I eased "Old Ugly" out of the lot, I took a few deep breaths to calm myself before going home to see my parents.

C H A P T E R   9

The weather held and on Saturday I was driving up the Heislers' driveway about noon. The garage door was open, so I drove in, parked the truck, and closed the door. They were waiting for me on the step, coffee mugs in hand, and offered one to me as I walked up. I took it in both hands and drank slowly, allowing my mouth to cool the coffee a bit before I swallowed. The warmth felt good after a morning of hunting in the cold.

We went into the house and sat down to a lunch of a hot hamburger casserole and fresh, warm, home-baked bread. We kept the conversation light during the meal, filling each other in on the details of our week's activities. It felt good to be in their company again.

"I'll get the coffee pot," Erika said as she started to get up.

"No, sit, sit," insisted Kurt. "You made the meal, so I'll be in charge of coffee refills."

While he was going over to the stove, I pulled out my notebook and pen. I knew coming into this weekend that I was pressing my luck with the weather and might not see Kurt and Erika for a long time, so I had to move things along. I started with a question about the subject closest to my heart. "Kurt, do you think there's such a thing as a moral war? I mean, Germany was a predominantly Christian nation, yet look what happened."

Kurt didn't seem surprised by the directness of my question. "I've given that question a lot of thought myself, Tom. Cultures have been attacking each other under the guise of morality since the beginning of time. Christians and Muslims, Protestants and Catholics, Jews and Arabs, Hindus and Muslims, people have been killing people for all kinds of reasons—religion, natural resources, greed—the examples are endless. In most cases opportunistic leaders convinced followers that theirs was a just and moral cause by appealing to an exaggerated pride in their country and instilling the fear that it was being threatened by an outside force. Can you name one war where the aggressor didn't claim that it was 'just' or 'moral'?"

I figured the question was rhetorical—and I couldn't think of a war to disprove his point, anyway—so I just let him keep talking.

"So it's no surprise we Germans reacted the same way under those circumstances. What patriot doesn't want to defend his country and its way of life? At the time we really believed that we were defending ourselves from the inevitable takeover by the Slavic hordes, that our very survival as a nation was at stake. So we thought we had to attack the Poles and the Russians before they attacked us. At about the same time on the other side of the world in Japan, their military leaders were convincing their citizens that they had to attack China and the United States if they wanted to survive as a nation. Unfortunately, millions died believing they were morally justified in starting those wars, and I'll bet you can find some Germans and Japanese today who still believe their cause was just."

"Kurt, I can maybe understand Germans falling for Hitler's warning that Poland and Russia were a threat, but what about Germany's wars against England, France, the Netherlands, and Norway? I'd say it was a war of aggression, which you say is wrong."

Looking absently into space, Kurt acted as if he failed to understand my question, or was choosing to ignore it. Finally, his answer came in the form of a confession. "Man is a magnificent creature with enormous potential for good, but he also has an equal capacity for evil. Devious rulers like Hitler know that and exploit it. I'm living proof of what happens when evil dominates good, and religion is used to further the ends of extreme nationalism. The Nazi state, especially the SS, succeeded in somehow giving honor and nobility to cruelty and inhumanity. Over time—even though I'd been raised in a strong Christian family—I became the ultimate evil, a basically good person who adopted a way of life contrary to the laws of God and civilized man."

I kept looking down at my notepad, fearful that I would interrupt Kurt's thought process if I made eye contact.

"So, Tom, do you think there is such a thing as a moral war?" Kurt continued. "If so, here's the question you really should be asking: Who gets to decide what's moral? And how can the word 'moral' have any meaning when it's subverted by such men as Hitler and Stalin? I've come to believe that the only moral war is one fought in defense of your country against unprovoked attacks. I don't think wars of aggression are morally justifiable under any circumstances."

Thankfully, Erika showed up with dessert before I had to respond. "Tom, I didn't want you to think that I wasn't following our rules, so here's the apple pie and real whipped cream, as ordered. Which one of you would like the check?"

"Cute," Kurt said. "Please sit down and join us. I'm trying to answer Tom's question about whether there can be a moral war, but I'm not sure we're making a connection."

We made short work of the pie, and Kurt continued what was starting to sound like a lecture. "Tom, maybe it would be easier if we made this discussion more personal. You say you'll serve if you get drafted, but you haven't told us whether you believe in this war in Vietnam. Do you have any doubts, or are you a real patriot who can hardly wait to serve your country?"

By now I knew Kurt well enough to realize that his last remark was tinged with sarcasm. I can't say I was surprised that he brought up Vietnam. I had hoped to avoid the topic because I still had mixed feelings about it, but given the direction of the conversation, I felt obligated to give him an answer. "I believe in supporting my country and its leaders, especially in time of war. I know this sounds corny, but I remember President Kennedy's inaugural address when he said, 'Ask not what your country can do for you, but, rather, what you can do for your country.' I believe there's something to that. I'm not a coward, and I don't want to let my country or my friends down."

Kurt gave me a puzzled smile with a slight headshake and started to talk, but stopped, as if he had thought twice about what he wanted to say. "Are you saying that this is a moral war, then? Do you believe that the communists in Vietnam are a serious enough threat to America that you would die for that belief?" Kurt's tone wasn't harsh or unkind, but he knew he was putting me on the spot.

"Do you find this amusing, Kurt? Are you making fun of my beliefs?" I couldn't prevent a defensive tone from creeping into my voice.

"Tom, I'm not criticizing your beliefs at all. I'm just smiling because you are missing the obvious here. What is that American expression, 'You can't see the forest for the trees'? Can't you see the similarities in our situations here? You've been skeptical about how I could join up to help my country when Hitler said we were being threatened, yet here you are considering it because President Johnson is telling you the same thing. What's so different about your situation? "

"Kurt, I can't believe you're comparing President Johnson to Hitler or the American way of life to that of Nazi Germany. How can you even defend such a thought?"

"I'm not comparing the men or the ideologies; I'm just comparing the situations—two young men going to fight for their countries because they believe their way of life is being threatened. Remove the personalities and the politics, and what's the difference?" Kurt paused and waited for my response.

I thought for a moment and couldn't come up with an answer without sounding defensive, naïve or both, so Kurt just continued. "Maybe it isn't fair to compare Nazi Germany and the United States under these circumstances, but I believe that a country should only go to war to defend itself from imminent danger, not some vague, distant threat. Countries shouldn't go to war for their benefit or to impose their ways of life on another society. Those kinds of wars only sow seeds of resentment. So is this a war of necessity for America or is it a war of choice?"

"Are you saying that we are fighting this war under false pretenses, that there really is no communist threat?" I knew I was being baited, but I couldn't help myself.

"I think there is some justification for the idea of containment and the domino theory, but in the case of Vietnam, I think the United States is overreaching. I followed the French-Indochina War closely. Many former members of the Waffen SS joined the French Foreign Legion and died at Dien Bien Phu, where the Vietnamese defeated the French. I believe that Ho Chi Minh and his followers are totally committed to the establishment of a united Vietnam, and they will do whatever it takes for as long as it takes in order to win."

"So you don't think we can win in Vietnam? Didn't you see that we just committed more troops to get the job done—we're up to almost 500,000 now—and President Johnson says we'll do whatever it takes to win? Apparently you've already forgotten what we did to your country not so long ago." I wasn't about to let him kick America around, no matter how stupid I sounded.

"Tom, I'm not trying to upset you by questioning America's ability, but please remember, you only studied World War II history; I lived it. I'm just trying to give you the perspective of a former military officer who knows something about fighting on someone else's homeland. Clearly, America has the resources and ability to win this war. I just don't know if it has the will to do so, not in a country that is so foreign, so remote and poses no immediate danger to them."

Kurt was right. There are times when book knowledge is no match for worldly experience, and this was one. Intellectually, I felt out of my league. No amount of theorizing on my part could counter Kurt's personal observations. I felt ashamed that I couldn't make a better defense of my country's policy, but I just didn't know where to take the conversation.

Kurt continued gently. "Tom, we all want to believe in our countries and our leaders, and there is no shame in that. Like you, I once felt an obligation to help my country achieve great things. I'm just bringing this up so you can think things over now while you still have a choice. You're older and better educated than I was when I had to make the decision, and I think you should take advantage of that. There's nothing cowardly about taking your time and looking at your options. I never even had the chance to think about whether I was doing the right thing. By the time I was old enough to enlist, nothing—not even my mother's pleadings—could keep me from it. She was one of the few who questioned Hitler's direction for

Germany." He thought for a few seconds before continuing. "Speaking of parents, what about your dad? He was in the military. What does he think you should do?"

"The same as you—check out law school—which kind of surprised me a bit, because he enlisted without hesitation," I said. "But I know my situation isn't exactly the same as yours or dad's, so maybe I'll give it a little more thought. If I go to law school, I want to go because my heart is in it, not just to get out of the draft."

"Tom, I can't judge how you choose to best serve your country, not with my past and the mistakes I've made," Kurt said softly, "and I'm sure you'll come to the decision that's right for you. But here's one final thought. Regardless of the circumstances, war needs constant justification; it should always be the last resort."

We sat in silence for a moment, and then Erika, who had been listening quietly for a long time, finally broke her silence. "As a mother who survived one war, my heart goes out to those mothers who are sending their sons off to Vietnam. It's bad enough losing your children when they are defending their country, but it would be especially difficult for me to send my son off to Vietnam. Does your mother worry that you might go off to war?"

"Hell, Erika, my mother still worries about me crossing a street by myself. Worrying is her full time job. She'll worry whether I stay here and go to grad school or go to Vietnam. Right now she's sitting there hoping I get home soon so I won't have to drive in the dark. That's just the way she is, and it wouldn't change if I were fifty and living in a monastery. As far as my mom is concerned, her children are never safe."

Erika smiled softly. "I think I understand your mother perfectly, Tom."

"Speaking of driving in the dark, I better pack up and hit the road soon. Thanks for giving me so much time today. This is a lot more interesting than sitting in the library reading history books."

CHAPTER 10

The next week a severe storm hit, freezing all the ponds and chasing the ducks and geese south, so I stayed in Grand Forks. Then Thanksgiving and Christmas came and went without another opportunity to see the Heislers. I made it home for both holidays—my brother and sister were there—but there was no way I could get away either time without arousing suspicion.

The Christmas visit actually turned out pretty well. One night during the Christmas holiday before my brother and sister had arrived, I caught dad in a mellow mood sitting alone in the family room watching television after mom had gone to bed. After a little small talk about the day, I asked him if we could talk about his war experiences.

"Why now?"

"Because when I was a kid you kept putting me off whenever I asked you what it was like in battle. You said I was too young to hear about that stuff. Well, I might be heading off to war myself soon. You think I'm old enough to hear it now?"

Dad paused for a moment, sighed heavily and sank back into the couch. He didn't look relaxed, just resigned.

"I guess you're right. If I can't talk about it with my own son now, who could I ever tell?" He sat silent for a minute. "It wasn't just that you were too young then. Living through that war was bad enough, but retelling

those stories was just more than I could bear. That's why I've never talked to anyone about what happened over there. People who weren't there
would never understand, and I just wanted to put it behind me and get on
with my life."

"Have you been able to put it behind you?"

"No, I don't think anyone can," dad said. "There are days the memories
are so fresh and raw that it feels like it happened yesterday, but then sometimes when I try to recall something specific, I can't bring up a single clear
memory. The hardest thing is when out of the blue a random scene comes
flashing back that's so real that I have to work to get myself out of it."

"Like what?"

"The other day I was walking down the street and caught a whiff of
diesel fuel from a utility truck driving by," Dad began haltingly. "Just like
that, I was back in a forest near Hatten, Germany, and I could see and hear
and smell the Tiger tanks come crashing through the trees, throwing up
snow, snapping tree limbs and crushing everything in sight. I was sitting
back to back in the foxhole with my buddy, and I could feel his warmth
seeping through me as we sat in the cold. I saw my best friend get shot and
ground up by a tank in a foxhole down the line. I felt an instant surge of
adrenalin, but worried that my legs were so cold and stiff I wouldn't be able
to run fast enough to get away. For that second, standing on that sidewalk,
I couldn't move. Then the memory passed, and I went about my business."

"Jeez, Dad, I'm sorry. I had no idea. Do these flashbacks happen
often?"

"It kind of goes in streaks. It won't happen for a long time, and then I
may get two or three of them in a week or so." He paused and closed his
eyes before continuing. "Then there's this one recurring dream I have.
I'm alone in my foxhole as the Germans come pouring out of the forest in
front of me. I just start picking out individual targets—one at a time like
we were trained to do—and I start squeezing the trigger on my M-1. Men
are falling all around me, and then, almost in slow motion, I clearly see the
look in the eyes of one young German just as I shoot him. It isn't a look
of pain or anguish—just total surprise—like he had never ever considered
that he might be one of the ones who would get shot. That's when the
dream ends. That look is frozen on his face, and he never hits the ground."

"So you killed Germans, then, and saw Americans killed?" I asked softly.

"Yes."

"Was it hard for you to kill people?"

"I didn't have time to even think about it. If I had, I suspect I'd be buried over there with a bunch of my friends. That's what we were trained to do as soldiers. They shoot at you, and you shoot back. In combat you can never start thinking about enemies as anything other than targets or you'll be dead. Fortunately, your training takes over and you just react. It was only later when I was back home that I started wondering about the German soldiers I killed—not questioning whether it was right or wrong, because given the circumstances of that war, I never doubt that—but just curious about who they were and whether they had wives and kids."

I paused for a few seconds to let that sink in before I remembered some things I wanted to follow up on. "If I can backtrack, Dad, you mentioned the Hatten Forest, and I'm a little confused. Weren't you involved in the Battle of the Bulge?"

"No, we just missed it. We landed in southern France on December 9, 1944, and we never got far enough north to actually take part in the Battle of the Bulge, but we were close enough."

"Were you aware that the SS executed American prisoners at Malmedy during the Battle of the Bulge?"

"Hell yes!" dad said, fire in his eyes. "That news spread like wildfire, and all of us on the line were aware."

"Did you ever see Americans shoot German prisoners?"

"I didn't see anyone do it, but I heard it happened sometimes, though nothing like the Malmedy massacre. You hear all kinds of stuff in a war zone, and you never really know what's true and what's scuttlebutt. I'm thankful for one thing, though ... that I wasn't guarding any German prisoners right after the news came down about Malmedy."

"Do you really think you could have shot prisoners in cold blood?"

"I don't think so, but I'm glad I wasn't put to that test. I saw guys do a lot of terrible things, things they didn't think they were capable of doing. When you see your best friends get blown to pieces in front of you day after day, and you don't think you're going to get out of the war alive, you just get numb to it. After a long time on the line, life doesn't seem so precious anymore, so it didn't surprise me when I heard rumors that stuff like that happened."

I couldn't believe how much dad was sharing. I felt as if I'd just opened Pandora's Box, so I pressed on. "I just found out by accident from mom that you were awarded the Bronze Star. I know that's a big deal, that they don't just hand those out like candy. What did you do to get that? And how come you never told me about it earlier?"

"What'd I do? The same thing as everyone else there, fight for my life! Our outfit was in an exposed position during the fighting in Hatten Forest. We were ordered to hold the line as long as we could to buy some time. Germans came at us from everywhere, and we fought them off as long as we could before most of my group was killed. Hell, everybody there was a hero, and I didn't do any more than the rest of the guys. I don't think I deserve a medal just for surviving."

"I'm sure it was much more than that," I pressed, hoping to get more details.

"Son, I've gotta' tell you that's about as far as I can go tonight," Dad sighed softly. "I never intended to bend your ear this long, and I sure as hell never thought talking about it would affect me like this. I'm sorry you had to be the one to hear all this."

For the first time in my life I saw tears in my dad's eyes. I sat speechless for a while, but as he struggled to continue, I gently broke the silence. "Dad, have you ever talked to anyone about this?"

"You mean, like a psychiatrist? No, I never wanted to get into any of that psychological mumbo jumbo. We all paid a price for that war. I just figure this is mine, and it's a much smaller price than many of my buddies paid. Regardless, I don't want you thinking that I'm some sad sack with guilt feelings about being in the war and doing what I had to do. I'm proud that I served, and I'd do it all over again if I had to."

CHAPTER 11

Back in Grand Forks after Christmas I was going crazy not being able to continue the meetings with Kurt and Erika. Our time together had become addicting, but I couldn't find a way to force another meeting. I did take advantage of the free time, though, by organizing all my notes and tapes and getting everything in a coherent order.

I also decided to just take my chances with the draft. I had seriously considered applying to law school and even started studying for the LSATs in my spare time, but eventually I decided against it. Part of me just couldn't muster up the passion for three more years of school, but the biggest reason—surprisingly, since I had never really considered it as a career choice—was that I discovered I really wanted to be a teacher. Initially I was fulfilling my student teaching requirement just to get the degree, but the more I taught, the more I enjoyed being in the classroom. Unlike the law, it gave me the chance to fulfill my desire for attention in front of an audience without landing someone in prison for my mistakes. And I thought I might even change a few young lives for the better in the process.

Unfortunately, graduating in the middle of the school year put me at a severe disadvantage in trying to find a teaching position. The best I could hope for would be to fill in for someone on medical leave, and schools rarely hired first-time teachers to fill those openings. Most likely I would have to wait until the next fall to start, and by then I would be drafted, so I just decided to accept my fate.

Once I made the decision I felt great relief. I figured I could do my two years of military service and come back to Grand Forks and work my way into the system. So, in anticipation of getting drafted after graduation in January, I started getting my affairs in order. I decided to spend my last few months in Grand Forks having fun with my friends rather than moving back to small town life in New Rockford. I went to a month-to-month lease on my apartment and lined up a bartending job that would start right after graduation so I could make a little money while I was waiting. I went through my closets and got rid of anything I didn't want to store and boxed up the stuff I was keeping. I even found a classmate who wanted to buy my car when I left. Despite Erika's prodding, I still didn't have a girlfriend to fuss over my leaving, so, all in all, I felt like I was in pretty good shape to make a clean break from everything.

There's an old joke that goes something like, "If you want to know if God has a sense of humor, just tell him you have a plan." Well, just when I was feeling comfortable with my plan, someone—I can't confirm it was God—stepped in. In early January, 1967, I received a phone call from the Grand Forks School District asking if I would be interested in applying for a teaching position opening up in January. A social studies teacher at Central High School in Grand Forks had become pregnant and had to resign. (There was no such thing as maternity leave in North Dakota in 1967.) Her resignation went into effect the middle of January, the day after my graduation. Even though I knew I couldn't take the position because I was likely to get drafted before I could finish out the term, I figured I had nothing to lose by going for an interview. It would just give me practice for the real thing when it came along.

Preparing for my interview confirmed my decision to be a teacher, and I started imagining myself in a classroom of eager high school students poised on my every word. During the interview I explained my draft situation and thanked them for considering me. I felt I did well, and at the interview's conclusion—to my utter amazement—I was offered the position. The principal explained that the draft issue would not be a problem. He told me to write to my local draft board immediately and request a teaching deferment, known as a IIA classification. I had no idea such a draft classification even existed, but I saw an opportunity to do something I wanted to do, plus buy some additional time to think about my obligations to my country. I mailed the request that day.

I felt like I needed to tell my parents about my decision in person, even though I had just been home during the Christmas break. I called mom and dad and told them I was coming home for the weekend and had some good news. Mom tried to coax it out of me, but I didn't give up a thing. The timing of the job offer presented one problem, though. I wanted to make a special visit to Bremen to share the news with Kurt and Erika, but there was no time to contact them by letter first, since I had to start the following Monday. I tried to give them a warning call, but there was no listing for any Heislers in Bremen, so I figured their number must be unlisted. I decided to take a chance and just drop in on them.

On the road from Grand Forks to New Rockford I speculated about what my parents' reaction would be. I figured mom would be happy knowing that I would be safe from the dangers of war, but I wasn't sure how dad would respond. I arrived home about six-thirty, and Dad greeted me at the door. "What are you doing back already? I haven't paid off the food bill from your last visit."

"Dad, I haven't laughed at that joke in five years. Do you think it gets any funnier with age?"

"Just ignore your father, Tom. You know we're always happy to see you. And I made your favorite raisin sour cream pie."

Over mom's typical child's homecoming meal—pot roast, potatoes and creamed corn—I explained the reason for my unexpected visit. My mother's reaction was exactly what I had expected; her glow of approval lit up the whole room. Dad's reaction was typically straightforward. "Tom, I only have one question. Are you getting a deferment so you can teach or so you can avoid the draft?"

"Dad, I think you know me better than that. I really want to teach, and this is a chance to try it out for a semester. There's no guarantee I'll get a permanent job in the fall, so I might just be putting the draft off for a few months. I admit, I'm still not certain about military service, and this will give me some extra time to think about it."

Even Dad couldn't keep from smiling. "Well, it is a good chance to get your career started. Grand Forks is one of the biggest school districts in the state, and you'll be able to stay in North Dakota to hunt if you get hired on full-time."

The next morning I told my parents I wanted to drive out by Bremen to check out my duck sloughs. My mother thought I was crazy, but dad understood. Mom packed me a lunch, and I left about eleven. As I was walking out the door Mom couldn't resist getting in one last dig. "You really are crazy to want to look at all that snow and frozen water. How do you ever manage to shoot any ducks when they seem so much smarter than you? Right now they're all down south swimming in warm water."

"That's clever, Mom. Thanks for the lunch. See you around four."

I drove to dad's store and traded my car for "Old Ugly." It took me about thirty minutes to get to Bremen, a little longer than normal because of some ice patches and drifting snow. County roads during a North Dakota winter are not for the faint of heart, so I was thankful I could navigate the terrain around Bremen from memory. I drove through the tiny village and headed north for about a half-mile, where I climbed a hill and turned left at the old cemetery. I continued west until I reached the end of a long shelterbelt.

Soon I was looking over the valley that marked the boundaries of my favorite hunting spot, the Bremen Slough. Glistening before me was a five-mile river of ice imprisoning a forest of weeds in a frozen vise. The frigid Canadian winds had blown the snow off the ice and piled it along the banks. I turned onto an approach, put the truck in park and unpacked my lunch.

As I stared out over my private winter landscape, I recalled the visit where Kurt had graphically described his life during the Russian winter of 1941-42. Sipping coffee and scanning the vast expanse of bleakness, I imagined myself with Kurt and Das Reich fighting through the deep snows of the Istra Reservoir near Moscow by day and then struggling every night to survive the mind-numbing cold. I wondered if I would ever have to make a sacrifice like that for America, or could.

After about ten minutes of daydreaming, I focused on my immediate dilemma. I was about to break my promise never to visit Kurt and Erika except during the hunting season. I could only hope they would understand the special nature of my visit and that they would be reassured by my vow to never break my word again.

———

"Tom, what the hell are you doing here?" Kurt looked surprised and concerned.

Before I could answer, Erika's voice called, "Kurt, who's there?"

"Come to the door and see for yourself."

Erika greeted me with her best thousand-watt smile. "Tom, what a pleasant surprise! You must have really missed me for you to break your promise."

Erika's flirtation angered Kurt even more. "This is not the time to be cute. Tom has some explaining to do. Let's go inside. And let me do the talking, Erika."

He waved me in and stepped outside the door, surveying the landscape in every direction before following me in. There was no offer of coffee or dessert, and soon we were sitting in the living room staring at each other. After a long silence, Kurt spoke sternly. "Well?"

In a semi-coherent string of rambling explanations interrupted by frequent apologies, I managed to explain the circumstances of my unscheduled visit. By the time I had finished, Kurt's scowl had vanished, and Erika, smiling broadly, got up and gave me a hug. "You were right to share this with us. We've been worried that you'd go off to war without even saying goodbye. We're so happy for you. And for us, because we'll get to see you more."

Thankfully, Kurt also looked less likely to kill me. "It's great news, Tom. We must celebrate your first real job. I'll get some brandy." He left the room and returned shortly with three glasses and a bottle of Courvoisier.

After a congratulatory toast, Erika asked, "So how does it feel to know you aren't going to Vietnam?"

"Temporarily relieved, I guess, but there's no guarantee of anything after this semester ends in June. If I don't find a permanent job by next fall, I'll be in the same situation with the draft, but at least this gives me some time to think. I'm still a little torn. I have friends who are already in Vietnam and others who'll be going soon, and they didn't have this hard of a time making a decision. I don't know why it's so hard for me."

Kurt looked as if he were about to say something, but before he could, Erika took my arm. "Well, let's look on the bright side and talk about important things. Now that you have some more time in Grand Forks, are you finally going to get a serious girlfriend? You know, a semester is plenty of time to get married and get started on that family deferment. A wife and baby would certainly keep you out of the war. Maybe it's something you should work on."

On cue, Kurt and I rolled our eyes, shook our heads and groaned in unison before breaking up with laughter. Then we sat down and talked and laughed for an hour or so before I had to head home. It felt good to just sit and converse as friends without having to take notes or think about where to take the conversation. I was relieved that the visit had gone well. Before leaving, we agreed that I would let them know via letter as soon as I knew my teaching status for the next year. I also promised never to break our agreement by showing up unannounced again.

CHAPTER 12

SATURDAY, SEPTEMBER 30, 1967

I could barely contain myself as I approached the Heisler farm. I had so much that I wanted to share with Kurt and Erika and so much more that I wanted to ask them about that I didn't know where to start. I had written Kurt and Erika with some good news—along with a request for apple strudel—so they were expecting me. The teacher for whom I was subbing had decided not to return, and the Principal offered me the job. I accepted on the spot and was now a full-time history teacher at Grand Forks Central High School.

So just like that the whole issue of my being drafted and going off to Vietnam went away. I thought that would make things easier for me, but, ironically, the war became an even bigger force in my life. Up until the time I had met Kurt and Erika, I had never critically examined America's reasons for being in Vietnam. I assumed I'd go and do my duty, because that's what loyal North Dakota men did, no questions asked. But now, as an objective history teacher, I felt obligated to learn more about all aspects of the war. Kurt's comment about whether Vietnam was a war of choice for America kept coming back to me, especially when I saw napalmed kids and dead and wounded GIs on the news every night and I pictured my students in their places. So before I even had a chance to think about whether I wanted to be a mentor or role model, I was one. Quite honestly, it scared the hell out of me.

The Heislers' garage door was up, so I nudged "Old Ugly" into its designated spot and pulled the door down. When I got to the house, the main door was ajar, so I opened the storm door and yelled, "Anybody home?"

There was a squeal of delight from behind the door, and Erika literally ran into my outstretched arms, a blur of blond hair and perfumed softness. She hugged me tightly for a long time, her tears of happiness dampening my shirt. "Tom, it's so good to see you! We've missed you so much. It's been a long eight months."

Kurt came walking down the hallway with an ear-to-ear grin and surprised me with a big bear hug rather than a handshake. "Tom, congratulations on the teaching job. We knew they'd hire you full-time once you got a chance to prove yourself. We're so relieved you didn't wind up in Vietnam."

"Man, what a welcome. I didn't get this roughed up playing football. If I'd known I'd get this kind of treatment, I'd have worn my rib pads. I'm going to be sore for a week."

"Oh, you poor boy. Don't tell us you've already gone soft now that you're a working professional. Come, sit down and tell us all about what you've been up to since January. Kurt, I'll cut some strudel if you pour the coffee."

We sat, ate and talked for an hour or so, catching up on things and just enjoying each other's company. Erika was disappointed to hear that I still didn't have a steady girlfriend and scolded me for not trying hard enough. I told her that seeing her and Kurt together had spoiled me, and I was holding out for perfection, like he had done.

"I think we better talk about something else because the bullshit's getting pretty deep—even for a farm," Kurt said. "All kidding aside, now that we've caught up on things a bit, tell me, how do you like teaching?"

"I love it. I'm much more comfortable teaching than going to law school, and I feel like I can make a difference. I've gotta' admit, though, that once in a while there's still a part of me that feels like I'm letting my country down. Anyway, here I am again with a list of new questions. So, are you still glad to see me?"

"Sure, you don't think a few more questions are going to scare us off, do you? We'll probably have some for you, too. We've done a lot of thinking and talking in the last few months, and it's amazing how many memories have come back to us now that we've started speaking openly about that part of our lives. So where would you like to start today?" Kurt was leaning back in his chair, coffee mug in hand, as relaxed as I'd ever seen him.

"Something's been bugging me all summer, and I can't believe I didn't ask you this before. If you came over to the States in '46, where were you for those twenty years before you got here to Bremen? There has to be some interesting history there, and I'd sure like to know about it."

Kurt started laughing before I even got the question out. "We can't believe you didn't ask us that, either, but you're not going to like the answer. Remember when we said we couldn't tell you our real names? Well, one reason is because we don't want you to try to trace our movements over those twenty years. I know you're tired of hearing this, but it's for your own protection that we can't give you that information. I hope we get a lot more time together in the future so we can share that with you, but we really can't talk about it yet."

"Do you have any idea how frustrating this is? I feel like I'm trying to put together a jigsaw puzzle, but someone keeps hiding some of the pieces. I like you two, and I really enjoy our time together, but my patience won't last forever, you know."

"We like our time together, too, and you can't believe how much we look forward to seeing you," Kurt said. "We promise, someday you'll have all the pieces. But surely you've thought of many other things to ask us about during our time apart."

"A lot of things, actually, but there's one area where you could really help me out immediately. I'm going to be teaching a unit on World War II later this semester, and I'd like to show my students that there was a lot more going on than just America's involvement. Kurt, I remember you telling me that you think Germany really lost the war on the Eastern Front against the Russians. Can we talk about why you think that, so I can put together a lecture with a little different angle for my kids?"

"Sure, as long as you don't plan on revealing your source," Kurt said, laughing. With that, he was off and running. Kurt talked—or at least tried to, with all of my interruptions—for a couple hours, getting into specifics about several battles and exactly where he thought Hitler had gone wrong. Kurt had obviously spent a lot of time thinking about the issue, and—based on my limited civilian knowledge—seemed to be a good military strategist. Erika provided some great insights about what it was like on the home front during that time, and how hard it was getting reliable information from the front lines. Together, their stories provided me with enough useful material for several lectures. About four o'clock I gathered my things and put them in my backpack. "Same time next Saturday?"

"That'll work, won't it, Kurt? Any special dessert requests?" Erika teased as she walked me to the door.

"Nah, just surprise me. You've never disappointed me yet … at least as far as desserts are concerned."

———

The rest of the fall was a blur of frantic activity for me. From a time standpoint teaching was more demanding than I thought it would be, and it took me a while to get into an efficient routine. Between preparing daily lesson plans (every one is new for a first-year teacher) and weekend hunting trips, I was constantly busy. I didn't get back to New Rockford as often as usual, and when I did, I often had time for only one day of hunting before returning to Grand Forks to prepare for my classes. In all, I only saw Kurt and Erika seven times that fall.

The visits followed our usual pattern except for a couple odd situations that further tested my patience. When I showed up for the third visit, Erika greeted me by herself and said Kurt had to go "out East" unexpectedly. She wouldn't tell me any more than that, and by now I knew there was no point in pressing the issue with her. It turned out rather well from a research perspective, though, so that somewhat eased my frustration. For three hours she captivated me with an uninterrupted account of her life in Nuremberg while Kurt was on the Russian Front. She recounted vivid details of her everyday home life, the gala parties for Nazi dignitaries, the tours of her father's factories, and the changing national mood as the war dragged on. I doubt I'd have gotten that much information had Kurt been there.

The other unusual occurrence came in late October. I drove up at the appointed time, but there was another car blocking the garage door. Before I could even get out of the truck, Kurt came hurrying out to greet me. His demeanor was very different; he seemed agitated and out of sorts, and was talking very loudly. "Tom, I'm sorry. Please forgive me. I forgot to call you and tell you that I can't go hunting with you today. We'll just have to try it again some other time."

As he was speaking, he rolled his eyes toward the house as if to warn me. Casually looking past him, I saw a man lurking behind the curtains in the kitchen window, so I just played along.

"No problem, Kurt. I've got plenty of things to do anyway. We can go some other time. Just greet Erika for me."

I swung the truck around and headed out the driveway and drove back to New Rockford, disappointed and curious. When we got together the next weekend, they wouldn't tell me who was there or why, so once again I had to let it go.

I continued to fill notebooks and tapes with information during the other visits and used what little free time I had to organize things in different categories—people, places, events, dates—so I could find them easily. I had no idea what I was going to do with all that information, but I wanted to access it quickly when the time came.

I spent my last visit that fall alone with Kurt on a Saturday afternoon while Erika was shopping. I couldn't help taking advantage of the situation by returning to my favorite subject. "Kurt, I've thought a lot about your explanation for ordering prisoners to be shot and hanging partisans, and every time I think I understand how that can happen, things seem to get cloudy. I see how people can get swept up in a patriotic frenzy on a collective level, but I still don't get how Christians like you could have strayed so far from your beliefs on an individual

level. I mean, acts like that just seem wrong under any circumstance. Can you help me understand that better?"

"I don't think I can possibly explain it to you any better than I have. The only real way to understand is to live it, and I wouldn't wish that on anyone. Did you ever talk to your dad yet about his battle experiences? I'm curious about what he had to face and some of the decisions he made."

"Actually, I did, and he surprised me a bit. That's kind of why I'm so confused."

"How so?"

"He said he was glad he wasn't guarding any German prisoners after he heard what happened at Malmedy. You don't know what kind of person my dad is, but I can't imagine him ever getting to that point. It shocked me that he could even doubt himself like that. He also said he heard rumors of Americans shooting prisoners, but he never actually saw it happen."

Kurt smiled ruefully. "I don't need to know your dad to understand why he thought that. I think at our core when our survival is in doubt, men can perform very base acts, and we all got to places inside of our souls that we never believed were there. And, yes, Americans shot German prisoners, too, but you don't hear much about that because, as the saying goes, 'The winners get to write the history.' I don't condemn them any more than I condemn myself, though. They viewed us as godless demons that deserved no mercy, and we thought the same of the Russians. It's much easier to kill people when you view them as inhuman monsters instead of men who are just serving their country."

"I don't know if I can ever get to that place, and I hope I never have to find out. Dad says he has flashbacks and dreams about the war often. Do you?"

Kurt's face was taut and pale as he stared off in space in silent contemplation for a moment. "Yes, all the time. Some of my actions were the ultimate distortion of conscience, and I feel like I've been condemned to live with those hideous images forever as my punishment."

"How do you deal with it all?"

"A strong faith and a loving wife get me through the tough days. Even though I don't belong to any organized religion anymore, I do believe in God, and my faith as a Christian gives me the power to lead a better life. I believe God forgives me for the sins I've committed, and every day I pray for his forgiveness. I don't know how I'd cope with it all if I didn't believe there was some way to redeem myself."

———

On my last visit in November I asked Kurt and Erika if they would modify the rules slightly for the coming year so I wouldn't have to wait until the next fall to see them. They relented and granted me two visits between January 1 and the start of the next hunting season. I immediately picked the weekend of my Easter break in April for the first visit and told them I'd pick a date later for a visit in the summer. It was a small victory, but I felt I was finally starting to make some progress toward a normal relationship.

CHAPTER 13

SATURDAY, APRIL 13, 1968

"Now that you've signed a contract for next year, does this mean you can keep getting this deferment as long as your school says it needs you?" Erika couldn't contain her excitement.

"Pretty much, from what I understand, so I think I can teach as long as they'll have me."

We were sitting around the kitchen table as usual, only this time we were enjoying some warm April sunshine rather than the cold fall temperatures that usually accompanied our visits.

"So this really means no war for you. You said once that you didn't want to feel like you were taking the coward's way out, that you wanted to do your part for your country. Are you comfortable with the way this turned out?" Kurt wasn't letting me off the hook easily.

"Depends on what you mean by comfortable. A lot of things have changed since last November. For starters, I now have seniors who are in exactly the same position I was in about a year ago—worried about getting drafted as soon as they graduate. And here's the scary part. They're looking to me for some guidance. Before you say anything, I already know what you're thinking, so hold the jokes, please."

I didn't wait for any sarcastic response. "So the whole thing's become complicated now that my beliefs don't affect just me anymore. To be fair to my students, I've had to objectively rethink this whole war, and I've done a lot more research. I have to admit it's not as black and white as it seemed to me a year ago. Here's my problem: How do I look a gung-ho eighteen-year-old in the eye when he tells me he can hardly wait to enlist and fight for his country's freedom and not tell him what I know about how we got into this war? And what do I say to a veteran who wants his son's favorite teacher to 'talk some sense into the kid' who wants to burn his draft card and join the peace movement? So, no, I don't think there's anything 'comfortable' about my position. You know, this responsibility thing can be a real pain in the ass sometimes."

"Tom, you've sure had a busy year, haven't you?" Erika said. "I sure admire you. I'm not sure I could handle being in front of a roomful of kids every day like that. It sounds like you're learning as much as your students, though."

"More, actually. I realize this time apart from you two has been good for me. When we first met, the excitement of discovering you was just too intense; I was trying to absorb so much information so quickly that I couldn't even think about what you actually said. Researching the war and organizing my materials from our visits has helped me calm down a bit, and the questions from my students have given me a fresh perspective. While I was reviewing the notes of our conversations, I was finally able to focus on your comments and think about things a bit more clearly."

"That's good to hear. What have you found in your research that's helped you?" Kurt asked.

"Some things that make me question our reasons for going to war. Are you aware that there was an attempt to repeal the Gulf of Tonkin Resolution in the U.S. Senate in March of '66? It seems there's compelling evidence that there were no North Vietnamese attacks on the U.S. destroyers as the administration claimed."

"Yes, I knew about it. Matter of fact, I recall trying to tell you a while back that there were a lot of questions regarding America's reasons for going to war. Seems you weren't quite so receptive then." Kurt said with a wry smile.

I flushed with embarrassment thinking about how much had changed since that meeting only a year and a half ago. "Well, it looks like a lot of Americans besides me are finally starting to ask questions about the war. The anti-war movement is really starting to take hold across the country, with hundreds of thousands of protesters in New York and at the Pentagon last year. There've even been a number of rallies at the U. I used to think most of those folks were a bunch of drugged-out hippies, but they've uncovered a lot of credible information."

"We're aware of some of the protests—we do get some news out here—but we're certainly not in the mainstream," Kurt said. "Are you telling us that you're now opposed to the war?"

"No, no, I'm not going that far. If, for some reason, circumstances change and I get drafted, I don't think I could say no to my country. I am, after all, a North Dakota boy who always feels obligated to do the right thing."

"Let's hope it doesn't come to that. Given your circumstances, I think the teaching deferment is a good break, and you're right where you should be. Erika, I can't think of anyone I would rather have responsible for my children, can you?"

"No, I think Tom's definitely the right person for the job."

"Thanks for the vote of confidence, but sometimes I really question myself. It's funny, a year ago I was afraid I'd be a coward if I didn't join the military and fight for my country. Now I have days when I feel like a coward if I'm not totally honest with my students about the war. I try to present both sides of the debate in the classroom, and I hope that's enough, but it seems like there's no middle ground when it comes to Vietnam. This is still a very conservative state, after all, and parents don't take kindly to public school teachers on taxpayer salaries challenging the government about a war."

"Well, we're very proud of you, and we're sure you're doing a great job. The school and your kids are lucky to have you."

"I'm not sure my students would agree with you, but thanks."

Before I left, we agreed that my next visit would be over the Fourth of July. I told Erika that since I was now a working professional that I was learning how to cook and take better care of myself, and I would make some cookies and bring them with me in July.

"Tom, your priorities are still all wrong. You should be spending that time finding a young lady to do that for you."

I was ready for her sarcasm this time. "Ich verstehen sie nicht, Frau Heisler."

She and Kurt were still laughing as I gunned my car down the driveway.

CHAPTER 14

As much as I loved teaching, I was ready for a break when June rolled around. I could hardly wait to hit Lincoln Park Golf Course with some of my teaching buddies. Between daytime golf, nighttime softball, and drinking beer afterwards, I didn't have much time for anything else, but it felt great to be totally irresponsible for a while.

I didn't speak with Kurt and Erika again before the July visit. We had agreed that I would show up on the morning of July 3 on my way back to New Rockford for the holiday. When I arrived, both garage doors were open and there were two different vehicles in the stalls. I got out and knocked on the door, and a total stranger answered. He said he had bought the farm from a government agency the last week in May, and he had never heard of the Heislers.

I was devastated. I left the farm in a total fog and drove to Bremen Slough, parked my car and stared blankly out across the choppy waters. I couldn't even begin to get my brain around all the questions I had. Who were Kurt and Erika really? Why had they disclosed such personal information to me and then disappeared without even saying goodbye? Was any of it even true? What did it mean that a government agency had owned the farm? Could I be in any danger? The phrase they had kept using—"for your own protection"—suddenly took on new meaning. And the worst thing was that there wasn't a single person I could talk to about it, no one to speculate with over a couple beers, no one to listen to me whine about all the wasted hours I had spent with two ghosts.

After bemoaning my fate for a half hour or so—while munching on the chocolate chip cookies I had baked—I collected myself and headed to New Rockford. Somehow I got through the next couple days with my folks without letting them know anything was wrong.

Over the rest of the summer I tried to track the Heislers down. I called the County Registrar of Deeds, and was told that the U.S. Government had owned the property from May of 1966—which was about when Kurt and Erika had said they'd moved in—until the sale to the current owners. The Bremen Post Office, Northwestern Bell Telephone and Tri-County REA had no record of the Heislers; it was as if Kurt and Erika had never existed.

By the time school started after Labor Day, my search had gone no-where. I hadn't heard a word from them nor uncovered a single person who could—or would—acknowledge their existence. The only logical conclusion I could come to was that the Heislers were working for the one entity capable of engineering a disappearance and cover-up of that magni-tude: the U.S. Government. But why would the Heislers be protecting me from my own government? It just didn't make sense. There was nothing more I could do, so I gave up the search, wondering if I would ever hear anything more of Kurt and Erika again.

C H A P T E R   1 5

FALL, 1968

Before school started in September I had packed all the tapes and notes from my visits with Kurt and Erika in a box and moved it into the back of the closet, hoping that the removal of the physical proof of their existence would also distance them from me mentally. It worked most of the time, and as the year progressed, I only occasionally speculated about their whereabouts.

My second year of teaching was going much easier. With a year's worth of lesson plans at my disposal and the knowledge gained from my rookie mistakes, I was spending less time worrying about whether I was a good teacher and more time becoming one. My weekends were free to hunt when I wanted or to just hang out, and I was enjoying teaching more than ever.

On the national front the Vietnam War was escalating rapidly, and it was becoming much harder for Americans to ignore. There didn't seem to be much middle ground; you were either for the war or against it, and neither side had much tolerance for the other. By now it seemed everyone knew someone who was in Vietnam, just returning or just about to go. Vets were coming back to attend UND and other state colleges on the GI Bill.

Many had been wounded, including some who had lost limbs; wheelchairs and crutches were becoming a familiar sight around campus. For other returning vets, the wounds weren't so visible and wouldn't show up for a long time. And then there were the ones who didn't return at all. I knew people in each of these categories, and I was still trying to make some sense of it all.

While I was glad to be teaching and felt that it was a worthwhile and rewarding profession, I still hadn't been able to resolve my ambivalence about the war or feel comfortable with my not being in it, and I often bemoaned my inability to form a justifiable position to defend. My teaching position pretty much guaranteed that I would not have to worry about being drafted as long as I stayed out of trouble, but many young men weren't as fortunate. The draft was now shaping the futures of an entire generation. Some men were enrolling in colleges they didn't want to attend, marrying and having families before they were ready and performing all kinds of unnatural acts to stay out of the service. Others dropped out of college, quit good jobs, delayed weddings and put off having children just so they could enlist and serve their country in its time of need.

As hard as I tried to put my feelings about the war on the back burner, events kept forcing them to the forefront. The first incident came one night at Frenchy's Bar when I ran into a younger football buddy of mine, Tim Lewis, whom I hadn't seen in a while. Tim had torn up his knee the year before (running back's disease, we fondly called it), had surgery and quit football. To make up for his lost athletic scholarship money, he took a chance and dropped out of school for a semester—which meant he gave up his student deferment—and went to Seattle to work for Boeing. While he was in Seattle his local draft board classified him as 1A, since he was no longer a student, and tracked him down and ordered him to report for his physical. Here's where the story really gets interesting. Before leaving he had become engaged to a girl back home, and her dad was a World War II veteran who had fought in Guadalcanal and was a real right-winger politically. Tim opposed the war and really didn't want to go to Vietnam, and he was dreading the conversation he knew he'd have with his future father-in-law. He assumed he'd get a rah-rah "God and country speech," and he was worried he wouldn't know what to say without jeopardizing his wedding. One night out of the blue the man calls Tim in Seattle and asks him what he's going to do. Tim hems and haws and finally says he'll report and do his duty if he has to. His future father-in-law asks him if he'd consider going to Canada and says he'd even help him financially if that's what Tim chose to do. Tim was speechless for a while, but finally asks why he'd want him to do that. The man says he doesn't want his daughter to become a widow because of some useless war in a country where we don't belong. Anyway, Tim wound up flunking his physical because of the knee surgery and didn't have to make the choice. The night I ran into him he had just received his official 4F draft status in the mail, and he was celebrating. The incident illustrated to me that even though there were two well-defined positions on the war, I couldn't make hasty assumptions about which side people were on.

The second event involved another friend, Pete Richardson, who wasn't so lucky. He was from Bismarck, North Dakota, and I knew him from playing American Legion baseball in the summer and from track meets in high school. Pete was one of the nicest guys I'd ever met— fun, laid-back, considerate, smart—and everybody liked him. One day in December I saw on the news that Pete had been killed in Vietnam. The story didn't provide many details, nor did the newspaper article the next day. I was curious about the circumstances of his death so I decided to do some digging. A week or so later I located one of his close friends who had moved to Minneapolis and gave him a call. We talked for quite a while, and he read parts of some letters he'd received from Pete. Listening to those letters, I couldn't believe it was the same person I knew. Pete's experiences in Vietnam had turned his personality upside down; he'd become remote, apathetic and bitter. He was a "tunnel rat" in Nam and actually enjoyed crawling around underground, killing "gooks," as he called them, and cutting off their ears as souvenirs. Apparently, Pete was killed in a tunnel himself. I couldn't even begin to fathom how Pete had gotten to that point. How could a man turn so drastically in such a short time? I thought of my conversations with Kurt and compared his circumstances to Pete's. Was it just inevitable that soldiers sunk to that level under the constant strain of combat, or was there something else involved? Of course, the real question in my mind was whether it would have also happened to me. I'm not sure I wanted to know the answer.

Another friend of mine, Ron Jenson, had gone on to graduate school and was the head resident of one of the men's dorms on the UND campus. We were playing golf one late September Saturday with a close friend of his who had just returned from Vietnam and enrolled in grad school. The friend had been a Navy pilot, and he announced to us that day that he was dropping out and returning to the Navy to make it a career. He said he missed the discipline and clearness of purpose of the military, and he couldn't think of a better way to serve his country. He also admitted that he was disappointed by the public's diminishing support for the war and the increasingly anti-war environment on campus. So even though he had just moved his wife and two kids to Grand Forks less than a month earlier, he was packing them up and moving them again. He asked me if I'd ever considered the military as a career, and I told him I was happy with the career I'd chosen. I breathed a sigh of relief when he didn't press me any further or ask me my opinion about the war. Later, when thinking about the situation, I questioned why I had felt so uneasy when I had nothing to feel guilty about. I had no good answer to my own question.

Another encounter a couple weeks later provided a totally different perspective. I ran into Keith and Brian—two guys I had known casually at UND—at a Sioux football game, and we chatted a while in between plays. I noticed Keith was limping and had some damage to an arm, so I asked him what happened. He smiled and mumbled something about "an error in judgment" and changed the subject. We decided to continue our conversation after the game and headed over to Whitey's Cafe in East Grand Forks. Over cheeseburgers and beers we traded stories about what we'd been doing the last couple years. At first neither of them wanted to talk much, so, to get things going, I regaled them with my harrowing tales of teaching history to surly teen-agers. As the beer flowed they started loosening up and talking more. It turns out they had both been medics in Vietnam. Both had opposed the war, and when they were denied Conscientious Objector status, they said they would only serve as medics. Brian didn't get very specific about events, but he said the war was a massive fuck-up with unclear objectives, no way to win and no end in sight. He said it was nothing like it had been depicted on television, and the administration was lying to the American public about our chances there. As Keith got drunker, his demeanor changed drastically; he became wild-eyed and cackled maniacally, yelling, "Stop shooting! Stop shooting! He's dead!" Through Keith's wild ramblings the story behind his injuries came out. He'd been shot up while the injured soldier he was working on was cut to pieces in front of him. Brian and I eventually calmed him down and got him outside and into the car. I was worried about letting them drive off, but Brian said this scene with Keith repeated itself often, and he had paced his own drinking to make sure he could drive. Again, I had been confronted by people who had faced similar choices as mine, but didn't have the means, as I did, to get out of serving. Yet they had stayed true to their beliefs and still found a way to serve their country.

As if these personal encounters were not enough to keep the war front and center in my mind, throughout the fall of 1968 the local anti-war rallies were becoming more frequent and more vocal. It seemed every time I picked up the *Grand Forks Herald* or the *Dakota Student,* I saw friends, current and former students and other familiar faces in the protest pictures. I was studying one such picture on the front page of the Herald on a November morning in the teachers' lounge on my break, and, as usual, I recognized several participants. As I was about to close up the paper, a face in the upper left corner of the picture caught my eye. She looked strangely familiar, but she hadn't been one of my students, so I assumed she was someone I'd been in a class with at the U or just seen around town somewhere. That's the reality of living in a city the size of Grand Forks; at some point you feel familiar with people you don't know just because you've seen them around a lot. I chalked this incident up to one of those times and forgot about it.

With my teaching position secure and a little more time to kill, my social life was becoming pretty active. I was still going out to the UND campus frequently to meet friends for a few beers or to do some research at the Chester Fritz Library, which was the best one around. I even had time for a few dates now and then, and I couldn't help but think that Erika would have been proud. One Saturday night as I was closing up Frenchy's with a few of my football buddies, I looked to the corner and saw the woman I had seen in the protest picture. She still looked familiar, only considerably more attractive (which might have been the beer talking), but I still didn't have a clue where else I'd seen her. I almost went over and asked her if we knew each other, but I still had enough functioning brain cells to realize how dumb that idea was.

Two weeks later, as I was leaving the UND library after putting together some notes on the Crusades for my third period class, I saw her again, sitting in a corner kiosk. I thought it seemed spooky, three encounters in only a few weeks. Still, I didn't know what I'd say to her, so I just left. I was halfway to my car when it hit me like a thunderbolt. She was the girl I'd seen in the picture in Kurt and Erika's bedroom two years ago, the one that I'd assumed was Erika when she was younger! I mentally kicked myself for not noticing the resemblance sooner. The girl's hair was longer, and she looked a little older now, but I was sure.

I took a couple deep breaths to calm myself and headed back to the library. I sat down at a table about ten feet away from her, aligned my sight angle, and opened my book so I could study her unobtrusively. She was a younger Erika, in the flesh. Kurt and Erika had told me that they couldn't have any more kids after Jochen had been killed, so what was going on? As I contemplated plausible opening lines, she started rearranging her books like she was getting ready to leave. I didn't know when I'd see her again, so I just took a chance and walked over to her. "Excuse me. You don't know me, but I think I know your parents, and I need to talk to you so I can ... "

"Now that's a novel pickup line. Has that worked for you this decade, Slick? That's a rhetorical question, by the way, so don't try to stumble through an answer. I can see how hard you're concentrating just to walk upright. Now buzz off and go see if you can impress some of the freshman girls. No, on second thought, with a line like that, try the high school."

"I'm not trying to pick you up; you're definitely not my type. It's just that I really do think I know your parents, and I want to ... "

"Not your type? Who're you kidding? I bet your type is anything with a pulse. You've been staring at me so long the janitor's going to have to clean the drool off your table. And that 'I know your parents' bit is really lame. I'm not from anywhere around here, so you couldn't possibly know my parents. Now, be a good little boy and disappear before you force me to get nasty." She turned her back to me and continued to fill her backpack.

"You mean it gets worse? That's also a rhetorical question, by the way. But, hey, if my parents were war criminals on the run, I guess I wouldn't want to talk to anyone either."

She snapped her head around sharply and glared at me coldly, then quickly surveyed the rest of the room.

I couldn't resist. "What's the matter? No snappy comeback? And we were off to such a warm start."

"You jerk, is this your idea of undercover surveillance? Why don't you talk a little louder? I think the students in West Hall might've missed a word. Can't you goddamn CIA guys do anything right? How many times do I have to go over this crap with you? Here, help me with my books, and let's go somewhere else to talk before everybody here knows who I am."

I was speechless. Fortunately, she didn't give me any time to respond, so she didn't notice.

"You know, you really are dumber than you look, which means you beat some terrific odds." She shook her head from side to side, muttering under her breath as she stuffed her notebooks into her book bag.

Regaining my composure, I decided to play along to see where this would take me. I picked up her bag and headed for the door, assuming the role of a haughty government agent, talking as I led the way. "Let's go to the coffee shop in the Union. It'll be busy, so there'll be a lot of background noise. Just do me one favor. If we run into someone I know, don't get cute and try to pretend you're my date or something. My friends would never believe I was this hard up."

"Yeah? Well, my friends know I'd never go on a mercy date just to make some loser feel good, so it looks like we don't have anything to worry about."

The Union was busy, but we found an open corner table that provided reasonable privacy. She was talking before we even sat down.

"You know, I've even seen you around campus a couple times, but I never guessed you were CIA. That dork thing you've got working for you is a great cover; you don't even have to pretend to be someone else. So what do you say we make this short and sweet? Just deliver your message, and then we can go our separate ways and forget we ever met, which will be pretty easy for me, but I'm sure you'll have to work at it; this is probably the most excitement you've had in months."

"That's pretty smart talk for someone so dumb. The deal was you were supposed to keep a low profile. Is this your idea of low profile? Getting your picture on the front page of one of the largest newspapers in the state at a war protest rally? What the hell were you thinking?"

"Is that all this is about, a stupid protest rally? I just got dragged there by some friends on the way to the Red Pepper to get some grinders. And you're worried that someone who knows me from out East would see this? Do you think there's such a shortage of newspapers around DC that everyone runs out to find a *Grand Forks Herald* first thing every morning to learn what's really happening in the world? I can't believe you risked blowing my cover in an open meeting just to talk about this. You know, if you're the best our country has to offer to keep me safe, I might as well slit my wrists now and avoid the suspense."

The flashing eyes suddenly hardened as she stopped and studied me more closely. "Wait a minute. You've never even told me your name or anything. Just who the hell are you? Show me some ID—now—or this conversation ends immediately."

I was laughing so hard at this point, I could hardly talk. "Oh, well, it was fun while it lasted. Now I know what James Bond feels like. Too bad I couldn't have held out a little longer. We never even got to his legendary interrogation techniques. Who knows what information I could've gotten out of you?"

She started to get up, so I kept talking.

"Okay, you're right, I'm not with the CIA, but you don't have anything to worry about. I wasn't lying when I said that I know your parents, and I wasn't trying to pick you up, but I don't blame you for being suspicious. I'm Tom Johnson, and I teach history at Grand Forks Central High School. And you're … ?" I extended my hand across the table.

"Extremely pissed right now!" She glared at me defiantly, refusing my hand. "How in the hell could you possibly know my parents? Tell me something that only they would know—and do it quickly—or I'll get a real CIA agent in here, and you'll wish you'd never met me."

"Too late. I was wishing that back at the library." I pulled out my wallet and handed her my driver's license. "You had a brother, Jochen, who was born on the same day I was, and he was killed in the Allied bombing of Nuremberg in 1945. Your father was a Waffen SS member, and your mother's father owned a factory in Germany, and her family was part of the Nazi elite. I can go on and on, but I hope that's enough to convince you that I know them. And please believe me, I won't hurt you, and I promise I won't do anything to blow your cover, which is what, a deranged college student?"

She sank back in her chair in utter disbelief. "Jesus, I can't believe this. Now we really do have to worry about the CIA." Her eyes darted around the room. "We have to get out of here, but first, tell me where you met my parents and why you're doing this. I need to know more before I can trust you."

"I met them in Bremen two years ago while I was hunting, and I got to know them over a number of visits. I knew that the symbol on Erika's ring was used by Das Reich, a division of the Waffen SS. When I confronted them with that and some photographs that I accidentally discovered, they trusted me enough to admit who they were."

"Wait a minute. Bremen ... you met them back in Germany? They said they'd never go back there? And Erika? That's not my mother's name, and my dad doesn't hunt, so I'm totally confused."

"Sorry, I forgot you're not a local ... Bremen, North Dakota. It's a little town a couple hours west of here close to where I grew up. I stumbled across your parents' farm when I was duck hunting. They never told me their real names. They called themselves Kurt and Erika Heisler because they were afraid I'd try to trace them."

"You met my parents two years ago in North Dakota? They're not supposed to be anywhere close to me. If they've been here all this time, that means they've been spying on me. And they couldn't be here without the CIA knowing about it. What's going on here? I'm so mad right now I can hardly think." She set her jaw and steeled her eyes into a pouty pose that was all too familiar to me. She was a carbon copy of her mother, and I could easily see why Kurt had no chance when he first met Erika.

"Well, they're not here anymore, if that makes you feel any better. They disappeared very mysteriously over the summer. That's one of the reasons I wanted to talk to you, to see if you knew where they were so I can contact them again. If you don't know where they are, then you're not the only one who's confused. Who are you people, and what the hell are you doing here? And who are you all hiding from? I think I need a scorecard and a rule book."

"Well, Tom—if that's your real name—if what you're telling me is true, we have to get out of here quickly. Write your phone number on a napkin, and leave it on the table and then leave. I'll call you within a half hour, and we'll set up a place to meet later tonight. Without being too obvious on your way home, check to see if you're being followed. You better be telling me the truth about all this, or I'll make your life a living hell."

"From what I've seen so far I have no trouble believing that. But just to show you I can make threats, too, if you blow me off this evening, I'll start telling the newspapers everything I know. A lot of folks would be interested to know that we have Nazi war criminals hiding out in North Dakota and their daughter is a student here. If you think your life is complicated now, you don't have a clue how much worse it can get. I am who I say I am, and I'll be waiting for your call."

"Gee, you sure know how to show a girl a good time. You gotta' love that old Midwestern hospitality. Just make sure you can find your way home without hurting yourself, and be ready for my call. Can you remember all that, or should I write it down and pin it to your mitten?"

"I think I can handle it. You know, this is just like old times. I'd be disappointed if I ever met a Heisler—or whatever the hell your family name is—without some clandestine arrangement."

I was out the door and in my car in five minutes. My adrenalin was pumping so fast I thought I could carry the car home faster than I could drive it. In spite of my excitement I had the presence of mind to observe if I was being followed. I drove a few extra blocks out of my way and doubled back again to make certain I was alone. As soon as I got inside my apartment, I popped a beer open, untangled the phone cord and moved the phone close to my chair. It rang halfway through my beer.

"Spies Are Us. Tom Johnson, at your service."

"God, you're even a bigger nerd than I thought. You ever wonder why you're still available to the dating public?" The disgust in her voice was palpable. "So, did anybody follow you, or were you too busy following bread crumbs to notice?"

"No. How about you?"

"No, and I'm pretty good at spotting tails by now. I'm also calling from a safe phone. This is probably the stupidest thing I've ever done, but I've got to hear more about your meetings with my parents. Where can we meet that's close and out of the way?"

"At the risk of being the butt of your sarcasm, I'll suggest the obvious. Why don't you just come to my place?"

"I'll pass on taking the cheap shot. Too easy. Actually, we can't take the chance of being seen together anymore, at least until I know what's going on. If certain people don't know anything about you yet, I sure don't want to lead them to you. Pick a place, and I'll meet you there in thirty minutes, and make sure no one's following you. This is serious, and these precautions are for your own protection."

"For my own protection? My God, I haven't heard that since the last time I saw your parents. Listen, if my ass is on the line like you all keep telling me it is, then somebody better tell me who I'm being protected from. Otherwise, don't even waste my time. I've about had it, and if I don't get some answers soon, I'm going to the FBI or the police or whoever to find out what's going on. Are we clear on that?"

"I can't promise you anything until we meet, so let's just get it over with. I'll tell you what I know, and if what you've told me so far is true, maybe we can figure this out together. Right now I don't know if I should just be mad as hell or worried about my own safety."

I gave her directions to a secluded spot not far from the UND field house where a few of the football players used to gather once in a while late at night to sneak a few beers. We described our cars and agreed that if there was anyone else there we'd keep driving, and she'd call me at home again later. After taking a circuitous route worthy of a Keystone Kops movie, I got there five minutes early and waited for her, contemplating the day's events. Once again a chance circumstance had turned my life upside down. If I hadn't seen her portrait on the Heislers' bedroom wall, I would never have recognized her picture in the paper, and the only reason I'd even given the newspaper a second glance was because I'd recognized a couple former students. The conversation with—I realized I still didn't even know her name—had energized me and gotten me curious again. As I watched headlights approaching, though, I wasn't sure I wanted the responsibility of keeping more secrets and introducing more uncertainty into my life.

She parked next to me and joined me in my car. I didn't give her a chance to speak. "Before you say anything, I've got to make some things clear. Ever since I stumbled upon your parents, I've had to keep part of my life secret from my friends and family. Now I've met you, and I'm already dreading where this could lead. I don't even know your name, or what you're doing here, or why your parents—if they are your parents—didn't tell me about you, or why they disappeared, or why the CIA is involved, and—here's the most important part—why everybody keeps telling me I'm in some kind of danger. If you can't be honest with me about any of this, just admit it, and I promise I won't tell anyone about you. I'll just go and try to live a normal life, regretting to my dying day, of course, that you and I can't spend more quality time together."

She gave me the first soft look I'd seen since we'd met. "Tom, I'm sorry, but it's already too late for that. Once you gave me that information about my parents, you started something I won't be able to control, but I'll do everything I can to keep you out of it. So here's the quick summary, and I can fill in the blanks later. My name here at UND is Sophie Anderson. The Sophie part is real, but Anderson is a cover, and that's all I can say. I came here to get away from my parents, and they're not supposed to know my whereabouts, so that's why I'm so concerned. The things you've told me have me mostly convinced that you did meet them. If you can give me a few more specific details—physical descriptions, personal habits, things like that—I'll feel better sharing information with you. I know you're un-comfortable with all this, but I have to make sure I'm not being set up. Can you live with that?"

Yet again my unquenchable curiosity overrode all other reservations. "Okay, but I have a request. How about we end our verbal sparring so we can figure this out together? Truce?"

"You call this verbal sparring? For me this is about as tough as playing checkers with a blind man. But, okay, since I want to know what's going on with my parents and the CIA, I accept your truce offer."

I gave her an overview of my meetings with Kurt and Erika, throwing in plenty of inside tidbits: Kurt's pronounced limp, the photos from the Russian front, Erika's teasing me about finding a girlfriend, the specific German desserts, the UND catalog and the photo in the bedroom.

She stopped me about ten minutes in. "Okay, okay, I'm convinced, they're my parents. I'm sure the UND catalog was no coincidence, but I've never seen them here, and they've never tried to contact me. If they weren't spying on me, I don't have a clue why they'd be here, or why they left so suddenly, or why the CIA didn't let me know about it, which was part of my deal with them."

"I know I'm going to regret asking this, but what does the CIA have to do with you and your parents?"

"You mean you haven't figured that out by now? Dad is CIA, recruited while he was in an Allied prison camp. I don't know the details, but, apparently, toward the end of the war the Americans were already afraid they might be fighting the Russians somewhere down the line. Because of dad's extensive experience on the Russian Front the CIA wanted to pick his brain about Soviet war tactics. That's how he and mom got to the States."

"The CIA ... damn! I knew they had something to do with the government. I just never thought it would be something as sinister as the CIA. No wonder they were so secretive about everything."

"I didn't even find any of this out until just a few years ago, which is what caused the big fight between us. Before that I'd been told that dad had been a soldier in the regular German army, and we'd come to America so they could get a fresh start. You know, land of opportunity and all that. I learned by accident that he'd been in the Waffen SS in Russia, and that's when things really hit the fan."

"When was the last time you saw them? And where?" I realized I was sounding like an FBI interrogator, but I couldn't help myself.

"Right after I graduated from high school in May of '66. I went to a private school in Virginia so dad could be close to DC for his government job as a foreign affairs liaison. At least that was his story, but I found out that was another big lie. Do you have any idea what it's like to find out at eighteen that your parents have lied to you your whole life? That you don't even know who they really are? That they've done horrible things that you don't even know about?" she said as she started to tear up.

"No wonder you're pissed. This makes me wonder how much of what they told me is true, and why they even wanted to tell me anything. They could have denied everything when I confronted them, and there really wasn't much I could have done about it, so I don't get it. But tell me, how'd you wind up way out here in North Dakota? There must be a connection to your folks living in Bremen, even if they never tried to contact you."

"I'm here courtesy of the CIA. After I found out that dad had been in the Waffen SS and realized how much he and mom had kept from me, I threatened to expose them. They pleaded with me to allow them to explain their side of things, but there was so much they couldn't tell me that I finally exploded. I told them I couldn't trust them anymore and wanted to get far away from them, someplace where nobody knew me. North Dakota sounded remote enough, and the CIA served as a go-between. They gave me a new identity and promised me they'd never let my parents know where I was without my permission. You can see how well that worked. Tell me, who can you trust when your parents and your government lie to you?"

"Well, look on the bright side. You wanted 'remote,' and you got it."

"Yeah, well this place would have to improve considerably just to be called remote. Next time I'll get a better travel agent."

"Trust me, it'll grow on you. But right now we need to figure out our next step. Where do we go with all this?"

"Next step?" she said defensively. "You're already assuming we're going to do something together. I'm not sure I'm there yet."

"Well, let's continue comparing notes until you get there. How'd you find out your dad was in the Waffen SS?"

"Totally by accident, or I'd still be back East believing he was just another Washington bureaucrat. I was working on a project for a U.S. History class with a Jewish friend named Rachel. Her parents came over here from Russia right after World War II. When I mentioned to her that my folks were from Germany, she kind of clammed up. I didn't know a lot about the war, and I sure didn't know much about Russia's involvement.

As we got into the project and I learned more about Germany's invasion of Russia, I finally asked her if my parents' background was making her nervous. Turns out it was, but then she really opened up to me, telling me about how her parents barely escaped being executed by the Germans in a little Russian village. The Germans destroyed everything in their path—burning, looting, killing—literally wiping some villages off the map. Her parents had a particular hatred for the Waffen SS, who led the campaign. Rachel's folks gave her material for our project—Russian newspaper articles, pictures of devastated villages and murdered peasants—and one of them caught my eye. It was a picture of an SS officer standing in a Russian village beside some peasants who had just been hung. The SS insignia—double lightning bolts—was clearly visible on his collar, and the soldier actually looked like my dad."

"I can't believe this. Are you saying it was your dad?" I said incredulously.

"It was a grainy picture, and it could have been a thousand different men. It's not like there was a shortage of young blond, blue-eyed Germans back then, is it? I didn't give it much thought at the time. But here's where the real coincidence comes in. I was stunned when you mentioned mom's wedding ring, because that was one of my clues, too."

"What do you mean?"

"As I was studying the picture, I saw a symbol on a tank parked behind the soldier, and I realized I'd seen that same symbol someplace before. It took me a while to put things together, and it finally hit me that it was the same symbol that was on my mother's ring. Once I made the connection, I asked her if the design had any significance, and she said, 'Not really. It's just something we saw and liked, so I put it on my ring.'"

"What'd you do then?"

"I started researching the history of the SS and confirmed Rachel's stories about the Russian front. Then, using my class project as the excuse, I started asking dad and mom specific things about the war—like where dad had served, exactly, and what battles he'd been in—easy stuff. Their answers were always vague, and they kept trying to change the subject, or they'd ask why I wanted to know. One night I just confronted them with everything I'd found out: Rachel's pictures of the Russian front, the connection with mom's ring and the Waffen SS symbol, the whole thing. And I asked dad if he was the soldier in the picture."

"Really? How'd that go over?"

"They kept looking at each other and stuttering, like they were making it up as they went along. Finally, I got so irritated I just demanded to know if dad had been in the Waffen SS. After a lot of stalling, he reluctantly admitted that he had. He said he'd felt guilty about it, especially given the SS's reputation in America, and didn't want people to know. He just wanted a fresh start in America after the war. I asked him about what he'd done with the SS, and he said he didn't want to talk about it, that it was a part of his life he regretted, and he'd moved on. He did admit that he'd fought in Russia, but said he wasn't the soldier in the picture because his unit never fought in that part of the country."

"So how'd you find out he was CIA?"

"It's a long story, so I'll just give you the *Cliff's Notes* version for now. Once I learned they'd been hiding things from me, I started paying more attention to details, like how long dad was gone, where he said he'd been, stuff like that. A lot of times things didn't make sense. He'd say he was in Mexico, but I'd see him unpacking heavy winter clothes when he got back home. Or he'd say he'd been in Canada in January and come home with a slight tan, and he's sure not one to sit in a tanning booth. So one day during a school break when I was staying overnight with friends, I got up early, parked down the street from our house and followed dad to work. He drove to the CIA building—Langley—and was waved straight through the security gate, so I could tell he wasn't just visiting. I was stunned!"

"Let me guess what happened next. You calmly confronted him and asked for a logical explanation?"

She actually laughed for the first time.

"Yeah, right. I went ballistic, threatened to tell everyone I knew that dad was in the CIA and demanded that he tell me the truth about what he was doing. Which, of course he couldn't do, because that's the whole point of the CIA, isn't it, to do things in secret? It was stupid and childish on my part, but I couldn't believe how I'd been lied to. I mean, why did dad lie all that time about the Waffen SS? Certainly the CIA knew about his past, so there has to be some connection there that I still don't know about.

And how many other things have my parents been lying about? Anyway, I threw a fit, the CIA stepped in, and here I am. So, Tom, aren't you glad you got to meet the rest of the family?"

———

After the chance encounter with Sophie my roller coaster life was back again. The problem was, after one meeting I didn't know if she was the "up" part or the "down" part of the ride. There was no question she'd inherited Erika's spirit and sense of independence and was not to be taken lightly, but, given everything that had happened over the last couple years, I wasn't about to take anyone's story at face value. We had ended the first meeting with the agreement to meet again in two days, with each of us bringing a list of questions. By the time we met, my list ran about two pages.

The second meeting was disappointing and surprising. Disappointing because she refused to reveal the real family name, and surprising because she said she didn't ever want to see her parents again; she just wanted to know what they were up to so she could give the CIA a piece of her mind (and I would have loved to have been there for that little meeting). She hadn't forgiven her parents yet and didn't seem about to any time soon. She was still regarding me with a cautious level of suspicion and wanted to know why I was seeking her parents again, and what I would do if I located them. Unfortunately, my friendship with her parents and my historical curiosity were not strong enough reasons for her to cooperate with me. She insisted—or, rather, demanded—that I give up my search and forget about them. She also refused to tell me how the CIA responded to her questions about what her parents were doing in Bremen and why she hadn't been informed of their presence. As exasperating as the situation was, though, I had to admit that since I had met Sophie, I wasn't spending much time worrying about my conflicting feelings about Vietnam.

I thought I had gotten Kurt and Erika out of my system, but learning about Sophie only made the Kurt and Erika mystery more tantalizing than ever. By now I was way past the point of intellectual curiosity about their roles in the war. I wanted to know everything about them, only I was back at square one with even more questions. Without Sophie's help, though, I had no way of following up on the significance of my new discovery. I felt like a man with a pocketful of money and no place to spend it.

The only plan I could come up with to get Sophie's help was to pester her until she agreed to meet with me again. After a couple more out-of-the-way sessions—preceded by security precautions that bordered on the comedic—she relented enough to help me on a limited basis. She agreed to listen to my summaries of the Bremen meetings and confirm the parts of the Kurt and Erika story that she knew to be true. We knew it would be slow going, because they had lied to her about so much of their past, but at least it was a start.

The few secret meetings Sophie and I had during November and December were devoted entirely to her parents. Scattered bits of small talk periodically interrupted our discussions of Kurt and Erika, but all elements of our personal lives remained closed. Most conversations centered on the time I had spent with Kurt and Erika at their farm near Bremen. Sophie knew little about her parents' real lives prior to 1946, and what she knew after 1946 she considered too false to be useful.

Sophie and I met only once in January, but that meeting proved eventful. She finally unburdened herself about the deep hurt and denial caused by her parent's web of deceit. We were sitting in my car in the Student Union parking lot, and I had just finished telling her something her dad had mentioned concerning the nature of war.

"Sophie, I do think I understand something about your parents, and I think you should give them a chance to explain their side of the story. I can only tell you bits and pieces of what they could tell you. You need to hear the whole story."

I expected a tongue-lashing, but instead I saw a look of vulnerability cross Sophie's face. She was sitting with her back resting on the car door, her knees curled up under her chin, and her feet were resting on the car seat. She had taken her shoes off and was observing me with her eyes bigger and bluer than ever before.

Actually smiling, she said, "Tom, why don't you turn the heat down a little. I know it's ten below outside, but it's getting too hot in here."

I did as directed, wondering what was coming next.

"Tom, I know you mean well, but I can never forgive my parents for hiding their past from me. I've studied a lot about the Holocaust, and I can't understand how a sane person could possibly have any connection to such an event. I wish my parents would have tried to explain their involvement to me and allowed me to judge their past based on the truth. Once I found out about their true backgrounds, I had no interest in listening to any further explanations; their lies had destroyed that opportunity. Right now I couldn't even tell you my real last name because I don't know what it is. Can you begin to understand how betrayed I feel?"

I remained silent, mesmerized by the level of Sophie's emotion. I turned the radio off and waited. Sophie had turned her face away, and when she turned it back toward me, her eyes were full of tears. She didn't apologize for crying or wipe her tears away. She just began to talk.

"It was my mother's lie that hurt the most. When I was growing up, dad was gone a lot, and I grew very close to my mom. Everyone commented on how much alike we were; 'kindred spirits' they called us. I idolized my mother and wanted to be just like her, to make her proud of me. I can't forgive her for her deception. I can't and I won't."

I actually wanted to hold Sophie and comfort her, but I decided that might be a dangerous act. Instead, I offered a verbal hug. "I'm sure your mother loves you, and she had a good reason for keeping her past from you."

"Nice try, Tom. It's even kinda' cute. But if you ever want to see me again, don't pursue the good Nazi line again."

CHAPTER 16

Two weeks later I received a phone call from Sophie, which was a first. Her preferred means of communication had been a coded note telling me when and where to pick her up for one of our talks.

"Hi, Tom. Can you meet me at the Chester Fritz reading room at eight-thirty on Tuesday night?"

"I thought we weren't supposed to be seen in public?"

"I'll explain on Tuesday. Can you be there?"

"Sure."

"Good. See you Tuesday night."

I spent the next few days thinking about Sophie's request. There was a certain fascination in trying to guess what she was going to tell me, and I found it difficult to focus on anything else. I was also curious to see if Sophie's lack of secrecy regarding our encounters was for real.

As I walked to the Chester Fritz Library on Tuesday evening, I was once again captivated by my surroundings, even though I'd walked the UND campus a thousand times. The Gothic-style red brick buildings with their cream-colored window and door surrounds provided a cozy feeling of warmth and closeness, an Ivy League flair on the northern plains. I got to the library's reading room early, about eight-fifteen, and sat in the most conspicuous spot I could find. The reading room—defined by a high ceiling and walls of windows that showcased a large mural depicting scenes of North Dakota's history—is divided into sections of table and chair ensembles and private study areas. It's one of the campus hot spots; students flock there to be seen and search for new talent, academic and social.

At exactly eight-thirty Sophie entered the reading room. She was wearing a powder blue parka with white fur trim around the sleeves and hood; her blond hair mingled with the fur trim. Seeing me, Sophie marched straight to my table, took her parka off and sat down. Watching her every movement, I was struck by the fact that I'd never paid much attention to Sophie's physical appearance, yet I'd been infatuated with her mother.

"Hi, Tom. Why do you look so serious? Tough day at school?"

"I'm just a little tired. Guess I'm getting old. You look happy. What's the occasion? Did the CIA pay you to leave them alone?"

Sophie flashed a satisfied smile. "Funny you should ask. I did have a little meeting with my CIA contact and we ironed out a few things. Actually, you and I were really stupid. We missed something so obvious I can't believe we failed to see it. Can you guess what I'm talking about?"

"I usually don't know what you're talking about even when I know what you're talking about, so how can I make a guess when I don't know what you're talking about?"

"I think that's clever, but I'm not sure," she said feigning a frown. "Anyway, I'll give you a hint. Why do you think the CIA knows about us?"

"I'm sure it's because I screwed up somehow."

The room was full of people, and it was a study room, so Sophie stifled what started out as a loud chortle.

"No, Thomas, think again. What event in your past have we failed to factor into our dealings with the CIA?"

"Why don't you just tell me?"

"No. You have to figure it out, or I won't tell you the rest of the story."

I pushed my chair back and started to get up, but then I sat back down. "This is ridiculous. Let's go some place where I can yell at you without making a scene."

"Do you want to come to my apartment? My roommates are gone."

Before I had a chance to make a witty response, Sophie leaned across the table and whispered, "I'm done teasing, so here's the full story."

I moved face to face with Sophie. "Thank you."

"The CIA knows about our meetings not because they're watching me, but because they're watching you. You're the one who discovered my parents and blew their cover. You're the reason they had to leave North Dakota. You're the one doing all the research on the Waffen SS and trying to find out about my parents. Duh!"

Sophie was right. As she sat smugly staring at me, I tried to remember anything unusual that would suggest CIA surveillance. "I don't see how they ever connected the two of us. We never talked on the phone. We were never in public together. We ... "

"I wish you wouldn't interrupt. I'm not done yet. Get your coat and let's go to the Union and you can buy me a coke. People are starting to stare."

It was a short walk from Chester Fritz to the Student Union. We found a semi-private booth, and I went and got two cokes, came back and unloaded on Sophie.

"Just how much does the CIA know about me? Should I check with my principal to see if I'm being investigated? Am I in trouble because I found out about your parents? Why hasn't the CIA contacted me personally?"

"Slow down, Tom. Just take a deep breath and let me finish." Sophie took a long drink of her coke. As she gazed at me with dancing eyes, her lips formed a perfect circle around her straw. "This could take a while. Do you have work to do for your classes tomorrow?"

"I'll manage. You said you were going to finish."

"The CIA leaves me alone, and I leave them alone unless something unusual happens. When you told me my parents were living in North Dakota until last summer, I contacted my handler. He told me that we needed to meet, but first he needed to do some more checking on you. Apparently your file wasn't thick enough. We finally held our meeting last week. My handler explained that my dad was doing CIA work in North Dakota and it had nothing to do with me, and that's all he would say on that issue. Most of our conversation was about you, your interest in my parents, what you knew about them, and what you intended to do with your information."

Sophie paused to sip her coke. She was about to continue when she saw me shaking my head and muttering to myself.

"What's so funny, Tom? Am I boring you?"

"I don't believe this. Two students I had during my first year at Central just walked by and gave me the thumbs up. One of them has a sister I'm teaching right now. Do you know what that means?"

"That your students will think you're one lucky guy?"

"No! I mean ... well ... oh, shit, it's all kinda' funny. I suppose it comes from growing up in a small town."

Sophie shook her head. "My, my, you're really a man of the world, aren't you?"

"You'll never know. Now finish your damn speech."

Sophie had a smug, smart-ass look on her face, and I could tell she was going to enjoy what was coming next. "Oh, it gets much, much better, or worse, depending on how you look at it. I'll give you a condensed version of my visit with Mr. CIA, and, if need be, I'll fill in the details later. Let's just say I told him you were not a problem, that your interest was solely centered on World War II history, and whatever my parents did after the war was of no interest to you. The CIA really isn't too concerned about people knowing my dad works for them; they just don't want people making the connection between my dad working for them and what he did during World War II. I guaranteed them that you would not divulge any knowledge you had concerning that issue. They were also interested in what you and I were doing seeing each other, what we talked about. I admitted that I was interested in finding out about my parents and to throw them off the track, I said you had the hots for me, and I was leading you on to find out more about my parents. They seemed satisfied—at least for the present—and they made me your handler. I'm to report any suspicious behavior on your part to them. I'm sure the CIA knows it's only a matter of time until the story of people like my dad working for them leaks out, but for now, my job is to watch you."

Sophie was so pleased with herself it was sickening. I was dumbfounded. I sucked on my coke and then pretended to bang my head on the table as I began my rebuttal. "So, that was an edited version? Thank God for that. I'd assumed you were intelligent, if a little aloof and overbearing, but I see I was wrong on the first point. How can you guarantee anything about me? And what's this crap about having the hots for you? We can hardly stand to talk to each other."

I could see Sophie was fighting the urge to call me a series of unpleasant names. However, after a calculated pause, she calmly replied, "Tom, I know we have no romantic plans. You're much too old for me, and I'm much too mature for you. Like I said, I needed to say something to get the CIA off our backs. I still want to talk with you about my parents. Maybe it would be good for us to learn a little bit about each other so we'd be able to converse more comfortably and not make stupid statements like you just did."

"If I offended you, I'm sorry. This CIA stuff has me a little spooked."

"Tom, what kind of music do you like? Who are some of your favorite singers?"

Without saying anything I got up and went to get two more cokes. I needed a little time to gather myself and get ready for another journey into Sophie's world. Sitting back in our booth, facing the object of my turmoil, I felt confused, but I had to say something. "I like most music. I like Bob Dylan, Peter, Paul and Mary, Marvin Gaye, the Beatles, Roy Orbison, Neil Diamond, CCR, Sam Cooke, Bob Seger, Dusty Springfield, Neil Young … Aren't you going to stop me sometime?"

"Why? I like all your choices. I saw the Beatles at Shea Stadium when I was a junior in high school. It was fantastic. Do you like Frankie Valli and the Four Seasons?"

"Yeah, they're okay."

"Did you see them at the Fieldhouse last fall?"

"No."

"Too bad I didn't know you then. I had free tickets. I've got a friend on the Board of Governors Entertainment Committee, and he gave me two tickets. I might even have asked you."

"I'd have been afraid to go. Some of my students might've seen me and thought I was picking up extra babysitting money on the side."

Sophie laughed, but quickly recovered. "Funny you should say that now that I'm babysitting you for the CIA." Then, without giving me a chance to speak, she was off on another tangent. "Do you like teaching? Are you a good teacher? I'll bet you are. I'd love to be teaching social studies right now. 1968 was such an unbelievable year. I hope we can get out of Vietnam and start to rebuild LBJ's Great Society. I hate Nixon. I'm afraid he has no morals when it comes to what's legal and what isn't. I heard a comment that his policy was 'If the government does it, it's legal.' I can only guess where ideas like that might lead us. Anything under the guise of national security will be justified."

I threw both my arms in the air. "I surrender! That's the most amazing speech I've ever heard. You asked two questions and answered one. You condensed a year's worth of current events into one sentence. You attacked one President and praised another while offering a plan for the future, all without taking a breath. I'm in total awe."

"See how fast we're finding things out about each other. What single event do you remember most about 1968?"

"Okay, I'll play your game: Bobby Kennedy's assassination. It was the last day of my first full year of teaching, and I was driving to Lakota the next day to meet my dad to go fishing in Canada. I was in my apartment packing when the news started coming across the TV. I stopped packing and stayed up all night watching the news. I never went to sleep. About nine in the morning I threw some stuff in a bag, got in my car and drove to Lakota. It seemed like time froze for twelve hours. I was in a trance until I started talking with my dad over breakfast. It was surreal."

Sophie looked at her watch. "Tom, I'd like to continue, but I need to go and study. I have a test in an elementary education class tomorrow morning. I'm interested in your opinion on world affairs, teaching, President Nixon, Vietnam and a lot of things. I'd like to find out more about you, and maybe by understanding you I'll be able to see why my parents trusted you, and I can figure some other things out. Would you like to go to a movie on Saturday?"

"With who?"

Sophie coyly puckered her lips in a pouty posture. "Hmmm. I hope that was just a feeble attempt at humor. I don't take rejection well, because I'm not used to it."

"Okay, let me take you out for dinner, and then you can take me to a movie. I suppose I'd better do as my handler tells me or I'll be in trouble with the CIA."

"I'd worry more about me than the CIA. Have you seen *The Producers* with Zero Mostel and Gene Wilder? Any movie about a musical called *Springtime for Hitler* has to be outrageous."

———

Saturday night I picked Sophie up at her apartment. We drove to Mike's Pizza for dinner and then to the Empire Theater for *The Producers*. After the movie we went to the Westward Ho for a drink, where Sophie produced a fake ID because she was not quite 21. She laughed and said the CIA gave it to her. I was a little apprehensive about her age, but I didn't want to seem too unworldly, so I went along with it. We actually had fun as we continued to get to know each other. Later that night, though, I made a major tactical error. I'm not sure how I failed to diagnose the situation correctly, but I attempted to kiss her goodnight at the door to her apartment, and the consequences were immediate and drastic. She turned away, and with a voice frostier than the frigid North Dakota air, said, "Tom, don't call me, I'll call you."

CHAPTER 17

JANUARY 17, 1998

The irritating jangling of the phone interrupted my nostalgic journey into the past. My wife was already talking as I picked it up, and I had a hard time getting a word in edgewise. "Yes dear ... I understand dear ... Shop as long as you want ... I know you run into lots of people you need to visit with ... Let's just go out to eat tonight ... Yes, I think you'll need it ... I love you ... Have fun."

My responses had been perfected by years of practice. My better half refused to admit that she was a shopaholic, but a closet stuffed with shoes proved otherwise. I deliberately neglected to mention Erika's phone call. I wasn't sure what my wife's reaction would be. Gazing at the piles of memorabilia scattered across the floor of my study, I realized it was time to escape from the past and wonder about the future. What did Erika want after such a long absence?

I put everything back in the box, returned it to the shelf and then headed back upstairs. I made myself a pot of coffee and assumed a position in my upstairs recliner (Can a guy have too many recliners?), turning so I could peer out the picture window. Looking at the bleakness of my backyard—barren trees, snow mounds, and a frozen stream bordered by cattails bending in the wind—I contemplated the coming rendezvous.

My conversions with Kurt and Erika in Bremen seemed like ancient history, but the feelings they kindled in me were still alive and vibrant. Who were they really? What did they represent? If my mom and dad belonged to "The Greatest Generation," what label could be applied to Kurt and Erika? I remembered teaching a unit on the Holocaust and staring at my hand, knowing it had shaken the hand of a person who was a member of the organization that ran the concentration camps. What generation did I belong to? Why had I become so captivated by Kurt and Erika? I'd spent thirty years trying to answer that question, and maybe Erika would finally provide an answer.

I poured myself another cup of coffee, took a sip, and tried to relax. It was going to be an interesting week.

The sound of the garage door opening brought me back from my nap; I had dozed off for about an hour. My wife was home, and I headed to the garage to help her unload the car. If she were true to form, the car would be crammed with irresistible bargains. I could hardly wait to hear how much money she'd saved me. I reached the kitchen just as she came in from the garage with several Norby's sacks.

"You can't believe the fun stuff that was on sale. Half off on all the winter clothes. I got some really cool outfits."

"Great. I can always use some more sweaters this time of year. My sacks must still be in the car."

"Don't be silly. You never like anything I get you, so I don't even try anymore. Did anyone call while I was gone?"

"No, it was pretty quiet … Oh, wait, I almost forgot, we did get one call you should know about."

"Who was it? Do I have to call back right away?"

"Your mother called, Sophie. She wants to meet us in Fargo on Saturday. I told her we had something else planned and didn't think we could make it, so she hung up on me."

"What? Mom called? Really? This better not be another one of your sick jokes. Where was she calling from? Is she really going to be in Fargo? Is dad with her? Tom, you've got to tell me everything. I can't believe I'll finally get to see her again!"

Sophie actually forgot about her shopping spree, paced around the kitchen table and began to ramble. "We've got a lot of catching up to do after thirty years apart. I can't believe it's been that long. Where do we begin? How long will they be in town? It wasn't supposed to work out this way, but fate has a way of altering our destinies. I can't wait to finally see mom and dad again!"

"Well, before you get your hopes up too much, she said she was coming alone and would explain Kurt's absence when we got there. That's all I know. It was a very short conversation."

"I hope nothing's happened to dad. You never know with all that CIA stuff they were involved in. I have so much I want to say to them, and I want to make sure dad hears it, too. You mean she didn't say anything more about him?"

"No, Sophie, and the answer won't change no matter how many more times you ask me. We just have to see what happens Saturday. I know it's hard, but just be thankful you even have one parent to talk to, given everything that's happened."

"I can hardly wait to see mom. I'm going to spend all my time thinking about what to say to her. I hate to give you any credit for this, but I wouldn't even be looking forward to reconciling with them if it weren't for that meeting you had with them back in '79. So I guess you do earn your keep once in a while."

"Wait a minute, did I hear that right? I get credit for something? Quick, let's mark this date on the calendar and have you sign it."

"Can't you be serious for one minute? I'm going right now to start writing out questions and preparing a list of things I want to discuss with mom on Saturday. I can't believe we're actually going to be together in the same room. And we have to remember to bring … "

"I'm way ahead of you. I told her it'd be waiting for her at the Holiday Inn. I'll put it in the mail today."

"Great. I hope she approves. I've been waiting for this day for a long time."

Sophie hurried off to the bedroom and left me to reminisce about my last meeting with Kurt and Erika in 1979, the meeting that had left Sophie and me in emotional limbo ever since.

CHAPTER 18

OCTOBER, 1979

It had been a pleasant week, weather-wise, and I was looking forward to another weekend of duck hunting. The season had been good so far and promised to get even better. I had already been to New Rockford for two weekends and Sophie and the kids had come along once to visit my folks, but this weekend I was going alone. I got home from school before Sophie, as she usually picked up Bruce and Sara from daycare. As I went through the mail I came upon a strange envelope, one that had been metered, not stamped. It had no other identifying characteristics except my address, and my name was underlined in red. I had only seen such an envelope once before, and that one had contained a congratulatory message from Kurt and Erika regarding our wedding. I separated the envelope from the other mail and left it unopened on the kitchen table. Opening a bottle of Jack Daniels, I poured myself a drink, sat down and stared at the envelope, apprehensive about its contents. Half way through my Jack and water, I opened it and found a small piece of paper with a typed, semi-cryptic message:

Remember the old days? Let's go hunting! Bring pictures of children. Bremen Catholic Church. 9:00 am this Saturday. See you. K/E.

Taking a slow sip of whiskey, I digested the request. I was to come alone to a remote church in the middle of nowhere to meet two people I hadn't seen in over ten years. These people—who just happened to be my wife's parents—were brought into the United States by the CIA under mysterious circumstances. To further complicate matters, Sophie had rejected them and vowed to never see them again. Nothing unusual or scary about any of this!

"What could they want? What could they want?" I kept repeating the phrase to myself as I walked into the basement to hide the note in my Kurt and Erika file. My parents would be in Minneapolis at a hardware convention, so it was a perfect weekend for a secret reunion with Kurt and Erika. I wouldn't need to make an excuse to anyone except myself. I knew I had to go, and I decided not to mention anything to Sophie until I returned from the meeting.

———

I was very familiar with the Catholic Church—a distinctive, brown-brick structure that integrated modern and Gothic architecture—as I had driven by it a few miles south of Bremen many times on my hunting excursions. I arrived at the large empty parking lot a few minutes before nine and parked on the north end next to three large box elder trees. I could see miles in every direction and there were no vehicles in sight. As I sat I wondered if Kurt and Erika would miss "Old Ugly." The object of so much abuse had been laid to rest, replaced by a green 1978 Chevy pickup, a "normal" green that no one could make fun of.

A few minutes went by before a black sedan suddenly emerged from behind the church and slowly glided up beside me. The electric window glided down, and a smiling Kurt motioned for me to get into the back seat. I joined them as a beaming Kurt shook my hand and said, "Congratulations, son."

Erika leaned over the front seat, kissed me on the cheek, hugged me tightly, and squealed, "Oh, Tom, we're so happy for you and Sophie. We love you and miss you both so much. I'm so excited for you!"

"I'm happy to see you again, too. I was starting to think this would never happen."

Before I could say anything else, Kurt asked, "Did you pack a lunch?"

"Yeah, but only for me. I really have no idea what's going on, but I assumed I'd be hunting this evening and I … "

"Still thinking about hunting first? Some things never change. Tell me, has Sophie adjusted to being in second place?" Kurt asked.

"I know you haven't seen her in a long time, Kurt, but did Sophie ever like being in second place for anything? Sorry, I could've packed a lunch for all of us, but let's face it, I didn't think you'd be dressed to go hunting, and it looks like I was right. Besides, I thought you two would at least have a pie and a thermos of coffee to celebrate our reunion tour. Things must really be serious to bring me out in the middle of nowhere for a meeting like this."

"Tom, funny you should joke about that," said Erika. "I wanted to bring a pie, but Kurt did say this was a serious trip, and a picnic wouldn't fit in. Right, Kurt?"

"Don't make me the villain. I just didn't think you had time to bake a pie and haul it all the way from … oops, end of sentence."

Erika continued, "I'm not sure which one of you has the worst sense of humor, but neither of you is funny. Tom, what Kurt was getting at is the fact that we only have about three hours to visit, and we can't go into a restaurant to eat because the CIA only allowed this visit if we promised not to contact anyone else. We'll just drive around until noon and then drop you off back here. We anticipated you'd be hunting this afternoon and hoped you'd pack a lunch. Now, go lock up your truck so we can start our little adventure."

"Just where are we headed during our drive around, back to your old home?" I asked after I'd rejoined them.

"I'm sure we'll drive past it, but we won't stop. We don't want to draw any attention to ourselves." True to form, Kurt was carefully surveying the terrain as he eased the car out of the parking lot.

As usual, I went right for the jugular. "You have a lot of explaining to do, so let's get right into it. When we were having our discussions back in the Sixties, you never told me you were in the CIA. Why not?"

"I assume Sophie has told you about her rebellion and the arrangement we have with the CIA?"

"Obviously!" I said.

Erika leaned across Kurt and honked the horn. "Excuse me. The CIA talk can wait. We've a lot of other catching up to do. Kurt, start to drive. I don't care where. Tom, tell us all about yourself, about our daughter, and our grandchildren that we've never seen. I still can't believe that the nice young man who discovered us in Bremen wound up marrying our daughter. Life is very strange."

For the next hour we slowly plied the remote gravel roads of central North Dakota. It was a beautiful, sunny autumn day, and Kurt jokingly accused me of scouting out new hunting spots while he chauffeured us around. For a while I did most of the talking as I caught them up on my family life, about Sophie and her love of teaching, about my teaching career, about Bruce and Sara. Then we talked about life's ups and downs, and they poured their hearts out describing the pain they felt because of Sophie's alienation. They were still holding out hope for reconciliation.

Kurt asked, "How bad is it, Tom? Does she have a better understanding of who we are or does she still hate us?"

"I'm afraid nothing has changed there, and there's not much I've been able to do to make it any better. To keep the peace I mostly just avoid the subject."

"Kurt, pull over on the next approach," Erika suddenly ordered, taking some photographs right out of my hand. "I think I've shown the proper restraint so far, but now I want to look at my grandchildren's pictures without being jostled around."

"Okay, but not for long. We don't want to be conspicuous."

"Apparently you've forgotten what it's like around here," I said. "This isn't exactly a rural rush hour, and I'm sure the lone car we might see won't suspect much."

Erika wasn't listening to either of us. She was mesmerized by the pictures of Bruce and Sara I had given her. "Tom, they're adorable! Blond hair, blue eyes ... Why they're perfect little Aryans." Looking first at me and then at Kurt, she sheepishly added, "I mean that in a good way, and I do hope we get the chance to meet them some time."

Kurt took the pictures from Erika and studied them for a long time. "They're beautiful, Tom. I can see resemblances to both you and Sophie. Perhaps Jochen would have looked just like Bruce at that age, but ... " Kurt's voice trailed off.

We sat in silence for a moment before Kurt broke the spell. "Why don't we all get out and stretch? The serious part of our reunion is about to begin."

As we stepped out of the car Erika pretended to look around. "I can't see you, Tom, where are you?"

Kurt and I simultaneously spun our heads to look at each other, and Kurt said, "If I were you, Tom, I'd stay hidden to avoid any more stupid comments. Let's get back in the car and get down to business."

"Well, I thought camouflage clothing was supposed to make you invisible." Erika was still giggling.

"If that was the case dear, I'd wear camouflage clothing all the time," Kurt said.

"Now who's trying to be funny? I thought you wanted to get down to business."

"I do, if you'll let me, Erika. Tom, why don't you sit in front with me? Erika, I'm sure you'll add anything I might miss."

"You see, Tom, nothing's changed. I still have to keep him on track," Erika teased, her blue eyes flashing.

Kurt put the key in the ignition and turned to me. "Do you have any questions before I get started?"

"Hell, yes! For starters, who are you really? And where the hell have you been for the last ten years? And why are you here again now? And what's the purpose of today's meeting?"

"I'm sure you've already figured out that we can't really answer all of those to your satisfaction, but I'm going to cover a lot of other information today, so listen up," Kurt said as he started the car and steered it backed onto the road. "Pretty much all of what I'm about to tell you is public record, and I'm sure you know a lot of it. The tragic thing about public records, though, is the public hardly ever asks to see them, and even if they do, the government has lots of ways to stall the process. So what I'm going to do today is tell you where we were at certain times and describe certain events. Then, using public records, even a history teacher ought to be able to put two and two together. Are you following me so far?"

"I am, as long as the math doesn't get any harder than putting two and two together."

By now Kurt was all business. "Good. Did you follow the Senate investigation of the CIA headed by Frank Church? It was commonly referred to as the Church Committee Hearings of 1975."

"Yeah, I watched it a little on TV and read about it in Time magazine. Some of the information seemed a little far-fetched."

"When the Church Committee made its report everyone got all excited about the evil things the CIA was doing. The problem is, most people only pay attention for a few days, and soon everything is glossed over and forgotten about. When something like this happens a few heads roll, and Congress threatens reform but nothing really changes. Thirty years from now everything will be the same. Funny, thirty years ago I was just beginning my career in the CIA, and now I'm speculating on 2009. I'm afraid we haven't made much progress in all these years."

"Just how did you get into all this stuff? Where and what did you do?" I interrupted.

Kurt admonished me with a stern look and drove in silence for a few minutes. By now the smell of freshly-turned earth was seeping into the car as we drove past a farmer on a tractor doing his fall plowing, and I breathed in the familiar scent as I waited for a response.

"From now on, listen, don't ask. It'll all be here; you just have to put some pieces together," Kurt said pointedly. "In 1949 I started as an advisor to Frank Wisner, who created the clandestine branch of the CIA. I was his expert on Soviet military tactics, and the job evolved into a participatory role in covert activities. I got my start in covert operations in Guatemala in the early Fifties, when we staged a coup and installed a new government there. It was one of the CIA's best success stories. In those days Wisner's covert ops section pretty much had free reign. We didn't bother to tell the rest of the CIA what we were doing, but we had access to a lot of hidden money. In Guatemala I worked under Tracy Barnes and another guy you might have heard of, E. Howard Hunt. In 1954 Barnes became the station chief in Frankfurt, Germany, and Hunt and I went with him.

"Tracy Barnes was a real character. He'd been a Wall Street lawyer before World War II, and when the war broke out, he wanted action. He was recruited by the OSS and got involved in the Jedburgh Program, which trained agents to be dropped into Nazi-occupied France and help the Resistance. Barnes was a true patriot, well-meaning and charismatic, but our British colleagues thought he was arrogant and naïve and didn't like to get his hands dirty doing real spy work. I had a special connection with Barnes because when I was with Das Reich in France, I met a friend of his from the Jedburgh Program, a Captain Anderson, who had been captured by the Gestapo, but that's a story for another day."

I raised my hand like a schoolboy. Kurt nodded, and I asked, "So you were over in Germany again. I thought you told me once that you could never return to Germany."

"Things change, priorities shift, precautions were taken. I wanted to help defeat communism, and this was the best use of my abilities to help win the Cold War."

"I know this is supposed to be a lecture, but can I ask a few more questions?"

"I thought all these years of teaching school might teach you some patience, but you're still as impulsive as ever. I'm sure I'll get to your questions, but go ahead."

"I remember the Church Committee reporting on CIA involvement in using LSD and mind control experiments to create a perfect spy, a 'Manchurian Candidate' so to speak. I think the code name for these programs was Monarch. Did you know anything about Monarch?"

"Not until the early Seventies," Kurt said. "The CIA is extremely fragmented, and many parts are not aware of what the other parts are doing; that's the nature of the beast. The units that dabbled in the Monarch experiment were among the most mysterious, always searching for a magic potion to control the human mind. I'll just say they considered and experimented with any possibility. Early groups even studied secret Nazi mind control experiments conducted in the concentration camps. They paid special attention to the experiments that Dr. Mengele performed on the inmates. These secret groups went under a number of different names, such as the TSS, Bluebird and Artichoke, finally culminating in a group called MKULTRA, headed by a Dr. Sidney Gottlieb during the Fifties and Sixties. The CIA was worried that the Soviets had already been successful in mind control experiments, and the Monarch guys were working feverishly to catch up. Lots of weird stuff went on; some experiments were even conducted at prestigious American universities, with CIA approval, of course. It's striking how many scientists are willing to serve those in power if the money and prestige are there. Ethical barriers were often crossed, and if things became really dangerous, the experiments were conducted in foreign countries, usually in South America. Most of the subjects were prisoners, unknowing students, the unfit or other malcontents. My brother Jurgen actually worked with Mengele in South America and was somehow connected with Dr. Gottlieb until he was found out and escaped to Syria, but, again, that's another story."

"Tell me more about your brother Jurgen," I said.

Kurt gave me a fatherly look. "You know enough already. Please don't ask me about Jurgen again."

"Sorry. I remember reading that, according to the Nuremberg Trials, things like medical experiments can't be conducted without the permission of the subjects, and they can't be placed in serious danger."

Kurt raised his eyebrows and shrugged. "Like I said, ethical barriers were crossed. Besides, who enforces rules like that, especially when the acts are committed in secret? It's funny how circumstances change things. Nazi doctors were condemned to death for performing experiments that … well, you get my meaning. Don't get me wrong, I believe we need to do what's necessary to win the Cold War, but sometimes I wonder how far we need to go to do that."

Kurt turned to me with a question. "In all your research did you ever read about Operation Paperclip? "

"Sure, I've read about it. Why?"

"You're one of the few, then. I'll bet not one in a thousand Americans knows anything about it." Kurt paused and gave me a wink. "Why do you think we're here? Do you think America could defeat the Soviet Union by themselves?"

I just looked at him blankly.

"Starting in May of 1945 there was a race between the Soviet Union and the United States to secure the services of Nazi rocket scientists. Operation Paperclip brought about seven hundred Nazi scientists to the United States to help build the American space program and win the Cold War. President Truman approved letting them in, but said no one connected with any crimes or with a Nazi background should be included. Well, the OSS covered all that up for anyone who was valuable, including Werner von Braun, the father of the American space program. Hell, by 1958 von Braun was on the cover of *Time* magazine and proclaimed a hero, even though he'd been a Nazi and a favorite of Adolf Hitler, which just proves my point that governments forgive and forget when it suits their interests."

"I thought I just read somewhere that some of those scientists will be sent back."

Kurt laughed, "Yes, earlier this year Germany abolished the statute of limitations regarding Nazi war criminals, and the U.S. is not as protective as it used to be. Maybe Erika and I will eventually be in trouble, too."

I was curious about another can of CIA worms and couldn't contain myself. "What about Cuba, Castro, and the Bay of Pigs? The CIA seems to be tied to all of them."

Kurt kept looking straight ahead at a cloud of dust being raised by an approaching car. "Apparently, I've lost control of my agenda, but I'll try to continue," he stated sarcastically. "After Castro took over Cuba in 1959, our same group that had engineered the coup in Guatemala was put in charge of getting rid of Castro. Some of the things we tried to do to Castro make James Bond seem extremely tame. The Bay of Pigs was our biggest failure, and in some ways we've never recovered. The Kennedys wanted Castro gone, and we failed. People were demoted or lost their jobs. Robert Kennedy was furious with us. I could go on, but what's the use? I'd better stop before I get carried away, and you can take that a number of ways. As I mentioned, all this stuff is in the Church Report, which only a few people seem to care about anymore. But I do know for a fact that Congress did not get all the details, especially about MKULTRA. Richard Helms, who was head of the CIA in 1973, and Sidney Gottlieb, the head of MKULTRA, destroyed the files when they felt the heat from Watergate."

A voice interrupted from the back seat. "Enough, I can't take any more of this stale history lesson. If I have to learn about secret agents, I'd rather go learn something firsthand from Sean Connery."

"And what would you like to discuss with Mr. Connery, dear? Perhaps you could start by showing him those pictures of your grandchildren. That would get his attention."

"Oh, I'm sure I could find a way to pique his curiosity!" Erika leaned forward across the seat. "Tom, where are we? Are we close to some town? I need to find a bathroom."

Kurt pulled over, parked on the side of the road, winked at me and said, "We don't need a town for that, dear. There's the ditch right here."

Ignoring her husband's comment, Erika looked at me with fire in her eyes.

"Well, I'm not exactly sure, Erika, but I think we're about ten miles north of Fessenden. I hunted around here a couple of years ago."

"I can make it. Tell Kurt how to get to there, and maybe we can even pick up a snack or something."

"Okay, but I've got a lot of relatives in Fessenden," I warned, "so maybe Kurt and I should stay in the car. We could stop at a bar or a gas station."

"I don't care, but let's get going."

We got to Fessenden, a town of about 800, and made it to a gas station in time to solve Erika's emergency. I decided to take advantage of the stop myself, after looking around carefully to see if there was anyone there I knew. It was a busy Saturday morning, but the coast looked clear, so I used the men's room before we headed back.

"How long does it take to get from Fessenden to Bremen? We only have an hour left, and my wife's extra side trip got me off schedule."

"Oh, dear, please get rid of your anal German perfectionism. We have plenty of time."

"I think I asked Tom a question. Will you let him answer it?"

"Yes, dear, I'm sorry," Erika said as she patted Kurt on his shoulder.

"Take Highway 15 east out of Fessenden until you come to a sign that says 'Bremen,' then turn left on a gravel road and you'll eventually come to the church. It's about twenty miles. The way you've been driving I'd say about a half hour."

As we started the last leg of our prairie tour, Kurt announced he had one more CIA story to relate. "In 1954 the CIA produced a secret study called the Doolittle Report, which reached one major conclusion: If the U.S. wanted to win the Cold War, we needed to resort to the Machiavellian tactics employed by the Soviet Union. The agencies interpreted this as justification for using whatever means necessary to achieve our ends, and I got into stuff I never thought I'd get involved in again. Back then I thought it was necessary, but as time goes on, I question whether anything like that is justified. Now I wonder where our country is headed. Anyway, that's the end of my sermon. Do you have any other questions?"

"Here's one thing that has me kind of curious," I said, "A couple of years ago—I think it was July of '76—Waffen SS Colonel Jochen Peiper was murdered in France where he was living. His home was bombed and burned. I know Peiper was the leader of the Waffen SS troops who massacred American soldiers at Malmedy during the Battle of the Bulge. You mentioned him once, and told me you named your son after him. Can you tell me a little more about him and whether you know anything about who killed him?"

"Good to see you're still keeping up with your research. Colonel Peiper served in the Leibstandarte; I didn't know him very well, but he was a good friend of Jurgen's. He was a real enigma, a charming, intelligent man, but a devoted follower of Hitler. Peiper was an excellent soldier, one of the dynamic, young officers who personified the daring and ruthlessness of the Waffen SS, and everyone looked up to him."

"Sounds a little like you."

Kurt gave me a funny look. "Only a little, I hope. Peiper was a few years older than me, closer to Jurgen's age. He was eventually sentenced to death for his war crimes, but his sentence was reduced to life in prison, and he was released in 1955. Apparently someone felt his original sentence should have been carried out, and he was probably murdered. The survivors of the Waffen SS—especially someone as well known as

Colonel Peiper—have many enemies." Kurt looked at his watch. "You know, Tom, we're running short of time, and I promise you, if you have any other questions, you'll get lots of answers when you write the book."

"Book? What book? What the hell are you talking about?"

For the first time in over a decade I felt Erika's hand in mine as she reached over the seat and squeezed my hand. The sensation made me shiver.

"Tom, we want you to write a book about us so maybe Sophie will understand and forgive us. You know she'll never believe it if we write it, but she might believe you. We also hope that someday Bruce and Sara might want to know who their German grandparents really were, and this will explain things for them. We know it's a lot to ask, but we assume you've kept all your notes from the old days at Bremen. With those and all the research you've done, you've got enough material for a good start. To help you finish our story, we've spent the last five years writing down our experiences and arranging them in chronological order. Here is everything we have—our notes, the pictures you found in Bremen on your first visit, and Kurt's pewter statue." She reached over the seat and handed me a duffle bag, stuffed so full the zipper barely closed. I didn't even try to open it.

"We want you to treat us fairly, so don't sugar-coat anything," Kurt said. "We are what we are, and we did what we did, so people can come to their own conclusions. To make it more readable, though, we think you should make it a novel, not some dry documentary. We spent so much time together talking about these things that you know us pretty well, so I think you should write the story from my viewpoint."

Erika scoffed. "Just like a man! He wants everyone to think he did all this by himself, but you'll see differently when you start reading."

Kurt smiled his familiar bemused grin, but didn't add anything to Erika's remark, which I took to mean the relationship was as strong and unpredictable as ever.

We drove in silence for a few minutes while I collected my thoughts and contemplated my next step.

"Well, say something," Erika pleaded as we entered the parking lot and pulled up next to my truck.

I couldn't help but smile smugly at this new turn of events. "You know, I've kept my notes from our conversations because I'd always planned on writing something about the two of you, even if it was just for my own peace of mind, so this may not be as hard as you think."

"What do you mean? And why are you smiling like that? Is there something you're not telling us?" Kurt looked mildly anxious.

"Well, kind of. Way back when I was still concerned about my safety, I felt I had to do something to protect myself, so I started taping all of our conversations."

"Taping? How could you have done that? We never saw any recording equipment or anything. What's going on here?" Kurt's voice was rising with each word.

"I didn't tape the actual conversations; I just taped as much as I could remember afterward." I then gave them a quick explanation of my system and let them absorb the information before I continued. "There's no way I could have written all that stuff down accurately, and taping seemed like a faster, more reliable way to keep a good record of the conversations. And you guys kept warning me so often that you couldn't tell me stuff for my own safety that I realized I needed some backup material in case something actually did happen to me. I mean, who'd ever believe me without some kind of proof of your existence?"

They leaned back in their seats and started laughing. Kurt said, "Well, I guess we can't blame you for that, and in the end, it'll work out for the best. But once again, Erika, our young college friend was more devious than we thought. Are you sure you're just a high school history teacher, Tom? Maybe you're working for the CIA!"

"Don't worry. Teaching is about as much stress as I can handle; that and living with Sophie. Anyway, I hate to rush these final minutes, but I know we don't have much more time, so let's finish this talk about the book. How soon do you expect it to be done?"

Kurt smiled understandingly. "I'm planning on retiring in three or four years, and, given your family obligations, we thought that timetable seemed realistic. Maybe between the book and my leaving the CIA we can finally make peace with Sophie. Eventually, we'd like to read the book and discuss it with her. Do you think that'll work?"

"I'll do my best. Just remember, though, I'm a history major, not a creative writer, so don't expect some Hemingway masterpiece."

"You'll do fine," Erika said. "You're way more creative than you give yourself credit for. But given the circumstances, it might be best if you don't tell Sophie about the book until you're done. But if you do decide to tell her about this meeting, tell her we love her, and we hope she'll forgive us some time. We love you too, Tom, and we can hardly wait to read the finished product some day. Do you have anything to add, Kurt?"

Kurt just shrugged and smiled.

We got out of the car and exchanged tearful, lingering hugs in silence. Finally, I broke away and eased into my pickup. Over the whining of my engine Kurt yelled, "Good luck hunting, but don't leave your lights on, and try not to fall into a pond!"

I sat and watched the sedan disappear across the prairie in a surreal haze of dust.

———

My Saturday hunt was short. I was too preoccupied thinking about Kurt and Erika to concentrate on ducks. I was a little mad at myself for not asking about some things on my list, like Kurt's opinion about some of the foreign policy decisions facing President Carter, or what to do about Iran. There were a lot of other things I was curious about, too, but the visit with Kurt and Erika had been like one of my trips to the grocery store; I always think of a dozen things I need before I get there, but once I'm walking the aisles, my mind goes blank.

After stopping off at my uncle's for supper on the way home, I stayed alone at my folks' house that night. I called Sophie, but didn't mention my meeting with her parents. I fell asleep wondering what to tell her about Kurt and Erika.

Sunday morning I was back to normal. I bagged my limit and was back on the road to Grand Forks by twelve-thirty. Arriving home about three, I shocked Sophie as I opened the door leading from the garage into the house.

"What's the matter, are you sick? You never come home from a weekend of hunting in New Rockford this early. Let me guess, mommy wasn't home to baby you, so you came home to me."

"Yeah, it's good to see you, too, dear. Where are Bruce and Sara?"

"Sara is taking a nap and Bruce is at Joey's birthday party. He'll be home about six. Remember, it's Bruce's birthday next Wednesday."

"I know. Guess I'll have to take him hunting next year."

Sophie was standing in the kitchen preparing lasagna. She turned and pointed a long, fork-like utensil at me. "Oh, wonderful. Then I can worry about two little boys out playing in the swamps with guns. How can I contain myself?" She leaned in for a kiss. "Glad you're home. Why don't you clean up and get all your stuff put away so we can actually have a Sunday supper on time."

I went downstairs to complete my hunter's ritual: clean the ducks, oil my Remington, hang up my waders (feet up, of course) and sort my dirty clothes for the laundry basket before taking a shower.

Entering the kitchen wearing only my robe, I put my arms around Sophie from behind. "How long before Sara wakes up?"

Sophie tilted her head and gave me a sarcastic smile. "Pretty big talk from a tired old hunter ... not long enough for what you're thinking about. Try your luck when the kids are in bed, big guy. Now go get dressed so you can help around here for a change."

After a noisy dinner with Sophie and the kids I went down to my office. As I began to read Kurt and Erika's story, I knew there was no way I could refuse their request. I also knew that the book would probably never be published, and that I might be the only soul to ever read it. But I had to write it for three reasons: One, to keep a promise to two people who affected my life in a way I couldn't even explain; two, to see if I could find out who Kurt and Erika really were; three, to record my in-laws' story in the hope that my wife and children would someday want to welcome them back into the family.

I started the book two months later during Christmas vacation. The first thing I discovered as a writer was all the work that goes into getting ready to write. Before I could tell Kurt and Erika's story, I first had to piece it together from a variety of sources: notes and audio tapes of our Bremen meetings, the materials that Kurt and Erika had given me, and my World War II research. My work was made even more difficult because I couldn't tell anyone what I was doing, which meant I couldn't enlist help for typing, transcribing or other tasks. Oh, and there was one other thing. I couldn't let Sophie know what I was doing. I decided that if she did happen to stumble upon some of my work and became curious, I'd just tell her I was working on a new unit for my U.S. History class.

So, working on weekends while Sophie was gone and late at night after she was in bed, I spent almost two years getting to the point where I actually felt like I could begin writing. To try to make sense of things, I built a wall chart that cross-referenced all the people in an event timeline, assigning them code names in case Sophie discovered it. Transcribing the audio tapes was unbelievably tedious and time consuming. Eventually, I got all my ducks in a row (It doesn't get any better for a hunter!), and I was ready to start the book in earnest.

CHAPTER 19

SATURDAY, AUGUST 22, 1981

As hard as the organization had been, it seemed a breeze compared to actually writing the story itself. I didn't know how to start, what approach to take, how to fill in the knowledge gaps, or how to correctly and fairly tell a story that wasn't mine. The fact that there was no sense of urgency to the project didn't help, either; after all, I didn't know if I would ever even see Kurt and Erika again, much less have them read the finished product. Those things—combined with my natural tendency to procrastinate—made the odds of my ever finishing the book look slimmer and slimmer as the days passed.

But one Saturday in 1981 something happened that renewed my enthusiasm for finishing Kurt and Erika's story. It had been almost two years since I had last seen them in Bremen, and Sophie and the kids were gone for the weekend. It was the first time I'd been able to enjoy a cup of coffee and linger over a *Sports Illustrated* in months. I was sitting in the kitchen enjoying the deafening silence when I heard a car door slam out front. I peeked out the window and saw a stranger walking up to the front door. Sensing a sales pitch coming, I mustered up all my resistance and greeted him at the door.

"Mr. Johnson?"

"Yes."

"My name is Claude Brossard," he said as he extended his hand. He was stocky, about late forties, with straight black hair, beady eyes, and a dark complexion accented by a pencil-thin black mustache. "I have some important information about the Heislers to share with you. May I please come in?" Intense and businesslike, he projected an air of confidence and menacing strength.

Completely off guard, I hesitated, scrambling to buy some time. Who the hell was this guy, and how did he know about the Heislers? His accent sounded French, not German. Should I deny all knowledge of the Heislers? What should I tell him?

"Mr. Johnson, I know you know who I'm talking about, the two people you visited on a farm near Bremen a number of times in the late Sixties? I believe you know them as Kurt and Erika Heisler, although those are not their real names."

Brossard was clearly well-schooled in the shock technique of ambush interviewing, and he had me totally flustered. As I stood there, he studied my face, analyzing every detail. I was sure that without saying a word, I had already given this strange man the answer he wanted.

"Mr. Johnson, I think we need to go in so we can sit down and talk in private."

Warily, I opened the door and let him walk in.

"Thank you. Before we sit, could I trouble you for a glass of water?"

I pointed him toward the kitchen and had him lead the way so I wouldn't have to turn my back on him. I poured him a glass of water, refilled my coffee cup and motioned for him to sit down. I sat directly across from him.

"Thank you. I know we won't be bothered because your wife and children are in New Rockford with your parents, so let's get down to business," he said matter-of-factly.

My stomach churned at that statement, and I leaned forcefully across the table. "Now how would you know where my wife and kids are? And why would you tell me that? Are you threatening me with something?"

Without flinching a muscle he continued evenly, "I'm sorry, Mr. Johnson, I don't mean to frighten you. You have nothing to fear from me. I just want some information and I'll be on my way."

"Well, since we're in my house, why don't you give *me* some information? Just who the hell are you to come here and question me? What business is it of yours whether I know these Heislers, anyway?"

Brossard calmly took a drink of water and gave me a faint smile, which turned out to be his only pleasant gesture of the visit. "Okay, if it makes you more comfortable, I'll tell you about myself before I ask you my questions. That will give you time to compose yourself and think carefully about what you should tell me about the Heislers. I was born in France in 1934. I lived in a little village called Oradour until I was ten. In June, 1944, a unit of the Waffen SS Division Das Reich destroyed Oradour and slaughtered its inhabitants, including my family. I survived only because I was visiting a friend in another village and escaped the massacre. I need not go into the gory details. Many of the men of Das Reich who participated in the destruction of Oradour were killed during the war, but most of those who survived were captured, put on trial and given death sentences. Unfortunately, most of those sentences were reduced to prison terms because of political pressure, and virtually all of these criminals were released by the mid-Fifties."

Brossard paused. "Am I boring you, or do I have your attention?"

"I always love a good war story. Continue."

"Your friend Kurt Heisler was an intelligence officer with Das Reich. He was captured by the Americans during the Battle of the Bulge, and somehow he seems to have disappeared in the United States."

"Apparently he didn't totally disappear. You found out about him."

Smugly satisfied with himself as he warmed to his topic, Brossard proceeded. "That, Mr. Johnson, is my life's work. I am, for all intents and purposes, a professional Nazi hunter, and I have devoted my life to bringing the murderers of Oradour and other deserving members of the SS to justice."

"How lucky for you there's a career path for this sort of work. You mean you actually make a living at this?" I couldn't keep the sarcasm out of my voice.

"Let me assure you, I have the backing of some very influential people, so money is the least of my concerns."

"How do I know that any of what you're telling me is true? You could be just another nut case trolling for information. I don't have to tell you anything."

"Still playing coy, eh? That won't work for very long, Mr. Johnson, but I certainly understand your reluctance, so I'll continue. I'm sure you can understand that, given the nature of my work, I carry no credentials, but I will share some information that will verify my activities. You can check names and dates at your leisure, which should be easy for a history teacher. I spent most of the Fifties in the French Foreign Legion, just so I could track down former members of the Waffen SS hidden in their ranks. I worked in West and East Germany during the Sixties. Then I moved to France during the Seventies, but I had to leave there in 1976. It seems there was a little fire at the home of a certain Waffen SS Colonel, and he didn't make it out. Then I was in South America from 1976 until I focused my attention on America. I don't know if Kurt ever mentioned a friend of his called Otto Weber? If you get a chance to talk to Kurt again, tell him Weber died in South America. I'll just leave it at that."

I stared back at him blankly.

Brossard gave me a knowing smile. "I sense you are still uneasy with all this, Mr. Johnson. Would it help if we relaxed a bit and called each other by our first names? Please call me Claude."

"Okay, Claude, let's just try that. Yeah, yeah, you're right, now I feel much better about having a total stranger threaten me in my own house." Trying to buy some time, I got up, opened the refrigerator and pretended to look for some cream for my coffee. What I really wanted to do was crawl in and hide behind the milk, but I regained a bit of my composure. "But you still haven't told me how you know of my family's whereabouts."

Brossard continued in an almost fatherly tone. "Tom, you and your family have nothing to fear from me. You're not on trial, and I'm not here to hurt you. If that were my purpose, I'd have done it long ago without anyone ever knowing I was involved. I just want some information, and then I'll be on my way."

I was now in a full panic mode, but trying not to show it. I stood over him and attacked. "Are you crazy? How do you even dare expose yourself like this? You've just confessed to murder! What's to stop me from calling the police?"

Brossard cackled in smug self-amusement. "Oh, Mr. Johnson—I mean, Tom—most people would call me a hero, not a murderer. I have no fear in telling you whatever I want, because I don't exist, at least not in your world. Who would believe you if you told them any of this? Besides, anything you say could be dangerous to your German friends. They already know I'm looking for them, and extra publicity would only add to their problems. No, I don't think you'll be talking to anybody about this."

I sat down, fearing I was beaten. Brossard calmly checked his notebook and then continued. "I will get back to your meetings with the Heislers in a minute, but first let me finish my resume. If you need any further proof of my abilities, let me give you a glimpse into the future. Do you know of Dr. Josef Mengele, the infamous 'Angel of Death'?"

"Claude, you know I'm a history teacher, so, of course I know of him."

"Do you have any idea where he is?"

"Hiding somewhere in South America is the rumor."

"Mengele is dead. He 'drowned' off the coast of Brazil a few years ago. The officials have made no announcement yet because they are still trying to verify that the bones they found in a shallow grave are Mengele's. I can assure you, they are. The official statement will come out in a year or two, but now you know something almost no one outside of government intelligence agencies knows about."

I looked out my kitchen window at the early afternoon sun, realizing I was being sucked into a world that I knew nothing about. I gave Claude a look of resignation. "I know it's a little early, but I need a drink. If you came here to get me rattled, you've succeeded. I need some time to think."

"It's never too early for a glass of red wine. Do you have any good Cabernet?"

"On a teacher's salary with two kids? The best I can do is some cheap Rosé. I think there's some left in the jug from our last potluck card party. But I need something stronger than a glass of wine. I'm having a Jack and water."

"You Americans always go to extremes. You have to learn to relax and enjoy the pleasures of a good wine. But considering the limited choices, I'll join you with the Jack Daniels. Make mine straight up, please."

Seated again at the table with drinks in hand, we stared at each other for a while. After a long swallow, I broke the stalemate. "What do you do for fun when you're not hunting down old Nazis? No, wait—let me guess—that is your fun."

"I pick my times to relax, but this isn't one of them, and you're wasting my time. Let me give you some names. You might want to write them down so you can research them to verify my credibility."

I got a notepad and pen from the hutch beside me, and Brossard started reciting names:"Odessa, Skorzeny, Barbie, Gehlen, Monarch, and Paperclip."

"I know something about all of them except the last two." Actually, Kurt had told me about Monarch and Paperclip, too, but I didn't want to admit my knowledge for fear of giving Brossard more information than he needed about my familiarity with Kurt and Erika.

"My compliments. You're more informed than most people. There are many other names I could give you, but these are enough to get you started. Immediately after World War II ended about seven hundred Nazis and SS men came to the United States under the protection of your government. They came to work in various capacities to help win the Cold War. Then two years ago West Germany eliminated the statute of limitations on Nazi war crimes, so now many of these men are being exposed and deported, and I want to get them first."

I poured myself another drink and held out the bottle. "Another?"

"Thank you, no. I have too much to do yet this afternoon. Now that you know a little about me and what I do, what can you tell me about your visits with the Heislers?"

I shook my glass in a circular motion, clinking the ice against its sides. "Forgive me, Claude, but this is just too absurd. Here I am sitting in my house in Grand Forks talking with a French version of Simon Wiesenthal about people I haven't seen in over ten years and events that happened forty years ago. I feel like I'm in a movie, a really bad movie, by the way. But if it helps to get you out of my house faster, yes, I knew some people around Bremen by the name of Heisler way back when I was in college. Why are they of interest to you?"

Claude looked at me with what I assumed to be his best attempt at a smile. "Finally, some cooperation. They say truth is good for the soul, Tom. Now I have just a few simple questions for you. If you answer them, I'll be on my way, and you can get on with enjoying your Saturday alone and forget we ever had this conversation."

The second drink was starting to relax me, and I decided to tell him everything I knew—or almost everything—but not because I wanted any harm to come to the Heislers. I realized that nothing I could tell him could harm Kurt or Erika; in fact, my information might even help them. I was more worried about Sophie. Maybe Brossard was just testing me, but it appeared he really didn't know who she was. Either way, I didn't want to take the chance of exposing her identity by prolonging the meeting.

"Gee, Claude, or whatever the hell your real name is, it's going to be a disappointment not to get together with you and do this again real soon, so get your pencil ready, and I'll tell you what I know. I'm sure you know more about Kurt and Erika than I do, or at least about their public lives. I did visit with them a number of times during the period you men- tioned. Our first meeting was a total accident; my truck stalled while I was out hunting and theirs was the closest farm. It was just coincidence that I gained their confidence. I was a history major and a World War II buff, and we connected when I noticed a piece of Waffen SS jewelry. We talked mostly about their lives in Germany, both before and during the war. I have no knowledge of what they did when they got to America or why they were living in North Dakota, and I don't have a clue about where they are now or what they're doing. I have received a few short notes from them over the years, none with a return address or a way to contact them. The notes contained greetings and occasional comments about current events, but never any information about their whereabouts."

"May I see the notes, Tom?"

"No, I threw them away. I'm not the sentimental type who saves stuff like that, and there was never a return address, so there was no point in keeping them."

"And your wife never got suspicious about these mailings?"

"I get stuff all the time from old football buddies, former students, teachers who left for greener pastures, you name it. She doesn't read my mail or even ask me about that kind of stuff. Even if she did, what's there to tell? That I met a couple from Germany while I was hunting their sloughs and got to know them a little bit? There were lots of German farmers around Bremen, and I got to know many of them. They all have a story to tell if you spend time with them. Believe me, the last thing my wife wants to hear is another one of my hunting stories."

I paused for a reaction, and Claude, ever the stoic interrogator, remained silent and expressionless, so I soldiered on. "I believe Kurt and Erika are good people. I know Kurt did some evil things on the Russian Front, and Erika supported the Nazi party, but it makes it easier to understand if you consider their circumstances. Like many other Germans, they got caught up in situations they weren't prepared to handle. They believed they were misled by Hitler and seemed genuinely sorry for some of their actions. But if you're suggesting that Kurt participated in the incident you describe at Oradour, well, from what I know of him, I just can't believe that."

"Tom, you're either very naïve or a fool. I'll give you the benefit of the doubt and call you naïve. I'm sure there were some normal people among the Waffen SS, but they were the exceptions. Moral beings couldn't do what the Waffen SS did. War brings out the beast in all of us, but even beasts have limits. The Waffen SS had no limits."

"And just what are your limits, Claude? Are contract killings for revenge more honorable than wartime atrocities? Do the executions come easier if they're justified by your political beliefs? Especially if they fatten your bank account?"

Brossard didn't answer. We sat and stared at each other for a few minutes. Then he jotted a few final comments in his notebook, stood up and said, "Thank you, Tom, for your time and for the drink. I'm convinced you don't have much more to offer me, so I doubt you'll ever see or hear of me again. Here's a bit of parting advice, though. I assume you know that Kurt has a brother named Jurgen. He's an evil man, and I suggest you never mess with him. I'm also on his trail, and you should hope that I find him before you ever get the chance to meet him. By the way, have you ever been contacted by the Runic Butterfly?"

"No, I've never heard of them. Who are they?"

"Just be careful if you ever hear from them," he said solemnly.

"Thanks for the tip, and I have a final question for you. Kurt and Erika did keep telling me that there were a lot of things they couldn't share with me, that it was for my own protection. Are you what they were protecting me from?"

I got the tight, smug smile one more time before he walked out the door.

"Goodbye, Tom."

I watched him drive away, relieved that he hadn't pressed me further on the letters or on Sophie's involvement. Maybe the CIA really did know how to keep a secret. Nevertheless, I couldn't take the chance that Brossard really knew Sophie's identity. I had to let the CIA boys know about Claude Brossard immediately. Over the years I had met a number of CIA staff as they periodically checked on Sophie, so I called her most recent CIA contact and left a message about Brossard's visit as soon as he was out of sight. I got a return call within five minutes.

"This is Ronald Wolfe returning a call to this number. Who am I speaking to?"

"This is Tom Johnson, Sophie's husband. You and I met briefly about six months back, Ron. Thanks for returning my call so quickly. The visitor who just left made me very nervous."

"Tom, are Sophie and the children there now?"

"No, they're at my folks in New Rockford, and this Brossard guy told me that as he sat in my living room. How the hell would he know that? Should I contact Sophie just to touch base? Should I be worried?"

"No, hold on while I have someone alert the authorities there and ask them to do a few inconspicuous drive-bys at your parents' house just to make sure everything's okay. I don't really think they're in danger, but I'll get back to you if we hear anything different. Hold on a sec."

I waited while he put me on hold, hoping I had done the right thing by alerting the CIA. Given Brossard's creepiness, it didn't take much for me to imagine all kinds of gruesome scenarios as the seconds ticked by.

"Okay, it's done. I'm sure you know there's a state trooper who lives in New Rockford, and he's going to check things out right away and also contact the local police. Right now I need you to fill me in on the details of your meeting with Brossard."

"I will, Ron, but first I need to know, is he who he says he is?"

"Yes, from your description, it sounds like it really was Claude Brossard, and he is exactly who he claims to be. Give me a rundown of the meeting while it's still fresh in your mind. Take as long as you need, and don't leave anything out, even seemingly minor details."

I recounted the day's events while Wolfe took notes, assuming that our conversation was probably being recorded as well. We were on the phone a good hour—interrupted once by the trooper's call to Ron telling him everything was fine in New Rockford—before he felt satisfied that I had given him everything I knew.

I jumped in when he paused to review his notes. "So, do I have to be worried here, Ron? Is he as dangerous as he makes out to be?"

"Unfortunately, he is, and this meeting fits his MO exactly. He's a fierce Nazi hunter and an alleged killer. We don't get too concerned about his killing Nazis; we just want to make sure he's not killing the Nazis who work for the CIA. He usually comes out of nowhere, catches people off guard, does his thing and disappears. We've been tailing him on and off for years, but he's a slippery devil with powerful friends and a lot of money, and he knows every trick in the book when it comes to moving under the radar screen. We knew he'd been in the States for a while, but we lost him in Boston about three weeks ago. The one good thing I can tell you about him is that he's never been known to harm civilians, so I'm quite sure that there's no threat to you or Sophie or the kids, at least as long as he doesn't know she's Kurt and Erika's daughter. Even then it would be totally out of his MO to harm them; he'd just try to bluff information out of them like he did with you. Right now I'm confident that he doesn't know who Sophie is."

By now my heart was racing, and my calm demeanor had totally vanished. "That's easy for you to say sitting safely in an office somewhere, but I need a little more convincing." My voice was rising as I spoke. "If you didn't even know he was here until I called, how the hell can you be so sure that he'll leave Sophie and my kids alone?"

"Because he's a creature of habit, and subtlety is not his strong suit. From your description of the events, you probably got a good idea of his personality and how he operates. Believe me, if he knew who Sophie was, he'd have gone right after her and not wasted time on you. The fact that he came at you first leads me to believe that he's really just fishing. He didn't get what he wanted, so he'll probably move on to new territory. Guys like Brossard are like sharks; if they quit moving, they die. Just to be on the safe side, though, we have to bring Sophie in on this so she can be on the lookout if he returns. I want to meet with the two of you as soon as she gets back. In the meantime if you think of anything you left out, call me right away."

I hung up and contemplated the implications of the day's events. There was no way I could keep the book from Sophie any longer. I would have to come clean on everything. My biggest problem would be deciding whether to tell her about the book before we met with Ron or after, as each choice presented its own risks.

To reassure myself I called Sophie while she was in New Rockford to make sure everything was okay. I told her I couldn't find the checkbook and then held my silence through the predictable verbal abuse regarding the male gender's inability to function without a female around to take care of them—with my mother cackling approval in the background—but it was worth it just to hear that everything was okay. Then, on Sunday morning, after rethinking my strategy about what kind of fake excuse to use for calling again, I phoned before Sophie was about to head back and told her to have dad check the tire pressure on the left front tire because it had been leaking. She thought it was kind of sweet that I would think of their safety, so I didn't have to suffer through any more slights to my gender.

They got back home around three. I asked Sophie how the trip went, and she said, "I can't believe all the Highway Patrol cars we saw today. They must have had speed traps set up or something, because we hardly ever see them on that road. I was lucky, though, and saw them all ahead of time, so I saved you some money ... no ticket." She was cute and adorable in her smugness.

Sophie and I put the kids to bed around eight o'clock and retired to our own room around nine, where we lay in bed for a while watching television. In between commercials I finally got up the nerve to tell her about Brossard, and I shut the set off. "Sophie, we need to talk about something that happened over the weekend. And before you get pissed at me, which I know you will, you need to really hear me out, because we have a potentially dangerous situation on our hands, and your being mad at me is only going to make things worse. Now, can you agree to listen to what I have to say before you start?"

"What, did you go out and get drunk with your softball buddies again and embarrass yourself? I swear, if you don't get away from some of those bums, they're going to … "

"Sophie, you're not listening to me. This is serious! A man came to our house yesterday looking for your parents, and he knew where you and the kids were. He's a Nazi hunter, a killer that the CIA has been trying to get for a long time, and he was here in our house grilling me about your parents. I called the CIA as soon as he left, and they had the New Rockford cops driving by mom and dad's house just to make sure nothing unusual was going on. He's the real deal, and we're meeting Ron Wolfe tomorrow night to talk about this whole situation."

"A killer! Oh my god, Tom, here in our house? How'd he find us? Does he know who I am? Do we have to take the kids and get out of here? How come you didn't tell me when we were on the phone? He could have been after us, and we wouldn't have even known!"

"I'd never have done things this way if I'd thought you were in danger. The CIA is convinced he doesn't know who you are, or he'd have gone right after you, and I think they're right this time. He somehow got my name and found out I had known Kurt and Erika back in Bremen, and he wanted to know if I knew where they are. Fortunately, I didn't have to bluff him, because we don't know where they are. I think he left satisfied with my answers, but I didn't dare take any chances, so I got the CIA involved. Now, if we can talk about this rationally, I'll fill you in on the details so you're up to speed when we meet with Ron tomorrow night."

"Rationally? A killer in the house and you think I can just sit here and talk about it like an old friend dropped over for a chat? How did you expect me to react? Dammit, Tom, give me a break!" There was a long, suspenseful pause before she spoke again. "Why don't you get me a glass of wine to help calm me down a bit, and then you can fill me in."

"I think the wine is a good idea, because I haven't even gotten to the part where you're going to be really pissed at me." By now her eyes were smoldering, and I had to turn away a bit to dampen the effect, or I wouldn't be able to get my story out. "You know that project I've been working on for my class? The one about World War II that you've been complaining is taking so much of my time? Well, that's really a book that I've been writing about your mom and dad. I saw them in secret one weekend in 1979, and I promised them I'd write a book about them so you and Bruce and Sara would know more about their real lives. I've barely started the book itself, and now this Brossard thing has added a whole new dimension to the story."

Sophie started to speak, but couldn't get a complete sentence out. She looked shocked, angry and confused all at the same time and just sat there sputtering.

"I think now is a good time for me to get the wine," I said as I retreated to the kitchen.

Over the next three hours and a bottle of chardonnay I walked through the whole episode with Brossard and my follow-up call with Ron Wolfe. Sophie eventually calmed down enough to listen, although she pointedly reserved the right to stay mad at me about the book and to bring it up again at a time of her choosing. We ended the discussion by making a list of questions for our meeting with Ron the next night.

———

We got a baby sitter for Monday night and met Ron at a small, nondescript office building in downtown Grand Forks. There were no signs on the front of the building, and neither Sophie nor I had ever been inside it before. Ron was waiting for us in the parking lot and immediately steered us into a small office. The office was as sparse as the rest of the surroundings, just a few chairs and a desk. There was nothing on the walls, and not a single item in sight that revealed anything about the occupants.

We sat down in front of the desk. Ron took the chair behind the desk, leaned forward and starting talking. "I know this is frightening, Sophie, but I want you to know that we've taken extra precautions to protect you and Bruce and Sara. Tom's probably told you that we had the authorities in New Rockford checking on you, but we also alerted the Highway Patrol, and they monitored your trip back to Grand Forks."

Sophie and I exchanged a quick glance, and she started laughing and said, "So that's what that was all about. I thought I was just lucky!"

"We couldn't take the chance that Brossard would go after you," Ron continued, "but here's the good news. We learned last night that he boarded a plane in Minneapolis under a different name and then connected in New York to a flight to Europe. He was one step ahead of us again, but at least we know he's not around here anymore. Brossard handles a lot of cases about missing Nazis, and my guess is he got a hot lead on another one. Just the same, we're going to have a few extra folks around keeping any eye on your family for a while. Do you two have any questions about anything before I let you go?"

"I've got one," I said. "How do you suppose he connected me to Kurt and Erika and tracked me to Grand Forks? They left Bremen in the late Sixties and no one here even knows anything about my relationship with them other than you guys."

"He probably snooped around and tracked you down the same way we did. Don't forget, he's one of the best in the business. I've got to tell you, though, Tom, a rank amateur could have sniffed this one out. Everybody in a ten-county area knew that ugly green truck you drove back then. Hell, we interviewed farmers who couldn't pick Hitler out of a lineup, but they all knew the Johnson kid from New Rockford who drove a butt-ugly Chevy pickup and hunted their sloughs. Trust me, Brossard didn't have to do much work to find you; we're just amazed he or someone else didn't show up sooner. But we do think you convinced him that you didn't know any-thing. He's a tenacious bloodhound when he gets a whiff of opportunity, and he'd never have left if he thought there was more to the trail here."

Sophie gave me a relieved look, sighed and then looked at Ron. "Well, we sure hope you're right. Just tell your guys not to be so obvious when they're checking up on us. Usually I can spot them a mile away, and I don't want my kids to see me get upset and have them wonder what's up."

Ron was a little taken aback and struggled with a comeback, but Sophie pressed on. "By the way, you don't know where my parents are, do you? Brossard wasn't here because they'd been here recently, was he?"

"Sophie, you know I couldn't tell you even if I knew where your parents are, but, in truth, I really don't know, and I don't know anyone else in the agency who does either, but that's not unusual. I don't believe Brossard's being here was because of anything like that. I think he happened to be in the Midwest checking on someone else and decided to follow up on a cold lead regarding Tom's relationship with your parents. But I guess we won't really know that until we catch him. Or maybe your parents can fill us both in if they ever show up around here again."

We shook hands with Ron and headed home, relieved, but determined to be cautious.

CHAPTER 20

After Brossard's visit, everything was out in the open, so working on the book became easier. I realized more than ever that I wanted Sophie, Bruce and Sara to be able to learn about Kurt and Erika in a new way, hoping they could all reconcile before it was too late. Plus, the added twist of Brossard hunting down Kurt and Erika inspired me to finish their story before he might catch them.

Armed with this renewed sense of purpose, on my first free weekend I pulled Kurt and Erika's box out of the closet once more to see if I could find a starting point for the book. I had already decided to follow their advice about writing their story as a novel rather than a documentary, but I chose not to write it from Kurt's viewpoint as he had suggested. I also determined there was no way I could include all of their material in one book, so I needed to pare it down. My final issue, then, was to decide on the book's viewpoint. From my own research I knew there were many books detailing Nazi atrocities, but few that actually described how Germans reached the point of acceptance for such evil acts, but I wasn't sure how to bridge that gap.

As I stared at the artifacts, hoping for some inspiration, Kurt's pewter Nordic warrior—the one I had knocked over the first day I met the Heislers—caught my eye. I placed it on the desk and studied it for a while, questioning why it was the only object Kurt had kept from his childhood. I tried to conjure up all the feelings the statue had evoked in Kurt as a young boy from a good Christian family growing up in pre-war Germany. I recalled my conversations with Kurt and Erika in the Bremen farmhouse and my efforts to reconcile my feelings for them with their earlier acts. In short, how could such seemingly good people do such terrible things? I contemplated the concepts of good and evil and the question of what constitutes a moral war, and after much internal deliberation I concluded that in order for us to determine how good people can be seduced by evil, we must first understand what attracted them to that evil.

With these thoughts in mind, I chose to write the book as an impartial observer, integrating Kurt and Erika's personal stories involving real events with my knowledge of World War II history in an attempt to provide a proper historical perspective. Most of the people, events, and dates depicted in the book that follows are as accurate as I can make them, except for family names and a few minor characters I added to move things along. The conversations are as I imagined they might be based on the many hours I spent with Kurt and Erika. Despite my best efforts to be impartial, I'm sure I subconsciously injected myself into the story as Kurt's alter ego from time to time. Here, then, is Kurt and Erika's story presented as a work of historical fiction. My goal was to do justice to their story and to history, and I hope I've succeeded. Knowing Kurt and Erika as I do, I think they would approve.

KURT AND ERIKA'S STORY: "THE BOOK"

CHAPTER I

A Knight Returns

In 1937 Germany was alive again, compliments of Adolf Hitler and the Nazi Party. Germany had been united by this one man, a myopic dreamer who had hypnotized the nation with promises of revenge and future greatness. For years Hitler had been holding the nation's citizens spellbound, blanketing Germany with a torrent of passionate rhetoric and a steady diet of parades, speeches, and rallies to keep the fires of the faithful kindled at an emotional peak. Everywhere, Germans were in a constant state of excitement and adoration, and everyone and everything was engaged in the relentless task of constructing the Third Reich. As a result, the economy was continuing to rebound from the effects of the Versailles Treaty and the Great Depression. To Germans, prosperity and Hitler were synonymous. The fact that certain groups, like the Jews, were being used as scapegoats for past woes was largely sublimated for the greater good.

Kurt and Erika's story begins in Ansbach, a small city southwest of Nuremberg with a history stretching back over 1,200 years. During the Ninth Century Ansbach had become the capital of middle Franconia, the predominately rural section of Northern Bavaria. During the Middle

Ages the Margraves of Brandenburg had made Ansbach their home, building their unique, Baroque-style residences alongside the historic Castle Gardens and the churches of St. Johannis and St. Gumbertus, giving Ansbach its classic German fairy-tale look. During the 1930s, however, Ansbach's claim to fame was its nearness to Nuremberg, the host city for the annual fall Nazi Party Rally. During this "season of spectacle" the entire region was a blur of flying banners, helmeted warriors and marching feet, accompanied by omnipresent, blaring loudspeakers.

———

On a lazy summer afternoon in August, 1937, a friendly sun extended its warm, paternal rays over Ansbach as two boys walked leisurely along a narrow, winding street between tall, thin buildings.

"Hey, Kurt. I heard your brother Jurgen's coming home tomorrow. When can I come over and talk to him about the army?" Ernst Meyer's handsome face radiated a luster of inner intensity.

"Ernst, you idiot, how many times have I told you? My brother's not in the regular army. He's in the SS," said Kurt Heisler.

Ernst, a robust youth of seventeen, was a prototype German boy: blond hair and blue eyes, just a shade over six feet tall, well built with finely-chiseled features. Kurt, the boy lucky enough to have an older brother already serving the Fatherland, was a little taller than Ernst and not as well built, but he was trim, athletic and possessed the same desired Aryan features. Ernst was a young man of strong emotional impulses, while Kurt was more reserved and introspective, yet they were great friends. Truly, these eager lads with the fire of youth burning in their souls had all the makings of future knights in Hitler's legions.

Kurt grabbed Ernst by his shoulders. "How did you know Jurgen was coming home? No one knows but our family."

"Are you kidding?" Ernst replied in a slightly mocking voice. "When one of the town heroes comes home, everybody finds out."

"What do you mean 'hero?' We aren't at war. Jurgen hasn't done anything heroic that I know of. So far, he's just my brother."

Ernst looked at Kurt in youthful amazement. "Kurt, you don't understand how lucky you are. If I had a brother in the Leibstandarte—Hitler's personal bodyguard—who had marched into the Rhineland and made the French back down, why, I'd be bragging all over Ansbach."

"Well, he's not your brother, he's mine, and I guess what Jurgen's doing is okay, but I'm not sure I'd pick the SS over the regular army."

"I bet you'll pick the Leibstandarte. We all will. You and me, and Walter, and Klaus, and Horst. Anyway, I don't want to get you going about the SS. You get too damn serious. Let's go over to Walter's and see if his mother's baked anything today."

As Kurt and Ernst continued down the street to the home of Walter Kruger, the third member of their boyhood gang, they engaged in typical, carefree, adolescent conversation. Yet, tangled among his outward laughter and verbal banter with Ernst, feelings of doubt simmered within Kurt. He could not stop thinking about Jurgen. Talking with friends, Kurt usually gave the impression Jurgen was a distant stranger who was largely forgotten by his family, but, secretly, Kurt burned with a desire to talk to his long-lost brother. Ernst would be surprised if he knew how proud Kurt really was of Jurgen's membership in the Leibstandarte Adolf Hitler.

Kurt's parents, however, didn't share Kurt's enthusiasm for Jurgen's military choice. As Catholics, the Heislers were not exactly avid Hitler supporters, and they differed in their opinions of him. Herr Heisler, a librarian, was a soft-spoken, mild-mannered intellectual who had studied the rise of Hitler and the Nazi Party. Twice he had gone to Nuremberg to witness firsthand the spectacle of the annual Party Rally and had come away impressed by Hitler's oratory and his ability to captivate his audience. Nevertheless, Fritz Heisler was not the type who made his mind up quickly, and he was still evaluating Hitler's abilities and ideas. All the pomp and ceremony surrounding the Nazis might be enough for some people to surrender their souls to Hitler, but Fritz, a distinguished, rational thinker in his early fifties, had to make up his own mind. He still maintained some reservations concerning the Third Reich, but so far he had given Hitler a rather guarded nod of semi-approval, subject to how future events might unfold.

Eva Heisler, a small, soft-spoken woman in her late forties, had no such ambivalence about Hitler; she was against him and everything he stood for. Fritz and Eva often discussed the political situation in Germany, and Fritz would sometimes point out all the economic and political good the Nazis had accomplished. He told Eva that she was overly emotional concerning Hitler, that he was not as evil as she proclaimed. Such analysis carried no weight with Eva, a tender, compassionate woman who had a love for all people. The idea of a "master race" was foreign to her character, and she considered Hitler and his ideology to be barbaric and inhuman.

Eva had tried to influence Jurgen, but he had somehow disappeared into the folds of Nazidom before she even realized he was leaning in that direction. Jurgen, a strong-willed young man who believed what he wanted to, was concerned about his place among other men, so the benefit of belonging to a group that espoused the philosophy of the superiority of the Aryan Race and defended the "Holy Grail" of Germanic purity was not lost on his ambitious nature. Jurgen had left home to seek his fortune in the summer of 1930 and had not been home since, casting his lot with the Nazis when he was only sixteen. During his time away he had joined the Nazi Party and become a member of the elite SS formation that served as Hitler's personal bodyguard, the Leibstandarte Adolf Hitler, or LAH. Now, after an extended absence, Jurgen was coming home, and Eva was worried.

Eva had tried to keep Kurt from dwelling on the life that his older brother was leading, but she was afraid she wouldn't be able to limit Jurgen's influence once he arrived. During his seven years away Jurgen had written only sporadically, but these letters were Eva's greatest concern. She could trace the development of Jurgen's hardness and lack of conscience by simply arranging his letters in chronological order. Each letter contained more praise for Hitler and the Third Reich than the one before. Eva hated to admit that her oldest son was a Nazi and a member of the SS, and, regretting her failure with Jurgen, she had vowed to keep

Kurt from falling under the same evil Nazi spell. In Kurt, Eva saw all the qualities that she valued: compassion, sincerity, tenderness, intelligence and respect. Surely, she thought, a boy possessing these qualities could never become mesmerized by Hitler's hallucinations. Until now Eva's efforts to shield Kurt had been successful, or so she thought, as she had managed to keep him from the influences of the party until the last possible moment. Although Kurt was a member of the mandatory Hitler Youth Program, he had not joined until late in 1934 when he was fourteen, even though his friends had all joined when they were nine or ten.

In 1937 there were nearly six million participants in the Hitler Youth Program. After Hitler had assumed total control of Germany upon the death of President Hindenburg in 1934, the Program had grown dramatically, eventually displacing a lot of the formal education of German youth. Catholic and Protestant schools were closed, and by 1936 enrollment in the Hitler Youth had become mandatory; parents faced heavy fines or imprisonment for keeping their children out of the Program. Over time the original academic aspects of the education had been supplanted by an indoctrination that promoted emotional devotion to Hitler and the State and an emphasis on physical fitness. This indoctrination spanned all phases of life and included prayers and oaths of allegiance to Hitler and the State. Hitler Youth summer camps, bike excursions, and campouts were designed to create an enjoyable combination of play and training. Group identity replaced individuality, so a great deal of time was spent on games and athletic contests to improve fitness and teamwork. By stressing emotional nationalism through game-like activities, the Program promoted extreme bonds of loyalty to Germany and to one another. To further expand the team concept, the Nazi Party placed special emphasis on training young members of the Hitler Youth to recognize and report enemies of the State, like the Jews. Organizationally, there was a distinct hierarchy in the Hitler Youth, from the smallest local unit on up. Ten-year olds commanded eight-year olds, twelve-year olds commanded ten-year olds and so on, and special leadership schools nurtured members who exhibited strong potential for command. Most German youths during this period had no real childhoods; they were in constant training to serve the state, become good soldiers, and follow orders without question. In this environment the State quickly became the religion of the youth of Germany, and many parents willingly forfeited control of their children.

Frau Heisler was not one of those parents; she remained steadfast in her struggle to keep Kurt from joining the dark side. It worried her that all the propaganda forced upon the Hitler Youth would eventually inundate Kurt and overpower his resistance, and she felt it was her job to keep things in perspective by balancing the Nazi indoctrination with reason. She had been unable to prevent Kurt from joining the Hitler Youth, but she countered this program of pagan misinformation with one of her own based on Christian principles. Eva hoped that by doing so she could establish a middle ground whereby Kurt could participate in the activities of the Hitler Youth without losing sight of the dangers that the Nazi philosophy presented.

Despite her precautions, Eva had underestimated both the effectiveness of the Hitler Youth Program and Kurt's ability to placate her about his moral development. Unknown to Eva, Kurt's internal scale had already tilted to the side of the twisted cross. Initially, Kurt enjoyed the camaraderie and competition connected with the Hitler Youth, but he was skeptical about some aspects of the program of indoctrination. Over time, though, given the enthusiastic attitudes of his friends and the constant bombardment of propaganda from youth leaders and Nazi officials, Kurt slowly slipped under the spell of the Nazi mystique. He had succeeded in rationalizing his own conscience to the degree that he felt he was still in total control, even though he was not.

On this August day Kurt and his friends had spent most of the afternoon just lounging in Walter's backyard talking about sports, hunting, and Jurgen's homecoming. Kurt had secretly read two of his brother's letters, and he was bursting with questions to ask him. He kept wondering why his mother was always degrading the Nazis. After all, they had regained much of Germany's lost glory, restored order, and revived the economy. The only people who seemed to suffer at the hands of the "New Order" were groups detrimental to the overall good of Germany.

To restore some order to his internal chaos, Kurt had decided on a course of action. The confusion caused by his mother's advice on the one hand and the pull of his peers on the other needed to be addressed. Kurt had decided that he must first talk with Jurgen, alone, and then attend the next Nuremberg Rally and see Hitler for himself. Then he would sit down, evaluate all aspects of the Nazi philosophy and make a decision about his future. Kurt had gone to the 1936 Nuremberg Rally with his father, but this time he wanted to go by himself. He had never been selected to be a Hitler Youth participant in the Rallies, but his friends had, and their stories filled him with dreams of glory.

"Hey, Heisler, you're dreaming again," Walter shouted.

"I guess I'm just bored listening to you, Walter."

Ernst chimed in, "Well, I'm dreaming about supper. Let's go eat and meet again tomorrow. I'm heading home."

Ernst and Kurt started for home, and when their paths separated, Ernst implored, "Kurt, I want to meet Jurgen. Don't you dare keep him to yourself!"

A few minutes later Kurt was walking up the steps to the front door of his home, a modest building that looked much like the surrounding houses—tall, narrow, and neat. As Kurt opened the door, he heard his mother yell, "Kurt, where've you been? Do you know what time it is?"

Kurt looked at his watch. "It's six o'clock. Why, is something wrong?"

"Wrong! Didn't you remember that we're eating early tonight?"

"Sorry, Ernst, Walter and I were fooling around, and I just forgot."

"Well, hurry up and get ready. We're eating in five minutes."

They were eating early because Frau Heisler wanted to discuss the coming visit of her long absent son. Increasingly concerned about the effect Jurgen's visit might have on Kurt, she wanted to make sure he understood the danger that Jurgen represented. Kurt knew that his mother was preparing to bombard him with warnings about Jurgen and the evil SS, but, surprisingly, supper passed with only normal conversation, so he relaxed. But as soon as the table had been cleared, Eva sprang into action.

"Fritz, Kurt, let's go sit in the living room and talk about Jurgen's visit."

Once they were comfortably seated, Eva came straight to the point. "Kurt, I know you have a certain admiration for your older brother, even though you can hardly remember him. Please don't be fooled by his appearance, his uniform, or his words. He represents an evil force in Germany!"

"Why do you say that, Mother? What has the SS actually done besides lock up a few enemies of the State and try to keep the Jews from ruining our country?"

"Kurt Heisler, where do you learn such stupidity? At your Hitler Youth meetings? These 'enemies of the state,' as you call them, have done nothing wrong except oppose Hitler in some way, and the Jews, tell me, what have the Jews done wrong to merit such scorn from the Nazis?"

Fritz interrupted, "Eva, maybe we should wait and give Jurgen a chance to talk before we form any conclusions about his role with the SS."

Eva shouted at her husband. "Why? You've read his letters. You know how he feels. I don't need to talk to him to understand how he feels about the SS."

"Mom, Dad, Jurgen's not really with the part of the SS that arrests Jews and people like that. He's with the Leibstandarte. Jurgen's role is more like that of a soldier, a special type of soldier whose duty it is to guard Hitler."

Kurt's comment suggested that he had moved more toward the other side than Eva had suspected, and she was white with rage and fear. "Nonsense, utter nonsense," she screamed. "Kurt, you'd better go to your room and pray to God that he forgives you for saying such horrid things. Spend some time thinking about the real significance of the stupidity you've just uttered. I don't think you really understand the reality of Jurgen's situation. We'll finish our talk tomorrow."

After Kurt had gone to his room, Fritz gently admonished his wife. "Eva, I've never seen you become so angry so quickly. I think we should have let Kurt stay and continued our discussion. We didn't solve anything by punishing him for speaking out."

"You're right, Fritz. I shouldn't have acted in anger. But I can't help myself when Kurt talks like he did tonight. He doesn't usually defend Hitler or the SS, so I thought I had things under control. I'll bet that all that trash he has to listen to at his Hitler Youth activities is having an effect. Then again, maybe he's just excited about seeing his brother for the first time in seven years. I'll calm down, relax, and get ready for tomorrow."

Upstairs, Kurt had begun reading a book on Norse mythology. His room was small, but pleasant. Framed hunting scenes and family portraits lined the walls, and a simple crucifix adorned the wall next to the bed. Kurt had always been somewhat of a dreamer, totally captivated by stories dealing with folklore and Teutonic legends, and as he lay on the bed thumbing through the pages, the images of warrior maidens flying through the sky on their winged steeds seemed only too real. He looked up from the book and stared briefly at the crucifix. As he searched for a cause to champion amidst a society steeped in the glorification of a dark, heroic past, the line between religion and fantasy became hard to distinguish.

Kurt got up and walked over to the open window. It was dark as death outside, and the blackness provided a perfect background for the stars to parade their brilliance. Gazing up at the stars, Kurt felt himself being magically transported into the heavens. The sparkling dots of light filled the room with an unearthly glow, and the universe appeared to be painted on the ceiling. Transfixed by this illusion, Kurt felt like he could touch a star just by reaching out his hand.

He looked down and picked up a small pewter statue from the bookshelf and placed it on the windowsill. The miniature Nordic warrior from the Dark Ages wore a pointed, winged helmet and held a raised sword in one hand and a shield in the other. His head was tilted backward as if he were invoking the Gods to hear him. The rough leggings binding the boots and the full, bushy beard completed the image of the powerful warrior. As Kurt stood spellbound, conjuring up heroic deeds, feats of grandeur, and acts of knightly honor, the statue seemed to grow as it reflected the magic starlight. As a barking dog outside the window jarred Kurt back to reality, his final image was of Jurgen and the statue merging into one surreal symbol of Teutonic greatness.

Kurt finally forced himself to lie down, but sleep did not come easily that night. He was bursting with questions about his older brother. What would Jurgen be like? How much had he changed since he had left home so long ago? What would it be like to actually talk with someone who was one of Hitler's personal bodyguards? It was hard to imagine his own brother as a member of the Leibstandarte, the most elite group of the SS.

Kurt shot up in bed. A bright sun was already well on its way to its noonday position, which could only mean he had overslept. A noise had interrupted his deep sleep, and before he realized he was awake, he was looking out the window. It promised to be a beautiful summer day, but Kurt wouldn't have noticed if the trees were growing upside down. His eyes were riveted on a majestic figure removing a suitcase from the trunk of a car in front of the house.

As the car drove off, Jurgen Heisler turned slowly around and gazed unemotionally at his old home. Suddenly a window on the second floor caught his eye. Jurgen heard his name being called by a frantic figure nearly falling out of the window. In mid-wave, the figure disappeared, as Kurt was already running down the stairs. About halfway down the stairs, he realized it would not be proper to meet one of Hitler's elite guards looking like a child who had overslept and hadn't dressed. Turning in mid-stride, he ran back to his room to put on some clothes. As he fumbled with his buttons, he surmised that his dad would soon be home for lunch and his mother must be really concerned about Jurgen's arrival in order for her to let him sleep so late. Kurt couldn't let go of the image he had just seen outside, a tall, black-clad German knight looking as strong and imposing as an ebony statue.

After he'd made himself presentable, Kurt hesitated before going downstairs. What should he say to Jurgen? Should he call him Jurgen? Brother? Lieutenant? Kurt threw back his shoulders and descended the stairs two at a time to meet a protector of Aryan purity. As he reached the kitchen, Kurt could hear voices, so he approached cautiously. Before entering, he stopped to listen to the conversation between his mother and his brother. From the little that he could make out, Kurt decided that everything seemed to be okay. Eva and Jurgen were talking politely, although in a rather cold, matter-of-fact manner, certainly not what you would expect between a mother and son who had not seen each other for seven years. But they weren't yelling. Hearing a pause, Kurt entered the kitchen.

Jurgen, who was standing only six feet away, was a magnificent physical specimen, well over six feet tall and slightly over 200 pounds. He stood in black, immaculately polished boots that extended to his knees, pants tucked neatly inside. Pants, jacket, belt and tie, all were black with white and silver accent trim. Everything was spotless, pressed, and perfectly arranged, but the small symbol on Jurgen's right collar fascinated Kurt the most. Stamped on the black background of his brother's right collar tab was a silver rectangle, inside of which were the twin lightning bolts that symbolized the SS. Kurt gazed at the silver streaks as if they had been handed to his brother by an ancient God on a mist-shrouded mountain-top. Never before had Kurt seen anything to inspire such respect and admiration, such fear and uneasiness, such pride and patriotism as the figure before him. Jurgen turned and gave Kurt a cold, penetrating glance.

Kurt froze.

"Heil Hitler, little brother. How do you like my uniform? By the look on your face, I'd say you think I'm the devil himself. Well, don't be shy. What do you have to say to your long lost brother?"

Kurt managed to stammer, "Welcome home, Jurgen. It's good to see you. How long are you going to be here?"

"Not very long, I'm afraid. I have to go to Nuremberg shortly and take part in preparation for the great Party Rally in September. As a member of the Leibstandarte Adolf Hitler, I'll be marching past der Fuhrer. You should all come to Nuremberg and participate in the Rally. It is the duty of all true Germans to do so."

Kurt simply stood before Jurgen in awe. Truly, this magnificent man before him was a symbol of German greatness! Kurt was bursting with pride as he basked in the glow of his brother's presence. All thoughts of the danger Jurgen represented disappeared as Kurt tried to win his brother's approval.

"How long did you say you were going to stay with us?"

Eva's question produced an immediate, cold response from Jurgen. "Dearest Mother, I assure you, you will only have to endure my evil influence for a day or two. A couple of my friends are going to pick me up in a few days because we need to rejoin the Leibstandarte."

"Then you won't be here for church on Sunday?" replied Eva.

"No, and if I were here on Sunday, I wouldn't be going to church. Religion serves only as an ointment for the weak. Church is a place for women, the old and the sick. The future of our country does not lie in some simple sermon uttered by a village priest, but in the message of our leader, Adolf Hitler. What did the church do to regain our lost power? What did religion do to build up Germany and make it strong again? Nothing! Now that we are again taking our rightful place in the world, the church would have us be kind to the same ones who caused us to suffer in the first place, people like the Jews. Germany can only fulfill her destiny if she assumes control over the dark, ignorant races of the world, the barbarians who are constantly trying to taint our pure Aryan blood. What good is a race of superior beings if they allow inferiors to have equal status and pollute society? The only proper place for Jews, Slavs, or other such malcontents is as servants of their masters, the true Aryan Germans."

Jurgen paused for a moment to let the significance of his oratory sink in. "Religion would have us treat these inferiors as equals. How ludicrous that such filth could be equated with the Teutonic races. You should read Darre's book *Blood and Soil* so you would be better able to understand the logic of what I'm saying. The SS, the Leibstandarte, is an order of German Knighthood that is being created to guard the German people from such lesser races as the Jews. In order to get into the Leibstandarte, a person must be able to trace his ancestors back hundreds of years and prove no trace of Jewish blood exits. We are our own religion, and we certainly don't need one that is shared by lower beings."

Eva, flushed with rage, could contain herself no longer. "Do you think you're all Gods? Do you think you really are supermen, a master race? Do you think nothing can harm you? I've never heard such ridiculous conceit in my life. I'm tempted to kick you out of your own home! Obviously, during the last seven years you've lost any degree of morality that you ever had. I've failed as a mother and as a Christian."

"Mother, you're being overdramatic. I'll say no more about this matter while I'm at home, at least to you. Suffice it to say that someday you'll be proud to say your son was an early member of the Leibstandarte. Please show me to my room. I wish to clean up."

Kurt had not moved an inch since Jurgen had begun to speak, and he watched in amazement as his mother, jaw clenched in anger, led his brother out of the kitchen. As they left the room, Jurgen turned to Kurt and said, "My brother, I'd like to talk with you later." Mother and son then disappeared from sight.

Kurt stood in a state of total confusion and conflicting emotions. He loved his mother and had just seen his older brother treat her as if she were an ignorant child, yet he had been mesmerized by Jurgen's speech. The image of the black knight who had just stood before him was reaching into Kurt's soul. He felt an almost swoon-like desire to follow in the steps of his brother. Surely, the destiny of Germany must be in the hands of men like Jurgen! As stirrings of patriotism and service to the Fatherland swept over Kurt, he looked at the finely-carved cuckoo clock on the wall and realized he needed to go outside and get some fresh air. Kurt knew his father would soon be home for dinner and his mother would be getting the meal ready. As long as Jurgen was upstairs cleaning up and Eva was busy elsewhere, Kurt decided it would be best to stay away from both of them until dinner. Outside, allowing the warm rays of the sun to calm his excited sense of impending conflict, Kurt wondered what events might unfold during the next few hours. He knew now, more than ever, that he must have a private talk with Jurgen, and he must go by himself to the Nuremberg Rally.

"PSSST! Hey, Kurt!" Ernst Meyer whispered from around the corner of the neighbor's house, "Where's your brother?"

Kurt turned to see four wide eyes peering at him from the shrubbery about twenty feet away where Ernst and Walter Kruger were hiding. Kurt laughed at the sight, and the tension of the past few minutes temporarily faded. Still laughing, Kurt asked, "And what are you two agents of the Gestapo up to? You look like a couple of spies, and very stupid ones at that. Jurgen is right behind you."

"Oh, God!" Ernst yelled as both boys turned around and saluted, screaming "Sieg Heil."

Herr Reuter, the Heisler's neighbor, was just walking up the sidewalk and had witnessed the fervent salutations of the young Nazis.

"And Heil Hitler to you, my young lions, but you'd better not have damaged those shrubs, or even the Fuhrer himself won't be able to save you from the wrath of Frau Reuter."

"Yes, Herr Reuter. We're sorry," stammered the bumbling boys. As soon as Kurt's neighbor had entered his home, Ernst attacked Kurt. "Very funny. How can you make jokes when we're on such a serious mission? We want to meet Jurgen."

Walter quickly added, "Yes, we know he won't be around very long, and how often do we get a chance to talk with a member of the Leibstandarte? We want to talk with him, and you just make jokes. Some good German you are!"

"Well, I'm not so sure my brother wants to bother meeting you two clowns."

Turning serious, Kurt called his buddies aside and whispered, "I really don't know what's going to happen. You both know how my mother feels about the Nazis. She and Jurgen are not getting along very well. I'd hoped that Jurgen would be able to talk to all of us about his adventures, but I don't know if that can be worked out. Why don't you go wait at home and I'll call you if ... "

Kurt stopped talking and stared at his friends. Ernst and Walter were both looking past him as if he didn't exist. Mouths open, eyes enlarged, bodies shaking, they tried to present themselves with some semblance of military bearing. Wondering what could be causing such peculiar behavior, Kurt turned to see Jurgen approaching. His black uniform contrasted with the bright sun and blue sky, which made him appear larger than he actually was. He was now wearing his cap, and the Death's Head symbol above the brim added a sinister focus to Jurgen's powerful image.

"Well, what do we have here? I find it hard to believe, but could these two young men be Herr Meyer and Herr Kruger?"

Walter and Ernst almost exploded with satisfaction upon Jurgen's recognition of them. Ernst, being a little bolder than Walter, responded. "Sir, could we possibly visit with you about your experiences in the Leibstandarte? We've never had a chance to talk with someone like you before. What was it like when you re-occupied the Rhineland? Have you ever talked with Hitler?"

"Relax, Herr Meyer. I think we can arrange a solution to your problem and also solve one of mine at the same time, because I need to talk to my brother about some things in private, and this is not the place to do it. I just talked to a very good friend of mine, Lieutenant Helmut Ziegler, who's also a member of the Leibstandarte. He has access to an armored scout car, and he's coming over this afternoon. How about we all take a little ride in the country this afternoon?"

The trio of young adventure-seekers could not believe their good fortune and mentally thanked the gods for whatever they had done to deserve such a wondrous reward. Before Kurt was able to respond, Walter and Ernst were screaming "Yes!" and asking where and when. As soon as Jurgen set the time and place, Kurt's friends were bounding down the street, heading home to get ready without saying another word to Kurt.

Looking up at Jurgen, Kurt could already feel the wind blowing in his face and telephone poles whizzing by as he raced across the countryside with the Leibstandarte. He wondered what his brother wanted to talk to him about.

Jurgen turned to Kurt. "Why don't you go inside and help your mother? Father's coming home soon, and I'd like to talk with him before dinner. Hurry now. I'll talk with you later this afternoon."

Kurt went inside without saying a word. Finding his mother in the kitchen, he was surprised to see a smile on her face.

"I'm glad to see you're in a good mood, Mother. I hope we all get along at dinner."

"I hope so, too. Jurgen's my son, and I love him, but I don't understand him. Hopefully, everything will work out. Please help me set the table."

During the meal it soon became apparent to Kurt what Jurgen had talked to his father about: avoidance, as in the avoidance of any conversation during the noon meal regarding Hitler, the Nazi Party, or Jurgen's involvement with them. Eva seemed to be in agreement, and the meal passed in pleasant conversation about past Heisler family events. Toward the end of dinner Jurgen politely asked his mother's permission to take Kurt, Walter, and Ernst for a ride that afternoon.

"Jurgen, you can take Kurt on a drive if you want, but don't try to persuade him to become a member of the SS like you. I will not have Kurt follow after you!"

"Thank you, dear Mother. I can assure you that Kurt will have to make up his own mind regarding his future, and if he can see at all, I won't have to help in that decision."

Fritz prevented further trouble from developing by quickly turning the conversation back to more pleasant topics. Kurt, however, had already mentally left the dinner table. He was sitting in a German war machine tearing across the open plain with the twin lightning bolts of the SS pinned to the collar of his jacket!

After lunch Fritz and Jurgen retreated to the study to discuss the world situation while Frau Heisler finished cleaning up the kitchen. Kurt went to his room, where he anxiously paced the floor and checked his watch, whose hands suddenly seemed to be made of cement. When the doorbell finally rang, Eva answered it and admitted Walter and Ernst. Kurt was still upstairs trying to accelerate time when his friends burst into the room.

"Hey, Kurt," Ernst blurted out, "guess who we just talked to?" Before Kurt even had a chance to make a guess, Ernst excitedly continued. "You know that Willie and Klaus are Hitler Youth leaders? Well, they get to go to Nuremberg and march past Hitler. Isn't that something?"

Willie von Skirch and Klaus Deichmann were the last two members of Kurt's inner circle of friends. Millions of German boys belonged to the Hitler Youth, but only about 50,000 would be selected to actually participate in this year's Rally, so it was something indeed.

Walter now interjected, "We all know what a fantastic feeling that will be, to march past der Fuhrer in front of all those screaming people. Maybe we can feel the same today, riding with the Leibstandarte. When is this friend of Jurgen's going to show up?"

"I'm not sure," replied Kurt. "Jurgen said he'd be here about two-thirty, and he's five minutes late right now."

On cue, a pulsating roar answered the boys' questions. Peering out the window, the three future soldiers of the Reich beheld another black-clad model of perfection seated at the wheel of an armored scout car with the familiar German cross on its side. Without saying a word, the trio darted downstairs and ran into Jurgen, who was pulling his boots on.

"Apparently you're ready to go," laughed Jurgen.

Such a statement seemed rather ridiculous to the three boys, but they all agreed that they were indeed ready. As they tripped over each other trying to get outside, Ernst turned to Kurt. "Why don't we ask Jurgen if he can help us get into the Leibstandarte? Since you're his brother, it might just be possible."

"Shssst! Be quiet, Ernst. We're only seventeen, and, besides, the Leibstandarte is small and very hard to get in. Besides, if I do try to get in, I'll do it on my own, without anyone's help."

"Yeah, right," Ernst replied.

"After I talk with my brother we'll talk about this again, but for now let's just wait and see what happens."

Soon Jurgen was introducing Kurt and his friends to the driver of the armored car. "Lieutenant Ziegler, here are three future fighters for the Fatherland. This is Walter Krueger, this is Ernst Meyer, and this young lion is my brother, Kurt."

Helmut Ziegler was nearly a carbon copy of Jurgen, just a little shorter with a fuller face. Otherwise, they looked exactly alike, a pair of strikingly sinister twins.

Helmut spoke in a deep, gravelly voice, "Heil Hitler, young soldiers of the Reich. Climb aboard my chariot, and we'll see if we can run down some Jews."

Ernst and Walter laughed at Helmut's comment, but Kurt only smiled. Kurt could not believe that Helmut was really serious. Or was he? Splices of Jurgen's speech began to replay in Kurt's mind. Were the Germans really a superior race? Was his mother buried in the past, refusing to face reality? Did other groups, like the Jews, really need to be controlled by the true Aryan Germans?

"Kurt, stop daydreaming, and let's go," scolded Jurgen.

As the armored car lurched forward, Kurt felt a surge of immense power, and he experienced a deep, emotional sense of duty to the Fatherland. The wind on his face blew away all his misgivings concerning the ideology of the Third Reich. For the rest of the afternoon he just wanted to enjoy this time of adventure and exhilaration.

The Heisler home was located near the edge of Ansbach, so the scout car only had to travel down a few narrow streets before reaching the open spaces of the lush, green countryside. Soon "Special Force Heisler" was roaring down a quiet country road. As they sped along in the sunshine, Kurt felt a merging of nature, man, and machine. A few stringy clouds dotted an otherwise clear, pale blue sky. Sunlight saturated everything and intensified the vivid colors of the meadows and woods of northern Bavaria. The distinctive clarity of the day extended the skyline seemingly into infinity. Kurt began to swell with a renewed pride, a sense of satisfaction, and an acceptance that he was honored to be a German, a member of the master race. He looked at Jurgen and Helmut—bursting with delight that his brother was in the Leibstandarte—and felt an overwhelming desire to follow Jurgen's path.

Given the circumstances, who could blame an impressionable young lad for falling under the sinister spell of extreme nationalism? All of Germany was living in a state of exaggerated excitement, and the people of the Reich were in love with their newly-discovered importance. Floating through the scenic beauty of his country in a German war machine with two stallions from Hitler's elite, it was impossible for Kurt to suppress his dreams of performing heroic deeds for Germany. Surveying a scene that could inspire poets to new heights, Kurt began to surrender his soul to the myth of Nordic glory.

After a half-hour of driving, Helmut pulled off the road and angled across a field toward an area of dense forest. Reaching the top of a small hill, he shut off the engine and announced that the destination had been reached, adding, "Now, lads, how about some lunch?"

Jurgen responded, "I didn't know we were going on a picnic. You must really think this is a holiday."

"And a 'Sieg Heil' to you, brother soldier. All fighting men must eat to keep their strength up, so let's see what old Helmut confiscated last night. We have cheese, ham, bread, sausages, and the mainstay of every soldier's diet: beer."

"Ha!" laughed Jurgen, "Where did you steal all this from?"

"Steal is such a coarse word," an indignant Helmut answered. "Why, I was given these morsels by a young fraulein for my services last night."

Helmut and Jurgen laughed heartily as they exchanged wisecracks about Helmut's escapades the previous evening. The three young boys just stood in awe, paralyzed by the wonder of being among the chosen.

"Well, come on, let's eat," yelled Helmut.

The five adventurers sat down on the virgin green carpet of the mead-ow and proceeded to devour Helmut's treasures. Jurgen drew a black-handled dagger adorned with a swastika on one side and the SS symbol on the other and sliced the bread, cheese, and ham. Helmut opened the cans of sausages and doled out the provisions to the group. As a final touch, Helmut produced a small keg of beer and, with a flourish, placed it on the ground in the middle of the gathering.

"You're a great host, Helmut, but what are we supposed to drink from?"

Helmut stood up and looked proudly at Jurgen. "Just you wait. Soon you'll be sipping the nectar of the gods from vessels worthy of SS hands." He walked to the back of the vehicle and returned with a large cardboard box. He opened it, reached in, picked up a silver object and tossed it at Jurgen. "Well, what do you think?" asked Helmut, with a very pleased look on his face. "Are these not befitting the proud protectors of der Fuhrer?"

"Fantastic, simply fantastic! Where did you get these, Helmut? I must have some," proclaimed Jurgen as he held the silver stein aloft, studying it as if it were the Holy Grail itself. The handmade stein was smooth and uncluttered, except for a circle of SS symbols around the middle. One set of lightning bolts was left plain, while the alternating set was painted black. The piercing sunlight radiated off the stein's carefully crafted edg-ing, further accentuating its elegance and craftsmanship.

"I had them made by my Uncle Herman. He's a silversmith, and a rather good one, don't you think?" Helmut asked.

"Good? He's incredible. What did you get them for?"

"My brother Erik just joined the Leibstandarte, and he's getting mar-ried in a couple months. I thought these would make a nice wedding present."

"I should think so!" replied Jurgen.

Kurt, Walter, and Ernst handled the steins as if they had been handed down from Thor himself. Kurt was in a state of euphoria, unable to be-lieve this was happening to him. Here he was with his two best friends, sitting on a hilltop drinking beer out of silver SS steins with members of the Leibstandarte Adolf Hitler, one of whom was his brother. The steins were large, and Kurt had never drunk this much beer so quickly, and after his second mug he needed to get up and move around a little. He walked over to the side of the hill facing the open meadow and surveyed the expanse of emerald grass. Munching on a sausage, he turned and faced the dense, dark forest. Maybe it was the beer, but Kurt began to see figures darting among the trees, heroic beings from Germany's dark past. Kurt raised his stein and saluted them.

Back at the circle Jurgen loudly burst into song, and Kurt returned to the group. For the next half hour they repeatedly sang the "Horst Wessel" song and a number of other Leibstandarte standards that Jurgen and Helmut taught their young admirers. Silver steins flashed in the sun as they saluted the Leibstandarte and Jurgen's and Helmut's deeds of glory. Kurt was beginning to feel as if he could conquer the world all by himself. He had never before, not even in the Hitler Youth activities, experienced such a feeling of power, comradeship and destiny.

"Kurt, walk down to the forest with me. I want to talk to you, and I need to take a piss," laughed Jurgen.

Staggering slightly, Kurt got to his feet.

"Are you sure you can make it, Kurt? You look a little sick to me."

"Yeah, well, I look better then you do, Walter. I bet you've already pissed in your pants because you can't stand up."

"Helmut, I hope you can take care of any emergencies. Kurt and I are going for a walk," Jurgen bellowed.

Leaving Lieutenant Ziegler in charge of Kurt's slightly intoxicated friends, the Heisler brothers descended the hill and strolled to the edge of the wall of trees. Jurgen leaned against a tree and became very serious. "Kurt, I'll be leaving soon, and it's impossible to say when I might see you again. I urge you not to be misled by our well-meaning mother. She's a good person, but she doesn't understand how things really are in this world. Germany has a mission to create a world of order and perfection. If we fail, a society of chaos run by misfits will rule the universe. It's your duty to aid the Fatherland in any way you can. If we're to reach our destiny, all true Germans must be willing to sacrifice themselves to the service of the Reich. I think it would do you good to see the great Rally in Nuremberg next month, and I've already talked to Uncle Konrad about your coming to stay with him during September. As you know,

Uncle Konrad is a supporter of Hitler, and he understands the situation our mother presents. Our uncle has agreed—in fact he was greatly in favor of the idea—of writing a letter to father inviting you to come and stay with him and Aunt Hilda. The rest is up to you, Kurt. Our Fuhrer needs all Germans to do their duty and to unite against our enemies. We have a chance to become the greatest power the world has ever known, a world ruled by a master race of superior beings. Remember, the future belongs to the strong and the brave!" Jurgen smiled and looked down at his brother, who was bursting with satisfaction.

"Jurgen, I am ready to do my duty." Kurt was not sure what he meant by his reply; he only knew that he wanted to earn Jurgen's respect and approval.

"Kurt, you speak like a true German. Once you've seen the spectacle at Nuremberg, once you've had a chance to experience our movement by yourself, I'm sure what your choice will be."

Extending his right hand, Jurgen simply said, "Come, little brother, let's rejoin the others."

Kurt took Jurgen's hand. He had never felt closer to his brother.

The remainder of the outing passed rather uneventfully. They were all in a good mood by the time the keg was finished, especially the three youngsters. Walter and Ernst were begging Jurgen and Helmut to get them into the Leibstandarte somehow. Jurgen told them to continue in the Hitler Youth, age a little more, and call him later when they were ready. Kurt said nothing about joining the Leibstandarte, but Jurgen's quick glance at him assured Kurt that such a possibility was within his reach. The ride home was a study in contrasts. Jurgen and Helmut were singing loudly, and Kurt and his friends were sleeping off the beer. As Kurt fluctuated between semi and total unconsciousness, he dreamt the dreams of the mystic warrior statue in his bedroom.

That night supper at the Heisler home passed without any trouble between Jurgen and his mother. Later in the evening Helmut came over, and Jurgen left with him for locations unknown. Kurt, tired and emotionally drained, went to bed early. Crawling under his blankets, he glanced at the ancient warrior. It seemed to smile at him and whisper, "Sleep well, young Siegfried."

The next morning Kurt woke up with a slight headache. Walking to his closet, he laughed at himself for being such a drunkard. As he was selecting his clothes for the day, Kurt noticed a piece of paper that had been shoved under the door to his room.

Suspecting it was a note from Jurgen, Kurt immediately picked it up and read:

"Heil Hitler, little brother. When you read this, I will be gone. Remember the things we talked about and look for me in Nuremberg. Kurt, follow your destiny. Jurgen."

CHAPTER II

The Princess of Nuremberg

Just as Jurgen had promised, Uncle Konrad invited Kurt to Nuremberg, and Eva Heisler consented to let Kurt go without offering any opposition. Surprisingly, she actually encouraged him to attend, hoping that the pagan spectacle would convince Kurt once and for all that the Third Reich lacked any real substance. During the weeks between Jurgen's departure and the Nuremberg Rally, Kurt stumbled through his days in a blur of eagerness and excitement.

Finally, the long-awaited day arrived, and on a cool, clear September morning Kurt began an adventure that would change his life forever. Just before he left with some neighbors who were also attending the Rally, Eva offered him one final challenge: "Please, Kurt, look beyond the ridiculous, emotional gibberish of Hitler's message and try to find an intellectual foundation for Hitler and the Nazis to stand on. I don't think you'll find any."

Kurt had been to Nuremberg many times before, but everything about this trip sizzled with a new vitality. All points of entry into Nuremberg were clogged with swarms of the faithful, all going to one place with one purpose— to honor der Fuhrer. The closer Kurt got to the city, the more fascinated he became with the scene unfolding before him. A nation was on the march, and the sea of humanity was devouring the landscape, yet there was no sense of confusion or disarray; everything and everyone moved in an eerie, pre-ordained pattern of precise organization. Soldiers, Nazi officials, and the SS were everywhere ... watching, herding, guiding. Nothing was left to chance, and nothing was allowed to disrupt the flow of the masses in their quest of homage.

Gazing out the car window as he entered the city, Kurt absorbed the spectacle through every pore in his body. Nuremberg was alive, and he could feel its pulsating energy from the throngs of people, all of whom seemed acutely aware that something momentous was about to happen. Nazi banners, flags, emblems and slogans decorated every surface, as if the entire city had been painted red, white, and black. Rows of houses showcased their walls of gleaming windows decorated with small, dirt-filled flower boxes, all sprouting countless small Nazi flags proudly proclaiming the rebirth of a powerful, vibrant Germany.

Such a display would have given any city a sense of the supernatural, but even without the festive Nazi trappings, Nuremberg appeared as if time had stopped during the Middle Ages. The artifacts from the Dark Ages—fortified walls, a moat, a castle, even a medieval torture chamber—intermingled with the city's Gothic architecture and gingerbread style cottages, reflecting the city's experience with both innocence and evil. Within, a maze of narrow streets, open markets and tall, gabled buildings joined together to form the heart of the city. As a crowning touch, the church spires stretching above stood as silent sentinels keeping watch over the magic city.

On this day Nuremberg had been turned into a place of worship, a surreal, feudal acknowledgment of the new religion, Nazidom. As Kurt felt himself being swallowed up by the maniacal wave of patriotic fervor, Nuremberg closed around him, pulling him to her bosom in an embrace that transcended reality, transporting him into the unknown. The 1937 Nuremberg Rally was about to begin.

"Well, here you are Kurt. I believe that's your uncle's house."

Kurt was startled by Herr Bauer's remarks. He had been so engrossed in absorbing the scenery of the city that he had failed to notice they had arrived at Uncle Konrad's.

"Yes, yes, it is my uncle's house!" As he reached beneath the seat to get his suitcase, Kurt thought to himself, "Heisler, that's a really intelligent comment, you dumbhead!"

Tumbling out of the back seat, Kurt said, "Thank you for the ride, Herr Bauer."

"You're welcome, Kurt. Enjoy yourself and appreciate the festivities. I'll call when we're ready to return to Ansbach in about a week. Heil Hitler!" As Herr Bauer drove off, Kurt stood motionless on the sidewalk, watching the car disappear.

A trance held Kurt, and all he could do was stare and marvel at the vividly-colored swastikas splashed across the walls of Nuremberg. Standing by himself among the Gothic splendor and Nazi panorama of Hitler's chosen city, Kurt felt small and alone. A tall, thin house with many windows had nearly half its side covered with one enormous Nazi flag. The red flag, with its white circle surrounding the black swastika, burned its image into Kurt's soul. A pulsating wave of red seemed to generate heat as it pulled Kurt's consciousness toward its reservoir of glowing evil. Contemplating his future, Kurt was lost in daydreams and fantasies.

"Excuse me. Are you lost?"

Kurt spun around and found himself facing a young girl about his own age. The girl repeated herself. "Are you lost? You've been standing there holding your suitcase for quite a few minutes. Maybe I can help you."

A confrontation of this type was the last thing Kurt needed. He'd dated a few girls, but had never been seriously interested in the opposite sex. Facing this beautiful creation, however, Kurt experienced an unfamiliar feeling. Already overwhelmed by the majesty of his new surroundings, he lost what few social skills he had and simply responded, "I ... well ... I ... no, I'm going into that house."

Totally in control of nothing, Kurt clumsily turned and bumped into the girl—almost knocking her over—before walking up the steps to his uncle's house. Then, suddenly overcome by gallantry, he turned and said,

"Thank you," and disappeared into the house. Once inside Kurt turned and peered out the small window near the top of the door. The cause of his anxiety was walking down the sidewalk. She did not appear to be bothered in the least by her encounter with the idiot from Ansbach. Kurt watched every step, each movement, and consumed every possible detail as the object of his bewilderment floated away. When she reached the end of the block, the girl crossed the street and entered a large house. Kurt calculated that the young fraulein apparently lived only a few houses away from his uncle. Maybe his aunt and uncle knew her, maybe they ... reality landed on him with crushing cruelty. "What the hell am I thinking?" Kurt swore at himself. What a complete moron he had been! As the trance began to lift, Kurt began to shudder at the thought of how he had acted. How could he have behaved like such a country bumpkin? All he could think about was the total lack of sophistication he had displayed in his encounter with the girl.

Suddenly, a voice boomed from behind Kurt, "Ha, ha, ha, ha! Well, my dashing nephew, I see you've come to Nuremberg with more on your mind than the Rally. My goodness, you certainly seem to have made quite an impression on young Erika von Klugemann. I'll bet she's already telling her parents about the handsome lad she just met."

Uncle Konrad, a short, barrel-chested man of forty-two with cropped, reddish hair, continued to enjoy himself at his nephew's expense. "Yes, I shall certainly have to call and invite the von Klugemanns over for dinner so they can all meet the gallant young Siegfried from Ansbach."

Thinking Konrad's merriment excessive, Kurt tried to set the record straight. "I assure you, Uncle, frauleins have no bearing on why I came to Nuremberg. I'm here to see the events of the Great Rally and to visit with you and Aunt Hilda. I'm only checking on that girl to see if I hurt her when I accidentally bumped into her while turning to come up your steps."

"And I assure you, Kurt, that your aunt and I are very happy that you've come to visit and participate in the Rally. It will be a great opportunity for you to experience for yourself the power and might of the Nazi movement. Nonetheless, the girl you bumped into is a fine young fraulein. Why, if I were your age, Erika would certainly be on my list of things to see while I was in Nuremberg." Konrad's round, jovial face seemed to get redder with each sentence.

Uncle Konrad led Kurt into the kitchen, laughing and teasing all the way. Upon entering, they encountered Aunt Hilda, who gave Kurt a hug while proclaiming, "My, Kurt, you've certainly grown since we last saw you. How are your mother and father? We should get together with them more often, since we are only a few miles apart."

"They're fine, and they send you their best wishes, Aunt Hilda."

Kurt couldn't figure out why adults—at least aunts and grandmothers—always had to comment on children's growth. Wasn't it natural for young people to grow? And, as far as getting together more frequently with his parents, Kurt knew the answer to that; his uncle and his mother were politically incompatible. Uncle Konrad was a very cheerful person, but whenever he confronted Kurt's mother about her attitude concerning Hitler and the Nazis, a verbal war was the inevitable result. That is why Kurt had been surprised that his mother had even agreed to let him stay with Konrad and Hilda while he was in Nuremberg. But, in truth, his mother's feelings were one of the main reasons Kurt had come to Nuremberg. He wanted to try and see if his mother was right, while so many other people—good people like his uncle—could be so wrong.

"Are you hungry, Kurt?" asked his aunt.

"Hell no!" blasted Konrad as he crossed his large, hairy arms. "He lost his appetite outside a few minutes ago."

"What?" exclaimed Hilda.

"Never mind," Kurt answered in a flustered voice. "Uncle is having a joke at my expense, and I don't see any humor in it because there's nothing to it."

"All right, I'll be good. For a while," laughed Kurt's fun-loving antagonist.

"Well, I have no idea what in the world you two are talking about, and at the moment I don't care. What do you want to eat?"

It occurred to Kurt that it was the middle of the afternoon, and he hadn't eaten since early morning. Just as he was about to make his request, Aunt Hilda sent his heart into a state of adolescent meltdown. "You might want a snack because we'll be eating dinner late tonight;

I've invited the von Klugemanns over. Kurt, there are only four of them, Frederick and Maria, their daughter, Erika, and their son, Hans. Maybe I shouldn't have invited them tonight, it being your first night here and all, but I felt I had to. They're so busy making preparations for all the dignitaries who'll be stopping at their home during the week of the Rally that I just thought I should help them out."

Uncle Konrad looked at Kurt and howled with laughter. Hilda stopped for a moment to observe the strange behavior of her husband and nephew. Konrad had a smug, sly smile carved from one side of his red face to the other, while Kurt looked as if someone had just beaten him senseless.

"I don't know why you two are acting so crazy, but that's enough!" scolded Hilda. "What is wrong with you two?" Kurt's aunt was a commanding figure of womanhood, tall and well-proportioned, like a singer from one of Wagner's operas. Even though she could be a little imposing at times, everyone loved Hilda because of her warm, open personality and her desire to stuff people with food and make them happy. However, when she became angry, even the Gestapo would hesitate before advancing. Now Frau Heisler stood, waiting for an answer.

Finally, Kurt summoned enough courage to speak. "Aunt Hilda, after my ride let me off, I stood on the sidewalk admiring the city, and a girl thought I was lost and asked if I needed help. After telling her I was not lost, I bumped her as I turned to enter the house. I guess I acted a little foolish. Uncle saw me staring after her as she walked away, and for some reason he thinks it's all very funny."

"Well, that doesn't sound funny to me, either. What's so funny about that Konrad?"

"Hilda, Kurt has left out a number of things. That girl happened to be Erika von Klugemann, and you should have seen the look on Kurt's face as he watched her walk down the sidewalk, like a little puppy seeing his new master. The fact that Erika is coming over for supper tonight only adds to the irony and excitement."

"Shame on you, Konrad! Kurt, your uncle often thinks he's humorous, when in reality he's just being dumb. Besides, Erika's a lovely young lady, and I'm sure the two of you will get along just fine."

"Okay, I'll be good," laughed Konrad. "I promise not to mention anything about the incident ... at least tonight!"

"Enough! Let's go have some lunch," ordered Hilda.

As Kurt made small talk with his aunt and uncle, he appeared calm on the outside, but inwardly he was an emotional mess. "Why," Kurt thought, "did this have to happen now?" He was not ready to deal with Erika so soon after he had made a fool of himself. Trying to subdue his anxiety, Kurt told himself to forget about what had happened on the street, which was easier said than done. As he fumbled with his food, Hilda said, "Kurt, I thought you were hungry."

"I guess I just don't want to spoil one of your wonderful suppers," Kurt bravely responded.

"I think I know why Kurt has no appetite," Konrad added gleefully. Even Hilda smiled at her husband's last remark. Kurt was so nervous he was almost sick, and he hated himself for it. Here he was—a man in search of his cause—and he was being incapacitated by a little girl he had really never even met. Ridiculous! Kurt decided he needed something drastic to snap himself out of his swoon-like state and channel his uncle's energies in another direction.

"Uncle Konrad, I'm thinking of trying to join the Leibstandarte. I know you have some connections. Could you help me?"

Hilda and Konrad exchanged wide-eyed looks of surprise. Both were aware of Eva Heisler's crusade to keep Kurt out of any service to the Nazis, especially the SS.

"That's quite a bold statement, Kurt, considering how your mother feels and how young you are."

"I'm not so young, and I need to make up my own mind about my future!"

Uncle Konrad paused thoughtfully for a moment, and then began to spell out his predicament. "Kurt, I know your mother resents the fact that I encouraged Jurgen to join the Leibstandarte, and I don't think I want to offend her any further. I'm sure you can find other people to help you if your mind is really made up. Germany needs the best, the bravest, the purest young people to serve the Fatherland, and I think you possess those qualities. That's all I'll say at this time. Maybe we'll talk about the Leibstandarte later, but right now let me show you to your room."

As his uncle led him to his room, Kurt was rather proud of himself. In one sentence he had stopped Konrad's teasing about Erika and suggested the possibility of following in Jurgen's footsteps. He still wasn't sure he wanted to join the Leibstandarte, but there was a chance. Kurt knew his uncle was an important businessman with some rather powerful connections to the Nazi Party. Having a brother already in the Leibstandarte and an uncle with some pull certainly would help his chances for getting into Hitler's elite guard. At least Kurt hoped so.

After unpacking and cleaning up, Kurt's fear of meeting Erika returned in full force. His thoughts about the Leibstandarte quickly receded, forced out by a vision of female perfection. Every time he tried to think of something else, he saw an enormous pair of deep blue eyes peering up at him and the sexiest lips he had ever seen saying, "Are you lost?" Kurt could not understand why he was so infatuated with someone he had seen for only a few minutes. He chastised himself for being such a complete fool, but he couldn't help himself. Trying desperately to think of something else, Kurt began to reflect on his aunt's comment regarding why she felt obligated to have the von Klugemanns over for supper. If they were busy preparing for lots of important people coming over during the Rally, Herr von Klugemann must be an important Nazi. Maybe Herr von Klugemann would even be able to help someone trying to get into the Leibstandarte.

"What an idiot!" Kurt actually muttered out loud. All this time he had been concerned about meeting Erika. What about her father? Kurt could imagine him laughing as his daughter described her meeting with the dimwit on the sidewalk. Envisioning a great, powerful member of the Nazi Party looking down at him with contempt, Kurt broke out in a cold sweat. As Kurt ground his teeth in frustration, Hilda knocked on the door and said, "Come down in a few minutes, Kurt. We'll be eating in about an hour, but the von Klugemanns will be arriving soon." Kurt walked across the hall, combed his hair and splashed some cold water on his face. Looking in the mirror, he tried to tell himself it was time to be a man and put away childish emotions.

Before he knew it Kurt was downstairs being introduced to the von Klugemanns. Frederick von Klugemann—medium height, slight of build, balding, with thick eyeglasses—was physically not the type of man one

would usually associate with power and politics, but his demeanor reflected his stature. He dressed elegantly and conservatively, and his man-
ners were perfect. Frederick's father had developed a business empire
consisting of coal mines, railroads, and an industrial complex. After his
father's death Herr Klugemann had expanded the family business, largely
by helping the Reich rebuild and being helped by the Reich in return. The
Nazi Regime courted his favor, and he was flattered enough by their attention to succumb to the great advantages of being one of the chosen.
All in all, Frederick enjoyed the role of a successful businessman and was
happy with his position in life.

As the introductions continued, it took Kurt only a moment in the
presence of Frederick and his wife to discover the dominant social force
in the von Klugemann household. Maria von Klugemann was the embodiment of the pure Nordic warrior maiden; tall and slender with long, flaxen
hair, she displayed a remarkable figure at fifty, and her pale, wrinkle-free
skin was that of a woman in her thirties. She was alluring, seductive,
graceful and powerful, all at once. When Maria von Klugemann walked
into a room, she owned it. And she knew it.

As Kurt was being introduced to Maria, her eyes held him in a beam of
cool softness. All he could think about was how exactly alike Maria and her
daughter looked, especially their eyes, so soft and inviting, yet so mysterious and deep. Flashing brilliantly, Maria's eyes could change from a soft,
pale azure to a deep, sinister indigo in a heartbeat. She was obviously used
to attracting stares, so Kurt's unabashed reverie did not faze her. "How do
you do, Kurt? I assume you're here for the Great Party Rally?"

The sound of his name, as spoken by Maria, sent chills over Kurt's
skin. Her voice had a mysterious, inviting quality that could neither be described nor forgotten; when she spoke, Kurt felt as if an actual angel were
summoning him to listen. He knew he wanted to impress this woman, but
he managed to maintain his composure. "I am pleased to meet you, Frau
von Klugemann. Yes, I'm here for the Rally, and to see my brother march.
He's in the Leibstandarte Adolf Hitler."

"Well, well," smiled Maria, "so you have a brother in the SS? We shall
have to be careful around you, won't we?" Maria teasingly eyed Kurt as
she let her last words trail off into the distance.

Turning to Hilda, Maria explained, "Dearest Hilda, Hans won't be coming for supper. I hope it won't inconvenience you too much. I only found out a few moments ago. He has a special Hitler Youth meeting that he has to attend. He does send his apologies, and he regrets having to miss one of your marvelous meals."

"What about Erika?"

"Oh, she's coming in a few minutes. I had a few surprises baking in the oven, and she's waiting to bring them over."

Hilda said that such a gesture was not necessary, and soon the two women were lost in conversation. Kurt talked briefly with Herr von Klugemann after being introduced, but soon Frederick and Konrad were engaged in their own discussion. Kurt suddenly found himself in the middle of two separate adult dialogues. Maria, seeing Kurt's situation, came to his rescue.

"Kurt, we live four houses north, on the other side of the street in the house on the corner. Why don't you walk over and help Erika bring over the surprises. I believe you've met her."

"Shit!" thought Kurt. "She's already told her parents what a clumsy fool I am."

"Yes, Frau Klugemann, I'd be glad to help. I hope Erika won't object."

"Why should she?"

"Well, I guess we had a little mishap when we met."

"It couldn't have been too serious. Erika never mentioned anything to me. Hurry over, or you'll lose your chance to be of help to her." The twinkle in Maria's eyes and the intent of her comment was obvious to everyone in the room, but even Konrad remained silent. Kurt sensed that Maria could—even among total strangers—confidently establish dominance without seeming demanding or offensive.

Now that he had admitted his fumbling with Erika to her mother, Kurt felt a wave of relief spread throughout his body, and he acquired a new feeling of confidence. He was actually excited to renew his relationship with Erika. As he hurried out the front door, Konrad could restrain himself no longer and bellowed, "Good luck, Kurt."

Kurt slammed the door and headed down the street. For the first part of the short journey he was surprised by his own self-assurance.

Moments earlier he had been dreading his next meeting with Erika, but now he found himself walking with eager anticipation, at least until he got to the door of the von Klugemann home. There, absolute and complete terror suddenly possessed Kurt. His legs felt like they were bolted to the ground, and, in a state of near paralysis, he was scarcely able to raise his arm to the door. His new confidence quickly plunging into pessimism, he wondered if he dared knock. Only the greater fear of Erika coming to the door and finding him standing like a scared child enabled Kurt to knock on the front door. He struck the door twice, softly, but to him it sounded as if he were trying to knock the house down, a death knell that made him shudder. Kurt waited, every sense acutely attuned to the slightest movement inside the doorway. After what seemed like a decade, the door opened.

"Are you lost again?" asked Erika.

Kurt was about to plunge into a frantic explanation, but before he embarrassed himself in a sophomoric, oratorical frenzy, Erika saved him with a smile and a handshake. "Hello, Kurt, I'm Erika. My mother phoned and said that you were coming. Please come in. I'm sorry about my little joke about being lost."

Kurt's heart was now in a zone it had never before inhabited. "Please, God," he muttered to himself, "let me be calm and in control." Kurt fully appreciated the absurdity of his feelings, but he didn't care. Tingling with anticipation, he began his first real conversation with Erika. "I'm sorry I was so rude this afternoon. I guess I was daydreaming, and you did surprise me."

"Nuremberg can do that to a person, especially this time of the year. Let's just forget about it and start over."

Kurt and Erika faced each other blankly for a moment, and Kurt thought he detected a little sign of nervousness in Erika's face, but it vanished quickly. "Come into the kitchen, Kurt, and I'll load you up with some goodies to take over. I understand you're in Nuremberg to participate in the Rally. Have you seen Hitler in person before?"

"Not yet, but I'm really looking forward to it."

"He was at our house once," Erika boasted proudly. "My brother and I snuck out of our rooms and took a peek at him." There was a pause, and then Erika continued, "Do you belong to the Hitler Youth?" Before Kurt had a chance to respond, Erika was talking again. "My brother Hans is a Hitler Youth Leader in charge of planning for the youth activities during the Rally. I think he'll soon be joining the Leibstandarte. That's Hitler's body guard of special SS soldiers you know!"

Seizing the opportunity to impress Erika, Kurt answered, "Yes, I'm in the Hitler Youth, and I have a brother already in the Leibstandarte. Someday soon I expect to join him."

"You'll have to meet Hans for sure," squealed Erika. "I wish I were a man so I could do something glorious for our country. You men are so lucky."

"I'm glad you're not a man!" As soon as his last words had passed his lips, Kurt desperately wanted them back. He knew his face was red as Erika smiled at him.

"And why is that?"

That simple question nearly unglued Kurt. Thankfully, the phone rang, and as Erika went to answer it, Kurt had time to collect himself.

"That was really smart, Heisler," Kurt scolded himself. Here he was, having his first conversation with a beautiful, young, aristocratic socialite, and he was sounding like a ten-year-old.

Erika returned, announcing, "That was my mother. She told me to hurry and come over before the food gets cold. She said we'd have plenty of time to visit over there. I heard your uncle laugh and yell something in the background, but I couldn't understand what he said. Everyone laughed, though."

Kurt felt a sudden desire to choke his humorous uncle. All he needed now was Uncle Konrad to do his comedy routine about the "flustered nephew," and Erika would realize, if she hadn't already, what a wreck she'd made of a future hero of the Reich.

"Kurt, please take those two pans, and I'll carry the other one."

Erika continued their conversation as they walked over to the Heisler house. "Kurt, you must come over tomorrow and meet Hans. He can show you around and maybe get you into some of the Hitler Youth activities."

"I'd like to meet him."

"Have you had a chance to meet my parents?"

"Just briefly, before your mother suggested I come help you."

"I don't know if you've had time to tell yet, but my mother and father are very different. They're both wonderful people, but my father is rather quiet and reserved. Mother, on the other hand, likes to be the center of attention. I'm just telling you this so you'll understand if she talks about my brother and me a little boastfully. Mother is a favorite of Hitler and many high-ranking Nazis. I sometimes wonder if she really believes all that Nazi stuff, or if she just likes all the attention."

Erika never had a chance to finish, for standing on the steps was Kurt's uncle, who shouted, "Hurry up, you two. Goodness, Kurt, do Hilda and I have to worry about you already? I'll have to call your father and tell him you're too much of a ladies' man for us to keep track of!"

Kurt blushed, but was surprised to also see a trace of color in Erika's face. He was not sure if that was a good sign or a bad one.

"Herr Heisler," Erika replied, "I shall tell my mother that you are making fun of me."

Erika began to laugh as Konrad faked a seizure. For once even Kurt had to chuckle at his uncle's antics.

Supper passed slowly for Kurt. The adults dominated the conversation, and Kurt and Erika only spoke when asked a question by one of the adults. Talk centered on one main subject, the Nuremberg Rally, and Maria von Klugemann was the focal point of the discussion. She clearly enjoyed her status as one of the social leaders of the Nazi Party in Nuremberg. More than once she mentioned some of the dignitaries who would be stopping at their house. She also managed to talk about her son's role in the Hitler Youth activities planned for the Rally. Suddenly, Frau von Klugemann gave a little speech that Kurt felt was directed straight at him.

"Germany has been made to suffer the burden of World War I long enough. We have been the scapegoat for countries that today are becoming afraid of us. Now is the time to move forward and claim our rightful place in the world. The men of Germany must be iron-willed and as strong as the steel from Frederick's factories. No other race possesses the qualities, the purity, the will to lead that we Germans do. We must let no one stand in the way of our rise to power. Someday, the rest of the world will thank us for saving western civilization from the Jews and the Bolsheviks. Ours is a sacred cause, and we must not fail."

At the finish of Maria's proclamation, Kurt was ready to jump up and scream "Sieg Heil!" For an instant Kurt's eyes caught Maria's, and he felt his soul being stamped with a big swastika. Even before he could start sorting out his future, Kurt was falling under the spell of two dazzling Aryan beauties—mother and daughter, no less—both deeply committed to the service of the Reich. During Frau Klugemann's patriotic pronouncement, Kurt had watched the look of admiration on Erika's face. It was obvious that Erika adored her mother. Frederick, however, was able to keep things from getting too emotional, and in his dry tone he said, "Congratulations, my dear. That was a stirring speech, but I doubt we can rule the whole world by next year."

No one but her husband would have survived such a comment, but Maria only shrugged it off. "Shush, Frederick, you know what I mean. I know I get a little carried away at times. Let's have some more wine to celebrate the beginning of the Rally."

Kurt laughed to himself at the new variable that had been added to the problem he was already struggling with: whether to follow after Jurgen or not. He wondered if he still had a choice after meeting Erika and Maria. "Yes, I can still sort this out," he said to himself.

After supper the adults retired to the living room. Kurt volunteered to help Erika wash the dishes and, for once, Uncle Konrad made no humorous comments. As she was leaving the kitchen, Frau von Klugemann said to Kurt, "In case Erika fails to ask, you must come over tomorrow and meet Hans. I'm sure the two of you will get along famously. Don't forget, now."

"Thank you, Frau von Klugemann. I'd be delighted to meet Hans. I hope I might be able to go to some of his Hitler Youth activities."

"I'm sure that can be arranged," smiled Maria as she departed.

"Erika, your mother is the most fantastic woman I've ever met!"

Mockingly, Erika asked, "And how many women have you met?"

"Well, enough to know that your mother is not an ordinary woman. She's ... she's ... she's indescribable."

"Yes, Mother is unique. I think I know her very well, and she still surprises me. She should have been a politician, the way she likes to be the center of attention and promote her point of view."

Changing the subject, Kurt asked, "Will you be home tomorrow when I come over to meet your brother?"

Teasingly, Erika responded in slow, measured words, "I don't know, Kurt. What time will you be coming over?"

"Actually, I have no idea."

"Well, how would I know if I'll be home if you don't even know what time you're coming over?"

Kurt couldn't tell from her tone if she was flirting, teasing or just playing hard to get, and he admonished himself for leaving her such an opening. Before he could answer, though, Erika continued. "I'll make this easy for you. Why don't you come over for lunch? I know for sure I'll be home then."

By this time the von Klugemanns and the Heislers were engaged in a deep dialogue near the front door, but Maria, ever on the alert, heard Erika's invitation. "Yes, good idea, Erika. I should have thought of it. It will be a good time for Kurt to meet Hans. I'll send him over about eleven to get you, Kurt."

Another voice joined the conversation. "Ha! I'll bet Kurt would rather have someone else come and get him."

Kurt turned to Erika to say something, but this time Erika came to his rescue. "Don't worry, Kurt. I know Herr Heisler and his childish sense of humor very well. He's a close family friend, and I often call him Uncle Konrad."

A few hours later Kurt was in his room trying to analyze the day's events. It was almost midnight, but he was wide awake. He had been dissecting every word that had passed between him and Erika von Klugemann. Finally, Kurt surrendered to the inevitability that it was too early to make any judgments except one. He knew she was the most enchanting girl that he had ever been fortunate enough to meet, and he wanted to get to know her better. Plus, her parents were well connected with the Nazi Party, and if he decided to .... Stopping in mid-thought, Kurt just shook his head. With all the turmoil and decision-making he was about to experience, Erika was not entering his life at the most opportune time. But then again, maybe she was. Kurt was also a little confused by the apparent approval he had been given by Maria von Klugemann.

Drifting asleep, Kurt decided Maria's attitude had just been a matter of politeness and courtesy. His last thought before entering the dreamscape of sleep was to wonder what type of person Maria would expect her daughter to date. "Probably a damn general!" was Kurt's final conscious thought.

———

The next morning Kurt awoke to dust particles dancing in the beams of sunlight that filtered through his bedroom window. As he lay watching the erratic movements of the tiny specks, he decided it was going to be a very eventful day. After performing his usual morning rituals, Kurt went downstairs and found a note on the kitchen table from Konrad and Hilda explaining that some emergency meeting had been called regarding the Rally, and they had to be there by eight-thirty and would be back late in the afternoon. The note also explained where to find milk, rolls, cereal and other breakfast necessities. Glancing at the clock, Kurt saw that he had missed their departure by just a few minutes.

"This should be rather relaxing," Kurt mused. "I've nothing to do until eleven o'clock except eat breakfast and wait for Hans." Just as he was about to butter one of his aunt's gooey caramel rolls, the doorbell rang. Wondering who it could possibly be, Kurt went to the front door. As he cautiously opened it, a friendly voice exclaimed, "Good morning. I'm Hans von Klugemann. I know I'm early, but my mother told me that your aunt and uncle went to a meeting this morning, and as long as you have nothing to do, she thought you might like to go with me to my Hitler Youth meeting. How about it?"

The young man standing in the doorway was not exactly what Kurt had expected Hans to look like. It was very evident than Hans looked as much like his father as Erika looked like her mother. Hans and Frederick were very similar in appearance, except Hans was taller, had lots of reddish-brown hair, brown eyes and a somewhat darker complexion. The Hitler Youth uniform he was wearing seemed to enlarge his proportions, and as Kurt was to discover, Hans had inherited his mother's dynamic personality.

"Are you sure it's all right? I'm not marching in the Hitler Youth Parade."

"Don't worry. You'll be fine as long as you're with me. Did you bring your uniform along?"

Pleased with himself for being prepared, Kurt answered, "Yes, just in case I'd need it for something like this."

"Good planning. I have extra ones, but they'd be a little small for you. We need to leave in about an hour. The meeting should be over just in time to be back at my house for lunch."

"Do you want to join me for breakfast?" asked Kurt.

Hans looked around, sniffed the air, and said, "Are you kidding? For some of Aunt Hilda's caramel rolls I'd skip the whole meeting." It was becoming apparent to Kurt just how close his aunt and uncle were to the von Klugemanns.

During breakfast Kurt and Hans got to know each other a little. Kurt found out that Hans was an avid member of the Hitler Youth busy with responsibilities connected to the great Rally, but he was also a typical, fun-loving teenager concerned with some rather typical adolescent tensions. Hans' current predicament revolved around a girl named Helga. Although Kurt listened patiently, he was not as interested in hearing about Helga as much as he was interested in learning Frau von Klugemann's feelings about the kind of people her children should date.

"Kurt, you absolutely would not believe Helga. She looks just like one of those big, fat opera singers, blond pig tails and everything."

"I doubt she's that bad."

"Well, maybe not quite, but she's definitely not my type. Mother just wants me to go out with her because she comes from a very important family. Her father is a very well-connected general in Berlin. I think my mother feels dating Helga might help my career, as if mother didn't have enough influence already."

"I think your mother is really a unique woman. I certainly wouldn't mind having her help." Kurt waited for Hans to make a response, but

Hans continued his lamentations regarding his mother's plans for his future.

"I love my mother, and I do plan on joining some special military formation, but she can be a little bossy at times. I'm sure if I'm not a general by the time I'm twenty-five, she'll be very disappointed. Wanting me to date Helga is going too far. My friends tease me about having to take her out, and I can't stand it. What makes the problem even worse is that I have another girl I would rather date, and I need a date for our Hitler Youth event tomorrow. Tomorrow!"

"What kind of event are you talking about?"

"Tomorrow afternoon our local Hitler Youth Group is having a social gathering to reward our members for all their hard work preparing for the Rally. We also want to have some fun. The party is going to start in the afternoon since we can't stay out very late because of the curfew."

"Why don't you just take the other girl you like?"

"Because my mother doesn't like her mother. Let's just say their political views are different, and leave it at that."

"I'm sure there are a lot of girls who would love to go out with a Hitler Youth leader. How about your sister? I bet Erika has a number of friends who'd love to go with you tomorrow."

"Have you and my sister been talking about this? Has Erika told you about Kristin?" Hans was visibly angry, and he was practically shouting.

"Told me what?" replied Kurt defensively.

"'Told me what! Told me what!' I'll tell you what! If my dumb sister has been shooting her mouth off again, I'll break her stupid neck." Pausing in his tirade, Hans walked up to Kurt and stuck a finger in his chest. "Erika told you all about Kristin and me, didn't she?"

"No. I just met your sister. Why would she tell me anything at all?"

Slowly, Hans began to calm down. For a few moments, nothing was said as Hans paced back and forth. Then, dramatically, Hans grabbed Kurt by the shoulders, smiled broadly and said, "I'm sorry for being so rude. My sister knows I see Kris secretly without my mother knowing, at least most of the time. Erika likes to tease me about Helga, and sometimes she overdoes it."

"I understand," was all Kurt could say.

"As for my sister, Kurt, I can tell she finds you interesting. Mother also likes you. Don't ask me why, but both of them tend to make up their minds very quickly about people. But, I'll warn you, they both like to show off and collect things."

"I'm not sure what you mean."

"I mean I have an idea. I have a great idea that could solve a lot of problems and also lead to a lot of fun. I think you should attend our Hitler Youth Party with my sister as your date."

Kurt had just been getting ready to ask Hans why he thought his sister was interested in him when Hans proposed his idea. Excited by the prospect that Erika had confided something about him to her brother, Kurt was both elated and petrified at Hans' suggestion. He wanted to speak, but was in a state of shock. Hans was so engrossed in his idea that he failed to notice Kurt's semi-comatose look, and he continued to explain his plan.

"We could work it out so Erika would have to go with you, and I could take Kris, and we could all go together. Erika just broke up with her last boyfriend, and she doesn't like to be without a companion. Since you're a guest, she'd have no choice. As far as Kris and I are concerned, I have a plan where we could trap mother into allowing me to take Kris."

Kurt finally snapped out of his stupor. "Hans, you make it sound as if you just want to use Erika and me so you can take Kris. I don't want to take your sister unless she wants to go with me."

"Oh, for God's sake, don't be so sensitive. I've already told you Erika likes you."

"Really? What makes you think Erika even knows who I am, and why do you think your mother already approves of me? I know my uncle must have told your mother about how my mother feels about Hitler. If your mother is against Kris because of a political difference with her mother, what about me? I can't see your mother letting her daughter go out with someone who has a parent that is anti-Nazi."

There was an uncomfortable silence, and then Hans began to laugh. The harder he laughed, the more frustrated Kurt became until Kurt blurted out, "What the hell is so funny? I see no humor in any of this!"

"It really is funny, and a little stupid. Think about it. The two of us only met a few minutes ago, and here we are talking about my mother and my sister like a couple of old friends scheming about how to handle women. I must be worse off than I thought. Let's just say I'm loyal to my sister and wouldn't do anything to hurt her. She's very capable of handling herself and controlling her own affairs, and I can tell she does see something she likes in you. I'll leave it at that. As for how my mother judges you based on the political leanings of your mother, I think that the feelings of your uncle and you brother Jurgen more than make up for that."

Hans checked his watch and exclaimed, "It's later than I realized. We'd better get going, or we'll be late for the meeting. Go put your uniform on so we can leave."

As Kurt departed to change, his mind was a whirlpool of questions. Hans had satisfied his question about Maria von Klugemann, but not about Erika. In fact, Hans had really just succeeded in creating a host of other questions. Kurt wanted to ask him about his sister, but now was not the time.

Ten minutes later, Hitler Youth uniform in place, Kurt looked in the mirror to adjust his tie. Looking back at him was a mini-storm trooper---a blond-haired, blue-eyed little storm trooper dressed in brown pants, black belt, brown long-sleeved shirt and black tie. The specially designed Hitler Youth swastika armband completed Kurt's transformation.

As Kurt and Hans walked into the Hitler Youth meeting, their conversation shifted from girls to service to the Fatherland. Kurt tried to concentrate on such lofty goals, but he continued to fantasize about Erika's fingers crawling up the back of his neck. He managed to partially repress Erika's image by reminding himself that his true mission in Nuremberg was to decide his future. Yet, every now and then, the name Erika would come ringing into his mind like a sword clanging off a steel shield. Kurt began to feel that Erika was somehow tied to his destiny, along with Maria, Hans and the strange, mysterious city that surrounded them all.

The Hitler Youth meeting went about as Kurt expected. There was less propaganda than usual because of the many organizational details that needed to be finalized for the Rally, but the atmosphere was electric as the cream of German youth prepared for the coming of der Fuhrer. At the start of the meeting Hans took it upon himself to provide the attendees with some background on Kurt. Hans' introduction impressed them all and greatly surprised Kurt. Hans introduced Kurt as a friend from Ansbach who was in Nuremberg for the Rally. However, Hans did not stop with a simple introduction; he added—in glowing terms—that Kurt's brother was a decorated member of the Leibstandarte and that Kurt was heavily involved with the Hitler Youth in Ansbach and was also destined for the Leibstandarte. By the time Hans had finished listing Kurt's credentials, it sounded as if Kurt was the ultimate Hitler Youth.

Surprisingly, Kurt found himself to be less irritated at Hans' exaggerations and more at home at the meeting than he had expected, and he rather enjoyed his exalted stature among the chosen children of the Third Reich. The meeting was short, since most of the planning had already been done; all that remained was a final review of everyone's responsibilities. Kurt never ceased to be amazed at the organization and precision that permeated all levels of the Nazi state.

It wasn't until the meeting was over and Kurt and Hans were walking over to the von Klugemann home that they had a chance to talk about the day's events. "Say, Field Marshal Heisler, you certainly seemed to enjoy yourself at the meeting," Hans began. "I think I'll call Hitler and see if I can get you assigned to the General Staff."

"Well, what could I do? You're the one who made me out to be such a fantastic young Nazi. How was I supposed to act? I should've told all your friends what a damn liar you are."

"I didn't lie at all," replied Hans, "but I might have stretched things a bit."

Kurt looked at Hans and began to laugh. Hans began to laugh. Soon the young adventurers were arm and arm walking down the street. A new friendship had been forged between Kurt and Hans that would soon be strengthened by two common interests, frauleins and service to the Reich. Although each hopeful hero dreamed about deeds of glory performed on some future battlefield, at present they had more mundane goals.

"Kurt, I hope you're still planning on taking my sister to our party tomorrow."

The question brought Kurt quickly back to reality. He realized the time for dreaming was over. He actually had to confront Erika, in person, and ask her for a date. Fuzzy creatures began to cavort in his stomach. "Do you really think Erika will go with me?" Kurt looked at Hans with the face of someone in dire need of positive reinforcement.

Hans—a broad smile lighting up his face—said nothing.

"Well, if I do ask her, how do you think I should do it? I mean should I just ask her straight out, or should I do something with her tonight and then ask her? I mean, when are you going to ask Kris? I suppose you need to know about me and Erika before you can ask Kris. I mean, for God's sake, what do I mean?"

Hans brought Kurt to his senses. "Don't panic. Just shut up for a minute and listen. We need to do a little planning so we don't screw anything up. My whole family will be home for lunch in less than an hour. My guess is that mother will seat you between Erika and me. During lunch I'll casually mention that it would be nice if you could attend the Hitler Youth Party, but that you need a female escort. Since you don't know any girls in Nuremberg and you're our guest, what could my mother do but offer Erika as the solution? Now, I ask you, what could Erika possibly say but yes, sitting right next to you?"

"But, I don't want to force her to go with me."

"It's better this way. Let me explain my reasoning. If my mother suggests that you take Erika, it proves mother likes you. That's important to find out right away. Second, you don't want Erika to think you're too anxious to take her out. I know my sister, and she thinks she's pretty desirable. If she thinks she has you dangling already, well, all I can say is good luck, buddy. My way, she won't know if you really want to take her, or if it's just mother's idea."

Kurt was amazed by his friend's cold, calculating manner, especially regarding his own sister.

"Hans, I think Erika will see right through your plan."

"Maybe, but she won't be sure. That's the important part."

"Hans, I hope you never get mad at me for some reason. With a mind like yours, I hate to think of what evil revenge you'd come up with. You're really devious."

Hans grinned broadly, and then slyly answered, "Well, I'm not doing this just for you. Wait until you see Kris, and you'll understand my motivation."

As the boys neared their destination, Kurt wondered if he had been afflicted by some spell emanating from the depths of Nuremberg. He had only been in the city for a little more than a day, and he had already collected a week's worth of contacts and experiences. Walking up the steps to the von Klugemann home with Hans, Kurt wondered what possibilities lay behind the door.

As he stepped into the house, Kurt realized how nervous he must have been the night before when he had met Erika here. He had been too preoccupied with one of its inhabitants to even notice the magnificence of the home. Now, however, his eyes were overwhelmed as they tried to take in everything. The exterior presented no real clue to the quality within; the house was slightly larger than the surrounding ones, but looked much the same. Inside, however, the von Klugemann home was a mansion befitting a family counted among Germany's social and political elite. It bore the stamp of people of wealth and taste, resplendent with exquisite furniture, art masterpieces, rare books, lush carpets, and sparkling chandeliers. Scattered about the home were Nazi symbols and artifacts that clearly informed guests of the political affiliation and influence of the residents, but it was in the main dining room where two dominant items loudly proclaimed the von Klugemanns' connection with the Third Reich. On one wall a large Nazi flag served as a tapestry, stretching to the high vaulted ceiling, while a large, beautifully-framed, autographed picture of Adolf Hitler hung above the massive fireplace. Kurt had been impressed with the home of his aunt and uncle, but he was awed by the magnificence of "Castle von Klugemann."

During Hans' quick tour, Kurt noticed there were no household staff around and asked Hans about it. Hans explained that a cleaning lady came in once a week and on special occasions extra help was hired, but normally Maria von Klugemann ran her home and did her own cooking. At first Kurt thought this to be rather odd, a woman of Maria's stature not having a household of servants, but after some thought Kurt decided that the idea of Frau von Klugemann doing her own household chores made perfect sense; not only was she a natural born leader, but she also did what she wanted, regardless of whether it fit others' expectations.

After the tour the two boys retired to Hans' room so Hans could complete the final pieces of his master plan. Hans explained that his mother felt a boy headed into military service should live in rather Spartan surroundings, so, in contrast to the rest of the house, the room was rather plain and unadorned; it contained only a few pictures of his family, Hans in his Hitler Youth uniform, and a picture of Hitler.

"Before I lay out the final maneuvers of 'Operation Kris-Erika,' I guess I should ask you a question" Hans said dramatically.

"What?"

"I've been assuming that you'd like to take my sister to our party, but maybe you don't have any real interest in her. Do you? Maybe I've been so anxious to take Kris that I've made some assumptions I shouldn't have."

Kurt was trying to answer, but Hans just continued to talk. "I can tell you this. Erika is a special person, even if she is my sister. She's good looking, smart, athletic and basically a nice person. I think she's fun to be with, although sometimes she can be a little stuck on herself. She knows she's special, and she can be a snob once in a while, but she's usually down to earth. I want you to know I love my sister, and I wouldn't set her up with someone unless I trusted him."

Finally, Kurt got a chance to respond. "Hans, I think you know I find your sister beautiful and fascinating, and you can trust me. I hope I can help you out with Kris, but the main reason I'm willing to go along with your plan is so I can spend time with Erika."

"And that's the way it should be. Now that that's settled, let's get down to business. Kurt, here's how my plan will work."

"Hans, I already know how the plan is supposed to work, how your mother will suggest I take Erika, and she'll have no room to get out of it. What else is there to figure out?"

"I've neglected to tell you the most interesting part," Hans paused, and then continued in a devious tone of voice. "So far, all we've worked out is how you can get Erika to go with you, but that's only half the plan. Getting my mother to let me take Kris is far trickier. Here's how I've worked out that scenario. Assuming everything works out between you and Erika, the key ingredient of phase two is Kurt Heisler. As soon as Erika has agreed to go with you, I want you to express your opinion that it would be great if you and Erika could go with Kris and me. You will then explain that you met Kris this morning, and she seemed so nice and very comfortable to be around."

"What! Are you crazy? Hans, I've never met her, and I obviously know nothing about her, even what she looks like. I won't say something that is going to get me caught in a lie."

Hans looked calmly at Kurt. "Relax. I have that figured out, too. I'll show you some pictures of Kris and tell you about her personality, likes, dislikes and how we happened to run into her this morning. The tricky part is that you'll need to trust me to misdirect any questions my mother asks that I don't think you can answer."

"Don't you think your mother is too clever to fall into your trap?"

"Maybe, but I'm counting on her being so excited about Erika going with you that she'll let her guard down a little."

Getting frustrated at Hans' rather dubious solutions to everything, Kurt defiantly replied, "I don't think your mother is overly concerned about me after one day. You're just grasping at straws if you don't think your mother will smell something rotten in Nuremberg."

"Cute, Kurt, very cute," Hans said sarcastically. "But you have to do it for both of us. Don't worry. My plan will work." He glanced at the clock located over his bed. "We have about twenty minutes before someone will yell at us to come and eat. Wait here."

Hans left the room but returned before Kurt really had time to worry about what he was up to. "I think we both need to relax a little, so I snuck a few beers out of the basement. Maybe they'll ease the pain a little."

Soon Kurt and Hans were fortifying their courage with the amber liquid while Hans produced the promised pictures of Kris. After a beer and more discussion, Kurt started feeling a little more confident about the plan. About noon, a faraway voice yelled, "Hans, you and Kurt can come on down to eat in five minutes. Please don't be late."

"Hans, is there a bathroom up here?"

"Yes, right across the hall. Splash some cold water on your face, and put on some of my cologne."

"Good idea. You do the same after I get back."

After both conspirators had freshened up, they shook hands and proceeded to lunch to put "Operation Kris-Erika" in motion. Entering the kitchen, they found Erika putting the finishing touches on the table settings.

Erika spoke first. "Hello, Kurt. How are you this fine day?"

The liquid courage had produced the desired effect, because Kurt answered boldly, "A lot better now that I have a chance to see you again."

Hans slapped Kurt on the back, grinned at his sister and loudly asked, "What are you doing tomorrow, Erika? Nothing important, I hope."

Getting suspicious, Erika exclaimed, "Why?"

"Well, my friend Kurt and I are making some plans, and if you're lucky, we might just include you."

Kurt continued, throwing caution to the wind. "Erika, I think it would be great fun to do something together."

Erika gave them an icy stare. Then, in a stern, yet sexy voice, she replied, "I don't need you two clowns to have a good time. If you're planning something, I hope you'll tell me so I can have a good laugh."

The sarcasm in Erika's voice instantly dissolved Kurt's newfound courage. In a few short seconds he had been reduced to a pile of frazzled nerve endings. Sensing his friend's faltering fortitude, Hans came to Kurt's rescue. "Erika, please finish setting the table. I want to show Kurt something in the study. I promise you'll find out soon enough what we're planning."

Quickly leading Kurt into the study, Hans shoved him into a lush, leather chair and said, "Take a few deep breaths and get your bearings. For God's sake, she's only a girl. Don't be so intimidated when she acts a little aloof. She's probably just as nervous as you are."

"I seriously doubt that. I don't see anyone coaching her on what to say next. I'm not sure I can go through with this."

Yanking Kurt out of the chair and heading him back toward the kitchen, Hans hissed, "You'd damn well better for my sake. Now go in there and be a man!"

As it turned out, "Operation Kris-Erika" was a resounding tactical success. About halfway through the meal, Hans managed to maneuver the conversation to the next day's Hitler Youth social event. He even worked in how everyone at his Hitler Youth meeting that morning had been extremely impressed with his friend Kurt. The first trap had been set.

"Everyone at the meeting said Kurt should find someone to accompany him to the party tomorrow. It's too bad Kurt doesn't know anyone in Nuremberg."

Frau von Klugemann took the bait without a moment's hesitation. "Erika, you're not attending with anyone. Why don't you go with Kurt? It would be fun for both of you."

The circumstances left Erika with little room to maneuver, but she had anticipated her brother's scheme and reacted accordingly.

"Why, yes, Mother, that's a good idea, but only if Kurt really wants to take me."

"I'd be honored to take you, Erika."

Smugly, Erika turned a vengeful smile on her brother. "Hans, wouldn't it be nice if Kurt and I could go with you and Helga?"

Now it was Hans' turn to panic. Maria's beaming face signaled that Erika's suggestion was about to get her hearty endorsement. Hans managed to give his sister a hateful look as he turned to Kurt and signaled it was time for Kurt to rescue him. Kurt's response sealed their friendship forever. "I'm sure Helga is very nice, but Hans and I ran into his friend Kris this morning on our way to his meeting. I think I'd be more comfortable being with someone I've already met. Kris seemed like a lot of fun, and we kind of talked about all of us going to the party together."

Frau Klugemann knew she had been outmaneuvered, but under the circumstances there was nothing she could do except approve Kurt's suggestion. However, to show her disapproval, she immediately changed the topic of conversation.

"Kurt, have you ever attended a Nuremberg Rally before?"

"Yes, with my father last year. But we were only here for two days, and I didn't see that much."

Maria's face began to glow, and her children could see a speech coming. Even Herr Klugemann, who up until now had appeared to be rather disinterested in the whole conversation, raised his eyebrows and looked sideways at Hans in resignation. They were not to be disappointed.

"We'll have to change that on this trip, Kurt. You can't imagine the feeling of pride generated by being part of a Nuremberg Rally; you have to experience it. When a million throats begin to scream 'Sieg Heil' as der Fuhrer stands to address the faithful at the great Luitpoldhain arena—amidst a backdrop of giant Nazi eagles, flags and swastikas—it will take your breath away. Kurt, if you haven't already, you will surrender yourself to the service of Hitler and the Reich during the next week."

It was at this moment that Kurt realized how much be wanted to impress Maria von Klugemann and her daughter. Without really thinking about what he was saying, he blurted out, "I'm quite sure I'll be following after my brother Jurgen and joining the Leibstandarte. I know it's very hard to get in. Maybe you can help me?"

"You've chosen a worthy goal, Kurt. Our country needs the flower of its youth—young men just like you—to champion our cause. Later, when the time comes, I may be able to help you get into one of the more prestigious military organizations."

As Maria turned her attention to Frederick for a minute, Hans nudged Kurt and whispered, "See, I told you my mother makes up her mind about people very quickly. I also told you I knew she liked you."

A smile of glowing warmth spread across Maria's face, and her eyes flashed with a radiant wave of blue approval as she looked back at Kurt. "I'm sure you will make us all proud some day, Kurt."

Kurt felt like a giant. Everything was going almost too well, and too fast, and he could feel every hair on his body standing at attention. He was beginning to understand the enormous feeling of satisfaction Frau von Klugemann could bestow on a person. Seeing her this way, Kurt understood why she counted many younger men among her legion of admirers.

The discussion quickly turned to other topics, and after the meal Herr Klugemann visited briefly with Hans and Kurt before hurrying back to work. Erika went to her room to change clothes so she could leave with her mother to run some errands. Before they knew it, Kurt and Hans were alone in the kitchen.

"Man, that worked out perfectly," boasted Hans. "I told you my plan would work, didn't I? Planning and execution, that's what separates Germans from the rest of the world."

Kurt smiled back at him. "Well, maybe a little luck and a friend to bail you out also help."

"Okay, I'll admit it, after Erika offered her suggestion, you came through and really saved the day."

"Do you think Erika will hold it against me?"

"No. She likes Kris better than Helga. She's just trying to get back at me for setting her up. In case you hadn't noticed, Erika likes to be in control, and she hates being backed into a corner. I loved it."

Giving a salute to Hans, Kurt said, "With your skills as a master planner, I imagine we'll all be saluting you in a few years."

"That certainly works for me," laughed Hans.

"As long as you've planned everything in such great detail, General von Klugemann, would you mind explaining the rest of the campaign to me?"

"Sarcasm will not help with your promotion, Private Heisler. I might share further details concerning 'Operation Kris-Erika' at a later date, but, unfortunately, I need to go to work. Seriously, Kurt, I almost forgot, but I need to help with something at one of father's factories. After I'm done, I better see Kris and make sure she knows all about tomorrow. I don't know exactly when I'll get back, but if I don't see you again today, I'll call you tomorrow morning. I'll give you all the specifics about the party then, but for now all you need to know is to wear your uniform, and I'll have a chauffeur pick you up at two. I apologize for leaving you so abruptly, but if I don't get this job done, I'll be in real trouble with my dad. Say, why don't you go down to the study? On my way out I'll tell Erika that she should show you around. That would be a great chance for you to get to know her a little better."

Kurt suddenly felt like he was walking in a wind storm, just trying to stay upright. He desperately wanted to get back to his uncle's house and digest the day's events, but before he could offer any objections, Hans had dragged him to the study, slapped him on the back, wished him luck and disappeared. It suddenly dawned on Kurt that he was about to confront Erika alone for the first time since her brother's plan had trapped her into a date with him. A sense of foreboding engulfed him, followed by a rush of nausea, and he felt the hot sweat generated by the fear of the unknown. What was he doing trying to impress a girl like Erika? Who did he think he was to believe that after two days he could impress the most desirable fraulein in Nuremberg? Pin-sized dots of perspiration formed on Kurt's forehead as he contemplated the absurdity of his situation. He desperately needed something tangible to regain his sense of equilibrium.

As Kurt paced in nervous circles, he began to closely examine some of the pictures hanging on the walls. Eventually, his eyes came to rest on a picture of Hitler descending the steps from an airplane at an earlier Nuremberg Rally. A Leibstandarte honor guard surrounded Hitler, and Kurt recognized his brother as one of its members. Seeing Jurgen standing at attention near der Fuhrer, Kurt could feel his brother's presence, and he recalled Jurgen's words about serving the Fatherland and being strong. Kurt had found his pivot point back to reality.

"You seem rather pleased with yourself, Kurt."

Turning around slowly, Kurt saw Erika standing a few feet behind him. Kurt took one more look at his brother's picture and decided it was time to act like a man.

"I suppose you're a little mad about what happened during lunch."

Erika left the question hanging over his head like the Sword of Damocles. Without uttering a word, she walked over to the large window looking out on the city, and paused for a second. Then she turned and gave Kurt a smile, not just an ordinary smile, but one of those beguiling gazes that only a coy, beautiful young girl like Erika can give. The silence was thunderous. Kurt couldn't begin to guess Erika's next move. He had prepared himself for any response, hot or cold, but not for silence. Erika's haunting "maybe" of a smile had him immobilized. He could neither re-treat nor advance, and he didn't know what to do. What he did know was that Erika was enjoying his discomfort, and he had to act.

"Erika, please come over and look at this picture."

Erika sauntered slowly over to where Kurt was standing and waited for an explanation.

"The third soldier from the left is my brother Jurgen. He's in the Leibstandarte, you know."

"Obviously."

Erika stepped closer to Kurt and asked, "Do you need his help, like you needed my brother's?"

Erika had now taken the sword hanging over Kurt's head and driven it into his phantom courage. Sensing Kurt's wounded condition, Erika pressed her attack. "Just because I agreed to attend the Hitler Youth party with you means nothing. I choose my own escorts. My brother thinks he's pretty smart. Well, I hope he doesn't get mother too upset, or he'll be in big trouble again. I'm glad he came up with his stupid plan, though. I did want to go to his party, and Kris is a lot of fun."

"What kind of a person is this?" Kurt thought. "How could anyone so beautiful be so cold, calculating, and cruel? And what in hell did she really mean?" Kurt tried to analyze each word Erika had spoken, but he could find no clues as to how she really felt. He only felt confusion and self-doubt. Finally, acting far braver that he actually felt, Kurt confronted Erika head on. "Erika, if you don't want to go with me, I'm sure Hans can find someone else to escort you."

Erika answered tartly, "I'm not sure about the girls in Ansbach, but in Nuremberg, we don't usually go out with strangers. As for my brother's abilities as a matchmaker, don't worry. He's not that persuasive. I told you, I choose my own escorts."

Kurt was starting to think Erika really was a little elitist snob, but she quickly changed course again. "I'm sorry, Kurt. Maybe I'm being a little too uppity, but I don't appreciate being used by my brother. I really would like to go with you tomorrow. I'm sure it will be interesting and fun. Why don't you come over tonight? We can visit and get to know each other a little better. Most of what you know about me has come from Hans, and most of what I know about you has come from Uncle Konrad, certainly not the two most reliable sources on earth."

Erika's last comment succeeded in relaxing both of them, and they began to laugh at the circumstances surrounding their first date.

"I'd like to come over tonight, and I'm especially curious to hear what my uncle has told you about me. Good or bad, I'm sure it's greatly exaggerated."

"I hope so," teased Erika with mock fear. "I need to leave soon with my mother. Do you have something to do this afternoon?"

Kurt looked at his watch and was surprised to see it was already two o'clock.

"I've been in Nuremberg for two days, and I've barely talked with my aunt, so I think I'll just go back home and visit with her."

Erika walked Kurt to the front door, and as they said goodbye, she touched his hand. "See you tonight. Come over right after supper."

Elated, Kurt floated the short distance to his uncle's house, desperately trying to prolong the sensation of Erika's touch of his hand. He was still unable to comprehend Erika's conflicting words and actions, but at least the future held hope. What else could he ask for?

Kurt found the Heisler household empty. His aunt and uncle had apparently not been home since Kurt had left early that morning. Kurt headed straight for the kitchen and began pillaging the contents of his aunt's refrigerator, not caring what morsels passed his lips as long as there was a steady flow of food to calm his nerves. After all, how many emotional dilemmas could a young man be expected to deal with in such a short time? Kurt had never really been interested in any one girl before, and this enigma known as Erika was an entirely new phenomenon. He needed time to relax.

As Kurt sat pondering the "why" of Erika von Klugemann, he heard the front door open. Next he heard his aunt ask, "Is anyone here? Kurt, are you home?"

Uncle Konrad added, "If you're in there with a girl, I'll tell her father. Unless it's Erika, of course."

"I'm in the kitchen alone, so you don't have much of an audience, Uncle Konrad."

Hilda and a beaming Konrad entered the kitchen and sat down with their nephew. After they discussed the day's activities for a few minutes, Kurt asked a question that he feared would invite his uncle's teasing, but that didn't stop him.

"Aunt Hilda, do you think Erika could come over for supper tonight? I guess I'm escorting her to Hans' Hitler Youth party tomorrow, and I'd like a chance to get to know her a little better."

"I'm sure you would!" cackled Konrad.

"Shush, Konrad. Why of course you can, Kurt. I think it's a great idea."

Hilda's admonishment had no effect on Kurt's uncle, who continued his assault on Kurt's social life. "Can your aunt and I be present, or would you prefer to dine alone?"

Kurt had decided that the best way to deal with his uncle's distorted sense of humor was to agree with everything Konrad said. "Why, thank you for asking, Uncle, and yes, we would like to dine alone."

"If you two want to continue to make jokes, go somewhere else. I have to plan supper."

Acting hurt, Konrad addressed Kurt. "Come on, nephew. Let's go have a visit. Even I can take one of your aunt's subtle hints."

Kurt and his uncle went into the living room for their first private talk, and Konrad was as serious as Kurt had ever seen him. He philosophized about the Rally and what it stood for, about the Nazi movement and its importance to the future of Germany, and the fact that he had been an avid supporter of Hitler since the late 1920s. Uncle Konrad also praised Kurt's mother as a good, but misguided, person who just did not understand the essence of Aryan supremacy. Kurt felt like he was listening to his brother Jurgen all over again. Kurt also learned that his uncle not only worked for the von Klugemanns' industrial empire, but that he and Hilda were their good friends. Although they did not travel in the same social circle as Frederick and Maria, they saw each other quite often.

At one point in their conversation Uncle Konrad even restrained himself enough to become serious about Erika. "Kurt, I'm sure I'll continue to tease you about Erika, but let me say this one time. She's a wonderful girl, an ideal example of Teutonic perfection. If I were your age, I'd chase after her until she accepted me or told me to go away forever. My advice is to treat her well, and good things may happen, not the least of which is the influence the von Klugemanns could have on your career."

"Uncle, I thought if I needed influence, all I had to do was tell people I'm your nephew."

"Okay, I guess I deserved that. Let's call it even," laughed Konrad.

The talk ended with a brief discussion of religion and the obvious contrast between the teachings of Christianity and the "master race" philosophy of the Third Reich. It was easy for Kurt to see that, like many Germans, Kurt's aunt and uncle still believed in God and maintained a selective adherence to basic Christian principles. But they had rationalized their beliefs to the point where their old Christian values had been subjugated to accept the necessity of a belief in Hitler and all he stood for. If a conflict were ever to arise between the two elements of their moral makeup, Kurt believed Konrad and Hilda would just ignore it or justify it in favor of the good of the Fatherland. Listening to his uncle's rants about religion, Kurt said little and learned nothing new, except for two comments his uncle hammered home: "God helps those who help themselves," and "You've been overprotected by your mother."

After the conversation Kurt went back to his room. He pondered his Uncle's comments and worried about his supper with Erika. He'd called the von Klugemann house twice, but there had been no answer, and he was afraid he'd be unable to reach Erika in time to invite her for supper. It was getting late and Kurt was getting nervous. Then there was a little knock on his door.

"Come in."

Kurt's aunt entered the room. "I'm sorry, Kurt. I forgot to tell you that Frau Klugemann called some time ago, and when she mentioned that she and Erika were going to be gone until after five, I took the liberty of asking Erika over. I hope you don't mind."

"No, Aunt Hilda, I'm glad you did. Thank you"

"And another thing, Kurt, Hans just called and wants to talk to you before you bring Erika over, so you'd better go over there pretty soon. We'll eat about six, so you have about an hour."

"Thanks. I'll go right over."

Before Kurt even touched the von Klugemanns' door, Hans opened it and whispered, "Come in. Let's go up to my room."

"What's the hurry?"

"Wait until we're in my room."

Safely in Hans' room the boys sat down, and Hans began speaking very rapidly. "I just wanted to tell you how great everything is going. I'm going over to see Kris for a little while tonight and confirm all the arrangements. I hear you're taking Erika over to your aunt's for supper. That's great. My mom and dad are sitting in the living room, and I'll take you down, and you can visit with them while you wait for Erika. Butter my mom up a little. She loves to be compliment-ed. Remember, don't act too anxious with my sister. Just play it very matter-of-fact."

"For God's sake, Hans, calm down and catch your breath. Have you talked with Erika today?"

"No! I haven't even seen her. That's your job, and don't screw it up!"

Before Kurt could question Hans further, he found himself in the liv-ing room, with Hans still talking. "Mother, Father, Kurt is here to escort Erika. I'll leave him with you until she's ready. I'm off to see Kris. Don't worry, I'll be home early. Goodbye and good luck, Kurt."

Frederick and Maria offered Kurt a chair.

"Well, Kurt, how has our city been treating you so far?"

"Fine, Herr Klugemann, except I haven't had a chance to see much of it yet."

"Oh, don't worry, you will," smiled Frederick.

Maria gave Kurt one of her "approval" looks and said, "You look very nice tonight, Kurt. I hope you and Erika have a nice time with your aunt and uncle. Don't let her eat too much. She's very partial to your aunt's cooking. I'm not sure what you young people are planning to do after sup-per, but I think you should both be in early. Tomorrow will be an exciting day, and you'll want to be rested for all the activities that will take place at the Hitler Youth event."

"Oh, Mother, don't worry about us. Kurt and I can take care of our-selves." Erika had appeared from nowhere and was now standing right behind Kurt.

"I know, but remember, there is a curfew. Run along now, or you'll keep Hilda waiting."

CHAPTER III

Hitler's Children

For Kurt the walk back to Uncle Konrad's house was short, but the journey was long: house to house, but childhood to manhood. Despite the short trip, Erika had enough time to get Kurt thinking. "Well, Kurt, what are you planning for the future? Did Hans tell you that he's joining the Verfugungstruppe soon? Do you know what that is?"

"I'm not exactly sure. It's like the Leibstandarte, right?"

"Yes, but the Leibstandarte is only one of the regiments making up the Verfugungstruppe. Together they form what is really going to be an SS army. Hans hopes to eventually get into the cadet school at Bad Tolz and become an officer in the Leibstandarte."

Kurt could see that if he was going to impress Erika von Klugemann, there was only one correct response.

"I'm quite sure I'm headed in that same direction. My brother Jurgen can probably get me straight into the Leibstandarte."

"I doubt it. It's not that easy. My parents know Sepp Dietrich, the commander of the Leibstandarte, and even with those connections, he's not giving Hans a free pass."

"I'd like to talk to Hans about it."

"Well, maybe I can put in a good word for you with Hans and my mother and father."

As they paused at the Heislers' front door, Kurt issued Erika a serious warning. "Don't believe anything my uncle says about me, and don't let him embarrass you if he acts stupid about us."

"Why should he embarrass me? Why should he even talk about us at all? We don't even know each other."

"I know, but I think my uncle would like us to ... well, you know."

"Unlikely, I would say!" Erika proclaimed in her haughtiest voice. But, immediately switching roles, she coyly stated, "I guess anything's possible, though."

Kurt almost laughed out loud, except he was too exasperated and amazed at Erika's ability to keep him confused. She had done it again, given him two conflicting signals and then left him hanging.

The door opened, and Uncle Konrad loudly ended Kurt and Erika's doorway discussion. "Are you two going to come in, or shall I set a table for two on the front steps?"

"Now, Uncle Konrad, don't be sarcastic. It doesn't become you." Erika's comment silenced Konrad, at least temporarily.

Kurt just shook his head. He could see it was going to be an interesting evening, sitting with the jokester of Nuremberg and a princess of the city's social elite. Aunt Hilda had prepared a feast for supper, but the conversation made the meal secondary. The main topic of conversation was, of course, the Nuremberg Rally. Nonetheless, at every opportunity Uncle Konrad found a way to bring up the possibility of a relationship between Erika and Kurt.

"I just love the month of September, don't you Erika? It's such a romantic month in our city."

"And what possible thing do you know about romance, you old troll?" asked Hilda.

"Well, in my younger days I was quite a ladies' man."

"That must have been long before I met you and took pity on you."

Konrad was unfazed. "What about you, Kurt? Don't you think Nuremberg has a romantic air to it on a cool autumn evening, say, like tonight?"

Erika actually knew Kurt's uncle far better than Kurt did, and she never let him get the best of her if she could possibly help it. "Maybe you and Kurt should head down to the local Rattskeller. There might be some lonesome frauleins in town for the Rally. I mean, it's such a romantic night."

Aunt Hilda had a generous portion of potato salad in her mouth and nearly choked as she squealed with laughter at Erika's rebuttal.

Konrad responded, "Well, we just might. Right, Kurt?"

"I have enough on my mind without having to chaperone you, Uncle. I'm sure I wouldn't be able to keep up with you anyway!"

Everyone had a resounding laugh at Konrad's expense, and Kurt was surprised at the cleverness of his comeback. But Uncle Konrad was far from done. "I don't want to embarrass anyone, but if I was an eligible young lad in the presence of a young beauty like Erika, I would know what to do."

"Enough of such silliness, Konrad. You're making everyone uncomfortable. I'm sure Erika and Kurt can take of themselves without your constant meddling."

Kurt looked at his aunt and said, "Thank you."

The rest of the meal passed without another "Konradian" incident, and the conversation remained centered on the coming Rally events. After supper Erika and Hilda did the dishes while Kurt and his uncle retired to the study.

"Kurt, what exactly are you taking Erika to tomorrow? A Hitler Youth what?"

"I'm not exactly sure, Uncle. I think it's a combination picnic and rally for the local chapter of the Hitler Youth, kind of a kick-off for the coming week's activities."

"Hans is a leader in the Hitler Youth. I assume you know that."

"Yes, it's hard to forget. I've been told many times already."

"And did anyone tell you that he is soon to join the Verfugungstruppe?"

"Yes, in fact Erika just told me that on the way over here."

"Kurt, you're a young man who needs to make up his own mind about things, but I can tell you that if you're interested in Erika, you'll never have a chance with her unless you follow after Jurgen and Hans." Konrad paused and tamped some tobacco into his pipe. "Hilda and I couldn't have children of our own, and Erika is like a daughter to us. I have known her nearly her whole life. She's a very strong-willed, proud person, but she's also a very good person, and that is enough on that subject."

Just as Kurt was about to ask his uncle what advice he could give him about getting into the Verfugungstruppe, Hilda and Erika entered the room.

"Well, don't you two look comfortable? I hope you haven't worked too hard sitting in those nice soft chairs."

Kurt's uncle looked at his wife, exhaled a puff of smoke and replied sarcastically, "Why don't you go back in the kitchen?"

"Why don't you and I go for a walk, and let Kurt and Erika visit alone for a little? I'm sure they don't need old people hovering over them all the time."

Erika looked surprised. "That's not necessary, Aunt Hilda. Kurt and I can visit tomorrow. We came to visit with you tonight."

"Well, Konrad needs to go for a walk. Look at how fat he's getting," laughed Hilda.

"Yes, and I suppose you think you look like a movie star," grumbled Konrad.

Soon Kurt found himself alone with Erika, except for their frequent companion: silence. Erika just sat in her chair, a tiny smile forming on her lips while she watched Kurt struggle with his uneasiness. Finally, she took pity on the poor soul sitting across from her, shattering the brittle stillness. "Kurt, tell me about your family and Ansbach. I don't think I've ever been there."

Thankful to Erika for ending the wordless vacuum, Kurt recited a short history of his family and described the highlights of his hometown. Feeling better after finishing his genealogical journey, Kurt asked Erika, "What about your parents and Hans? Have they always been such ardent followers of Hitler?"

"I think we as a family have supported Hitler for quite some time. I know that my father's business has been helped by his contacts with the Nazi Party, but I really believe the reason we've supported Hitler is because we think he's the best hope for the future of Germany. Look what he's done already."

"I don't think everyone feels that way," replied Kurt.

"Well, you can never make all the people happy."

"What about the people that oppose Hitler? They never get a chance to offer any opposition. They just get sent away."

"During hard times it takes a strong leader and strict measures to survive, and at times people who stand in the way have to suffer."

"What about the Jews? Why are they being made the scapegoat for all of Germany's problems?"

"Hitler's not the first person to recognize the Jews as a divisive force in the world. What has he really done to them? Deprive them of German citizenship and make them second-class people in Germany? They should all just leave Germany, and everyone would be happy."

Erika paused, gave Kurt a formidable stare, and continued, "I thought you were a follower also, or are you just a mommy's boy?"

Indignantly, Kurt replied, "Excuse me! My mother's entitled to her opinion, and so am I. I'll make up my own mind, and I don't need you or your brother or your parents to do it for me."

Kurt would never know it for many months, but it was this moment that began to kindle Erika's serious interest in Kurt. She'd never been challenged by a potential suitor before, and it enticed her.

"I'm sure you will, Herr Heisler. I only hope you make the right one."

"And what's the right one?"

"As you just so defiantly stated, only you can decide how Kurt Heisler can best serve the Fatherland. But—and this is only the opinion of a young girl—if you choose to ignore Hitler and his dreams, I think you'll find yourself on the outside looking in, if you know what I mean."

Kurt looked at Erika and smiled, but inside he was debating the ending of her last sentence. Did she mean "on the outside looking in" at Hitler or at Erika von Klugemann? Mulling that question over in his mind, Kurt decided it was time to change the tone of the conversation. "Erika, I hope you aren't still mad about being forced to go with me tomorrow."

"I already said that I wasn't. We'll have fun, and maybe the Nuremberg night will seduce you into becoming a more ardent member of the Hitler Youth. Right now, though, I think we should walk back over to my house.

It's only about thirty minutes until curfew, and maybe Hans is home, and we can talk about tomorrow."

Hans was not home yet, and Frau and Herr von Klugemann were busy, so Erika and Kurt found themselves saying goodnight on the von Klugemanns' front steps. There, Erika boldly positioned herself face to face with Kurt, tantalizing him with an intimate glimpse of the face of temptation. "Be on guard tomorrow night, Kurt. When the bonfire licks its way into the Nuremberg night, strange things can happen. I'll see you tomorrow. Good night."

Before Kurt had a chance to say or do anything, Erika had spun around and entered her house. Kurt walked home in his familiar daze, visited briefly with his aunt and uncle, and retired to his room. Sleep, as was its recent custom with Kurt, came slowly. He agonized over Erika's every word and fantasized over the face that had almost touched his. He finally drifted off with visions of bonfires dancing in his head.

———

Morning came with all the splendor and promise that a new day brings to those in search of their destiny. The sun slowly crawled from the depths below the horizon before starting its blazing arc across the heavens. The fresh, slightly-chilled air of early autumn introduced vigor and vitality to the dashes of color in Mother Nature's bouquet. Amidst all this stimulation, Kurt's spirits were tingling with anticipation as he sat down to breakfast.

"Well, nephew, did you sleep okay, or did you dream about Erika all night?"

"Uncle Konrad, even your teasing can't harm me today. I can just feel the excitement of the Rally all around, and it hasn't even started yet."

"Oh, it's begun, but we won't be going to anything until tomorrow. Today, you just concentrate on your party. The rest of the week you'll be dazzled and amazed by what you see and hear."

"Eat your breakfast, Kurt," scolded Aunt Hilda.

"I'm not very hungry, but I guess I'll need my strength. Right, Uncle?"

They all laughed and happily chattered their breakfast away, engaged in the conversation of the disciples awaiting the arrival of their savior. Soon, however, Kurt's uncle had to leave for work, and his aunt began her household chores. Kurt was left to await the phone call Hans had promised he would get that morning.

By eleven o'clock Kurt was getting nervous. He was starting to think about a myriad of things that could go wrong, and imaginary catastrophes filled his head. As the noon hour approached, there was still no word from Hans. Just as a state of panic was about to consume Kurt, salvation arrived in the form of Hans von Klugemann in his Hitler Youth leader's dress uniform, ringing the front doorbell.

"Aunt Hilda, is Kurt ready to go?"

"I don't think so. I think he was waiting for you to call to tell him when to be ready and what to expect."

"It's my fault. I've been so busy I forgot to call. Can I talk to him?"

"Yes, you can," yelled Kurt as he came down from his room.

"Good morning, Kurt. I hope you slept well."

"Morning. Hans, it's nearly noon, and why is everyone so concerned about how much sleep I got last night?"

"I just told Aunt Hilda I forgot to call because I had so many things to take care of. Anyway, we'll pick you up exactly at two o'clock and then go straight to the Hitler Youth games. Erika and Kris will be with me, and you'll be that last one being picked up. Do you have any questions?"

"I guess not. You've already told me what to expect."

"Well, then, I need to take care of some last minute details. See you at two. Heil Hitler!"

"Heil Hitler!" saluted Kurt.

Kurt and his aunt had a quick lunch, and then Kurt went to his room to put his Hitler Youth uniform on and get ready. It was already a little after one, and Kurt was starting to realize that the moment was nearly at hand, his first date with Erika.

Fully dressed in his uniform, Kurt slowly walked over to the bed and sat down. He continued to think about his image. Is this what he really

wanted to be? He knew that being with Erika, Hans, and their friends singing Nazi songs around a campfire during the beginning of the Nuremberg
Rally would not be a time for objective reasoning, only emotional feelings. Familiar questions again hijacked Kurt's thinking, and he felt an urgency to answer them once and for all. Should he leave home and try to
join the Verfugungstruppe and follow after Jurgen? Is that what he really
wanted, or was he just trying to impress Erika? Was he being influenced
by his friends and not making his own rational choices? Had he overly ro-
manticized Nordic mythology and wrongly connected it to Hitler and the
SS? Would the grandeur and pageantry of the Nuremberg Rally push him
in the wrong direction? Unfortunately for Kurt, the questions came much
faster than the answers.

Kurt breathed deeply and made a decision—almost. Yes, he admitted
to himself, all of the factors he had considered were influencing his decision about trying to join the SS, but he felt fairly sure that he wanted to
join the Verfugungstruppe because that is how he wanted to best serve
the Fatherland.

"Kurt, are you ready? It's almost two o'clock."

Hilda's voice startled Kurt out of his examination of conscience, and
he realized he had been conducting his soul searching far longer than
expected.

"How do I look, Aunt Hilda?"

"Very impressive, Kurt. I think a certain young lady will be swept off
her feet."

"Not you, too. Uncle Konrad is enough."

Hilda smiled, patted Kurt on the shoulder, and then gave him a moth-
erly hug. "I hear a car. Kurt, you'd better go. Have fun, and we'll see you
later tonight."

"Thanks. See you later."

Kurt strode out the front door and into his future with the Third Reich.

A large, black touring car driven by a chauffeur was idling in the street.
As Kurt walked toward it, the chauffer came around and opened the door
for him. Leaning over to get in, Kurt peered inside and saw Erika sitting
demurely on the far side of the back seat. In the front seat Hans and Kris
were urging him to hurry up. As Kurt sat down, Hans introduced him to

Kris. "Kris, this is my friend, Kurt, from Ansbach. Kurt, this is Kris. Kurt, I've already told Kris all about you."

"Only good things, I hope."

"Mostly," Kris replied cheerfully.

Erika said nothing, and Kurt was almost afraid to look at her. As the chauffeur headed the car toward their destination, Hans and Kris began their own conversation, and Kurt turned to Erika. She and Kris were dressed in the uniform of the League of German Girls: dark navy skirt, white blouse, and black kerchief held closely at the neck with a woven leather ring. The League of German Girls was, in effect, the female branch of the Hitler Youth. Like the boys' program, the League stressed physical fitness and team activities, which accounted for about two-thirds of their time; the rest was dedicated to various forms of propaganda and indoctrination. While the Hitler Youth's main purpose was to prepare ardent soldiers for the Fatherland, the League's goal was to provide proper wives and mothers to administer to the needs of the male members of the Reich. Erika enjoyed the competition and camaraderie of the League program, but she was much too independent to become very zealous about the indoctrination aspect. Consequently, Erika—unlike Hans—was not in an exalted leadership position. Whenever her mother rebuked her for her lackluster performance, Erika would respond by saying, "Well, Mother, I guess I'm just too much like you."

Kurt started the conversation. "It's funny, but I never thought of you as a member of the League of German Girls. It just doesn't seem like you."

"I guess there's a lot you don't know about me."

"I hope that will change."

Erika studied Kurt as she contemplated his last comment, and then said, "If you're on my team today, you'd better play well, or you won't have a chance to find out any more about me. I always win."

"I think I just found out something else about you, didn't I?"

"What?"

"That you're always trying to be as dominant as your mother. You want her to be proud of you."

"My, my, aren't we a little Freudian expert all of a sudden? Don't try to analyze me, Kurt. You'll just confuse yourself."

"Kurt," Kris said, looking at him from the front seat, "Hans tells me you're joining the Verfugungstruppe with him in a few months. Is that true?"

Kurt turned away from Erika and faced his questioner. Hans had been correct when he had described Kris as being "unbelievable." She was a prototypical Aryan female: blond, blue-eyed, full-breasted, and physically fit. Kris was a little taller and heavier than Erika, and her features were not as exquisite, but she presented a robust, healthy look that made her instantly likable. Before Kurt had a chance to answer Kris' questions, Hans offered an explanation. "Sorry, Kurt, I haven't had a chance to talk with you about it, but I think it would be great if we joined together, and I think it's very possible. If you're interested, I'll explain my idea in more detail later."

"Sure, I'd be interested in listening to your idea, and maybe we can ... "

"You two joining the SS army," Erika snickered. "Now that's a scary thought. Why, if Hitler knew I bet he'd be overcome with excitement."

"Erika, shut up!" exclaimed Hans.

Abruptly, the chauffer stopped the car and announced that they had reached their destination. A large, tree-filled park surrounded Kurt and his friends as they exited the car amidst a panorama of activity. About four hundred members of the Hitler Youth and the League of German Girls were milling about the various playing fields lined with picnic tables heaped with food. In one corner of the field a large pyramid of wood stood ready to be torched.

The party was intended as both a reward and a call-to-action for the local youth leaders connected to the Nuremberg Party Rally. A few resident dignitaries made speeches, but the local Hitler Youth leaders were mainly in charge. Kurt had been involved in similar activities back in Ansbach, but he had never seen such a level of fervor and enthusiasm as he was witnessing in this Nuremberg park. When Hans gave a short speech promoting service to the Fatherland, Kurt actually got goose bumps on his forearms. At the speech's conclusion, one excited young lad got up and yelled, "Let the games begin!"

During most of the ensuing activities the sexes were separated into teams competing against their own gender, but in one event, the relay race, they were combined. Nearly thirty teams—each made up of two boys and two girls—were entered in the relay event. The running order was girl-boy-girl-boy, and each runner had to run one hundred meters and then hand off to a teammate running back in the opposite direction. The four fastest teams from the preliminaries would be in the finals.

After listening to the instructions, the teams got together to position their runners and plan their strategies. As part of the planning committee, Hans had worked his magic to ensure that Kurt, Erika, Kris and he were on the same team. Kurt had not seen Erika since the beginning of the games, and as Hans read aloud the order for the relay, Kurt couldn't keep his eyes off her. Any reservations he might have had about wanting Erika evaporated as he gazed at the lithe, athletic goddess across from him. Erika was totally immersed in the pursuit of victory—hair in disarray, face flushed and glistening with the sweat of battle, and unwavering eyes gleaming fiercely.

"Kris, you'll run first. I'll go second and hand off to Erika. Kurt, you'll run anchor. Any questions?" Hans said in clipped, authoritative tones.

No one spoke.

"Remember, in the preliminaries we're competing only against the clock. We have to be among the four best times to make the finals. In the finals we're running strictly against the other three teams," Hans added.

"I know three of us are good runners. I hope you are, Kurt," Erika warned.

Kurt smiled as he bent over to stretch. "Assuming I don't get the baton too far behind, we'll win, Fraulein von Klugemann."

Before Kurt had time to even think about it, the race was over. Hans was a steady runner, Kris was a powerful runner, Kurt was a fast runner, and Erika was a gazelle. After the preliminaries were completed, Hans joined the other team captains to find out the results, leaving his teammates to ponder their status.

"I hope we make the finals."

"Don't worry Kris, we did. Our anchor ran much better than I expected." Erika gave Kurt a fetching, mysterious expression of approval and continued. "If we run that well again, I think we'll win."

Hans returned with the information that confirmed part of Erika's prediction. "Well, we made the finals, but two teams had better times, so we need to run better if we want to win."

Erika then gave Kurt her first real compliment as she assessed the situation. "We'll be able to see everyone we're running against, so all we need to do is make sure Kurt's close at the last exchange, and we'll win. Let's go!"

Kurt felt as if he had been knighted by Hitler himself. He dare not fail.

Kris and Hans ran well, but by the time Erika got the baton, she was fifteen meters behind. She was a flash of blond lightning, and when she finished her leg, she got the baton to Kurt only about five meters behind. Running as if his future depended on it, Kurt caught the lead runner at the tape … victory! An overly excited Erika jumped into his arms and gave him a sweaty hug, kissed him on the cheek, and yelled, "Kurt, we won! We won!"

Savoring her kiss and feeling Erika's hot, moist cheek next to his, Kurt experienced a level of delirium he never knew existed. As Erika's breasts pressed firmly against him, and her rapidly beating heart pulsated into his chest, he felt as if he'd been transported to Valhalla to visit with the Gods.

Erika quickly regained her composure. "I'm sorry, Kurt. That was inappropriate of me. I just get so excited sometimes." Kurt mumbled something about it being okay as she turned to join some of her other friends, but he was unaware of anything else for a few minutes. Eventually, the blood started flowing back into his brain, and he could function again, but he retained a flush of excitement for the rest of the day, which proved to be anti-climatic.

Kurt rejoined the group and ate, drank, and laughed with his new friends. A little after eight o'clock the entire group of the young faithful gathered around the pyramid of wood. The pyre of timber was set ablaze, sending fingers of light darting into the growing darkness. The group formed an enormous circle around the fire, and as they held hands and sang songs to the Fatherland, Kurt put his arm around Erika's waist, and she accepted it naturally. He remembered her admonishment from the previous day. "Yes," Kurt thought, "it is a magic night, and I am under Nuremberg's spell. Truly, I am among the blessed."

As the fire burned down, Hans announced that curfew was nearing and the party was over. As the crowd dispersed, Hans came over to Kurt and told him that the chauffeur would take Hans and Kris over to her home but would drop Kurt off at the von Klugemann home so Kurt could say good night to Erika and walk home.

During the ride back to the von Klugemanns, Kurt's heart was beating nearly out of control. How should he say good night? Had he already been too forward? Was Erika just having fun with him? Should he try to kiss her? Everything was happening too fast, and Kurt was floating outside his own body. Suddenly the car stopped to let Kurt and Erika out, and as it drove away Hans yelled, "I'll call you sometime in the next few days, Kurt. Be nice to my sister."

Standing in the front entryway, Kurt and Erika looked at each other. Erika spoke first. "See, I told you it would be fun. I'm glad you took me."

"I'm glad you agreed to go with me."

"I better go in now."

Kurt's mind was whirling. Why was Erika so abrupt? Was she worried about the curfew or did she just want to get rid of him? What should he do?

Sensing Kurt's plight, Erika floated to his rescue, at least a little. "Kurt, I'd like to see you again before you go back to Ansbach. Would you like to see me?"

"I think you know the answer to that."

"Good night, then, and I'll talk to you later this week."

Erika held out her hand, and Kurt gently squeezed it and said, "Goodnight, Erika."

———

Kurt did not see or talk to Erika for the next three agonizing days. The spectacle of the Nuremberg Rally, however, provided enough distraction, even for a love-struck teenager. Kurt had tried to prepare himself for the intense propaganda and extreme nationalism he knew the Rally would incite in him, but he soon realized nothing could have prepared him for an event of this magnitude. To Germans, the Rally was a pilgrimage, and Nuremberg was its Mecca.

The sheer size and the organizational precision of the event were beyond description. Kurt would not have believed it himself had he not been there to observe it directly . To house the influx of people, tent cities had been erected in parks and open areas, their canvas structures spaced in exact, carefully measured rows to maximize ease of movement. Thousands of latrines were strategically placed throughout the city to facilitate the human traffic. Even the food was distributed with strict military precision. At night thousands of neon-lit Nazi eagles, floodlights, loudspeakers, flags and banners created a swirling atmosphere of light, sound, power and motion that enveloped the crowds overrunning the stadiums and streets. To prevent unnecessary loitering, the police had declared certain city sections off limits and enforced strict curfews. As further insurance, Nazi Party officials, regular army soldiers, and SS troops were stationed throughout the city to ensure nothing disturbed the well-rehearsed flow of the Nazi program. The organizers' absolute attention to even the smallest detail—this nearly neurotic control of people's movements—left Kurt dumbstruck.

As the Rally progressed, two unforgettable events carved particularly deep impressions in Kurt's young psyche, creating a phenomenon comparable to religious ecstasy. The first occurred the night Kurt and his aunt and uncle went to the Zeppelinwiese Arena to hear Hitler. As Kurt entered the stadium, the overwhelming spectacle sucked his senses right out of him. The arena was aglow with searchlights shooting brilliant beams straight up into the black sky, piercing the darkness with a ring of man-made fire. Focused streams of light bathed the massive swastikas and golden images of eagles atop the flags throughout the stadium. Wagnerian anthems—musical salutes to stir the Teutonic soul—blasted from the loudspeakers, arousing the blood of every German. The massed flags, the klieg lights, the banners, the blending of darkness and light created a mystical ambiance. The scene was so overpowering that Kurt had trouble walking; Uncle Konrad had to keep pushing him forward to his seat, where they joined the eager faithful who were already jammed into the stands and focused on the events on the field.

The crowd roared as thousands of Nazi flag-bearers moved eerily in and out of the light on the stadium floor as they performed intricate drill maneuvers. Suddenly, the action stopped and everyone snapped to attention as a hush enveloped the arena. The lights went out, plunging the silent crowd into utter darkness. Then, slowly, one by one, a few lights flicked on and started sweeping the stage randomly before centering on a lone figure. As the mob recognized their master, they erupted in a thundering chorus of "Sieg Heils!" The effect of two hundred thousand voices—all screaming in total darkness—gripped Kurt's soul in an emotional vise. The roar became deafening, and Kurt found himself waving his arms and screaming with everyone else, as if to extend the limits of the universe. The faces of the swelling multitude contorted into crazed, maniacal masks as they continued to cheer. Women looked as if they were gazing at the Messiah, with wild, adoring looks that defied description. Kurt marveled at the intensity of feeling that poured forth from the spectators. "What kind of man could create such a wave of emotional abandonment?" he wondered. Gradually, the chorus died down and Hitler began to speak. As der Fuhrer continued, Kurt's heart pounded harder and harder until it reached a dangerous crescendo, his desire to serve the Fatherland growing with an irrational will of its own. Kurt felt his skin tingle and draw together as he no longer felt like an individual; he had become a part of the collective that existed now as one and would last through the rest of the program. (Later, back at Uncle Konrad's, Kurt was still so caught up in the fervor he couldn't even remember how he got home.)

Kurt's second baptism into the ranks of Hitler's legions took place the next day at the massive concrete structure called the Luitpoldhain. Sitting in the stands with ninety thousand spectators, Kurt noticed that every inch of usable space sported some type of Nazi symbol, just like at the Zeppelinwiese. Huge concrete eagles glared down upon the spectators as they sang their salute of praise to der Fuhrer. At one end of the arena where the Nazi dignitaries were displayed, three enormous, rectangular Nazi flags stretched far into the sky. In the stands the crowd sat mesmerized by the activities of two hundred and fifty thousand participants on the stadium floor. Preening troops packed shoulder to shoulder goosestepped around the stadium, the thunder of their boots echoing across the arena, accompanied by the roar of tanks and the drone of planes passing overhead. As the crowd roared its approval, Kurt found himself renewing the zeal he had exhibited the night before, even though the experiences were totally different. The Zeppelinwiese event had been a mystical, religious experience, while the Luitpoldhain rally was a naked display of military might. Both, however, demonstrated Hitler's ability to create a hypnotic mastery over his followers and showcased the brilliant organizational and theatrical abilities of the Nazi state. And both worked their magic on Kurt. Zeppelinwiese captured his soul; Luitpoldhain secured his allegiance.

Days later when Kurt tried to recall what Hitler had actually said during his speeches, he found that he could remember very little. There had been the predictable references to the hated Jews, the lowly Bolsheviks, the dangers of communism and, of course, appeals to all true Germans to do their duty for the Fatherland, but nothing specific. Like the Germans before him, Kurt learned that falling under Hitler's spell was an emotional response, not an intellectual one. Germans found Hitler with their hearts, not their minds.

During these head-spinning few days Kurt had not forgotten about Erika, but he had been preoccupied to the point that he had shuffled her into the background. A call from Hans three days after the Hitler Youth outing forced Kurt to face the stark reality that he would be leaving Nuremberg in a few days. Hans mentioned in passing that Erika wanted to see him before he returned to Ansbach, but said he was calling for a much more important reason: Did Kurt want to try to join the Verfugungstruppe?

If Hans had asked the same question even a few days earlier, Kurt would have hesitated. For months he had existed in the grey world of doubt and indecision, straddling the abyss, one foot on his mother's side and one foot on Jurgen's, but during the last few days Kurt's soul had been captured by the pagan spectacle he had witnessed. There had been so many experiences pulling at his emotions that he didn't know exactly when he had reached his decision, only that he had. By challenging his core, the Nuremberg Rally had etched its image on his soul, and he had accepted his brother's way of life. His answer to Hans regarding the Verfugungstruppe was by now a foregone conclusion; he couldn't say "yes" fast enough. Hans told him he would call him in the morning with further instructions.

Kurt sat in his room the next day waiting for Hans' call. By now he had recovered enough from the emotionalism of the last few days to realize how badly he wanted to see Erika again. Just as he was about to give up on Hans, the door to his room opened and in walked Hans, talking excitedly, as usual. "Your aunt told me just to come up and surprise you. I hear you're really impressed with the events you attended. So was I, but we can compare notes later. Right now I have some information to give you, and we need to go over some things."

Kurt shook his head and said, "No, not another one of your famous plans, please, no."

"No jokes. This is serious stuff. First of all, you did agree to try to get into the Verfugungstruppe with me, right?"

"Yes."

"Okay. Now here's the good news. My mother and father are having a big party tomorrow night. I'm going to arrange it so you can come over and meet some of these important people—and see Erika, by the way—but I haven't worked out all the details yet. I definitely have some ideas that might help us get into the Verfugungstruppe. I'll call you tomorrow with more details, but make sure you keep tomorrow night free."

With that final order, Hans left as quickly and as noisily as he had arrived, and Kurt decided it was time to share his decision with Uncle Konrad and Aunt Hilda. In the past few days Kurt had spent a lot of time talking with them about the implications of the Rally and the inherent duty of all Germans to follow a path of service to the Reich, so his announcement about joining the Verfugungstruppe with Hans came as no surprise to them.

"Please, don't tell my parents. I'll do that, but I'm not sure when. I suppose it depends on if and when I get in, and what the circumstances are at the time."

"Don't worry. I won't let your blabbermouth of an uncle say anything," promised Hilda.

Konrad was as serious as he had ever been with Kurt. "I'm very proud of you, Kurt. You're quickly becoming a man, a man that Germany needs. This is even better than I had hoped for when we first learned you were coming. I don't want to get ahead of you here, but just how are you planning to apply?"

"Hans has a plan, but he hasn't told me what it is yet. Tomorrow night his parents are having a big party, and a number of high-ranking Nazis will be there, including Sepp Dietrich, the head of the Leibstandarte. I doubt Hans will have any trouble getting in with all the connections his parents have. I hope Jurgen's being in the Leibstandarte will help me. Maybe Hans' parents and you could also help by speaking up for me?"

"Have you forgotten that I've already mentioned those possibilities to you? Of course we'll speak for you," reminded Konrad. Assuming an academic tone, he continued. "You'll have to take a very demanding physical. Plus, there'll be a background check to see if you have any distant relative with impure blood. I hear the SS goes back at least a couple hundred years to check that no inferior strain contaminates your pure Aryan blood. But Jurgen's already passed that test, so you won't have a problem. "

"By the way, Kurt, I almost forgot. Herr Bauer called this afternoon and said he'd pick you up promptly at ten o'clock the day after tomorrow. Your time here has certainly gone fast."

"Yes, it has, and I haven't seen Erika since ...." Kurt tried to suck his words back into his mouth, but it was too late.

Surprisingly, Uncle Konrad was rather compassionate. "Kurt, my nephew, I think you should do something about that very soon, don't you? Does your fair maiden know of your plans?"

"I was just going to talk to you about that. I invited Hans and Erika over for lunch tomorrow afternoon. I hope you don't mind. Also, Hans asked me to sleep over at his place tomorrow night. His parents asked me over to their party to meet some of the dignitaries, and by staying over I don't have to worry about the curfew. I can also help out with the party."

"And, conveniently, also have a little extra time with Erika. What do you say, Hilda? Do you think my brother and his wife will forgive us if we let their son stay overnight at his new girlfriend's house?" The familiar leering Konrad was back.

"Konrad! Enough of your silliness!" Hilda gave him a look that only a wife can give, and Konrad shrunk meekly into his chair.

Hilda beamed at Kurt. "I think it's all a wonderful opportunity for you, both to see Erika and to help your career. But the best news, Kurt, is that your uncle and I cannot attend the von Klugemanns' party."

"Thank you, God," Kurt responded, looking skyward as Konrad feigned disappointment.

———

As Kurt prowled around the house waiting for Hans and Erika to come for lunch, he thought about Ansbach for the first time in over a week. It dawned on him that he would soon be back with his own family and friends. He had only been gone from home a week and hadn't traveled very far, but time and distance had existed in another dimension during the Nuremberg Rally. He wondered if he should tell anyone about Erika, but worried more about the effect his joining the SS would have on his mother. Small seeds of doubt still inhabited the deep corners of Kurt's mind, but he was sure he had made the right decision to serve the Reich. Even as a fleeting twinge of conscience lightly pricked Kurt's reasoning as he rationalized away his doubts, he felt confident about following in his brother's footsteps. Thinking so hard that he was actually sweating, Kurt gradually broke out of his trance of self-approval and noticed that it was nearly eleven-thirty. Full of confidence, he went upstairs to freshen up a little. After splashing some water on his face and toweling off, he straightened his clothes and combed his hair. Kurt liked this new person staring back at him from the mirror, especially when he mentally replaced his civilian clothes with a sleek, black SS uniform.

Kurt Heisler walked down the stairs with the stride of a young man on a mission.

———

Kurt knew this day could prove to be one of the most significant days of his life, and he needed to take advantage of every opportunity. Uncle Konrad wasn't coming home for lunch, but Aunt Hilda still produced enough food to feed the entire block. By the time Kurt reached the kitchen, she had already set the table, stacked the various meats, breads and cheeses on plates and was lighting two candles.

"Aunt Hilda, there are only four of us. Who's going to eat all this food?"

"Just never mind."

"And what are these candles for?"

"Well, I just thought that this might be your last meal at my house for some time, and with Hans and Erika over, I thought candles would give it a special atmosphere."

"Aunt Hilda, you're a special atmosphere all by yourself."

"My, aren't we in a charming mood today."

"I guess I just take after Uncle Konrad."

"For God's sake, don't even joke about that. Konrad and charming should never be mentioned in the same sentence."

As Kurt and his aunt laughed heartily at Konrad's expense, there was a knock on the door. Aunt Hilda opened it and admitted Hans and Erika, both of whom seemed overly eager to escape to the Heisler household for lunch.

"Thank you so much for getting us out of our house. You know what mother's like when she's hosting such a big event, and Hans doesn't help matters much by continually getting in her way."

"What do you mean?" Hans asked indignantly.

"What do I mean? Every time mother turned around you were there asking her who was coming and whether you could meet them."

"Oh, shut up or Kurt will see what you're really like."

Aunt Hilda stepped in. "Ok, enough sibling babble! Sit down and eat before your mother calls and I send you home for causing a disturbance."

Kurt had not uttered a word to this point. He was being reminded of just how striking Erika von Klugemann was.

"Kurt, are you ready to meet Sepp Dietrich?" Before Kurt could answer, Hans started listing the names of some of the people who would be attending the von Klugemann reception, but stopped midway through. "I see by that dumb look on your face you're more interested in seeing Erika than in anyone I've mentioned. Kurt, you are one very sorry individual."

Kurt knew he'd been busted, and misdirection was his only defense. "That's certainly an impressive list, Hans. How are the two of you, and what parts of the Rally have you been able to attend?"

The three quickly started comparing notes about the Rally, and what had impressed them the most. Hilda's sumptuous spread and the stirring conversation kept them going for an hour before the topic switched from the Rally to the upcoming evening's activities.

"I'm guessing that everyone will be dressed very formally tonight. What shall I wear?"

Hans responded immediately. "Sorry, I thought you knew. Just wear your Hitler Youth uniform."

Hans stared at Aunt Hilda, who read his mind. "Don't worry. I've already washed it."

"Well, I'm not going to wear my pretty little German girl uniform. I'm getting more dressed up than that."

"And who are you trying to impress?" kidded Hans.

"Nobody in this room, that's for sure," Erika paused teasingly. "Well, maybe someone."

Kurt said nothing, but thought to himself, "Ok, now what does that mean? Should I even take the bait?"

Hans started for the door. "Contrary to what my sister thinks, I'm a very helpful person, and Erika and I should get back home to help out. Thank you very much for dinner, Aunt Hilda, but we'd better go."

"Yes, thank you very much," Erika said to Hilda as she looked at Kurt. "Kurt, we'll see you about seven o'clock, then?"

"The guests won't start arriving until after eight, so you can help get things ready and maybe help keep mother calm," Hans explained,

As brother and sister headed out the door, Erika turned and smiled. "Don't be late, Kurt. It'll be a great event, and you'll have fun."

———

Kurt arrived at the von Klugemanns promptly at seven o'clock. Dressed in his crisp, spotless Hitler Youth uniform, he was ready to be pressed into service by Maria von Klugemann. The von Klugemanns' dining area was dazzling, highlighted by fine wines, hors d'oeuvres and the two most attractive women Kurt had ever seen. Maria von Klugemann, in a stunning silver evening gown, greeted Kurt warmly. "Good evening, Kurt. You look very handsome in your uniform. Hans has told me of your decision to join him in attempting to get into the Verfugungstruppe. I'll do what I can to help both of you. I can already imagine how dashing you both will be in your SS uniforms. Can't you, Erika?"

Erika was dressed in a low-cut, black evening gown that clung to her slender, athletic body like it was painted on, revealing more cleavage than anything Kurt had seen her wear before. A delicate silver necklace accented the contrast between the stark black dress and her creamy skin. Erika's blond hair was fluffed up more than normal, and she presented Kurt with an image that would be seared into his memory for the rest of his life. Clearly, Erika was the only woman in the room who could take men's eyes away from her mother.

Erika had not responded to her mother's question concerning Kurt's appearance so Kurt spoke first. "Thank you for the compliment, Frau von Klugemann, and you ladies both look extremely lovely tonight. As for getting into the Verfugungstruppe, I would appreciate any help you could give me."

Kurt had attained a new level of confidence and resolve during his days at the Nuremberg Rally, and he felt compelled to act on it. Smiling boldly, he said, "Erika, you look a little different than the sweaty little runner who jumped into my arms after we won the relay at the picnic. I must say, you look especially grown-up tonight."

Maria turned to her daughter with a rather surprised look, and in a semi-scolding tone asked, "Erika, what's this about jumping into Kurt's arms? How unladylike!"

Erika glared at Kurt and then faced her mother. "Mother, we'd just won a race, and I was so excited I just jumped into Kurt after he ran the last leg of the race. You know how carried away I get during competition."

Maria laughed. "Yes, that I do know."

Kurt was bursting with surprise and satisfaction. He had actually turned the tables on Erika, and she was the one feeling uneasy. Sensing his opportunity, he seized the moment. "Frau von Klugemann, I would be happy to assist you and Herr von Klugemann in any way that I can tonight."

"Why, thank you, Kurt. That's very nice of you. Actually, you and Hans can bring up some more wine from the cellar and then help set up a few more chairs in the reception area. I think Hans is already in the cellar. Let me take you down there. Erika, I'll be right back."

Kurt looked at Erika. "I hope we'll get a chance to visit later."

Maria answered for her daughter. "Oh, I'm sure you will. Now let's go because I have a lot to do. In fact, Erika, you show Kurt where the cellar is, and then hurry back so you can help finish touching up. Hurry now!"

Erika shot Kurt a quick glance before answering, "Yes, Mother."

Walking down a long hallway that led to the wine cellar steps, Erika unleashed her indignation at Kurt. "I suppose you think you're pretty clever embarrassing me in front of my mother. Well, don't think you're going to get away with it."

"Relax, Erika. I was only having a little fun. You're too worried about being perfect all the time."

"Oh, really? Well, I guess that's not your concern, is it, Herr Heisler? Here we are." Erika opened a door and pointed down a flight of stairs.

"Do you think you can find your way down, or would you like me to take you by the hand and lead you down?"

Using whatever charm he could still muster, Kurt responded, "Yes, Erika, I'd like you to take me by the hand, and actually, I do think you're perfect."

Without saying a word, Erika took Kurt's hand and started down into the darkness. A light shone weakly from somewhere below, but neither Kurt nor Erika bothered to turn on the stairway light. About halfway down the steps, Kurt stopped and prevented Erika from leading him any further. Kurt could not believe his boldness, but the setting was just too all- consuming. It was the culminating moment of Kurt's venture into the absorbing magic of the Nuremberg Rally. The pagan splendor of the city, the intensity of his decision to join the SS, the grandeur of the von Klugemann home, and, finally, his growing attraction for Erika created a situation he could no longer control. Standing on the stairs, Kurt wondered if he was headed into the darkness or toward the light. Caught in this mysterious void, he put his arm around Erika's waist and pulled her to him. She did not resist. In the semi-darkness they searched each other's eyes, and both saw something that foretold a future together. One short, tender, youthful kiss was exchanged. Only one, but it was enough!

"I hope you're not offended by my forwardness."

"I wouldn't have kissed you if I hadn't wanted to. We'd better find Hans."

Before they could move another step, Hans found them. "Hey, what's going on up there? Who's there?"

"I'm bringing Kurt down to help you."

"In the dark? Good move, Erika. Look out, Kurt!"

"Shut up, Hans!" yelled Erika.

As she gave Kurt's hand a squeeze, Erika whispered, "If you tell Hans about our kiss, I guarantee you'll never get another one."

Erika delivered Kurt to Hans at the bottom of the stairs and returned immediately to help her mother.

"I hope you didn't take advantage of my sister."

"Are you kidding? She thinks I'm just a country boy straight off the farm."

"I don't think so. Here, help me carry up the wine. I don't know how many people are coming, but if they drink all these bottles, it'll be some party. Did you visit with my mother?"

"Just briefly."

"Did she mention anything about joining the SS or about Sepp Dietrich?"

"Just that she'd help if she could."

"That sounds good, and I'll remind her when we get upstairs."

Kurt and Hans hauled up three loads of wine and distributed them at strategic locations among the tables. The guests would be arriving soon, and Maria was flying around checking on last minute details. Hans slowed her down just long enough to remind her to talk to Sepp Dietrich about them.

"Why, yes, I'll mention it to General Dietrich. I'm sure he'll be able to help you. I think you're both making a wise choice. The Leibstandarte and the other units of the Verfugungstruppe are the finest groups of soldiers in our great country. I'll try to introduce you to the General if I get a chance, but there will be many people coming and going, and it may be too hectic for a formal introduction. If I can't arrange it, I'll put in a good word for you. After the first couple of groups arrive, the three of you should probably go upstairs until the crowd dies down. Then you can come down for a snack. Hans, take good care of Kurt."

As soon as Maria was out of earshot, Hans turned to Kurt with an enormous smile on his face and shouted, "We're in! When mother says she'll do something, she does it. We're in!"

"I think you've been in all along, but thanks for bringing me along."

"My goodness," Erika exclaimed as she interrupted the happy twosome. "What could make you two so happy? Did mother make both of you generals?"

"Mother just said she'd get Kurt and me into the SS army. Can you imagine that?"

"Yes, especially since you already told me that earlier."

"Well, I wasn't really sure before, but now I am," answered Hans.

Erika turned to Kurt. "Congratulations. I'm sure you'll make a fine soldier."

"What about your own brother? Don't you think I'd make a fine soldier too?" grumbled Hans.

Before the three could engage in any further banter, Frau von Klugemann informed them that the guests were arriving, and that they should make an appearance, be introduced, and then disappear upstairs.

Kurt didn't even have time to get nervous. Before he really realized the significance of what was taking place, he was in the process of meeting some of the most powerful people in Germany. Later, he would remember shaking hands with von Ribbentrop, the German Foreign Minister; Bormann, Hitler's closest advisor; Goebbels, the Minister of Propaganda, and the man dressed in the black and silver ceremonial dress of the SS, General Sepp Dietrich. The entire grandiose scene passed quickly, like a fleeting dream, and within a few minutes Kurt and the two von Klugemann children were upstairs.

Erika, Hans, and Kurt went into Kurt's room and began to visit about the whole wonderful world that they were becoming a part of, the world of power that was Nazi Germany. Then, out of nowhere, Hans did something that earned him Kurt's friendship forever. "Erika, Kurt, I know you two would like to be alone for a little bit, so I'm going out for a short time, say about twenty minutes. Make your plans to see each other again. And, Erika, remember, I was nice to you at least this once."

Hans left, and Kurt and Erika were awkwardly alone. Erika was somewhat embarrassed about the affection she had already shown to a stranger, and she had decided to act proper and aloof.

"I hope your stay in Nuremberg was all that you'd hoped for, Kurt."

"It was much more than that. Everything I wanted to see, I saw. Everything I wanted to decide about my future, I did. Plus—and I mean this sincerely—I met you."

"I'm glad I met you also. You'll have to come to Nuremberg and see us all again before you leave for basic training."

"Well, I don't know if I'll get into the Verfugungstruppe, but if we do, Hans thinks it would be about January before we'd leave."

"I hope Hans is still here for Christmas. If he is, maybe you could come and visit us then?"

"That would be great. I guess now we'll just have to wait and see how things work out. If Hans and I go in together, I'm sure we'll want to get together a couple of times before we actually leave." Kurt knew what he wanted to do next, but he didn't dare. It took all the courage he had to just blurt out, "Erika, I'll miss you. I'd like to see you again and get to know you better."

"I agree. We do need to get to know each other better." Erika got up and walked toward the door, making sure there would be no kiss this time. "We should go and find Hans and see what he's doing. I'm sure you and I'll see each other again."

Before Erika had a chance to open the door, it flew open and Hans burst into the room.

"Kurt, we're in! I just talked with my mother, and she said the two of us would be joining the Verfugungstruppe together, assuming we pass all the tests. She just told me Sepp Dietrich said the SS was increasing the size of its army branch, and that with our credentials, he didn't see any problems. Man, isn't that fantastic?"

Hans paused a second to catch his breath. "And if that news isn't good enough, my dad gave me two bottles of wine and a few snacks to celebrate. He even gave me a glass for you, Erika."

Hans poured everyone a glass, and they quickly toasted the occasion before Hans reverted to his usual bluntness. "Say, you two better have a quick goodbye kiss. Erika, mother wants you downstairs in a few minutes to start helping with something."

Defiantly walking toward the door, Erika said over her shoulder. "I'm sorry, Hans, but Kurt and I need no advice from you on saying goodbye. See you both downstairs."

"Women!" laughed Hans.

Kurt and Hans attacked the remainder of the two bottles of wine like the two novice drinkers they were, which quickly produced a quick case of light-headedness in the two young supermen. By the time Maria called for them to come downstairs, the wine was gone, along with their coordination. As they clumsily tried to negotiate the stairs, Herr von Klugemann looked up and commented, "Hans, I think you and Kurt have done enough celebrating for tonight."

"Don't be such a worry wart, Frederick. Would you boys like something more to eat?" Frau von Klugemann motioned to the well-stocked table.

Kurt thanked her, but excused himself to go to his room, knowing that he needed to get to sleep before he did anything stupid.

Kurt and Hans woke up the next morning with slight headaches after their celebration, and neither went down for breakfast. By the time Kurt ventured downstairs, Erika had left to run some errands for her mother. Before Kurt had a chance to ask Frau Klugemann when Erika would be home, Aunt Hilda called to tell Kurt that his ride would be picking him up in one hour. Accepting that fate had determined he wouldn't see Erika again on this journey, Kurt had some final words for Frau von Klugemann. "I can't thank you enough for all your hospitality and for helping me get into the Verfugungstruppe. I hope you'll never have cause to regret helping me."

"I'm sure I won't, Kurt. You'll have to come back soon to visit us. Our home's always open to you. I know that you and Hans will need to keep in touch concerning your coming adventure."

Hans, who had now joined them in the kitchen, added, "I'll call you in a few weeks when I find out more about the selection process. I think another member of our family will be anxious to see you again, even if she doesn't always act like it."

Maria said nothing, but Kurt detected a slight smile. She and Hans walked Kurt to the door, and as Kurt exited, he turned and asked, "Would the two of you please say goodbye to Erika for me? And thank you both again for everything."

Hans shook Kurt's hand as Maria exclaimed, "You're very welcome, Kurt, and we shall look forward to your return."

Back at his uncle's, Kurt quickly packed his belongings and visited with his aunt for a while. Then, before he fully realized that his stay in Nuremberg was over, he found himself seated in the back seat of Herr Bauer's car heading back to Ansbach. Kurt's mind was a logjam of competing thoughts and images that rendered him speechless. Physically and emotionally drained, he tried to visit with the other passengers as little as possible. Eventually, wrestling with ideas of how to deal with the anticipated conflicts with his parents when he got home, he fell asleep.

CHAPTER IV

The Nazi Elite

Kurt's parents expressed a quiet joy at their son's return from the Nuremberg Rally. Frau Heisler was relieved that he had arrived home without any noticeable signs of change from his attendance at the pagan ritual. They peppered him with questions about the Rally, his impressions of what he had witnessed, his new acquaintances, and Uncle Konrad and Aunt Hilda's health. Somehow, in all his descriptions Kurt neglected to tell them about the von Klugemanns, or about being captivated by the spectacle of the Nuremberg Rally, or about his decision to try to join the Verfugungstruppe. He had decided that the best approach was to wait a few weeks and let things settle in a little before making his announcement, and he hoped his aunt and uncle kept their promise not to say anything about it to his parents before he did. But the more Kurt witnessed the relief on his mother's face at his apparent escape from the clutches of the Third Reich, the more he realized how difficult it was going to be to tell them his plans.

During his first few days home Kurt was surprised at his newfound self-assurance and confidence. In Nuremberg he had often speculated about whether his attitude about the Reich would change when he returned to Ansbach. Now, whenever he questioned the choice he had made in Nuremberg, he always reached the same conclusion: His decision to join the armed SS was right for himself and for Germany. He admitted that there was a degree of rationalization in his logic, but he didn't care.

The first people to learn of Kurt's plans were his close friends, Ernst Meyer and Walter Kruger. As soon as they could get their hands on Kurt, Walter and Ernst dragged him into Walter's basement and bombarded him with questions. Acting nonchalant, Kurt matter-of-factly recounted his experiences during the Rally. Finally, when he had created the proper level of awe in his friends, Kurt dropped his bombshell. "By the way, I was at a party where I was introduced to General Sepp Dietrich of the Leibstandarte. He's going to help me get into the Verfugungstruppe, and I think I'll be leaving sometime in late December. I haven't told anyone but you guys yet, so please don't tell a soul, especially my mother or father. I'm waiting for the right moment to tell them."

Walter and Ernst were speechless, eyes wide in astonishment. When Ernst finally found his voice, he practically shouted, "You lucky bastard! It's almost impossible to get into that part of the SS. I don't suppose there's any chance you could try to get us in?"

"I'm not in yet, but with help from my brother and some people I met in Nuremberg, I think I have a very good chance."

"What do you mean 'some people'? Sepp Dietrich is hardly some people."

Kurt laughed at Walter's analysis. "I mean some other people besides General Dietrich. You're right, though, I guess I am a lucky bastard. Seriously, guys, what branch of the military are you going to apply for?"

"I'd like to follow you into the Verfugungstruppe," answered Ernst. "I don't have your connections, but I think I'll try anyway, maybe in a year or so."

"My dad wants me to join the Luftwaffe. Can't you just see me flying an airplane?" Walter said with an exaggerated frown on his face as he imitated a pilot behind the controls of plane.

"No way," laughed Ernst, "but I guess anything's possible." Soon the three friends were lost in friendly teasing about their futures, each predicting how he would perform greater deeds of glory than the others.

From late September until early November Kurt was gone from Ansbach, working on a farm helping with the harvest as part of the Hitler Youth program. He enjoyed working outdoors with other boys his same age, and, although the work was hard, it was a satisfying time for him. He liked the physical labor, and the job provided him a temporary respite so he could plan an acceptable way to tell his parents about his decision to join the SS.

Returning home after his agricultural adventure, Kurt finally felt ready to confidently explain his decision to his parents. After allowing himself two days to get back into his usual home routines, he felt the time was right and decided to make his announcement that night after the evening meal. The meal and conversation were proceeding pleasantly when the doorbell rang. Frau Heisler went to open the door, and as she opened it, Kurt heard her gasp and in a resigned, feeble voice say, "Come in."

After walking through the front door, two officers in full dress uniform of the Leibstandarte Adolf Hitler positioned themselves in front of Kurt and his parents. Jurgen Heisler introduced Captain Karl Deutsch, and Kurt knew by the boastful grin on Jurgen's face what his brother was about to announce, but there was no way for Kurt to stop him.

"We're only going to be here for a few minutes. Captain Deutsch has other stops to make in the area before returning to Berlin. I will let him give Kurt the good news."

The Captain, in a very official voice, addressed Kurt. "Kurt Heisler, you have passed the SS genetic background check, and assuming you pass the physical examination, you have been accepted as a member of the Verfugungstruppe. Congratulations! Heil Hitler." Both Leibstandarte members clicked their heels together and saluted. Then each shook hands with Kurt. Captain Deutsch handed Kurt a packet. "Here is an official letter from SS Reichsfuhrer Himmler, information for your physical examination, your reporting date for basic training, and an introduction to the program of physical and mental training you will undergo. Please review them, report on time and arrive prepared. Do you have any questions?"

Not daring to look at his parents, Kurt replied, "Heil Hitler, Captain Deutsch. I'm proud to be given such a great honor. I only hope I will be able to live up to the standards of the Verfugungstruppe."

Jurgen added, "My special congratulations, Kurt. I'm extremely proud of you. You are soon to be a member of the most magnificent military unit in the world."

Fritz and Eva Heisler had remained motionless and silent ever since Jurgen had first started to speak. They looked stunned, especially Eva. Sensing his parent's predicament, Jurgen said, "Kurt, I can guess by the look on our parents' faces that you haven't told them about your desire to join the SS." Turning to face Fritz and Eva, Jurgen continued, "Mother, Father, I congratulate you on having two sons engaged in such a noble profession. I'll let Kurt explain why he made his choice after we leave. By the way, I've been promoted to First Lieutenant. I'm sure that makes you proud."

Fritz Heisler recovered enough to visit with Jurgen briefly while Kurt talked with Captain Deutsch. Eva was still in a state of shock. She wanted to scream, to cry, to run out of the room, but all she could do was remain transfixed like a statue. As Jurgen and Captain Deutsch prepared to leave, Eva gave Jurgen a very mechanical hug, said goodbye, and left the room. As soon as Jurgen and the Captain were gone, Eva reappeared.

Before giving his mother a chance to explode into a tirade of disappointment, Kurt boldly took the initiative. "I know you might not understand why I'm doing this, but before you disown me, I'd like to say a few things. First of all, I love you both very much. I know that both of you, especially you, Mother, are somewhat opposed to the Nazis and what they stand for. You have a right to your opinions, but I have a right to mine. I admit I still have a few questions about some of their teachings, but overall I accept the goals of the Third Reich, and I want to be a part of it. The future of Germany depends on the willingness of her citizens to sacrifice themselves to the Fatherland, and I can think of no better way for me to serve such a calling than to join the Verfugungstruppe. I think I can still observe the fundamental Christian principles that you've taught me, and I promise I won't do anything to dishonor you."

Fritz's responded, "You're right. It's your choice, Kurt, and you'll have to live with it. I hope it turns out to be what you want."

Eva, in a voice already drained of emotion, added, "Kurt, I love you and I'll always love you. There's nothing more that I can say. You already know my feelings about the Nazis, especially the SS. I had hoped that you wouldn't choose the path that has consumed your brother and distorted his attitude about the dignity of all human life. I can say no more to you, except, 'May God have mercy on your soul.'"

The next few days were spent in an atmosphere of tension and denial. Nothing was said about Kurt's choice or his coming departure, except for his explanation of why he was going back to see Uncle Konrad and Aunt Hilda so soon. Kurt told his parents about some new friends he had made in Nuremberg, and that he needed to see them again. That was all the explanation that was given or expected. Within this strained undercurrent, life went on as normal at the Heislers. Then, without fanfare or tears—but under a cloud of parental dejection—Kurt left for Nuremberg and a long-awaited reunion.

Any misgivings Kurt had created by betraying his parents quickly disappeared upon his return to Nuremberg. Uncle Konrad, in his typical carefree mood, picked Kurt up at the train station and informed him that everyone was anxious to see him again. It was the middle of November, and the "magic kingdom" was wearing its white carpet.

In the midst of such a romantic setting Kurt wanted to see as much of Erika as he could, but it didn't take him long to figure out that things weren't going to work out the way he had hoped. To begin with, he hadn't anticipated that the physical examination and other activities related to joining the Verfugungstruppe would be so time-consuming. He also hadn't given much consideration to Erika's normal schedule, which was quite full, to say the least. Combined with the shortness of his stay, these circumstances afforded few opportunities for romance.

Kurt knew Erika was popular, but he hadn't thought about how much that committed her to social events, especially at this time of the year. Erika said she wanted to spend time with him, but it seemed that whenever he called, she was already gone or was just leaving for some special event with her friends. While he was proud of her popularity, he was also bothered that she had so much time for her friends, but not much time for him. Still, he didn't want to overreact. After all, they had just met in September and had only been together a few times. So rather than getting frustrated and doing something rash, Kurt decided to confide in Hans about his concerns. Hans assured Kurt that Erika was still interested in him and that this was just a normal schedule for Erika at this time of year.

That satisfied Kurt for a while, but after a few days he felt a real need to find out more about Erika's social life. One day as he and Hans were lounging around alone at Hans' house, Kurt began to question him in more detail. "Hans, I really don't want to be a nosy old lady, but just how much does Erika date? I mean, I admit I really do like your sister. Do I have a chance with her?" Before allowing Hans to respond, Kurt added a quick condition. "Anything I ask or you tell me stays between us and goes nowhere else. Agreed?"

"Relax, friend, you're too nervous. First of all, I won't tell Erika anything, and second, yes, you definitely have a chance. Erika's very popular, and she likes being the center of attention, but there's no one person she's really interested in except you. She won't admit it to me, but I think she finds you special. But you just met her, and you aren't around much. Someone like Erika is not just going to sit around. The most important thing you have going for you—besides your good looks, of course—is that my mother likes you. If we're successful in the SS, she'll push Erika in your direction. Don't worry, Erika doesn't do anything she doesn't want to, but mother's influence will help. Trust me, just be nice, polite, show her some interest, and it'll work out. Remember, she's my sister, and I love her. If you weren't a good guy that I trusted, I wouldn't be saying this, okay?"

"Okay, but I still feel like I'm a little out of my league going after someone as popular as your sister."

"Nonsense! Quit that kind of thinking, and be a little confident in yourself. Think of your good qualities and what you're going to become. Women like men who are strong-willed and dominant, like men of the SS."

How could Kurt argue with such logic? "Yes, Herr General," was his snappy reply.

Taking Han's advice to heart, Kurt decided not to even try to see Erika alone during his stay in Nuremberg. He visited with her once when Hans was around and again with the whole von Klugemann family, but most of his time was spent fooling around with Hans. Kurt and Hans had decided to leave for the Verfugungstruppe together on January 2, 1938, so the von Klugemanns had planned a small party as a sendoff on New Year's Day. Maria and Frederick told Hans and Erika they could have some friends over on New Year's Eve for a little party of their own, including Kurt, of course.

Thinking ahead to that night, Kurt realized it didn't take a tactical genius to see the intriguing possibilities that a New Year's Eve party presented: a young soldier's last encounter with his sweetheart before he left for SS military training and a future filled with uncertainty. Could there be a better time for a young suitor to make a move? Kurt headed back to Ansbach with that scene firmly implanted in his mind.

Back home Kurt spent his last weeks mending the relationship between himself and his parents and dealing with the tasks necessary to complete the general preparation for his new life. He was only partially successful in his campaign to gain his parents' acceptance of his decision to join the SS. His father tried to understand Kurt's reasoning and did give Kurt credit for wanting to help his country. Eva, however, would not yield an inch in trying to understand Kurt's choice. She told Kurt she would always love him and pray for him, despite the fact that he had quite certainly chosen an evil occupation. Kurt remained firm in defending his decision, but he defended it as softly as he could, vowing to bring only honor to the Heisler name.

Kurt also spent time with his gang of friends, who all promised to keep in touch and get together again whenever possible. When he had left Nuremberg in the middle of November, Kurt had anticipated a long, tedious wait until he could return. Instead, the days flew by, and it was soon Christmas Eve. Kurt attended church with his parents, followed by a quiet family celebration at home. On Christmas Day some friends came over to celebrate and say goodbye, and the next day Kurt had a final supper and emotional visit with his parents, knowing there wouldn't be another for a long time. There were many tears and lingering hugs before Kurt retired to his room. Early the next morning, after a final salute to his Nordic figurine, he hugged his parents and departed for Nuremberg.

———————

On December 27 Uncle Konrad picked Kurt up at the Nuremberg train station and informed him that the von Klugemanns were still visiting relatives and would not be home for two more days. Kurt spent the free time visiting with his aunt and uncle and traveling about the city. During one of his walks, he came upon some Jewish businesses that had been boarded up and closed. The Nuremberg Laws of 1935 had taken German citizenship from Jews living in Germany and made them second-class people in their own country, and the signs clearly demonstrated that Nuremberg was a center for Jewish hatred. "Jews not wanted" and "Away with all Jews" had been painted on the buildings.

As he continued walking, Kurt pondered the Jewish question more seriously than he ever had before. After all, he was joining an organization that specialized in getting rid of the Jews. He didn't really understand why the Nazi Government considered the Jews such a menace, but he had placed his trust in Himmler and Hitler and felt they must be right. Kurt liked his feeling of Aryan superiority, and, because he liked the idea of a superior, untainted Nordic ancestry ruling Germany, he agreed with the order that Jews and pure Germans should not marry or intermingle. Besides, the world was divided between those who ruled and those who were ruled, and to Kurt, with his over-romanticized view of German history, it was obvious who should fit into each category He recalled the beliefs that had been drilled into him in school: "The strong have always dominated the weak," and nature dictates that "only the fittest survive." Kurt reasoned that if Germany were to take her rightful place among the nations of the world, organizations like the Verfugungstruppe would have to be strong and keep lesser peoples in a state of subjugation. Besides, as long as the Jews caused no more trouble, things would work out. Kurt had been over this ground before and nothing of dramatic significance resulted from his musings this day, but he did reaffirm his hope that his role in the SS would not require such minor assignments as locking up dissident Jews. He had much more to offer the Reich than being a low-level policeman. Arriving back at his uncle's, Kurt felt a renewed sense of purpose, convinced that he had made the right decision.

It wasn't until December 29 that Kurt finally went over to visit the von Klugemanns after dinner. As it turned out, he spent most of his time with Frau von Klugemann and Hans, who eagerly greeted Kurt at the door. "Come in, Kurt. Are you ready to leave? I can hardly wait!"

"Yes, I'm ready, but we do have a few days to celebrate."

"Obviously, and New Year's Eve will be a real celebration. And I know we'll get a grand send-off on New Year's Day."

"Is Erika home?"

"Well, yes and no. She's upstairs getting dressed up for some friend's party. Don't worry, she'll act coy, but she doesn't have a date; she's going with a bunch of her friends. I suggest you don't pay much attention to her. You'll get your chance on New Year's Eve. By the way, tomorrow night we're going to a party at one of my friends, and Erika is not invited. As they say, 'All's fair in love and war,' right?"

"Whatever you say, General. I'll follow you anywhere." Kurt hoped his enthusiastic response concealed his disappointment.

Soon Kurt and Hans were sitting in the living room with Maria, discussing the boys' upcoming adventure. "It's certainly an interesting time to be going into military service," Maria commented. "Challenging times are ahead, and groups such as the Leibstandarte will be in the forefront. There's the question of what to do with all the Germans living under Czechoslovakian rule in the Sudetenland, as well as the status of our relationship with Hitler's native Austria. Also, sometime in the near future I feel certain we'll need to do something about Stalin and the threat of Bolshevism."

"Mother, you really should be on the General Staff, helping to plan future campaigns."

"Don't be sarcastic, Hans, or I won't let you go and join the Verfugungstruppe," laughed Maria. "Besides, I'd rather just sit home and tell everyone what they should do."

"We know, we know," mocked Hans

"Why, hello, Kurt. When did you come over?" Erika was standing in the entryway to the living room, dressed for a night out.

Maria answered before Kurt had a chance. "Kurt's been here for about a half-hour, and I don't think it's very nice that you're going out when he's over to visit."

A slight crimson glow passed over Erika's face, but she quickly regained her composure. "I'm sorry to be leaving Kurt, but my friends and I have had this get together planned for a long time. I'll see you before you leave." Erika walked over and gave Kurt a brief, polite hug and said, "I'm glad you're here."

Erika then hugged her mother. "Bye, Mom, bye, Kurt. See you later."

"What about me?" Hans said as he feigned a hurt look.

"Good question. I've been asking that for a long time. What about you?" Erika taunted as she left the room. Kurt realized he hadn't said a word during Erika's entire performance and quickly commented, "Your daughter is certainly popular. She must take after her mother."

Maria gave Kurt a bemused smile. "You don't need to charm me, Kurt. Save your energy for Erika. If you ever get serious about her, trust me, you'll need all of it."

"He might not have to worry about it, Mother. After we get back on leave, Kurt can probably do better than Erika. The girls will be crawling all over us," interrupted Hans.

"Hans, be nice," cautioned Maria. "You know very well Kurt would be hard-pressed to find anyone better than Erika."

Maria left the boys to themselves, and for the remainder of the evening Hans and Kurt talked about the next night's activities and the plans for New Year's Eve. Kurt went back to his uncle's before Erika came home, so he didn't get to see her again that evening.

The next day Kurt and Hans had lunch with Frederick von Klugemann at one of his factories. Kurt was starting to appreciate Herr von Klugemann more and more. He was obviously a very intelligent man, and Kurt was beginning to understand why he could hold his own with Maria. After lunch Frederick gave Kurt a tour of the von Klugemann industrial complex and amazed him with his business acumen and his dry sense of humor. "A business is like a woman, Kurt. Just when you think you have everything mastered and under control, she comes up with some unexpected emergency that needs immediate attention. If you fail to address her problems, you'll lose your ability to command respect and loyalty in both areas."

Kurt gave Herr von Klugemann a confused look. Frederick laughed and responded, "Pay attention to her needs, and she'll pay attention to yours."

Kurt still wasn't sure how to interpret Herr von Klugemann's comment, but he acted like he did. "Tell me, Herr von Klugemann, how do you understand women?"

"Young man, that's one of mankind's oldest questions. The best answer I can give you is, 'Don't try.' The more you try to guess what they really mean, the more you usually mess things up. Just be consistent and forge ahead."

Kurt left the factory with a new image of Maria's husband and some added insight on how to interact with Erika.

The party at Hans' friend's home that night was nothing special. Many people were away for the holidays, and most of those present were waiting until New Year's Eve to do any real celebrating. But enough toasts were made and "good wishes" consumed to put Kurt and Hans in very good humor. They arrived back at the von Klugemanns about eleven o'clock. Both Maria and Frederick were already asleep, but Erika greeted them from the study. "Who's making all that noise? How do you expect anyone to sleep?"

Hans led Kurt into the study to confront their antagonist.

"Well, sister—or maybe I should say, Mother, since you're so worried about us—what are you doing up so late? And don't tell me you were trying to sleep here in the study, although you should be. Don't you need your rest for another party?"

"You two look like you've been having fun. What brings you home so early? Let me guess. Hans couldn't find anyone who'd listen to him."

"I won't dignify that with a response. Kurt, you can visit if you want, but I'm going to bed. See you tomorrow night." As Hans walked past Kurt, he gave him a wink and a knowing grin, and suddenly Kurt was alone with Erika.

For a change, Kurt opened the conversation. "I'm surprised you're home."

"Really? Did you think I'd just sit around and wait for you?"

Kurt reminded himself of Herr von Klugemann's advice—"Be consistent and forge ahead"—and said, "Erika, that comment's a little too sarcastic, even for you. I know you know I'm interested in you, but if you don't feel the same, let me know. I'm sure I'll survive."

Erika was momentarily stunned by Kurt's frontal attack, and it took her a few seconds to respond. "It depends on your definition of the word interested, doesn't it?"

Now Kurt was forced into a defensive situation. Erika had seized the high ground and was waiting to see how Kurt would counter her question.

"Do we have a date for tomorrow night, or are you with someone else?"

"Are you asking me for a date?"

"Yes!"

"Well, it's really not a date party. Everyone will be together in a big group just having fun."

"Well, can we have some fun together then?"

Erika gave Kurt a delicate smile, and after a measured pause said, "Yes, Kurt, I'm sure we can."

"Thank you. Now, if you'll excuse me, I'm going to bed."

New Year's Eve day was one of nervous anticipation for Kurt. It had finally hit him that this would be his last night with Erika for a very long time. He had no grandiose intentions of making a major conquest, but he hoped to achieve a few lesser objectives. He did not go over to the von Klugemanns until eight o'clock that evening, and when he arrived, Frau and Herr von Klugemann had already left to celebrate elsewhere. Kurt was introduced to many people, and as the hours marched toward midnight, most of the evening's activities unfolded as Kurt had expected, drinking, eating, and playing games. Gradually, as the night progressed, people began pairing off, and Kurt sought out Erika. During the evening's ebb and flow, Kurt had noticed one certain young man always seemed to be around Erika, and when Kurt found her around eleven-thirty, she was in his company again.

Erika had been involved in running the party, and she had not given Kurt any indication that she wanted him with her at the magic moment when 1938 arrived. Kurt hesitated for a brief couple of minutes and pondered the possibilities. Was he a boyfriend or just a friend? Should he make a move? Panic—a feeling Kurt had not dealt with in a long time—suddenly appeared like an old friend. Kurt began to alter his intended route toward Erika. Apparently she had made her choice. As Kurt began to turn away, he again remembered Herr von Klugemann's words of advice. Admonishing himself for being so timid, Kurt renewed his march toward Erika. The time had come to make a stand. Then, as was her modus operandi, Erika seized the moment and said, "Kurt, have you met my cousin, Karl? He's from Bremen and is staying with us tonight."

Feeling utterly disgusted at himself, Kurt shook hands with Karl and exchanged a few pleasantries before grabbing Erika's hand and leading her to a corner of the large basement room where the party was being held. Kurt was straddling that strange, uncomfortable zone between youthful innocence and adult worldliness. He fully understood that he'd been swimming in the quagmire of adolescence, but he badly wanted to join the world of men, and right now an unfamiliar force was pulling him into adulthood. What really was he? How should he act with Erika?

"Erika, I want to be with you at midnight."

"Why? Do you think you'll get a kiss?"

"What do you think?"

"Find me then, and we shall see, my soldier." Erika smiled at Kurt, pressed a finger softly on his lips and then spun around and returned to directing some last minute details for the midnight celebration.

Soon people gathered in small groups and began to sing songs—a few traditional ones mixed with patriotic Hitler Youth standards—to pass the time until midnight. Erika returned and she and Kurt joined Hans and Kris and a few other couples, forming a circle and holding hands as they sang. Kurt held Kris' right hand with his left hand, but he barely noticed. All his attention was centered in his right hand, which was holding Erika's. It may have been simple handholding, but the feeling of Erika's flesh against his was enough to generate an electrical impulse that far exceeded its innocent touch. When the magic minute struck, the room filled with cheers of celebration, wishes of good fortune for the New Year, and long embraces. Hans yelled, "Sieg Heil," and the room erupted in a chorus of "Sieg Heils" in response. Kurt then left the world of mortal man and entered a world of pure pleasure and ecstasy. He wrapped himself around Erika, devouring her with a kiss well beyond his expertise. Erika's soft, wet lips were not shy in their response to his aggressiveness, and they lingered for a few long seconds before retreating.

"Can we be alone somewhere for a few minutes?" Kurt implored achingly.

"Come with me!"

Erika led Kurt down into the wine cellar. They were alone among the countless bottles of wine, and the only light came from a small fixture at the bottom of the stairs. Kurt took both of Erika's hands and held them as they stood in silence gazing at each other. Finally, Erika spoke. "I'll miss you, Kurt, and I'll wait for you to come and see me when you get some leave."

"I'll miss you too, Erika. I know we're very young, and we really haven't had much time to get to know each other, but I can't help feeling there is something special between us."

"I suppose you think that line will get you another kiss?" Erika stretched up on her toes as Kurt pulled her to him, feeling the softness of her breasts against the front of his shirt. Another tender kiss ensued, followed by a longer, even more passionate one.

"We'd better go back before Hans makes some stupid comment," Erika said, breathing heavily and backing away with a sigh. "Remember, we do have something special, but only time will tell us what that is. Let's hope it's something worth waiting for."

With that hopeful declaration Erika led a flustered Kurt back upstairs and into the real world again.

The next afternoon, January 1, 1938, the von Klugemanns had a small farewell party for Hans and Kurt before the two young "supermen" headed off to become members of the Nazi elite. Uncle Konrad and Aunt Hilda were there, along with many social and business acquaintances of the von Klugemanns. Maria had decorated her house with every imaginable symbol of the Third Reich. She even had a large cake adorned with the appropriate frosting, white icing with dark chocolate SS runes spread across the top. A large banner with twin lightning flashes hung from each end of the dining room, congratulating Hans and Kurt on their selection to the SS. Strains of Wagner's *Magic Fire Music* permeated the house. In such an atmosphere even Winston Churchill would have clicked his heels together and shouted "Sieg Heil!"

Everyone was in an extremely exuberant mood, and the alcohol flowed freely as the afternoon progressed. During one congratulatory speech a neighbor exhorted Hans and Kurt to perform great deeds of valor for the Fatherland. Uncle Konrad added that he also was very proud of the two new warriors, but he continued on a more cautionary note. "I'm sure Hans and Kurt will serve our country with distinction, and if needed, great bravery. But they have not yet proven themselves on the field of battle, so let's not pin any medals on them yet, although I'm sure any relative of mine has the blood of heroes surging through his veins."

Konrad was immediately subjected to a crescendo of abuse and laughter. Kurt, who was in good humor by this time, asked, "By the way, Uncle, which branch of the service did you become famous in during The Great War?"

"What?" exclaimed Uncle Konrad. "Haven't I told you the story of how I almost captured the entire French Third Army by myself? I was just a lad of ... "

Konrad's historic fable was cut short by loud screams of protest. Shouts of "No, not again," and "I've heard that lie a hundred times," filled the room. Trying to silence his detractors, Konrad's stoically replied, "Now you know why there are so few heroes. This is the thanks you get."

Kurt basked in the group's acknowledgement that he was becoming part of something special. Joining an organization that epitomized the Aryan elite and placed its members above other men caused Kurt to feel superior, like he was some sort of a superman. How could he not? Hearing Maria von Klugemann's constant praises, seeing Erika's recurrent smiles, and listening to the lofty expectations of the guests, how could he not?

By the time the celebration drew to a close, Kurt was barely coherent. It was a good thing that he and Erika had shared a tender moment and private goodbye the night before, because by night's end he was in no condition to talk intelligently to anyone, especially Erika. A gleeful Uncle Konrad eventually helped Kurt stagger home.

———

Far removed from the party scene of Nuremberg, Kurt quickly comprehended the seriousness of his commitment as the reality of Verfugungstruppe basic training engulfed him. The steady stream of propaganda he had experienced in the Hitler Youth paled in comparison to the incessant drumbeat of Nazi indoctrination he was experiencing in the Verfugungstruppe. The job of the Hitler Youth had been to force young Germans like Kurt to not only accept, but to embrace the concept that the state was everything, that the individual existed only to serve Hitler and the Fatherland. It was designed to accomplish this objective through a number of strategies: First, the training subordinated religion and replaced it with adoration of the state; after all, Germany did not need God when it had Adolf Hitler. Second, the program glorified team sports where athletic ability was seen as proof of one's superiority. These activities served to dull the intellect while instilling a psychological acceptance of teamwork that could later be transferred to the battlefield. Finally, a special emphasis on games of a brutal, violent nature further promoted physical perfection and created a caste of young men willing to accept the idea of "survival of the fittest." These strategies—combined with the doctrine of German racial superiority—produced a violent, aggressive, godless youth who harbored no feelings of tenderness or tolerance for weakness, youth who believed they were destined to lead and conquer. So by the time Kurt and his comrades started training in the Verfugungstruppe, they were not only in good physical condition, but, without their realizing it, the battle for their minds had already been won. They had arrived for training remarkably similar in body and mind: physically perfect, racially pure, predictably malleable, and unwavering in their commitment to the Fatherland.

The Verfugungstruppe continued the heavy emphasis on sport and physical fitness and capitalized on the natural aggressiveness of the cadets to train them as assault forces. To simulate real combat to harden these troops, the Verfugungstruppe often used live ammunition during military training, which occasionally resulted in casualties. Typical of the SS mindset, the commanding officers viewed the losses as a small price to pay for the superior soldiers that were being produced.

In order for the SS training to work, discipline had to be paramount, even for the minutest details; obedience was required without question or hesitation. Fortunately for the training staff, blind obedience to the cause was assisted by the low educational level of many SS members, especially in the ranks because of the strict racial and physical requirements. But what really held the group together was the spirit of mutual respect cultivated by the Verfugungstruppe throughout the SS. In the regular German army, the Wehrmacht, the gap between officers and men was very well defined and seldom crossed. In the SS the gap existed, but it was often bridged by this special comradeship among all SS men, officers and enlisted men alike. This unique SS structure created a special commitment to each other in support of their common goals of unmatched loyalty and courage under fire. The final product of this special training was, in effect, the perfect soldier, a man of unmatched physical qualities and unquestioning obedience willing to undertake any order to help the team. The SS became a hard, ruthless band of warriors with supreme confidence in their own destinies and no tolerance for inferior beings. Unfettered by conventional rules of war, the "supermen" answered only to their own code of conduct.

———

After their basic training and a few months of active duty, Kurt and Hans finally received four-day passes, which they spent in Nuremberg. Kurt continued his relationship with Erika, but at an even slower pace. She was not about to capitulate to Kurt just because he was now a member of the SS, and Kurt had gained enough confidence in himself that he felt secure with the progress between them. Kurt did not even bother to visit his parents on this leave. He had entered his basic training with a small, deeply-hidden sense of doubt, but step by tiny step, that doubt was being erased. Kurt would deny it, but as far as his parents were concerned, he was becoming a carbon copy of Jurgen.

———

In September of 1938 Kurt and Hans were again in Nuremberg participating in the last and greatest of the Rallies. Only this time they were marching past der Fuhrer as a part of the SS Special Forces, not watching from the stands. As he goose-stepped past Hitler's reviewing stand, Kurt swelled with a new sense of destiny and power.

During this short stay in Nuremberg a momentous event occurred for both Kurt and Hans: early acceptance to the SS officer cadet school at Bad Tolz. Normally, a two-year period of service in the Verfugungstruppe was required before a candidate could even be considered for admission to one of the SS cadet schools, but Maria von Klugemann didn't want her shining knights-in-training to have to wait that long. She had used her influences with Sepp Dietrich and other important Nazis to get Hans and Kurt into Bad Tolz after only a year of membership in the SS forces. So, Hans and Kurt again found themselves at a reception at the von Klugemanns, only this time they were honored guests, not teenagers to be hustled upstairs and out of sight. And, he got to be alone with Erika again, even though it was for a brief moment one evening.

The meeting didn't go nearly as smoothly as Kurt had anticipated, however. Having been out of contact so long, Kurt had no way of knowing that Erika was struggling with her feelings about him and his newly-acquired SS attitude. Encouraged by the news of his admission into Bad Tolz and fortified with a little too much wine, Kurt became too forward with Erika and was immediately rewarded with a strong rebuke. "Kurt, I don't know what you were expecting from me, but I hope your training hasn't convinced you that the only thing women are good for is to produce babies for the Fatherland. I know that's the attitude of Hitler and his followers, but my mother and I are exceptions. You seem to have forgotten that we barely know each other, and, even though we agreed that a future together holds some promise, it isn't guaranteed. I still expect to be courted and not taken for granted."

That strong reprimand quickly brought Kurt down to earth. After some serious soul-searching on the trip back to garrison duty, he realized his arrogance and the emergence of his superiority complex, while helpful in conquering Germany's enemies, would not serve him well in conquering the woman of his dreams. As soon as he returned to duty, he wrote a sheepish letter of apology to Erika. He received a quick acceptance from Erika, full of innuendos, and ending with the coy tease, "Remember, Kurt, SS men are only to marry women who are pure and chaste. I'll wait for you, my soldier."

CHAPTER V

Bad Tolz

In January of 1939 Kurt began the final phase of his transformation by starting officer cadet training at Bad Tolz, a castle-like retreat of the SS Junkerschule nestled at the foothills of the Bavarian Alps. The setting—idyllic meadows, deep valleys, plunging icy rivers and snow-capped mountains—was spectacular, but it belied the darkness of its purpose. Here, handpicked by Himmler and his subordinates, the elite of German manhood were trained to become the ruling class of the new order, Teutonic knights dedicated to defending the grail of Germanic purity and perpetuating the Reich for a thousand years.

The underlying assumption behind the training at Bad Tolz was that war with the Soviet Union was inevitable; further, it would be a war unlike any other, a war of racial survival. To this end, training was savagely simplistic. A typical day at Bad Tolz started at six o'clock with an hour of demanding physical training, followed by a Spartan breakfast of porridge and mineral water. The rest of the day consisted of weapons training, field exercises, military tactics, history and strategy, with very few breaks in between.

But it was not the military schooling or extreme physical condition-ing that set Bad Tolz apart from other officer schools; it was the fanatical ideological indoctrination and the relentless emphasis on comradeship among fellow cadets. The simple rule that lockers had to be left unlocked subtly reinforced the concept of complete trust that the cadets were to have in each other. To promote the concept of Aryan supremacy, three times a week the cadets received ideological instruction based primarily on two sources: Rosenberg's *Myth of the Twentieth Century* and Darre's *Blood and Soil*. Additionally, the cadets were infused with a strong dose of anti-Bolshevism to reinforce Hitler's belief that Germans were superior humans and that certain other races—notably Jews and Slavs—were in-herently inferior.

By training's end Kurt and his fellow cadets would be transformed into hard, coldly-efficient masters of the art of war, convinced that they were empowered to save European civilization from the sub-human bar-barians of Slavic Russia. Cadets entered Bad Tolz as eager, young, naïve officers, but would leave as part of the new SS generation, a generation from whom the rest of the world would shrink back in horror. Truly, a breed apart.

———

Kurt was resting in the austere barracks he shared with his three best friends at Bad Tolz, Horst Rikker, Kurt Mueller and Werner Nitz. They were stretched out on their bunks, sharing a last moment of conversation before the nightly curfew. The cadets were entering their fourth month at Bad Tolz, and by now had formed deep, but competitive, friendships.

"We really are a bunch of splendid, blond beasts. I relish the thought of being part of such a group, and I can't wait to lead such men into com-bat," said Werner.

"What you say is true, Werner, but some of us are more splendid than others, especially those of us from Prussia. We were born to lead," said Horst.

Werner rolled over on his side to get a better look at Horst. "Obviously, you're a leader. If you weren't, you wouldn't be here. However, I see nothing about you that automatically places you above the rest of us."

Before Werner or Horst could continue their friendly rivalry, Kurt Mueller interrupted, "Why don't both of you keep quiet? We must all be special, or we must all be crazy. I still can't believe all the shit they put us through. I thought basic training was bad, but this school is getting ridiculous. Who the hell thought of using live ammunition during training exercises? I saw some slow-footed grunt killed this afternoon."

"I heard that the officers decided it was the only way to get you to keep your big ass down low enough to get under barbed wire."

"Very funny, Heisler. Speaking of asses, yours is always dragging during our morning wakeup exercises, so you'd better get to sleep. I don't think you can cut it here much longer."

"Actually, Cadet Mueller, I'm just resting so I won't spoil my breakfast. You know how I love that porridge and mineral water." Kurt was immediately bombarded with abuse from all directions.

"Yeah, right, Heisler."

"Anyone who enjoys that same shit every day is crazy."

"Heisler, it's against our code to lie, you know."

"If Reichsfuhrer Himmler ever goes into the restaurant business, he'll go broke. That's why they work us so hard before breakfast, so we won't know what we're eating."

Kurt rolled over on his back and folded his hands together. "Okay, okay, I get the point. But I really don't mind the porridge."

Werner added, "I heard porridge is good for your brain, so with all the strategy stuff they throw at us, I guess we should be glad to eat it every day."

"Somebody better re-think that theory, because I sure don't see you guys getting any smarter," said Horst.

"Yeah, well, I might not be your equal in the classroom, but who's the best one here in weapons training and field exercises? Book learning only goes so far. You also have to be able to perform under fire." Werner sat up in bed and pretended to aim and shoot a rifle, adding sound effects. "We perform better than other soldiers because fear is not in our vocabulary. No other army can match our standards for courage and excellence in combat. Remember the code; nothing is impossible for us to accomplish."

"Well spoken, Werner, especially for someone who's never fired a shot at anything that fired back. But I want to remind you there is one exception to your code. It will be impossible for your team to beat mine tomorrow."

"I accept your challenge, Horst, and you better get to bed soon so you can be at your best in the morning," snorted Werner.

Horst smiled and rose up on his elbows. "Don't get me wrong, Werner. I agree that competing in contests against each other helps strengthen our loyalty and trust. But if we're to be invincible, we need to harden ourselves in battle conditions against enemies who are our equals ... each other."

Horst got out of his bunk and walked a few steps to Werner, who was still sitting up in his bunk. Looking squarely at Werner, Horst said, "Loyalty and comradeship are fine, friend, but tomorrow I'm going to kick your ass."

Kurt found it impossible to experience the SS indoctrination at Bad Tolz without aspiring to become the superman of Nietzsche's dreams. It might seem improbable that a person of Kurt's background could surrender to such an ideology, but given the confluence of circumstances in his life, it was understandable. After all, he was an impressionable young man searching for a cause in Germany's crusade to pull itself out of poverty and despair, and he was courting a girl from a family of Nazi zealots who spurred him on. His friends were joining the crusade faster than he could count, and no one other than his mother was providing a counter-balance to Hitler's rhetoric. Yet, even with all these external influences weighing on him, it was the intense comradeship created with a hundred similar young men at Bad Tolz that finally succeeded in erasing the remainder of Kurt's conscience. The music, the singing of marching songs, the feeling of brotherhood, all these created a union among Kurt and his comrades that only death could interrupt. To a man, Kurt and his friends embodied the Waffen SS code: "The SS man's basic attitude must be that of a fighter for fighting's sake; he must be unquestionably obedient and become emotionally hard; he must have contempt for all racial inferiors and for those who do not belong to order; he must feel the strongest bonds of comradeship with those who do belong, particularly with his fellow soldiers, and he must think nothing impossible."

The SS training had drilled the code into every fiber of Kurt's being, and there in the Bavarian wonderland, he crossed over. It was as if he conjured up a black box, put his conscience in it, and buried the box in the deepest recesses of his soul. The confused, hesitant adolescent had become an ardent, loyal soldier of the Third Reich.

———

The speculation about which country Germany would invade ended abruptly in September of 1939 when the German armies attacked Poland. The victorious campaign was over so quickly that Kurt and his fellow cadets were deeply disappointed that they couldn't finish training in time to fight for the Fatherland. They knew they wouldn't have to wait too long for another chance, though, because France and England had responded to Hitler's invasion of Poland by immediately declaring war on Germany. Kurt and his Bad Tolz comrades anticipated that Hitler would send his legions against France next, but they didn't know where or when. The cadets didn't care about the details; they just wanted to be involved. They ran through their daily drills with such zeal that their instructors' grim faces began to crack with smiles. The harder the cadets were pushed, the better they liked it, because they knew the accelerated schedule meant they would soon be sent off to combat.

Graduation for Kurt's cadet class at Bad Tolz was February 3, 1940. Kurt and his best friends—Kurt Mueller, Werner Nitz and Horst Rikker—all graduated with the rank of Second Lieutenant in the Waffen SS. They had originally been told they would receive two weeks of leave before reporting to their new assignments, but this changed with an announcement at the end of the graduation ceremony. The commandant, Colonel Deutsch, announced with regret that all leaves had been cancelled because the troops were urgently needed to prepare for an upcoming campaign. But instead of complaining about their lost leaves, the new officers cheered the immediate opportunity to begin their service in a combat operation for the Fatherland. They were given that evening to celebrate, but were to report by ten o'clock the next morning to receive their assignments, to which they would be posted immediately.

Kurt screamed his approval just as loudly as his fellow officers, but he was somewhat disappointed; he had wanted to see Erika before being dispatched to his assignment. After hearing the news, he walked over to a quiet spot and began to recall his last visit with Erika. In July, 1939, he had taken his only break from cadet school and had spent most of his six-day leave with Hans in Nuremberg. Hans and Kurt were still close friends, but at Bad Tolz they had each acquired new friends. Predictably, Hans' friends tended to be more aristocratic than Kurt's, so he and Kurt hadn't spent much time together during training. When they did get together in Nuremberg, it was good for the old friends to hang out again and trade lies about how much tougher it had been for each of them at Bad Tolz.

During this vacation Kurt arranged to see his parents in Ansbach, and the results were unsurprising. He was as polite and agreeable as possible, but the same gap now existed between Kurt and his parents that Jurgen had experienced. Conversation was strained and artificial, funneled mainly into mundane musings about the past. Politics and the Reich were avoided, if possible, but points of discussion inevitably arose. Fritz had grudgingly accepted Kurt's new life, but Eva was totally despondent about her failure with both her sons. Kurt knew it was fruitless to offer any further explanations on the subject, but he tried to maintain a happy, carefree attitude about everything. Given the circumstances, Kurt only stayed one day and night in Ansbach before hurrying back to Nuremberg to see Erika.

Kurt again stayed with Uncle Konrad and Aunt Hilda, who treated him like royalty. Frederick and Maria von Klugemann also lavished praise on Kurt and fussed over him whenever they were together. Such were the rewards of the elite among the faithful. Erika, however, remained very coy in her flirtations. But one gorgeous July evening Kurt and Erika had walked to a nearby park, and it was this night that had Kurt musing about the past. He could recall every word, every action and every feeling from that night ...

"Do you want to make the military your career?" Erika asked. She was sitting on a picnic table while Kurt leaned against a nearby tree. The sweet smell of flowers mingled with the other summer fragrances arising from the finely-trimmed bushes and grasses of the park. It was about eight-thirty, and the sun was slowly surrendering to the night. A reddish-yellow haze hung over the park, stubbornly trying to forestall the descending darkness.

"I guess I've never really thought about a long-term career. Things have been happening so fast that we all seem to be just living for the moment. The enlistment period for an officer in the Waffen SS is twenty-five years. Does that meet with your approval?"

"You don't need my approval, Kurt. You must seek your destiny based on your own goals and convictions, not on mine or anyone else's."

"Agreed. But I hope someday our destinies will be linked, and I hope you feel the same way."

Erika pulled her knees up under her chin and sat looking at Kurt, a half-smile crossing her face. "My, you're making some bold assumptions, don't you think?"

"Not so bold, Erika. Why, what are you planning to do with your future now that you're grown up?"

There was an ominous pause as Erika pondered her response. Her answer surprised Kurt. "You know, Kurt, when you used the term 'grown up,' it made me realize that we're both really living in the adult world. It just seems impossible, but I'm eighteen years old and will be starting school at the University in the fall and will also help my father with some of his business matters. You'll soon be twenty and an officer in the Waffen SS. Sometimes I wonder where the carefree days of childhood went. It seems all I can remember about my growing up is an endless series of parades, speeches, ceremonies, and games promoting the Reich. I just hope our country prospers and that we do establish a stable government that will last for a thousand years."

Kurt stared at Erika in amazement. He walked over to the picnic table and sat down beside her. Before he had a chance to respond to her comments, Erika continued. "I want to make something special of myself. I don't know exactly what, but I don't want to just get married and raise babies for the Fatherland like most of my friends."

"Erika, you're a very special person already."

Kurt pulled Erika closer, cupped her chin with his hand and lifted her face toward his as he gently kissed her. Erika wrapped her arms around his neck and kissed him with a deep passion. Kurt could feel the moist sensation of Erika's lips and could hear her words ringing in his ears, "I hope we do share a common destiny."

Erika's next statement forced Kurt to face the reality of their relationship. "Kurt, I should tell you that I've had some dates since we last met, and I'm sure I'll have more while I'm attending the University. Life there does have its social side, and I like to be involved in everything. You know me."

"Well, I'm not sure how well I know you because we're apart so much, but I hope I'm still at the top of your list."

Erika smiled teasingly at Kurt. "At the present time, Herr Heisler, I'd say your position at the top is secure. I miss you all the time, and when I'm out with someone else, I'm usually thinking about you."

"I'm not sure that's the kind of compliment I want to hear right now. Just how much do you go out with other men?"

"Not much, especially alone. We usually go out in groups and socialize together."

"I thought all men our age were in some form of military service."

Erika laughed and answered, "Well, I suppose my choices will be limited, but I'm sure there'll be enough so life at the University won't get too boring. How about you, Kurt? Have you had any dates?"

With a look of exasperation, Kurt said, "What do you think? I've been a little too busy with my training to dabble with frauleins."

"Does that mean I'm still at the top of your list?"

"I won't even pretend to be coy here, Erika. You are my list."

"If you're saying my only competition is the SS, then that's still more competition than you have . . ."

"Daydreaming about Erika again, huh?" Kurt turned to find a taunting Horst Rikker standing beside him. "Well, you'd better forget about her for a few days. Men of the SS can't have a conscience, but that doesn't mean we can't have a love life, you know."

"What are you talking about?" Kurt asked.

"Second Lieutenant Heisler, let's find some young Bavarian beauties, confiscate some beer, and proceed into yonder majestic mountains. We do have one night to celebrate."

Kurt thought about Erika's comment that she was going to continue to date at the University and quickly responded, "An excellent suggestion, Second Lieutenant Rikker. I hereby give you command of this mission. Please place Second Lieutenants Nitz and Mueller under your command. I assign you the task of securing the necessary beverages and frauleins to carry out the major objectives of the operation. I'll secure a method of transportation and some food."

"Up your stupid ass, General," laughed Horst. "See you outside the barracks in two hours."

"Agreed," Kurt shouted as he saluted Horst.

He did not know exactly why, but Kurt felt like getting drunk. He felt very good, and he liked the idea of being a "superman." Why shouldn't he test his superior qualities out on a mere mortal, like a young mountain damsel? Although Kurt's morality had been buried under the weight of the SS indoctrination, he still found it necessary to rationalize at times, and this was one of them. He loved Erika, and he wanted to remain faithful to her, but he also needed some experience so he would be prepared when the time came to have sex with her. The more Kurt pondered his logic, the more he became convinced he was right, until a chilling thought struck him. What if Erika should find out about this excursion from Hans? Hurriedly, Kurt checked with one of Hans' friends and found out that Hans would be spending the night at a festival in one of the local villages. All clear.

It didn't take Kurt long to solidify his decision to enter the land of the sexually experienced. Maybe it was the nature of the female companions his friends had secured, or maybe it was the romantic panorama of the glorious Bavarian countryside, but Kurt became a willing participant. Right on time, Horst, Werner, and Kurt Mueller had come roaring up with a half-track filled with beer, wine, food, and three frauleins. Apparently they had just driven into a nearby village, stood up in the half-track and offered any young woman the opportunity to spend an evening with some of the "chosen." The allure of the SS uniform had not reached a point where the average fraulein would publicly throw herself into such a precarious position, but three daring damsels had accepted the challenge and were quickly helped into the SS war machine.

Soon they were headed off into the spectacular Bavarian winter scenery. The half-track was a good method of transportation because it could navigate the snow-filled trails of the rural area around Bad Tolz; it was a cold mode of travel, though, so they wrapped blankets around themselves as they began their journey. Horst was the driver, so he was the one left temporarily without a date.

"Do you have any idea where in the hell you're going?" Werner yelled at Horst.

"Don't worry. I know exactly where I'm going. Just shut up and wait and see. Besides, a man of your slovenly tastes shouldn't be too concerned about the accommodations."

As Horst guided the half-track down a snow-covered path leading into a dense forest, the others were downing schnapps to keep warm. Luckily, the evening was not excessively cold, and, between the blankets and the schnapps, the ladies were staying warm and beginning to enjoy themselves. The half-track soon came to a jarring halt, and Horst yelled, "All right, you vermin. Crawl out of your holes, and let me join the fun. See where I have brought you?"

Throwing off their canopy of blankets, Kurt, Werner, Mueller and the three frauleins saw a quaint cottage tucked away at the base of a hill in a dense maze of fir trees. Smoke floated in thick clumps from a chimney as beacons of light extended from the windows of the elfin structure. While everyone else gawked in amazement, Horst walked up to the cottage and knocked on the door. An old man answered, talked with Horst for a few minutes, put on a large fur coat and walked to the rear of the building. He soon reappeared, driving an ancient truck that sputtered off loudly into the surrounding whiteness.

"Okay, you horny bastards, bring in the refreshments and the women, and let's start to celebrate," Horst shouted from the doorway.

The cottage was actually much bigger than it appeared from the outside. It had a main room, a small kitchen and two small bedrooms. A massive stone fireplace dominated the living room, which held two couches, two large chairs and an oak table with four wooden chairs. A large elk head hung over the fireplace, and a trio of candles glowed on the table, which was soon covered with provisions. Kurt Mueller saluted Horst and exclaimed, "My God, Horst, how did you have time to line this up?"

"Planning, my dear Mueller, planning. But mostly luck and some cold, hard cash. Let's just leave it at that."

As the revelers made themselves comfortable, Kurt made his choice for the evening. The three young ladies were all about eighteen years old and fairly good looking, but one was quieter than the other two and not as rowdy, and Kurt focused on her. He could sense she was uneasy as the carefree fun soon began to degenerate into more ribald behavior. Grabbing some food and a bottle of wine, Kurt staked his claim by seizing the girl of his choice and heading toward one of the bedrooms. "I'm going into this bedroom, and I don't want to be bothered by any of you animals. I guess you'll just have to do some sharing. I'll be out later to get some more wine. Have fun, boys."

"Hey, who said you could be such a prima donna? I thought this was supposed to be a group venture."

"Sorry, Werner, but I like to conduct my business in private. You still have two women, this large room and the other bedroom. If that isn't enough, you can always use the kitchen. Good night." Kurt shut the door and wedged a chair under the doorknob for extra security. Turning around, Kurt encountered a sight that quickly shattered the veneer of his SS hardness and superiority.

Sitting on the bed, already nearly undressed, was the pretty young girl, trembling and nearly in tears. Kurt surveyed the scene quickly and came to two conclusions: He did not want to betray Erika's trust, and he could not take advantage of the innocent creature shaking on the bed. "What's your name?"

"Gretchen," came the nervous reply.

"How old are you?"

"Eighteen."

Kurt was curiously amused by the fact that both of them were basically the same age, yet Gretchen seemed about ten, and Kurt felt about forty in comparison.

"Please put your clothes back on, and let's talk. I'm not here to rape you."

Gretchen looked at Kurt in amazement and stammered, "But I thought we came here to . . ."

"Please, get dressed," repeated Kurt.

Kurt turned his back and went to a small dresser and opened the bottle of wine and poured two glasses. Glancing in the mirror on the dresser, he could see Gretchen getting dressed. The thought occurred to Kurt that he had already seen more of Gretchen than he had ever seen of Erika. A strange sense of satisfaction swept over him as he strengthened his resolve to remain celibate for the evening. He no longer felt a need to prove his manhood. Regardless of the possible pitfalls, Kurt decided on a course of action that would allow him to save face, and also let Gretchen escape the predicament she had gotten herself into and was now regretting. Later she could deal with her friends however she wanted.

"Here, have a glass of wine, and let's just talk."

Gretchen was now fully dressed, sitting on the edge of the bed. The bedroom was small, but warm and cozy. A floor vent connected to the fireplace provided gentle heat to the room. Above the bed a small window framed in white curtains was almost completely frosted over. Besides the bed the only pieces of furniture were a creaky wicker chair, a dresser and a nightstand next to the bed, all white.

Kurt handed Gretchen a glass of wine and sat down in the chair. Surrounded by the room of white, Kurt stood out like an evil black knight. "Gretchen, why'd you agree to come with us? Didn't you know what we were coming here for?"

"Yes, but I thought it was my duty. At least that's what my friends told me. They're more experienced than I am, and they convinced me it was time I became more patriotic. Paula and Annette aren't my best friends, but I was with them when your friends made their offer, and I just went along on an impulse. As soon as we got here, I knew I'd made a mistake. I'm still a virgin."

"Let me get this right. You were told it was your duty to have sex with soldiers?"

Gretchen gave Kurt a rather incredulous look. "You and your friends are not ordinary soldiers. SS school cadets at Bad Tolz are special men and are to be treated accordingly. Many of you will die in future battles because of your extreme bravery, and before that happens, young German girls must offer their services to you so your heroic qualities can be passed on."

Kurt returned Gretchen's look with one of even greater astonishment. "Who told you that? It sounds like something Horst would say in order to get laid."

"No, he didn't say it. I'm not sure where I heard it. Girl talk, I guess."

"Well, it's certainly an interesting idea, and I know a lot of people who'll likely take advantage of it, but I plan on being around to pass on my 'special qualities' for a long time, so you don't need to be patriotic with me."

They sat in silence for a moment, and then Kurt continued. "I have a girlfriend I'm very serious about, and I'd feel guilty cheating on her. That's just how I am."

For the first time Kurt saw Gretchen smile. "So, Kurt, if that's your attitude, why did you come on this adventure? Didn't you know what we came here for?"

"I guess I deserve that," laughed Kurt. "Let's just say I went on an impulse like you did, and leave it at that. By the way, there are two Kurts in our group, you know."

Gretchen was still smiling as she answered, "No last names, then. Kurt and Gretchen will be enough for the rest of the night. Can I have another glass of wine?"

After pouring Gretchen another glass of wine, Kurt outlined his plan. They would act as if they had sex and let their friends draw any conclusions they wanted. If further explanations were required, they could deal with it on their own later.

Suddenly, there was a horrendous banging on the door as Werner screamed, "Hey, it's too quiet in there. Kurt, what the hell's going on? Come on out and join the party!"

"In a little bit. Are you done already? I knew you had no staying power! Go away and stop bothering me."

Werner tried to open the door, but failed, and soon drifted away in a torrent of vile language.

"Gretchen, you need to smear a little lipstick on me."

"How? With my lips?"

"That would be the most realistic, but be careful. I'm human, you know." Kurt sat down on the bed next to Gretchen, and she mechanically kissed him on the check and neck, making sure to leave visible signs.

By now Kurt and Gretchen were feeling the effects of the schnapps mixing with wine, and Kurt realized his plan for remaining celibate was in jeopardy. "Maybe we'll have to continue this when I get back. It felt awfully good," Kurt joked as he stripped down to his shorts. "I'll bring back a couple more bottles of wine. You're a lovely young woman, and if I get drunk and pass out, we both might be safer."

"Naughty, naughty, Kurt. Don't tempt me too much. I've never had a chance to sleep with a superman before."

"I'm going out to make sure we're left alone for the rest of the night, and I'll pick up some more supplies. Strip down to your bra and panties and get under the sheets, and mess up your hair a little, just in case one of my friends decides to check on us."

"For heaven's sake, Kurt, don't let one of them come in here when you're gone. Promise?"

"I'll do my best. Don't worry. I'll be back in a few minutes."

Kurt walked over to the mirror and rearranged himself to look like he had just escaped from a sexual circus: lipstick stains on his face, hair disheveled and wine stains on his bare chest. He staggered out of the bedroom into a scene straight from ancient Rome.

The participants in the pagan orgy didn't even notice Kurt's entrance. The room was decorated in flesh tones, as everybody in the main room was naked. Mueller had one of the frauleins bent over a chair and had mounted her from behind. The other girl was sitting in a chair with Horst's head in her lap. Werner was standing behind the damsel and was slowly pouring beer over her right breast. The amber liquid ran down her breast, paused as it encountered the dimpled surface of the nipple, and then dripped rapidly into Horst's mouth.

"Excuse me, everyone. I'm just out to get some more wine. Don't let me stop anything important. By the way, we do need to report for duty at ten in the morning, remember?"

"Shut the fuck up and crawl back in your hole, if you know what I mean," snarled Werner.

"Don't worry about tomorrow," gurgled Horst through his waterfall of beer. "We'll all be passed out by midnight, and that'll give us plenty of sleep."

Kurt grabbed two more bottles of wine and scurried back into the safety of his room. Although the screams from the sexual extravagances in the next room were rather apparent to Kurt and Gretchen, they tried to take little notice. Gretchen wrapped a blanket around herself and sat on the edge of the bed while Kurt curled up in the chair with another blanket.

They drank and ate and talked. They talked about Germany and the world, about Hitler and the SS, about Erika, and about boys Gretchen had dated. They talked about everything, until they finally reached the point where they needed to confront the dangerous situation they were in.

"Gretchen, the wine is gone. I think we need to go to sleep. I don't hear a sound coming from the next room. They must all be asleep or passed out. Do you want me to sleep in the chair?"

By now both Gretchen and Kurt were fairly drunk, but not to the point that they failed to recognize the bond of affection that had grown between them.

"Come to bed, Kurt."

Kurt crawled under the sheets wearing only his wine-stained shorts, and Gretchen remained in her bra and panties. Without any hesitation, they cuddled together and relaxed in the warmth of each other's body.

"Gretchen, would you mind if I kissed you?"

"I was hoping you would."

They fell asleep in each other's arms.

———

When Kurt woke up the next morning, his head was pounding, and his mouth tasted like his army socks after maneuvers. Gretchen was already dressed and had picked up the room.

"Good morning, Kurt. How do you feel?"

"I've felt better. What time is it?"

"About seven-thirty."

"Have you detected any signs of life from next door?"

"I heard somebody groan a few minutes ago, but it's been pretty quiet."

Kurt quickly got dressed and helped Gretchen make the bed. Next, he took Gretchen by her hands and sat down on the bed with her.

"Gretchen, did I do anything I shouldn't have last night after we went to bed? I hope not, but I can't remember too much after a certain point."

Gretchen squeezed Kurt's hands. "You didn't do anything I didn't want you to do. Kurt, I'll never forget you or last night. Erika is a very lucky girl."

"Gretchen, last night was special for me also. I learned a lot about myself that I couldn't have without your help."

As they started to leave the room, Kurt and Gretchen stopped and hugged each other. They wished each other good luck and happiness and said goodbye with one simple kiss.

As Kurt and his companions left the cottage, he had a strange feeling of lost innocence, not of sexual innocence, but of childhood innocence. He had just experienced his first night of sleeping with a woman and was now heading into another world totally unknown to him. Kurt's transformation was nearly complete. He was about to become a well-honed part of one of history's most prolific killing machines.

CHAPTER VI

A Taste of War

The surrender of Poland in the fall of 1939 ushered in a period called the Phoney War. England and France had declared war on Germany, which had signed a cynical, non-aggression pact with the Soviet Union, and the United States was remaining neutral. Despite the war declarations, nothing happened for months. The French sat confidently behind their Maginot Line, feeling secure that this series of fortifications could keep any German force at bay. England, feeling safe in its island fortress, sent some troops to France to help repel any German invasion.

Hitler waited until May 10 of 1940, when, suddenly, the term Phoney War was displaced by a new word: Blitzkrieg! German forces pounded the Maginot Line at its weakest point just south of the Ardennes, hoping for a quick breakthrough. Simultaneously, Hitler launched a diversion into Holland and Belgium to draw British and French forces away from the main attack. In this battle Second Lieutenant Kurt Heisler of the Standarte der Fuhrer of the Verfugungsdivision of the Waffen SS was among the Nazi legions going to war. Most of his friends from Bad Tolz were with him, except for Hans and a few others who had been sent to the Leibstandarte Adolf Hitler.

Hitler's Army Group A was given the main task of breaking through the Ardennes into France, while the secondary force of Army Group B was attacking Holland and Belgium. The Verfugungsdivision was assigned to Army Group B, with the Standarte der Fuhrer as one of its spearheads. Growing up in Ansbach Kurt had often gazed at his statue and dreamed of performing feats of glory on the field of battle. Now the opportunity was at hand. He was in charge of a full platoon—men trained to be among the best soldiers anywhere—and he was in a state of shock. As he waited for the signal to attack, simultaneous thoughts scrambled his mind. How would he react in his first combat, to his first sight of death on the battle-field? Would he be scared? Would he be killed? How would he feel when he killed someone?

The Dutch were entrenched in an area called the National Redoubt, a series of rivers and canals that formed a natural defensive strongpoint that was easy to defend and difficult to attack. The first objective of the Standarte der Fuhrer was to cross the Ijssel River. Crouching in their jumping-off point, Kurt and his men were edgy with anticipation. At the commander's whistle, however, all doubts disappeared. A rush of adrena-lin surged through him, and his head pounded from the excitement. He had no time to worry or fear death; he just reacted. Kurt jumped up and screamed, "Let's go!" as he led his men into death's world for the first time.

As the accompanying artillery barrage grew into a constant roar, large chunks of the enemy line in front of them disintegrated into giant erup-tions of earth and flesh. The static vibrations of German MG-34 machine guns and MP-40 sub-machine guns joined the chorus of battle sounds that rattled out a song of death. The ground exploded everywhere, in little puffs and large geysers. Bodies were shredded, and the screams of wounded and dying men pierced the air in the lulls between explosions.

The first soldier Kurt saw killed up close was his friend from Bad Tolz, Second Lieutenant Kurt Mueller, who was leading the platoon on Kurt's left. Kurt saw his friend dashing across an open space between two groves of trees when suddenly Mueller's face exploded like a tomato hitting a white fence. Nothing was left of his head except a soft piece of unidentifi-able mush. Kurt had often wondered what his reaction would be when he saw death for the first time, especially the death of a fellow comrade. It might have been the excess of adrenalin flowing in Kurt's blood or the hypnotic excitement of battle, but when he saw Mueller go down, he felt only anger and revenge. He kept advancing.

During the course of the day's action Kurt was introduced to all of war's gruesome images, the horrific sights and sounds of men being turned into something else. Thankfully, he did not have to kill anyone at close range that day. He fired at distant forms only, as if in a surreal game. His intense training, coupled with man's natural survival instinct, had directed his actions as he fired at anything in a different uniform. By day's end many of the soldiers who had stepped onto the battlefield that morning were no longer living, but Kurt had survived.

In the next week Kurt's leadership and killing skills improved, and he quickly became accustomed to a soldier's constant companion: death. After all, Waffen SS members were trained not to think about dying, and sacrificing their lives for the Fatherland was one of the things they had signed up for.

The German war machine continued to tear across France, Belgium, and the Netherlands. German Panzers roared across great expanses of foreign real estate, churning the earth into towering clouds of dust. Stuka dive-bombers screamed hideously and rained death on the enemy below. As the Germans advanced, part of the Verfugungsdivision was on Kurt's left flank engaging the French First Army. The other half—Kurt's half—joined the Leibstandarte SS Regiment and continued to drive toward Rotterdam. Although the fighting was fierce, Kurt saw no atrocities committed by either side, and he made sure that any prisoners who fell into his care were treated according to the Geneva Convention. It was easy to be gracious when you were the victor and the enemy was nearly your equal. This battle with the Dutch, French, and English was like a deadly game about who was superior in the art of making war, but it was not a struggle for racial superiority, so it was conducted according to the rules of war.

By May 14 everything was going well for the forces of the Reich as Kurt and his Standarte stood before the city of Rotterdam. Here, for the first time, Kurt beheld a sight that tempered his joy ride with Hitler's victorious legions. The opposition suddenly stiffened, and to show the world the dreadful consequences for those who resisted the Reich, the Luftwaffe bombed the entire center of Rotterdam into a fine, powdery mist. The bombing numbed the surviving residents into helplessness, and they had no choice but to surrender. Observing the devastation from a distance, Kurt felt a momentary sense of remorse at the loss of civilian life as he began to realize the immensity of the Blitzkrieg's awesome destructive power. As he reflected on the morality of the bombing, Kurt decided that in this case the end had justified the means because many of his comrades would have been lost trying to take the city with a ground attack.

Kurt and his comrades had little time to celebrate Rotterdam's surrender. The Verfugungsdivision abruptly turned around and headed into France to help drive the British Expeditionary Force to the beaches of Dunkirk. It was during this drive toward Dunkirk that Kurt's comradeship with his Waffen SS brothers was sealed with blood. The British were entrenched in a series of fortifications around the La Bassee Canal and the upper reaches of the River Lys. Ideally situated defensively, the British caused heavy casualties among the Standarte der Fuhrer attempting to storm the positions. During this battle Kurt's platoon left their cover and were advancing toward a British strong point. As the fire grew more intense, Kurt and his men were forced to crawl toward their objective, cutting their way through a circle of barbed wire. Suddenly a British grenade rolled straight at Kurt, and he froze. Without hesitation, a private in Kurt's platoon dove on the grenade. His body muffled the explosion and absorbed the deadly force, rising slightly into the air; the private died without making a sound. As Kurt knelt over the dead comrade who had saved his life, a British bullet hit Kurt's sub-machine gun and quickly spun him around. Silently saluting the fallen warrior, Kurt turned and led his men toward the British and took the strong point. Afterward, in a quiet moment, Kurt reflected on the honor of serving with such men, men whose sense of loyalty to one another was greater than life itself.

In this battle, as in many that followed, Waffen SS casualties were greater than those of other German units. The Waffen SS had been trained to attack relentlessly, which they certainly had done, but it was often at a terrible cost. These mad dashes of daring drew criticism and ridicule from the regular army officers, at least early in the war. Later, especially in Russia, they would thank God for the recklessness of the Waffen SS. Kurt's appreciation, though, was more immediate, as his comrade's disdain for death had just saved his life.

———

Hitler did not want to waste his best mobile forces in the trench warfare of Dunkirk, so Kurt's division was ordered south to chase the French, and as one of his men remarked, "It was a picnic." The French soon surrendered, and the British escaped back to England in one of the most daring rescues in history, as an unlikely flotilla of British ships plucked their soldiers off the beaches. Despite the daring English rescue, the world now knew that Germany was supreme on the European continent.

All in all, it was a good time to be a German soldier. There were victory celebrations everywhere, and those who had achieved such a swift and decisive victory were lavished with praise. Everyone expected it would only be a short time until Germany invaded England, but for the time being, it was a moment to trumpet Germanic pride.

Before getting a leave for Nuremberg to receive the congratulations he desired most, Kurt was stationed in France. There, during a conversation with a fellow junior officer in the Verfugungsdivision, Kurt was asked if he had heard anything about a massacre at a place called Le Paradis.

A rumor was circulating that a Waffen SS officer had supposedly shot a number of British prisoners in cold blood. Kurt scoffed at the suggestion. He could not contemplate that an organization that fought with such great valor could possibly stoop so low as to execute unarmed prisoners. He realized that war was filled with terror and danger, but it was the terror and danger of the warrior filled with excitement and glory, not cowardice and criminal activity. Kurt never heard about it again, and the incident quickly faded from his memory.

Because they were small in number compared to the regular army, the Waffen SS was acknowledged only briefly in the official army reports about the defeat of the Allies in the spring of 1940. The name Waffen SS first came into official use to denote all the various units of the SS Army in March 2, 1940, but they were only recognized because they were motorized and had the best equipment. But their numbers were growing, and, with every battle, so was their reputation.

In August Kurt was finally granted a two-week leave, and he began his tour of triumph by spending two days celebrating in Berlin with Horst. Then he went home to see his parents for a few days. For a conquering hero Kurt entered his home with a certain amount of trepidation. However, his parents were happy to see him, and the visit went better than he had expected. His mother was so glad that Kurt had not been injured that she ignored the fact that he was a member of the Waffen SS. Fritz was proud of his son, and the family reunion was the best they had experienced in a long time. Even a quick call from Jurgen to his parents saying he was also fine failed to dampen Kurt's homecoming. As Kurt was leaving for Nuremberg, his mother did give him a short lecture on being careful—and being a Christian—but she was not as harsh as she had been in the past. Unfortunately, none of Kurt's close friends had been home. They were all engaged in some form of service to the Fatherland, but Kurt went to visit most of their parents and was able to find out what his friends had been doing and accept hearty congratulations from everyone.

In Nuremberg Kurt went straight to Konrad and Hilda's house and was treated like royalty. Uncle Konrad asked Kurt a few questions about the war in France, but told him he would wait until everyone was together at the von Klugemanns before getting into too much detail so Kurt wouldn't have to repeat himself. Mostly, Konrad filled Kurt in on the experiences of Jurgen and Hans. Kurt knew that all his friends except Kurt Mueller had survived the war, but he had heard very little about Jurgen and nothing about Hans. Uncle Konrad, realizing he possessed information new to Kurt, capitalized on this fact, and, in true Konrad fashion, dragged the stories out interminably. Finally, Kurt learned that Jurgen had been promoted to Captain and had been awarded the Knight's Cross, one of only a handful of the Leibstandarte to receive the prestigious honor. Captain Jurgen Heisler was now one of the rising stars of the Waffen SS. Hans had also distinguished himself with the Leibstandarte and had been awarded the Iron Cross, First Class. However, he would not be home for another three weeks. Kurt was disappointed that he would be unable to see Hans, but his absence allowed Kurt to be the first hero welcomed home, and he did not have to share the attention with anyone else.

The very night Kurt arrived in Nuremberg the von Klugemanns held a celebration in his honor. He had also been awarded the Iron Cross, First Class, for his exploits in combat, and as soon as Maria saw his impressive medal, she squealed with delight. "Kurt, you are a true hero of the Reich." Erika did not say a word, but she walked up to Kurt and threw her arms around him and kissed him in front of everyone before they all retreated to the dining room. The group at the dinner table was fairly small, but they were proud Germans ready to pay homage to one of Hitler's finest. Included were the von Klugemanns and some of their selected friends, Kurt and his aunt and uncle, and a few of Frederick's business associates. By the time Maria got through with her hero's welcome and toast, Kurt felt as if he had defeated the French all by himself.

Kurt played the part of the dashing Nordic warrior very well. Resplendent in his black, silver and white uniform, he charmed everyone at the table with stories about the victory over the Allies. The twin lightning bolts on his collar and the medal around his neck reflected the light, providing gleaming props for his tales of heroism. Finally, there was a break in the retelling of war stories, and Erika, who had barely had a chance to visit with Kurt, nudged him under the table. "Do you realize it's over a year since we've seen each other? Time has disappeared much faster than normal. I've missed you!"

"Yes, I know exactly how long it's been, as I've counted every day away from you, and I've missed you on every one."

"Then why didn't you write me more letters or call me a few more times?"

Erika's question caught Kurt off guard. "I guess I'm just not much of a letter writer, and I have been pretty busy, you know. Being a hero on the front lines is pretty much a full-time job."

Even Erika's smirk was bewitching as she responded. "So I'm hearing, Lieutenant Heisler. By the time my mother gets done singing your praises, I won't be able to compete with your ego."

Kurt squeezed her hand and looked softly into her dazzling blue eyes. "I hardly think so. We need to spend time alone together soon. A lot of time!"

Before Erika could respond, Maria seized center stage by proposing another toast. "Ladies and gentlemen, I offer a toast to one of the finest examples of German manhood, and a symbol of future German greatness, Waffen SS war hero, Lieutenant Kurt Heisler."

Amid the cheers and the clinking of glasses, Kurt could feel Erika's leg rub against his. That touch meant more to Kurt than any medal ever could. Erika whispered in Kurt's ear, "I guess I don't have to worry about praising you. Mother's doing enough for both of us. But I am proud of you, and I want to be alone with you soon."

Kurt continued to visit with Erika whenever possible during the rest of the evening, but he was forced to retell his war stories until he was getting annoyed. He was learning that there was a downside to being a war hero, a glorious, but tedious downside.

Finally, by eleven o'clock all the guests had gone except Kurt and Uncle Konrad and Aunt Hilda. Kurt was figuring out how to sneak a few moments alone with Erika when Maria made a surprise announcement. "Kurt, tomorrow night Frederick and I are taking you and Erika out for dinner and the opera. It will be a very special night."

"Thank you very much, Frau Klugemann. I'd be delighted to attend the opera with you and your husband."

"What about me?" asked Erika.

After the laughter died down, Kurt asked Maria, "What shall I wear to the opera?"

"Exactly what you have on now. I need to show you off a little." Looking at her daughter, Maria could see that going to the opera with her parents was not exactly what Erika had planned for tomorrow night. "Don't worry, Erika. You'll have plenty of time to see Kurt without your parents around. Don't pout now."

Erika glared at her mother, but made no reply. Sensing a conflict brewing, Uncle Konrad came to the rescue, "Well, thank you all very much, but it's late and we should be going. Kurt may be able to stay up all night on the front lines, but I've seen this opera, and I can assure you, he needs to rest up so he can stay awake during this one."

———

About noon the next day Maria called Kurt with a distressing message. Erika had slipped and sprained her ankle while coming down the stairs, and she was refusing to go to the opera. The sprain was not serious, but she was in some pain. Kurt immediately went to see Erika and was soon reminded of how similar Maria and Erika were, both proud, determined, stubborn women. When mother and daughter clashed, it was a supreme test of wills, and Kurt had not witnessed it firsthand until now.

Maria met Kurt at the door. "Come in, Kurt. Erika is pouting in the study. Why don't you go in and see if you can do something to convince her to go to the opera? We're still going out to dinner and to the opera, whether Erika goes or not. I've worked very hard to set this evening up, and you simply cannot refuse to go. After all the buildup, I would be deeply humiliated if I didn't have my war hero to show off to my friends."

"Good morning, Frau von Klugemann. Yes, I can see your dilemma. I don't suppose it would help if I found another war hero to take my place?"

Maria's withering look said it all.

"That's what I thought. I'll see what I can do."

When Kurt entered the study, Erika was seated on a couch with her back to him, reading a book. Sensing his presence, Erika spoke without turning around, "Kurt, have you been talking with my mother?"

"What do you think?"

"Well, I'm sure she's told you that I'm a big baby, but I'm not limping my way into a fancy restaurant and then hopping around an opera house. I will not be helped along like a cripple. If I can't stand on my own, I won't go."

"Not even for the opportunity to spend the evening with me?"

Returning Kurt's sarcastic inflection with an equal dose of her own, Erika replied, "Kurt, that's not a fair question, and, what's more, it's beneath you. Why don't you stand up to my mother and refuse to go to the opera so you can stay here and take care of me?"

"I've tried, but your mother is not going to give me that option."

"Oh, I see. One of Hitler's wonder soldiers is afraid of a middle-aged woman. How did you ever earn that medal for bravery anyway? You're sure pretty meek around her."

"It would take a much braver man than I to confront your mother, Erika. Hell, I think the whole Reich is afraid of her. Seriously, are you hurt that badly that you can't go out this evening?"

Giving Kurt another withering glare, Erika huffily responded, "Let's just say I'm hurt badly enough that I don't want to go, and that's final!"

"Well, I'll try again to convince your mother that you need my special attention and that she and your father should attend the opera without us."

"I wish you luck, Lieutenant Heisler, but I think you have your work cut out for you. When mother has her mind made up, she can be very stubborn."

"I wonder if you could possibly have inherited any of your mother's temperament."

"Don't try to be clever with me, Kurt. I'm not in the mood."

"Speaking of being in the mood, I only have a few days of leave left. Considering the fact that we haven't seen each other in a year, and who knows when we'll see each other again, maybe we should spend some time together, if you know what I mean."

After a static pause, Erika used her most alluring voice and motioned to him. "Kurt, come here and sit next to me."

Being careful not to jostle her right leg, Kurt sat down beside her. She reached out and grasped Kurt's hands in hers and looked at him lovingly. "Yes, we do need to spend as much time together as possible."

Inches away from the face he had fantasized about for many months, Kurt couldn't resist the temptation and pulled Erika firmly toward him. She flinched in pain and yelled, "Ouch, my ankle! Don't be in such a hurry, Kurt. I'm not going anywhere."

Ignoring her complaint, Kurt encircled her in his arms.

"Just where are we going, Erika? It still seems like we're standing on the steps of my uncle's house three years ago when we first met. Do we really have a future together?"

Without another word being spoken, Kurt and Erika embraced in a series of short, tender kisses. Erika slid her hands up the back of Kurt's neck and into his hair. "Stay with me tonight, Kurt. We'll discuss our future."

Just as Kurt was about to respond, there was a knock on the door and Maria entered the room.

"Well, Kurt, have you convinced my daughter to come with us tonight?"

"Kurt is staying with me tonight, Mother. I need company to ease my pain."

"Excuse me, daughter, but you don't know what pain is … yet. Kurt has a commitment to fulfill, even if you won't. I assume, then, that you absolutely are not coming tonight?"

"No! I just can't go."

Maria wheeled away from Erika and confronted Kurt. "Kurt, I shall find you another companion then, a really cute one. Let's see, I think Frau Steinar's daughter is available, and if … "

"Mother, don't try to be so damn dramatic. Besides, you wouldn't dare!"

"Really, my dear? Do you think I would allow myself to be the laughingstock of my social group? We'll just see if I dare."

Erika was starting to get a little nervous.

"Mother, I know you too well. You're just doing this to try to force me to go."

Kurt sat pinned between mother and daughter, forced to fight a war on two fronts with no one protecting his flanks and not daring to offer an opinion. Then Maria made a pronouncement that shocked Kurt and stunned Erika into temporary speechlessness. "I realize that the two of you are not even engaged, but I'm assuming that you'll get married someday. The two of you are a perfect fit. Therefore, I'm not going to forfeit a chance to show off my future son-in-law, especially after his victorious participation in our defeat of the French. Actually, Frau Steinar's husband, General Steinar, is currently in Berlin, and she would be glad to serve as your stand-in, Erika. I know you very well, too, so I've already checked, and there is nothing she would like better than a young war hero as her escort for the evening."

Maria paused to allow the full impact of her announcement to sink in. Then she continued, "Unless you tell me right now that you're going tonight, I shall inform Frau Steinar that she will be going with us."

Erika was not sure which of her mother's comments had surprised her the most, the fact that she had already made arrangements for someone else to take her place or her assumption that she and Kurt were perfect for each other and would get married. "Mother, I think you're speaking out of place and are being far too presumptuous. I will make my own decisions about these matters, and I'm still not going tonight. Now that your question has been answered, please leave Kurt and me alone."

"Certainly, dear. Kurt, please be ready by five-thirty. We'll pick you up. Frau Steinar is a charming and entertaining woman, and you'll have a wonderful time. As the wife of a general, she has many insights and stories about military life that should interest you. I'll talk with you later, Erika." Her victory accomplished, Maria exited the room. As Erika sat sulking, Kurt could not help but begin to laugh.

"Do you ever win an argument with your mother?"

"Sometimes, but I'm the only one who does."

Maria had given Kurt a huge opportunity, and he proceeded to take advantage of it. "So, your mother thinks we're a perfect fit. That must mean I have her approval to do some serious courting."

Erika scowled at Kurt with a sinister dark blue in her eyes. "I have my own agenda for the near future, and marriage is not included. I plan on enjoying life at the University, and I'm just starting to get involved with father's business dealings. I'm still dating a little, but I do miss you and want to be with you. I can't understand mother's marriage comment, because we really need to see more of each other. In between my activities and your being gone playing soldier, I just hope we can find time to spend together."

Overcoming a great temptation to do some romancing, Kurt decided that he could also play Erika's game of aloof affection. "I can't decide if you're punishing me or your mother for your decision to stay home, but I'm going back to my uncle's for lunch. I hope you recuperate enough so that we can see each other before I leave in a few days. Enjoy your solitude tonight."

As Kurt left the study, a slightly befuddled Erika said, "Have fun tonight, Kurt. Hopefully, I'll see you tomorrow."

———

Kurt's evening at the opera with Frederick, Maria, and Frau Steinar was an exercise in excessive showmanship as Maria paraded him around like her personal trophy. He was introduced to more people than he could possibly remember, all the while being acknowledged as a hero of the Reich. Of course Maria made sure to mention to her friends that Kurt and Erika were definitely an "item."

The evening's highlight was Wagner's *Die Walkure*, a dazzling performance that swept the audience away on the wings of Teutonic power, past and present. Many an eye turned toward the von Klugemanns' prominent box and took notice of the black knight in their midst. Throughout the evening Frau Steinar captivated Kurt with stories of her husband's experiences in the military, and Kurt charmed her with tales from Bad Tolz and his battle experiences in France. Unfortunately, Kurt's enjoyment of the evening was dampened by Erika's absence and the image of her sitting home alone. He wondered if he had been a little too cold in his exit from Erika earlier in the day. Kurt's contemplative state didn't escape Maria's attention, and near the middle of the final act she nudged him and whispered, "Are you thinking of Erika?"

"At times. I have a feeling she's not too happy with me at the moment."

"Don't worry. She'll be awake when we get home, and we shall all have a glass of sherry. Then Frederick and I will go to bed, and the two of you can be alone for as long as you like. Enjoy the opera!"

The evening passed quickly enough, and before he knew it, Kurt was sitting in the limousine with the rest of the opera party headed for home. At the Steinar residence he got out and escorted Frau Steinar to the door while the von Klugemanns and their chauffer waited in the car. "I had a wonderful evening, Frau Steinar. Your husband is a very lucky man."

"Thank you, Lieutenant. I will return your compliment by saying that you are a handsome, charming young man. If I may be so bold, I hope everything works out between you and Erika. I can't think of a more perfect couple. She's a lovely young woman."

Kurt clicked his heels together and he kissed her outstretched hand. "Heil Hitler! Thank you, and good night, Frau Steinar." As soon as he was back in the car, Kurt was inundated with a salvo of compliments from Frau von Klugemann.

"Kurt, Frau Steinar certainly gave you her stamp of approval. She's not easily impressed, and you can take her praise as a very high endorsement. A number of my other friends also thought you looked very dashing." Maria began to laugh at herself, and then added coyly, "Of course, none of their endorsements is nearly as important as mine, which you obviously know you have."

"Maria, I think Kurt has had enough prompting for the evening," admonished Herr Klugemann. "Everything will work out in time."

"Oh, dear Frederick, relax. Right now, I think a glass of sherry is in order."

The chauffer stopped at the van Klugemann residence and helped his passengers out. As the trio walked up the steps, Maria exclaimed, "My goodness, the night has gone so fast. Let's hope Erika is in one of her good moods. We don't want anything to spoil such a glorious evening."

Entering the house, Maria yelled, "Erika, we're home. Come and join us for a glass of sherry."

A voice floated out of the study, "Come in and join me. I'm already having a glass of sherry."

Upon entering the study, the von Klugemanns and Kurt beheld a sight that shocked Frederick, infuriated Maria, and numbed Kurt. Predictably unpredictable, Erika had seized the initiative and was already having her own party. She stood in nothing but a sheer, black nightgown, blond hair in fluffy disarray, her blue eyes ablaze with a mischievous glow. Holding a glass of sherry in one hand while resting the other on the back of a couch, she swayed ever so slightly. A tray with a bottle of sherry and three glasses sat on a dark oak table, and Erika's white robe lay over one of the four heavy oak chairs surrounding the table. "I thought we might toast your night at the opera," Erika stated in an air of feigned innocence.

Frederick responded first, "I see by the level of the bottle you're not on your first glass of sherry. You know young lady that we find this behavior ... "

"My God, Erika, you look like a common tramp!" Maria barked. "Put your robe on right now! How dare you embarrass us like this?"

"Mother, I'm not a child anymore, and I'm not dressed inappropriately." Erika was now standing defiantly with her hands on her hips, chin jutting forward. "This is my house, and I'm home alone relaxing in comfort. And since you've already decided that our war hero here is already my intended, what's the big deal about how he sees me?"

Maria became even more furious with Erika's flippant response. "I know what you're doing. You're staging a little protest because you didn't get your way and were left alone. Well, I don't care how old you are. As long as you live in our house, you will act like a lady. Now put your robe on!"

Frederick turned to Kurt. "Kurt, let's have a glass of sherry, and then you should probably go back to your uncle's. I apologize for my daughter's shameless behavior. Based on the sherry missing from the bottle, I would say Erika should go to bed."

By this time Erika had put her robe on and was trying to act as sober as possible.

"Mother, Father, can't Kurt stay and visit with me for a little bit? I've hardly seen him since he's been in Nuremberg."

There was no forgiveness in Maria's response. "You should have thought of that before you made such a fool of yourself."

Kurt was desperately trying to figure out some way to be with Erika, but he sadly concluded that the present circumstances made that impossible. He had to accept the situation Erika had created and make the best of it. "Thank you, Herr von Klugemann. I'd like to enjoy a glass of sherry with you before I'm on my way."

"Don't you have anything to say to me, Kurt?" asked Erika.

Kurt knew he had to give her some words of support, but that he was treading on dangerous ground, so he measured his words carefully. "I must say, Erika, you do look rather fetching in your choice of evening attire. I only hope that someday I shall see you dressed the same way, but in a more correct situation."

"If you mean like on our honeymoon, you may have a long wait, Lieutenant Heisler, no matter what my mother has already decided for us."

"That's it, Erika. I'm escorting you to your bedroom. Good night, Kurt. Erika will apologize tomorrow."

After Maria and Erika had left, Frederick actually smiled and offered Kurt some advice.

"Again, Kurt, I'm sorry for how my daughter behaved. It certainly was not proper, especially for someone with her upbringing, but then she's her mother's daughter. If you plan to continue courting Erika, her behavior is a variable you'll need to take into consideration."

"I already have, Herr von Klugemann, and with your permission, I plan to continue to see your daughter whenever I can. I must adhere to the SS code—no retreat, no surrender."

Frederick laughed heartily as he and Kurt found their way to the couch. They sat and enjoyed some light-hearted exchanges about life with the von Klugemann women over a few glasses of sherry, and then Kurt departed for his uncle's.

Later, lying in bed, Kurt could not fall asleep. A hauntingly beautiful creature in a sheer, black nightgown looked down at him seductively, keeping him awake, contemplating what might have been.

———

The next day Erika called over to the Heislers and asked to talk to Kurt. Her apology was half-hearted, and after talking with Kurt about her bad behavior, she asked him to come over so they could make plans to be together for the rest of his leave. Stupidly, Kurt asked her how she would be dressed, and Erika slammed the phone down and refused to answer Kurt's return calls. Seeing no other alternative, Kurt walked over to the von Klugemanns and knocked on the door. No one came, so Kurt concluded Erika was home alone. Trying the door, he found it unlocked and entered the house.

Walking in a few steps, Kurt yelled, "Is anyone home?" Hearing no reply, Kurt changed the tone of his voice and softly called out, "Erika, I'd like to talk to you, however you're dressed." He heard a burst of laughter in the next room, and Erika soon sauntered into the entryway.

"I must admit, Kurt, you're developing a sense of humor. I thought you men of the Waffen SS were supposed to be rather dull, unfeeling robots devoted solely to the art of making war."

"Are you saying I need help in the art of making something else?"

"Don't get too funny or this conversation will be a short one. Come, let's go sit down and talk."

Sitting next to Erika on the sofa, Kurt asked, "How's your ankle?"

"Much better, thank you. The swelling has gone down, but I'm still limping a bit."

"I'm glad you're starting to heal up. I'm sure you'll be back to normal in no time. Are your parents home?"

"No! And I'm sure my mother doesn't want you over here alone with me. She's probably afraid I'll try to seduce you. After the scene I created last night, I'm afraid she thinks I'm rather shameless. I'm a little embarrassed by my behavior, Kurt, and I'm sorry. I was depressed about not being able to be with you at the opera, and I guess I had one glass of sherry too many. I stepped over the boundaries of good taste."

After her momentary lapse of humility, Erika resumed her seductive mode. "Despite that, I hope you weren't too disappointed by anything you saw last night."

By now Kurt was able to play Erika's game on equal footing. "I'm not sure. I think I need a better look."

"I think I need a good look also. I've always wondered what a superman really looks like, and I think I deserve a vote."

"I think it could be arranged so both of us could get what we want."

"Possibly, but not yet, my eager young Lieutenant, not yet."

"Well, when then? I leave tomorrow, and who knows when we'll be together again, or if I'll make it back alive. Besides, this dance we're doing has been going on for a long time, and I really think it has to reach a conclusion soon. The band can't play on forever, you know."

Erika crossed her legs demurely. "Is that just a line to get me out of my clothes?"

"You already did that last night."

"Last night is over. We're talking about today and tonight."

Getting serious, Kurt said, "I really do need to leave tomorrow and report back to my division. I thought I had a few more days, but the last couple days of my leave were cancelled for some reason."

"Well, then, let's not waste the time you have left. Let's go to a movie, and then afterward we can drive somewhere and be alone for a long time."

Kurt could not pass up the opportunity to needle Erika one more time. "Well, that sounds fun. Do you promise to be good?"

"I can assure you, Kurt, I may be a lot better than you want me to be!"

"And just how do you mean that? After all, your mother's already planning our wedding."

"Oh, shut up, Kurt."

Kurt leaned into Erika, put his arms around her and gave her a soft kiss. She looked up at him mockingly, "Can't you do better than that?"

Kurt responded immediately and did much better.

"It appears your training wasn't a complete waste. You take orders well, Lieutenant. Now stop before my mother comes home."

"I don't think I'll take orders very well tonight, unless I agree with them."

Erika did not respond. He could tell she was planning something, so he remained quiet and let her think. After a few moments, Erika asked Kurt, "Can you get your uncle's car for the evening?"

"I'm sure I can. What time shall I pick you up?"

"No later than six-thirty," answered a still contemplative Erika.

"If something changes, call me. I need to pack and make some phone calls today because I need to leave early in the morning. Having the afternoon free will allow me to get everything done, so nothing will spoil tonight."

"Except me," mocked Erika, as she leaned into Kurt for a goodbye kiss, which turned into several, each longer than the last. Finally, Erika pushed Kurt away, saying, "That should keep you interested until tonight. Now, go do your errands so you can hurry back to me." Kurt left reluctantly, and Erika limped into the kitchen to make lunch.

The afternoon couldn't pass quickly enough for Kurt. He had been waiting for this night for over a year, and he had no idea when another chance like this might come again.

———

That night Erika met Kurt at the door. "Change of plans. Go park the car in the garage and return to the house." Kurt turned without saying a word, and as he was parking the car thought, "What in the hell does this woman have planned now?" He knew better than to try to guess.

As soon as Kurt entered the house, Erika danced over to him, gave him a preview kiss and began to explain her plan for the evening. "Kurt, unless you disagree, I've made a change in our plans for tonight. I want to be alone with you and talk about our future. We can't talk much sitting in a movie theater."

"I agree so far. Tell me more."

"Father and Mother won't be home until ten at the absolute earliest, so we can be totally alone until they get home. When they get here, we can visit with them until they go to bed, and then we can be alone some more."

"Okay, so why'd I drive over here? I could've walked. And why'd I put the car in the garage?" Kurt was still cautiously curious.

"I wanted everyone to think we went to a movie. I just don't want my mother on my back for having you over here alone. Sometimes I just don't understand her. She thinks I'm too forward at times, but then out of nowhere she tells us she thinks we'll get married like it's some foregone conclusion. Tell me, do you think I'm too forward?"

"In certain situations, maybe, but certainly not in regard to our being intimate together, if you know what I mean."

"You wouldn't want me if I were easy, would you, Kurt?"

"That's not a fair question for a soldier who's just spent a year with a bunch of men," Kurt said with a laugh. "For now I'll just say 'maybe,' so don't press me too hard on that issue. But getting back to your plan, why did I park in the garage, and what do we tell your parents when they get home?"

"Don't you trust my plan, Kurt? I had you park in the garage so your aunt and uncle wouldn't see the car and know that we were here alone. As for my parents, when they get home we'll tell them we just got back from the movie and that we wanted to visit with them. If they ask any questions about the movie, just let me do the talking and you just agree."

"Sounds okay to me, but I feel like I'm fourteen years old again," shrugged Kurt.

Erika laughed and took Kurt's hand to lead him into the living room. "I can tell you're definitely not fourteen. Please sit down and get comfortable. Would you like some coffee?"

"I'd rather have a beer."

"Later. We're going to do some serious talking first. We have lots of time. It's not even seven yet."

"All right, I'll have a cup. What exactly do you want to talk about?"

"Our future . . . yours, mine, and Germany's," Erika said as she poured two cups of coffee from the steaming pot on the mantle. "I listen to my father and his friends talk about the war. I read the newspapers and listen to the speeches on the radio about how our country is doing such wonderful things. Now I want to hear you tell me what you think will happen next in this war."

"If this is your idea of foreplay, Erika, I'm not sure it's working for me. What's next? A few tender passages from *Mein Kampf* to set the mood?"

Erika looked genuinely hurt, so Kurt realized it was time to back off. "You really are in a serious mood, aren't you?"

"Yes, I really do want to have a serious discussion about our future, and I want to hear your assessment of where things are going."

"All right, Erika, I guess that's a reasonable request, and I'll treat it seriously." Kurt paused and set his coffee cup on the table. "First of all, I doubt we'll try to invade England any time soon. Crossing the channel presents too many problems. If the air war is successful, an invasion may be possible, but that's still much in doubt. Anyway, England is isolated and no threat to us, and we really have no need to defeat the English more than we already have; they're still trying to rebuild their army after Dunkirk. Second, it's only a matter of time until we'll need to smash Russia and destroy the threat of Bolshevism before they attack us and destroy European civilization as we know it."

"I've heard friends of my father say that Hitler would never fight a two-front war because that mistake led to our defeat in the last war."

"Well, we have no threat in the West now that France has surrendered and England has been isolated, so there's nothing to worry about in that regard."

"What about the United States?" Erika asked, surprising Kurt.

"What about the Atlantic Ocean?" Kurt replied.

Erika gave Kurt a stern look. "I'm serious, Kurt. What about the United States? They're the ones who turned the tide against us in the Great War. Don't you think they'll come to the aid of their friends again?"

"Where would they land? We control the continent. Our U-Boats have a ring around England, preventing most ships from getting into English ports. But even if we did go to war with America for some reason I can't think of, by then we'll have destroyed the Soviet Union."

Erika pressed on. "Kurt, I think you're making it sound too easy. If I remember my history, Russia has never been successfully invaded. Do you recall Napoleon's disastrous invasion of Russia?"

"Sure, but Napoleon's experience isn't relevant because there's never been an army like ours before. Besides, we have no alternative. Eventually it will be them or us."

"So you're saying we're going to invade Russia?"

"Not exactly. I'm just saying that sooner or later we'll be at war with Russia, regardless of who starts it. The current non-aggression pact between our countries is only a temporary agreement of convenience. Hitler and Stalin are both well aware of that. The conflict may be far in the future, but I have a feeling it'll be sooner rather than later."

"Do you think you'll have to go when it happens?" Erika said with a look of concern.

"I'm pretty sure of it. When I was at the Junkerschule at Bad Tolz, we were trained to be the spearhead to slay the Russian Bear. No other group is better mentally equipped to defeat the Soviet barbarians than the Waffen SS."

Erika had never before witnessed Kurt being so forceful regarding another race of people, and she became melancholy. "Kurt, I don't want you to go to Russia. I fear them as enemies. I fear for you if you try to conquer the vastness of Russia."

"It's what I've been trained to do. A soldier follows orders and does his duty. Our duty in the Waffen SS will be to help Germany save the world from the Red Menace. Don't worry, if it comes to war with Russia, I'll return to you, I promise."

Erika laid her head on Kurt's shoulder. They did not speak for minutes, lost in their private musings about the future. Kurt eventually broke the silence. "Erika, do you agree with your mother that we're a perfect fit?"

"I don't think my mother should have made any reference to a marriage between us, but it does show how much she likes you. As for us, I think we like each other, get along well together, and complement each other. I'm not sure that means we'll get married, not because we're not ready, but because of our circumstances. I think everything depends on what occurs during the next year or so. What do you think?"

"I guess I agree, reluctantly. My life as a soldier is so fluid and dangerous right now that it makes it hard for me to ask you to wait for me, knowing that you'll constantly be worrying about what might happen to me."

"Don't you think I'll wait and worry whether you ask me to or not?" Erika said softly.

Simultaneously, Erika and Kurt reached for each other and were soon locked in a passionate embrace. As their kisses grew in intensity and duration, their tongues began to probe, sparingly at first, and then relentlessly. Lost in passion, they began to devour each other, interrupted only by longing sighs. Kurt's right hand tenderly unbuttoned Erika's blouse as she panted her approval. Slowly, Kurt began to rub the outside of Erika's bra with one hand as his other hand began releasing her breasts from their last vestige of modesty. Erika continued to attack Kurt with a sensual barrage of kisses, covering him from neck to forehead. Suddenly her bra slipped off her breasts, but she caught it before it fell off completely. Turning away from Kurt, Erika replaced her bra and sat up very rigidly. Regaining her composure, she turned to Kurt and spoke in a soft, faltering voice. "Kurt, we must stop now. I want to go further, and I don't want to be a tease, but for right now, this is as far as I'll go. Please don't make me go any further, please!"

Kurt was not in a totally rational state, but, sighing loudly, he retreated back on the couch. "I hope you know this isn't easy for me."

"I know, and I thank you."

In his state of frustration Kurt almost asked Erika if she stopped all her dates at this point. He held his tongue when he recalled her earlier comment that all of her dates had been very casual and that no one but Kurt really mattered to her. He tried to make some small talk to prolong the evening, but they soon realized that spending any more time together would be frustrating to both of them. Reluctantly, they parted with a

series of desperate, soulful goodbye kisses, not knowing when—or if—
they would see each other again.

———

Early the next morning, with the lingering scent of Erika's perfume still on
his shirt, Kurt left to rejoin the Verfugungsdivision. Shortly after arriving
he learned his group was to become part of a new German combat force.
During the resting period for the German Army after the fall of France,
Reichsfuhrer Himmler had convinced Hitler that the Waffen SS should be
expanded in size and given better equipment. Consequently, the combat
divisions of the SS were being reorganized into bigger, more powerful
units, both in the number of divisions and in the quantity and quality of
their support equipment. In January Kurt's division was officially renamed
Second Waffen SS Motorized Infantry Division, Das Reich.

CHAPTER VII

Crusade in Russia

During the fall of 1940 Hitler decided not to attempt an invasion of England. Instead, he focused the military on planning a Holy War against Russia, which would break Germany's non-aggression pact with Stalin. Hitler convinced Germany that the barbarians of the East, the lowly Slavs, were trying to erase the culture of Europe. Operation Barbarossa, as the invasion plan of Russia was called, was an ideological campaign designed to destroy this threat of Bolshevism forever, a crusade to save Europe from another "Dark Age." This couldn't be accomplished with a campaign like that waged against France, which was conducted with military correctness according to the established rules of war. In order to exterminate the Slavic horde, the war against the Soviet Union had to be fought by another set of rules, the survival of the fittest.

There were, however, serious misgivings among many members of the German General Staff regarding an attempt to conquer Russia. First, they believed that a two-front war ran counter to the philosophy of the German military experts regarding how to conduct a modern war. Second, the Wehrmacht leadership wasn't convinced of the political strategy of a "Holy War" against Russia; they clearly saw it as another war to be won by superior strategy and tactics. Finally, the specter of Napoleon's debacle in the Russian wasteland continued to haunt the generals. But Hitler was the leader, so, once again, politics prevailed over military expertise, and the generals were ordered to perfect a plan to conquer Russia.

SS Reichsfuhrer Heinrich Himmler saw this war in the East as a special opportunity to showcase the unique skills of the Waffen SS. Trained in the ideological mold of Nietzsche's superman, the SS was ideally suited for ruthless combat between two enemies struggling to completely destroy each other, and Himmler lobbied heavily for the SS to play a leading role in the invasion of Russia. Not surprisingly, when the final plans for Operation Barbarossa were drawn up, Kurt's prediction to Erika would prove to be correct, and the Waffen SS would be at the front of the battle line.

———

In early February of 1941 Kurt managed to get a short leave to go to Nuremberg and see Erika. Because he only had a few days, he did not take the time to go to Ansbach to see his parents. In Nuremberg Kurt stayed with the von Klugemanns, although he did spend time with Konrad and Hilda. Maria visited often with Kurt and updated him on Hans' recent activities. Everyone sensed that something was in the air, that some momentous event was about to take place, but no one really knew where or when. They all grilled Kurt for answers, but he could only say that Das Reich was a mobile force that was constantly being upgraded to undertake whatever task they would be assigned. This vague response, of course, only convinced everyone that Kurt knew more than he was revealing. In truth, Kurt knew nothing about his next assignment.

In the few days they had together Kurt and Erika were almost inseparable. They walked together, laughed together, and planned together. Whenever possible they were intimate together, but only to the extent allowed by Erika. She continued to keep Kurt at bay sexually and admonished him to respect her wishes. Even Kurt's pleas that she might never see him again failed to soften her resistance. Erika's parting plea, however, gave Kurt a hope, a dream that would help sustain him through the darkest days of his young life. "Come back to me, my love, my hero. Come back to me well and whole. Come back to me having served Germany well, but come back to me. And your prayers will be answered."

———

Hitler's timetable for the invasion of Russia suffered a setback in April of 1941 when he was forced to send troops into the Balkans to subdue the enemy there. Without Hitler's knowledge Mussolini and the Italians had attempted to conquer Greece and failed; it was left to Germany to clean up the mess. Das Reich was one of the German formations sent to stabilize the situation caused by Mussolini's failure. Germany sacrificed some soldiers, but the victory was quick and efficient, and the legend of German invincibility continued to grow. The Waffen SS also added to its reputation as a group of fearless, unstoppable fanatics. The only drawback of the Balkan campaign was that it delayed Operation Barbarossa from May 15 until June 22, 1941.

With each military success Kurt's confidence in Hitler and the Fatherland continued to grow. Life as a member of the Waffen SS was full of excitement, and, luckily, he had escaped any injury or wounds. So far, it was good being a superman. Then, in the early summer of 1941, the German war machine faced its greatest challenge. When the Fuhrer's address announcing the invasion of Russia was read to the German troops on the eve of Barbarossa, Kurt's heart burned with the passion of a pagan warrior. He and his friends in Das Reich were confident they would be in Moscow by the end of the summer.

———

On the morning of June 22, 1941, Kurt was one of three million German soldiers stationed along a front that stretched over nine hundred miles, north to south, along the German-Russian border. The German plan was to advance into Russia until the German Army controlled a front extending from Archangel in the north to Astrakhan in the south, which would leave Moscow inside the German side of the line.

The German attack forces were divided into three major groups: Army Group North, aimed at Leningrad; Army Group Center, aimed at Moscow; and Army Group South, aimed at Kiev. Das Reich was an integral part of the most powerful of the three Groups, Army Group Center. Unlike most Wehrmacht units, the Waffen SS divisions were motorized, so Das Reich was placed with the fast Panzer Divisions leading the breakthrough. Field Marshal von Bock commanded Army Group Center, which comprised two armies and two Panzer groups. Colonel-General Heinz Guderian commanded the Second Panzer Group, which included Das Reich, led by Waffen SS General Paul Hausser.

———

Second Lieutenant Heisler was pacing back and forth in a wooded area a little southwest of Brest-Litovsk, the former Polish fortress now under Russian control, awaiting the word to move his men up to their jumping-off point. The beginning of the crusade against the evil empire of Bolshevism was only minutes away. The troops were confident of victory, and an electric tension sizzled in the early morning air. Kurt was unsure of what the next few weeks would bring, but he knew Germany must strike the Soviet Union a quick, devastating blow. He thought back to his statue in Ansbach and realized that he was on the threshold of fulfilling his boyhood dream. He sensed his life was about to change forever.

Kurt was anxious to get started, and he was waiting for First Lieutenant Paul Streicker to return from the company meeting with instructions.

Peering at his watch, Kurt noticed that his heart was pounding much faster with each passing second. While he waited, his mind began to wander from the upcoming battle, and he thought about his friends. Walter Kruger, his old friend from Ansbach, was somewhere in the Second Panzer Group as a member of the Twenty-Ninth Motorized Infantry Division. Brother Jurgen, now a Captain in the First Waffen SS Motorized Infantry Division, Leibstandarte Adolf Hitler, was with Hans van Klugemann in the southern sector with Army Group South. Ernst Meyer, having just joined the Waffen SS, was back in Germany starting basic training. Horst Rikker, Kurt's friend from his cadet days at Bad Tolz, was in charge of a platoon alongside Kurt. And then there was Erika. He envisioned Erika, smelled her, felt her presence, and wanted her more than anything he'd ever known. During the battles in Holland and France he had never really worried about dying, but the eerie calm before the start of Barbarossa seemed more ominous. Kurt wondered if he would ever see Erika again.

"Lieutenant Heisler, move your men down to the river, quietly now." The quest to protect Germanic purity was about to begin. Although by now Kurt was a hardened soldier who had experienced the terror of war, nothing in his past could have prepared him for the magnitude of human suffering, slaughter, and sacrifice that was about to unfold.

"I don't believe this fucking country or these crazy Russians," yelled Private Kuntz. "We just keep rolling forward, killing them by the thousands, and what happens? More land to cross and more Russians to kill. It never seems to end. I'm afraid we may be shooting the bastards all summer in order to finally get rid of them."

Someone shouted, "Shut up, Kuntz! Get some rest while you can."

Kurt was too tired to even smile at the brief exchange. The attack on Russia had been in progress for over a week, and he had already witnessed more destruction than he thought could take place in a century, much less nine days. Despite their swift progress, still lying before the Germans was a savage, yet beautiful, land; virgin forests, green-rolling hills, vast fields of wheat and sunflowers interrupted by foul swamps and recurrent rivers. Above it all the blue summer sky extended into eternity. To Kurt, the dominant feature of Russia's geography was its endless space, a vastness that made men feel totally insignificant.

Kurt and five Das Reich comrades were wedged together in an armored half-track as it raced along with other vehicles attempting to keep up with the tanks of Guderian's Second Panzer Group. The race into Russia had been swift and successful for the German Armies, but devastating and disastrous for the Russians. Nonetheless, the Russians had proved to be much tougher fighters than the Germans had anticipated. They were not well led, and their armor tactics were un-coordinated, but the Russian soldiers exhibited great tenacity and bravery. They had no fear of death, and there seemed to be an endless supply of them. This unexpected Soviet heroism had resulted in heavier than anticipated German casualties, especially among the eager men of the Waffen SS.

Another unwelcome surprise for the Germans had been the condition of the Russian roads. During the Blitzkrieg across France the German mechanized forces had been able to take advantage of a fine network of roads, but Russian roads were barely navigable, even in good weather. They were often nothing more than dirt trails that produced clouds of fine dirt that gagged men and clogged machines. Anticipating what these roads would be like during heavy rains or winter snowstorms, the soldiers of the Reich pushed even harder to finish the Russian Campaign before the severe arctic winter took hold.

———

As the weeks went by the infinite Russian sky changed from a soft blue to a dirty, greasy, blackish-gray from the uncountable fires. Dark columns of smoke spiraled upward in every direction, as if the whole world was on fire. Some fires were large, as entire cities burned to the ground. Others were only single tanks or trucks, but each pyre marked a death site like a floating tombstone. Accompanying the fires was the unceasing roar of planes, tanks, trucks, horses, motorcycles, marching men, explosions and the screams of dying soldiers that created a cacophony that even Dante could not have imagined. Whether they were next to dead comrades or behind the front lines, combatants couldn't escape this nonstop symphony of agony. Silence simply didn't exist anywhere along the entire front of Operation Barbarossa.

"Hey, Lieutenant. Do you have any idea where the hell we are? Everything has started to look the same around here—lots of dirt filled with dead Russians."

A laugh went up from the occupants of the half-track.

"I think we're pretty close to Minsk," answered Kurt.

Another solider exclaimed, "For God's sake, I thought we'd be in Moscow by now. It seems like we've been driving and fighting forever."

As the men with Kurt continued to express their bewilderment at not already forcing a Soviet surrender, their Second Lieutenant was looking intently through his field glasses.

"Corporal! Stop this damn machine!" shouted Kurt. As the half-track came to a lurching halt, Kurt continued to scan the horizon with his binoculars. Slowly, two large hulks began to appear in the east. A soft whistle escaped from Kurt's mouth as he said, "Sergeant, would you look at what the hell is coming our way now? Have you ever seen anything like these tanks before?"

Sergeant Blumersbonn grabbed the glasses from Kurt and took a look. "No, Lieutenant, but I'd guess it's what our troops in the Southern sector have already run up against, the new Soviet T-34."

"My God," exclaimed Kurt, "they make our tanks look like toys. I thought those Russian KV1s and KV2s we ran into two days ago were scary, but they were slow and clumsy, thank God. These devils seem to be much faster and more maneuverable."

A German motorcycle came tearing across a field already stitched with tread marks and stopped beside Kurt's half-track. The driver sat on his cycle and yelled at Kurt, "Lieutenant, Captain Hartman and the rest of the company are under attack a little way back. The enemy has new super tanks and a lot of infantry. The Captain intends to hold until reinforcements arrive. He figures the Russians are coming out of those woods over to the left. He wants you to hold this flank in case they try to get around him from your side. You'd better dig in."

"I don't even have a full platoon right now. And what in the hell am I supposed to stop those tanks with, prayers and spit?"

"Captain Hartman is sending you an anti-tank gun crew and a squad from the motorcycle battalion, but I sure wouldn't give up on the prayers. Good luck, Lieutenant."

"Wait up a second. Where's the rest of the Regiment? Why are we cut off?"

As he turned his motorcycle around to return to Captain Hartman's company, the cyclist yelled over his shoulder, "They've already gone east. These Russians hid in the woods and let them pass, and now they're trying to break into our supply columns and destroy us from behind. Heil Hitler!"

The Germans were learning—often at great cost—what a dangerous adversary the Russians were. During their headlong rush, the rapidly moving Panzer Forces often bypassed Soviet forces, leaving them for the following infantry to clean up. These Russian units would frequently hide until an opportune time and then spring a surprise attack on isolated and unsuspecting German troops. After the resulting battles of encirclement had been won by the German Panzers and vast hordes of Russian men and material had been annihilated, the slower moving infantry would then need to spend days clearing out pockets of fierce Russian resistance.

While Kurt contemplated his predicament, an explosion tore open the nearby ground, knocking him over and showering him with dirt. Quickly picking himself up, he screamed, "Head for that depression over by that farmhouse."

The half-track gunned its way toward a shallow, sunken strip of land that had been a farmer's crude attempt at irrigation. A short distance from the ditch, the tilting remains of an ancient farmhouse struggled to remain upright. A few sparse trees were scattered randomly about the farmstead, and the rest of the surrounding landscape was flat except for a few small, hilly areas off to the right and some ominous woods to the left. Brown-clad figures were emerging from the woods, scurrying behind the Soviet T-34 tanks. Kurt had the half-track drive down into the deepest part of the ditch so only its top third was visible to the Russians, leaving its heavy machine gun with a clear field of fire.

"Those damn Ivans don't seem too worried about us the way they're strolling right at us," yelled a private.

"Halsdorph," yelled Kurt, "take a man and set up your MG-34 in that clump of trees. Then we'll have a cross-fire between you and the gun on the half-track."

"Yes, Lieutenant.'

Kurt continued to bark out orders. "Some of you get in the rubble of the farmhouse. Fritz, Karl, man the gun in the half-track. Everyone else spread out in the ditch."

"Lieutenant, we can stop the infantry, but how are we going to stop those tanks?" As if in answer to Private Sturm's question, the promised anti-tank gun, its crew, and a group of twelve motorcyclists came roaring up. But just as the cyclists scrambled into the protection of the shallow ditch, a direct hit from a T-34 turned the antitank gun and its crew into torn, tattered chunks of flesh and steel. The gun and the personnel-carrier that had been towing it were smoking pieces of junk. Kurt could see only two bodies. The others had disintegrated or become part of the twisted metal sculpture.

"What a fucking lucky hit. Those tanks are a long way off to score a direct hit like that. Now we're screwed!"

"Shut up, Krueger. As long as I can hear you whining, I know we're not dead yet. Let's keep calm and remember our training."

Corporal Reisbeck added, "I don't recall getting trained on how to fight a T-34 hand-to-hand, so we'd better hope those tanks run out of gas before they get here."

A young First Lieutenant hopped off his motorcycle and came running up to Kurt. "Lieutenant," he addressed Kurt, "It's too bad about the anti-tank gun, but it wouldn't have made any difference against those T-34s. Our 3.7 millimeter guns are just too small against them. I saw one of those monsters hit at least ten times by a 3.7 anti-tank gun the other day, and the tank didn't even seem to notice. We finally blew it up with satchel charges under the treads. That's why we're here; we have satchel charges in our sidecars. You try to keep the Russian infantry occupied, and we'll buzz around on our cycles and blow the treads off the tanks so we can finish them off. It's our only hope."

Fortunately for the troops under Kurt and Captain Hartman, the main Russian attack was farther to the west in the area of the Tenth Panzer Division. The enemy infantry attacking Kurt's force numbered about 100 men, plus the two T-34s. Kurt commanded just twenty-seven men in his stronghold, including the twelve cyclists, to hold off the Russians. Kurt's group did have a couple things working for them. One of the motorcyclists had brought along another machine gun, so the Germans had three that were well positioned in their defensive alignment, and the Russians had to advance across open ground to take Kurt's position.

As the Soviet troops moved into range, Kurt's men sent a constant stream of steel tearing into them. Some of the Russian troops tried to hide behind their tanks for protection, but most just kept coming, firing from the hip in their familiar half-crouched running position while yelling the now familiar Russia battle cry, "Urra! Urra!"

The clattering of automatic weapons signaled death for many of the advancing Russians. Empty cartridges flew though the air like angry hornets as Kurt's men continued to pour fire into the Russian ranks. Small dirt geysers leaped into the air in front of Kurt's position as Soviet small arms fire began to seek out the German defenders. Motionless brown forms dotted the open field, some vainly trying to rise before they were permanently silenced. A shell from one of the Russian tanks hit the old farmhouse, and the German defenders there ceased to exist. Rolling ever closer, the T-34s fired in Kurt's direction. Luckily, most of them missed their mark as Kurt's men burrowed into their trenches. By now most of the Russian infantry had been killed or disabled, and Kurt was wondering when the cyclists would mount their attack. The tanks were only a few hundred yards out and showed no signs of stopping.

"Wish us luck, Lieutenant," smiled the leader of the suicide squad as he roared past. "If we aren't successful, you'll have to use your imagination to stop Ivan."

For a few seconds Kurt was spellbound by the drama unfolding in front of him until he remembered he was supposed to be providing cover fire for the cyclists. They raced out of each end of the trench and flew toward the T-34s, zigzagging to outguess the tanks' machine guns. One cycle was struck and exploded almost immediately. Soon three others joined the burning wreckage of the battlefield. As the riders became intermingled with the Soviet forces, Kurt's platoon ceased firing so they wouldn't hit their comrades racing among the tanks. A few of the motorcycles had side-cars attached, and the men in them gunned down the few remaining able Russia infantrymen, making this a battle between the two Soviet tanks and the five remaining SS motorcycles.

The turret guns and the machine guns of the T-34s tried to keep up with the speeding cyclists, but they managed to destroy only one more German machine. In the end the gallantry and self-sacrifice of the SS cyclists decided the outcome. By reaching a momentary blind spot in the rear of the Soviet tanks, two cyclists jumped off and placed satchel charges in critical areas on the T-34s before being shot dead. The Soviet tankers attempted to open their hatches and remove the charges, but fire from the German half-track killed any Russian who exposed himself. Soon two burning hulks sent dark smoke twisting upward, as if to honor the heroism of their fearless destroyers. Kurt had never witnessed such bravery; only four cyclists survived the ordeal.

One survivor was the Lieutenant who had talked with Kurt. He drove up as Kurt was walking among his men, checking on casualties. "Well, Lieutenant, our men performed admirably and managed to prevail, at least for today. How many casualties do you have?"

"It looks like five dead and three wounded, but yours were even worse," answered Kurt. For a moment Kurt and his fellow officer surveyed the devastation in front of them. Burning tanks, smashed motorcycles, scores of dead Russians and several dead Waffen SS soldiers littered the battlefield. Here, in this small, insignificant corner of the earth over a hundred human beings had been snuffed out in a matter of minutes.

"That was quite a mess out there, Lieutenant." Kurt said. "We couldn't have survived without you. Your men's brave performance truly exemplifies the spirit of the Waffen SS."

"Thanks. Unfortunately, it looks like the Fatherland will require many more such sacrifices in the days ahead, but no burden is too great to bear as long as we destroy the hated Russians. I pray they never learn how to use their tanks properly in massed formations. If they do, it'll make our crusade much more difficult. I've seen too many scenes like this already; we have to stop T-34s with sappers, artillery, or anti-aircraft guns because our tanks and anti-tank guns just don't have the firepower."

"Then we have to adjust quickly," Kurt responded ruefully. "We've lost over half our force, killed or wounded. We can't continue to absorb those kinds of losses."

"Yes, but the Russians lost all their men," said Kurt's comrade in arms as he sped off to join another battle.

———

At the start of Barbarossa the fastest German formations—the Panzer Divisions and the Motorized Infantry Divisions—stopped for nothing, advancing as fast as possible to prevent the Soviet forces from reorganizing into strong defensive positions. The German command had intended for the trailing regular infantry units to contain and finish off any pockets of isolated Russian forces that the motorized forces left behind. However, the initial strike force had advanced so rapidly that the slower-moving German infantry couldn't keep up, so some of the troops intended for the vanguard had to stop their advance to seal off Russian troops trying to break out from their pockets of encirclement. These assignments were called "picket duty."

Soon after the fierce battle with the T-34s, Kurt's men rejoined their main Das Reich Company and were promptly sent to take part in picket duty on the southern edge of the Bialystok-Minsk Pocket, where a large number of Russian troops had been cut off and were now struggling to find an escape route out of the circle. Kurt's group was sent as a temporary replacement force for the Twenty-Ninth Motorized Infantry Division, which had been ordered forward to start the race for the first major objective of Army Group Center: Smolensk.

Kurt knew that his friend Walter Krueger was with the Twenty-Ninth, and Kurt quickly saw evidence of the effectiveness of Walter's division, a scene that would stick in his mind for a long time. The Russians had attempted to escape by using an old dirt trail, and in several days of horrible combat the Twenty-Ninth had decimated them. The earth was barely visible beneath the dense, brown blanket of Russian soldiers. Anything man could destroy—vehicles, horses, supply wagons—lay twisted and burned across the landscape. Bodies or parts of bodies littered the fields, hung from trees, sprawled from tanks and trucks, and lay intermingled with horse carcasses. In front of one German trench thousands of Russians lay linked arm-to-arm, row-by-row, clearly illustrating the Russians' fanaticism in their failed attempt to breach the lines of the Twenty-Ninth. The overpowering smell of rotting human flesh would stick in Kurt's nostrils for weeks.

When Das Reich was relieved from picket duty and ordered forward toward Smolensk, Kurt's division crossed the Berezina River with other Panzer and motorized divisions and raced for the Dnieper River, the last natural barrier before Smolensk. Each day seemed exactly like the day before: long days and nights of combat, relentless forward movement, little sleep, constant physical exhaustion, cold food, daytime sweats and nighttime chills, and penetrating dust. This was life for the German forces during Operation Barbarossa. Running on sheer adrenaline, the Germans pressed on across the enormity of the endless country with the goal of a quick victory serving as their driver. Pushing toward Smolensk, Das Reich was combined into a Panzer Corps with the Tenth Panzer Division and the Grossdeutschland Motorized Infantry Regiment; together they fought across the stretch of land between the Berezina and Dnieper Rivers, finally crossing the Dnieper on July 11.

But the worst fighting was yet to come. For twenty-five consecutive days the forces of Hitler and Stalin waged an unrelenting battle of epic proportions for Smolensk. The immensity of the conflict and the loss of life in the Smolensk campaign is almost impossible for the human mind to comprehend. In less than a month Russia lost more men killed and captured—over a half-million troops—than most countries' entire military force. The Germans, knowing such losses would have finished any other nation, kept wondering how the Russians could keep fighting, thinking that Russia must be nearly out of soldiers. But Russia had a nearly inexhaustible supply of men and was willing to sacrifice them to buy the precious time needed to organize defensive positions, train more soldiers and produce more of the terrible T-34s. Finally, on July 16 the Twenty-Ninth Motorized Infantry Division captured Smolensk, achieving the first major objective of Army Group Center.

———

A few days after Smolensk fell Kurt was bouncing along in a half-track heading even deeper into Russia amid an endless column of vehicles. He stared blankly at the hollow faces of the men with him. At times the dust was so thick he could hardly see the face of the soldier next to him. Half sleeping, slumped over, they looked like starved animals. Kurt realized he must be a sight himself. The Waffen SS sometimes wore the traditional field-gray of the regular Wehrmacht, but they also had distinctive camouflage smocks, a battle uniform unique to themselves. They often wore the smocks over their regular uniforms and covered their helmets in the same multi-blotched material, but by this time their clothes were so covered in grime and dirt that their camouflage had turned to a grayish-brown mess. After a month of perpetual combat, the troops of Army Group Center were reaching a breaking point. They needed sleep, showers and clean uniforms, but they were too tired to notice their own condition. As he lay in his half-track, Kurt wondered what special spirit kept his men going. "We really must be supermen," he thought.

Spearheads of the German Panzers were now well past Smolensk, flying along the motor highway that led straight to Moscow. However, their troop numbers were seriously reduced and their equipment was badly in need of repair. Though the end was in sight, the constant dust created serious problems for the German vehicles, and mechanical failures were reaching dangerous levels. Army Group Center had advanced nearly five hundred miles into enemy territory, and Moscow, "The Soul of the Soviet Union," was less than two hundred miles straight ahead.

In their push toward Moscow Das Reich and the Tenth Panzer Division succeeded in driving the Russians from a strategic area of the Desna Bend near Yelna in a fierce, bloody battle. The Bend extended fifty miles into the Russian lines east of Smolensk and dominated the high ground in the surrounding steppe, thereby creating an excellent launching pad for the final push toward Moscow. The Soviet High Command was also aware of the importance of the Yelna Bend, and they forced Das Reich to sacrifice even more men to hold the position they had already paid dearly to occupy.

On July 20 the men of Das Reich and the other Divisions were ordered to prepare defensive positions in the Yelna Bend. Das Reich dug in, camouflaging their anti-tank guns and 88s and establishing fields of fire between the machine gun emplacements. They assembled the self-propelled assault guns in the rear to be used as fire brigades, ready to be rushed to any danger spot to stop potential breakthroughs by Soviet tanks. Infantry units dug in extra deep, knowing what was coming. "Those stupid fucking Russians" was no longer a phrase of disrespect or a joke, but a term used in frustration and desperation. The German armies in the east had learned that the Russians had an endless supply of men, and that the longer the war lasted the more this numerical advantage would become a factor.

The countryside around Yelna was similar to the hundreds of miles the German troops had already conquered, areas of green and brown open space and miles of the Russian steppe, broken intermittently by swamps, forests, and hills. The one difference was that the terrain of the Yelna area was higher, so it was easier for Kurt's group to defend. There, dug into the Yelna hills, Das Reich waited for Ivan to begin his attack.

———

Kurt had been nervously awaiting the expected attack for three days. A few skirmishes had taken place, but it was obvious to the Waffen SS that they were only Soviet probes testing for weaknesses in the German lines. Kurt walked over to a foxhole where a few of his men were engaged in a game of skat.

"Lieutenant, if Ivan gives us another day of rest, I think I'll take a bath. I'm so clogged with dirt, I haven't seen my skin in weeks." Corporal Dietz was doing the talking.

"Really, Corporal?" the soldier next to Dietz responded. "From what I've heard, you looked pretty much the same when you joined up."

"Shut up and play. The way you smell, you're the one who should be taking a bath, and I just might be the guy to give you one."

"Relax while you can, men. Baths are the least of our worries. I'm sure our little vacation will end soon." Kurt watched his men play cards for a few moments and wondered how much longer they could keep going. Every soldier in sight wore at least one bandage somewhere, and their uniforms, besides being caked with grime, were torn and ripped by shell fragments and barbed wire. The men themselves were ghost-like from lack of sleep, little food and the constant strain of war. Regardless of their physical appearance, the men of Das Reich were still confident of victory and had maintained their special comradeship.

One of the men looked up at Kurt and exclaimed, "Don't worry, Lieutenant, we may look like shit, but when the Russians attack, we'll turn them into shit. In a few weeks we can all bathe in comfort in Moscow."

"Without a doubt, Private. In fact I hope the Russians attack soon, because it looks to me like you're all getting fat and lazy." Then Kurt looked directly at Corporal Dietz and laughed. "By the way, Corporal Dietz, you really should clean up a little. If you get killed, the burial detail won't even touch you."

"Ha, Ha," replied the corporal.

Whoomp! Whoomp! Whoomp! The shells of the infamous Russian "crash-boom" field artillery pieces (the Germans had given this particular piece of Russian artillery its name because they saw the crash before they heard the boom) began slamming into Das Reich positions. The rest period was over.

"Hit the trenches!" yelled Kurt as he dove into a trench.

The shelling lasted about thirty minutes, followed by an attack from tanks and infantry. Kurt was crouched in a trench with about fifteen infantrymen. Behind them in another dugout was a heavy mortar crew flanked by machine gun emplacements and Panzerjager (tank killer) squads. Behind these basic defensive formations were secondary lines of defense, mobile assault guns, and the heavy artillery. Numerous configurations like Kurt's were strung out and manned by Das Reich for miles in both directions.

"Fire, dammit, fire!" Kurt muttered to himself as he watched the Russians advance through his trench telescope. Black clouds of dirt and smoke began to obscure the advancing infantry as the German artillery found the range. The Russians were charging with their customary disdain of death, and Kurt became a fascinated spectator as he observed human beings being tossed into the air like cartoon characters. Whole groups of Russians disappeared as if swallowed up by the earth. Soviet soldiers fell to their knees, trying to hold in the contents of their gaping stomachs. Others, dismembered beyond recognition, were writhing in agony on the ground. Still, the brown tide rolled forward like a force of nature, straight at Nazi Germany's elite.

"Fire!" officers of Das Reich yelled up and down the line.

Kurt was rapidly firing his MP-40 when the soldier on his right fell to the bottom of the trench as he screamed, "Shit, I'm dead!" A tall, blond German near Kurt was neatly decapitated, and he showered everyone around him with blood.

"Keep firing! We have to kill all those bastards!" screamed Kurt. " Kill every damn one of them!" That was much easier said than done. The first attack by the Soviets was smashed, but they made two more attacks that day with the same results. The next day the Russians made three attacks and four more the day after that. After it all, a huge pile of shattered, smelling flesh lay rotting in front of Das Reich positions. "The God of War is having a feast," Kurt thought.

Clearly, losing Smolensk had not impaired the Russians' willingness to keep fighting.

———

Another hot summer day unfolded on the Eastern Front, where the battlefield extended from the Baltic Sea to the Crimea. Nearly every foot of ground in the immense theater of war was a private tableau of death. No place, however, was a greater panorama of destruction and carnage than the area of the Yelna Bend defended by the Second Waffen SS Division. As the first glimmers of sunlight slowly revealed the ghostly killing fields, the battered soldiers of Das Reich began to prepare for another day at the killing factory.

Kurt had taken command of what was left of the platoon when his First Lieutenant had been hit in the stomach with a high explosive shell and now lay honored with a wooden cross. Kurt spied his company commander, Captain Hartman, making his way to Kurt's position, so Kurt crawled over to meet him in a shell hole a few hundred yards behind the front line. Walking upright was tantamount to committing suicide, as Soviet snipers had a nasty habit of creating a neat hole in the head of anyone foolish enough to expose himself during the daylight.

"How are you and your men holding up, Lieutenant Heisler?" Captain Hartman inquired.

"Good, Captain, considering what we've gone through the last week. How much longer can the Russians continue to attack like this? The ground is so full of dead bodies it's hard to see over them."

"The barbarians have no concern for human life, that's for sure," replied Captain Hartman. "How are your casualties, Lieutenant?"

"I'd guess about thirty percent killed or too injured to fight. Just about everyone else has some sort of minor wound, but nothing to keep them out of action."

"Well, Lieutenant, you're luckier than most units. A number of platoons have been reduced by sixty percent. I heard of one entire company about a mile to our left that's been virtually wiped out. If these animals continue to come at us like this for another month or so, we'll lose most of our division, but they'll lose a million men. But, hey, if this job was easy, they wouldn't have sent us. Keep reminding your men of that, Lieutenant. Good luck."

"Thank you, Captain. We'll not fail to do our duty."

As Captain Hartman disappeared into the next trench, the Russian artillery started its morning wake-up barrage right on schedule. One shell scored a direct hit on a Panzerjager squad in the middle of a trench. The anti-tank gun flew into the air and landed on a wounded soldier, crushing him to death. Two other soldiers were blown completely out of the trench and died in pieces. One soldier was buried under a mound of dirt. Another soldier jumped up with his trenching tool to run over and dig him out, but was immediately shot dead by a sniper. By the time the buried soldier could be uncovered, he had suffocated. As the attack continued to develop, someone yelled the words most feared by a German soldier, "T-34s coming! A lot of them!"

All the German artillery pieces—88 millimeters, assault guns, flak batteries—opened up on the advancing Soviet armor. Swirls of dust clouded the bright, clear morning as German Panzerjagers hunted down the mechanical monsters of Russian steel. It was a scene that Kurt had already seen too many times—bursting shells, burning tanks, and screaming soldiers caught in a deafening inferno. Most of the tanks were stopped, but a few broke through the German trenches and had to be finished off with satchel charges and sticky bombs. Before they were finally destroyed, the T-34s had mangled and killed thirty Waffen SS soldiers, including one of Kurt's best friends, First Lieutenant Paul Streicker. Kurt watched in horror as Streicker led a charge at one of the tanks and suffered a direct hit from the tank's turret gun. He disappeared in a fiery red mist. Rage overcame Kurt, and he experienced great joy at seeing another wave of Russian infantry torn to pieces as they charged into the massed firepower of Das Reich. At this point there was hardly a Russian soldier standing upright and alive without leaking blood or missing body parts.

The Russians attacked only twice more that day. Kurt felt like he was swimming in a pool of blood, but felt no remorse or guilt at his participation in the slaughter. The Russians had to be eliminated, but the soldiers of the Reich were becoming emotionally numbed by the staggering statistics of death. To make matters worse, there was no respite from the butchery, inside or outside of the trenches. The overpowering stench from the dead sickened even the battle-hardened veterans. Men frequently fell to their knees retching in the trenches, with the smell of their vomit only furthering their nausea.

The crucible of Yelna lasted nearly five weeks. During one ten-day period Das Reich fought off thirty-seven Soviet attacks. The Soviets had made a supreme effort to break the German lines at the Yelna Bend and had failed. Hitler's elite Waffen SS had risen to the challenge and broken the Russians in the dust of Yelna, but the victory exacted a heavy toll on Das Reich. Kurt's division suffered alarmingly high casualties, proof that extreme bravery in combat corresponded to an excessively high rate of attrition. But the reputation was growing—among friend and foe alike—of the undaunted courage and fighting ability of Hitler's private soldiers, the Waffen SS.

———

Near the end of August Kurt and Das Reich were taken off the line at the Yelna Bend for a few days of rest before being sent into battle again. This time, though, they did not go east to Moscow. Hitler had decided to capture the heartland of southern Russia rather than advancing further on the Soviet capital, so Das Reich was ordered south toward Kiev, the cornerstone of the Ukraine. Many of Hitler's generals strongly disagreed with his decision, but, as always, the Fuhrer prevailed. For the next month Das Reich engaged in the giant dash to encircle the Soviet Armies in the Ukraine, where the magnificent steppe was even more endless, ideally suited for tank warfare and rapid movement.

Despite the change in scenery the daily routine for Kurt and his men remained the same: endless hours of traveling, fighting, dying, killing, eating dust, and straining to achieve victory over the hated Slavic horde. The German Panzer Divisions and the Motorized Divisions sped toward Kiev, fighting their way across immense, ocean-like fields of wheat and sunflowers. By September 26 the forces of the Third Reich captured Kiev, wiping out entire Soviet Armies and capturing six hundred thousand prisoners in the process. Surely, Russia had to be near surrender, or so thought the soldiers of the Reich. But instead of getting time off to rest, Colonel-General Guderian's Panzer Group—which had formed the northern wedge of the giant pincers that had slammed shut around Kiev—turned around and headed back to the area between Smolensk and Yelna, the site of their previous battle.

"Headed back for what purpose?" was the question everyone in the Panzer Group was asking. The troops were anxious, and they could only guess what was coming next, but the one word on everyone's lips was "Moscow."

As Guderian's Panzer Group roared its way back from its glorious involvement in the enormous victory at Kiev, Kurt wondered if he would live to see the mysteries of Moscow. He usually did not worry about such things. He had seen so many men killed that he had a rather unfeeling attitude regarding the possibility of his own death. During actual combat he had little time to think, but in more reflective times he was forced to admit that the odds were not in his favor. He had not even been seriously wounded yet, and he wondered how long could his luck hold out.

Thinking about his mortality triggered painful thoughts of home, a world that was totally foreign to him after all his experiences in Russia. It was impossible for the mail to keep pace with the extremely fluid nature of the early stages of Operation Barbarossa, so correspondence from home was always delivered to the front line troops very late. Kurt had received a couple of letters from Erika, which he read and re-read often, but he rarely allowed himself the temptation of dwelling on their future prospects. He had written one letter to his parents and a few to Erika, but conditions did not allow time for much more than that. Besides, he didn't even know what to say to anyone. How could he sound positive about his fate or provide hope and comfort to anyone after all he had been through? Home, family and friends were just illusions and distractions to

Kurt now, and he tried to chase their memories from his consciousness. But sometimes at night, looking up into the Russian sky, he would drift away into the land of his lost youth, dream of Erika and implore, "Please, God, let me see her again."

CHAPTER VIII

The Professor

While Kurt was stalled with the mass of men and machines awaiting the final push to capture Moscow during the fall of 1941, Erika was attending the University of Nuremberg. One of her classes, "An Analysis of the Writings of Friedrich Wilhelm Nietzsche," was taught by Dr. Johann Ruger. Tall and athletic, with black hair graying slightly at the temples, Professor Ruger carried himself with boldness and confidence. Not surprisingly, the distinguished professor—a brilliant intellect and a charismatic personality—was very popular with his female students, even at forty-two years of age. He was also an ardent Nazi who used his class as a vehicle to champion the cause of the Third Reich.

The first day Erika entered the classroom she became infatuated with the class and its instructor. Students were required to read Nietzsche's six major works: *The Birth of Tragedy, Thus Spake Zarathustra, Beyond Good and Evil, On the Genealogy of Morals, The Antichrist,* and *The Will to Power.* The main component of the grade for the class was a paper demonstrating how Nietzsche's philosophy had come to fruition in the Nazi State. Most of the class was pure lecture, but unlike many other classes at the University, Professor Ruger sometimes allowed for exchanges between class members and himself. During these exchanges, Ruger followed Aristotle's teaching technique of answering a question by asking another question. The lecture hall was constructed like a Greek amphitheater, with the students sitting above the main stage, which reinforced the dramatic atmosphere of the exchanges. It was during one of these student-teacher interactions in late September that Erika and the professor first made contact, when Dr. Ruger stopped in mid-lecture, and asked, "Why do you think Nietzsche proclaimed 'God is dead'?"

Erika, sensing that that rest of the class was too intimidated to respond, waited only a few seconds before asking, "What God was Nietzsche referring to?" Her question immediately created a connection between teacher and student, between older man and younger woman.

"What God do you think he was referring to, Fraulein von Klugemann?"

"I think he meant God in the Christian sense, the God who sent his son to die on the cross for us."

"Do you think that it really makes a difference which God Nietzsche meant? Maybe he meant that all Gods are dead because they no longer serve any useful purpose for modern man."

"If that is the case, Professor, what morality guides modern man? Doesn't man need a higher authority to answer to in order to achieve nobility?" Erika felt more empowered with each exchange with Professor Ruger.

Ruger paused thoughtfully near the lectern, which his vanity never allowed him to use; he didn't want anything obstructing his students' view of him. Ninety students gazed down on Professor Ruger, breathlessly awaiting another of his acclaimed oratorical performances. He didn't disappoint. He began speaking slowly and softly so students had to strain to hear his well-rehearsed monologue. "What morality guides man, you ask? Well, Nietzsche says religion is a system used by the weak to keep those stronger than themselves under their control. He says there is no God, no all-judging being who determines who goes to heaven or hell, so there is no universal morality and no deity to answer to. The concept of heaven is escapist garbage, and without heaven and hell there is no escape from this world. So, in the absence of any universal morality, man—the strong man—needs only to answer to himself."

He stopped to let his hungry students absorb his brilliance, holding the pause until the room was deathly silent. Then, his voice slowly and melodically rising, Ruger began again. "Who, then, decides what is moral, what is right or wrong? The masses, perhaps? Nietzsche tells us that the masses are rendered powerless by their traditional religious values of compassion, pity and tolerance, that human compassion is man's greatest weakness; it serves only the weak and retards the growth of the strong man. In Nietzsche's words, 'The will to power is the will to life.' So life, then, is beyond mere good and evil; it is the need for power. The weak exist only to serve the will of the strong, to be exploited and dominated so the strong can be free to reach their creative potential. It is only the strong and the fit, then, who possess the power to determine what is moral."

Professor Ruger's voice was now almost a shout. "Class, you must accept that there is no delayed gratification awaiting us in heaven or no eternal torture in hell. There is only the here and the now, only this life on earth. *We* must become the strong men ... *We* must live every moment to achieve our inherent freedom in this world, for there ... *is ... no ... other!*"

The class sat spellbound for several seconds before breaking into thunderous applause as Professor Ruger strutted off the stage.

———

From September until early November Erika continued to be Professor Ruger's favorite student, even daring to challenge him in class. On one such occasion she boldly asked, "Professor, don't you think that the idea of the Aryans as a master race can be carried a little too far at times? We're all proud to be Germans, and we're a great people, but can we be so much better than everyone else?"

The lecture hall fell silent. Everyone was amazed and shocked that Erika dared to confront the professor in such a manner; everyone except for

Professor Ruger. "Fraulein von Klugemann, I appreciate the courage it took for you to ask such a question. It proves you are strong. Your question allows me to expand on one of Nietzsche's most important concepts—the overman or superman—which I have mentioned only briefly in prior classes."

Professor Ruger, back in his element, assumed his most professorial pose at the center of the stage, standing motionless until he had everyone's eyes upon him. "Who exactly is this overman?" he began in his soothing lecture voice. "In short, he is a higher form of being, a man of power whose sole purpose is to dominate. In some ways he remains a primitive, blond beast, celebrating the joy of his existence and the ultimate truth of his superiority, but he answers to a new set of values, the values of the strong man. The more interesting question, though, is how does this overman, or superman, come to be? First, he must erase all traces of his weak human attributes—pity, tolerance, compassion—and deny the existence of the afterlife. Then, liberated from all values save those he deems valid and secure in his own independence, overman can finally be free to concentrate on this world—the real world—and not on future rewards in a world that doesn't exist. At this stage of his transformation, no longer affected by suffering or pity, his independence and creativity allow him to determine his own morality. Overman becomes master of his own fate."

Professor Ruger paused dramatically, hands clasped at his waist in mock humbleness. Then, ever so slowly, he scanned the audience, left to right, to make sure his message was being properly received. On cue the students stopped breathing, as if some unseen force had sucked all the air out of the room. When the professor was sure he had their rapt attention, he continued. "What, then, is the sum of all these parts, this overman, you might ask? Let me introduce him to you. Overman possesses complete power over himself and others. He feels deeply, but rationally, and is always in control of his own destiny. He questions all doctrines that drain his energies or challenge his right to dominate. But he is no rigid automaton; he is constantly changing his assessment of the world as he proceeds in an affirmation of life in the real world. Most importantly, overman doesn't allow religion or society to determine what is good or evil; he decides, thereby creating his own morality.

"Once you grasp the concept of overman, it is only logical, then, to ask where the loyalties of such strong, independent men lie. Here is

Nietzsche's answer: Overmen have only one sense of loyalty beyond self, and that is to others of their own kind. When supermen bond together, they create a state of supreme power and authority that is all-powerful and unbreakable. The nation created by supermen is the ultimate achievement of the strong over the weak, which is the natural order of things. So, to your point, Fraulein von Klugemann, other countries contain nationalities who are nearly our equal, but you must always remember that we Germans are the strongest of the strong, and the Slavs and the Jews are the bottom of the bottom. We owe loyalty only to other Germans."

Later that night at home, reflecting on Professor Ruger's extended answer to her question, Erika smugly congratulated herself on her boldness and shrewdness. She had actually set the professor up with her question, and he had eagerly taken the bait. Earlier in the week she had decided to discuss the concept of overman for her class paper, and not wanting to risk possible embarrassment from Ruger's unpredictable ridicule, she sought his approval of her topic through her question about overman. The idea had come to her one evening while re-reading Kurt's letters; one from his early days at Bad Tolz provided General Felix Steiner's prototype of a Waffen SS soldier: "An individual who combined the outdoor skills of a hunter with the physical stamina of a trained athlete, one who could function in any environment and take over for immediate superiors killed in battle with no loss of combat effectiveness." This certainly sounded like a superman to Erika. As far as she was concerned, Professor Ruger had publicly confirmed the viability of her already-titled paper, "The Waffen SS as the Embodiment of Nietzsche's Overman."

Erika was waiting in the hallway outside of Professor Ruger's office. Standing there, she shivered as she felt a cool November draft, which quickly turned her thoughts to Kurt on the Russian front. She knew the winters there were fierce, and she was feeling somewhat guilty for attending classes while he was stranded somewhere in Russia. She wondered how he was holding up, or if he were even still alive. As the minutes ticked away, her thoughts slowly migrated from Kurt to the Waffen SS and then to her paper. She felt confident that her paper was well done; she hoped she had impressed Professor Ruger.

Erika could not understand why, but she felt a strange attraction to the professor, even though he was married, arrogant to the point of rudeness, and often preached a philosophy she could not accept. Maybe the attraction was just the result of the special attention he showed her in class, but over the last two months a unique awareness had been growing between teacher and student. Erika had sensed by Ruger's demeanor that he also felt something for her, but she wasn't sure what. The situation made her excited, uncomfortable and somewhat ashamed of herself, all at the same time.

Erika tried to think about Kurt and drive the unholy image of Dr. Ruger from her mind, but without success. The more she dwelt on Ruger, the madder she became with herself, but disgust was not a strong enough antidote for her affliction. She was unable to understand her feelings, and that new sensation was, in itself, unnerving to her. She knew Professor Ruger was not a man she could ever love, but she felt an almost overpowering need to please him. A special duty to the state seemed to be calling Erika into a symbolic union with Nietzsche himself. Compounding Erika's bewilderment was the fact that she disagreed with many of Nietzsche's teachings.

An office door opened, and Professor Ruger said, "Please come in, fraulein. My secretary's gone for the day, and I have to answer the door myself."

He led Erika through a small office into his study. "Sit down, Erika," Ruger commanded as he went behind his desk and seated himself. Erika was rattled by the professor's use of her first name, but she had no time for interpretation.

"Let me congratulate you on your paper. It is excellent. Having a brother and a friend in the Waffen SS enabled you to bring a special perspective to your analysis. However, I detect a degree of skepticism in the tone. You seem to question the absolute abandonment of the superman's need to be responsible for the needs of those of a weaker nature. The strong need to have no conscience in their quest for power. Sometimes a woman's maternal instincts obscure objective reasoning regarding some of Nietzsche's concepts, but I thought you had moved beyond that stage."

Erika responded in a nervous, shaky voice, "I agree with most of what Nietzsche says, but I still feel we need to show some compassion to weaker people. Why do we need to crush them so completely? As long as they accept the fact that we are superior and they cause no trouble, shouldn't that be enough?"

"At times, perhaps," responded the professor. "Erika, you are seeking truth and knowledge. According to Nietzsche, 'Truth is nothing more than the invention of fixed conventions for practical purposes.' As for knowledge, it should never be allowed to stand in the way of the joy of life."

Professor Ruger gave Erika a stare that made her feel naked. Struggling to keep her composure, she asked, "Why is war necessary for the strong to dominate?"

"Nietzsche said, 'War and courage have done more great things than charity,'" the professor explained, smiling. "What he means is that war is the method by which the strong are best able to eliminate the inferior, and thus create a state where perfection and order exist. The ultimate order—the supreme strength—comes into existence when overmen form a union called the state. The merging of the individual wills of strong men into one supreme will ensures that the state of the strong will dominate all of society."

Erika managed a weak laugh. "I'm afraid you're losing me, Professor Ruger."

"Erika, would you consider me an overman, a superman?"

"Yes."

"Am I thus only responsible for my own code of conduct?"

"According to Nietzsche, yes."

"And where do you fit into Nietzsche's superman scheme? What are women to do in order to be strong and dominate?"

"I'm not sure. Women aren't allowed to be soldiers and ..."

"You are to be the superman's helpmate, to care for him, bear his children and provide maternal stability for the State. Are you prepared to do your duty?"

Erika was shaking, but she managed to reply, "What do you mean, Professor?"

"Come and sit on my lap."

Fluctuating between erotic fantasies and fearful reality, Erika did as the professor asked. She rested her head on his shoulder as he stroked her hair. They began to kiss, and Erika knew she was entering a dangerous world, one beyond her youthful experience.

"Erika, stand up and get undressed."

Erika was frozen in a state of shame and shock as she watched Professor Ruger begin to finger his zipper. Simultaneously, crushingly, but with a wave of liberation, she experienced disappointment with herself, disgust for the professor, and exhilaration at her own strength of will.

"No, Professor Ruger, I will not undress, and I'm not your helpmate or plaything. I am strong enough to stand up to you. I thought I was at the foot of the master, but I was only fooled by my youthful immaturity. Thank you for helping me see the real meaning of a superman. I will drop your class if necessary, but I won't tell anyone of our encounter. Good day, Professor."

After leaving the building and getting into her car, Erika was too emotionally distraught to go straight home. She drove a short distance and parked under a canopy of branches that formed a tunnel over a side street. She sat, pondering the purpose of her existence. The confining space of the car added to the feeling of suffocation of her shattered state. Even though she was not dressed for the late afternoon chill, Erika left the car and walked to a small bench. As the hours passed, Erika remained lost in thought. People walked past and stared at her, she became cold and hungry, and she knew she would incur her mother's wrath for missing supper, but she did not care. Only two things mattered to Erika, her love for Kurt and her search for herself.

During the next month, Erika appeared to live a normal life, continuing her classes at the University, including Professor Ruger's. Apparently his ego was so enormous that her rejection was only a minor blip in his string of conquests. He never talked with her again except in class, where everything functioned as before.

When time allowed, Erika went to work with her father to continue her education in the family business. She enjoyed both settings, but her mind was often elsewhere, seeking Kurt somewhere in Russia. Erika had not seen Kurt since February—almost a year and counting. She knew his living conditions were inhuman and he faced death constantly, and she prayed that he would survive.

Contrary to Nietzsche's philosophy and Professor Ruger's teachings, she did not believe that God was dead. Quite the opposite, she was seeking her identity with God, with Kurt, and with the teachings of the Third Reich. She was not sure what God she prayed to, but she was convinced there must be something more than this earthly existence. She felt pride in what Germany had accomplished, but she was concerned with some of the methods of the Nazi State. Erika gradually came to the conclusion that she would need to wait and see how things developed before reaching any final judgments. She was consumed by an awareness of her heightened feelings for Kurt and wondered what effect the war would have on him. Had he succumbed to Nietzsche's superman mentality? Would he retain any degree of mercy or tenderness after the massacres at the Eastern Front? Would a true overman allow himself to possess these attributes? Erika felt secure in her belief that Kurt was a good person and that he would never totally lose his soul to the teachings of Nietzsche, but only a reunion would be able to validate her feelings.

By Christmas, 1941, Erika was in agony over Kurt's fate. It had been months since she had received any news from him, and the festive nature of the holiday season only added a twist of irony to the void created by Kurt's absence. Disaster had descended on the German Armies in Russia, and the calamity accelerated Erika's worries. Erika poured out her love to Kurt in a letter, but she had no idea if he would ever receive it, or if he were even alive. Writing the letter did help her feel better, however, and she convinced herself that Kurt was alive and that they would soon be together.

CHAPTER IX

"I Can See the Spires of Moscow"

In late September, 1941, Hitler and his generals met to debate whether to risk a final dash to capture Moscow before winter arrived. Their biggest obstacle was time. The German forces had been entrenched only two hundred miles from Moscow since mid-July, but it was questionable whether they could mount an offensive that would capture the Russian capital before they were caught in the grip of winter. The importance of the precious weeks lost fighting in Greece earlier in the spring was now magnified.

After much discussion Hitler and his staff decided to make a daring push for Moscow and seize the city before the Russians realized what had happened. The campaign—Operation Typhoon—was scheduled to commence on October 2. To augment the depleted Panzer forces of Army Group Center, the entire Panzer Group operating around Leningrad was transferred to participate in the operation. Colonel-General Hoepner, who commanded the German tank forces around Leningrad, was placed in charge of the newly formed Fourth Panzer Group, which included Kurt and Das Reich. Hoepner was to lead the opening phase of the attack by striking south of Yelna near the Smolensk-to-Moscow motor highway. The highway was the best and most direct road into Moscow from the west, and both sides clearly understood that this would be a battle for control of the roads.

From September 30, when Colonel-General Guderian began his attack, until October 14, the double battle of Vyazma-Bryansk raged. To the exhausted German soldiers it appeared to be a carbon copy of the earlier battles of encirclement at Minsk, Smolensk, and Kiev. Fast-moving German Panzer forces punched holes in the Russian defenses and poured through, surrounding numerous Soviet armies. Horrible fighting raged without letup for two weeks, with the fighting often reduced to hand-to-hand combat with knives, bayonets, and trenching tools.

In another brilliant example of military expertise, the German forces performed a series of classic battles of encirclement and annihilation in the area of Vyazma and Bryansk. Some of the Russian forces managed to escape by mounting suicide charges through the German lines, but most were either killed or marched into captivity. By battle's end—only three weeks after the fall of Kiev—another nine Soviet Armies and their twelve hundred tanks had been destroyed, and seven hundred thousand Russian prisoners were taken. These shattered Soviet forces had been charged with the responsibility of defending Moscow, and now they were gone, leaving a huge hole in the Soviet defensive line in front of Moscow.

Everything, however, did not go perfectly for the German forces of Operation Typhoon. On October 7 the first snow fell, and when it melted, the roads became impassable rivers of mud. German fighting troops had to be removed from battle to clear roads and get traffic moving, which slowed combat efforts to a snail's pace.

It was a gray, cloudy day, and an unmistakable gloom hung in the air. Russia had been foreboding in the sunlight of summer, but now, in the chilly charcoal of mid-October, the landscape of the steppe had become truly menacing. Earlier, when the German troops were still fresh, Russia's sunny expanse seemed an exciting challenge. Now this same vast sea of grass had assumed the frightful aura of a possible Armageddon.

Lieutenant Kurt Heisler was propped up against a small tree, trying to get some rest. Das Reich had been taken out of the line for a special assignment, and he was taking advantage of the brief respite. Everywhere around him the tools of war were being readied for another battle. The men looked worn-out and filthy, but, surprisingly, had renewed energy and confidence, perhaps out of desperation. They wanted to spend the winter in Moscow, not in the open steppe freezing to death, so they didn't want to waste a day needlessly. As usual, no one had any reliable information, but everyone sensed this assignment was going to be their most important to date.

Kurt kicked at the mud with his boot, wondering if the roads would hold until the Russians were beaten. He longed for a shower, a decent meal, and one night's sleep in a real bed, but his primary wish was for silence. He wished that for one day he would hear no sound of war, nothing to remind him of the constant killing. He tried to conjure up images of Nuremberg and Erika, but even that was difficult. He had started several letters to her in the past few weeks, but could not finish them. He was too consumed with the horror of war. How could he ever explain it to her? Kurt was trying to recall exactly how Erika had looked in her black nightgown when he was rudely interrupted by one of his new friends, Lieutenant Wohl.

"Kurt, get your ass up. Captain Hartman has just come back from getting his orders about our next cushy assignment. He wants to meet with all his officers. Now!"

"Oh, good. I was afraid we might get a couple days of rest, and it would take away our fighting edge. After all, why would we need sleep to fight a war?"

Paul laughed. "Well, you can rest up when we get to Moscow. As our reward we'll have our pick of all those beautiful Russian women, and then you'll need all the rest you can get. Wouldn't it be fun to do something to a Russian beside kill it?"

"Paul, I doubt if any Russian woman would submit to your charms unless she was already dead. Someday you'll get too excited about a piece of ass, and you'll go running after some wench with your pants down and a sniper will shoot your balls off."

Wincing, Paul grabbed his crotch. "Don't even say that. It's not even funny to joke about."

Kurt and Paul were rudely interrupted by Captain Hartman calling his Lieutenants to join him around a scout car. As soon as everyone was assembled, the Captain laid a map over the hood and stuck a finger on some coordinates. "Soldiers of the Fatherland, tomorrow, October 14, Das Reich has been given the opportunity to open the gate to Moscow."

Paul nudged Kurt and whispered, "Oh, shit! We're in for a real ass-kicker tomorrow. Whenever old Hartman starts out with 'soldiers of the Fatherland,' it means one dangerous mission is at hand."

"Don't be so cynical. You heard the man. It's an opportunity."

Captain Hartman continued, "Here, at Borodino, on the Smolensk-Moscow highway, only sixty miles from Moscow itself, Das Reich will get the honor of breaking the core of the Soviet capital's first line of defense. Borodino is the focal point of Moscow's entire defensive scheme. It will be our greatest opportunity to demonstrate the superiority of the Aryan race, and, especially, the qualities of the Waffen SS. I say this because our intelligence informs us that Stalin has brought up his best division to defend Borodino, the Thirty-Second Siberian Rifle Division. They are equipped with many T-34 tanks and are dug into very strong defensive positions. Tomorrow will be no ordinary battle. It will be Hitler's elite versus Stalin's elite. Germanic purity will fight the barbarians from the Far East. No member of the Waffen SS will flinch from his duty, no matter how difficult the task. We shall prevail, whatever the cost. Sieg Heil, comrades."

Kurt was surprised to find himself yelling back a loud "Sieg Heil" as the chants rang out up and down the ranks of the entire Das Reich Division. Tomorrow would definitely not be an ordinary day. Four months of continuous combat had not blunted the zeal of the Waffen SS, and their special taste for battle was becoming their trademark. Tomorrow would be the ultimate test, and Kurt believed his men were up to the challenge.

Kurt and Paul walked slowly toward the trench where they had left their gear. "Well," muttered Paul, "I hope we both make it through tomorrow. The Russians we've fought so far have been tough enough. If these Siberian bastards are tougher yet, tomorrow should be a real interesting day."

"I'm sure we can take anything they send our way. They may be good fighters, but they haven't had to fight us yet."

Kurt grabbed Paul by his shoulders and boastfully declared, "I predict we'll kick their Siberian asses all the way back to Siberia. They'll rue the day they challenged Das Reich."

The two young Lieutenants wished each other luck and went to join their men.

Kurt slept little that night. Pacing in his trench, he looked up at the stars and wondered if these same stars could be seen in Nuremberg. He dared not even think of Erika. If he survived the ordeal with the Siberians, he would allow himself to think of her again. For the first time in weeks he thought of Ansbach, his parents and home. He hoped someday he would return. Somewhere far away a tiny Nordic statue held its sword high in honor of a warrior about to join the ultimate conflict.

———

Nothing in Kurt's prior experience compared to the nightmare at Borodino. It seemed as if the bowels of the earth opened up, and the legions of hell seized control of the universe. The soldiers of Das Reich and their companions of the Tenth Panzer Division ran headlong into the fierce, unyielding tenacity of the Siberian Thirty-Second Rifle Division. The reports on their courage and fighting ability had been well-founded.

The Siberians were tall, magnificently built warriors who fought like devils and never surrendered. Their tall fur caps and fur boots gave them a giant, awe-inspiring appearance. Stalin's elite from the far side of the Soviet Empire were among the best-equipped units in the Soviet Army, and the soldiers of Das Reich paid dearly for every step they advanced toward Borodino.

Kurt was lying in a ditch. Two dead Siberians lay nearly on top of him. One was headless, and the other had a head, but no face. Kurt had smashed it into nothingness with his trenching tool. Covered with blood and panting for breath, he hugged the ground as a horrendous scream tore the air apart. It felt as if all the oxygen had been sucked off the face of the earth. As trees began to fly and showers of debris rained upward, hundreds of deafening explosions pulverized the advancing Germans.

"Stalin's organ pipes" were playing a refrain of death for hundreds of Das Reich soldiers. The Soviet Katyusha mortar-rocket batteries had been given that nickname by the German troops, and the organ pipes were among the most terrifying weapons of World War II. The rockets took off with a hideous whine and flamed across the sky like comets with long tails of red fire before crashing into the earth with machine gun rapidity. One battery could launch three hundred and twenty rockets in twenty-six seconds, and the ensuing terror unnerved even the most experienced troops.

Kurt tried to scream, but no sound came out. He could only hear the whine of screaming rockets and their thunderous explosions. Advancing SS troops evaporated in large bunches or were tossed about like rag dolls. Men, bleeding from the ears and nostrils, cried for the terror to stop as the concussions from the incessant bombardment drove them insane. Soldiers tried to dig deeper into the hard Russian soil, but there was no escape from the tongues of fire. But on this day they did not stop Das Reich. Somehow, Kurt and most of his comrades survived the rocket attacks, only to face a charge by the Siberian Infantry. Screaming "Urra! Urra!" they advanced like great waves of fur-covered giants.

Kurt screamed at his platoon, "Kill them all … keep firing … kill them all," as he fired into the Siberian mass. "Die you stupid bastards, die, or get the hell out of our way."

Kurt was frustrated that his gun could not fire faster. Everywhere along the German line the Waffen SS were trying to hold the advancing Siberians before they engulfed the Germans in a sea of blood. Suddenly three burly, fur-capped figures were on top of Kurt. He managed to eliminate one with a burst from his MP-40. He then caved in another's face with the butt of his gun, but the third stabbed him in his right arm with a bayonet. Kurt felt a sharp, slashing pain and then forgot about it as he fell to the ground in a death struggle with the tall Siberian. Kurt was about to discover if there was a heaven or hell, but just as his adversary was about to drive a dagger into his chest, a German soldier ran past and blew the Siberian's head apart. Kurt wanted to rest and fix his wound, but a pause meant certain death.

"Lieutenant Heisler! Over here."

Kurt turned to his left, and saw Paul Wohl leading some men across the unimaginable destruction of the battlefield.

"Where's my platoon?" yelled Kurt. "I got isolated in that fucking rocket attack."

"I don't know, but gather up anyone you can find. We have to take a Russian strongpoint. Come on."

Kurt surveyed the terrain. The Siberians had established themselves in deep, cunningly-constructed trenches that extended in all directions. Even with their super-human effort, Das Reich had so far barely made a dent in the Soviet defenses. Kurt quickly rounded up a few men and joined Lieutenant Wohl. "We need some artillery fire on line. If we don't have some covering fire, it'll be suicide to attack it."

Lieutenant Wohl managed a wry smile. "I thought that's why we joined the Waffen SS."

Kurt could only shake his head at Wohl. "Is there a radio man nearby?"

"Everyone I've seen has a nice round hole in his head, compliments of a Russian sniper."

Apparently someone in the rear sensed the situation confronting Kurt and Paul, because German artillery shells immediately began to pound the Siberian stronghold.

"Let's go!" Kurt and Paul yelled simultaneously as they jumped to the attack.

As German troops began their advance against the Siberian fortifications up and down the line, Kurt wondered how men could move into certain death with such total commitment. Soldiers of both sides died in great numbers, some screaming, some in silence, but all with great courage. As the battle raged, Kurt was soon engaged in hand-to-hand combat with a hulking Russian. Through sheer adrenaline Kurt succeeded in gaining the upper hand and plunged his knife into the Siberian's throat. The dying soldier's escaping air made a soft gurgling sound as it mixed with his blood. Kurt began to offer up a silent prayer of thanks, but quickly realized how foolish that seemed. If there really was a god, how could he allow such bloodshed and suffering? And why would he choose to answer Kurt's prayers above all the thousands of others that were surely being offered that day?

Seeing a pile of Russian bodies just beyond his trench, Kurt fired a burst into the mound to make sure it contained nothing still living. The bodies jumped slightly as his bullets passed through them, and Kurt heard a few death moans. A nearby Waffen SS officer yelled, "We need more artillery support. Call for some 88s." Another voice, in a state of panic, yelled, "Tanks—T-34s—coming over the hills. We need help now!"

Kurt looked up in time to see dozens of Soviet tanks advancing right at their position. Behind him German assault guns, Panzerjagers and some tanks from the Tenth Panzer Division charged into action. Explosions, smoke, fire and an overpowering clamor smothered the landscape. As Kurt fired at the Soviet infantry mingled with the T-34s, tanks exploded and turrets catapulted high into the sky, like great metal fireworks. Soldiers and soil, men and metal, blended together in a hideous, reddish paste. A number of T-34s had to be finished off by German infantrymen using satchel charges, but the men of the Waffen SS withstood the Siberian tank attack.

A private came running down to Kurt's trench and announced, "Lieutenant Heisler, what's left of your platoon is over here. Follow me."

Kurt hollered at Lieutenant Wohl, "See you later, Paul. Good luck." Running over and around stacks of bodies, Kurt arrived back with his platoon just in time to be greeted by Captain Hartman with some replacements, all of whom looked even worse than Kurt's men. "Lieutenant, I'm giving you a few replacements. I know it doesn't come close to the number you've lost, but it's the best I can do. I can't imagine fighting being any worse than what our company has been through, but these replacements are from the Third Regiment. They got chewed up so bad that their Regiment is being disbanded and divided up between us and the Deutschland Regiment."

"My God, Captain, I can't imagine what they must have gone through. This battle is getting beyond ridiculous," said Kurt.

"Well, they must be good men to have made it, so make the most of them. And may I say you look like hell, Lieutenant? You'd better get your wounds looked at if this hell ever stops."

"Thanks, I will, but In case you hadn't noticed, you wouldn't win any beauty contests yourself."

"No shit! The only contest I want to win right now is the one for my life. Good luck, Kurt, and keep going for the good of the Fatherland."

The three new men—Private Herman Schmidt, Private Otto Weber, and Corporal Karl Schneider—were hurriedly incorporated into Kurt's platoon and the attack continued. All day and into the night the furious battle raged, ebbing back and forth in a supreme contest of wills. High ground, trenches, woods, and pillboxes were taken, lost and re-taken. The dead began to pile up like leaves in late autumn as the two elite forces battled each other to a standstill. Neither side would give an inch without being blasted from it.

For three days the struggle continued without pause. A hideous scar—an earthen wound stuffed with dead soldiers—had been carved across the countryside surrounding Borodino, and a choking gray smoke hung over the battleground. Both the Germans and Russians were in utter disbelief, wondering what more they could endure, but neither would give in. Nothing but the complete destruction of the enemy would satisfy them. It was as if some insane, sinister deity was staging a celebration of slaughter, a tribute to man's inhumanity.

By the end of the third day Kurt had been slightly wounded two more times, and it seemed the only thing holding his uniform together was blood, dirt, and sweat. He was facing total exhaustion, as were most of the soldiers of Das Reich. Kurt and what was left of his company were huddled in an area of small hills and deep ravines, catching their breath before making a last desperate attempt to break through the Siberian stronghold. As he gazed out over Borodino, Kurt could easily see why the Siberians had picked this place to make a stand. The city was a crossroad in the Smolensk-Moscow main highway, and the intersections of roads formed a natural defensive barrier which the Siberians had used to establish a nearly impregnable defensive gauntlet of barbed wire, machine gun emplacements and minefields.

As Kurt checked the bandages on his wounds, one of the replacements, Private Weber, came crawling over. "Lieutenant, I heard a rumor that all our artillery is going to concentrate on one small point of the enemy line and try to blast a hole in it, and then we're going to try to get enough stuff through to finally win this damn battle. Is it true?"

"That's the rumor, private. Captain Hartman is over at Regimental headquarters now, so I guess we'll find out soon enough."

Weber was only eighteen years old, a farm boy from the small town of Freudenstadt in the Black Forest. Although he had received the obligatory SS indoctrination about being a superman, Private Weber was still able to feel fear. "Lieutenant Heisler, sometimes I get damn scared out on the battlefield, especially against soldiers as crazy as these Siberians, so please just shoot me if I fail to do my duty."

"Relax, Private. It's best not to think about it. Just do what you've been trained to do, and everything will turn out. Remember, the Siberians are worse off than we are. We only have to fight them, but they have to fight us."

Weber managed a smile. "Thanks, Lieutenant. I never thought of it that way before. I really feel sorry for those Siberians now."

Captain Hartman soon returned and confirmed the rumor; the men would get a short rest to reorganize, and then every piece of German artillery within range would barrage a targeted section of the Russian line. When the firing stopped, all functional Das Reich men and machines would commence a shock attack.

The final struggle for Borodino was indescribable. Watching their massive artillery barrage, the German troops believed no living thing could survive it. As soon as the artillery attack ended, Das Reich attacked with their normal ferocity, only to discover how wrong their assumptions had been. The Siberian defenders greeted the Germans with a fanatic determination in a last attempt to slam the gates of Moscow shut. Germans and Russians stood side by side and hacked each other to pieces. A man running alongside Kurt stepped on a mine and shot upward like a Roman candle. In one section of the battle the Germans used flamethrowers to burn the Russians out of their strong points, and human Russian torches ran a few feet before crumbling into charred, smoldering heaps.

At one point Kurt and Paul Wohl's platoons attempted to destroy a series of machine gun nests that dominated a series of small hills creased by shallow ravines. The men slowly worked their way up the ravines until they were stopped by barbed wire. "Cut that wire," commanded Kurt, and a young soldier with wire cutters dashed forward. He managed to snip one strand before falling face first into the wire, his body riddled with bullets. Several soldiers followed and suffered the same fate. Eventually, enough bodies were stacked up that the Germans could use them as a foundation to clear the wire, and they poured through the breech. Wohl's platoon went first, and most were cut down by machine-gun fire. Kurt's platoon fared little better, and the hillside and ravine were soon covered with twenty camouflaged forms. After two more attempts, enough Waffen SS made it through the ravine to silence the Siberian machine-guns.

Inside one of the enemy strong points, Kurt saw his first Siberian captive, who had been dazed by a mortar shell. Before Kurt had a chance to take a good look at him, a Waffen SS corporal walked over and emptied his Luger into the Siberian's face. Kurt felt nothing. His indoctrination defining sub-humans and the magnitude of the inhumanity he had witnessed had left his emotions numb.

The elimination of the Siberian Thirty-Second Rifle Division provided Army Group Center with a great victory. The gates to Moscow had been smashed open by the soldiers of Das Reich and the Tenth Panzer Division, but the toll was steep. The General in command of Das Reich, Paul Hausser, had been severely wounded and had to be replaced. Also, because Waffen SS officers were trained to lead from the front, many were casualties at Borodino, leaving severe leadership gaps in the ranks.

Despite fighting past the point of exhaustion and enduring staggering losses, Das Reich had little time to savor their victory. Borodino was just the gateway to Moscow, so they pressed onward. On October 19 they captured Mozhaysk, which was less than sixty miles of good highway from the capital. Then the Russian winter did what its armies could not; it stopped Operation Typhoon in its tracks.

A white carpet quickly blanketed the Russian landscape, soaking into the ground and turning the soil into a brown, clingy impenetrable muck. The German tide rolling toward Moscow became mired in mud, a victim of what the Russians called "rasputitsa" (the roadless season). The advances of the past few weeks had been accomplished in spite of extreme hardships caused by the muddy roads, but further progress was impossible until the ground became frozen solid. Soldiers of the Reich had already used much of their limited strength to pull machines and supplies through miles of mud, and now, caked with sludge, they resembled shaggy, unkempt beasts of burden. Even their toes hurt from the strain of endlessly extracting their jackboots from the deep muck.

Fighting these demoralizing conditions as well as the Russians, Das Reich somehow managed to continue the advance until late October. Morale and effectiveness were still high—the troops could sense the nearness of Moscow—and the thought of final victory spurred them on to superhuman efforts. The men cut down trees and used the timbers to form roads of wood imbedded in the mud, but this soon became just another task that further drained the troops and robbed them of their stamina. The combination of continuous battle and miserable weather conditions eventually forced the German armies to halt within a few hours of Moscow.

Das Reich would soon face another hardship. Because Hitler had assumed that Barbarossa would be over before the onset of winter, the German forces had not been provided with winter clothing. The temperature was still not far below freezing at night, and conditions remained bearable. However, the troops had heard stories about the severity of Russian winters, and they anxiously awaited warmer clothing. Actually, they would have appreciated any change of clothing. The snow, rain, and mud mingled with the lice running rampant inside their dirty, smelly tunics, creating a very dismal life for men who had done nothing except fight, sweat, and bleed since June 22.

The Russian snowfall completed the bleak picture of gloom. Nothing broke the colorless monotony except the reddish muck of the roads. To make matters worse, the only vehicle that could navigate in the muddy conditions was the Soviet T-34, which had a wider track than German tanks and was better able to stay on the slippery roads. All too often the last thing a tired German infantryman heard as he lay in the mud counting the lice on his chest was the sound of a T-34 bearing down on him.

Operation Typhoon ground to a halt at the Istra Line, the last line of defense before Moscow. This final barrier, which extended into the center of Moscow itself, included every possible type of defensive obstacle. Here, less than an hour's drive from their ultimate objective, the German Forces were forced to halt until the temperature dropped enough to turn the mud to cement. They spent the next three weeks trying to keep warm and regain their strength for one final attempt to capture Moscow. As Army Group Center waited for reinforcements, supplies, fuel, ammunition and winter clothing, they were continually harassed by Russian troops. Soviet T-34s terrorized isolated pockets of German troops, leaving trails of carnage in their paths. Soviet ski patrols, camouflaged in white, silently glided in out of nowhere, swiftly attacked and disappeared back into the void of winter whiteness.

While the Germans waited out the weather, they huddled together wherever they could find warmth. One of their objectives was to occupy Russian villages, but an earlier tactical error was making this more difficult. Early in the Russian Campaign Hitler had directed his soldiers to be hard and merciless in their treatment of the Russian sub-humans, and now the German Army was paying for this error. Initially, many peasants had welcomed Hitler's legions as liberators from Stalin, but their hopes were soon dashed by the cruelty and arrogance of the German troops, especially that of the Waffen SS. Their treatment of the Russian peasants had quickly turned potential allies into bitter foes.

———

By the second week in November it was getting much colder, especially for men still in summer uniforms. Kurt's company had managed to take over a village after many of the inhabitants had fled. The small, dirty, smelly peasant huts were nothing more than thatch, sod and who knew what else, but compared to an open trench, they provided heavenly warmth. The villagers that remained were treated harshly, crowded into a small number of huts in one corner of the village and forced to share what little food they had with their German "guests."

Kurt was crammed into a fairly large hut with fifteen other soldiers, huddled together to generate as much warmth as possible. A few were playing cards, some were trying to sleep, and others just stared at the roof with hollow, red eyes. The night air was still, with an icy feel; outside, it even smelled cold. The chimney smoke rose in dense columns and drifted into the nothingness of the bleak Russian darkness.

A weary, grumpy face stuck itself into the hut and announced, "Weber, you lucky bastard, it's your turn for guard duty. Be careful you don't fall asleep and let some T-34 run our asses over."

Private Weber groaned and refused to get up, saying, "Say Schmidt, how about doing my shift? I'll pay you back later."

"Fuck off!" boomed Private Schmidt.

Kurt yelled, "Let's go, Private. We all need to do our duty." Kurt hated to send anyone out into the frigid night, but at this point all the German troops had left to keep them going was discipline and a desire to get to Moscow. For some unknown reason Kurt had formed a special attachment to the three replacements he had received during the hell of Borodino, Schmidt, Schneider and Weber. Perhaps it was because nearly all the original members of his platoon were dead or back somewhere recovering from their wounds. During the days of relative inactivity preceding the final push to Moscow, Kurt had taken some time to discover more about the three men, and they had become close, which was pretty common among soldiers in extreme conditions.

"Yes, Lieutenant," said Weber as he shouldered his rifle and left the warmth of the hut for the cold of guard duty.

"You know," remarked a soldier from another platoon, "I've got so many lice that they're actually helping me keep warm. The little bastards chase each other around and the friction keeps me warm."

A chorus of abuse greeted the remark, with Corporal Schneider's voice being the loudest. "I'd give my right arm just to taste some good bread. This hard, black shit they give us is so stale and tough we should use it as bricks and kill Russians with it." Schneider was somewhat older than most of the group; he'd been a baker from Berlin before joining the army and had served in the Wehrmacht for a few years before joining the SS in 1939. He also had a wife and six children back in Berlin, which, along with his bald head, made him the butt of many jokes from the eighteen to twenty-one year olds that dominated Kurt's platoon, who referred to him as the "old man."

"And speaking of killing Russians," Schneider continued, "my old bones tell me that it's going to get real cold, real soon, and you know what that means."

"Yeah, Schneider," a private mumbled, "your old, shriveled balls are going to freeze off."

Although they all laughed at the joke, everyone in the hut knew what Schneider meant. Colder weather equaled frozen soil, which meant a renewal of Operation Typhoon.

"Lieutenant," asked a soldier named Rickter, "do you really think we'll attack as soon as the ground freezes solid?"

Rickter had been in Kurt's platoon since the holocaust of Yelna. He was somewhat of an enigma for being a Waffen SS member. Courage and bravery were holy words among the Waffen SS, but not with Rickter. He was an ardent Nazi, but was as careful as possible in combat and never took unnecessary chances. The rest of the men disliked him and could not understand how he had gotten into the Waffen SS. They assumed he must have had some connection high up in the chain of command. Surprisingly, it did not seem to bother Rickter that he was not well liked, and he had managed to survive a host of horrible battles.

Kurt answered Rickter. "We're too close to Moscow to stop now. If we can use our tanks successfully after the ground freezes, we can be in Moscow in a few weeks, before the Russian winter really hits."

Rickter responded, "I've heard a rumor that we might dig in where we are, and wait until spring before resuming the attack."

"Shut up, Rickter!" screamed Private Schmidt. The third member of the Borodino replacements, Schmidt was the most reckless and daring soldier in an army that specialized in such behavior. If ever there was a man born to be a warrior, it was Private Schmidt. He was an awesome physical specimen, six feet, four inches tall, two hundred and thirty pounds, every ounce rock-hard muscle. His battlefield exploits were already legendary within the Waffen SS: how he had strangled two Russians at the same time, one in each hand, and how he had demolished five attacking Russians with only his trenching tool. Private Schmidt was the exact opposite of Rickter. If the Waffen SS ever needed a perfect recruitment tool, Schmidt was their man.

"God dammit, Rickter," continued Private Schmidt, "the only way we can defeat these stupid Russians is to smash them right now. I don't know about anyone else, but I'm spending Christmas dining in the Kremlin. We haven't come this far and gone through all this shit to be stopped right on Moscow's doorstep. How many of you want to freeze your balls off spending the winter in a fucking hole in the ground? Not me."

Sensing the need for a little humor, Corporal Schneider added, "I'll bet young Weber will agree. He's probably out in his foxhole playing with himself, dreaming about screwing the entire female population of Moscow, young and old, ugly and beautiful. It's the only thing keeping him warm."

Everyone laughed, because they all knew Weber as the ladies man of the company. He was also a great practical joker with a natural, easy-going personality, but his number one hobby was women. Thanks to his movie-star good looks, his exploits in the bedroom were as legendary as Schmidt's combat feats. After a few stories about some of Weber's sexual conquests, the conversation drifted back to Rickter's last statement, and a young private asked, "Lieutenant Heisler, what are our plans? Do you have any real information?"

"Not officially, but I've heard that the Corps Commanders—Hoepner, Hoth, Guderian—all want to make a final attempt to capture Moscow before winter really hits."

Most of the men muttered agreement with Kurt's response before re-treating back into silence. An outside observer, walking into the smelly hut and seeing the collection of tired, filthy soldiers would not have thought them possible of mounting any sort of offensive military maneuver. And he would have been wrong.

As horrible as the fighting had been in Russia, Kurt had not seen evidence of any sadism or torture by either side. During combat with the hated Russians, prisoners were routinely shot by both sides, but front line troops had neither the time nor the inclination for torture. But, for partisans, torture seemed to be a recreational pastime. Kurt had heard stories about what the partisans had done to captured German soldiers. Whenever this happened, the Germans would retaliate, which created a cycle of escalating gruesomeness. Kurt had also heard stories about tens of thousands of Russian soldiers being allowed to die of starvation in German POW camps, but he didn't pay attention to such talk. He had enough to do just trying to stay alive at the front.

On November 15, however, Kurt and his men faced the horrors of a racial war firsthand; one of his company's reconnaissance patrols had not returned, and Kurt and part of his platoon set out to find them. Kurt's squad was dog-tired and irritable over the extra assignment because the temperature was already down to fourteen degrees, and they still had no winter clothing.

"Fuck this damn country," cursed Private Schmidt. "After we finally conquer this piece of shit, we ought to burn the whole fucking place to the ground and leave it for the wolves. No people in their right minds could want to live in this dung heap."

"People don't, the Russians do," cracked Corporal Schneider.

"You know," mused Otto Weber, "I'm not even sure I could screw a Russian woman if she was lying naked in front of me."

"If that becomes a problem, Private Weber, I'll order you to screw her. That way if anyone rides your ass about it, you can say you're just following orders and fucking for the Fatherland."

By the time the laughter died down, Kurt's squad was approaching no man's land, so the men walked on in silence. They trudged for miles over small hills covered in shallow snow, through patches of skinny trees and brush, through peasant villages—some empty, some not—but they found no sign of the missing patrol. Finally, as the squad was skirting the edge of a large area of virgin forest, Private Schmidt, who was on point, yelled, "Oh my God! Oh my God!"

Quickly the rest of the squad caught up to Schmidt, who was on his knees vomiting at the horrific scene. Five men of the Waffen SS had been nailed to separate trees and grotesquely mutilated. The dead men hung on the trees like pieces of butchered cattle, their naked bodies sliced with gaping wounds full of frozen blood. Five white faces were etched in icy agony, each projecting a picture of total barbarism. Each man's penis had been cut off and shoved in his mouth. Blood had frozen in rivers of red from the nail holes in the men's feet and hands, and an unholy mixture of blood, foam, and vomit cemented the ghostly anguish on the faces of what had once been living flesh. The gruesome scene sent tremors of anger and revenge surging through every man in Kurt's squad. His voice shaking with emotion, Kurt yelled, "Cut them down and bury them as best you can. Now!"

Not a single word was spoken as the men performed the sickening task, made difficult by the frozen, unyielding turf. Each man dug furiously, reciting whatever prayer he still knew while planning revenge. When the disfigured bodies had finally been laid to rest, Private Schmidt approached Kurt and said, "Lieutenant, can we make a sortie into the Russian lines to demonstrate to them what happens when members of the Waffen SS are desecrated like this?"

Kurt didn't hesitate. "We have a few more hours. Let's go."

No one thought about the morality or the possible consequences of their actions as they sought out the closest Russian village. The grisly specter of their defiled comrades provided all the inspiration the squad needed to push through the frigid night. They came upon a village of about a hundred peasants, and, finding no readily identifiable Russian partisans upon whom to exact their revenge, they made the villagers pay anyway. Kurt ordered twenty randomly chosen men, women, and children to be hung. The bodies were left swaying in the icy air as a warning to the partisans. That image—twenty men, women and children dancing a deadly dance in the winter shadows—would be seared into Kurt's memory as a permanent reminder of what he had become.

———

On November 19 the Germans began the final sprint for Moscow. A deep frost had finally hardened the Russian soil enough to enable the mechanized forces of Army Group Center to begin their desperate drive to seize Moscow before the full force of winter descended on the Eastern Front. A light blanket of snow had briefly concealed the scars of war, but the now familiar battle remnants quickly destroyed the purity of the newly-fallen snow. Red blood merged with the filthy grime of smoke, oil, and upended earth to defeat Mother Nature's attempt to cleanse her battered soul.

The German objective was to gain control of the roads leading into Moscow, and the SS attacked with a seemingly impossible fury from such a tired and depleted force. The Fourth Panzer Group attacked north of the Smolensk–Moscow motor highway, while the troops of Army Group Center tore into the final Russian line of defense before Moscow. Every inch of Mother Russia was dedicated to stopping the invading Germans. Russian defensive positions were strategically placed all the way into the capital. Soviet barbed wire and minefields lined every open space, artillery and anti-tank guns covered every road, and machine gun emplacements dotted the landscape like animal burrows.

By now the Second Waffen SS Motorized Infantry Division and several other divisions had been merged into the Fortieth Panzer Corps, creating a special motorized battle group. They were to smash their way into Moscow by way of Istra and the Istra Reservoir about a half hour's drive northwest of Moscow. At the town of Istra the soldiers of Das Reich again displayed fanatical courage and bravery. Gazing upon the golden dome of the Cathedral of the New Jerusalem, the young soldiers pushed themselves toward Moscow.

As the battle raged into late November, the temperature hovered between zero and twenty degrees and still the German armies in the East had not received any winter clothing. A few greatcoats had been delivered, but most of the troops were still fighting in their summer tunics. Across the lines, however, the Russian soldiers were properly prepared to withstand the elements. Dressed in white camouflaged parkas, the Soviet soldiers looked like giant, deadly snowmen. A study in contrasts, the Russians wore large, fur-lined boots, while the Germans still wore their normal jackboots—many with no socks inside—whose nails provided an excellent conduit for frostbite. Hitler and the planners of Operation Barbarossa had failed to anticipate the possibility of a winter campaign, but it was the common German soldiers who paid the price. Many a German soldier who managed to survive his first winter in Russia left a few toes on the frozen steppes.

Crawling, cursing, scratching, and killing for every inch, the forces of Army Group Center somehow continued to move forward. Horrendous battles, large and small, were waged at hundreds of sites. Das Reich continued to struggle toward its objective and nearly bled itself to death during the struggle at Istra. Again they faced the dreaded Siberians, and again the two sides engaged in a conflict pitting fanatic against fanatic. The entire terrain before Moscow became shrouded in an unearthly haze of frozen whiteness, tainted dirty gray by the passage of thousands of machines and the struggles of more than a million men. Each night revealed a dazzling light display, with artillery shells illuminating the darkness of the frigid cold as they sought out the enemy. Men froze to death, unnoticed, as they slept. Courage was no longer the private domain of Das Reich. It was too commonplace among all the troops of Army Group Center to draw any special recognition.

The script of the battlefield was all too familiar to the weary soldiers of Das Reich, heroic Russian resistance and those splendidly awful T-34 tanks. Men were mangled into the frozen soil by tank treads, ignited by flamethrowers, obliterated by artillery shells, and beaten to death in hand-to-hand combat, but still Das Reich continued to advance. After struggling through waist-deep snow, crawling over hills of scrawny trees and brush, and fighting Russians continuously, Das Reich finally broke through the last line of defense before Moscow. But before the Germans could rejoice in their victory and take advantage of the open road to the capital, more Russian soldiers came pouring in. They flowed from Moscow as if there were an assembly line cranking them out by the thousands.

But Kurt's division—in fact, all of Army Group Center—was disappearing in the white fog before the gates of Moscow. So near their goal, the German Army began to disintegrate into small bands that looked like refugees. They bore little resemblance to the magnificent force that had invaded Russia in June. To keep from freezing to death, the ragtag German troops supplemented their uniforms with whatever articles could be made useful: clothing pulled from dead soldiers and peasants, tablecloths and bedding from huts, anything that would help them survive the numbing cold of the Russian nights.

The cold also took its toll on weapons and machinery. The oil in machine guns froze solid, firing pins snapped like glass, and the men often heated rocks and held them to their weapons to thaw the mechanisms. It took hours to get tanks started because no winter oil had been provided.

Logistical support was sporadic at best, and supplies for the troops had virtually run out. They were nearly out of ammunition and desperately short of food. Food that was delivered was frozen solid and had to be chopped apart with bayonets and licked like frozen ice cream. Medical supplies were as scarce as the Russian sunlight. The limited supply of frostbite cream was exhausted early in the campaign. Hygiene was nonexistent; men had been wearing the same uniforms for months. Skin and clothing were starting to become one, separated only by colonies of body lice, and the resulting smell was beyond description. The lack of proper food caused dysentery, which only added to the stench surrounding Army Group Center.

Somehow, amid misery and exhaustion and lacking proper support and supplies, large and small contingents of German troops advanced, spurred onward by the goal of being the first German troops to enter Moscow. But human endurance has limitations, and the men of Army Group Center were reaching theirs. By December 3, Das Reich had been through three weeks of frozen mayhem, and a majority of the German troops had simply lost the ability to advance; some soldiers were even going insane from the cold. A few small units, however, were still trying to push forward despite below zero temperatures. Kurt and what was left of his platoon had joined Paul Wohl and members of his platoon somewhere a little north of the suburbs of Moscow. The small group was huddled together around a self-propelled gun and a Mark IV tank that had joined up with them.

Desperately, the men did whatever they could to keep from freezing to death. The two vehicles had parked near a small clump of trees extending from the snowdrifts at the base of a small hill. Ignoring the danger of drawing enemy fire, someone lit a fire in a space carved out of the snow and brush, and the men gathered around, taking turns getting close to the warmth. Counting stragglers they had picked up and the crews of the tank and the self-propelled assault gun, Combat Group Heisler-Wohl numbered about forty men. The tank was low on gas and had only four shells left. The assault gun had six shells left and only enough gas to go another few miles. As men rotated away from the fire, they stomped their feet on the ground and kicked the tank treads to restore some feeling to their feet. For some it was already too late; blood and bandages decorated their uniforms, and their faces and lips—partially hidden by unshaved stubble—were cracked and bleeding from frostbite. As some cracked their teeth on frozen rations, their curses seemed to freeze and hang in the icy air.

About ten o'clock a council was called to discuss what action the combat Group should take the next day. Lieutenant Wohl began by asking, "I wonder where in the hell the rest of the Division is, or the whole goddamn army for that matter. We can't be more than a few miles from Moscow. You can see the church steeples for Christ's sake. We could be sleeping in Moscow tomorrow night if we make one more major assault."

As usual Otto Weber's mind was on something other than the fighting. "Hell, even if we got there I don't even think I could screw anybody. My balls are frozen rocks, and I haven't felt them for over a week. Even if I could get a hard-on, my dick would probably snap off."

The men were too tired to even respond to the easy opening that Weber had left them.

"I think we should make one last effort to reach Moscow," offered Private Schmidt. "The Russian defenses seemed a little softer today, and maybe we can cut through straight into the city. If we have to die, we might as well go down running through the streets of Moscow screaming, 'Down with Bolshevism!'"

Kurt wearily stood up and addressed the frozen collection of desperate men.

"I agree. It just seems futile to have come so far and suffered so much to give up now. In seven months we've fought our way through hundreds of miles of Russian territory, and it's only a few more miles to Moscow. How can we stop now?"

One of the tank crew asked, "Do you think there are many groups like ours, still trying to advance?"

"Of course there are, you dumb shit," said Schmidt. "Do you think we're the only Germans who don't want to freeze to death out in the open for the next four months? Besides, if there are enough groups like ours, one more kick might just be enough to knock the Russian shithouse over."

A soldier from the Nineteenth Panzer Division joined in. "I think we're all in agreement that we should continue to advance. Lieutenants, do you have a plan?"

Lieutenant Wohl wearily offered one. "We all go as far as we can. When the tank and the assault gun run out of shells or gas, we leave them and continue on, until we're dead or in Moscow."

"That's simple enough," someone muttered.

———

For a few hours Kurt tried to get some sleep as he lay in his bedroom of snow. Given his condition, sleep should have come easily, but it did not. The cold made him afraid to nod off. Too often soldiers who fell into a deep sleep never woke up. Kurt was convinced that he would never be warm again, that his carcass was frozen solid, like a side of beef in a meat locker. Numb physically and mentally, he was beginning to think he was living in a macabre illusion, an extended dream. In a real world no man could possibly witness what he had during the last seven months and still be sane.

The next morning the small group of German soldiers, led by Kurt and Paul, began their final agony as a fighting force. After advancing only a few hundred yards, the assault gun ran over a mine and was destroyed. An hour later they abandoned the Mark IV after it fired its last shell. The troops advanced another two miles toward Moscow, but that was the extent of their odyssey. The breaking point had been reached. Out of the forty men who had started out on the last surge from their group, only sixteen made it to the shallow ravine where their hopeless journey surrendered to reality. During their final two-mile advance, they destroyed three pillboxes, two tanks, and crossed two lines of Soviet trenches.

The Russian forces who had opposed them were ill-trained units, hurriedly rushed to the front as a stopgap measure to buy more time so additional experienced Soviet divisions could be brought up. This did not bode well for Army Group Center. If Soviet emergency units had been able to stop the final German spearheads attacking Moscow, what would be the fate of Army Group Center if they were counter-attacked by fresh, powerful Russian armies?

As the shattered remnants of the combat group lay exhausted in their little ravine, they looked longingly at Moscow. Kurt passed his field glasses around to anyone who wanted a clear look at the city. Someone muttered, "How could so much sacrifice have been for nothing? God must be on the other side."

A strong answer quickly rang out, "We aren't dead yet, and next spring we'll finish the job. All we need is some rest and reinforcements. Next summer all the hell we've gone through will be justified."

As the haggard men contemplated their fate, Kurt walked over to Paul and quietly asked, "What's in store for us now?"

Lieutenant Wohl just patted the snow, shook his head back and forth and said nothing.

"How are we to survive a winter on this barren chunk of frozen shit without supplies?" Kurt complained. "We need fuel, ammo, winter clothing and, well, everything. They have to pull us back soon, Lieutenant."

———

Kurt didn't have to wait long for his answer. Hitler said there would be no retreat from any soil where a German soldier had left a boot print, and he ordered the German troops to stand their ground to the last man.

The Russians were more than happy to accommodate Hitler's plan; in fact, they were eager to take the Germans down to their very last man. On December 6 the Russians launched a massive counterattack along a six hundred mile front, starting with a shattering artillery barrage. Before the smoke had cleared, white-clad Soviet ski battalions were slashing through the German lines, followed by hordes of Soviet infantry supporting T-34 tanks. The fresh, well-equipped Russians tore through the depleted ranks of the German Army as easily as vultures picking apart a road kill. Across the entire front T-34s rumbled over the snow like herds of hulking prehistoric beasts feasting on their prey.

The German troops, especially the Waffen SS, had always been trained to attack, so this defensive warfare was a new experience for them. Necessity proved to be a great instructor. As the cold froze guns into useless objects and rendered tanks inoperable, the Germans were forced to call on new reserves of courage and ingenuity. They devised strategies to attack Soviet T-34s with little more than satchel charges, Molotov cocktails and a fanatic fatalism, stalling the Russian advance wherever they could.

The reward for Kurt and his comrades who survived the daily onslaughts was the unbearable evening cold. Temperatures plunged to thirty degrees below zero, and winds blew with gale force. The men couldn't even dig foxholes; the ground was frozen so hard trenching tools only scratched the surface. The rare times they got near a source of warmth, they screamed in pain as feeling returned to frozen fingers, toes, and other extremities. No supplies or reinforcements were getting through, and food was so scarce that frozen horsemeat had become a prized delicacy. Men who were lucky enough to last the night awoke each morning to a new Russian attack.

Despite these appalling conditions, German units held back the attacking Russians for a short time, but they were eventually forced to retreat before they were overwhelmed. The withdrawal turned out to be haphazard and costly, however. Since there was no official order to retreat from Hitler himself, some unit commanders tried to hold their ground, fearing Hitler's wrath for disobeying orders more than they feared the advancing Russians. Many of these units were never heard from again, swallowed up by the Soviet counterattack or lost to the harsh Russian winter. Somehow, though, parts of units managed to fight their way toward the rear, where they regrouped and established a basic line of defense. The retreating German Army, with all these things against them, miraculously held together for a while in December of 1941, but once again Hitler and the German High Command had tried to do too much with too little, and the front-line German soldiers suffered the consequences.

Combat Group Heisler-Wohl had managed to fight its way to the rear and rejoin other retreating elements of Das Reich Division. During most of December and early January of 1942, Das Reich and the rest of Army Group Center continued to move slowly backward. The Russians and Germans attacked and counterattacked each other along a constantly shifting front line, and neither side really knew where the enemy might appear next.

In early January nine Soviet divisions broke through the German lines near Rzhev, crossed the frozen Volga River and gathered in the German rear. General Model—a daring, aggressive commander who seized the initiative whenever possible—was now in charge of the German forces operating near Rzhev, and he was determined to smash the Soviets in a series of counterattacks. Before he could do this, however, the Germans needed to close the gate on the Volga where they had broken through. This task fell to Kurt's Der Fuhrer Regiment, commanded by Colonel Otto Kumm. The assignment was as difficult as any given to a German unit during the entire war in Russia. With only six hundred and fifty men, the Der Fuhrer Regiment was to hold its position, whatever the cost. No matter how many Russian soldiers and tanks would try to cross the Volga, the Der Fuhrer Regiment had to stop them, or Army Group Center would be in danger of being cut off and destroyed. And even if Kurt and his comrades were successful in sealing off the entry point so these Soviet divisions couldn't be reinforced, the Germans knew the Soviets would stop at nothing in an attempt to re-open the supply line to their surrounded comrades.

As Kurt's men prepared defensive positions for the battle, he mentally assessed his regiment's condition and the enormity of the assignment. Even under the best of conditions holding off the Russians would be almost impossible, but Kurt's regiment had been severely depleted since the Russian counterattack had begun. Day after day, night after night, they had struggled to stay alive, to keep from being cut off and annihilated. By now Kurt had lost three toes on his left foot, and he had not felt his right foot for over a week. For others, things were much worse. Even for an elite unit like Das Reich, the price was becoming more than some men could stand; many committed suicide rather than face another night of frozen terror. Now they were being asked to do the impossible again and Kurt questioned if they could even mount a respectable defense. He knew that in the end there was nothing they could do but mentally brace themselves for the coming onslaught.

In preparation for the Russians Kurt and his company were struggling to dig defensive fortifications in the frozen soil of the barren landscape next to the Volga River. Cursing as they toiled in frustration, the soldiers tried to chip shallow indentations in the icy crust. "What the hell is the sense of trying to dig in this frozen shit?" exclaimed an exasperated sergeant. "I've broken three shovels, and I haven't made a hole big enough to hide a fucking ant."

Captain Hartman answered calmly, "You damn well better make a hole, or Ivan will make you wish you were an ant. Unless you make a nice deep foxhole, you'll wind up feeding the treads of a T-34."

"Captain, I heard that the men manning the 88 over on our right used mines and blasting cartridges to make some trenches," Kurt offered.

"Okay, Lieutenant, that's worth a try. I'll place you in charge. Send a few men to pick up some mines and cartridges, and let's see if it works."

Captain Hartman then yelled in the other direction, "Lieutenant Wohl, set up a machine gun at both ends of the trench, and get that anti-tank gun set up in the middle."

Using the explosives and their strong backs, Kurt's men finally constructed a series of trenches and fortifications out of the granite soil on the banks of the Volga. Even though they were small in number, Kurt's regiment had been well supplied with machine guns, anti-tank guns and some artillery, which provided them with a small measure of comfort. Kurt hoped that this strategically employed firepower would be sufficient to halt the inevitable Russian horde.

Colonel Kumm had set up regimental headquarters in Klepenino, a little village of about thirty houses about a half mile back from the front lines where Kurt and his men had established their trenches. The Colonel and his regiment then waited for the Russian attack that would test the strength of their defensive position.

They did not have to wait long. At the end of January the Soviets made their first attempt to break through the German bulwark. Kurt was huddled in his frozen home when the cry went out, "Movement across the river! Looks like massed infantry supported by tanks!" Kurt never ceased to be amazed at the Russian infantry's method of attack. The unnatural ability of Russian soldiers to endure pain, and their total disdain for death was astonishing, even to soldiers as reckless as the Waffen SS. Whether this courage was the result of their daily vodka ration, as some Germans suggested, was a moot point; clearly, they were a fierce and brave enemy.

The German batteries opened up, first the artillery and then the anti-tank guns. The crew of Kurt's 88 knew its job well, as evidenced by the seventeen kill rings painted on its long barrel. Very quickly, six Soviet tanks erupted into smoldering pieces of junk, black igloos marring the pallid snow carpet. Kurt opened fire with the rest of his regiment, and soon many white-clad Soviet infantry dotted the Volga ice, lying like giant dead rabbits. After this pounding the Russians retreated back across the Volga.

"I suppose they were just testing us," remarked Corporal Schneider.

"Yeah, they'll be back," cautioned Rickter. During the past month Rickter had assumed the character of a coward more and more. The ceaseless diet of death had unnerved him, and he had become almost too hyper to sleep. The other soldiers were trying to ignore him, fearful that his attitude would become contagious if they acknowledged it. More than one had toyed with the idea of shooting him. In fact it was generally expected that someone would eventually "take care" of Rickter before he gave the company a bad name.

Without being ordered, Rickter jumped up and said, "I'll go back to headquarters and see if any replacements are coming up." Before anyone even had a chance to tell him to shut up and stay put, Rickter started toward the rear. He hadn't gone ten steps when a Soviet artillery shell exploded at his feet, immediately transforming him into a grotesque statue of frozen black flesh. Rickter's lower body had been blown completely away, but his torso remained largely intact and fell straight to the ground, quickly freezing to the ice by the warmth of his blood. The three-foot monument stood as a grotesque warning to the Der Fuhrer Regiment, a reminder of what happened to the weak and unworthy.

The men quickly forgot Rickter as Russian shells began to fall like fiery meteors on the German positions. "Here they come again," yelled someone up the ranks, as if any warning were needed. The rapid, thundering explosions in the still, cold air was beyond deafening as hot metal bounced off the frozen ground, tearing large holes in German bodies.

More smoking tanks, more piles of dead Russians, more dead Waffen SS soldiers. The madness continued day after day, and the number of Kurt's friends became smaller and smaller. Captain Hartman was killed by a Russian sniper. Paul Wohl was bayoneted during a Soviet night attack. A large part of the company next to Kurt's had been overrun and hacked to death in hand-to-hand combat. Kurt watched his men disappear until his company was at quarter strength. Lieutenant Kurt Heisler was now in charge of his company for one simple reason: He was the only officer still alive.

On the sixteenth day of the Battle of Rzhev, Kurt was awakened from a short sleep by a worried Corporal Schneider. "Lieutenant, we have to cover the left flank quickly. HQ tried to contact the company to our left and got no response, so they sent a squad to assess the situation. They're all dead, every last man. Soviet tanks overran them last night. It's horrible! Men are squashed and blown all over the place. The Russians are massing on the other side of the river to push through the gap, and the regiment's sending all available manpower to plug the hole. Colonel Kumm radioed to tell you to send all the men you can possibly spare."

"Corporal Schneider, you stay here with third platoon and hold. Whatever happens, good luck."

Kurt gathered the rest of his company and headed over to help cover the large gap on his left flank, where they were immediately sent to defend the far right side of the gap. Kurt hurriedly began to organize a defensive position as the Russian artillery began to bear down on them. "Weber, set up your machine gun over there. Some of you men get those smashed anti-tank guns out of the way, and get the new ones in position. Neumann, take two men and set up the other machine gun in that corner of the trench, and set up the radio in there. Call for artillery as soon as the Russians hit the river."

Kurt was still screaming orders as the Soviet artillery began to walk shells in to find the range. Other hastily assembled groups were digging into positions on his left. As soon as the Russian infantry started to attack, the artillery from the German rear opened up on the advancing Russian columns to slow them down, but stopping the Russians remained the job of individual Waffen SS soldiers. They beat back the first two attacks, but the third wave of Russians rolled over the German defenses. An enormous Russian in a clean white uniform charged at Kurt, who wheeled and emptied his sub-machine gun into the white blur, painting the white uniform with red blotches.

Germans and Russians were intertwined in hand-to-hand combat for nearly an hour. Kurt saw Weber's machine gun post submerged under a flood of Soviet soldiers. Two Russians fell upon Weber, who managed to evade the bayonet aimed at his stomach while shooting the attacking Russian in the face with his pistol. The other Russian, however, caved in Weber's nose with a rifle butt before Weber could kill him. A tall German soldier jumped into Weber's trench, shooting one Russian and bayoneting another.

Another member of Kurt's company beat Kurt to Weber's trench and caved in a Russian head with a shovel. Kurt arrived in time to gun down the last three Russians. Weber's feeder was dead, the ammo belt still in his hands. Weber was bleeding profusely from his rearranged nose, breathing by spitting out huge rivers of blood between gulps of air.

"Shit!" yelled Weber as he mixed blood, breath and words, "My good looks are gone! I won't be able to get laid for a year."

As Kurt dropped his guard for a second to process Weber's comment in the heat of battle, a Russian with a gaping hole in his stomach lunged at Kurt with a knife but was skewered just in time by Private Schmidt's bayonet.

Miraculously, the reserve German line held. The battlefield before the Germans was a ghoulish frosting of blood and gore layered on top of the snowy crust. The few surviving Russians were retreating back across the Volga, leaving their wounded comrades crawling around on their hands and knees, slipping in the gory mess as they moaned and died.

But the attacks were far from over. Two nights later a company of the Der Fuhrer Regiment was attacked and endured four hours of brutal hand-to-hand fighting with the Russians. By daylight the German company was nearly wiped out, and the dead Russians littering the landscape marked where the attack had finally been stopped.

By the eighteenth day of the siege on the Volga there were only a few huts still standing in the village of Klepenino. Taking a short break from the action to report to Colonel Kumm, Kurt observed the devastation in Klepenino firsthand. While he was there he also caught a glimpse in a mirror and didn't even recognize himself. He had lost nearly twenty pounds since June, and he was starting to look worse than many of the starving peasants he had encountered.

"How are you holding up, Lieutenant?" was the Colonel's grim greeting.

"Colonel, I only have seven men left able to fight out of my entire company. We'll fight and die to the last man, but unless help arrives soon, the Russian numbers will get us."

"Yes, things are getting a little serious. The Russians silenced our 88 yesterday by running over it with one of their tanks. But the brave men of the SS made them pay dearly. They knocked out nine Soviet tanks before going under. I just talked with General Model, and he said the counter-offensive is working. Reinforcements are coming, and a few have already arrived. We have to hold out a little longer. Pull your men back tonight and dig in inside that hut over there. Get down as low as you can and make firing slits near the bottom of the building. Hopefully, we only need to hold out another day or two. Good luck, Lieutenant, and take care of yourself and your men."

"Yes, Colonel."

Under cover of darkness Kurt evacuated his forward position and moved into Klepenino, establishing a strongpoint in one of the five remaining huts. That night the Russians attacked what remained of the shattered village again and again and again. Tracers from Weber's machine gun outlined a path of death for the advancing Russians. Soviet tanks and German assault guns chased each other around in the dark, like angry blind beasts seeking prey. Wounded men fell in front of their own tanks and died screaming in the darkness. Inside their hut the last members of Kurt's company battled like demons possessed.

"I'm hit!" cried Schneider.

"How bad?" answered Kurt as he lay on the floor and continued to fire.

"I'm not sure. I'm so tired and numb I can't feel much, but there's a big hole in my side and a lot of blood."

"Shove a rag in it, and keep firing as long as you can. We'll fix you up in the morning."

The Germans barely survived additional Russian attacks over the next few days. The Russians managed to get within twenty yards of the huts of Klepenino, but they failed to break the thin line of the Waffen SS; the soldiers of the Der Fuhrer Regiment had held at Klepenino and stabilized the front.

Although Moscow had not been captured and the forces of Army Group Center had been forced to retreat many miles, they had not been eliminated. Stalin had hoped to encircle and completely destroy the entire German force that had attacked his capital, but his goal was thwarted by the tenacity, resourcefulness and courage of the German soldiers. By March the German armies were still deep in Russian territory, and, although battered, exhausted, and in need of equipment, they were still a formidable fighting force. And summer was coming.

By the time Der Fuhrer Regiment was taken off the line and reported to divisional headquarters on February 18, only thirty-five of the original six hundred and fifty men were able to report. Their losses were staggering, but they had done their job, and their sacrifices had saved Army Group Center. The Waffen SS's stature continued to grow among the ranks of the German military. The SS Divisions of Operation Barbarossa had performed with such bravery and distinctiveness that they were now regarded as some of the best units in the German Armed Forces. This recognition came at a very high price, however. In the attack on Moscow the Second Waffen SS Division suffered a casualty rate of nearly seventy percent, and by the end of February, 1942, Das Reich had lost approximately eleven thousand men killed or seriously wounded, which was roughly three out of every four men.

Capitalizing on his men's brave performance, Reichsfuhrer SS Himmler convinced Hitler that such fanatic devotion should be rewarded. Consequently, Kurt and the rest of Das Reich, along with the Leibstandarte and Totenkopf SS Divisions, were gradually taken out of Russia and sent to northern France for a rest, to be refitted as Panzer-Grenadier Divisions.

CHAPTER X

Restoration

As Kurt's train sped toward the recovery bivouac in France, he gazed absently out the window. He had rested up, recovered from his wounds and put a few pounds back on, but, emotionally, he was still in a trance. He was now a war hero, an elite among the elite. He had been awarded the Knight's Cross and promoted to Captain for his actions at Klepenino, remarkable achievements for someone only twenty-two years old. A captain that young was unusual under normal circumstances, but there was nothing normal about Operation Barbarossa. Das Reich had lost so many officers during the struggle in Russia that many young men had to be thrust into higher ranks with more responsibilities. Kurt's only close friends to survive the debacle in Russia were also promoted, Schmidt and Weber to Sergeants and "Old Man" Schneider to First Lieutenant. Everyone else was dead. The list was long and painful: Wohl, Streicker, Hartman, and all of Kurt's friends from Bad Tolz.

Crammed in among the rest of the troops, Kurt felt eerily alone, only now daring to allow himself to contemplate his future. Catching his reflection in the window, he still barely recognized himself; his face had acquired the sad, gaunt look of a middle-aged man who had seen and experienced too much. He had killed hundreds of men and had seen thousands die, and his emotions were dulled to normal human joys and sorrows. To survive the horrors and uncertainties of combat he had assumed an indifferent, almost aloof attitude toward life; now he wondered who and what he had become. He was looking forward to his time in France to see if he could find himself, to see if he could exist again in the normal world.

As for the war itself, Kurt was surer than ever that Russia must be defeated. What else could justify the horrific sacrifices they had made? Rarely had mankind seen a breed of young warriors like the Waffen SS officers who survived the wreckage of the war in Russia during 1941 and early 1942. They were a special group of soldiers who had not only been to hell and survived, but were now preparing to return for an even deeper and deadlier descent, for Russia is where Germany would win or lose the war. Kurt was firmly convinced that he and his Waffen SS brothers would achieve their ultimate goal of destroying Bolshevism, whatever the cost.

Unfortunately for Germany, events outside Russia were changing the course of the war. On December 7, 1941, while Das Reich was struggling in Russia, Japan had attacked Pearl Harbor, immediately drawing the United States into the conflict. The one thing Kurt had feared most, a two-front war, was now a reality. Kurt knew this would make their objective in Russia even more difficult, but he didn't want to dwell on that as the train moved closer to the safety of France. He was prepared to take the necessary time to recover, rebuild and accept the homage he was due, especially in Nuremberg.

As the reality that he was safe slowly took hold, Kurt gradually relaxed, and his thoughts turned to the fate of others. Whenever he ran across a member of the Leibstandarte, he asked about his brother Jurgen and Hans von Klugemann. After many such encounters he learned that Jurgen had survived the horrors of the Eastern Front and was still in Russia, along with most of his division. It took Kurt longer to learn about Hans von Klugemann, but at a rest stop he finally found a soldier from Hans' unit. Kurt learned that Hans had been killed during the early days of the retreat of Army Group South, to which the Leibstandarte had been attached. Kurt's informant was the only survivor of Lieutenant von Klugemann's group, and he guessed the date of Hans' death to be December 10 or 11. Hans had been leading the remnants of his company to the rear when a large force of Cossack cavalry overtook them. Hans had tried to organize a resistance, but the situation was hopeless. The Germans were exhausted, ill-equipped and on foot while the Cossacks were fresh, well supplied and on horseback, so there was no contest. Hans' comrade described how the Cossack horsemen had come screaming across the barren steppes like demons with wings, and how he had watched in horror as Lieutenant von Klugemann was trampled to death.

"Trampled to death," Kurt mused as he continued to stare out the window. "What a horrible way to die." He could almost feel the thundering hooves on his friend's writhing body. He remembered Hans telling him about his dream of someday becoming a general. Now Hans had disappeared forever, pounded into an unmarked piece of ground somewhere in the expanse of southern Russia. Kurt wondered if he should tell the von Klugemanns how Hans had really died. He knew the official notification would just say Hans had been killed, and the body had never been found, a fate that had befallen thousands of German soldiers during that horrible winter on the Eastern Front. Kurt decided to just let the official communication end the question of Hans' death. How could he possibly explain to Maria that her dreams for her son's future had been smashed into oblivion in one of the bleakest spots on earth, that her son's crushed body would never have a grave? Kurt decided it was enough that he had to live with the image of his friend's death; the least he could do was spare the von Klugemann family from seeing that same image.

One day the train stopped for a short time at a small depot somewhere in Poland. A train headed in the other direction was also resting there. Soldiers from both trains disembarked to stretch their legs, and as they intermingled, an eerie communion developed between the two sets of soldiers. One group was leaving the Russian cauldron; the other was heading into the meat grinder of the Eastern Front. One group comprised weary, battle-hardened veterans who needed a strong dose of rest and relaxation; the other was made up of eager, youthful fresh faces who wanted only to see action, confident that they could conquer Russia by the end of the summer of '42. As they waited, Kurt became involved in a conversation with a young second lieutenant from Berlin, who said, "So, Captain, you're going back to be re-fitted. I'll bet you can't wait to get back into action and help finish off the Russians."

Kurt smiled at the man's enthusiasm. "Well, I'm sure we can use a little rest first. My division has been in constant battle for close to a year, and even the German soldier needs to relax once in a while."

"They say that you soldiers of the Waffen SS were among the bravest of the brave during Barbarossa. I hope my division can match your courage."

"Thank you for the compliment, Lieutenant. All Germans must do their duty and be willing to sacrifice greatly if we're to prevail over the Soviets. They're not to be taken lightly. As you will soon find out, the war on the Eastern Front is rather simple. We must totally destroy the menace of Bolshevism, or they'll destroy our civilization. There are no other options. Russia is an enormous expanse of land, and she seems to grow soldiers by the millions. We must defeat her soon, as a long conflict favors the side with the largest numbers."

The idealistic, youthful face beamed. "Yes, sir, we will. I hope the Waffen SS gets back into the war as soon as possible."

"We still have some troops in Russia."

"From what I hear, not enough."

Looking intently at his new admirer, Kurt advised, "Even though he may be a sub-human and lacking the finer qualities of the Aryan Race, the Russian is a worthy opponent and a fierce fighter. He fights like a wild animal. You must be hard and ruthless in battle. The Russian gives no quarter, and if you hesitate or show him mercy, you'll be dead. Good luck to you and your men, Lieutenant."

A whistle blew and the troops boarded their respective trains. As Kurt sat listening to the hypnotic melody of metal on metal, he could not help but be amused at the irony of the conversation that had just taken place. An "old" veteran, needing a respite from the ravages of war, had been giving advice to a young warrior eager to see the face of death. They were both twenty-two years old.

In the spring of 1942 Northern France was alive with beauty and freshness. With its early spring fragrances and colors it was a lush utopia compared to the barren bleakness of winter in the wasteland of Russia. Amidst the tranquility of the French countryside, Das Reich was being reborn, rising from the ashes of war to transform itself into an even fiercer bird of prey. Their ranks were not only replenished, but enlarged and supplied with the newest and best equipment. They were also given their own tank battalions, and, as recognition for their outstanding valor, they were made special troubleshooters for the Third Reich, to be sent wherever the danger was greatest. As for the men themselves, each day away from the Eastern Front restored their strength and vigor.

By late May Kurt had been in France for nearly two months, but the part of his division that had remained in Russia had just returned, so Das Reich was finally reunited. One day while Kurt was checking over the new replacement roster, he discovered a very familiar name among the Waffen SS recruits reporting to Das Reich, a corporal named Ernst Meyer. By the fickle nature of fate, Ernst had been assigned to Kurt's company. After initially rejoicing at the prospect of being reunited with his boyhood friend, Kurt recognized the good and bad points of being his best friend's commanding officer. "Best friend? I haven't seen Ernst since. . . why, it must be over three years," Kurt thought to himself. But best friend or old acquaintance, Kurt could not restrain himself from planning a little extra for his address to the new replacements. As a wounded veteran of the Eastern Front, a decorated war hero, and a company commander, Kurt was quite proud of his accomplishments. Why shouldn't he strut a little before an old neighborhood friend?

"Corporal," Kurt commanded as he walked back toward the house that served as his residence, "find Sergeant Weber and tell him to report to me immediately."

"Yes, Captain."

Captain Heisler's headquarters were located in a large house in a pleasant little village located in the rolling hills of Northern France. Das Reich was encamped in and around the village, and Kurt shared the house with two other company commanders of his regiment, Captain Dieter Wolff and Captain Oskar Arntzen. Both officers were slightly older than Kurt. Dieter was twenty-four and Oskar was twenty-three. Both had graduated from Waffen SS Officer Cadet School and had lived through the rigors of the Russian campaign. Dieter and Oskar had been in the Deutschland Regiment of Das Reich, but now they were all company commanders in Kurt's Der Fuhrer Regiment. Even though they had all been in the same division during Operation Barbarossa, the three had never met until this posting. The confident young officers were quickly establishing that special solidarity that exists among leaders of an elite fighting unit.

Dieter Wolff had lost his left eye in Russia, and a black patch covered the empty socket. Otherwise, he was the typical Nordic SS type. He was from Frankfurt, where his father worked in a factory, and Dieter had joined the SS to escape the same fate. Oskar Arntzen came from a higher social class than either Dieter or Kurt. Oskar's father was a count with a large estate in East Prussia, and Oskar—true to his noble roots— could be overbearing at times. Usually, though, he was good-natured and relatively down to earth. A stickler for details and excessive neatness, he possessed a quick temper and liked to have things his way. In private when Dieter or Kurt wanted to tease Oskar, they would refer to him as "Count" instead of Captain. When they really wanted to get under his skin, they would call him "Count Clean." Oskar, slender and shorter than most Waffen SS men, had coal black hair, a pale complexion, thin lips and a small, bird-like nose, all of which gave him a rather sinister appearance. He had lost his left hand at Borodino, and he always wore a leather covering over the stump. As his equals, Kurt and Dieter got along well with Oskar, but his men sometimes became frustrated with his demanding nature. Captains Wolff and Arntzen were both excellent soldiers and zealous followers of Adolf Hitler. Captain Arntzen was a little more outspoken and fanatical when talking about Nazi teachings than Captain Wolff, who tended to be more low-key and humorous. Personalities aside, both would perform any action that would help bring about the German domination of Russia.

When Kurt arrived at his house to work on his special greeting for Ernst Meyer, he found that Dieter was gone, and Oskar was going over some work details. "Good afternoon, Herr Count," greeted Kurt.

"Good afternoon, Herr Peasant," came the reply.

"Oskar, have you heard anything about the extended leaves that we've been promised? Now that our companies are nearly back to full strength, we should be able to go. Hell, we've been back from Russia for over two months, and we haven't gotten to go home yet."

"Well, all the officers couldn't leave at the same time, and we did volunteer to stay and help with the early reorganization. But, to answer your question, I did mention it to Colonel Hauptner, and he said the three of us could probably get two full weeks of leave at the end of this month. That's only nine days away, you know."

"I can count, Count."

Oskar ignored Kurt's dig. "I propose that we all split our leaves into two segments. First, let's go to Paris and spend a few days celebrating together. Then we can separate and visit our families. Kurt, I know your idea was to take a quick weekend pass to Paris and then come back here and wait for a longer leave later in the summer, but after our first leave, I'm not sure we'll get another one for quite some time."

"What the hell?" said Kurt. "You don't think we're going back to help out in Russia already this summer? We aren't ready yet."

"You never know."

"Well, shit, I'm taking this whole summer off. I need to rest and raise a little hell."

"Go ahead. Our regiment did all the fighting in Russia anyway. I guess Dieter and I might as well do it all again."

"Say, Count, why don't you tell me how you really lost your hand? Someone told me you cut if off so you could go home and live out the rest of the war with your mother," Kurt said.

Kurt and Oskar continued to argue loudly about who had seen the most combat during Barbarossa. Actually, the three friends knew that all members of Das Reich had participated in more than their share of battles, but they still liked to argue the point. It was usually a verbal sparring match between Kurt on one side and Oskar and Dieter on the other, the Der Fuhrer Regiment versus the Deutschland Regiment. This time the game was temporarily suspended by a knock on the door.

"Come in," said Kurt.

"Sergeant Weber reporting, Captain."

"At ease, Sergeant."

"Yes, Captain."

"Sergeant Weber, I want you to post an order and make sure all the men in the company understand it. I want the entire company in full battle gear, wearing their camouflage uniforms, on the parade ground at nine in the morning. Do you have any questions?"

"Yes, Captain. Are we being inspected by someone special?"

"No, but we're going to show off a little for some new replacements. I want them to see what they're expected to become. If the men perform well, maybe I'll get you a pass to Paris."

"Sorry, Captain, you know I'd much rather stay here and drill the men, but if you insist...."

"Dismissed, Sergeant," laughed Kurt.

After Sergeant Weber left, Oskar asked, "What the hell are you up to now?"

"Just a little ego trip, my dear Count. One of my boyhood friends has just been assigned to my company, so I thought I'd strut a little bit."

"What are you going to do, storm the old folks' home at the edge of the village?" Oskar seemed rather pleased at his last comment, but the look on Kurt's face told him it was time to back off. "Well, good luck tomorrow, Captain Heisler. I need to get back to work."

Kurt went to his room to work on the next day's speech.

———◆———

As Kurt sat at his desk, mulling over his address to the new members of his company, he realized again how he really had become a believer in Hitler and the Third Reich. He was filled with a deep sense of pride in Das Reich and the entire Waffen SS. He had no doubts about the holiness of their quest to conquer the sub-humans of Russia and establish the dominance of the Aryan Race. Anyway, it was too late to turn back now.

Even the specter of the people he had hanged failed to do much damage to his conscience. Kurt reflected on the events surrounding that act of retribution for a moment and dismissed the hanging as an unfortunate necessity of total war. Then he went back to polishing his speech.

———

The next morning was serene and peaceful. Nature was standing at attention, and a noticeable stillness permeated the green pastures, rolling hills, and fully-budded trees. Pillow-shaped clouds drifted aimlessly in a spring blue sky slightly streaked by early sunlight. It seemed that even the elements wanted Kurt to make a dramatic impression on his old friend.

In the middle of the closely-mowed green meadow that served as a parade ground for Das Reich stood a company of camouflage-clad soldiers locked at attention, their postures revealing intense pride. As Sergeant Weber began to bark commands, the men's precision and exactness in executing the drills were awe-inspiring, confirming that this was no ordinary group of fighting men. Each set of bright, gleaming eyes followed the company commander's every move during inspection. As the drills progressed, Captain Heisler did not even look at the new replacements standing at attention off to one side. After his inspection was over, Kurt motioned to Sergeant Weber, who barked, "Parade rest!"

Captain Heisler then walked between the two sets of soldiers now facing each other. One was a small group of new replacements, and the other an entire company composed of battle-hardened veterans and well-drilled replacements. As Kurt got to the middle of his company, he wheeled to face them and gave the Nazi salute, "Sieg Heil!"

Back from his company came a roar of "Sieg Heil!"

Kurt turned around to address the new members of his company. His black dress uniform formed a striking contrast to the brown camouflage background provided by his men's uniforms. He paused and slowly examined the new men.

"Soldiers of Das Reich. What you have just witnessed is what you are now a part of, the Waffen SS, the best soldiers in the German Army, which makes you the best soldiers in the world. You've been told during your training that you're special soldiers, and that you must follow a special code, the code of the Waffen SS. You must live the code with every fiber of your being. You are the hope and the future of the Fatherland. Nothing asked of you by your superiors can be seen as too great a task. Nothing demanded of you by your comrades-in-arms can be refused. Nothing. You have formed a friendship that is greater than life itself. In the Waffen SS we live and die together, officers and enlisted men alike. We eat the same food, sleep in the same tents and fight the same foe side by side. The only difference is that your officers give the orders, and you must follow them. Never doubt or question an order. Follow it immediately and exactly. Remember that all Germany is depending on you. We shall conquer and rule or be turned into ashes, depending on how you fulfill your duty to the code. Become familiar with your fellow soldiers, because from this moment on, you owe your lives to each of them. You are now a member of the Second Waffen SS Panzer-Grenadier Division, Das Reich, and, as such, are above other soldiers. Act like it at all times."

Kurt saluted the new replacements and then strode off the parade ground.

———

After getting back to his quarters, Kurt decided that he needed to have a talk with Ernst. Having his boyhood friend under his command presented some interesting circumstances, and Kurt decided it was best to get them out of the way as soon as possible. He sent a message to Corporal Meyer to report to his company commander. The rendezvous began a short time later with a knock on Kurt's door.

"Come in."

"Corporal Meyer reporting, Captain."

"Come in and make yourself at ease, Corporal."

"Thank you, Captain."

"Why do you think I sent for you, Corporal?"

"I don't know, Captain."

"Sit down and relax, Ernst, and until you leave the room, call me Kurt. How are you?"

"I'm fine, Captain, I mean, Kurt. I just can't help calling you Captain."

Kurt laughed and said, "That's good, because after you leave here, that's the only way you'll address me, at least under normal circumstances. But for now, I order you to call me Kurt."

Ernst allowed himself a slight grin. "Yes, Kurt."

"How long has it been since you've been in Ansbach?" Kurt asked.

"About six months, I guess. How about you? My folks said they haven't seen you in quite a while, but that's not unusual with this war."

Gradually, as the two old friends reminisced, the stiffness between them disappeared. Ernst informed Kurt that out of their old circle of friends, only one had become a victim of the war. Klaus Deichmann had joined the navy in 1940 and become a submariner on a U-Boat. His submarine never returned from its last mission in March of 1942. The other members of their group were both in the Wehrmacht. Willie von Skirch was with the Third Panzer Division, and Walter Kruger was a member of the Twenty-Ninth Motorized Infantry Division.

"Willie was just home on leave, but I never got a chance to see him." Ernst said. "I talked with his father before I came here, and he said that Willie was being sent to join the Third Panzer at the front. He's a replacement like me. Willie will be seeing action this summer, I suppose, probably before I do."

"Don't worry, Ernst. I guarantee you there are plenty of Russians to go around. What about Walter? Have you heard anything about him?"

"Boy, he must have had it almost as tough as you did. He went right through all of Barbarossa. I remember his dad telling me that it was Walter and the Twenty-Ninth who captured Smolensk."

"Well, they had a little help," chuckled Kurt. "The Twenty-Ninth is certainly a good outfit, though. We saw evidence of that outside of Smolensk."

"Walter was wounded last October and was home for a while, but he's back on the Eastern Front now, somewhere near Willie's division," Ernst said. "Do you think we'll be sent to the front this summer? I certainly hope so. I can't wait to see some combat."

Kurt pondered a bit before answering, debating how much to tell Ernst. "I really haven't heard anything about when we'll be sent back to Russia. I would think that if our division was going to be sent this summer, we'd know by now. The assumption is that we won't be sent anywhere until we're totally ready, and then we'll be sent where we're needed most, as it should be. The Colonel is guessing that once this resting period is over, it'll be a long time before we're allowed such a luxury again."

"Have you heard from your brother, Jurgen?"

"No, and I'm not sure exactly where he is. The Leibstandarte stayed in Russia longer than we did, but I just heard that they're coming to France to be refitted, just like we are. I'm sure my brother will have some fantastic stories to tell. I know he made it through Barbarossa okay because my parents got a letter from him explaining that he was safe."

"Have you been able to see your parents yet?"

"Not yet, but soon. We've been so involved in getting the division refitted that I haven't even been to Paris yet. I've written a few letters, though, and I've gotten a few."

"I talked with your parents just before I left to join Das Reich. Your dad is pretty proud of his two sons, even if he doesn't talk about your heroics very much, especially around your mother."

"How is mother's attitude? Still the same, I suppose."

"I really can't answer that, Kurt. When I was talking to her, I could tell that she was worried and concerned about both of you, but she tried to let on that everything was fine."

"Did she say anything about the Waffen SS?"

"Only that I was about to make a bad mistake, just like you had, and that after the war Germany would be punished for the crimes committed by the SS."

Kurt stood up, but remained behind his desk, staring down at Ernst.

"Since when has it been a crime to defend your country? If the Russians ever get a chance to destroy us, they'll obliterate every trace of our culture. We're fighting a war to save all of western civilization from the Slavic hordes of Russia. Ours is a noble cause, not one to be questioned by anyone!"

Ernst could see that Kurt was visibly upset and tried to take the conversation down a notch. "Your mother is a good German and a good person, Kurt. She just doesn't understand."

"Understand what? I suppose she thinks kindness will win the Russians over, and they'll just accept the fact that we're superior. Listen, Ernst, I could tell you stories that would make your toes curl. Ivan is not an enemy to be treated with kindness. He may be inferior to us, but it's that same animal quality that makes him such a fierce opponent. A Russian soldier has no fear of death and shows no mercy, nor asks for any. I remember the battle at Boradino during our final sprint toward Moscow. I saw hundreds of Siberian soldiers stand, fight, and die with all the emotion of a bunch of rocks. The hills of Boradino were absolutely saturated with blood and gore, but neither side would give an inch. Entire companies stood belly to belly and hacked each other to death with trenching tools and bayonets. In the end we won because we killed all of them before they killed all of us. To show weakness to a beast of prey is to invite your own destruction."

There was a long pause as Kurt seemed lost in the recent past, and Ernst sat in awe of a friend who had survived such a struggle.

"Someday my mother will understand," Kurt said with his jaw firmly fixed. Then he sat down behind the desk and with a softer tone said, "It's good to see you, Ernst. Now report back to your platoon, Corporal Meyer."

The three young captains had been presumptuous in their hopes for an extended leave in early June. Das Reich had received a severe mauling in Russia, and restoring it to full strength was a difficult task. They spent June drilling and assimilating the new soldiers and coordinating the new complement of tanks with the motorized infantry to create a Panzer-Grenadier Division. The fresh troops were anxious to head straight to Russia to prove themselves, but the veterans were content to wait. Even as they enjoyed the soft, warm breezes of the French summer, the veterans shivered at the memory of the bone-penetrating chill of the Russian winter.

On the Eastern Front the German Armies were again smashing deep into the Soviet Union, this time in the South, and new city names and places were creeping into the German vocabulary: the Caucasus, the Don Bend, Rostov, and even an occasional Stalingrad. But the three main Waffen SS Divisions—Leibstandarte, Das Reich, and Totenkopf—were still in France continuing their convalescence and rebirth. Kurt, Dieter, and Oskar were offered a few weekend passes, but they gave them up for the opportunity of longer leaves later in the summer. Many veterans of Das Reich had taken leaves soon after they had returned from Russia, but Kurt and his two friends had volunteered to remain behind and help during the transition period.

By the middle of the summer Das Reich was becoming an even more impressive fighting machine than it had been before Barbarossa. All summer long a constant influx of fresh troops, new tanks, assault guns, half-tracks, anti-tank guns and other tools of war swelled the ranks of Das Reich. The Second Waffen SS Panzer-Grenadier Division still was not quite ready, but by the end of July it had reached a point where it could spare three captains for an extended leave.

"Forty days," exclaimed Captain Dieter Wolff.

"Forty days," echoed Captain Kurt Heisler.

"Forty days of relaxing, drinking, and women," cheered Captain Oskar Arntzen. "We must plan each day to take maximum advantage of every minute."

"I guess it was worth giving up our leaves these past few months. Forty days!" repeated Dieter. He looked directly at Oskar. "After we get back from our long vacation, do you think we'll be headed for combat right away?"

"Hell no," bellowed Oskar. "The division still has a long way to go before it's at peak strength. I'd say it won't be until the beginning of January before we're sent back to Russia."

"I'll take your word and relax then," commented Kurt.

Ever the organizer of their triumvirate, Oskar produced paper and pens and began to create a detailed plan for the most efficient way to spend their leave. "All of us must list where we have to be on certain dates, what cities we're going to be in, and how we can be reached. Then we'll work out a schedule so we can raise hell together for at least a couple of weeks."

Kurt agreed to participate in Oskar's proposal, but said his plans would be affected by a long-awaited letter he had just received from brother Jurgen, who was now a Colonel in charge of a regiment in the Leibstandarte. Jurgen had said that he would be in Paris the entire month of August, and he gave Kurt an address and a phone number where he could be reached if Kurt ever got to Paris. Silently giving thanks for the timing of his good fortune, Kurt scheduled the first part of his leave in Paris, then a few days with his parents and the remainder in Nuremberg with Erika.

Oskar and Dieter left to make travel arrangements, leaving Kurt alone with his thoughts. Now that the leave had become a reality, Kurt allowed himself to seriously think about Erika for the first time in many months. It had been so long since he had spent any time with her that she seemed like a dream he had created. He hardly dared think about her for fear she might have changed in some way. During the long months of the Russian campaign, Kurt had often fallen asleep thinking of Erika, wondering if he would ever see her again. What little correspondence there was between them had been shallow and unsatisfying. Even after arriving in France, Kurt had been unable to get in touch with reality regarding his feelings for Erika. Pounded physically and mentally by the devastation and death of the Eastern Front, Kurt had been slow to gain a sense of normalcy. He needed to find out if he had any remaining capacity for the natural human emotions of tenderness and kindness, or if he had become one of Nietzsche's supermen. He needed to regain his bearings before his next face-to-face encounter with Erika.

Kurt had actually seen Erika briefly in April under terrible circumstances; he had traveled to Nuremberg to attend a funeral service for Hans von Klugemann. The casket contained no body, and the ceremony was gut-wrenching in its sadness. Erika and Kurt shared a few embraces and many tears, but the situation and the setting were so poignant and brief that they had no extended opportunity to be together. Kurt had offered what support he could, but both Maria and Erika were overcome with grief, and his words were insufficient solace to mend the deep wounds caused by Hans' death. Maria did manage to embrace Kurt and tell him that he would now have to carry her standard into battle against the hated Soviets to avenge Hans' death. Erika had only nodded agreement at her mother's words, tears running down her face as she squeezed Kurt's hand.

Kurt only stayed for the funeral, but before leaving he had a short visit alone with Erika. During their fleeting reunion Erika expressed her joy at receiving Kurt's letter informing her of his safe return to France, and she told him she bore no grudge that he had made no effort to see her. "I assume, Kurt, that we'll soon be able to celebrate your safe return under more pleasant circumstances. I've missed you terribly."

"I do apologize for seeming so indifferent about seeing you. I've missed you greatly, and I need to be with you, but I need time to heal and to find myself and to discover what I have become."

"And what have you become? Are you saying you can't love me because you only love the SS, that supermen have no room for such trivial things as romance?"

"Those are not fair questions, Erika. I can't even begin to describe what we went through in Russia, and I've only been back resting for a month. We'll see each other soon, I promise."

As he sat at his desk reading one of Erika's letters, Kurt pondered her parting words in Nuremberg. "We shall soon see each other, again, my Captain, and you will have your patience rewarded" Suddenly, Kurt felt a sharp pain in his back. "Ouch! You stupid bastard! Why'd you hit me?"

"Dreaming about Erika again?" Oskar responded. He and Dieter had returned while Kurt was lost in thought.

Dieter added, 'I suppose we'll have to go to Paris without you."

"Oh, shut up, both of you," snarled Kurt.

Unruffled, Oskar continued. "I'm sure you'll be able to see Erika enough. Now let's talk about more important things. Get your schedules out so we can compare them to see when we can spend time together and raise some hell."

Oskar's planning succeeded in establishing an itinerary where the three friends could spend the first week of their leaves together in Paris. Most of the rest of their leaves would be consumed by individual commitments, but according to Oskar, they needed to get together at the end of their vacations for a special treat. Oskar refused to elaborate, but he gave Dieter and Kurt an address in Bavaria and told them to meet him there during the last week of their leaves. Kurt and Dieter both promised to show up; it sounded too mysterious to refuse.

Kurt's final itinerary consisted of a week in Paris with his friends, a week in Ansbach with his parents, at least two weeks in Nuremberg with Erika and concluded with the mystery trip to Bavaria.

———

Paris, the "City of Love," is reputed to be the most romantic in springtime, but for Kurt and his fellow soldiers who had recently experienced a Russian winter, Paris in August also turned out to be pretty spectacular. There were still enough beautiful women, charming cafes and breathtaking scenery to soothe the tattered emotions of the war-torn soldiers of Das Reich. Kurt and his two brother officers had secured lodging in a large, well-equipped chateau that also housed some Waffen SS officers who had gone to military school with Oskar. Their not-so-humble quarters contained all the expected French accessories: a well-stocked wine cellar and exquisite furniture, tapestries, crystal chandeliers and tasteful works of art adorning every room.

After settling in, the trio decided to spend their first couple days just touring Paris. As Dieter put it, "We have plenty of time to drink and chase women. Let's just relax for a couple of days and explore the city." With a Volkswagen at their disposal, the trio drove off to experience the soothing charms of Paris.

"I'll tell you one thing," remarked Oskar. "We sure haven't done any damage to this city, but I bet that if those vile Russians ever gain control here, they'll turn it into a pigsty in a matter of days."

"This really is a special city. There's no doubt about it." said Dieter.

"I'd actually feel guilty if I had to fire on Paris. Such beauty should not be destroyed."

"Why, Oskar," needled Kurt, "for a fleeting moment there you almost sounded like you have a conscience."

"Shut up, you Bohemian farm boy. What do either of you know about art and the appreciation of classic beauty? Come, let us explore the museums of this fine city, and I shall attempt to explain some of the elements of class to you of the ignorant masses."

Kurt and Dieter just rolled their eyes and shook their heads. Kurt could not help recalling the stories Dieter had often told him about Oskar. During the campaign in Russia, except when things were at their worst, Oskar always tried to dress immaculately. He even attempted a regular dinner routine, acting as much like an aristocrat as was possible within the confines of the Waffen SS code. Yet, during combat he behaved like a man possessed, leading his men in fanatical attacks against the enemy. Oskar fought like he was immortal, showing a remarkable disdain for death, even by Waffen SS standards. It was hard to imagine this frail-looking, aristocratic intellectual as a fierce, merciless fighter, but during battle that was exactly the transformation that Oskar experienced.

In honor of his expertise—but mostly because they didn't want to waste precious time in a prolonged argument they couldn't win—Kurt and Dieter allowed Oskar to assume total command as the tour guide. And Oskar didn't disappoint, displaying the same enthusiasm and zeal for creating cultural experiences that he had exhibited fighting on the Russian Front. In short order he produced an itinerary that mapped out—almost to the hour—their first four days in Paris. From the requisite museums to the best cafes and restaurants (complete with menus and wine lists, of course) to the evening shows, the schedule was a cultural tour de force. As expected, given Oskar's elite upbringing, he pulled the entire adventure off with class and grace. Also, as expected, Kurt and Dieter refused to give Oskar any recognition for his efforts.

At the end of the fourth day of their grand adventure, Oskar expanded his role as tour guide and cultural disseminator to include the position of social director. After speeding their borrowed VW around a sharp corner and screeching to a halt in front of their chateau, Oskar proudly announced, "Well, gentlemen, I have something special in store for you tonight. It has nothing to do with art or culture, so there's a slight chance that both of you should actually be able to comprehend it."

"Finally!" mocked Dieter.

Ignoring the comment, Oskar continued. "Some friends who reside in a chateau not far from here are having a party this evening, and we're invited. We're to appear in full dress uniform in the main dining hall by seven o'clock. A stately feast of champagne, caviar, pheasant, and all the trimmings will be served, and I've also been told that entertainment will be provided by the cast of one of those quaint little shows where women disrobe to music. What do you commoners call it?"

"Shakespeare?" offered Kurt.

"To screw or not to screw!" mocked Dieter in his most theatrical voice.

"Four days of culture and this is the result? Enough, fools. As is the custom, these ladies will be available for private performances later in the evening. I suggest that we retire to our rooms to prepare ourselves for the evening's festivities, although from what I've seen of you two so far, there could never be enough time for you to make yourselves look civilized."

Kurt lay on his bed admiring his lavish surroundings. He had a room to himself, and he was resting on a giant, four-poster bed crowned with a canopy of exquisitely embroidered lace. The room was so ornate and richly adorned that Kurt was almost afraid to walk around in it. Surveying the opulence around him, he marveled again that he had been able to survive the struggle of Barbarossa. Here he was, resting in a room fit for a king, while only months before he would have killed for a few hours of rest in a grimy, reeking peasant hut. Kurt speculated about the living conditions he might find himself in during his next tour at the front and marveled at man's ability to adapt to his surroundings.

For some reason Kurt had not given much thought to the events planned for the evening. He was so eager to see Erika that the opportunity to sleep with a prostitute did not really appeal to him. Recalling the escapade in the forest cottage after graduation from Bad Tolz, Kurt could not think of a reason to repeat that scenario. Nine straight months of war had taken a severe toll on his emotional structure, but sitting in this chateau retreat, he was overcome with an all-consuming passion to be with Erika. Closing his eyes, he conjured up the smell of her, felt the softness of her skin on his fingertips and heard the longing in her voice during their last tender moment. No whore, no matter how charming or experienced, could substitute for Erika. Tonight he would have a good meal, get drunk, and watch others make fools of themselves. He had a much purer goal in mind.

At seven o'clock sharp Kurt entered the dining hall and took a moment to soak in the ambience of the room. Crystal chandeliers dangled like giant shiny Christmas ornaments from the high, mural-covered ceiling. Plush tapestries accented the mahogany walls, and white marble statues posed in sharp contrast to the dark surroundings. One large table, graced with candles, SS symbols, and the finest cuisine and wines, stretched majestically across the middle of the stately dining hall. Seated at the table in their now infamous black and white dress uniforms were fifteen members of the Waffen SS, the most feared fighting force in the world. Most of them were from Das Reich Division, but some were from the Leibstandarte Adolf Hitler Division. Looking over the room, Kurt was overcome with the same feeling of pride he had first felt long ago when he saw his brother Jurgen in his SS uniform.

Kurt didn't have much time to bask in the glory of the moment because Dieter, who obviously had started celebrating a little earlier, saw him and yelled for him to come join him at the table. Kurt complied and was soon cradling a glass of fine wine and sharing stories with his brothers-in-arms. Conversation and drink flowed freely, interrupted only by the frequent toasts offered to their fallen friends. At some point in the evening Kurt found himself standing and offering his own toast. "Gentlemen, I ask you to honor the memory of Waffen SS Lieutenant Hans von Klugemann, a young knight of the Leibstandarte who lies somewhere in Russia. May we all have the good fortune to take our last breath in defense of the Fatherland."

As glasses clinked and cheers echoed off the enclosing walls, a young officer from the Leibstandarte stood up and added to Kurt's eulogy. "To all the fallen warriors of the Waffen SS and to a renewed dedication to avenge their sacrifice and to protect the purity of Germanic womanhood as personified in Hans von Klugemann's sister, Erika."

Once Kurt gathered his senses enough to comprehend the speaker's words, he froze in stunned disbelief. Who was this bold bastard, and how dare he utter Erika's name in his presence? Was he an old boyfriend, a new boyfriend, a family friend? Kurt needed to find out! Stealing a look at the source of his consternation, Kurt thought he detected an evil smile.

"I'll kill you, you insolent prick!" Kurt swore inwardly as his brain swirled in uncontrolled confusion during the meal. Several courses of gourmet food passed Kurt's lips, but he wouldn't have noticed if it had been gruel. His mind was so fixated on learning the identity of the stranger that he blocked out all other avenues of thought. Kurt held out his champagne glass for a refill, repeatedly, during the remainder of the meal.

As the evening progressed, Kurt succeeded in creating more internal confusion by contemplating various theories about the possible relationship between Erika and the stranger. By the time a fluffy French pastry was served as dessert, Kurt was ready to walk over and confront Lieutenant "Asshole," but just as he was about to move his chair back, one of the hosts stood up and announced, "Gentlemen of the Waffen SS, we have some entertainment for you." The speaker paused until the room became quiet before continuing. "Before presenting the members of our classical dance group, I've been instructed to inform you that for a slight fee they will be available later to give you an individual performance."

A series of expletives and lewd laughter greeted the announcement. Dieter Wolff, who had been engaged in a conversation with an officer from Frankfurt, Dieter's home town, noticed Kurt's unstable condition and yelled, "Heisler, if you don't watch yourself you'll be the first member of Das Reich who can't get it up under perfect battle conditions."

"Fuck off! At least I've got something to get up."

"Touchy, touchy, Kurt, what's the matter? Are you afraid we'll tell Erika?"

Kurt raised his glass for a refill, ignoring the taunt.

Spinning off in yet another angle of contemplation, Kurt felt a melancholy quiver envelope his body as he hazily examined the reality of his relationship with Erika. What now seemed centuries ago he had been a youngster of seventeen held spellbound by the princess of Nuremberg. Now he was an old man of twenty-two who had survived hell and returned to recapture this vision of perfection he had seen only once in over five hundred days. "My God," Kurt daydreamed, "it really has been an eternity since Erika and I have been together. How can I expect that she's been faithful all that time? It was easy for me not to date anyone. I was too busy killing Russians or passed out from exhaustion, but how could I have realistically expected Erika just to wait for me?" Kurt knew he was rationalizing, but he had almost convinced himself that he would understand if the soldier who had made Erika's toast was her new boyfriend.

"Hey, Kurt, have you seen so many perfect tits in your life that you don't even notice anymore? I mean, there are some nice ones bouncing around right in front of you, and you haven't even looked up."

Jolted out of his stupor by Dieter's question, Kurt laughed at how deep his trance had been. The entertainers were performing practically on top of the wildly cheering SS men seated at the dinner table. Six female dancers were in various stages of nudity as they gyrated across the floor. Surprisingly, most of the women were attractive and could actually dance. The men hurled bawdy suggestions at the dancers, who were pairing off with the revelers who made the most creative proposals. Kurt smiled, and even yelled a few cheers himself, but even the sight of bare female flesh did nothing to arouse him, and he felt no desire to actively participate.

Kurt was not the only abstainer. A few other members of the group were too drunk, too married, or just too disinterested to indulge in the main attraction of the evening. Kurt's interest was centered on the Lieutenant from the Leibstandarte who had instantly become his rival. Without warning, Kurt's antagonist waved at him and motioned him into the hallway. Wondering what could possibly be the stranger's intentions, Kurt hesitatingly followed him out the door. The hallway was empty, and Kurt initiated the conversation.

"Why aren't you enjoying yourself like the others?"

Instead of answering, the stranger asked Kurt, "Why aren't you?"

Kurt fumbled a little and then explained, "Well, to be honest, I'm a little drunk and I just … well, it just doesn't seem like the thing to do at the moment. I guess I'm a little reserved about these types of things."

"So am I," answered the Lieutenant. "Besides, I got a hell of a case of the clap in Russia, and I'll be damned if I'll screw a stranger again. By the way my name is Karl Lang. I'm a Lieutenant in the Leibstandarte and an aide to your brother Jurgen. I hope my mentioning Erika was not in bad taste, but you should have seen the look on your face. You looked like you wanted to kill me!"

Kurt didn't know if he wanted to laugh and shake Karl's hand or simply smack him in the face, but he recovered quickly. "You're right, there were a few evil thoughts running through my head, but, hey, no hard feelings. What made you do it? How do you even know about Erika?"

"Your brother told me about how you're going with the daughter of some important Nazi industrialist, and how they all think of you as their son now that Hans is dead. Jurgen also said that Erika is really gorgeous and that if he were a little younger, he might date her himself."

"Jurgen has never seen Erika. How the hell does he know what she looks like?"

"Didn't he tell you? This damn war. Even brothers can't keep in touch. He was at the von Klugemanns for a dinner honoring the officers of the Leibstandarte who'd been awarded the Knight's Cross. General Sepp Dietrich himself conferred the Knight's Cross with oak leaves on your brother. Jurgen is now a Colonel in charge of a regiment and is a real favorite of General Dietrich." Lieutenant Lang paused and waited for Kurt to respond, but as Kurt said nothing, he continued, "I see you also have the Knight's Cross. Congratulations! According to Colonel Heisler, your exploits in Russia are legendary."

"Thank you, Lieutenant. I think my brother might be exaggerating a little, but I don't think you brought me out here just to tell me that."

"True, Captain. I'm here to invite you over to Colonel Heisler's chateau outside of Paris. The Colonel wants you to have dinner with him tomorrow evening and then stay overnight to enjoy a very special surprise he has for you. Captain Heisler, you are to bring a suitcase packed for a week's journey, including your best dress uniform and the other necessary items. There will be no cost involved. Everything is being taken care of by your brother and someone else."

"What do you mean by someone else? Why is this all such a secret?"

"I'm just following orders, Captain. You'll have to wait and talk with your brother to get your questions answered. I'll pick you up at noon tomorrow, and you can have lunch with the Colonel. Then he can fill you in on all the details."

"I should have asked earlier, but these events have taken me by surprise. How is my brother?"

"Excellent! He looks quite splendid as a Colonel, and as I said, he is General Dietrich's favorite, who happens to be one of Hitler's favorites. Consequently, your brother is highly regarded in some rather important circles."

"Were you with my brother during Barbarossa?"

"For most of it. He's quite a soldier. His men worship him, and the Russians fear him. During the last stages of the Battle for Rostov ... on second thought I'd better let the Colonel tell you about his exploits himself." The conversation was suddenly interrupted by the smashing of glass and the shrill screeching of angry females from inside the main dining hall. It was so jarring that Kurt joked, "Maybe England has launched an invasion, using prostitutes as the first wave."

"Let's go see if we can help," laughed Karl.

Entering the dining room, Kurt and Karl were treated to a scene of chaotic comedy that sent them into spasms of ribald laughter. Several of the female performers were getting dressed and spewing insults that would have made any drill instructor proud. Apparently the officers hadn't delivered on the dancers' suggested performance fees.

"Fucking Nazi Pigs!"

"You dumb assholes will pay for this!"

"I'll talk to the Paris commandant, and you sons-of-bitches will be castrated if they can find your puny balls!"

One of the members of the Waffen SS responded to the last outburst of the angry women by yelling, "You didn't seem to have any trouble."

Another soldier added, "You swine should actually pay us for our services. Not every fraulein gets to have sex with Hitler's elite guard." The SS officers were beside themselves with laughter as the ladies stomped out of the room.

The rest of the evening was spent drinking and recalling deeds of valor performed for the Fatherland. Kurt told Oskar and Dieter that he would be cutting his participation in their Paris leave short due to his brother's invitation. Both of them were too drunk to care, but Oskar did manage to remind Kurt of their rendezvous in Bavaria. Kurt promised to be in attendance, and around midnight he asked Lieutenant Lang to give him a ride home. By this time Kurt had sobered up enough to realize that he should escape the party before things got out of control. He had not seen Jurgen in a long time, and he did not want to be impaired by a severe hangover at this reunion; he wanted to be totally alert and at his best. Kurt went to sleep wondering what special treat Jurgen had in store for him.

———

"Heil Hitler, Captain Heisler. It's been a long time."

"Heil Hitler, Colonel."

"My, my, Kurt, you certainly became a captain in a hurry. I suppose by next year you'll be a general."

"Very funny, Colonel. You know why I got promoted so rapidly. Das Reich had virtually no officers left by last February so all junior officers were moved up to fill the void."

"Das Reich was in Russia last winter? You mean you've actually seen combat?" Seeing that Kurt wasn't very amused by his joke, Jurgen quickly embraced him and invited him to sit down and relax. Kurt took a second to take in the surroundings, which must have been a king's chateau. The room they were in was not large—it was apparently a private study—but it was furnished lavishly. A large, darkly-stained oak desk dominated the room, resting on a red carpet that also supported three soft leather chairs, hand-carved bookcases and a small oak table. Even though the room was small compared to the others in the house, a large, spectacular chandelier dangled from the ceiling.

Jurgen's additions to the room were readily apparent: large pictures of Hitler and Sepp Dietrich on opposing walls, a large Nazi flag on the wall behind the desk, and a Leibstandarte flag on the remaining wall. Sitting behind the desk, Jurgen Heisler looked spectacular as a colonel in the Waffen SS. He showed no signs of physical damage from the war, and he carried himself like a true knight of the new order.

"I'm certainly glad to see you, Kurt, and I want you to know that I'm very proud of you. I know all about your exploits, and the Knight's Cross around your neck is proof of your heroism. Of course, you know I was just kidding about Das Reich. Your division ranks with the Leibstandarte as a fighting machine, which means it's one of the very best. Tell me, were you at all of the major battles involving Army Group Center?"

Kurt related his experiences during Operation Barbarossa and his activities since Das Reich had arrived in France. When he finished, he asked Jurgen to tell him about his experiences with the Leibstandarte in Southern Russian during Barbarossa.

"Well, little brother, we both know that Ivan is an inferior being, but I think we now also understand that these same qualities that make him a sub-human also create a deadly foe. He's not smart enough to be afraid or know when he's beaten. I swear the Russian soldier can live on a diet of dirt and snow. Any other nation on earth would have been wiped out by Operation Barbarossa; we killed, captured, and incapacitated more Russian soldiers than most countries have people, and yet we were stopped short of victory by the weather and a lack of supplies. Anyway, I don't see much sense in re-enacting my war stories at this time. My experiences were much the same as yours, except in a somewhat different environment. The steppes of Southern Russia really are quite spectacular, but I suspect before too long you'll get a chance to see them for yourself. What I'd prefer to discuss, Captain Heisler, is the surprise I have in store for you."

"You'll get no argument from me," replied Kurt. "I don't know about you, but I'm to the point where I'd almost rather kill more Russians than have to talk about it again to a group of strangers."

"I know what you mean. How can you explain the horrors of combat to a group of civilians over a seven-course meal every night? That's what they ought to be giving us medals for." They both laughed at the absurdity of their situations.

"Well, then, let me give you the basic details about my surprise," Jurgen continued. Tomorrow we'll be in Berlin, and the next night you'll be waltzing and dining with a certain young lady. I think her name is Erika. You will be my guest at a very important dinner and ball. Hitler himself may make an appearance. Many influential people, military and civilian, will be attending, including the von Klugemanns. Apparently their daughter needs an escort for the evening. Are you sufficiently rested to handle the responsibility of this special mission, Captain Heisler, and are you willing to sacrifice yourself for the Fatherland?"

Kurt was thunder struck! Having sublimated his desires for longer than he could remember, Kurt could barely contemplate the possibility of a normal encounter with Erika, especially one that would take place with only two days' notice. Could it really be true that in two days he would be holding and looking into Erika's spectacular eyes again? The opportunity that Jurgen had just presented seemed too good to be true, and perhaps too sudden. Kurt was still vexed by the mysterious, inviting goodbye Erika had given him at their April meeting in Nuremberg.

Eventually, Kurt collected himself. "I... ahh ... well, that would be ... ahh, well, quite nice, actually."

"Oh, bullshit," laughed Jurgen. "Don't act so nonchalant. I know how you must feel. My God, man, you haven't really been with Erika for ... well, since before Barbarossa. Just take advantage of this gift and enjoy it to the fullest." Jurgen walked over to a liquor cabinet and grabbed a bottle and two glasses before continuing. "Not only that, Kurt, but we haven't seen each other at all in the last few years and very little before that. Clearly, we need to get better acquainted. Here, let's enjoy some cognac and talk like brothers again."

Jurgen did all the talking for the first fifteen minutes, philosophizing about the SS, the Nazi movement, the crusade in the East, and duty and sacrifice in the Waffen SS. He emphasized how proud he was of Kurt and how he had tried to keep track of him. Jurgen had also lost friends; Helmut Ziegler, who had accompanied Jurgen to Ansbach in 1937, had been killed as the LAH was evacuating Rostov during the Russian counterattacks in early '42.

"Jurgen," Kurt finally interrupted, "that picnic in the forest with you and Helmut seems so very long ago. It's only been five years, but so much has happened. It makes you wonder about all the sacrifice so many fine men had to make. Can their sacrifice be worth all the misery? Can our goal of world order dominated by Germany really be achieved? Sometimes I wonder. Then I get mad at myself, and I know if we all do our duty we'll succeed, but it's an enormous task."

"Never doubt that Germany will conquer Russia, never!" Jurgen forcefully proclaimed. "No sacrifice is too great to achieve that end. As you know, our forces have been smashing into the Ukraine and the Caucasus, and we'll deal the Russians a mortal blow. The summer offensive has been a great success, and it's only a matter of time until we join our forces in the East."

"I didn't mean to imply it's impossible, the victory in the East. I know what must be done."

Jurgen raised his glass. "Heil Hitler, little brother."

Over the next hour the two brothers talked about the war, their experiences, their mother and father and life in general. Jurgen explained that he had only been home once in the last four years, but both parents seemed to have finally come to terms with his role in

Germany's great resurgence. Eventually the conversation centered on Kurt's friends from Ansbach and their whereabouts. When Kurt mentioned that Walter Kruger was a member of the Twenty-Ninth Motorized Infantry Division, Jurgen informed him that the Twenty-Ninth was with the Sixth Army headed toward Stalingrad.

"Stalingrad," exclaimed Kurt. "Why, that's halfway across Russia."

"Well, not quite, but it's certainly a long way from Germany. I'm not sure they actually intend to attack Stalingrad, but I know they're getting very close to the outskirts of the city."

Kurt changed the subject abruptly. "Jurgen, what about America entering the war? What effect will that have on our situation?"

"I really don't know. I'm not sure what Americans are like, or if they have the will to tackle a challenge like this when they aren't threatened at home. I think it would be good for us to knock out the Russians before America can become involved in the war. Our resources would be stretched quite thin with major battles on both fronts. That scenario is exactly why the Waffen SS is becoming more important in the planning and execution of the battle plans. After our refitting is completed, we'll be fully mobilized with our own tanks, and we can swiftly move from one theater to another to crush the enemy wherever Germany is threatened."

Jurgen looked at his watch and blurted, "We've been talking like two old women. Do you realize what time it is? We need to catch a plane for Berlin in about three hours. I think we've deviated from our immediate plans long enough. If I may be so bold as to ask, just how well do you know the von Klugemanns?"

"Fairly well. I was around them quite a bit during the Nuremberg Rally of '37 and a few other times. The last time I saw them was late April when I went to offer my condolences for Hans' death. Did you know Hans? He was in the Leibstandarte."

"Yes, I knew Hans," replied Jurgen. "He was not in my regiment, but I'd met him and visited with him a few times. He was a fine soldier. He also spoke fondly of you and your time together at Bad Tolz and about you and Erika. He really thought you two were destined to be together."

"It's rather tragic the way he died," answered Kurt.

"Tragic, but not in vain," came the hard reply from Jurgen. "Do not fear, Captain Heisler, the Leibstandarte will get its revenge for our comrades who now reside in Russian soil."

"Don't forget the rest of us. You aren't the only unit to have lost friends in the East. I have only a handful of friends left that I knew before Barbarossa. Being so dedicated to war has its drawbacks, especially if you want to reach old age."

"A warrior's life tends to be dramatic and dynamic, but short. That is our lot as soldiers."

Kurt changed the conversation back to the von Klugemanns. "How well do you know the rest of Hans' family?"

"Only a little. I've been to a few social functions where they were present. Sepp Dietrich is a favorite of Maria von Klugemann's and vice versa, and as I've moved up in rank, I've been around them a few times. Erika certainly looks and acts like her mother. She's a little firebrand. I'm not sure you can handle such a Valkyrie. Do you want me to help you out?"

Jurgen sensed that Kurt's laugh was only out of courtesy, so he quickly moved on. "Seriously, Kurt, Erika's the embodiment of a true Nazi Princess, and if I were you, I'd certainly be in hot pursuit. Maria seems to like you, and with the death of Hans, Maria and Erika seem to have selected you to take his place, even if you're in the lowly Das Reich."

"Very funny, brother."

"Well, that's just my humble advice on your love life. Right now, I have some administrative details to take care of. My orderly informed me your bags are downstairs. We leave in three hours, so be in the chateau entrance with your gear a little before three. Until then you're free to roam around and do whatever you want. If you need anything, just ask my orderly." Jurgen's words were now quick and to the point, like a man who expected his orders to be followed.

As Jurgen walked Kurt to the door of his study, he stopped and hugged Kurt one more time. "I'm glad we had this private chance to visit, little brother. We can continue it on the plane, but once we get to Berlin things will be a little more formal. By the way, don't forget your Knight's Cross.

Women are always impressed by a man in uniform, especially an SS uniform with the Cross. See you in a few hours."

Kurt clicked his heels together and saluted with a "Heil Hitler, Colonel," and left. As he was descending the stairs to the main floor, Kurt spied Jurgen's orderly. "Corporal," shouted Kurt.

"Yes, Captain?"

"I'm going out into the courtyard to relax. Could you bring me a stein of beer and a few pretzels?" asked Kurt.

"Certainly, Captain."

———

Sitting on a stone bench among courtyard shrubs, Kurt marveled at the exquisitely-maintained greenery around him. It was about one-thirty, and the heat of the sun reflected off the living sea of vegetation surrounding him. Surveying the grounds, he fixed his gaze on the leaves of a finely-clipped hedge and began to visualize Erika's face among the leaves. Kurt took a deep drink from his stein and began to daydream. He saw the leaves slowly begin to part. Their intricate branches began to separate to create a passageway in which a form appeared, a Teutonic goddess, blond hair flowing, her blue eyes setting fire to the leaves. The vision's clothes began to slowly melt away, and she stood there in all her perfect Nordic nakedness, a woman-child of the master race. The apparition floated slowly out of the castle of green and stood before Kurt. Erika's image stretched out her arms, offering an object in her right hand. At first Kurt could not make it out. Then, slowly its blurred image came into focus. Cradled in the palm of her hand was the statue from Kurt's room back in Ansbach, with his Knight's Cross dangling from its neck.

"Captain Heisler! Are you all right?" Jurgen's orderly broke into Kurt's trance.

"Yes, Corporal. I was just dozing a little. Maybe that last beer on such a nice warm day was too much for an old soldier."

"Captain, can I get you anything else?"

"No, Corporal. You may go."

Kurt laughed inwardly at himself for indulging in such childish fantasies, but he wondered if the vision was trying to tell him something. Had he become the statue he'd spent so much time contemplating? Was this phantom Erika his reward, the culmination of his boyhood fantasies about being a Teutonic knight accomplishing feats of greatness? Just how did Erika fit into his dreams of grandeur? What was in store for the future? Had fate selected them to be together?

Kurt got up and began to walk among the hedges. Deep in thought about the future, he no longer even noticed his surroundings. How could he become seriously involved with Erika, armed with the knowledge that he could soon be back on the Eastern Front? Remembering the devastation and horror that he had been through and knowing he would return to that world, how could he expect or even want someone to wait for him? The more he thought about the future, the more morose he became. He realized how lucky he had been to survive the war to this point, but how long would his luck last? He questioned whether it was okay just to live for the present with no regard for the dismal prospects looming in the near future. How should he approach Erika and their relationship, especially after the tragic death of her brother? Kurt paced and considered such questions without keeping track of time.

"Captain Heisler, your brother's leaving in thirty minutes. May I help you get ready?"

The orderly's statement snapped Kurt out of his reverie.

"No, thank you, Corporal. I'll be downstairs on time."

———

Sitting like royalty with Jurgen in the back seat as they sped away from the chateau—the Leibstandarte flag snapping in the wind on the driver's side—Kurt once again felt special. He really was a knight of the Third Reich. He had become his statue. Here he was, a captain of Das Reich, sitting next to his brother, a colonel of the Leibstandarte, representing two divisions in the Waffen SS, Hitler's personal army. Kurt realized he was entering the world of Nazi aristocracy, power, and romance. Now he had to live up to his position and bring honor to his division and his country.

"Captain, are you ready?"

"For what? I still haven't seen our actual itinerary. Until then, I guess I'll have to wing it."

"You're right. I really haven't told you, have I?" replied Jurgen. "Well, we'll be checking into a suite at the hotel where the dinner will be held. After check-in we'll get together with some of my fellow officers for supper. Later, we'll do whatever suits our fancy. By the way, Erika and her parents won't be in Berlin until tomorrow, but they're staying at the same hotel. I guess you can relax until tomorrow."

———

Upon their arrival in Berlin Kurt continued to be impressed with Jurgen's importance, and his own. The role of the Waffen SS was expanding and becoming more of a focal point of Hitler's military planning. Consequently, two young officers of such an elite group were given preferential status, especially in the German capital. An aide greeted Kurt and Jurgen at the airport and chauffeured them to their hotel, where gigantic Nazi flags swathed the hotel's facade, and SS soldiers guarded the entrance. Kurt and Jurgen strode into the lobby like young Caesars, accepting salutes from the various guards along the way. Inside, German eagles, banners, swastikas and other pagan tokens mixed with the marble and mahogany of the luxurious hotel.

Jurgen and Kurt were escorted to a suite on the fourth floor. After unpacking and freshening up, they headed down to the bar for a drink.

As soon as they entered the bar, a short, barrel-chested man wearing the uniform of a Waffen SS General approached Jurgen. It was Sepp Dietrich, the commander of the Leibstandarte.

"How was your flight, Colonel Heisler?"

"It was fine, thank you. General Dietrich, may I present my brother, Captain Kurt Heisler of Das Reich Division?"

"So this is the dashing young Captain I have heard so much about. Maybe I should try to get you transferred to the Leibstandarte," laughed General Dietrich, "since you seem to rival your brother's reputation as a soldier, at least in the eyes of a certain female acquaintance of mine."

"Thank you, General. I only hope I can live up to such compliments."

"Well, I'm sure we'll all get many chances to prove our bravery in the coming months. I'm glad you're both here. Colonel, we need to visit about some divisional business tomorrow before the dinner. I'll have someone call you about noon. Until then, enjoy yourselves."

Kurt was a little stunned. Sepp Dietrich, one of the most important men in the Waffen SS had just paid him a compliment, but more importantly, Maria von Klugemann had been singing his praises. Then a thought occurred to Kurt. Would Erika feel like her mother was pushing her at him? Would Kurt simply be a replacement for Hans? Kurt again remembered his brief visit with Erika in April at her brother's funeral. Erika's mysterious comment, "Wait until we see each other again," lingered in Kurt's mind. The realization hit Kurt that this would be the first festive time he would be with Erika in well over a year. He wasn't even sure how he would feel about her. His boyish infatuation had been extinguished in Russia, and he questioned whether he had retained any softness or tenderness. Would he be able to recapture the emotions he had experienced for Erika before Barbarossa?

These thoughts were soon pushed aside as a large group of SS officers gathered in the hotel bar and began the familiar routine of drinking, singing and storytelling. They spent most of the evening in a spirit of lighthearted camaraderie and celebration, bragging about past exploits and predicting greatness for future campaigns. Everyone agreed that it would only be a matter of months before they would be back in action in Russia. The most persistent rumor circulating the ranks was that the First, Second and Third Waffen SS Divisions would be organized into a special Panzer Group under Kurt's old divisional commander in Barbarossa, General Paul Hausser. The young officers were all excited about the possibility of joining such a special group.

One handsome officer appeared particularly eager to get back to the Eastern Front. "Gentlemen, a toast to return to our destiny, the destruction of the Soviet Union." Amid salutes of approval the officer walked over to Kurt and Jurgen and said, "Colonel Heisler, somehow I've not been introduced to your brother, the hero of Rzhev."

Jurgen replied, "I'm just saving you for a special moment, Jochen, and, apparently that moment has arrived. Major Peiper, may I present my brother, Captain Kurt Heisler?" As Kurt and Jochen shook hands, Jurgen continued, "Kurt, Major Peiper will soon join me as a colonel in the Leibstandarte. He's the most daring soldier I know."

"Considering the company my brother keeps, Major, that's quite a compliment. It's a pleasure to meet you," Kurt said.

"I think your brother might be exaggerating a bit, Captain," laughed Major Peiper. "Can you believe a soldier would do such a thing?"

Kurt and Jochen visited for a few minutes before another officer came and dragged the Major away.

"Kurt, Major Peiper's my best friend. From what I saw of his performance in Russia, I think you'll be hearing a lot about him in the future."

"He's certainly charismatic. I hope to see him again some day, Colonel."

Jurgen responded, "I'm sure you haven't heard the last of Major Peiper, and your paths will cross again."

CHAPTER XI

Paris

"Wake up, Captain! You have an exceptional day awaiting you, and you've already spent a good part of it asleep."

Kurt slowly rolled over onto his back and struggled to open his eyes to view his antagonist. Slowly the fuzzy figure standing over the bed came into focus. It was Jurgen's orderly, Corporal Schmidt. "I'm just following orders, Captain. Your brother left for a meeting with General Dietrich and the main officers of the division. He told me to let you sleep no later than two o'clock."

Kurt struggled to get his bearings, still unsure of his strange surroundings. Slowly, the fog began to lift, and he realized it must have been a very hard night; he'd never slept this late in his life.

"Do you need some coffee, Captain? And maybe something to eat?"

Kurt nodded feebly, groaned, and rolled back onto his stomach. He didn't care about anything except the turmoil in his stomach and the parade in his head. Gradually, he was able to assemble a few concrete thoughts in sequence and began to realize what a poor human specimen he currently presented.

"I'm coming in, Captain," proclaimed Corporal Schmidt. The large, ornate door to Kurt's bedroom swung open, and a silver serving tray rolled in, seemingly pulling Corporal Schmidt along with it. "I have very strong coffee and an assortment of eggs, ham, toast, and pastries. Do you require anything else, Captain?"

Kurt was painfully regaining complete consciousness and replied with a grunt, "Maybe a new head, Corporal. Thank you."

"Ring when you're done, Captain. Heil Hitler!" Schmidt saluted and exited, his clicking heels echoing in Kurt's throbbing brain.

Surprisingly, Kurt was not overly excited about the evening's upcoming adventure. As he gingerly sipped his coffee and gnawed on a roll, he collected himself enough to ponder the mystery known as Erika. As a mental exercise he traced every moment of their relationship from their first meeting in front of his uncle's house in Nuremberg in September of 1937 through the sad events of April of 1942. "My God," he thought, "in nearly five years I've only seen Erika about twenty times, and nearly a third of them were during the 1937 Nuremberg Rallies." He struggled to recall every moment of their last real time together, his final leave before the invasion of Russia in June of 1941. "Unbelievable, simply unbelievable," Kurt muttered to himself. The last year seemed like an eternity. As if on cue, Kurt was soon lost in his recurring cycle of internal questioning. Who was Erika von Klugemann, really? How had she changed since her brother's death? Did he love Erika? Did he really love her as a person, or was it partly her surroundings and the power she and her family represented? Or was it simply because, like a mirage in a desert, she had been his only vision of survival during his dark days? How much true emotion could a Captain in the Waffen SS allow himself to feel for another person? Was the bond he felt for his fellow brothers in Das Reich stronger than what he felt for Erika? These random, disconnected thoughts ran together as Kurt's mind manufactured endless, confusing questions about his future. How much longer would the war last? What would life be like for a member of the Waffen SS without war? Who was Kurt Heisler, and how had he changed since 1937?

The coffee finally kicked in, and Kurt managed to snap out of his spell with just enough time to finish his brunch. By the time he had showered and freshened up, he was starting to recover from the past night's revelry. He remembered that dinner would begin at eight o'clock with a social hour at seven, but that was all he knew about the schedule. He laughed to himself, "Well, I guess anyone who's been through combat in Russia can handle the surprises at a dinner party."

By five o'clock Kurt had regained mastery of his senses, but a slight sense of panic had set in, and he really wanted to know at least a few details concerning the night's events.

"Captain Heisler, your brother is downstairs and requests your presence," Jurgen's orderly announced.

Kurt walked downstairs and was surprised to see Jurgen sitting with a very striking woman in her early thirties. It occurred to Kurt that Jurgen had never discussed or even hinted at a love life. Kurt knew Jurgen had never married and that his life was the Leibstandarte, so it was a bit of a shock to see him with a female companion. Kurt berated himself for his thoughts. Obviously, Jurgen had a personal life; why wouldn't he need female companionship?

"Countess Louisa von Steinmetz," began Jurgen, "may I present to you my younger brother, Captain Kurt Heisler? Kurt, this is Countess von Steinmetz, my companion for the evening."

Gallantly, Kurt took Louisa's outstretched arm, kissed her hand and said, "I'm delighted to meet you, Countess."

"And I'm delighted, also, to meet such a dashing young soldier of the Reich. Jurgen tells me you are one of the rising young officers who will lead Germany to her ultimate victory."

"I would be honored to do so, but I think the Colonel may be a little boastful as to my abilities."

"Where's your date?" asked Jurgen.

"What?"

"Where's Erika? Haven't you contacted her yet?"

Kurt knew he'd been out of it for part of last night, but he didn't think he would have forgotten that detail. "I didn't know I was supposed to! I just thought I'd meet her at dinner. I don't even know where ... "

"Just kidding, brother. I know it was a late night for you, and ... "

Countess von Steinmetz intervened. "Jurgen, you're not being very nice. Don't worry, Captain, Erika won't be able to meet you until just before seven o'clock. I know the von Klugemanns quite well, and they won't be able to get to the dinner any earlier. Actually, Jurgen just picked me up at the airport, and as I'm staying in the same hotel, we thought it would be nice for us to meet before the dinner."

"Well, that's very nice," Kurt responded, "but as a matter of fact, I didn't even know Erika was my official date. I just thought we'd both be at the dinner and get together afterwards."

"I wasn't sure you could handle everything about the evening, so I only told you the details on a need to know basis," kidded Jurgen. "You'll be Erika's escort for the evening and will be seated with the von Klugemanns at one of the main tables. The dinner will be very formal. I'm not sure what dignitaries will be present—Hitler himself might make an appearance—but there will be many speeches and toasts during the meal. Afterward, however, the dance and evening activities will be purely social, and you should make the most of it, Captain."

"Is that the last of your 'need to know' details? You were right, it sounds like much more than I can possibly handle," Kurt replied sarcastically.

"Don't worry," cooed the Countess. "You'll do fine. I can tell you the von Klugemanns are very fond of you, and I don't have to tell you how Erika feels about you."

"Kurt, Louisa and I are going out for a little while to see some friends, and then we'll be back to get ready. We'll meet you in the Great Hall a little after six. You know what to wear."

"It was nice to meet you, Captain, and I look forward to dancing with you this evening," Louisa said with a smile.

"I look forward to our dance with great anticipation, Countess. See you both at six. Heil Hitler!" Kurt returned to his room to rest and collect his emotions.

Kurt walked over to his suitcase and removed a small leather case, which he slowly opened. Reverently, his fingers lifted the shiny object most prized by every German soldier, the Knight's Cross of the Iron Cross. Someday, he thought, he would add the oak leaves, or even swords, to the Cross, but for now he was particularly proud to be such a young recipient of this award. Placing it around his neck and straightening it in the mirror, he thought of what he had been through to earn it. He saw the faces of fallen comrades he would never see again, heard the deafening thunder of battle, and recalled the unforgettable stench of death. Even though the face in the mirror was still youthful in appearance at twenty-two, his countenance had acquired the edge of one who had been through the crucible of combat; he wondered what he might look like if he survived another trip to the front. Abruptly, Kurt saluted himself in the mirror, clicked his heels together and headed toward the Great Hall.

———

Waffen SS Captain Kurt Heisler strode into the Hotel's Great Hall like a character from a Wagnerian Opera, and he couldn't help but notice the number of eyes that followed him. Aptly named, the Great Hall was enormous, adorned with mosaics and heavy, dark wood that dominated the ceiling and walls. Everywhere, Nazi and Waffen SS paraphernalia overpowered the surroundings, making the Hall look like a miniature Nuremberg Rally. It was just after six o'clock and the room was filled with guests. Kurt did not recognize anyone yet and was looking for a familiar face when he heard a voice behind him exclaim, "Heil Hitler, Captain Heisler. How are you?"

Kurt turned to see his commanding officer from Barbarossa, General Paul Hausser. Hausser's approach—a high-ranking officer initiating conversation with a lowly captain—exemplified the special esprit of the Waffen SS. General Hausser also had a special reason to remember Kurt;

he had recommended Kurt for the Knight's Cross at Borodino the same day that he had been seriously wounded himself. General Hausser continued, "I see you're wearing your Knight's Cross. I remember well the deeds you performed to earn it. Wear it proudly. Please allow me to get you some champagne." The General waved at a waiter, who immediately rushed over with a silver tray topped with glasses of champagne.

"Thank you, Herr General. I'm honored that you remember me. Have you fully recovered from your own wounds?"

"Yes, thank you, Captain. Certainly well enough to lead you and the rest of Das Reich into Russia soon. But, what do you say we suspend the war talk and enjoy the evening?"

"A wonderful idea, General. I'll let you go so you can talk to some of the really important people."

"Rest assured, Captain, you men of the Waffen SS are my most important people, but, unfortunately, even war has its politics," the General said as he rolled his eyes toward a group of senior officers. "Enjoy your evening." With a nod and a click of his heels, the General was gone.

Gazing around the vast hall, Kurt spied Jurgen and Louisa laughing with a small cluster of officers and female companions. Grabbing another glass of champagne as he strode across the floor, Kurt advanced toward Jurgen's group. Before he was able to announce his presence, Jurgen noticed him and yelled, "Kurt, over here."

Kurt joined them and Jurgen made introductions all around. Soon they were proclaiming toasts to the glory of the Fatherland, the Waffen SS, and each other. At seven o'clock Jurgen turned to Kurt and pointed to the other end of the hall. "Well, I suppose we'd better find our places. I think the von Klugemann table is over there somewhere. See you during the dance. Good luck, Captain."

Just as Kurt was turning to make his way to the other side of the room, he noticed a stunned look on Jurgen's face and that of his fellow officers. Even the women of the group became strangely quiet. Turning completely to see what they were staring at, Kurt's heart stopped. He paused, transfixed, turned to stone by a figure of such great beauty that he simply could not breathe. Approaching Kurt was a tall, slim beauty encased in a shimmering, silver evening gown that exposed bare, white shoulders gently brushed by flaxen hair. A sharp v-shaped neckline outlined a pair of perfectly shaped breasts, and a delicate belt accentuated the athletic figure. Clearly, Erika von Klugemann was the most dazzling person in the room.

Erika pulled him to her and gave him a long, soulful kiss. She then gently clasped his hand and said, "Kurt, please join us at our table."

Kurt was in a state of partial paralysis, not just by Erika's physical appearance, but also by her attitude. She did not even acknowledge Jurgen, Louisa, or anyone in their party as she turned and started toward the table without releasing Kurt's hand. After five years of teasing and playing the role of the unattainable, haughty princess, she seemed to be saying, "I'm yours!" Stumbling across the room to the table where Fredrick and Maria von Klugemann were seated, Kurt struggled to gain some measure of composure. All he could think about was the improbability that such a heavenly being could possibly be interested in him. As they arrived at their table, Maria hugged Kurt and greeted him warmly, "Oh, Kurt, we're so happy to see you again. My, you certainly look dashing, especially with the Knight's Cross. Erika, don't you think Kurt looks just splendid?" Erika said nothing, but her soft, longing eyes never left Kurt as they sat down at the table.

The meal was a gastronomic delight, a fitting banquet to honor members of the Nazi elite, and for the next two hours Kurt met dignitaries, endured speeches and joined countless salutations for fallen comrades. He engaged in small talk with Frederick von Klugemann, mainly about his business and what effect the war was having on production. Seated between Maria von Klugemann and Erika, Kurt knew he couldn't ignore Maria and engaged her enough to be courteous, but he really wasn't taking in much of their conversation. He was totally under the spell of the enchantress whose adoring eyes continued to hold him in a state of euphoric numbness. The intense, deeply mysterious blue of Erika's eyes that Kurt was used to seeing had been replaced by an inviting softness.

Maria, as usual, dominated the proceedings and tried to snare Kurt into her web of captured subjects. She detailed the exploits of Hans during the war, exalted his memory, and secured a promise from Kurt to avenge Hans' death on his next tour of duty in Russia. Kurt was in a precarious position. He wanted to talk exclusively with Erika, but one simply did not ignore Maria von Klugemann. But before Kurt could come up with a plan, Erika came to the rescue. "Mother, enough! Kurt and I need to talk without your constant interruption. Thank you." It was the first time Kurt had ever seen Maria upstaged.

Maria gave Erika a brief look of indignation, but quickly recovered her smile. "I understand, dear. I know you two really need some time together, so I guess Frederick will just have to listen to me, but, Kurt, you must save a dance for me."

As he promised Maria some dances, Kurt marveled at how a mother and daughter could be so much alike. Whatever the reason, Kurt was eager to investigate Erika's new attitude, but amidst all the festivities, they were unable to have any real privacy. Most of their conversation centered on how much they had missed each other, their families, the war and the evening in general. Continuing to surprise Kurt, Erika made the first bold statement about where the evening might be headed. "Kurt, when we're on the dance floor, we need to talk about our future. I didn't realize how much I missed you until after you left Nuremberg in April. I've ached to be with you so much since then that I physically hurt."

"Erika, we have so much to talk about I don't know where to begin. This war has changed so many people in so many ways, but I've never stopped hoping that we could be together someday. Sometimes, during the misery of war, you wonder if you're trying to escape that horror by retreating into a dream world, and it gets hard to separate reality from fantasy. Now that we're finally together, I ... "

Erika pressed a delicate finger to his lips, brushed his ear with her own lips and whispered, "Shush, Captain. Say no more until we're on the dance floor."

The heavens seemed in concert with the two young lovers as the orchestra began to play. On the dance floor Erika and Kurt finally found enough privacy to speak without worrying about eavesdroppers. Holding Erika, drinking in her perfume, feeling her softness and warmth, swaying with the music, Kurt sensed that his fantasies were about to come true. Erika was now as bold and direct as she had previously been coy and mysterious. As they danced, she slid both hands gently up the back of Kurt's neck and pulled his face down toward hers. As her intense eyes burned a hole in his, she said, "Kurt, do you want me?"

An electric current surged through every molecule in Kurt's body. Placing a soft, tender, lingering kiss on her lips, he replied, "Erika, I've wanted you from the first time I made a fool of myself in front of you."

To prove she hadn't totally lost her naughtiness, Erika laughed. "And which time would that be?"

"You know, in Nuremberg when we first met, and you thought I was lost."

"Well, you did act pretty stupid then, but we were both just kids."

Kurt returned to Erika's first question. "What do you mean by do I want you? I can take that statement a number of ways."

Erika responded with a tantalizing, drawn out, "Well?"

"I think we need to be alone soon, very soon," Kurt blurted out in a sense of urgency. "Where are you staying? I think Jurgen told me, but I can't remember."

"We're here at the hotel."

"How can we be alone with everything that's going on?"

"It just depends on how things work out during the evening. An opportunity may present itself."

Again, Kurt found himself reading double meanings into whatever Erika said. Did she have a plan, or was she just teasing him again? As they danced around the ballroom of the Great Hall, the way Erika held Kurt and the looks she gave him erased any doubts Kurt had about her intentions.

"Excuse me, Captain. May I cut in?"

"Only if it's a direct order. Otherwise, not on your life," laughed Kurt to Jurgen's request.

"Well, I'm sorry to have to pull rank on a family member, but it is an order!"

Soon Jurgen was dancing with Erika and Kurt with Louisa. The Countess dressed and carried herself with class, and Kurt found her to be charming and down to earth as well. Tall and slender, with long brown hair and brown eyes, Louisa had an oval face dominated by a prominent nose and a brilliant smile. She was a little older than Jurgen, about thirty-two, and had been married, but her husband had been killed in North

Africa, and she was just now dating again. Jurgen was interested in Louisa, but, as yet, any real relationship was in the early stages. Kurt enjoyed talking with her, but found it hard to sustain any real interest in polite conversation except when the talk centered on Erika.

"Your Erika is absolutely lovely, Kurt. Do you plan to get married?" Almost before she had asked the question, the Countess apologized. "I'm sorry. That was a stupid question, and very vulgar of me to ask. I guess I just made an assumption, what with all the rumors."

"What rumors?"

"Well, as you know, the von Klugemanns are what you would call the new aristocracy, the Nazi aristocracy. By the way, just so you know, I'm not one of the old aristocrats who resent such people. Just like any group, the new aristocracy has some members who are hard to take, but the von Klugemanns are very nice people." Louisa paused, and looked slyly at Kurt. "Don't say anything, but the rumor is that Maria is making plans for a massive wedding that will be the social event of the decade, and I think you can figure where you fit in."

"What?" an indignant Kurt almost shouted. "Are any traditions sacred anymore? It would be nice if I was allowed to ask her to marry me first!"

"Don't get too excited, Kurt. I'm sorry I said anything. Really, Maria is such a great planner and organizer that she's just anticipating. She always likes to be ahead of things." Louisa smiled and said gently, "One thing is certain, Kurt. Maria must surely approve of you and want you as a son-in-law, or else she'd be taking a very different approach concerning your relationship with her daughter."

"I'm sorry I yelled, but you certainly surprised me. Thanks for sharing the information with me, and by the way, what about you and Jurgen?"

Louisa blushed slightly, "Are you trying to get even with me, Kurt?"

"No, seriously. I'm just now getting to know my older brother, and I never really pictured him with a woman. He's so dedicated to the Leibstandarte that I didn't think he had time for anything else."

"That's a fact. It's good to hear his own brother say that, so now I know it's not just me. But we'll see what happens." Her brown eyes were twinkling as she finished speaking.

As the dance continued, Kurt remembered he had promised Maria von Klugemann a dance, and with Louisa's information that dance now presented more interesting possibilities. Soon Jurgen and Erika came over to switch partners, and Kurt was back dancing with Erika. As they maneuvered about the dance floor, Kurt contemplated his next step. Should he ask Erika about her mother's wedding plans? Should he wait and see what Frau von Klugemann said when Kurt danced with her or should he say nothing to anyone?

"Kurt, you've gone silent on me. You must be thinking about something important, because I can't believe you've already run out of things to say to me when you haven't seen me for so long. Maybe you're working on a secret plan to end the war?" teased Erika.

"I'm thinking I need another glass of champagne to work out the final details of Russia's demise. Let's go sit down for a while, and you can help me with the plan."

"Okay, I like making plans."

Frederick and Maria were out dancing, so Erika and Kurt were alone for the moment. After the banquet the larger tables had been removed, and small circular tables adorned in fine linen tablecloths now surrounded the dance floor. A single candle embellished with an SS symbol provided a soft, romantic glow for each table. Kurt held his glass of champagne to the candlelight and gazed at the glowing reflection as the flame danced among the bubbles.

After a few minutes of silence, Erika interrupted his digression. "What do you see in the champagne, Kurt?" Without pausing for an answer, she hit Kurt with another shock. "Kurt, do you love me?"

Kurt decided it was his turn to be in control. "I'm not really sure. That's a tough question."

Erika sat back in her chair. "What? How can you say that?"

It was obvious that Erika had not expected Kurt's response. She was not used to being the one toyed with. "Captain Heisler, if you find me undesirable or unattractive, I guess I should look elsewhere for a male companion." Glancing around the room, she said. "I don't think I'll have much trouble finding someone."

"My, aren't we touchy." Kurt's comment enflamed Erika even more, so he decided to continue his charade a little longer. "How do you know when you're really in love?"

Erika was not prepared for Kurt's attitude, and she failed to notice the sly smile on his face. "Well, if you don't know, I guess you're as dumb as I first thought you were. I just don't … "

"If you ask a stupid question, sometimes you get a stupid answer. Of course I love you, and I know you know I do, so why did you even ask?"

Erika gave Kurt one of her icy blue stares. "You understand women about as much as I expected!"

"Apparently you like to tease, but you don't like it when the situation is reversed, and I understand you better than you think."

Erika and Kurt stared at each other for a moment. Then, simultaneously, they exploded in giddy laughter. When they finally calmed down a bit, Kurt reached across the table and caressed each of Erika's hands with his. "Yes, Erika, I do love you. Now, what shall we do about the fact that we love each other?"

"That, my dear sir, is very simple. Let's get married."

"I thought it was the man's job to propose."

"It is, Kurt, but hear me out. I know you'll be leaving in a few months, and I want us to be married before you go off to war again. Also, I just want the two of us to go off and get married. We can tell everyone later when things are more settled. I know what my mother will do if she has a chance. She'll turn our wedding into such a spectacle that it'll take at least a year of planning. She'll probably even try to arrange a cease-fire so all of her dignitary friends can come. I don't want to wait that long, and I don't want to be part of all that pageantry. Well, what do you think?"

"I guess we can sort out the details later, but, first, let's make it official," Kurt said as he pulled a ring off his finger. The silver ring with Das Reich's symbol on it was obviously a few sizes too big for Erika, but he put it on her finger and solemnly asked, "Erika, will you marry me?"

"Yes, yes, yes, yes … "

They leaned into each other and kissed, a long, simmering, forever and ever kind of kiss. When they had recovered their senses and returned to planet Earth, Kurt said softly, "I'll get you a real ring soon, but for now keep that one as our sign of commitment."

"I will, I will," came Erika's soft reply.

"You know, you've never even met my parents."

"I know. Why don't I meet them when you go to see them during the rest of your leave? I know your aunt and uncle have told them a lot about me, even if you haven't."

It was true. Kurt had only mentioned Erika occasionally in his letters home, as the war had interrupted any normal exchange of information. But that was only part of the reason; not knowing whether he'd survive, he didn't want to burden his parents by introducing them to anyone of significance. Sitting at the table with Erika, Kurt felt something he had not felt for a very long time, a need to see his parents and restore a relationship that had been strained by the war. "That's an excellent idea. I'll call them and let them know I'll be bringing you along when I come home. Can you arrange your schedule?"

"I don't think there'll be any problems."

"We'll need to do some planning. I'm going to spend some more time in Paris with Jurgen, and after that I should have about four weeks left."

"In your last letter you said you'd be going somewhere in Bavaria with your friends during the last week of your leave. Is that necessary?"

"I don't know, maybe not. I'm sure I could make an excuse and not go. Let's see how things develop. I have no idea what Oskar has in mind." Kurt paused as a thought came to mind. "If you come to Ansbach with me, do you think your mother might get a little suspicious that we're planning something?"

Erika deliberated for a moment and then offered her assessment. "Mother knows I've never met your parents, and she knows we're getting serious about each other. I don't think she'll see anything unnatural about my going to meet them. But we shouldn't give her any reason to think we're engaged by having our parents get together."

Kurt agreed and gave Erika a broad smile, and with all the gallantry he could inflect into his voice, proudly stated, "You know, it just really hit me when you just said it. We're engaged!"

"Don't get any ideas," huffed Erika with an air of aloofness. "We're engaged, not married."

"Let's see what the evening brings. We may have to go somewhere very private to do some more planning."

Erika giggled, but quickly got more serious. "Kurt, how long will you be in Berlin?"

"Jurgen and I go back to Paris tomorrow. But, no matter what happens tonight, we'll be able to spend at least two weeks together very soon."

"Why don't you fly from Paris to Nuremberg, so when we go to Ansbach to see your parents, we can take one of our cars? And don't stay with your aunt and uncle. Stay with us, stay with me."

"Not a bad idea, not bad at all. I was thinking of getting the use of a staff car, but flying would be much quicker, and I'm sure Jurgen could line me up with some military flight into Nuremberg." Kurt's mind was racing, and he realized he needed to ask Erika some important questions before her parents returned. "Erika, a couple of quick questions before I encounter Maria. First, what shall I say to your mother during our dance if she asks about us?"

"That's not a tough question. You should be able to answer that one yourself. Just say we're dating and leave it at that. If she says anything— and I mean anything—about a wedding, act shocked and say we can't consider something like that until you're back from the next campaign in Russia. What's the next question?"

"Okay, I'll make this one a little harder. Are you really serious about getting married soon?"

"You'll find out Captain Heisler, and soon."

"What the hell does that mean?"

Erika just laughed and said nothing.

"Well, if you won't say anything, let me ask the question in a somewhat different manner. What kind of private ceremony, if we have one, are you thinking about?"

"A very quick one," squealed Erika.

"I'm serious! Do you want a church wedding, an SS wedding, or just a simple civil ceremony? You know, we've really only talked about religion once or twice in all of our conversations. I know your parents were Lutherans once, but the Reich has pretty much become their church and yours. My parents are Catholic and still go to church when they can, but I know my mother would be greatly offended if we had a pagan wedding."

Erika's demeanor changed completely, and she became very serious. "Kurt, I believe in God. Do you?"

Her statement stunned Kurt. Thinking it over, Kurt realized how long it had been since he had really thought about such a moral puzzle. He wondered how many layers of indoctrination and human suffering lay piled on top of his answer. Finally, after a long pause, he responded. "Yes, I think so, but I'm not sure exactly what form God takes. I wouldn't call myself a Catholic anymore, or even a very religious person, but I do believe there's a 'being' to which we all must answer. I believe a 'God' demands that we live an honorable life and do our duty and ... "

"Kurt, you're not in danger of betraying the Reich if you tell me you believe in God. I know you do, so a simple 'yes' is all I need. Now, to answer your original question, let's have a simple civil ceremony. I think a church wedding would create far too many complications. Besides, under the present circumstances it would be slightly hypocritical and largely impossible. But I don't want one of those SS ceremonies where everything is so totally godless and centered on producing children for the Fatherland. I've had a few friends tell me about them, and I couldn't stand that. I want to marry you, not the SS."

Kurt was seeing a new side of Erika. He had always perceived her as this Aryan Nazi aristocrat, devoid of any feeling of religion except for the state, and he didn't know this side existed. Time was running out, though, so he had to press on with his final question. "Next question: I'm going to ask Jurgen if we can use our suite uninterrupted tonight from eleven until midnight. Can you get away from your parents?"

"After what we've been talking about, you're asking if I need my parents' permission? I thought the dress alone would convince you that I'm an adult, Kurt. Now I don't know whether to be disappointed or insulted. I guess I'll have to make things a little clearer for you; I can take care of myself, and the answer is yes."

"Okay, I guess I deserved that, but things have happened quickly tonight, and my mind hasn't caught up with everything yet." Kurt looked at his watch. It seemed as if he and Erika had been talking for hours, but it had only been about fifteen minutes. "I'm sure we'll be separated at times during the next hour, but let's make sure we meet back at this table about ten-thirty. That'll give us some time to make a discreet departure."

Erika was not wearing a watch. "What time is it now?"

"About nine-thirty."

Erika smiled and said, "See you later, my husband-to-be, and good luck."

Kurt turned and discerned the reason for Erika's warning. Maria von Klugemann was heading purposefully in their direction.

"Captain Heisler, I believe you owe me a dance, and I'm here to collect."

"It shall be my great honor, Frau von Klugemann, to have you make my evening complete."

For the next twenty minutes Kurt was held captive by the social leader of the Nuremberg Nazis. Maria presented her usual propaganda about the state of affairs and the responsibilities of all Germans, but Kurt found he wasn't as spellbound as he used to be by Frau von Klugemann. He was too preoccupied with thoughts of her daughter and what he'd be doing at eleven o'clock. Finally, Maria brought up the question of Kurt and Erika's relationship. "Captain Heisler, I hope you and my daughter are getting along well. I see a fine future for the two of you. I think you and Erika are the absolute embodiment of German superiority and perfection. Young people like you will ensure our special culture will live on."

"I thank you for such a high compliment, Frau von Klugemann. I can only answer for myself, but I'll do my best to ensure that the Reich will survive and prosper. However, it won't be easy."

"I don't want to waste time talking of Russia and the war right now. I know you warriors of the Waffen SS will ultimately smash the Slavic hordes of the east. I want to talk about you and my daughter."

Kurt began to respond, but he decided to let Maria expose her plans before he spoke.

"Kurt, I'm beginning to love you like a son. I couldn't ask for a better son-in-law. I know this is a little bold and direct, even for me, but I think you and Erika should get married before January."

"Why before January?"

"Let's just say I have information that after January Das Reich will be gone for some time. You probably already know why and where."

"I have a good idea, but I'm not sure I should be comforted that my girlfriend's mother has better intelligence sources than I do."

Maria laughed and gestured more freely as the excitement built in her voice. "Captain Heisler, it would be such a great wedding, a fantastic, elegant wedding with such a guest list. Why, the Fuhrer might even attend."

Before Maria could continue her glorification of the wedding, Kurt decided to terminate, at least temporarily, her mental matrimonial fantasy. "Frau von Klugemann, Erika and I have not really talked about a marriage. We're just starting to realize how much in love we are, and I think after I return from Russia, say about a year from now, a wedding is very possible. It would also give you sufficient time to complete all the details necessary for such a wedding."

Maria gave Kurt one of her ultra-dazzling smiles, ones she saved for special occasions. "I've never been corrected in such a polite and clever manner, Captain, and I must accept your proposal. You're right; some of this is up to you and Erika. But mind you, young Captain, treat my daughter well. She's my greatest treasure, and woe to the man who would harm her."

Kurt was not sure how to take Maria's last comment. He hoped she was just being Maria von Klugemann and toying with him just a little.

As they walked back to their table, Kurt said quietly, "Erika is a treasure to both of us. I'll always treat her as such, and I'll never do anything to bring shame on the house of von Klugemann."

Maria beamed and softly kissed Kurt on his cheek. From a short distance away Erika yelled, "Mother, he's mine. Hands off!"

"Yes, he sure is, Erika," laughed Maria.

Erika had been dancing with her father, who quickly engaged Kurt in conversation about the situation on the Eastern front. Kurt wondered if he should bring up his engagement to Erika with Herr von Klugemann, and actually ask his permission, but decided against it. Kurt looked at his watch. It was exactly ten. Soon his rendezvous with Erika would begin.

As Kurt and Frederick continued their small talk, a wave of intense excitement began to sweep through the other end of the Great Hall. Dignitaries scuttled in all directions, and extra security personnel appeared out of nowhere as a surge of exhilaration engulfed the room. Adolf Hitler was making a surprise appearance.

Kurt was simultaneously excited and dejected. He knew he now had a good chance to personally meet Hitler, but he feared his chance to be alone with Erika was in danger. He felt a tug on his sleeve, and he turned and saw Erika looking up at him with inviting eyes. "Don't worry, Kurt, we'll still find time for an embrace. I promise."

"Let's go shake hands with Uncle Adolf," giggled Erika. Then, gripped by a sudden realization of the flippant nature of her remark, she whispered in Kurt's ear, "For God's sake, Kurt, don't ever tell mother I joked about Uncle Adolf."

"Don't worry. I won't tell anyone."

The special people being allowed to meet der Fuhrer, people like the von Klugemanns, had already formed a long reception line. Normally, a mere captain would never have been able to approach Hitler, but as a friend of the von Klugemanns, Kurt was invited into line with them.

Kurt's heart was pounding and his hands were sweaty. He was so nervous that he was glad the line moved slowly so he had time to collect himself. He could not believe his luck. He was actually going to shake hands with Adolf Hitler! Kurt remembered being mesmerized by Hitler during the Nuremberg Rally in 1937, and back then he could hardly have imagined meeting him in person. As the von Klugemann entourage inched toward Hitler, Kurt observed the guests filing past der Fuhrer. Some lingered a moment and visited, others were quickly dismissed with only a nod of the head. Some shook hands, others went away untouched. Kurt was in a state of numbness when Frederick shook hands and said something to Hitler. Next, Erika smiled and shook Hitler's hand as he gave her a broad smile. Then came Maria, who curtsied, and before she could utter a word, Hitler had seized one of her hands with both of his. "Ah, my dear Maria. And how are you? I hope things are going well." Hitler and Maria exchanged pleasantries for a few seconds, and then Maria introduced young Captain Kurt Heisler to the man who had changed the destiny of mankind.

"Fuhrer, I would like to present to you Captain Kurt Heisler of the Waffen SS. If things work out as I expect, he will soon be my son-in-law."

Hitler stared at Kurt, quickly noticed the Knight's Cross around Kurt's neck and spoke, "I think your daughter is making a wise choice. Keep up your heroic defense of the Fatherland, Captain Heisler, and I must say, you are a very lucky man."

Kurt was able to mutter a few words of homage and a thank you, but he couldn't even remember exactly what he had said. A strange feeling infected Kurt. After meeting Hitler, Kurt came away with a vastly different impression than he had expected. In front of the multitude Hitler seemed God-like, a messiah who carried a nation on his shoulders. Yet in a face-to-face meeting, Kurt found him very commonplace and ordinary, not at all what he had expected.

An hour later Hitler left as suddenly as he had appeared, but the Hall buzzed from the excitement of his visit long after he was gone. Everyone seemed so stirred up that Kurt wondered why he had been so lukewarm in his personal reaction to meeting Hitler. The orchestra began to play again, and as the dance renewed, Erika clutched Kurt by his shoulder and said, "Dance with me." As soon as they were wrapped in each other's arms gliding across the ballroom, Kurt said, "Are you thinking what I am?"

"About Hitler? Yes, pretty impressive, isn't he?" teased Erika. "What did you think about meeting him face to face?"

"It was a great honor, but I'm thinking of someone else right now who's even more impressive."

"And who could that be? But before we change the subject, I bet you saw why I sometimes call him Uncle Adolf. It drives mother crazy, but that's what he seems like to me, at least when I'm around him."

"Let's disappear for a few minutes," Kurt said with a sense of desperation, "and let the others go home dreaming of Uncle Adolf."

"It's about time you started doing the asking!"

Soon Erika and Kurt were on the couch in the suite. The clock on the wall stood at eleven-thirty and Jurgen had only promised privacy until midnight. Kurt was a mass of nervous energy; he realized he had no experience at this, and for a brief moment wished he had taken advantage of some of the women he had been offered earlier. At least he'd feel more confident about what to do next. Then he thought, "This is Erika, the woman I have waited for my whole life. I'll just take it slow and everything will be ... "

While Kurt was contemplating, Erika threw her arms around his neck and kissed him with more passion then any mortal man could bear. Kurt reacted to Erika's aggression with total abandonment. His lips went from her lips to her ear, to her neck, down her shoulders and ever so slowly to her breasts. Erika pulled Kurt's head tightly to her bosom and then suddenly bolted and stood up. Her evening gown hit the floor, followed quickly by a slip and a bra. Suddenly, Erika stood naked from the waist up in all her Nordic purity. Kurt looked at the clock and began to undress in a state of frenzy.

"Wait! Stop just a minute," urged Erika. She sat down next to Kurt and began kissing him again, and he tenderly explored an area which he had tried to touch over a year ago, before he'd been stopped and severely admonished. This time, however, there was no denial, only moans of passion and pleasure. He had succeeded in unbuckling his belt before Erika had asked him to wait. Now Erika placed her hand on the outside of his underwear, feeling his hardness, and Kurt groaned and began to kiss her breasts. Kurt started to remove the rest of Erika's clothes as he feverishly complained about their lack of time.

Erika allowed Kurt a few more moments of exploration before grabbing his hands in her own. "Kurt, I'm sorry, but this is as far as I'll go until we're married. It has nothing to do with the time. If we had all night I wouldn't have sex with you, not until we're married." As Kurt groaned and leaned back against the sofa, Erika continued, "I'm not trying to be a tease, but please respect me. After we're married you'll have to beat me away with a stick."

"You know, I can't endure your game of sexual maybe much longer," Kurt said as he buckled his belt and helped Erika back into her evening gown. Then, both fully dressed, they held each other and engaged in a long, tender kiss. "Erika, I love you beyond measure, beyond time, beyond life itself. I don't know how I can wait until we're finally married."

"I love you, too, and you won't have to wait much longer. Do some planning on your own, and when we see each other later during your leave we can figure out how to get married, okay? "

"To hell with the planning! Why don't we find someone to marry us right now?"

"Patience, my Captain. I had to use all my feminine charms to prompt you to propose just a few hours ago, and all of a sudden we're looking for a pastor at midnight? Trust me, it'll be even more fun in a couple weeks when we have our wedding rings on our fingers. Right now we should get back to the dance."

The dance continued until one o'clock, but Kurt was so emotionally spent that everything seemed one large anti-climax of thank-yous and goodbyes. In one evening Kurt had become engaged to the woman he had desired for the last five years, had met Adolf Hitler, and had experienced a hint of what pleasure awaited him in the near future. It was a long time before Kurt finally fell asleep.

———

The next afternoon Kurt and Jurgen flew back to Paris, arriving back at Jurgen's villa by early evening. During the trip they talked about Louisa, Erika, the dance, Hitler's surprise appearance and Kurt's planned visit to Ansbach. Upon hearing about Kurt's Ansbach trip, Jurgen asked him to tell their parents he would try to visit later in the fall, provided this was acceptable to them.

Over the next few days Jurgen had to tend to a number of administrative duties, but the brothers continued to renew their growing friendship. They found plenty of time to discuss the war and what the future held for them. Not that Kurt had doubted it, but it became clear that Jurgen was a true fanatic who never questioned Hitler or the role of the Waffen SS. Although a loyal friend and dedicated companion to those who believed as he did, Jurgen was as equally harsh and unfeeling to anyone who opposed the principles of the Leibstandarte. As for himself, Kurt knew he was a true disciple of the Waffen SS, but occasionally during these discussions with Jurgen about racial superiority and its consequences, he could feel a few doubts creeping in. Whenever these concerns surfaced, Kurt reminded himself that only duty and the survival of Germany counted, and he immediately buried any doubts deep in his subconscious. Kurt wished he could see things as one-sidedly as Jurgen, and he acted as if he did, but small seeds of discontent were starting to germinate deep in Kurt's soul.

———

Near the end of his stay in Paris, Kurt decided to ask Jurgen to be the best man at his wedding. On their first day back from Berlin, Kurt had asked Jurgen to arrange a flight to Nuremberg for him on August 13, and Jurgen had been able to set it up, but not without a price; Jurgen taunted Kurt unmercifully about being so devoted a nephew to go to all that trouble just to see his Aunt Hilda and Uncle Konrad in Nuremberg.

The day before Kurt was to leave for Nuremberg the two brothers met for lunch on the balcony outside Jurgen's study. It was an absolutely gorgeous summer day. A slight breeze created a gentle sway among the trees and hedges down in the courtyard as the birds chirped their shrill songs back and forth. In this setting it was hard to imagine a war raging elsewhere in the world. As he sipped his coffee, Kurt said, "Jurgen, isn't it hard to comprehend as we sit here in this idyllic setting like two little princes that in a few months from now we'll give anything for a little warmth or a bath or some peace and quiet?"

"Enjoy it while you can, little brother. Such is the life of a soldier."

Without really contemplating his brother's response, Kurt blurted out, "Jurgen, would you stand up for me at my wedding sometime in late October? It will be a small private event. You can't tell anyone—not even mom or dad—and especially not the von Klugemanns or anyone connected with them."

Jurgen didn't even blink. He just studied his brother for a moment. "Why all the secrecy?"

Kurt explained the details of their wedding plans, and Jurgen agreed with their reasoning. However, he suggested a small SS ceremony. Kurt deflected that suggestion by explaining that Erika didn't want even that much publicity. Finally, almost as an afterthought, Jurgen smiled and said, "Yes, Kurt, I'd be honored to attend and stand up for you, but you realize I'm doing so at great personal risk."

"What are you talking about?"

"You do understand that when Erika's mother eventually finds out, she'll probably kill me for keeping your wedding a secret."

"Such is the life of a soldier," joked Kurt.

"Why the end of October?"

"Well, the date is fluid, for obvious reasons, but we had to pick a starting point. Do you even know where you'll be stationed then?"

"Probably still in Paris," said Jurgen, "but by then things should be gearing up for us to head back into combat. By the way, you realize that the SS has a very strict marriage code? A member of the Waffen SS actually needs official permission to get married, and it's necessary that the wedding be an SS wedding. Somehow I don't think anyone will question Erika's credentials."

"I hardly think so, and I'm sure that sometime later we'll have an official SS ceremony. As you can see, we don't have much time to put this together. Do you know what the plans are for the Waffen SS Divisions currently being refitted? I'd hate to get shipped out with little notice without being able to enjoy my wedding night!"

"Yes, I can see where that would be a tragedy. You probably know about as much as I do. I suspect after we're back to full strength and supplied with the best new material available, we'll be sent where the danger is the greatest. I think our assignment will depend on the outcome of the Sixth Army's attempt to capture Stalingrad."

Jurgen paused briefly before continuing in a concerned tone. "Kurt, sometimes marriage tends to make a soldier too careful during battle. I've seen it happen with some of my men. Don't let that happen to you, and always remember the code; we must think nothing impossible."

"Thanks for the concern, but don't worry. Erika knows the risk of being married to someone in our position, especially considering what happened to Hans."

"As long as both of you understand. Who else will attend the wedding?"

"We haven't really discussed those details yet. I'd like to ask my friends Oskar and Dieter, but they'd probably talk too much and give away our secret. I don't know what friends Erika might like to include."

"If your objective is a quiet, secret ceremony, then the fewer guests the better. There also would be fewer logistical problems. Let me offer a suggestion." Jurgen's idea was to hold the wedding in Paris, close to where Kurt would be stationed and where he would most likely be able to get at least a weekend pass. Jurgen was already stationed there, and Erika could say she was going to visit Kurt, who was staying with Jurgen in Paris. It would all seem very natural. And to keep everyone in the dark, Louisa could stand up for Erika.

"What do you think?" Jurgen asked.

"I think it's perfect, and I think Erika will agree."

"I'm happy for you, little brother, but I'm already worried for you."

"What do you mean?" asked Kurt with a frown.

"For you to even think you can predict how Erika will react to your logical suggestion indicates your reasoning skills are already seriously impaired."

"Touché, big brother, touché! But thanks for being there to protect me on my big day."

———————

As Kurt's plane landed in Nuremberg on August 13, he was curious about Erika's state of mind and any plans she had made in the week they had been apart. He had talked with her twice on the phone, but said nothing of Jurgen's idea. Kurt thanked the pilot for the lift and carried his luggage to the parking area where he and Erika had agreed to meet. He did not recognize anyone and sat down on his baggage to wait. He hoped it would be short, as a light drizzle was starting to fall. As Kurt watched cars come and go, he noticed a small amount of bomb damage around the airport, and he realized that the war was coming home to Germany. Although the damage done by Allied planes was mostly confined to coastal cities and the industrial sections of the Ruhr, a few British and American bombers were making their way deep into Germany. The Luftwaffe was still in control of the skies over Europe, but Kurt wondered about the future. He figured the Allies would land somewhere soon, and if they eventually invaded Fortress Europa, he was worried about whether Germany could sustain a two-front war. For the first time Kurt actually thought about the safety of his parents, the von Klugemanns, and Erika. The solution was obvious to Kurt. Within the next year the Soviet Union must be defeated, or Germany could be in serious trouble.

"Hey, soldier, need a lift?"

Kurt looked up to see a beaming blonde peering out from a large black Mercedes.

"I borrowed one of daddy's cars," shouted Erika. "Hurry up and get in, or we'll be late for supper."

Kurt got in and Erika drove about twenty feet before pulling sharply over to the curb. She slid across the seat, jumped into Kurt's lap and gave him one long, delicious kiss before hopping back behind the steering wheel and speeding off.

"A little shy aren't you?" Kurt said with happy sarcasm. "By the way, do you have any driving experience? I haven't been this scared since the battle for Moscow."

Erika kept a straight face. "You were probably much safer facing the Russians."

After an adventurous trip, Erika managed to successfully maneuver the Mercedes into the von Klugemanns' garage about five-thirty in the afternoon.

That evening Kurt was the guest of honor at a small family gathering with Frederick and Maria von Klugemann, Erika, Uncle Konrad and Aunt

Hilda. The last time Kurt had actually visited with his aunt and uncle was back in the spring of 1941, before the start of the campaign in Russia. During Kurt's last visit to attend Hans' funeral, there had been no time to see them privately.

Uncle Konrad was beaming with pride on two counts: First, he was taking all the credit for getting Kurt and Erika together; second, he was proud of the young German knight carrying the family name into battle. Aunt Hilda was concerned that Kurt looked too skinny, and she urged him to take better care of himself. As the dinner wore on, Kurt—to his dismay—was forced to recount his exploits during Barbarossa and give his opinion about what it would take to finally bring victory in the East.

"By heavens," shouted Uncle Konrad as he slammed his beer stein on the table, "it seems Ivan has an unlimited supply of men to sacrifice. How can we kill them all?"

"We'll do whatever it takes, Uncle," Kurt gallantly answered.

"Ah, maybe the Russians will be finished before you even get back there," replied Konrad. "The Sixth Army is at the gates of Stalingrad, and after Stalin's city falls, maybe they'll surrender."

"I hope you're right, but the Russians will defend Stalingrad with a fanaticism that matches our own. The fight for Stalingrad will not be easy, and even if the city falls, I'm sure that will not be the end of the war in Russia."

The next event took Kurt by surprise. Erika's father was usually quite unemotional and businesslike, but tonight he was nearly breaking down. Frederick von Klugemann slowly stood up, raised his stein and with faltering voice said, "I salute a fallen soldier of the Fatherland, my son Hans von Klugemann, and I welcome into our home and family his friend and fellow soldier, Kurt Heisler. Heil Hitler!"

They all clanged their steins together, loudly repeating "Heil Hitler." Then they all recounted stories about Hans. At one point Kurt thought Maria was going to have to leave the room, so at an appropriate break in the conversation, he shifted to a more pleasant topic. "You know, Uncle, you take a lot of credit for getting Erika and me together when all you did was laugh at my bumbling infatuation and make fun of me. It was really Hans who forced Erika to go out with me in the first place."

"Ha!" laughed an indignant Konrad. "I was just teasing you so you'd have the courage to ask Erika out. I knew the two of you were made for each other."

"Yes, dear, you're so smart," scolded Aunt Hilda.

"Yes, I remember well Hans' little scheme back in the fall of '37," Maria said with a shaky voice that slowly grew stronger. "But that event actually turned out well, and I hope someday soon I'll have another son."

"Mother!" was all Erika said.

Uncle Konrad gave one of his booming shouts and slapped Kurt on the back. "Don't be afraid, Kurt. There are worse things than being married, but I can't think of any at the moment."

Soon the room was again filled with laughter and good-natured teasing, but Kurt was somewhat ill at ease. He wondered if Erika had told her parents they were engaged. He did not see his ring anywhere on her, and she had not said anything during the meal to suggest she had revealed their secret, but he wasn't sure she'd been able to keep their secret given Maria's persistent badgering.

Hilda brought up a new topic. "So, you're going to see Fritz and Eva. They'll enjoy that. They're very nice people, and I'm sure they'll love you, Erika."

"Maybe we should come along. I don't see my brother as often as I should, and we can get together and ... "

Hilda's icy stare stopped Konrad cold.

"Just kidding, kids," he finished meekly.

"I think it's about time Erika meets Kurt's parents," Maria stated.

Kurt needed to ask Erika what prompted all this togetherness talk, but he would have to wait. Another hour passed before the meal and the conversations were finally finished. Thankfully, Aunt Hilda came to the rescue and asked Frederick and Maria if they wanted to play some bridge, which left Erika and Kurt alone for the remainder of the evening. As the adults went into the study to play bridge, Erika and Kurt stayed in the kitchen.

"Erika, what's the deal? Have you announced our engagement?"

"No, I haven't said a thing. I guess everyone's just assuming that we'll get married soon. The war just accelerates everything, including people's willingness to speak their minds; maybe it's because they don't know when they'll see each other again."

"I'm just glad you haven't let our secret out, but the way everyone's talking, maybe we should make an announcement and have a real wedding."

Erika glared at Kurt and stated emphatically, "No!"

"Okay, if you insist. It's your wedding, too."

"When you come back from Russia victorious, we'll announce that we're married, and explain why we did it in secret. We can have a spectacular celebration for your safe homecoming, Germany's victory, and our marriage. Why, it'll be so stupendous even mother may be unable to do it justice."

"Let's pray all those things occur," Kurt replied.

"They will, dear Captain. Come closer."

"Your parents are in the next room."

"I'm aware of that, and, besides, you know where I stand about sex before the wedding. But that doesn't mean we can't have some close time together." She motioned him over. "Come over here. No, wait, I'll come over there." Erika got up and gently lowered herself upon Kurt's lap. She put her right arm around his neck and laid her head softly on his shoulder.

"Do you still love me?"

"No, I've changed my mind since last week. I met this young woman in Paris and ...."

"Shut up, or I'll have Uncle Adolf send the Gestapo after you."

———

Kurt spent two days in Nuremberg visiting and relaxing. He stayed at the von Klugemanns, but spent quite a bit of time at his aunt and uncle's. Kurt and Erika were unable to spend any real time alone, but during one of their conversations Kurt was able to tell Erika of Jurgen's wedding suggestions, and she agreed completely with the plans. The next step was to see if Kurt could get a weekend pass as soon as he confirmed that everyone else could make it on that date.

Early on the morning of August 16, 1942, Erika and Kurt left Nuremberg for Ansbach. Erika had exchanged the black Mercedes for a VW convertible, and she insisted on driving. It was a clear, sunny day ideal for traveling. The china blue sky contrasted nicely with the emerald green grass of the meadows. As Kurt and Erika sped along the highway, Kurt tried to block out all thoughts of the war, but as he felt the air sweep through his hair, he could not help recalling the early days of Barbarossa when the German Panzers dashed across the open steppes of the Soviet Union. Speeding along with Erika, Kurt truly felt like a superman. Nazi Germany was at its zenith of power, Paulus and the Sixth Army were entering the outskirts of Stalingrad, and Rommel and the Afrika Korps were dashing toward Cairo and the Suez Canal. As those events were unfolding, Kurt was speeding through the scenic Germany countryside with a radiant beauty who was soon to be his bride and wondering if life could be any better.

After a short while the car entered some gently-wooded hills, and Erika swerved off onto a side road and began bouncing along a rutted, twisted trail.

"What the hell are you doing now?" shouted Kurt.

"Just wait, you'll see," a gleeful Erika answered.

After a few turns the VW rounded a corner and drove down a steep hill to the bank of a small stream and stopped. Erika was beaming. "Our family used to come here on picnics when Hans and I were little. I'd nearly forgotten about it. It hasn't changed at all."

Kurt surveyed the surroundings. Truly, Erika had taken him to one of the most romantic spots on earth. A canopy of lush evergreens enclosed a small open area where a swift little stream tumbled down a high, plateau-like rock formation. As the stream bent around the base of the rocks, it formed a small pond and then continued its journey out the other side, disappearing into the evergreens.

Still smiling, Erika opened the front of the VW and produced a blanket, picnic basket and bottle of champagne. "Time for breakfast."

Kurt just looked at her in amazement and realized—again—that being married to this woman was going to be quite an adventure. Erika spread the blanket out on a lawn-like section of meadow bordering the stream, just where it began its pooling. Opening up the picnic basket, Erika produced a small bowl of strawberries and a container of fresh cream.

"Nice breakfast," laughed Kurt. "Where are the glasses, and who's going to drive after we drink the bottle of champagne?"

Erika gave Kurt a whimsical, flirtatious look. "You're too worried about small details, dear. We can drink straight from the bottle, and a dip in the pool will sober us up."

Kurt opened the champagne as Erika dipped the strawberries in the cream and spread them on a plate. Laughing she said, "No, I'm not going to drop them in your mouth like I'm feeding a Roman emperor. You can feed yourself, I hope."

Erika lay with her head in Kurt's lap as he sat cross-legged and sipped champagne through strawberries melting in his mouth. For a time they engaged in no conversation, but just sat looking at each other—the beautiful Nazi princess lying with her Waffen SS knight—as they ate the fruit of paradise and drank the nectar of the gods. They were two perfect people at the perfect spot at the perfect time.

Finally, Erika sat up beside Kurt, and they rested on each other, shoulder to shoulder, as they finished the bottle. Then they slowly turned to each other and began a series of long, lingering kisses. Kurt gently pushed Erika to the blanket and partially lay on top of her as they continued their journey toward ecstasy. Erika softly grasped Kurt's wrist and pushed his hand away from her breast. "I think it's time for a swim. Close your eyes and promise not to peek as I undress. Promise?"

Kurt uttered an unconvincing, "I promise."

"You can't look until I yell when I'm in the water. It's deeper than it looks," warned Erika.

She went behind the VW, undressed, and ran into the water. "Help, Kurt, save me! The water is cold and I need someone to warm me up."

"Ok, I'm coming in, but you can't look, either."

"I won't. I promise, promise, promise," came Erika's response.

Kurt quickly disrobed and headed toward Erika, who broke her promise and then put her hands over her eyes until Kurt was next to her.

"You looked," Kurt said with as much indignity as he could muster.

"I just had to see what a nude superman looks like. Not bad, Captain."

"My God, this water is freezing. I'm stiff as a board."

Erika began to laugh almost uncontrollably, and as Kurt realized the significance of his statement, he actually blushed, but managed a brave, "Well, I am. What do you expect?"

The water was up to Erika's neck and about to the middle of Kurt's chest. Kurt wasn't sure if Erika just wanted to keep warm or if she wanted to be close to him, but she threw her arms around him and held him close. Kurt could feel two very hard nipples denting his chest, yet he remained motionless and did nothing. Erika reached up and kissed him and said, "Let's get dressed before anything happens. I came in first, so I'll get dressed first." Again, Kurt said nothing but watched as this Nordic nymph climbed out of the water and into the sunlight. As Erika disappeared behind the VW, beads of water glistening on her bare, beautiful skin, Kurt yelled, "I repeat my offer to get married immediately. I can't take this much longer."

"I must admit, what I've heard about you men of the Waffen SS—that you're totally controlled by duty and always disciplined—must be true. My, what a waste," said Erika.

"Don't press your luck, my shy little water fairy. Even the best soldiers have a limit, and I've about reached mine. One more episode like your water torture and even your Uncle Adolf won't be able to save your virginity."

Erika replied with just three words: "August, September, October."

Kurt got behind the wheel this time, and as they sped off, Erika had a panic attack. "Heavens, Kurt, I must look a mess after our little swim. I can't meet your parents looking like a farmer's daughter back from milking the cows. We'll need to stop somewhere so I can become more presentable."

"Sorry, it was your idea, so now you make the best of it. You tested me. Now let's see how you handle yourself in a delicate situation."

"You can't be serious. Kurt, don't you dare do this to me!"

Kurt hadn't been serious when he started teasing Erika, but the more he thought about it, the more he liked the idea of putting his princess on the spot. Anyway, contrary to what she thought, Erika looked stunning. The wind had dried her long, blond hair as it floated behind her like a lion's mane. Her complexion was still flushed from the crisp dip in the stream, and she truly looked like a goddess.

As he drove, Kurt became contemplative and completely changed the tone of the conversation. "You know, Erika, I don't really believe what's taken place in the last few weeks. We've shared many tender moments. We've professed our love for each other. We're planning to get married in a few months. Everything seems so wonderful and so normal, but things are not normal. I've done terrible things during the past year, and I'll need to again in the next year. This same person that you've been swimming and dancing and laughing with these past few days has killed hundreds of people, ordered prisoners shot, burned the homes of the helpless, and I will do it again to save Germany, our culture, and you."

Erika laid her head on Kurt's shoulder and said strongly "Captain, a soldier must do his duty. I know you're a good person, or I wouldn't be planning on spending the rest of my life with you. Do your duty, but make sure you don't lose your soul, except to me."

Kurt drew Erika closer with his right arm, and they drove onward to meet his parents.

—————

Kurt's parents were absolutely captivated by Erika. She immediately charmed Fritz and Eva with her explanation of why she was slightly in disarray; she simply told them the truth. Kurt smiled to himself and inwardly gave her credit for passing his test.

Their days in Ansbach were spent visiting, getting acquainted and re-acquainted. One day when they had some time between a picnic and a night out with Fritz and Eva, Kurt and Erika explored some of Kurt's boyhood haunts. None of Kurt's best friends were home. They were all either dead or off somewhere immersed in the war. Kurt did visit the parents of Willie von Skirch, who was in Russia with the Third Panzer Division and the parents of Walter Kruger, who was with the Sixth Army nearing Stalingrad. Both sets of parents said that as far as they knew, their sons were okay, and they spoke of how proud they were of them. Walter's parents were especially concerned about how far away Stalingrad was and how dangerous the coming battle would be. Kurt assured them that all would go well, and Walter would be part of a great victory for Germany.

One evening while Erika was visiting with his mother, Kurt had a long talk with his father. They reminisced about everything they had shared as far back as Kurt could remember, but kept the war talk brief. Fritz asked about Jurgen, and Kurt related the events that had recently brought the two brothers closer than they had ever been and mentioned that Jurgen would like to come home for a visit soon. Fritz nodded his approval, and then came as close as he could to expressing his support for Kurt's decision. "Son, I understand you're a man, and you've followed a path you felt would best serve Germany, but even though you're a member of the SS, I hope you still retain some of your religious upbringing."

Kurt answered as truthfully as he could without offending his father. "Yes, I've retained some of my religious teaching. You know, Father, the old soldier's expression still holds true, 'There are no atheists in foxholes.'"

Fritz gave a relieved nod, and that's where they left the subject.

The next afternoon a change of partners took place. Kurt had a long visit with his mother, and Erika talked with Fritz. Before Kurt could even ask Eva her impression of Erika, she began with a gushing barrage of compliments. "Kurt, I'm so pleasantly surprised. After hearing descriptions of Erika and her parents from Uncle Konrad, I half expected to meet a haughty, spoiled little aristocrat, but Erika is so genuine."

Kurt laughed and started to speak, but Eva continued her glowing appraisal. "Kurt, you're a lucky man. Erika is attending college and working in her father's business so she can be independent and control her own destiny. And she talks about how you both believe in God. She even offers to help with meals and chores. What more could a mother ask for? Kurt, Erika is simply beautiful. I love her! Maybe you should think of getting married before next summer."

At that point Kurt thought to himself, "Well done, my princess. You've certainly passed all the tests." He gave his mother his stock explanation. "Mother, you know we can't do that right now with me off to the front again soon. Besides, that wouldn't give our families enough time to properly prepare for a wedding."

Eva let out a long sigh. "Well, I guess you're right. We've waited this long, so I guess we can wait a little longer to have her in the family."

The talk then shifted to other things. Kurt had been expecting a stern lecture from his mother about the pagan philosophy of the SS somewhere during his visit, but Erika's statement about their belief in God appeared to have defused that issue. Like Fritz, Eva kept military discussions to a minimum, as if not discussing the war would counteract its effects on their lives. The mother-son talk ended with a discussion of Jurgen. "Mother, you really should write to Jurgen and tell him to come home and visit. We've become much closer now that we've had more time together, and he mentioned that he'd like to come and see you both."

"Jurgen can come home any time he wants; he doesn't need an invitation, but there will always be friction between us because of his total denouncement of religion."

Kurt asked, "How do you know I don't feel exactly like Jurgen?"

"A mother just knows, that's all." Eva then left him with a mother's universal plea. "Please try to be careful, Kurt, and don't lose yourself in this war."

As Kurt and Erika were driving back to Nuremberg the next day, they congratulated each other on how successful the trip had been and began to talk about the future. "Kurt, assuming things work out and we get married in late October, when do you think I'll get to see you again?"

"I can't answer that. It depends on what develops with the war and my division's role in it. I suspect that when we get our orders, I'll get one more leave, maybe around Christmas."

"This war must end soon, Kurt. I fear what might happen to our country if it just keeps going on. Get it over with and come back to me."

———

Kurt had two messages waiting for him in Nuremberg. One was a message from Das Reich Headquarters in France informing him that his leave had to be shortened a week because of "operational concerns." The second message was from Captain Oskar Arntzen stating that he and Captain Wolff would be in Nuremberg on August 20 to pick Kurt up and go to Bavaria as the three had previously planned. Oskar's message acknowledged how their timetable would have to be accelerated because of their new orders. As soon as he read both messages, Kurt knew that he couldn't join his friends in Bavaria, as the trip would use up the rest of his leave. Given his newly-engaged status, Kurt realized that nothing Oskar had in store could make that trip worthwhile, regardless of what the "special occasion" was, and the two words "Lebensborn" and "Steinhoring" in Oskar's message confirmed his decision. Kurt called Oskar as soon as he read the message, but it was too late. Oskar had already left, and there was no way to reach him until he and Dieter arrived in Nuremberg.

By now Kurt was very familiar with the Lebensborn program. Started in the mid-Thirties and kept relatively secret, it was a system of government-sponsored homes where unmarried, pregnant women of the proper Aryan background could stay during their pregnancies. To be eligible, women had to prove the father also had the proper racial background and membership in the SS. A few locations were even established so SS soldiers could meet German girls for the purpose of passing on their superior genes. As the war progressed and many racially pure soldiers like those of the Waffen SS were being killed in battle, such get-togethers became more urgent. A few places like Steinhoring actually had banquets and parties with special rooms, which Kurt thought was a little excessive. After what had transpired between him and Erika in the preceding days, there was no way he would consider going, but he thought he might have a little fun with Erika. Actually, Kurt thought he could also test Maria to see just how totally immersed she was in the philosophy of the Master Race.

Walking into the kitchen, Kurt found Maria and Erika with looks of concern on their faces. It was about three in the afternoon, and Frederick would not be home until about five-thirty, so Kurt had a free hand to play his little game.

"Bad news and good news. I have to go back to France and rejoin Das Reich a week earlier than I expected, but I've still got a few days left. My two friends I told you about, Captains Arntzen and Wolff, will be here tomorrow, and we're going someplace in Bavaria. Has either of you ever heard of a place called Steinhoring?"

Kurt watched in amusement as Maria von Klugemann reacted with a look of disgust and Erika with one of pure anger. Erika responded first. "Captain Heisler, don't you dare! Don't ... you ... dare!"

"Don't I dare what?" asked Kurt innocently.

Erika's face was crimson. "Oh, I suppose you don't think I know what those, those Steinhoring places are for. Well, I do!"

"I've heard a little about them," Kurt responded slyly, "and I thought you two would be pleased that I'd make such a sacrifice for the Fatherland."

"Sometimes Himmler gets a little carried away with some of his racial fantasies," spoke Maria. "He's on the right track most of the time, but some of his ideas and programs are a little far-fetched, and this is one of them. I suppose for some men and women under certain circumstances it might be satisfactory, but not for men of honor or women of any reputation."

Kurt continued his charade, "I think I heard somewhere about a League of German Girls and something about women with the correct background who are supposed to provide the Reich with as many babies as possible. The Master Race needs to grow, you know, and if all the men with the right characteristics are killed in the war, what will happen? Erika, weren't you a member of the League?"

As both von Klugemann women glared at him, Kurt could control himself no longer, and he exploded with laughter. "All right, all right, I wasn't really planning on going. I didn't even know the destination until I just read the message. Erika, I hope you know me well enough by now to know that I really wouldn't consider something like that. Or did you want me to do my duty?"

Kurt waited for a response, but getting nothing but frosty glares, he asked, "By the way, how do you two know so much about the Lebensborn program?"

"I know a couple of girls who have been to places like that, and that's all I'll say, except there is a limit to fulfilling one's 'duty to the Fatherland.'" Erika's color was returning to normal.

Maria added, "If you aren't going, Kurt, what will you tell your friends?"

"I'll tell them the truth. After they meet Erika they'll understand."

———

Kurt's assessment of his friends' reactions to his decision not to accompany them on their "journey of duty" turned out to be correct. Oskar and Dieter drove up to the von Klugemann house about mid-afternoon and politely asked if Captain Heisler was ready to go on their trip. Maria asked them to come in and refresh themselves, and she took them to the study to sit down and relax. Soon Oskar, Dieter, and Maria were drinking coffee and visiting. When Kurt entered the room, Maria quietly excused herself. Just as Kurt began to explain to his friends that he would be unable to participate in the adventure, Erika made a dramatic entrance.

Oskar and Dieter couldn't have risen faster if Hitler himself had entered the room. Dressed provocatively in a tight, black dress, she approached Kurt and gave him a lingering kiss. Then, turning to Oskar and Dieter, she introduced herself. "Captain Arntzen and Captain Wolff, I'm honored to meet such good friends of Kurt's. I hope you perform your duties well at Steinhoring, but I am the reason Kurt will not be joining you." Erika then turned elegantly and exited the room.

Kurt, working as hard as he could to contain himself, said casually, "Do either of you need any further explanations?"

"Captain, why don't you two go to Steinhoring, and I'll stay here?" offered Dieter.

"Good grief, she's stunning, Kurt," exhorted Oskar. "What's more, she appears much too sophisticated for a man of your simple charms. Clearly, she deserves someone with a more refined, aristocratic background. Someone like me, perhaps."

Soon the three friends were laughing and joking, and Oskar and Dieter couldn't even pretend to needle Kurt about staying in Nuremberg. Erika did not reappear, and Oskar and Dieter thanked Frau von Klugemann for her hospitality, told Kurt they would see him in France, and departed for Bavaria. Maria turned to Kurt and asked, "Where's Erika? She's not being very polite."

"No, she's just being Erika."

The remaining few days passed much too quickly, and soon Kurt was on his way back to Paris. He caught a military flight from Nuremberg to Paris, which allowed him the chance to see Jurgen for a night before catching a ride to company headquarters in Northern France. The two spent the evening planning the wedding, and they set a tentative date for the third Saturday in October. Kurt's assignment was to get a pass to Paris for that weekend and then contact Jurgen. If all went according to plan, Louisa and Erika would arrive in Paris on that date.

—

When he reached headquarters and reported in, Kurt could see Das Reich was definitely starting to resemble the military force it had been before Barbarossa; if anything, it was becoming even more formidable. Kurt arrived back for duty a day before Oskar and Dieter. He knew that with a week to plan their verbal assaults, he would be in for a barrage of good-natured ridicule, and when they arrived the next day, they didn't disappoint him.

"Hey, Heisler, I hope your little fraulein came through for you. You really missed every man's dream vacation."

Dieter quickly chimed in. "Oh, I don't know about that. I thought it was some pretty hard duty. In fact, I was hard for a week." Dieter could barely contain himself at his cleverness. "Captain, I figure the Reich will be supplied with a battalion of children in about nine months. And for your listening pleasure, we'll fill you in on all the details. It'll probably take several days, because there's so much to tell."

Oskar and Dieter laughed heartily as an amused Kurt silently withstood more descriptions of their masculine prowess.

"Now, mind you," continued Dieter, "these weren't just common whores we're talking about. They were young beauties doing their duty for the Fatherland, and I must say they really enjoyed their work. Their inspired dedication took me to new heights."

Kurt could no longer hold back. "For you, Dieter, that's probably three inches if you're hard. But I'm happy that you two could perform such honorable service for your country. I hope you were better lovers than you are fighters, or the German race is doomed."

"Listen to Captain Smug here," Oskar commented. "Just because he has the most beautiful woman in Germany waiting for him, he thinks he can ridicule our heroic deeds on the battlefield of love." He then paused for effect. "But I have to admit, if I was going to pass up an opportunity like we just had, it would have to be for someone like Erika. All kidding aside, Kurt, she is something special, and I can understand your decision."

"I can't argue with Oskar on that," said Dieter. "You're a lucky man, Kurt, especially for someone so ugly and uncouth."

After some more light conversation the business of war eventually took over. The time for rest was over, and the friends scattered to find their individual companies to prepare for the final extinction of Bolshevism.

———

As October approached, the officers and men of Das Reich talked constantly about the Battle at Stalingrad. Everyone had been hoping for a quick victory, but that was not happening. The German Sixth Army had reached the city, but progress was slow, literally block-by-block. True to form, the Soviet High Command was sacrificing lives to gain time, and the Russian soldiers were defending their soil with rabid fanaticism.

Kurt couldn't think about Stalingrad without wondering how Walter was doing and whether he was still alive. Recalling his own horrific experiences in Russia, Kurt said a silent prayer for Walter.

"I wonder if we'll be sent to Stalingrad?" Dieter asked as he, Kurt and Oskar were having a beer at the officer's mess hall one afternoon, digesting the latest news from the Russian Front.

"Probably," answered Oskar gravely. He then slammed his left arm on the table. Whenever Oskar really wanted to emphasis a point, he would take his left arm with the leather sling covering the stump where his left hand used to be and slam it on something. "The Division is nearly ready to go. I guess we're waiting for some new wonder tanks, Tigers, I think they're called. Then we'll go and kick Ivan's ass back to Siberia."

"It'll be interesting to see what things are like a year from now," added Kurt.

Dieter was also now serious. "I hope all of us are still around a year from now and celebrating the end of the Russian campaign."

"To the Division, the Fatherland, and the end of the Russians," toasted Kurt. The three friends banged their steins together as they saluted one another.

"Say, I heard you're leaving for Paris next weekend, Kurt. What's the occasion?" asked Dieter.

"I'm going to see Jurgen. It'll probably be the last time I have the opportunity to see him in Paris."

"Have fun. It might be a long time before you get such a chance again," said Oskar, as he and Dieter left Kurt with his thoughts.

Kurt hadn't really lied about the reason he was going to Paris, because, technically, he was going to see Jurgen. With a little finagling, Kurt had secured a pass to Paris for the third weekend in October. Although it would only be for four days, Thursday through Sunday, he would not have to report back until noon on Monday. Kurt had immediately contacted Jurgen and Erika and confirmed the date with them. Jurgen told Kurt he would set up everything, including an appropriate location, someone to perform the ceremony, and the honeymoon arrangements. Jurgen's last words were, "Have no fear, brother. It'll be secret, discreet and tasteful. The rest will be up to you."

———

Kurt tried not to be too preoccupied about Erika as he performed his duties during the days before his wedding, but he was losing his ability to concentrate. In addition to contemplating life with Erika, Kurt was recalling Jurgen's earlier warning and starting to wonder if being married would affect his performance in the "Russian Cauldron." Would thoughts of Erika waiting at home for him make him more careful? Thinking about such things was often the kiss of death for men in combat.

As Kurt tried to keep his emotions in check while he readied his men for their next assignment, he was thankful for one fortunate circumstance that had made his job easier since his promotion to Captain. His Company contained three veterans from the Barbarossa campaign who, besides being integral parts of the company command structure, were also Kurt's friends. Their experience and leadership took some of the load from Kurt's shoulders, and he didn't hesitate to involve them when necessary. Sometimes as Kurt watched Lieutenant Schneider and Sergeants Weber and Schmidt, he couldn't help but recall what they'd all been through together. As he watched them taking their unit through a precision drill, Kurt called Schneider aside. "Lieutenant, what do you think? Are we ready?"

"Yes, Captain, we're ready."

"Excellent. You know I'm leaving tomorrow for the weekend. Make sure Sergeants Weber and Schmidt don't get into any trouble," Kurt said with a smile.

"Don't give me an impossible order," Lieutenant Schneider stated with mock seriousness. "That's way too big a job for one man."

"Do the best you can, Lieutenant. Remember, nothing is impossible."

"Heil Hitler! Have a good trip, Captain."

Kurt finished his duties for the day. Then he packed and prepared to leave for Paris.

———

Paris was still Paris, and the weather was still enjoyable, but Kurt really didn't notice. He could only think of one thing: Erika. Jurgen had taken care of all the details, and he had done his usual thorough job. The brief ceremony was to be held at three o'clock Friday afternoon at the chateau

Jurgen was occupying. He had procured the marriage license, and it was ready for signing. Jurgen explained to Kurt that having a military chaplain would satisfy both military and religious concerns, and, somehow, Jurgen had found a Lutheran chaplain from an infantry regiment stationed in Paris to perform the ceremony. Jurgen had instructed the chaplain to keep the ceremony a secret and was able to keep all the paperwork to a minimum. He had made reservations for the wedding party at an exclusive restaurant on the Seine River immediately following the ceremony. Finally, Jurgen had secured a small villa just outside of Paris for Kurt and Erika's weekend honeymoon retreat; it would be well stocked with food and drink and there would be a car in the driveway in the event the couple wanted to venture out during the weekend. Standing in Jurgen's chateau on Thursday afternoon listening to Jurgen's review of the itinerary, Kurt was amazed at his brother's efforts.

"Jurgen, I can't thank you enough. I hope I can repay you someday."

"Maybe, but marriage is a long way off for me. Besides, this shows I do have a romantic, sentimental side, or at least the start of one," laughed Jurgen.

"Well, I'd say it's a great start. I have a couple obvious questions. Where's Erika staying tonight, and what about Louisa?"

"Funny you should ask. I have no idea."

"No humor, please. In my current state, I don't think I can handle many practical jokes. "

"Well, okay, if you must know, Erika and Louisa are staying at a friend of Louisa's tonight, and you can't see Erika until the wedding. Just a little romantic twist, you know. I haven't planned a bachelor party or anything for you, but tonight you and I will spend your last night as a free man together, and Erika will do the same with Louisa. What they do is their business, and what we do is ours."

"Can't I even talk to her?"

"No"

"This is a little ridiculous," grumbled Kurt.

"We need to build the anticipation!"

Kurt eyed Jurgen woefully. "You don't think five years is enough anticipation?"

"Okay, little brother, no more jokes. You have my word of honor as an Officer of the Waffen SS that everything is ready, and tomorrow you and Erika will be married as scheduled."

A look of relief passed over Kurt's face, so Jurgen added, "Now that we're clear on the arrangements, the night is yours, Kurt. What would you like to do?"

"If I'm going to have to wait until tomorrow afternoon to even talk with Erika, I think I'll require a little 'medication' tonight."

"I anticipated as much, and your wish is my command, Captain."

That night the two brothers enjoyed a gourmet meal with exquisite wine, followed by the finest Parisian nightlife. After sampling the entertainment at five different clubs across several hours, they began arguing about who should drive, and Jurgen finally wrestled the keys away from Kurt.

"Captain, I think we'd better put you to bed, or your performance tomorrow night might give the Waffen SS a bad name."

"That would be unthinkable," came an indignant and slightly slurred response.

"Let us take yonder chariot back to the chateau, have a cognac, and end the evening with a little brotherly camaraderie," offered Jurgen.

Kurt woke up bright and early on Friday morning, eager with anticipation; not even the excesses of the previous night could dull his senses on this day. He bathed and dressed quickly and went to find Jurgen, but had no luck. Even the orderly didn't know where he'd gone, so Kurt ordered some breakfast. He was relaxing with a cup of coffee and wondering what surprise Jurgen was cooking up when he heard a car stop in the driveway. In a few minutes Jurgen proudly pranced into the kitchen. "Well, my young Captain, you don't look too bad, but it's readily apparent that you're no match for your older brother."

"I think you've had a little too much practice. Besides, I'm a little nervous."

"I just picked up your wedding gift," Jurgen proclaimed proudly. "Since your wedding is such a secret, you won't be getting more than two gifts, so you'd better wait and open it after the ceremony. By the way, do you have a ring?"

"Thank God I remembered to do that. Let me show you." Kurt went to his bedroom and came back with a small, black box. "What do you think?" Kurt asked as he displayed the open box.

"Exquisite, tasteful, discreet, and very appropriate," applauded Jurgen.

The ring was a duplicate of Kurt's SS ring, only more delicately crafted of pure silver. It contained one notable addition, a small diamond located in the middle of Das Reich's symbol. "I like the symbolism. It seals the relationship between the two of us and our commitment to Germany," Kurt continued. "This one will fit her finger, so now I can get my SS ring back. I gave it to Erika as an engagement ring, but she was not to wear it. This one can be explained away as a gift, so it won't give away the secret of our marriage."

"Good thinking," Jurgen said as he started for the door. "I have to make some calls, but don't worry, everything is ready. I'm going to pick up the chaplain about one-thirty, and we should be back here by two-thirty at the latest. Louisa's bringing Erika over a little before three, and then the ceremony will commence. Any questions?"

"Commence? This is not a military operation, Jurgen," Kurt said. "For God's sake, don't make it one."

"I assure you, God has nothing to do with it either."

———

After checking to see that the wedding room was in order, Jurgen called Louisa to make sure things were on schedule at her end. Then he ordered a light lunch for himself and Kurt, as it was already approaching noon. While

Jurgen was obviously in complete control, Kurt was somewhat concerned about himself. He was getting nervous, and he chastised himself for being so immature, but he just couldn't help being apprehensive. After all, he hadn't even seen Erika for two months, and in the next few hours he would be marrying her; just cause to be uneasy, he decided. Even in his excited state, Kurt was painfully aware that after this weekend, the future was uncertain. He knew the chances were good that he could be killed or seriously wounded in Russia. He knew that Erika was also well aware of these dangers.

"Eat some food, Kurt, and stop worrying. Everything will be fine," Jurgen urged as he escorted the orderly in with lunch. Jurgen's admonishment snapped Kurt out of his self-imposed anxiety session, and the brothers sat down to eat. Jurgen made enough small talk to distract Kurt during the meal, and when they had finished, Jurgen left, saying he would be back to pick up Kurt in exactly ninety minutes.

———

The setting was simple, yet elegant. Jurgen's study was left unchanged except for a white linen cloth spread over a table graced with four tall, slender candles. The drapes were drawn, and the glowing candles provided the only light. Two tall, handsome men dressed in immaculate black uniforms stood to the left of the table, and an army chaplain—hands clasping a Bible—stood solemnly behind it. A door opened and Louisa and Erika entered and proceeded to the right side of the "alter." Louisa wore a black dress that matched the uniforms of the groom and his best man. Erika—without a doubt the most dazzling member of this handsome group—wore a shimmering white gown that illuminated the dim room.

Kurt had never seen her eyes so piercingly blue, her hair so brilliantly blond, or her face so radiant. Her glow almost made the candles unnecessary. The ceremony was brief, but beautiful. At the exchange of rings Erika looked with obvious approval at Kurt's selection, and before she slipped Kurt's old ring on his finger, she whispered, "Look inside." Kurt read the inscription inside the band: My love forever, Erika, 10-23-42. They exchanged rings and kissed to cheers from everyone. At the completion of the ceremony Jurgen's orderly joined them and took some pictures.

It was a splendid late autumn afternoon, and Jurgen had set up a private little reception on the balcony overlooking the courtyard. The short journey from the darkness of the wedding room to the sun-filled brilliance on the balcony provided a fitting symbolic climax to the ceremony. The trees and shrubbery of the courtyard were becoming bare, but enough foliage remained to provide a golden, reddish blush to the setting. Four black, wrought-iron chairs surrounded a white marble-topped table adorned with an array of cheeses, breads, nuts, fruits, and a very expensive bottle of champagne with four glasses. The table held two presents, one from Jurgen and one from Louisa. Jurgen poured everyone a glass of champagne and then offered a toast. "To Kurt and Erika. May you always be happy, healthy and successful in your life together."

The tinkling of glasses and the downing of the champagne was quickly followed by a succession of additional toasts. Fearing he would drink too much too quickly, Kurt put an end to the toasts by taking Jurgen's gift from the table and sitting down to open it. He carefully removed the paper and opened the box to reveal a magnificent pair of silver wine goblets inscribed with the Nordic runes of the SS. Kurt's mind momentarily drifted back to the ride with his friends and Jurgen and Helmut in the fall of 1937, vividly recalling the day he had decided to follow Jurgen's example.

"Thank you so much. They are simply gorgeous," Erika said.

"Yes, Jurgen, thank you. I remember the first time I saw some like this. I've wanted some ever since."

Then Erika opened Louisa's gift. It was a small, ornate, handcrafted music box that played one of Erika's favorite lullabies. As the newlyweds thanked her, Louisa said, "Now, Erika, when Kurt is gone defending us, you can listen to the music and remember this moment and feel his presence."

The two couples sat and talked for about an hour, whereupon Jurgen stood up and announced, "I see it is nearly five, and we have reservations for supper at six-thirty. I know you two are eager to be alone, and you soon will be. Just allow us to treat you to dinner. As soon as we finish, we'll drive you to your villa, and the rest of the weekend is yours."

Erika blushed slightly. "Gee, I'm in no hurry. Are you, Kurt?"

The statement drew a burst of laughter from Jurgen and Louisa, but Kurt could only give an unconvincing shrug of his shoulders.

———

The dinner setting was romantic, the music wonderful, the food fantastic and the conversation delightful, but Kurt and Erika were too anxious to be alone to really appreciate the surroundings or the company. They held hands under the table and nuzzled each other between courses and struggled to make conversation with Jurgen and Louisa. When the wedding meal was finally over, Jurgen ended the newlyweds' agony.

"I think we better take you two to your villa before you make a scene right here at the restaurant."

This time no one even snickered.

The villa was in a peaceful, wooded area just on the southern outskirts of Paris. Jurgen drove up to the front door, got out of the car, opened the rear door for Kurt and Erika and gave Kurt his final instructions. "Here are the keys to the villa and the keys to a car in the garage. Eat and drink whatever you want. Everything in the villa is at your disposal. When you leave on Monday morning, put the keys under the rock next to the mailbox. I know you'll enjoy the weekend. I love you both. Heil Hitler!"

The brothers hugged each other and shook hands, and then there were hugs all around. Jurgen and Louisa drove away, and Kurt and Erika were finally alone for the first time as man and wife. They silently watched the car carrying the best man and the maid of honor slowly disappear from sight. For a moment neither spoke nor looked at the other. Then Erika slid her arms around Kurt's neck and said, "Let's go inside."

Kurt struggled to get the door unlocked, but finally succeeded, and they floated into a charming cottage filled with earthly delights. Louisa had gone to the villa earlier in the day and decorated it with fresh flowers. Every room in the villa had at least one bouquet, and the sweet, fresh aroma permeated the interior. After setting down their luggage, Kurt and Erika began a quick exploration of their honeymoon hideaway. Erika squealed with delight, "Oh Kurt, it's perfect. I love everything about this place. It's so cheerful and happy. Let's never leave."

As they turned the lights on room by room, the villa blossomed into an enchanting array of bright pastels, with each room varying slightly in shade. The furniture was delicate, but not overly ornate, and the furnishings were tastefully coordinated, prompting Kurt to remark that the house was obviously decorated by a woman. The tiny kitchen had been stocked with all the necessities. After a tour of the main floor, the couple went upstairs to the master bedroom. An elegant, canopied, four-poster bed with a delicately embroidered bedspread of pure white stood as the room's centerpiece. A special bouquet of roses and a note of congratulations from Louisa rested on the main dresser. Outside the window was a small balcony with a panoramic view of the French countryside. A soft, luxurious carpet of white, accented by light blue walls, enveloped them in a dreamy romantic cocoon.

Almost to herself Erika said, "Kurt, you know what I like best about this place?"

"No ... well, me, I hope!"

"Besides you! I like the fact that there are no swastikas, no giant eagles, and no signs of the war or of the Reich. I'm so accustomed to seeing them everywhere that this is just refreshing."

"Speaking of refreshing, why don't we put our stuff away and then get into something more comfortable?"

"Why don't we just hop into bed?"

"I thought women wanted to have a lot of preparation before sex, especially the first time."

"Sweetheart, I've been preparing for five years. I knew the first time I saw you that you were the man I would marry."

"Well, why in the hell were you so hard to deal with? You really kept me in the dark about how you felt."

Erika assumed her seductive "come get me" look. "I had to be sure you deserved me."

Kurt embraced Erika and tenderly uttered, "I'm sure I don't, but I guess it's too late now." In his mind Kurt had played out how romantic he would make the initial act of consummation, but suddenly all his plans evaporated. Slowly, tenderly, passionately, he began to kiss Erika as he picked her up and laid her on the bed. As Kurt's hands began to undress Erika, she managed to murmur, "Did you lock the door? Are the lights still on downstairs?"

Kurt said nothing, and Erika forgot her questions. After undressing each other, they pulled back the sheets and fell into bed. Erika was lying on her back with Kurt lying on his side beside her. Kurt began to kiss Erika's breasts and then her lips and continued to alternate back and forth. He slowly slid his hand down to Erika's belly button and began to draw circles around it with his finger. Softly purring her approval and opening herself to him, Erika took Kurt's hand and guided it even lower.

———

Afterward, lying with her head on Kurt's chest, Erika said, "I can't tell you how many times over the last few years that I've imagined what sex with you would be like. Captain Heisler, it was even better than I imagined. I've decided I don't want to share you with the military any more. Can't you just stay with me forever?"

Kurt hugged her lightly. "I've often tried to imagine you completely naked, and I must say you look a little better with your clothes on."

With Kurt laughing and Erika's fists pounding him on the chest, Kurt grasped Erika's arms and pinned her to the bed. "You, my dear, are perfection, and I will spend my life adoring every inch of you."

With her arms still imprisoned in his grasp, Kurt began to kiss Erika's breasts again and then released her as he started down and kissed her stomach and then continued down until they were again lost in each other.

After completing a second round of ecstasy, Kurt dryly commented, "I suppose I really should go downstairs and lock the door. Can you wait that long to do it again?"

"If I have to, but don't be long."

Kurt put a robe on and went downstairs, locked the door, and then went into the kitchen to prepare a snack. Soon he was back in the bedroom with a tray of goodies and a bottle of wine. In his absence Erika had donned a white robe and almost blended into the sheets.

"I think we need a little sustenance. I'm getting a little tired. Maybe you're too much for me to handle."

"I doubt it. If you're a true warrior of the Reich, you'll do your duty, or I'll have Uncle Adolf ... "

Erika's sentence was cut short as Kurt started tickling her feet.

"Oh, please don't do that! I can't stand to have my feet tickled!"

"See, I've learned something new about you already."

"Give me a glass of wine, and don't touch my feet!"

———

Kurt and Erika spent the rest of the weekend in similar fashion, engaging in carefree fun and spontaneous lovemaking. They did take the car for a couple of rides through the French countryside and enjoyed a romantic picnic, but most of the time they relaxed in the coziness of their little villa.

On Sunday afternoon Kurt was relaxing on the couch in the villa's small living room, dressed only in his underwear. Erika had been outside taking a short walk, but when she entered the living room, she noticed Kurt had fallen asleep, so she seized her chance for revenge. Tip-toeing over to Kurt's outstretched legs, she grabbed his feet to tickle them, but as soon as she felt one foot in her hand, she screamed, "My God, Kurt, your toes are gone!"

Holding his right hand to his chest, Kurt jumped up. "You almost gave me a heart attack with that scream. That's not a nice way to wake someone up. I guess I forgot to tell you, I had those three toes amputated in Russia a while back."

"How could you forget to tell me something like that? It must have been horrible. Did it hurt much?"

Kurt gave her an exasperated look. "No, it actually was quite pleasant." "Sorry!"

"I'm surprised you've never noticed my slight limp. It takes time to get used to missing three toes on one foot. You never even noticed when we took that little skinny dip on the way to meet my parents?"

"I was too busy peeking at something else. I confess that I never spent much time fantasizing about the size of your feet."

"Funny girl."

"I'd say you've recovered well. I never even noticed anything when we were dancing."

"I suppose you were too interested in trying to get me to bed." Kurt was still lying on the couch and Erika was standing over him.

"Captain Heisler, do not speak or move until I'm done."

Erika undressed and knelt by Kurt's feet. She began to kiss the scars on his left foot where his toes had been, and then gradually moved her lips up his calf and beyond his knees. Soon he had forgotten about the toes.

———

Monday morning was bittersweet. Louisa picked Kurt and Erika up at nine o'clock and drove them to the airport where Kurt was catching a ride back to his division with another officer of Das Reich who was flying in from Berlin. As they arrived at the airport, Kurt saw that his traveling companion was already waiting, so he took Erika around the corner of a building for a lingering kiss and a tearful goodbye. Kurt promised he would see her before he left for Russia. Erika watched until the plane was out of sight, and then Louisa drove her to Nuremberg.

———

By mid-November Kurt had been back with his Division for nearly three weeks. Stalingrad was the main topic of speculation concerning their next assignment, as General Paulus and his Sixth Army had still not taken the city. The Germans controlled about ninety percent of Stalingrad, but could not dislodge the Russians from their last remaining foothold on the west bank of the Volga. In late November, without warning, the Russian Army went on the offensive, attacking the weakly held German line northwest of the city. This section of the long Russian front was held by Rumanian troops, who proved to be no match for the horde of Soviet soldiers and tanks that came pouring at them. The Russians also attacked south of Stalingrad, and when these two pincer movements joined up behind Stalingrad, the Sixth Army was cut off except by air. Conditions on the Eastern Front continued to deteriorate in December, and the Waffen SS elite divisions that had spent the summer and fall recovering from the previous year's campaigns were reaching a state of anxious readiness. As if the Reich needed anything else to worry about, General Erwin Rommel and the Afrika Korps had been stopped at the Battle of El Alamein and were now being pushed across North Africa by Field Marshal Bernard Montgomery and the British Eighth Army. To make matters worse, the Americans had landed in North Africa, so Rommel was being squeezed from two sides.

Sitting in their quarters in mid-December, Das Reich Captains Arntzen, Heisler, and Wolff were engaged in an intense conversation discussing strategy and various rumors about where and when the division might be heading. "Do you think we could be sent to Tunisia?" suggested Captain Wolff.

"No chance," growled Captain Arntzen. "We won't worry about Africa. We still have the Mediterranean to protect us, and, besides, it's not the Americans or British that we really need to worry about; they're at least civilized people. It's still the war against the Bolsheviks that will determine the fate of Germany."

"What really worries me is a two-front war," Kurt added. "Our resources are going to be stretched very thin, and the bombing of our cities has to affect both our war production and civilian morale."

"The German people are strong, and we'll prevail, whatever the obstacles," Oskar shouted as he banged his stump on the table.

"Do you think Hitler will allow the Sixth Army to fight its way out and reach our lines? I mean, as a last resort?"

"Dieter, you know Hitler's axiom that a German soldier never retreats," Oskar said in his best lecturing voice. "If we can't break through to them, they'll just have to hold out until spring when we can mount a new thrust to rescue them."

"What if they run out of supplies before then?" asked Kurt.

"Reich Marshal Goring has promised that the Luftwaffe can fly in enough supplies to sustain them," answered Oskar.

"Ok, General, then tell us when and where we'll be sent," Dieter asked Oskar.

"I'd guess sometime between mid-January to early February, and definitely to the Eastern Front, but exactly where depends on what happens at Stalingrad."

"I guess we better enjoy ourselves on leave next week, then," Dieter said in a resigned voice. "It may be a long time before we're home again."

The officers' last leaves had been staggered so only a few would be gone at one time, so celebrating Christmas at home was a luxury only a few would have. Oskar and Dieter had five-day leaves coming at the end of December, and Kurt had a four-day leave starting on January 3. But, except for the tradition of "Joy and Cheer" during the holiday season, many members of the SS failed to observe any religious ceremony at Christmas, so not having leave during the holiday wasn't a big sacrifice for them.

"When we're home again, things will be much better in the East, or we'll be dead. That's how important our next mission will be," pronounced Oskar.

"I have a bad feeling about my leave falling in January. What if we go early and it's cancelled? I need to see certain people one last time." Kurt's comment elicited much sarcasm but little sympathy from his friends. However, they were both sure he would get his leave and see Erika again.

———

Kurt got his leave. After spending one day with his parents, he went straight to the von Klugemanns in Nuremberg. The situation at Stalingrad continued to worsen, and even Maria von Klugemann was sounding a little apprehensive. As their marriage was still a secret, Kurt could not spend time alone with Erika like he wanted, but just seeing her lifted his sprits.

On the last night of Kurt's leave, however, luck was on their side. Erika's parents were conveniently gone until early in the morning, and Kurt and Erika were able to spend the evening alone. They made love, they cried, they talked about the future, and they rested in each other's arms for hours. The next morning, after saying goodbye to his aunt and uncle and the von Klugemanns, Kurt offered Erika only a one-sentence goodbye. "Erika, I love you, and I will return."

Keeping herself under control only by a supreme act of will power, Erika looked at Kurt with a small tear in each eye. "Whenever I get depressed with your absence, I'll do two things. I'll play Louisa's music box and think of our wedding night, and then I'll look into the diamond on my ring, see your face, and know you'll return. I love you."

They kissed, not knowing when their lips would touch again.

CHAPTER XII

Nordic Gods of War

Kurt and his Das Reich comrades arrived in Russia in early February, 1943, and they were immediately deployed to defend the city of Kharkov. Shortly after their arrival, a disaster of immense proportions befell the armies of the Third Reich. The Sixth Army under Field Marshal Frederick von Paulus was forced to surrender at Stalingrad, the first time that a major German force had suffered defeat during the war. Seizing the momentum, Stalin's armies were trying to encircle and annihilate all of the German Forces in the Ukraine and the Caucasus by trapping them east of the Dnieper River near Kharkov.

The brutal cold and deep snow made conditions dreadful for both sides, and Kurt and his men had to literally shovel through knee-deep snow to make any progress or mount an offensive. While tediously tramping through this endless world of white, Kurt often played mindless games of fantasy to keep his mind off the dreadful conditions. His favorite distraction was observing the small chunks of snow—"snow mice" Kurt called them—as they exploded forward with each new step, leaving faint tracks until they came to rest. He became an expert at estimating how far the tiny projectiles could go. On really cold days they traveled the farthest because the crust provided a harder surface; on warmer days they stopped faster as they penetrated the melting crust. Every time he snapped back to reality and realized how foolish his little game had become, the familiar phrase, "Such is the life of a soldier," popped into Kurt's head.

The marches drove Kurt and his men to the point of exhaustion, so adequate sleep was vital to their survival. Because the intense cold made it impossible to spend nights in the open, they commandeered huts in small villages to provide warmth. The men rotated time in the huts, and those outside kept small fires burning deep in the trenches—even though they risked drawing Russian fire—because the cold posed a greater threat than the enemy.

Often on cold February mornings, hunched close to the fire in the early dawn light, Kurt observed that even the smoke from the huts' crude chimneys appeared to freeze as it left the protective warmth of the inner world. It hesitated as it hung in dense, dirty white clumps above the huts, frozen globs of smelly soot inching their way across the sky. To Kurt, the soot's slow progress was symbolic of the German advance.

———

Hitler was intent on holding Kharkov, whatever the cost, especially after the debacle at Stalingrad. To Hitler, Kharkov—the political and industrial center of the Ukraine—had become another symbol in his war with Stalin. The task of defending Kharkov, however, proved to be impossible for the Germans. Russian forces outnumbered them in both men and equipment, and their recent victory had given them great confidence. The Russian armies had already advanced too far to be stopped, but Hitler still insisted that the city be held. Field Marshal Manstein tried to talk Hitler out of his unrealistic view of the Kharkov defense to no avail. Hitler firmly believed his Waffen SS legions would save the day because they would do whatever he asked and would never surrender.

General Hausser's Waffen SS Divisions tried mightily to defend the city, but he could see that if they did not fight their way out, they would be surrounded, and the Stalingrad disaster would be repeated. Hausser asked repeatedly for permission to withdraw, but the answer was always the same: "Kharkov will be held to the last man." By February 14 Hausser and his soldiers were nearly completely surrounded, so Hausser, exercising his battlefield prerogative, ignored his Fuhrer and evacuated the city of Kharkov.

Hausser's escape from Stalin's rapidly closing circle at Kharkov saved his divisions and many others. Even though Das Reich and the Leibstandarte had suffered serious losses during their Kharkov defense and subsequent retreat, Hausser's decisive action enabled them to retain most of their fighting capabilities. This act of disobedience infuriated Hitler, but Hausser was soon proven right. The Russians, seeing Hitler's Elite SS troops retreat, interpreted this action as proof that the Germans were beaten and were running to escape across the Dnieper River. Nothing could have been further from the truth. Field Marshal Manstein was regrouping, and he lured the Soviets into over-extending themselves so he could smash their advancing columns before launching his own counter offensive.

The first phase of Manstein's counterattack was designed to stop and isolate the spearheads of the various advancing Russian Armies. One of the Russian units posing a threat was the Soviet Sixth Army, which was making a mad dash for the Dnieper River. On February 19 Das Reich tore into the flank of that Russian force. Fighting was fierce and unforgiving, and after stopping the Soviet advance, Manstein decided to recapture Kharkov. He sent the SS Panzer Corp under Paul Hausser to accomplish the task.

The selection of the SS Panzer Corps to lead the attack on Kharkov represented a change in attitude that high-ranking Wehrmacht officers had held about the Waffen SS. Early in the war the Wehrmacht looked down on the SS as undisciplined wild men who suffered unnecessarily high casualties because of their excessive fanaticism. By the third Battle of Kharkov in March of 1943, however, the SS's outstanding performance had convinced officers like Manstein that the presence of the SS was a great advantage.

General Hausser and the Waffen SS Panzer Corps completed the final capture of Kharkov in six days. A savage battle erupted between Stalin's Guard Regiments and Hitler's Special Legions, but by March 15 the city was again in German control. Manstein saw the chance to encircle a vast number of Soviet armies in the area around Kursk and decided to press on with his attack. Unfortunately for the Germans, "General Mud" came to the rescue of the Russians. The spring rains turned the Russian roads into knee-deep mud, and all operations came to a standstill. Fighting both the Soviets and the mud, the SS Panzer Corps was able to take the city of Belgorod on March 18, but at that point Manstein's group was forced to a halt. The advance was stopped, but after six weeks of constant combat, numbing fatigue, blowing snow, freezing cold and sloppy mud, Das Reich finally had the opportunity to relax, heal its wounds, and get some mail.

Kharkov and the other German victories helped restore the Germans' reputation, but the Stalingrad loss clearly had tarnished the Nazis' superman image.

———

It was March 28 before the mail caught up with Das Reich. Kurt held Erika's letters in his battered hands and stared at the writing on the outside of the envelopes. He had finally regained his strength after a week's rest from combat, but the emotional strain still permeated his soul. He had become used to death and its ugliness, but any soldier who retained an ounce of humanity had to feel the loss, the terror, the unbelievable human suffering and agony produced by this war.

Leaning against his backpack and closing his eyes, a panorama of the last six weeks flashed before Kurt's eyes like images on a movie screen: frozen carcasses, dismembered bodies, men intertwined in mortal combat, and, always, the faces of friends he would never see again. The hardest loss to bear had been that of his best childhood friend from Ansbach, Ernst Meyer. Kurt recalled his little talk with Ernst back in France when Ernst had just joined his company, and in his first taste of combat, Ernst was killed. He had been charging across an anti-tank ditch in the outskirts of Kharkov during the drive to recapture the city and was caught by an enemy machine gunner and ripped to pieces. Later in the day Kurt had become nauseous as he passed the mutilated body of his boyhood friend.

Ernst's death was just one of many that Kurt privately mourned. The "old man," Lieutenant Schneider, had been blown apart by a T-34 shell, and Kurt's good friend and fellow officer Captain Dieter Wolff had simply disappeared as he led a squad of men into a building in Belgorod that disintegrated in a devastating explosion. Their faces mingled with countless others as Kurt mentally recited a litany of the dead.

Continuing his mental human inventory, Kurt moved on to friends who had survived, but had been seriously wounded. Sergeants Weber and Schmidt were recuperating in a field hospital, hoping to be back in action within a month, and brother Jurgen had lost an arm during the battle at Kharkov and was rehabilitating in Berlin. Kurt felt somewhat alone knowing his older brother was no longer nearby, and he wondered whether Walter Kruger, who had been with the Twenty-Ninth Motorized Infantry at Stalingrad, was dead or in a prison camp.

Emotionally spent, Kurt put down the letters from Erika without opening them and walked outside to survey the area where Das Reich was recovering from its battlefield ordeals. He viewed the mass of fatigued men and battered equipment and wondered whether it had been worth it. Amidst the bleak surroundings, Kurt felt a surge of pride in what he and Das Reich had done, knowing how well they had performed their duty. He still believed it was worth it if they could accomplish their goal of smashing the Bolsheviks to ensure Germany's freedom from Russian domination. Remembering Erika's plea to "end the war soon," he went back inside to read her letters. Before opening the first one, he paused, took off his ring and read Erika's inscription, "My love forever, Erika,

10-23-42." Then Kurt read her letters one by one, over and over until he fell asleep, dreaming of a little, far-off stream that flowed into a peaceful pond surrounded by evergreens.

The next day Kurt sent off letters to Erika, his parents, and Aunt Hilda and Uncle Konrad. Then he re-read Erika's letters. The pain of Erika's absence burned more intensely with each word. Kurt realized how lucky he had been for so long and wondered if he would survive to see her again. He calculated that since 1940 he had spent about four hundred and twenty days in a combat situation, and his only real injury was the loss of a couple of toes from frostbite.

"Captain Heisler, where are you?" laughed Oskar Arntzen.

"Someplace you've never been," grunted Kurt.

"What a mess this place is. Belgorod is shot to hell. You can hardly find a place to live. The roads are like tar pools. Our men spend more time pushing out stuck vehicles than fighting."

"Such is the life of a soldier."

"Oh, shut up!"

"Well, Oskar, you've said that to me how many times?"

"Apparently too many."

"How's your company shaping up?" asked Kurt.

"About as well as can be expected considering what we've all been through. How about you?"

"The same."

Captain Arntzen couldn't refrain from launching into one of his speculative speeches." "I figure in about two months, around June 1, we should be ready to deal Ivan the final blow. The roads should be dry, and we should be back to full strength and ready to go, and I say, the sooner the better. The more time the Russians have to build up their fortifications, the harder they'll be to dislodge. But, you never know about our High Command. They'll probably figure out some reason to delay things."

As usual, Captain Arntzen was correct in his judgment regarding the German High Command. April and May came and went, and by the middle of June the German Army had still made no move to attack the Kursk salient. The salient was a bulge in the German line occupied by the Russians that presented a tempting target for a classic Panzer pincers movement. Both sides knew it was only a matter of time before the Germans launched an attack, but the debate between Hitler and his generals about where and when to attack raged for months. Field Marshal Manstein had urged an attack as early as May 1. He and many other German generals warned Hitler that if he waited too long, two things were likely to occur. First, the Russian defenses would be too strong to attack; second, the Allies would land in Sicily or Italy, and the troops needed to attack the Kursk salient would have to be transferred to one of those areas.

General Guderian—who had led the fast Panzer divisions of Army Group Center in 1941 only to be sacked after his failure to capture Moscow—urged the German High Command to let the Russians attack first. Guderian had been recalled to help rebuild the depleted tank reserves and had produced remarkable results. He argued that the new Panther tank had not been battle tested and should not be sent straight into a major battle without first being given time to work out potential problems. By letting the Russians attack first and extend themselves, the Germans could buy some time so the newly refurbished German Army could then swoop in and annihilate them.

Finally, after months of debate, disagreement and vacillation, Hitler gambled Germany's fate on one roll of the dice and set the date for Operation Citadel for July 5, 1943. The Germans had assembled an awesome military force for Operation Citadel, which comprised two sectors, north and south. Field Marshal von Kluge assumed overall command in the north, and Field Marshal von Manstein led the south. For the north the Ninth Army under Colonel-General Model consisted of thirteen divisions for the attack, two divisions in reserve, six divisions in the line and about seven hundred aircraft from the Sixth Air Fleet for air support. In the south Colonel-General Hoth commanded an even more powerful force: fifteen attack divisions, four divisions in the line, two divisions in reserve and eleven hundred aircraft from the Fourth Air Fleet. Hoth's group also included a thousand tanks and four hundred assault guns for the southern front that was only fifty miles wide. The southern attack force was further divided into two parts: The Fourth Panzer Army, which was to strike north and join up with Model's forces to encircle the Soviet's Armies in the salient; Army Detachment Kemp, which was to strike east and cover Fourth Panzer Army's flank and intercept any Soviet reserves coming into the battle. German formations had been rehearsing their plans for months, and every detail of the offensive had been repeatedly reviewed. Never had such firepower been assembled in such a small area. German soldiers felt confident that no enemy could withstand such an onslaught.

The Germans knew that the Russians had amassed an even greater force of men and material and had constructed an elaborate system of trenches, anti-tank positions, minefields, artillery concentrations, tanks and air support. The Soviets' positions were echeloned in unprecedented depth and nearly impregnable. After breaking through one maze of trenches, the German forces would simply run into another. To counter this defensive line, the Germans were relying on the element of surprise and sheer brute strength to break through.

CHAPTER XIII

The White Rose

It was a good day, full of the freshness of spring. Erika was having coffee with her best friend at the University, Katarina Steen. Both ladies were in a cheerful mood and enjoying their time together. Erika had just received a long-awaited letter from Kurt telling her that he was healthy and resting somewhere on the Russian steppe, so she was able to put aside her worries for a little while. The two friends had been chatting happily for nearly an hour, catching up on things, when Katarina asked a question that was totally off the subject.

"Erika, have you ever heard of Sophie Scholl and the White Rose?"

"Of course, hasn't everyone?"

"Not really. I'm sure our government prefers that most Germans don't know the White Rose ever existed. Have you read any of their writings?"

Erika smiled sweetly. "No. Why would anyone read such treason? How can we survive as a nation if people are allowed to question der Fuhrer?"

"Exactly," agreed Katarina. "I talked with someone who'd read one of the leaflets, and he said it was just pure communist garbage, and no respectable German should bother with it."

Erika was becoming strangely uncomfortable, and she began to nervously twist her hair with the fingers of her left hand. She was about to change the subject back to more cheerful topics when Katarina made a comment that created a knot in Erika's stomach.

"I ask you, Erika, why would a smart young girl ever commit herself to an endeavor that would certainly lead to her death? Treason can never be justified, especially by people like Sophie Scholl. She got what she deserved."

At home that evening, Erika was still uneasy. She was, in fact, well acquainted with Sophie Scholl and the White Rose and wasn't sure why she had been less than honest with Katarina. For reasons unknown to Erika, someone had sent her a copy of all the White Rose essays. She had glanced through a few pages and then rather disinterestedly stored them in her closet without even mentioning them to her parents. Initially she was going to throw the leaflets away, but something compelled her to save them. Now she wasn't sure what was making her uneasy. She wasn't worried about being caught with treasonous material. Who would ever search the von Klugemann home for such an item? Was Katarina's question some kind of trap? Could Katarina have been the anonymous source of the leaflets? Erika decided that there had to be something about the papers themselves that was creating her uneasiness, so she got them out of the closet and read them one by one.

As she read the leaflets, Erika recalled the history of the White Rose. It had been founded in late 1942 by Hans Scholl and four other like-minded University of Munich students who began debating the morality of blindly accepting the views of the Nazi regime. During the last half of 1942 they published four essays entitled "Leaflets of the White Rose" and were then joined by a Professor Huber, who wrote the final two essays called "Leaflets of the Resistance."

Borrowing from the Greek philosophers, the White Rose leaflets championed individual freedom and responsibility while rejecting submission to the mob. The writers proclaimed that the State is never an end in itself, but exists to serve the development of the individual. The publications challenged ordinary German citizens to stop being complacent and urged them to protest the evils of Nazidom and rebel against tyranny.

In the middle of a world war, the White Rose dared the German population to stand up to Hitler.

The leaflets were cranked out by hand, placed in envelopes, stuffed into suitcases, and carried to various cities in southern Germany where they were mailed to people selected at random. All members of the White Rose participated in the distribution. The bottom of the last page of each essay contained the following request: "Please duplicate and distribute".

Predictably, the White Rose was short-lived. Hans Scholl and his sister Sophie were arrested at the University of Munich for distributing inflammatory material on February 18, 1943. They were questioned by the Gestapo for four days and guillotined on February 22. Remnants of the movement continued to surface for a while in Munich and Hamburg, but eventually all its members wound up in Nazi prisons and concentration camps. All six original members of the White Rose were executed by the Gestapo.

Sitting on the floor of her closet and feeling like a spy reading classified documents, Erika read all of the leaflets a second time. Still feeling uneasy, she stood up and paced back and forth in her bedroom and began a discussion with herself. "Erika Heisler, you're acting very childish. Why are you so troubled because of Sophie Scholl? Is it because you don't know who sent you the White Rose stuff? Is it because you don't understand why they sent it to you? Do you think it could be because of your father's business dealings with the Third Reich?"

Erika stopped in mid-stride and stood motionless. She tried to erase an image etched in her memory, but she couldn't. Staring at the ceiling, she renewed her internal interrogation. "Did Sophie deserve to die for protesting against the government? Was it the duty of the people to support their leaders no matter what? Was it possible that Hitler and the Nazis were wrong?"

Erika stomped the floor with her right foot, went to her bed, sat down and blurted out, "Erika, you're thinking treasonous thoughts, stop it."

Doubt had never been Erika's companion. She had always been sure of herself and her position in the world. Consequently, she was ill-prepared when hesitation, uncertainty and distrust began to creep into her consciousness. Erika wondered to herself, "Are these feelings of confusion and doubt because of the disaster at Stalingrad? Are they caused by my fear for the safety of my husband? What?"

Erika closed her eyes and saw an image that wouldn't go away, and realized it was the source of her uneasiness. It was the image of a young woman calmly waiting to be beheaded as she stood up for her belief in the dignity of man.

———

Captain Kurt Heisler was supremely confident. As he looked over the vast sea of military might of which he was a part, he felt that this was the best chance to fulfill Erika's plea to end the war in Russia. The SS Panzer Corps made up the right wing of the Fourth Panzer Army attacking Kursk from the south. Just west of Belgorod the three SS divisions—Leibstandarte, Das Reich, and Totenkopf—were poised to rip into the Soviet defenses. The three Waffen SS divisions included more than six hundred tanks and assault guns, and many of the new devastating Tiger tanks. The battle plan called for the heavy Tigers to form the point of a wedge that would penetrate the Russian defense; the lighter tanks would form the outer sides of the wedge, and the motorized infantry would occupy the middle.

On the Southern Front, Operation Citadel began a day early so the German forces could quickly capture a series of hills just inside the Soviet lines that would provide the German artillery spotters a clear field of vision. On the night of July 3 German engineers cleared a path through the Russian mine fields. Then, on the afternoon of July 4 the Fourth Panzer Army attacked and got a taste of what Operation Citadel would be like: pure hell. They succeeded in gaining the high ground, but the fighting was brutal, and they incurred heavy losses. That night as they rested and got ready for the climatic beginning of Citadel, Kurt and Oskar visited at the regimental briefing.

"Today went rather well," Oskar stated.

"We lost too many men," grumbled Kurt.

"Not as many as Ivan did, and by the time we're done, Ivan will be reduced to a pile of shit," Captain Arntzen's voice was almost a shout.

"Remember, nothing is impossible for the Waffen SS, and God help those who oppose us."

"Well spoken, Captain Heisler. I know the Russians think they're ready for us, but I don't think they really know what's going to hit them tomorrow."

Contemplating Oskar's statement, Kurt added, "These next few days will decide the fate of the Fatherland, and we must defeat the Soviets. We must, Oskar, we must!"

"That's why we're here, Herr Captain. You send the best to the most difficult situations."

"We also have some rather good help, like the Third Panzer Division, the Grossdeutschland Division, the ... "

"Yes, I agree, we aren't alone, but we're always in front, always."

The two young Captains embraced each other, wished each other well and went back to their men.

———

Early on the morning of July 5 the Luftwaffe met and defeated the Russian Air Force in the skies over the Southern Front of Operation Citadel. That left the Stukas and bombers free to rain a torrent of destruction on the Soviet fortifications facing Hoth's Fourth Panzer Army. A massive artillery barrage pounded the Russian forward positions into a state of chaos and confusion. Kurt looked at his watch—only five minutes before the signal for the attack. He took off his ring and stared at Erika's inscription, "My love forever," and then he thought of the statue of the Nordic warrior. The time to be the ultimate warrior had arrived.

"For the Fatherland!" Kurt screamed as he led his company of Panzer Grenadiers after the armored spearhead and into the steaming inferno called the Battle of Kursk. Resistance was fierce, but the air and artillery attack had succeeded in flattening much of the Soviet front-line positions. Two unexpected factors hampered the Soviets' ability to stop the onslaught of the Waffen SS. Stuka dive-bombers had been equipped with thirty millimeter anti-tank cannons and were being used on Soviet tanks with devastating effect, and the Germans' ground support aircraft were using a new type of high-fragmentation bomb; the bombs contained clusters of mini-bombs that exploded just above the Soviet anti-tank crews with horrendous results.

The Soviet trenches and bunkers were a different story, however; they had to be blasted and stormed by the Grenadiers. The maze of trenches had been developed in great depth, and Soviet fields of fire had been calibrated so their machine guns covered every step the German forces would have to cross. The day was already hot, and dust churned up from tank treads and explosions hung in the air before settling on the soldiers' uniforms and skin. Gritty furrows of sweat and dust creased the faces of Kurt's men as they tore their way through the Russian trenches.

"Schmidt," Kurt ordered, "take three men and knock out that bunker over on that mound at the end of the trench. We can't move forward until it's blown."

While Sergeant Schmidt grabbed a demolition charge and began crawling toward the Soviet bunker, Kurt motioned to another squad to attack a Russian machine gun nest at the other end of the trench. Two of the men providing cover fire for Sergeant Schmidt were quickly shot dead, but they had bought enough time for Schmidt to maneuver close enough to hurl his satchel into the bunker. After an enormous explosion Schmidt and the other soldier picked off the few dazed survivors as they staggered from the smoking bunker.

At the opposite end of the trench, the squad attacking the machine gun emplacement was having more difficulty. They had already lost three men and were pinned down. Without waiting to give an order, Kurt took off around a small ridge below the trench as he yelled to anyone in hearing distance, "Cover me." As he crawled through the grass, he was forced to cross over dead and mangled bodies. Stopping to catch his breath, he found his hand in the entrails of a corpse's stomach, but didn't even flinch. His hands and knees were soaked red with German and Russian blood.

A Russian rose up immediately in front of Kurt and leveled his gun at Kurt's head, but before he could pull the trigger his body was riddled with machine gun fire. Kurt turned and saw two privates from his company behind him. "Thought you might need some help, Captain. Let's go!" one of the men yelled. The trio ran forward about thirty yards and threw themselves into a slight depression to rest when a new threat arose.

"Tank ... coming around that hill!" yelled Private Kholler.

"Stay down," ordered Kurt. "Maybe they haven't seen us, and I've only got one demolition charge. We need that for the machine gun."

As the T-34 made straight for Captain Heisler's small group, there was a loud "kabooom" as the turret was blown straight up, and a column of smoke poured out of the lurching tank chassis. A Panzerjager squad had seen the advancing T-34 and had come to the rescue. Kurt barely had time to acknowledge his good fortune, but he signaled a quick "well-done" to the squad as it disappeared to hunt another Russian tank.

"Captain, give me your demo charge. Officers charge bunkers only as a last resort."

Soon Kholler was inching closer to the machine gun nest. When he got within ten yards, he stood up and charged the Soviet position, but was cut down within a few steps. Kurt assumed he was dead, but somehow Kholler continued moving forward and, while holding onto the charge, dove into the machine gun emplacement, blowing up himself and the Russian crew. Kurt quickly turned and yelled to his company to advance to the next series of trenches.

All day long, into the night and continuing the next day, Das Reich and the other divisions of the Fourth Panzer Army attacked with unrelenting fury. The deepest penetration made on the first two days was by the SS Panzer Corps, who advanced twenty miles into the Soviet defense by July 6. Hausser's Panzers had torn a large gap in the Soviet defense system, and he intended to exploit it. On July 7 his three divisions fanned out into open countryside. The Leibstandarte and Totenkopf turned to the north, in the direction of Kursk, while Das Reich headed northeast toward a town called Prokhorovka.

As Das Reich fought its way toward Prokhorovka, Soviet resistance grew stronger and stronger. The endless steppe was usually obscured in smoke and dust, except during occasional downpours that turned the streams into rivers and the trails into mud. Smells and sounds of war overpowered the men's senses, again testing their mental and physical limits to the point of exhaustion. German troops had been given food and ammunition for five days, and after a week of constant combat the forces of the Fourth Panzer Army were running short of everything. On the other side of the line, the Russians were replenished daily. To make matters even worse, the Germans were losing the numbers game. Only adrenalin and a euphoric feeling of invincibility kept the German forces moving forward, as they ignored their horrible losses of men and material.

Resting on the night of July 11, Kurt looked over his company. Its strength had been cut in half. Sergeant Schmidt, who had survived all the battles since 1940, was dead, blown apart by a grenade as he charged a Russian strongpoint. Kurt and Second Lieutenant Huber were the only officers left in Kurt's company. As he gazed at his exhausted, battered men, Kurt questioned whether they could continue to take such heavy losses. As he took a long drink of water, he felt a hand on his shoulder.

"Kurt, how are you holding up?"

Kurt turned to see Oskar, who had a bloody bandage around his left ear and another around his right shoulder. "Apparently much better than you."

"Well, at least I haven't lost any more body parts," laughed Oskar. "I don't know if I can look down another fucking Russian trench or blow up another bunker. This has to end. I've heard some rumors that don't sound too good, but maybe it'll force us to try a little harder. What the hell, we've only been going half-speed, right, Heisler?"

"What rumors?"

"I suppose we'll find out something at tonight's briefing, but a colonel told me he just heard the Allies landed on Sicily yesterday. He also said that Model's attack in the north is not going as well as expected. He's even in danger of being forced on the defensive, which is bad news for us. Do you recall any successful half-pincer movements from our military history class, Captain?

Kurt had to laugh at Oskar's attempt at humor. "No, Oskar, and I hope your info is wrong. Things are bad enough already."

"Shit, we'll just have to defeat Ivan by ourselves, then. Come on, let's go find out what light duties are in store for us tomorrow."

———

At the briefing Captains Heisler and Arntzen learned that the rumors Oskar had heard were basically true. Model's attack had stalled, and on July 10 the Allies had invaded Sicily. In addition, Army Detachment Kemp had not made the quick progress in the south that the German command had hoped for, and the Soviet Fifth Guards Tank Army was heading toward Prokhorovka without resistance. This turn of events forced the commanding generals to take a desperate, all or nothing gamble, and they introduced the new strategy at the meeting. The revised battle plan called for Model to make a final effort to break though the Russian defenses on July 12 and advance on Kursk from the north. Also on July 12 Colonel-General Hoth would unleash all his tanks to attack the Soviet Fifth Guards Tank Army near Prokhorovka. Meanwhile, Kemp's southern force, especially the Sixth Panzer Division, would push to Prokhorovka to join Hoth's group. If these three armored forces could link up in time to coordinate a major attack, they just might be able to smash all the Soviet forces in the area.

As Kurt and Oskar walked together back to their companies, Oskar said gravely, "Kurt, I hope to God, whatever he is, that I'm wrong, but I don't think we can win tomorrow. We've given everything, and we'll continue to do so, but I think we've tried to do too much, and history will be our judge."

Kurt had never seen this negative side of Oskar before and asked, "Meaning what?"

"I really don't know what I mean, except maybe we aren't as superior as we think that we ... Oh, what the hell's the matter with me? I've become morbid and stupid in my old age."

"I can't believe that you of all people would say such a thing, Oskar. You're the most avid Nazi I know."

"I'm sorry for sounding weak and sentimental, but I guess it's a feeling that just came over me. Kurt, I don't think I'll survive tomorrow. It's funny, I've never felt like this before, and it's like I need to make amends or something. I feel like saying I'm sorry, but I don't really know for what or to whom. I still believe in our cause, but I'm actually scared for the first time in my life. I suppose that can do strange things to someone who's never experienced it before."

"Oskar, we all get that feeling once in a while, but I bet you're going to be around to introduce me to all those Lebensborn children you keep bragging about. Hell, you'll probably be introducing me to their grandchildren some day, too. Tomorrow will be just another day for us."

The two friends shook hands and parted, both trying not to linger on the conversation any longer.

On July 12, 1943, Colonel-General Model never made his attack on the Northern Sector. A Soviet offensive to his rear forced him to call off the attack. To exacerbate the problem for the Germans, Army Detachment Kemp was unable to reach the battlefield at Prokhorovka, so the German forces that were already there were slightly outnumbered. The battle was waged between two elite armored forces, the Soviet Fifth Guards Tank Army and Hausser's Waffen SS Panzer Corps. Some fifteen hundred tanks and assault guns assembled on the field of battle on July 12, making it the largest clash of armor in history.

As Hausser's three Waffen SS Divisions advanced early in the morning, they ran straight into elements of the Soviet Fifth Guards Tank Army, and a battle of epic proportions was joined. The German Tigers were superior to the Russian T-34s in armor protection and in the range and firepower of their cannons, but the Soviet forces negated this advantage by charging right into the German formation, forcing the battle to be fought at close range. In effect, it was the equivalent of hand-to-hand combat between tanks.

Chaos and confusion were the orders of the day; clouds of dust, burning tanks, falling planes, artillery explosions, endless machine gun chatter and the constant screams of the dying created a battle scene of inconceivable magnitude. Hundreds of tanks chased each other across open fields, battled among small orchards, and roared through shallow valleys. As the forces collided, it became difficult to tell friend from foe. Communication and coordination among Waffen SS tank groups, which had always worked to their advantage in the past, became impossible. Overhead, the opposing air forces battled continuously for air supremacy.

Kurt and the Grenadiers of Das Reich had dug in on the southern edge of the battle and were trying to protect their right flank from repeated assaults by the Soviet Second Guards Tank Corp. Kurt's men had established a defensive position in a small depression and were firing at the advancing Russian infantry. To assist them, assault guns had been partially buried throughout the lines in fortified pits to be used as anti-tank emplacements. Other companies of Das Reich were on both flanks, and Captain Arntzen was in command of a company just to Kurt's left. Throughout the day the men of the Waffen SS had repelled wave after wave of massed Soviet armor, but as they gathered themselves to fend off the next attack, they were becoming desperate. Nine straight days of combat had sapped the strength of the SS, and many soldiers who had survived the ordeals of combat were collapsing from heat exhaustion.

As Kurt waited for the next attack, large hunks of turf suddenly exploded into fountains of dust as T-34 shells landed along the Waffen SS lines. A T-34 broke through the lines, and two men grabbed demolition charges and went after it. One was machine-gunned by the tank as soon as he cleared the trench. The other almost made it to the side of the tank before he met the same fate. Suddenly, the T-34's turret erupted, and smoke began pouring out of it. The two SS men had momentarily diverted its attention, allowing a passing Tiger tank to disable it, but it was soon replaced by two more T-34s and Soviet infantry that appeared directly in front of Kurt's company.

"Get those tanks now!" Kurt yelled to the Panzerjagers.

A shell exploded near one of the anti-tank guns, flipping it over on its side and killing the soldiers behind the gun's shield. Other soldiers immediately scrambled the gun back into position and began firing at the advancing Soviet tank in a race to see who could react first. The T-34 fired and destroyed the German anti-gun and its crew, but a shell from one of the German assault guns exploded the Russian tank, so, simultaneously, both adversaries became causalities of war. The resultant smell of flesh burning on hot metal added another sickening odor to the already stifling, foul smelling air.

"Infantry breaking through on the right!" someone yelled.

Kurt turned and fired his sub-machine gun into a dozen running Soviet troops, killing seven immediately. The other Soviet tank had been destroyed by a demolition team, so the remaining Soviet troops had no recourse but to surrender. There was no time for Kurt's unit to be hampered with guarding them, so he gave the order to shoot them. It wasn't the first time he had given such a command.

As the battle raged, Kurt sprinted to the right flank to check on Oskar's company. While directing fire at another wave of advancing Soviet armor and infantry, Kurt saw Oskar Arntzen moving into a forward position to better observe developments in front of his company's lines when a T-34 came crashing out of a gully and fired, killing everyone in the line of fire except Oskar. As he began to run back to the main defensive line, the tank's machine gun raked his legs, and he staggered to the ground. The Russian tank rumbled straight at the terrified Captain, who lay helpless, writhing in pain on the ground. Placing its right tread squarely on Oskar's feet, the tank paused, as if to make a point to all the watching SS troops, and then slowly moved forward and churned the screaming Oskar into a bloody pulp of earth, flesh and bone. A rage engulfed Oskar's men, and they quickly overwhelmed the

Soviet tank, pulled out the crew and brutally executed them on the spot.

Kurt, temporarily nauseated, fell to the ground and vomited before being quickly forced back into action. For the remainder of the day every time he killed a Soviet soldier, he fired an extra round into him in memory of his dead friend.

After eight hours of apocalyptic horror, the tank battles for Prokhorovka finally came to an end. The Germans and the Soviets had each lost about three hundred tanks. The Waffen SS had withstood the massed armored attempts to break their lines and forced the Soviets to withdraw from the field of battle, but the Russians had proved they could battle on even terms with Hitler's best. More importantly, Russia could replace the men and tanks they had lost, but Germany could not. Germany had spent the bulk of its armored force during the Battle of Kursk and would never again be able to match Soviet military strength. For the German Army on the Eastern Front, this battle would be the high tide of the Wehrmacht, and Kursk would become known as the German Waterloo.

On July 13 Hitler summoned the two commanders of Operation Citadel—Field Marshals von Kluge and von Manstein—to his headquarters in East Prussia. Hitler informed them he had decided to call off the Operation because of the Allied landing in Sicily and the Italian Army's failure to offer any resistance. Field Marshal von Kluge agreed with Hitler's decision, but Manstein wanted to continue to fight the Russians. He felt success had almost been achieved in the Southern sector, and if Kemp's group could link up with Hausser's Panzer Corps, victory could still be achieved. Hitler was swayed by the argument and allowed Citadel to continue in the Southern sector. The drought around Kursk ended abruptly, however, and Manstein had to continue the campaign in pouring rain. Seeing only limited success after a few more days, Hitler reversed himself. On July 17 he told Manstein that he was taking the SS Panzer Corps out of Citadel and sending them to Italy. Manstein had no choice but to shut down Operation Citadel.

General Hausser was replaced as the commander of the SS Panzer Corps, primarily for his failure to defeat the Soviets at the Battle of Prokhorovka, but also because Hitler still resented Hausser's act of disobedience by retreating from Kharkov the previous February. Originally, all three divisions of the SS Panzer Corps were to be transferred to Italy, but Soviet breakthroughs in the south changed that plan. Field Marshal Manstein needed some mobile troops with lots of dash and firepower, and he talked Hitler into letting him have two of the Waffen SS Divisions making up the SS Panzer Corps—Das Reich and Totenkopf—so only the Leibstandarte was sent to Italy.

The SS Divisions had been badly battered during the Battle of Kursk, but they still remained a powerful attack force and were sent south to the Donets region in late July. There, in a series of actions north of the Sea of Azov near Stalino, the SS Divisions were instrumental in halting the advancing Soviets and stabilizing the front. As a reward for their success, they were immediately sent back north to help stop a massive Soviet thrust breaking out around Belgorod and Kharkov.

By early August Das Reich was being shuttled back and forth plugging gaps as needed to dam the Russian tide. Once again, the soldiers were becoming drained by heat, daily combat, frantic movement, lack of sleep and continuous attacks from the Russian Air Force. In mid-August Das Reich was sent to help the Third Panzer Division stop the Soviet Fifth Guards Tank Army from reaching Kharkov from the north.

———

To stop the Russian advance the Panzer Grenadiers of Das Reich had established concealed positions along the Kharkov-Bugodukhov railway line. Beyond them to the north were endless fields of sunflowers and above them a vast, clear sky that provided no shelter from the scorching sun.

"Captain Heisler, what day is it? I can't keep track any more. Everything just seems like one big blur to me."

"Today, Corporal Kohmer, is the eighth of August, and, I hope, a day of rest. God knows we need one. Try to relax, but have your squad keep ready, because soon our old friends from Prokhorovka, the Fifth Guards, will come screaming out of those sunflowers."

"That's one hell of a pleasant thought, Captain."

"I'm sure the Russians feel the same way," Kurt said with a smile. "Corporal, make sure the men drink plenty of water. This sun really sucks the moisture out of you. And get some rest."

"Yes, Captain, and you get some rest, too."

Kurt tried to heed the corporal's advice as he lay down in the long grass on the railway embankment. He gazed up into the pale blue sky and, except for occasional planes, distant explosions, noisy tanks and the putrid smell of men who had not washed or changed clothes in weeks, it was rather pleasant. For a moment Kurt tried to forget the war and the bloodbath he had been a part of for the past six months.

While Kurt rested, his exhaustion carried him to a trance-like state. He imagined himself merging with the soil, allowing his essence to be absorbed by earth and transported out of the hell he currently inhabited. As the camouflage patterns of his uniform merged with the earthy hue of his surroundings, Kurt rolled side to side, seeing if he could somehow escape into the shadows his movements created in the grass. Minutes ticked away as he continued to drift in his reverie, but soon an errant shell down the line brought him back to the present.

He sat up to dwell on more pragmatic concerns, like how things were in Germany. He wondered if the Allied bombing raids were becoming more frequent and what their effect was on the German people, especially the special people in his life. "Erika, Erika, Erika," Kurt muttered to himself. During the long days of combat he hardly dared think of her because the pain of her absence was so great, especially when he considered the distinct possibility he would never see her again. For the first time in a long while Kurt allowed himself to dwell on his memories of Erika. He remembered his promise to her to end the war against Russia in the summer of '43. He remembered Oskar's comments about maybe not being "superior" and about "trying to do too much" as he replayed Oskar's horrifying death. Kurt had not prayed in earnest in years, but he began to pray. "God, have mercy on me, and forgive me for the evil I have done. Please keep Erika and her family safe. Keep my family safe. Please end this war and return the world to something better."

Kurt was drifting in and out of sleep. He was beyond total exhaustion, and his nerves had been replaced by a tangled mass of burned out circuits. He began to experience a strange, out-of-body sensation. He was a little boy again, holding the statue of his Nordic Warrior as he gazed down at this strange SS person lying on the Russian steppe. Who was this man? Who was Waffen SS Captain Kurt Heisler? And what had he become?

———

On August 19, 1943, the world exploded in front of the Third Panzer and Das Reich Divisions. At dawn the Soviet Fifth Guards came storming through the sunflowers and surrounding fields, and the resulting battle raged all day. The German forces held their ground and destroyed nearly two hundred Soviet T-34 tanks, but it wasn't enough to keep the Russians at bay.

The next day was a repeat as the Soviets attacked again and again. All the instruments of the German orchestra of war—tanks, flak guns, assault guns, 88s—sang their fatal songs as they hurled shells into the Russian ranks. Still the Russians advanced. The situation was beyond Kurt's comprehension. How much misery and pain could man be expected to endure? How much death could he see and remain sane? The

Russians attacked in waves, and Kurt was once again at the very center of the maelstrom. In the midst of the fighting late in the afternoon, a T-34 shell exploded a few yards from Kurt, and then, almost in slow motion, he felt himself flying through the air. He felt no real pain, only a sense of warm numbness, and then ... nothing.

CHAPTER XIV

Revelation and the Anti-Christ

For nearly a month Kurt lay in a state of suspended animation in a Berlin hospital. He had been quite lucky. A self-propelled assault gun had partially shielded him from the explosion. Shrapnel sprayed his lower legs, and flying debris from the exploding assault gun peppered his upper torso, but his vital organs had been spared. Doctors in the field hospital removed most of the shrapnel and sent him on to the Berlin hospital. There the doctors' biggest concern was the severe concussion that had sent Kurt into his deep coma.

To no one's surprise, Maria von Klugemann had stepped in and used all her influence to procure a private room to improve Kurt's chances for recovery. The doctors told Erika and Jurgen, who had rushed to Berlin as soon as possible, that there was really nothing else they could do for Kurt. He could wake up tomorrow, or he might never regain consciousness; if he did, he might suffer from amnesia or motor-control problems. The doctors' only advice was, "Wait and see."

Jurgen stayed only three days, alternating between visits to the hospital and to Countess Louisa von Steinmetz's country estate outside of Berlin before flying back to Italy. The Countess also had an apartment in the city close to Kurt's hospital, and she gave Erika the apartment keys and the use of a car. Erika spent most of her days sitting with Kurt or visiting friends of the von Klugemanns when she needed breaks from hospital duty; she and Louisa also strengthened their friendship during long conversations over dinners. Through it all Erika tried not to think about the awful possibility that Kurt would never speak to her again. It took all her strong-willed character to sustain her belief that everything would be all right, that she and Kurt would be able to hold each other again someday.

———

There was nothing dramatic about Kurt's re-entry into the world of the living. On the evening of September 22, 1943, he simply woke up.

Alone in his room, Kurt began to blink his eyes over and over as he surveyed his surroundings, trying to get his bearings. Next, with great effort, he raised his right arm and then his left, then his right and left legs, slowly inventorying his limbs and assessing his ability to function. His mouth was bone dry from a month's inactivity, and he craved water, but all he could do was work up some saliva and swallow a few times to lubricate his throat. He tested his voice and produced only a hoarse whisper, but everything seemed okay. Satisfied with his physical state and already tiring from this slight activity, Kurt tried to remember anything and everything. He slowly traced back events—his childhood, his marriage, Das Reich, the Russian Front, everything; he even remembered events right up to the explosion.

Transferring his observations outward, Kurt noticed that the wall calendar was turned to September, but no dates had been marked off. He tried to roughly calculate the days since his injury, but the mental effort was too much too soon, and he gave up. Just as he was about to call for someone and proclaim his return to the world, Erika entered the room.

Kurt quickly closed his eyes and remained motionless, trying to sort everything out. How should he announce his resurrection to Erika? As he lay there pondering his next move, Erika walked over to the bed and silently stood by him. She then bent over and gently kissed him on the forehead.

"Can't you do better than that?" Kurt croaked hoarsely as he opened his eyes.

Erika staggered backward in stunned disbelief. Speechless, she just stared at Kurt.

He tried it again. "Say, you look pretty good, fraulein. Why don't you get in bed, and we'll see if I can remember what to do?" The labored croak was still barely understandable to either of them. Erika's eyes were filled with tears, but she was still struggling to form a response, so Kurt pressed on. "I hope the rest of my body works better than my voice, or I'll have to have a serious talk with my doctors."

"Oh, my God, Kurt, I can't believe you're conscious! Thank you, God, for bringing my husband back to me. Thank you, thank you! Kurt, I was afraid I'd never get to talk to you again. I love you!"

Kurt's physical condition was no match for his bravado, however, as he feebly stretched out his hand to Erika, who took it and kissed it lovingly. She pulled a chair close to the bed, sat down and began to sob uncontrollably. She laid her head on Kurt's chest, and he gently stroked her hair. Kurt was still rather confused and disoriented, but he didn't want to return to the world of blackness, so he fought to continue the conversation.

"Erika, I love you so much. There have been many times I was afraid that I'd never see you again. How long have I been unconscious?"

"For over a month, and the doctors and I have been worried that you might not come out of the coma. I'm so happy that you're back with us. I've missed you so much. I was so afraid I'd lost you. Let me go get a doctor to check you over."

"No, wait. I know I'll be asleep again soon, and I want to enjoy you alone for a few more minutes. Just get me a glass of water for my throat. We have a lot of catching up to do. Maybe you can start by telling what's happened to me in the last month."

Erika's tears were flowing almost non-stop, but she composed herself enough to pour Kurt a glass of water and help him nurse it down. After he finished, she said, "Okay, I'll wait a minute or two before I get the doctor, but there isn't much to tell; you haven't moved from that bed since you got here. What's the last thing you remember?"

"Fighting the Russians north of Kharkov and then suddenly flying through the air and landing on my ass."

Erika was encouraged that he remembered that much, but she was apprehensive about asking her next question. "What do you remember about your life?"

"Pretty much everything, I think. You're my sister from Munich, right? Go ahead, ask me something else."

Erika couldn't help but laugh at Kurt's attempt at humor and was relieved that he had retained that part of his personality. Concerned that she might wear him out, Erika asked him a few selective questions, and it quickly became apparent that amnesia was not going to be a problem. Seeing that Kurt was drifting off, and knowing she was pushing her luck, Erika hugged him, kissed him, and said. "I'm so happy you've been returned to me, my love. We'll have lots of time to talk and get caught up, but I'd better run and get a doctor before you fall asleep again."

The doctors were elated at Kurt's recovery. They found no permanent damage, and his memory and other brain-related functions all seemed normal. But a month of lying in bed had left him in no condition to resume any strenuous activity. The medical staff was also concerned that sudden activity might return Kurt to a coma permanently, so they ordered him to stay at the hospital for another month to gradually recover his strength, to be followed by three months of home recovery.

Kurt's physical improvement was dramatic; he became stronger and more alert with each passing day, and the doctors were hopeful that he would recover completely. Erika was amazed at how quickly her future had turned from the unknown to the cautiously optimistic, and within a week of Kurt's awakening, she was immersed in her preparations for his return home. But now that she was convinced Kurt had shaken off death's grip, she worried that what she must soon reveal to him would jeopardize his remarkable progress. The doctors had helped her keep the secret by telling Kurt he couldn't have any other visitors until he gained more strength, and that any undue excitement might hinder his recovery, but he was well past that stage now. They had just told her today that the decision about when to inform him was up to her, but it should be soon because he was becoming suspicious about not having more visitors. Erika had kept her mother and Louisa from visiting Kurt, afraid that they might slip and say something before she did, but it wouldn't be fair to anyone to drag things out longer. She hated that the decision was totally in her hands.

When Erika reached Kurt's room he was sitting up in bed looking quite perky. "Frau Heisler, you're looking particularly splendid today. I must have been crazy to have chosen the army over you. If I'd known how good it is to see you every day and have you take care of me, I would've deserted a long time ago."

"Oh, sure, that's big talk coming from you in a hospital bed, but I distinctly remember someone who could hardly wait to conquer Russia for the Fatherland. How does the Russian Front look to you now?"

"Well, I like it a lot better from here. This scenery is much better, and so are the benefits. Just this morning the doctors told me that I can begin fulfilling my husbandly duties when I regain my strength, and I feel stronger every time I see you walk into the room. But, Erika, you look a little worried today. Are you afraid that I've lost that part of my memory? Maybe you should come a little closer and lie down beside me and see what happens."

"Kurt, that's great news, but for all your bold talk, I think we'd better wait a few more days. It's been a long time, and I'd hate to fuck you into another coma. How could I live with myself?"

Kurt shook with laughter at her crudeness. "Please don't hold back on my account. I'm willing to take the chance. It'd be a lot better than dying in combat."

"Relax, Captain, I'm just testing your sensibilities and trying to make you feel more at home by using a little trench language." Erika wanted to keep the humorous banter going, but she knew her mission was too serious. She walked over to the small table under the window and sat down. "But you are right about one thing; I am a little worried today. Kurt, now that you have come this far there are some things we have to talk about. Come here and sit by me, so we can talk."

"This sounds serious," Kurt said as he got up off the bed and pulled up a chair next to Erika's. "I know you've been troubled by something ever since I woke up, and you've been waiting until I got better to tell me. And the doctors have been strangely vague about why I couldn't have any other visitors. It seems odd that they wouldn't even let me see my family. Is it Jurgen? Did he get killed? Now is as good a time as any to tell me. Whatever it is, I have to deal with it, and you can't keep it inside forever."

Taking Kurt's hand, Erika looked into Kurt's eyes and started softly. "Jurgen's fine. He was actually here for your first three days, but he had to rejoin his unit in Italy. I've kept him informed of your progress, and he hopes to be able to see you soon." She paused and wiped away some tears before continuing. "Kurt, as soon as your parents heard you were here, they called me and made arrangements to pick me up and drive me here. While they were rushing to Nuremberg, their car was broadsided in an intersection, and they were both killed instantly. I'm so sorry, my love."

Kurt sat silently for a minute and then slowly stood up. He offered his hand to Erika and pulled her to her feet. He embraced her tightly without speaking, burying his face in her hair to hide his tears. They both wept softly for several minutes. Then Kurt gathered himself and staggered over to the bed and lay down. Erika joined him there, curling up with her head on his chest.

"When I came home on leaves, there was this unspoken agreement—especially with my mother—that we would not talk about my commitment to Das Reich and all it stood for. Over time I felt that my combat experiences helped me understand their beliefs better, and I was looking forward to telling them how much I respected them for holding fast to their values. I can't believe I won't get that chance. You know, I worried about you and Jurgen and all of my army friends and hoped nothing would happen to any of you, but it never occurred to me that something would happen to my parents, at least not something like a car accident."

After a pause to regain control of his emotions, Kurt continued. "Right now, I just can't comprehend the randomness of it all. I survive a dozen battles against all odds, and they get killed in a traffic accident. Where's the fairness in that? It seems like God is just playing with us!"

"I'm sorry you have to be told like this, Kurt. The doctors said we had to wait a while to tell you because they were afraid the emotional shock might send you over the edge. Jurgen flew home to handle the funeral arrangements while I stayed here with you. Your parents had a lovely service. It seemed like the whole town of Ansbach was there."

They lay in silence for a while longer. "What about your parents? Why haven't they been here to see me?" Kurt asked. "I can't believe your mother hasn't been here every day fussing over me and telling the doctors what they're doing wrong."

"It's not because she hasn't been trying. I made her promise she wouldn't show up and jeopardize your recovery, but I'm sure you'll be seeing her soon now that the news is out. I might as well warn you, I also told everyone we're married. I had to tell the doctors that I was your wife so they could discuss your treatment with me, and there didn't seem to be any point in keeping the secret from others any longer."

Kurt shook his head slightly and sighed. "Better you than me to tell your mother. And how did Frau von Klugemann take the news that her only daughter had deprived her of a showcase wedding?"

"She understood the circumstances, and she took it well. She was just as stunned as the rest of us at the loss of your parents. Their deaths and your injury certainly put things into perspective, and she's happy for us that we got to share the time together as a married couple that we did. She'd just like us to have a bigger ceremony for friends and family when you're up to it."

"Erika, I'm sorry you had to go through all of this and then be the perfect actress in keeping it from me. Are there any other secrets or things that I should know?"

"You should know that I prayed every day that I would give anything if I could have you back for just one hour to tell you how sorry I am that I've been such a spoiled brat at times, and that I love you, but that's no secret."

"And I love you, too, my dear Erika. There were many times I didn't think I'd live long enough to hear you say those words or be able to say them to you. And right now it's hard for me to believe that my mom and dad are dead, that I won't ever be able to tell them I love them and ask them to forgive me for my arrogance."

———

By October, 1943, the war was going badly in Russia. Anyone with a sense of realism understood that victory over the Soviet Union had been lost; at this stage just keeping the Russians from advancing into Germany was going to be difficult. The Western Allies had taken North Africa and Sicily and had landed in Italy in early September. British and American bombers kept increasing the magnitude of the destruction they were inflicting on Germany, and the optimism of the German people was being replaced with a grim determination.

The doctors had been right to worry that bad news could affect Kurt's recovery. The news of his parents' deaths had heightened the internal conflict that had been developing within Kurt, reawakening long-dormant feelings. Even prior to hearing about his parents, Kurt's mind had become a sea of turmoil, flooded with contradictions and changing tides of loyalties. On one hand, he was proud of the sacrifice and courage he and the Waffen SS had displayed on the battlefield and proud of the military success of the German Armies. He was proud of his status in an elite organization and his promotion to Major, with Oak Leaves adorning his Knight's Cross. But on the other hand, these accomplishments also fueled the fire that raged within his inner self. He felt guilty about some of the acts he had committed during the war in Russia and about the gruesome aspects of the SS reputation. He felt guilty about how he had neglected his parents for the past few years. Most of all, he felt guilty about the person he had become.

Outwardly, Kurt showed no sign of lessoning his intensity and commitment to the Waffen SS and the Nazi cause. He hadn't confided in anyone about his personal identity crisis, not even Erika, because he wasn't sure if it was an after-effect of his injury or a real shift in his beliefs. He hesitated to burden her until he had sorted everything out.

Kurt was thankful that his condition allowed him the luxury of being able to say he was tired and then feigning sleep whenever he felt he was close to revealing too much of himself. He could then just close his eyes and contemplate both sides of his situation. He wondered if he would be having the same misgiving about the war if Germany had defeated the Soviet Union and the war in the East had been won. Was he making excuses because things were starting to go bad or was he really having a renaissance of conscience regarding the morality of war itself? His internal self-examination went on for days without resolution.

One October day Kurt's musings were mercifully broken by the long-postponed visit from Maria von Klugemann. She arrived without fanfare, but in typical Maria fashion, quickly sucked all the air out of the room. This time, though, Kurt was thankful for Maria's overbearing exuberance.

"Major Heisler, can you believe the staff has kept me from seeing my own son-in-law all this time? Even after I told them I was a personal friend of der Fuhrer, they would not let me in. I may not be a doctor, but one would think that a veteran of the Eastern Front could certainly face his mother-in-law for a few minutes without slipping into a coma. How are you doing, Kurt? Are they treating you well? Do you need anything? Do you want me to talk to someone about getting you out of here sooner? I got you a private room, you know. At least they didn't interfere with that. And you and Erika are married! I can't believe she kept it from us all this time. But given the circumstances, you two did the right thing, and

Frederick and I are so thrilled to have you in the family. Now that you've recovered, though, we have to have a real wedding ceremony, and let me tell you what I've planned so far. To begin with … "

"Frau von Klugemann, I see you still don't need anyone else to carry on a conversation. But let me just say it's good to see you, especially knowing that I am now your son-in-law. Thank you for understanding our reasons for not telling you about our marriage and for taking such good care of Erika in my absence. Please forgive me if I can't talk too long, but I have this habit of falling asleep without warning. Why don't you continue telling me about the reception you're planning for us?"

"Why, thank you, Kurt. That silly Erika told me you didn't want to hear anything about this, but I was sure that a hero of the Reich would want to share his happiness with his brothers-in-arms. Here's what I was thinking about a guest list … "

Kurt trailed off after the third sentence or so, without even having to pretend he was sleeping.

———

Just about the time Kurt was feeling he would have to break down and confess his doubts to Erika, a new point of reference was added to his search for meaning, Count Gunther von Kresbach. By mid-October Kurt was physically well enough to take on a roommate, and Count Kresbach was moved into the same room. The Count came from an old, established line of Prussian aristocrats who had served in the military out of duty to the Fatherland rather than allegiance to the Nazis or Adolf Hitler. He was a Colonel in the Third Panzer Division and had been severely wounded during the Battle of Kursk. Kurt was glad for the company, if only for breaking the monotony of his recovery routines.

For the first few days the two German officers regarded each other with a degree of suspicion, engaging primarily in polite conversations about the war and comparing experiences from Russia. Colonel Kresbach had never had an occasion to visit with a member of the SS, and he regarded all SS personnel as members of a group without morals. During the course of the war on the Eastern Front he had come to respect the Waffen SS for their abilities as soldiers, but he had many questions about their other activities. Kurt was equally ignorant of the regular German Army's attitude about the SS, and he was interested in the Count's perceptions. Gradually, as they became more comfortable with each other, the topics of conversation between Kurt and the Count grew more intense and personal.

One morning after breakfast the Count took the conversation to a new level. "Major Heisler, if I may be so bold as to ask, why did you choose to join the Waffen SS instead of the regular army?"

Kurt surveyed the Count before answering. Count von Kresbach was much older than Kurt, about forty-two, with white hair and a white mustache. He had been shot in both legs and was slowly starting to walk again, but be was usually in a wheelchair most of the day. Kurt often pushed him around the hospital grounds, especially during their most private conversations, like today. Kurt stopped the wheelchair under a large tree. The ground was covered with brightly-colored leaves that loudly crunched as they crumbled under Kurt's feet and the wheels of the wheelchair. Kurt parked the Count so his chair was facing a bench next to the tree and then sat down facing him.

"To be honest, Colonel, I'm not entirely sure. I suppose it was a combination of things: my involvement in the Hitler Youth, my brother's membership in the Leibstandarte, my friendship with Erika and her family and my desire to impress them, but mostly the influence of my brother Jurgen"

"Yes, you've told me about Jurgen already. But how did he convince you? What did he say?"

"He never told me to join the SS in any overt way, but he was so confident and elegant when he came home that I wanted to look and act like he did."

"But he must have said something that provided you with encouragement or inspiration."

"Well, I remember a very short speech he gave me as he was going back to rejoin the Leibstandarte after his first visit home. He asked me what I was going to do to help the Fatherland. I said that I supposed I would become a soldier. Jurgen stared at me and said that if I was going to do that, I might as well join the best, the Leibstandarte. He said the SS Army was small in numbers, but would grow in time; he also said that with him already in the SS, I'd have no trouble getting in somewhere. Truthfully, though, I don't think he would have had to say anything; that black uniform said everything."

The Count stared intensely at Kurt. "Do you consider yourself a true believer of the Nazi doctrine?"

"Yes, I do."

"Are you sure, Kurt? I've visited many times with you during the past two weeks, and I cannot escape the feeling that you're searching for something. I think you're unsure of your present situation."

"Why do you say that? I've never voiced any second thoughts about my duty and honor as a member of Das Reich."

"True, but I think you're starting to look beyond your duty to the SS and are seeking answers to some much deeper questions that we all need to address."

Kurt got up from the bench and began to pace in front of the Count's wheelchair, loudly crunching leaves as he walked. In an agitated voice, he said, "The only question we need to address is how to win the war, and no one is better suited to do that than the Waffen SS."

"Well, as long as you want to start talking about the Waffen SS, let me ask you a couple more questions. First of all, what do you know about the Einsatzgruppen?"

"I know more about them now than I did back in '41 when they were functioning. They were SS thugs who killed Soviet political leaders, Jews and other undesirables behind the front lines during Barbarossa. Since we of the true Waffen SS were always in the most advanced positions on the field of battle, we were far too busy to be concerned with such stupidity."

Count Kresbach paused and seemed to be pondering Kurt's answer, but he soon persisted in his relentless quest to pierce Kurt's soul.

"I thought there was some exchange between front line SS troops and the Einsatzgruppen and that you often were detailed to hunt down and kill partisans in the rear areas, which is where many of your atrocities were committed."

"I'm not on trial here, am I, Herr Colonel? For the record, I don't appreciate your innuendos. I don't know anyone in my company who had any connection to the Einsatzgruppen, and, as for the partisans, they were a problem for every German soldier on the Eastern Front, including your Third Panzer Division. We all had to deal with the situation the best we could. We of the Waffen SS are not to be confused with other parts of the SS. We're first and foremost soldiers, soldiers who want to be in the most dangerous and pivotal places, soldiers who expect to do the impossible. War is cruel and unfair. It's not a place for the timid and merciful. We have a unique passion for battle, and our officers lead from the front."

"Maybe that's why you lose so many officers, and your casualty rates are so ridiculously high."

"Since when has bravery been a crime in the destruction of the enemy?"

Sensing he had pressed this particular issue far enough, Colonel von Kresbach jumped to another question. "I accept your answer for now, Major Heisler, but what about the SS running the concentration camps? You do know about the camps, don't you?"

"Again, I really don't know much, and I don't care to know. My job, and that of my division, is to fight. We don't run camps. I've talked to a few men who were wounded who said they spent some time as camp guards while they were recuperating, but there weren't very many, and I really didn't pay much attention to them. Ivan kept us as busy as we wanted. So why don't you tell me what you know about the camps?"

Colonel von Kresbach straightened up in his wheelchair. "I apologize, Major. I've asked you a question that I don't know a lot about, either, but I've heard from a number of sources that the final solution to the Nazi problem of what to do with the Jews is to send them to special camps where they're all to be exterminated."

"We're soldiers, not butchers. We need to stop the Bolsheviks, or they'll destroy our civilization as we know it, and many Jews are

Bolsheviks. I see no reason to kill German Jews, but they need to be carefully watched so they can't hinder Germany's growth." Kurt realized that he was shouting his response to Colonel von Kresbach, and he forced himself to calm down. "You seem to have put me on the defensive, Count, and I'm surprised by how agitated I've become. The true Waffen SS members have nothing to hide. Our record speaks for itself. But why are you asking me all these questions? I'm just a soldier who was wounded fighting for his country, just like you."

"I apologize, Major, for being so abrupt in my questioning. I admit I was testing you just a little. It goes without saying that no one can question the courage and tenacity of Das Reich and the other divisions of the Waffen SS. Let's talk again sometime about the solution to Germany's problems, but for now let's enjoy this beautiful fall day with more pleasant topics."

———

That night, waiting for sleep to rescue him from his mental torment, Kurt mulled over the discussion with Count Kresbach. Kurt knew he had answered all of the Count's questions honestly, but he wondered if he had deliberately avoided knowing about issues like the concentration camps. He had been so involved in the war and with Erika that he had not paid much attention to anything else, but was all this just a rationalization to avoid any personal responsibility?

Kurt was proud of Germany and its people, but he was unsure about parts of the Nazi doctrine and its leader, Adolf Hitler. Militarily, Hitler's interference in Russia had been a complete disaster, and Kurt had seen many of his comrades die as a consequence. It was becoming more and more apparent that Hitler was demanding the impossible while living in his own world of fantasy and illusion. Kurt still felt great loyalty and dedication to certain ideals of the Waffen SS and saw them as Germany's best line of defense against her enemies. He still believed the world needed order and discipline to prosper and that Germany offered the best hope for creating such order, but he struggled in defining what course of action he should take in order to help save Germany. He'd been struggling with the question of moral responsibility for nearly a month now, and he was reaching one conclusion: He could not change what he had done or failed to do in the past; his future was the only thing that now counted. He went to sleep on that realization.

———

Kurt was discharged from the hospital on October 20. He continued to talk with Colonel Kresbach until the end and promised to visit him at his estate outside Berlin as soon as the Count was back home. One unfortunate piece of information Kurt had learned from Kresbach was that Lieutenant Willie von Skirch had been killed during the Battle of Kursk. Combined with all the deaths he had witnessed, the news of Willie's death had a very depressing effect on Kurt. Seemingly, all connections with his childhood in Ansbach were gone. His parents were dead, and now the last of his boyhood friends was gone, too. Given these circumstances, Kurt was consumed by a need to see his home one more time.

Erika picked Kurt up at the hospital, and the two of them drove to Nuremberg. The plan was to use the von Klugemanns' home as their central point of occupancy and make visits from there to other locations, such as Ansbach, Louisa's chateau, and Count Kresbach's estate. Frederick and Maria von Klugemann welcomed their new son-in-law with an exceptional dose of affection. Frederick, who was not usually given to outward expressions of emotion, was very demonstrative in welcoming Kurt into the family, and Maria was absolutely frantic in her greeting.

"Oh, Kurt, you're looking very healthy, and we're so happy to see you," Maria said, giving him a warm embrace. "We're overjoyed you and

Erika are married. We couldn't have picked a better husband for her. And it's such a tragedy about your parents. I know they were very proud of you, and I'm sorry that we'll never get the chance to meet them."

"Thank you. I know my mother and father were already under Erika's spell, and they would have liked both of you as well," Kurt said. "Let's hope we're done with tragic events for a while. How are both of you doing?"

"Quite well, thank you, Kurt," Frederick answered. I've taken a couple of factories underground to avoid the incessant Allied bombing. The British pound us at night and the Americans by day, but we've actually increased production. Manpower is getting difficult to find, so we're starting to use Russian prisoners and other undesirables to replenish the work force. Surprisingly, the morale of the German people remains strong, and I think Germany can still prevail."

"Business, business!" Maria scolded. "Is that all you can talk about Frederick? That and this damn war? Kurt, what would you like to eat?"

"Anything other than cold army rations will be fine, Frau von Klugemann."

Abruptly contradicting her admonishment of Frederick, Maria asked. "How much longer will this fighting continue, Kurt?"

"I don't know, but we must survive. And we will, whatever the cost and whatever the sacrifice. Desperate times require drastic measures, and the German people must be prepared to meet any challenge. I know the Waffen SS will do its duty."

"Well spoken, Kurt," Frederick responded.

"You are our hope and our future," beamed Maria. "Now let's be a little more festive to celebrate your homecoming, your recovery, and, of course, your marriage. I hope you don't mind, but I've planned a small reception to celebrate your marriage."

"When, and how small?" asked Erika.

"This Saturday, and not as big as I would like, child. A lot of people can't come because of this damn war, so I suppose about fifty people."

"Well, for you, Mother, that is very small. Where do you want Kurt and me to stay?"

"In your room, Erika. It's the biggest bedroom available, and the most private." Maria had a sly grin on her face as she made the last comment, enough to actually make Erika a little flustered before she responded, "We are married, you know!"

"Yes, and by now Kurt should be fully rested," suggested Maria.

"Mother, I give up on you!"

Kurt, looking somewhat sheepish, just stood silently during the mother-daughter exchange, waiting to take their suitcases up to Erika's old bedroom.

Despite Kurt's bravado during his stay at the hospital, Kurt and Erika had not been able to have sex, mostly because Erika was never allowed to stay overnight. Now the situation had definitely changed, and as soon as they closed the bedroom door, Erika began to tease Kurt.

"Major Heisler, how's your stamina? Do I need to be careful, or can you still handle a German princess?"

Kurt, smiling wickedly, said nothing. It had been nearly nine months since they had made love, and, although somewhat apprehensive, he was eager to renew his physical contact with Erika.

"Do you still remember what I like, or do I have to retrain you?" taunted Erika as she rubbed up against him.

"I thought we might make it to the bed, but if you keep touching me like that, I guess the floor will have to do."

"Well, that's music to my ears, Major! Thank goodness I still have an effect on you. I'm sorry to be teasing you, but I just wanted to make sure that you're still interested in me. This has been difficult for me, too, you know. With all the doctors' warnings, I haven't dared touch you for fear of getting you excited and sending you into another coma. So this is good news. But we have to wait until later to finish what we've just started. Don't worry, I promise I'll make it worth the wait. After tonight you may want to call the hospital and see if they still have your bed available."

They went downstairs and joined Maria and Frederick for a short dinner and a review of the reception guest list. Kurt soon said he was tired, and he and Erika went to bed early. True to her promise, Erika made it very worth his while, and they were both convinced that Kurt's recovery was complete.

The reception was an enormous success, at least in the eyes of Maria von Klugemann. None of the high Nazi personnel were able to attend, but a number of second-tier party members and various city and business VIP's shored up the guest list. Maria delighted in parading Kurt around in his well-decorated uniform and introducing him as Erika's husband and her wonderful son-in-law. Erika became slightly miffed at being ignored by her mother, and after the last guest had finally left, couldn't wait to call her mother on her behavior.

"I'm glad you're so fascinated by men in uniform, Mother, but I'm your daughter, and you could have at least included me in a few of your introductions."

"Oh, don't pout, Erika, everybody knows who you are. Yes, you're my daughter, and you're just like me!"

"Really, Mother, you'll never grow up, will you?"

The two kindred spirits stared at each other for a few moments and then broke out laughing and shared a hug.

After a week with the von Klugemanns, Kurt and Erika drove to Ansbach for a look at Kurt's old home. The trip was bittersweet. They stopped at the little hidden pond where they had taken a swim on the way to meet Kurt's parents; that enchanting day now seemed like decades ago. This time it was far too cold for a swim, so they just sat in the car and talked. Lying with her feet up on the seat and her head resting on Kurt's shoulder, Erika reminisced. "Kurt, do you realize it's been over a year since we were at this spot? I can't believe all the things that have happened since we last visited our little pond."

They sat for a while, enjoying the peaceful setting, both lost in their own thoughts.

"Kurt, what would happen if we lost the war? I mean, I know we won't, but what would our enemies do to us if we lost?"

"What brought up a question like that, especially in a place like this?"

"I don't know. It just seems that things aren't going so well, and I hear all this talk of new weapons and future victories, but nothing seems to materialize. Remember, you said you'd end the war in Russia last summer. See, it's your fault." Erika turned, stroked Kurt's cheek with her hand and kissed him. "Just kidding, dear. I know how hard you all tried."

Kurt wondered if this was the time to tell Erika about his confusion regarding the course of the war and his allegiance to Hitler. He wanted to talk to unburden himself and confess everything, but decided it was better not to involve Erika, at least for the moment.

"We'd better go, dear. It's getting late." Kurt said as he started the car.

———

Kurt went to a neighbor and got the key to his old home. Jurgen was going to rent it out to some people he knew that had to be stationed in the area for a while, and after that it was just going to be locked up until things were more stable. Jurgen had gone through the house and placed all the family memorabilia in Kurt's old room. Kurt and Erika spent a couple of hours looking through various windows into Kurt's past. They had planned to spend the night in Ansbach, but Kurt felt such an intense cloud of melancholy that he decided to leave Ansbach and return to Nuremberg that same night. He took only one item from the house: his Nordic statue.

———

Kurt continued his convalescence at the von Klugemanns while awaiting his next assignment. His strength was returning, and he started some paperwork duties for Das Reich. He had been offered duty at a concentration camp, which convinced him of two things. Obviously, such places did exist, and members of the Waffen SS were involved. Kurt realized he needed to be a little careful in his opposition to matters of this nature, so he disguised his disgust for such an assignment by requesting regular duty as a soldier in a combat unit.

Kurt's request was granted, and he was assigned to the Headquarters staff of Das Reich as an intelligence officer and liaison with the German High Command. The position would allow him to observe what was going on inside the highest levels of the Third Reich while helping him decide how he could best serve Germany. The doctor recommended that Kurt not report for a few months, as he needed more time to fully recuperate, but, in the meantime, Kurt made a few visits to Berlin to familiarize himself with some of his new responsibilities.

On one such visit early in December Kurt and Erika visited their respective friends in Berlin. After dropping Erika off at Louisa's apartment in Berlin, Kurt drove to the Kresbach estate to take up the Count's invitation to visit. The December scenery was on the bleak side, but even the dreariness of winter couldn't hide the majestic beauty of the grounds of Bakenhall, the Count's family estate. Set among dense woods, the main residence looked like a medieval castle—which it basically was—with modern renovations.

As Kurt stopped the car outside the main door, a servant quickly approached, picked up Kurt's luggage and walked him into the main hall. The room was exactly what one would expect of a country manor: high-beamed ceilings, mounted animal trophies, family portraits and coats-of-arms adorning the walls, large wooden furniture framing a gigantic fireplace, and a stately stairway ascending to the upper floors. As Kurt gazed at some of the portraits, he heard footsteps accompanied by a tapping sound, and he turned to see Count Kresbach coming down the stairs with the aid of a cane.

"Welcome to Bakenhall, Major. I'm so glad you could come. We shall have a nice visit and relax for a couple of days. My wife and daughter are visiting relatives in Munich and, except for the staff, we have the whole place to ourselves."

"Thank you, Colonel. I'm looking forward to talking with you again. I'm glad to see you're out of your wheelchair."

"Yes, yes, I'll be chasing after my wife again soon. That's probably why she headed out of town," laughed the Count. "Come, let's go into my study. I have some excellent sherry, and we can catch up with each other."

Comfortably seated in large leather chairs with sherry in hand, the men reacquainted themselves. After some polite conversation and a second glass of sherry, Kurt got up and walked over to study the photographs on the desk. "A fine looking family, Colonel. I'm sure you're proud of them."

"Yes, Major, I am, and I hope they survive this war. And, naturally, I hope the same for you and all those you hold dear. I am so sorry about the loss of your parents."

"Thank you, Count. It seems life keeps handing us these surprises when we least expect them. But how are you doing with your recovery? Will you be reporting to the Third Panzer again soon?"

"It will be quite some time yet, or maybe never, at least concerning my old responsibilities. I guess time will tell. What about you?"

"I'm officially reporting for duty in late February or early March, but until then I'll be working as a liaison between the Waffen SS and the German High Command in intelligence, whatever that means. I hope I'll be back in combat by summer."

"I'm not sure I'd wish too hard for that."

Kurt pondered his next question. Should he ask it or not? "Count, during our talk at the hospital you'd begun to talk about our duty and responsibilities to save Germany. What did you really mean?"

The Count gave Kurt such an intense gaze that Kurt wished he'd never asked the question. After what seemed like an eternity, Count Kresbach responded, "I don't think I should be talking about such things with a member of the SS intelligence. Whatever I say could be used against me and my family, which, suffice it to say, really puts a damper on any frank discussion. Let's just enjoy ourselves and engage in pleasant conversation. How is your stay with Erika's family going?"

Kurt found himself talking with Colonel Kresbach, but thinking about something else. What was the Colonel really a part of, and how could he get him to share it?

During the next two days the Colonel gave Kurt a tour of his estate, took him to the opera in Berlin and continued to quiz him about his beliefs. Gradually, Kurt began to conclude that the Colonel was trying to see if he could be trusted, but Kurt couldn't figure why. Finally, on the last evening of Kurt's stay, the Count came to the point.

"Kurt, have you ever read the "Book of Revelation" from the *New Testament?*"

"No, I guess I haven't, at least that I can remember."

"Well, it talks about the battle at the end of the world, the struggle between the followers of God and the Anti-Christ: Armageddon. There are many people who are beginning to think of the present Apocalypse as the start of such a time and Hitler as the Anti-Christ. Kurt, to put it bluntly, that man is evil incarnate and must be removed from power for the sake of Germany and for all humanity."

Kurt sat in silence and let Count Kresbach do the talking.

"I'm taking an extreme chance talking to you about this, and I'm putting my life and that of my family in your hands. Even though I know of the oath you members of the Waffen SS take, I feel I've come to understand you well enough to trust you. I'm a Catholic, and I know you were once, and maybe you still retain some sense of Christianity. God teaches us that the deliberate taking of a life outside of war is wrong. This fact is at the center of one of the great philosophical and moral questions of all time. Does the end justify the means?"

Count Kresbach walked over to the credenza and picked up a picture of his family and studied it. After a tense pause of quiet anticipation, he slowly turned around and confronted his young friend. "What is our duty, Kurt? What do we owe Hitler and the Nazi Party? Our blind obedience is leading Germany to moral degeneration and the total loss of humanity. There's no doubt it will eventually destroy us. Is there not a higher cause, to keep our dignity as human beings and to end this madness and save Germany? We must eliminate Hitler and make peace with the Western Allies and then use all our forces to try to stop the Russians from invading Germany. There is no chance to make a peace with Stalin. He's even more godless than Hitler. I can't tell you any details, but plans are being made to remove Hitler from power. If you turn me in, my family and I will be killed. But I will not tell the Nazis anything, no matter what they do to me. So they will know nothing more than they already know, only you will have killed my family and me. I feel I can trust you with our safety, or I'd never have dared say this to you."

Kurt had expected something like this from the Count, but the straightforward announcement was much more than he had anticipated. After thinking things over for a minute, Kurt responded. "My, you've certainly given me a lot to think about, Colonel. But first, you have my word that I'll keep this totally secret from everyone, even my wife. As you might guess, I need to know where you think I fit in with this plan. If I agree to join you, what role would I perform in this coup?"

"I can't say where, when, or how this will evolve, but after Hitler is gone, we'll need someone to help bring the Waffen SS over to our side. We have someone in mind to bring the army over and to lead the military of our new government. We think you could be of help in bringing the SS troops on board; you and someone else that I won't name at present."

"Why me? How can you dare expose such information to a member of the Waffen SS? Do you and your organization have a death wish?"

"All good questions, Major Heisler. I can't answer them completely right now, but I can state absolutely that we do not have a death wish. Let me just say that we're looking for someone in your organization who is an officer, a war hero with a certain background and character. You matched all our requirements, so my being assigned as your roommate in the hospital was not an accident. All those hours we spent talking about the war, morality and duty had a purpose. I had to make a judgment about asking you to join us, and for my sake and Germany's, I hope I made the right one."

"You have, Colonel, you have. When do I have to decide, and what do I have to do?"

"We need an answer in a few months, and whatever you decide, you'll just go about your regular duties until I contact you. Do you have any other questions?"

"None that you can apparently answer now. I'll give your proposal a lot of thought. Thank you for your confidence and trust."

"I hope I've not misjudged you, Kurt. When things come together, a lot of people will be depending on you."

Kurt left the next morning to pick up Erika in Berlin. As if Colonel von Kresbach had not given Kurt enough to think about, on the ride back to Nuremberg Erika announced to Kurt that she was pregnant.

———

Outwardly, Kurt expressed great joy at Erika's announcement, and he was truly happy about the future responsibilities of fatherhood. But with Germany battling for her very survival, Kurt knew it was not an ideal time to bring a child into the world. Erika's news also complicated Kurt's internal debate about whether to talk with her about his possible involvement in a plot to overthrow Hitler. Kurt did not want to jeopardize the safety of Erika, her family and his unborn child. He knew that if the plot failed, repercussions against the plotters would be immediate, brutal, and all-inclusive. Between Colonel Kresbach's offer and Erika's announcement, Kurt felt even greater pressure to do something to save Germany, but what?

During the final weeks of his recovery Kurt debated whether to accept Count von Kresbach's invitation. He grappled with all sides of the question. Kurt had taken an oath to be loyal to Hitler until death. Up until recently he had believed that Hitler was the future of Germany, that the Aryan Race was superior, and that service in the Waffen SS was the best way he could serve his country. Kurt thought about all the Russians he had killed in support of his beliefs, some of them in cold blood. He could rationalize that war, by its nature, didn't allow for distinctions about how you killed your enemies—it was kill or be killed, right?—but that argument grew weaker with reason. The question was, what did he believe now?

In search of the answer, Kurt found himself gradually returning to his mother's long-suppressed Christian teachings, but not without a struggle. It took weeks of agonizing soul-searching, but eventually he realized he needed to answer to a higher oath than that of the SS; he needed to answer to God. Then, armed with the belief that there was a higher power than Hitler, Kurt prayed and asked for guidance to make the correct decision. Freed enough to think objectively, Kurt concluded that Hitler and Himmler were wrong and that Colonel von Kresbach's suppositions were correct; in order to save Germany, Hitler had to be removed. If Kresbach's plan succeeded, the Waffen SS would have to change their loyalties from Hitler to a new leader and a new type of government, and all resources would have to be focused on winning the war in Russia. Kurt calculated that the loyalty and zeal of the Waffen SS could be channeled to support someone else, especially if they were convinced the survival of Germany depended on it. That would not be a hard case to make, given the Waffen SS's experience in Russia. No one wanted to think of what would happen if Germany lost that war. Kurt knew that there were some contradictions in his new thinking, and it was still difficult for him to be totally repentant for what he had done, but he thought it was a good start.

Kurt decided not to tell Erika about his decision to become involved in the plot against Hitler. For starters, the hardship of the war and her pregnancy were enough for her to worry about. But the strongest reason not to involve her was her safety; if the plot failed and Kurt was found out, Erika's ignorance and her parents' standing with Hitler would help keep them from being executed.

Before reporting for active duty in early March, Kurt and Erika made a final visit to Berlin to celebrate and see friends. During the short stay Kurt saw Colonel Kresbach and told him that he would participate in the attempt to overthrow Hitler and form a new German government. Kresbach embraced Kurt and expressed his appreciation and respect for the struggle that Kurt had gone through to reach such a traumatic decision. As they parted, the Count told Kurt to patiently perform his duties and wait to be contacted.

———

At the von Klugemann home in Nuremberg Kurt and Erika had dinner alone the night before Kurt left to rejoin Das Reich. Erika was about halfway into her pregnancy, and she was trying to be humorous and brave, not knowing when they would be together again. "I suppose other women are starting to look pretty good to you when you look at my fat stomach?"

Kurt had a comment ready, but decided this was not the time for humorous sexual innuendo. "Erika, you'll always be the only one for me, and I'll always love you, even if you make Uncle Konrad seem skinny."

"Well, that's almost a nice, sweet comment. Almost, you Nazi pig!"

"You'd better not let your mother hear you talking like that, or she'll turn you in to Uncle Adolf."

"Uncle Adolf has enough problems to worry about, and I can take care of my mother and you by myself."

The irony of Erika's last few words tore at Kurt's soul as he turned the conversation in another direction. "You know I'm kidding, dear. I'm really looking forward to seeing our first child and being a father."

"Are you really, Kurt?"

"Yes, of course."

"I get scared at times, what with all the bombing and your leaving again. I hope our child enters a world that's a better place than it is now."

"We can only do our duty and hope for the best. We'll survive and our child will live in a better world."

Kurt and Erika held hands across the table and looked at each without speaking. Kurt felt Erika squeeze his hands a little harder as she asked, "Will you be there when I have the baby?"

"You know the answer to that, Erika."

"I know, but I can hope, can't I? I love you so much and want you by my side when I have our baby."

"I'll do everything I can to be here for you."

Then, as if she had a premonition, Erika said, "Kurt, I know terrible things happen during war, but I also know you're a good person and will always try to do what's right."

"What's right during a war? Are we right, Erika?"

"We need to do whatever is necessary to survive as a nation and a culture."

"Are you so sure our culture is so much better than that of other countries?"

Erika looked at Kurt with surprised disbelief. "Kurt, this doesn't sound like a major in the Waffen SS. What's wrong with you?"

Erika's statement solidified Kurt's decision, and he felt a sense of relief as he answered. "I'll do my duty to help Germany survive in the best way possible."

———

The next morning Kurt left for southern France. Most of Das Reich was east of Bordeaux near the town of Montaubaun. Kurt's division had been stationed in the area since early spring, trying to recover from the disaster that had befallen the German forces in Russia after the Battle of Kursk. The division was being refitted as a Panzer Division with the best equipment because Hitler felt the elite Waffen SS Divisions provided the best chance to produce a victory for Germany. When Kurt arrived at Divisional Headquarters, he was amazed at all the new faces and the absence of old ones. He received permission to visit his old company, and the shock of that visit proved even greater; there were virtually no familiar faces. Kurt searched among the men for someone to visit with, and he finally asked a young recruit if the company had any older veterans. Kurt was told to go and see Lieutenant Weber.

"Could it be Otto?" thought Kurt. Otto Weber, the young farm boy from the Black Forest who was so good-natured and full of fun? Could he possibly have survived all of the battles since '41? The answer to Kurt's question was yes and no. Lieutenant Weber was indeed the same person whom Kurt had last seen as a Sergeant in his company last August near Kharkov when Kurt was blown into a coma, but he was no longer a young, good-humored sergeant. He was a cold, old veteran who had seen far too much death to retain any sense of happiness or optimism.

"Lieutenant Weber."

Weber turned, ready to snarl a nasty reply to whoever it was that had disturbed his rest. There was only one person on earth that could have melted the crust of war off of Weber, and that person was now standing in front of him.

"My God, Captain, is it you? I mean, Major. I thought you were in a hospital in Berlin trying to remember who the hell you were." As the two old comrades hugged each other, they began to laugh and cry simultaneously.

"Why the hell did you come back, Major? You should've stayed back in Germany and spent the war in a comfortable nut house instead of coming to this nut house in the country."

"You still have your fine sense of humor, I see."

"Not really. Now that I'm an officer, I'm really an asshole. It seems to be a requirement."

"You were always an asshole, even as a private, so nothing's changed."

"It's good to see that being a Major with Oak Leaves and all that shit hasn't changed you, either," scoffed Lieutenant Weber. "Sincerely, Major Heisler, it's good to have someone back who knows what real war is like. These replacements seem eager and brave, but most of them are only seventeen or eighteen, and I fear the quality is not like the old days. Hell, half of the replacements in my company are Alsatians. I doubt if any of them could have gotten into the Waffen SS back in '41."

"Well, Lieutenant, war creates difficult circumstances, and we have to make adjustments. How have things been going for you since we were last together?"

"I've picked up a few nicks here and there, but I've been lucky so far. Being an officer has its good points, but I'm not sure it suits my personality."

Kurt and Otto visited briefly about the past, and then Lieutenant Weber asked, "Major, just what are your new duties with Das Reich?"

"I'm with the headquarters' staff. I guess they figure my head's still a question mark—no jokes, please—so they don't want to send me right back into combat. I have a number of responsibilities connected with intelligence, including being a liaison to the High Command for Allied invasion planning, rebuilding Das Reich, and countering the resistance movement."

"Excuse my language, Major, but that assignment's a crock of shit. It just proves what we fighting men always suspected; intelligence officers don't have any intelligence. As soon as we're in combat again, I hope they put you back where you belong, up front kicking some Allied ass."

"I hope so, Lieutenant. That's what we've been trained to do."

"And we still do it better than anyone else. Seriously, Major, what is your first real assignment?"

"I'm going to get you promoted so you can be an even bigger ass-hole," laughed Kurt.

"Stop by again soon, Major, and share some of your 'intelligence' with me, but right now I need to help some of these new supermen become what they're supposed to be."

"I will, Lieutenant. I'd like to stay and watch you perform as an officer, but I'm due back at headquarters for a briefing. Good luck, Otto."

"Heil Hitler, Major Heisler."

———

The next few months Kurt spent his time traveling to Berlin for war games, investigating reports of Maquis (French Resistance) activity, and working with the headquarters' staff of Das Reich. He learned that the Maquis comprised several components: one group under Charles de Gaulle, one communist group, and various other splinter groups. They were loosely organized, but eventually all aligned themselves under de Gaulle's group. Most units lacked training and equipment, but they were a deadly force to be reckoned with when they received outside help and supplies, which is why German intelligence intercepted and killed many British agents sent to organize the Maquis. Kurt came across reports of Maquis savagery in the treatment of German prisoners and of the hideous manner in which German forces retaliated. Predictably, the situation had expanded into a repetitive cycle of terror for each side. German intelligence also knew that it would only be a matter of time before aide for the Maquis began to arrive from the United States. The escalating atrocities forced Kurt to recall his experiences on the Eastern Front, and he realized something needed to be done soon to tame the Maquis.

While he was doing intelligence work on the Maquis, Kurt was also renewing his respect for the discipline, comradeship and unique attitude of the Waffen SS. He loved being a soldier. He loved being a part of a world of pure dedication. And he loved being in an atmosphere of order. Kurt's only feeling of remorse was for the disdain for human life that the Waffen SS preached. He was beginning to comprehend the magnitude of the fanaticism that bred such blind loyalty to obedience. Once again a cloud of rationalization confused Kurt; he succeeded in convincing himself that all of the past misdeeds of the Waffen SS would be forgiven if their zeal could be transferred from serving Hitler to saving Germany.

CHAPTER XV

Prisoner of War

On May 27, 1944, Kurt was sitting at his desk sifting through a stack of memorandums, organizing scattered pieces of information concerning a possible Allied invasion on the coast of France. Included among them were notes about local Resistance units. While poring over these piles of papers trying to establish logical connections, Kurt was interrupted by his adjutant.

"Heil Hitler, Major."

Without looking up, Kurt replied, "Heil Hitler, Lieutenant. What do you have to report?"

"One of our patrols has captured an American spy working with a local Maquis unit. Would you like to visit with him before we turn him over to the Gestapo?"

Kurt immediately looked up. "Yes. I've never talked with an American. Does he speak German?"

Smiling broadly, the Lieutenant replied, "Apparently a little, but I'm sure the Gestapo will get him to sing in a number of languages. The American is not long for this world. I'll have him here shortly."

After his adjutant left, Kurt pondered the Lieutenant's parting words. For some reason, it bothered Kurt that he would be talking to a dead man. Any enemy agent working as a spy or helping the resistance was shot, often after a lengthy session of torture. It had been accepted practice for the Waffen SS to shoot captured enemy soldiers on the Eastern Front, especially during the hectic swirl of combat, but this situation seemed very different. Sitting behind a desk in a non-combat area looking into the face of a man marked for death was unsettling and surreal.

Kurt wasn't normally involved in the interrogation of prisoners; standard Gestapo protocol was to pass any useful information gleaned from prisoners on to Kurt in report form, so he was not sure how to prepare himself for the American captive. He arranged a chair in front of his desk and ordered a fresh pitcher of water and a glass for the table.

Kurt leaned back and closed his eyes. What should he ask this American prisoner? Kurt remembered his vow to never shoot another prisoner, that he would only kill during combat to save his country. In his attempt to remain as honorable as possible in a world gone mad, Kurt had made this vow after his conversations with Count Kresbach. As Kurt pondered, an eerie feeling of empathy settled on him, and he wanted to help the condemned American.

As he waited, Kurt's old nemesis appeared, that moral puzzle that had been taunting humanity since the beginning of time. Does the end justify the means? Kurt's mind worked overtime with philosophical quandaries. Should all spies be shot? What danger was the American now that he was a prisoner? Did he possess information about the coming invasion that might save countless German lives? How many saved lives justified torturing a man to death? What if a tortured man produces no useful information? At some point wouldn't a tortured man tell you anything just to end the pain? Is the act of torture judged only by the significance of the results?

"Stop!" Kurt screamed to himself. He poured himself a glass of water and tried to remind himself of who he was and that he had a job to do. But who was he and what was his job?

A knock on the door ended Kurt's inner turmoil. The adjutant entered with the American prisoner, who looked looking worn and tired, yet defiant. His hands were tied behind his back, and, dressed in civilian clothes, looked like one of Hitler's master race: tall, blond, and blue-eyed.

"Heil Hitler, Major. Here's the American spy. Do you want me to remain in the room?"

"Heil, Hitler. No, Lieutenant. Untie him before you leave and have a guard posted outside my door. I'll call you when our visit is over."

"Yes, Major. You have thirty minutes before the Gestapo will be here to collect their prize."

Kurt had been unable to construct a plan to question the American; he had decided to see how things developed and make adjustments as the session progressed. Kurt motioned for him to sit in the chair directly in front of the desk. "I'm told you speak some German. Are you fluent enough to answer some questions or would you like me to get an interpreter?"

Speaking in German, the prisoner replied, "According to the Geneva Convention, all I'm required to tell you is my name, rank, and serial number. John Anderson. Captain. Number 67849308."

Kurt smiled. "Ah yes, the famous Geneva Convention. A piece of paper filled with noble intentions, but of little use during an actual war. What if one side does not believe in it? Does that give the other side the right to break its own rules?"

Kurt was pleased with himself. He could see that his question had caught the American off guard. Sensing an opportunity to get Captain Anderson to talk, Kurt decided to focus initially on a general philosophical discussion, rather than trying to extract information. "Captain, out of courtesy I'll call you by your rank, but you're really just a spy. Tell me, how can you make rules for war? By its very nature, war is the absence of rules, except one: win. The winners always decide the rules and punish the losers. Isn't the moral obvious? Do what is necessary to win?"

Captain Anderson became agitated to the point where he forgot the situation he was in. 'Major, I don't think you actually believe the garbage that's just come from your mouth. Rules are what set human beings apart from animals. I guess that's what sets us apart from you."

The game was on. Kurt saw an opportunity to pursue his quest to find justification for the horrors that he had participated in while serving the

Third Reich. Maybe he could also learn some valuable information from the American.

"You speak rather boldly for a man in your predicament."

Captain Anderson shook his head with a laugh of resignation. "Major, you and I both know I'm a dead man. Whatever you want to call me—spy, secret agent, member of the OSS, resistance fighter—I'll never leave Gestapo headquarters alive. Why should I worry about anything I say to you or what you say to me?"

Kurt stood up and walked over to the small table holding the pitcher of water.

"May I offer you a glass of water, Captain?"

"No."

"Let's continue then."

Kurt sat down on the front of his desk, only a few feet from Anderson.

"Captain, explain to me why America has assumed the role of the world's savior. What sets you apart? Your industrial capacity, your wealth, your faith in democracy? What?"

Anderson exploded. "You pompous ass! Comparing what you Nazis have done with what we're trying to do is beyond the scope of insanity. We're trying to save lives and cultures and you're destroying anyone who stands up to you or doesn't fit your distorted idea of perfection."

Kurt knew he no longer believed everything he was about to say, but the devil's advocate in him had taken over. "So, America has a plan for what's best for the world. Well, so do we. Ours may be more direct and brutal, but who's to say that a world run by the most able will not benefit mankind over time. Sometimes people die in order to achieve a greater good."

Captain Anderson's face was as crimson as the Nazi flag decorating the wall. Almost shouting he asked, "Can I have that glass of water now?"

Kurt poured a glass of water and handed it to him. Captain Anderson stood up and forcefully hurled the water into Kurt's face, shouting, "Wake up, you Nazi swine!"

Kurt jumped back and removed his Luger from its holster. Captain Anderson calmly sat down.

Kurt leveled the pistol at Anderson's head. "Captain, apparently you wish me to shoot you before the Gestapo get you. Being a civilized man,

I'm disappointed in your behavior. Don't move from your chair again. Do I have your word?"

Kurt walked over to the table, picked up a towel and cleaned his face. He then walked behind Captain Anderson and slowly put the Luger back in its holster. Walking back and forth behind Anderson, Kurt continued. "Let me ask you a hypothetical question. For the sake of argument, let's say you win this war. How long do you think America can exist as a friend of the Soviet Union? Stalin has murdered more people than Hitler, yet you're helping Stalin fight Germany. The Soviets are a dictatorship, as are we. So what's the difference? The odds are you'll have to engage the Soviets in war, and let's say you win and stand alone as the only super power in the world. What do you think you'll do if some day you find a country that's curtailing your growth or withholding resources from you and will not agree to your demands that it change its ways? Will you leave it alone or will you try to impose your ideas on its leaders by force? Does having all the power give you the right to decide the direction that all societies must eventually go? Is power the ultimate arbitrator, and if so, why are you so different from us?"

The American said nothing. Kurt walked around to his desk and was surprised to see a composed, almost tranquil look on Captain Anderson's face. Kurt stood looking at him, waiting for a response. When it came, it took Kurt by surprise.

"Major, I've misjudged you. You're obviously a man in search of himself, a man who's in the process of rejecting what he's been and struggling to find a new meaning for his life. There can be no other reason for the questions that you've just asked. Maybe there's hope for some of you supermen yet. The means can only justify the end if the means are a last resort to subdue a universal evil. That evil must be immoral beyond debate. Some people will have to die to erase that evil and save mankind, but it should be as few as possible. That's what separates us from you. We're willing to sacrifice our lives to help others; you sacrifice your lives to subjugate others."

Kurt was staggered. How did this condemned man know what he was searching for? Kurt poured himself a glass of water and tried to regain his composure by making a joke. "Don't worry Captain. I'm too much of an animal to waste water." After slowly draining the glass, Kurt shifted the topic. "Captain, if you could provide me some useful information about the resistance or plans for the invasion, I could help you with the Gestapo, maybe even save your life. I'm sure you've been working with the Maquis, advising them on how to delay us as we move to stop your planned invasion. Give me something so I can help you."

"I actually believe you're sincere, Major, but no matter what I tell you, you can't save me from the Gestapo. I won't tell you anything."

Kurt felt a great sorrow for the man he was coming to respect.

"May I ask you, Captain, what did you do in civilian life?"

"I guess I can break the Geneva Convention this one time. I graduated from Yale with a law degree, and I was working for a Wall Street law firm when the war broke out."

There was a knock on the door, and before Kurt could open it, two Gestapo agents entered, roughly grabbed Captain Anderson and hauled him away without speaking or acknowledging Kurt as his confused adjutant looked on from the doorway.

Kurt shrugged his shoulders, smiled at his adjutant and told him not to interrupt him for an hour. After a few seconds, Kurt got up, closed the door and then slumped down in his chair. He remained there a long time, staring blankly at a picture of Erika, grappling with a concern that had never really bothered him before. Kurt knew he needed to find out what Captain Anderson knew about any possible Allied Invasion plans, and he also knew that he had no taste for interrogation and torture. But, by association, was he just as guilty as the Gestapo? By allowing them to do the actual interrogation, was he just ignoring his own responsibility for the fate of Captain Anderson? Was there anything he could have done to save the American? Did he really have a choice? If he had a choice, would he have saved the Captain and possibly forfeited a chance to save Germany? Was he avoiding his conscience by allowing someone else to make these decisions? Once again Kurt's mind became numb from the endless circle of questions.

To put his mind at rest, Kurt concluded that Captain Anderson knew the possible consequences of working with the French Resistance. Unpleasant as a visit with the Gestapo could be, it was a by-product of working against the Third Reich. Kurt felt sorry for the American, but he had a job to do, and it was time to get back to work. He needed to help save Germany.

Two days later Kurt received a call to report to Gestapo headquarters in Toulouse. He left immediately, assuming the Gestapo had obtained some useful information from Captain Anderson. It was a tense drive for Kurt, filled with speculation about Anderson's fate. At Gestapo headquarters, Kurt was quickly escorted to the man in charge of Anderson's interrogation and given an apology.

"Sorry, Major, we tried to reach you to tell you we no longer need you. The American spy wished to speak with you. For some reason he seemed to respect you, and we thought you could help in the interrogation, but he died an hour ago. Unfortunately, he revealed nothing of real value. Let's hope future prisoners will provide information that will help our cause. You're free to return to your duties. We'll keep you informed."

Kurt knew he couldn't leave without making a request. "Could I see Captain Anderson?"

The Gestapo agent looked curiously at Kurt. "If you hurry. He's about to be disposed of. I think he's still in the basement in one of our special rooms. I'll take you there, but I warn you, he's not a pretty sight."

Kurt thought that his combat experiences had exposed him to enough ghastly human remains so he would never experience nausea again, but he was wrong. Outwardly, Kurt was able to maintain control, but inwardly, he was a mess. What had been Captain Anderson was tied to a chair, nude except for a pair of shorts. His feet were bloody and swollen. His fingers and thumbs were dislocated and black. His face was beaten almost beyond recognition, and his teeth were scattered about the floor. Deep furrows had been carved in his chest and back from the barbed wire that had been tightened around his torso. Blood drenched the Captain, the chair, the floor, and the surrounding walls.

As Kurt stared at the lifeless form hanging to the chair, the Gestapo agent said, "I'm surprised the American died. We hadn't even gotten to the good stuff yet."

"Apparently, it was good enough."

As Kurt turned and staggered out of the room, he made another vow to himself. He would never tell Erika about his involvement with Count Kresbach.

CHAPTER XVI

Fear of Discovery

"Major Heisler, report to General Lammerding's office in five minutes for a staff meeting. The Allies have landed in Normandy," Kurt's aide announced breathlessly before rushing off.

"So now it's begun. The waiting is finally over," Kurt said to himself, observing the date on his calendar: June 6, 1944. He gathered all his intelligence reports and reported immediately.

The staff meeting was brief because the invasion information was sketchy, and the conflicting orders from the German High Command were unclear. General Lammerding confirmed that there had been an Allied landing on the Normandy coast of France, but Hitler refused to release the reserve Panzer divisions to repel the attack because he believed Normandy was a diversion; Hitler was convinced the real invasion would occur further north. The General ordered everyone to begin preparations to move out and scheduled another meeting for late afternoon. Kurt hurried back to his office and was reviewing all his intelligence regarding routes to Normandy, available rail transportation for heavy equipment, and estimates of Maquis resistance strength in the area when a call came to report to General Lammerding again.

Kurt entered the lavish study that General Lammerding was using as his office and waited while the General finished reviewing a file. Lammerding handed Kurt a piece of paper. "Major, read this and tell me what you think."

Kurt scanned the letter. "I would say that your directive is specific and leaves no doubt about how our Division is to behave in dealing with any hostile actions by the civilian population. But why is such an order even necessary?"

"Berlin has ordered us to proceed to Normandy on June 8. However, instead of traveling by the shortest route, we're to head north and destroy the Resistance groups in that area to demonstrate the futility and consequences of their actions. As you know, Major, there are many factions making up the Resistance. The Maquis itself includes rival factions, such as the Communist wing, but they're all just terrorist groups, and we're to treat them as such. We must force the French people to recognize the danger that these gangs represent to France and its people. We also need to deal with British and American commandos who've been dropped into the area to work with the Resistance; they are spies, which means they can be legally executed. Please note that the directive says that no unnecessary looting or mistreatment of civilians will be tolerated. Lawful citizens will be respected, but swift, harsh treatment will befall anyone giving support to terrorists or spies."

"I've noted the directives, General. I agree that the burning of any house from which we're attacked is certainly justified, but executing ten civilians for every German killed by the Resistance seems unduly harsh. After all, France is a civilized country; it's not like we're still in Russia."

"I appreciate your opinion, Major, but there's only one way to deal with partisans. The civilian population must be made to understand that."

"Yes, but why not let some other group deal with the Resistance? A Panzer division shouldn't be wasting time with such activities; we should proceed to Normandy as rapidly as possible. Field Marshal Rommel has said that any invasion must be stopped on the beach."

"You're probably right, but you know we don't contradict orders, Major. Anyway, I doubt that the Resistance will cause us more than a few days' delay. I want you to monitor Resistance activity and any actions we take against them."

"Yes, General."

As Kurt walked back to his quarters, he again pondered the paradox of morality and war. He struggled with the conflicting nature of a soldier's duty to follow orders without hesitation against the dilemma of a soldier's moral choice to refuse an order. Was such disobedience ever justified? The Waffen SS had been built on the unyielding principle of absolute obedience and duty, whatever the consequences. Even though Kurt was progressing in his search for his conscience, he had been so thoroughly indoctrinated that it was hard for him to imagine himself tolerating one of his own soldiers willfully disobeying an order. Still, Kurt questioned whether shooting civilians would help Germany win the war. He had thought about these same questions in Russia, but at that time he was consumed by his SS training. Then he was an eagle of the Reich, flying into the Slavic hordes to save the Fatherland from the sub-humans. Now he was debating the application of total war against a civilized country; he was even wondering if his past actions in Russia were justifiable.

By the time Kurt was back at his desk, he had concluded that at some point a moral choice must be faced by a soldier, but he was not sure where that point was. Where did morality exist if your goal was to win the war and survive?

———

On June 8, 1944, fifteen thousand men and more than two hundred tanks of Das Reich began a four hundred and fifty mile journey to the Normandy battlefield. The constant Allied air strikes and the nuisance attacks of the Maquis added several weeks to the trip. On June 9 elements of Das Reich rescued the German garrison at Tulle, which had been under attack by the French Resistance. Forty mutilated German soldiers were discovered, and in retaliation ninety-nine Frenchmen were hanged from lampposts in the streets of Tulle. The action was seen as an acceptable consequence of war, at least by Waffen SS standards; it would take an atrocity of much greater magnitude at Oradour-sur-Glane to shame even the Waffen SS.

Oradour-sur-Glane was a small village of no real importance, except it was in the vicinity of Das Reich's line of march. Major Helmut Kampfe, the commander of the Third Battalion of the Der Fuhrer Regiment of Das Reich, had gone ahead of his battalion and had apparently been captured by the FTP, the French communists who worked with the Maquis. A rumor circulated among German troops that an SS officer was being held in Oradour and was to be executed, but the official report of the Der Fuhrer Regiment on the Oradour incident mentioned that some murdered German soldiers had been found in Oradour.

Major Kampfe's friend, Major Adolf Diekmann, commander of the First Battalion of the Der Fuhrer, was sent to Oradour to investigate. On Saturday, June 10, for reasons unknown, Major Diekmann ordered one hundred and eighty men of his battalion to destroy Oradour-sur-Glane and its inhabitants. Perhaps Diekmann felt frustrated at the delays caused by the Maquis. Maybe a report that his friend Major Kampfe had been killed by the local resistance prompted his decision. Or maybe he just wanted to make a statement to the Maquis. Regardless of the reasons behind it, Major Diekmann's order was carried out with a brutal coldness that was excessive even for the Waffen SS. Only a few villagers escaped the massacre; six hundred and forty-two men, women and children were slaughtered. Most of the men had been shot, covered with straw and then burned, some while they were still alive. The women and children had been herded into a church that was then torched into a raging inferno. By the end of the day the entire town had been razed.

Kurt learned about the action at Oradour while routinely sorting through various communications at headquarters. Immediately he went to see the commanding officer of the Der Fuhrer Regiment, Colonel Sylvester Stadler. Inside a field tent Colonel Stadler and his staff were poring over maps when Kurt was announced.

"Come in, Major. Be brief. We're on the move, as you well know," said a captain standing at a table.

Kurt looked at the others in the tent without responding. Colonel Stadler looked up from his maps and gazed at Kurt. Sensing the reason for Kurt's hesitation, Stadler motioned for his staff to leave the tent and waited until they were gone before speaking. "I can see by your face you have some questions for me alone. Let me guess, Oradour?"

Kurt was surprised that the Colonel was so open about the destruction of the French village. "Colonel Stadler, I've read the official report on Oradour. Can you explain how this could happen?"

"Major Heisler, Major Diekmann was ordered to go to Oradour to see if he could find Major Kampfe and rescue him. If he couldn't find him, he was to bring back some villagers to use in exchange for Kampfe, bargaining chips to use with the Maquis. Major Diekmann had no orders to destroy Oradour or to kill any of its inhabitants. There's some speculation that hidden stores of munitions caused the church to explode and burn, but that's irrelevant at this point. The Waffen SS does not murder women and children. I won't have the honor of the Regiment soiled by this incident. I've already talked with Major Diekmann and informed him that as soon as is possible, considering our current circumstances, I'll initiate a court martial. The men under his command were following orders, which, as you know, they cannot question. Consequently, only the Major will be court-martialed. Do you have any other questions?"

"I served with both Kampfe and Diekmann in Russia, and I can't believe Major Diekmann could've done this. I also can't believe that a soldier could burn innocent women and children. Obedience must have some limits."

"Major Heisler, this is an unsettling incident for everyone, and it will be dealt with at the proper time. Right now we have to worry about the Allies at Normandy, and I suggest you turn your attentions there. You're dismissed."

Kurt left Colonel Stadler's tent and walked a short distance to a parked motorcycle, which he used as a chair. As an entire division of men, material, and machines swirled around him, Kurt barely noticed. Many of the men were heading to what they knew would be their final destination on earth. Engines roared, officers shouted orders, and soldiers cursed their fates, but Kurt didn't hear a sound. Resting his head on his forearms, which warmed the cool handlebars of the cycle, Kurt was again lost in his personal hell. Words pounded his brain like hailstones striking a tin roof: brutality, honor, survival, Germany, loyalty, accountability, death, orders, discipline, God.

"Major, are you all right?"

Kurt bolted upright and stammered, "Yes, just catching a little rest."

"I'm sorry, Major, but I need my motorcycle. The faster I can get to Normandy, the quicker I can help send the Allies back where they came from."

Kurt looked into the youthful face staring at him, a teenage zealot of Das Reich, a newly-minted private burning with a desire to offer his life in service to the evil empire. Studying this example of newborn fanaticism, Kurt dismounted and watched him ride away, wondering how such blind, innocent dedication could be ordered to burn women and children. Suddenly, Kurt was struck with a revelation. "I must talk to my good friend, Otto Weber, who is in Major Diekmann's battalion."

It took Kurt a few days to find Lieutenant Weber, as his battalion, along with the rest of the Der Fuhrer Regiment, was finally nearing the Normandy battlefield. Das Reich was traveling mostly at night to avoid the deadly Allied air attacks. Resistance activity had finally abated; apparently the enormity of the destruction of Oradour had dampened the fervor of the Maquis. However, they had accomplished their mission by significantly delaying Das Reich.

Kurt caught up with Weber's Der Fuhrer Regiment as it neared Normandy on June 15. Colonel Stadler had just been ordered to assume command of the Ninth SS Panzer Division (Hohenstauffen), and Lieutenant Colonel Weidinger was now in command of the Regiment. It was about five-thirty in the afternoon, and the column was spread out for over a mile along a ditch. The vehicles were camouflaged, and the men were resting among the trees and tangled shrubbery of the hedgerows bordering the road. As soon as the protective cover of night arrived, the Regiment would spring to life and begin the final phase of its march to stop Operation Overlord.

Kurt found Otto Weber nestled comfortably on a mattress of hedgerow vines. Weber was nearly asleep, but he smiled broadly as soon as he recognized Kurt approaching. "Heil Hitler, Major Heisler. Glad to see that you are looking so fit. Are you here on official business, or is this just a social call?"

"I just wanted to visit with you, Otto. I'll bet that in a day or two, our chances will be severely limited."

"Hell, Major, they're already limited. As soon as it gets dark, we'll be on the move again. Apparently the entire fucking Luftwaffe is on vacation. I haven't seen one of our planes since we left our summer home. It's pure suicide to travel in daylight. We have so much camouflage on our vehicles we look like a moving forest when we travel."

"How's my old regiment doing? Are the replacements you were drilling last spring ready for their first taste of combat? Are they ready to uphold the traditions of the Waffen SS?" Kurt was hoping his questions would get his friend to comment on the incident at Oradour.

"They didn't flinch from their duty at Oradour. Since you're in intelligence, I'm sure you're aware of what happened there."

"Somewhat, but give me a firsthand account. I'm interested in hearing how the young recruits performed under stress."

Otto continued to describe the Oradour incident, unaware of the trap he was being led into. "We were given a rather distasteful task at Oradour. The village was obviously being used by the Maquis, some of our soldiers were missing, and an example needed to be made. Major Diekmann ordered us to eliminate Oradour to break the will of the people supporting the Maquis. I never saw or heard a single soldier hesitate to do his duty. As you know, shooting women and children is a very stressful mission, but the efficient elimination of the people and buildings of Oradour accomplished our goal; resistance diminished significantly afterward."

Kurt shook his head at Weber. "What do you mean, 'As I know'?"

"You fired on partisan groups in Russia. We all did, and they usually included women and children."

"What about herding women and children into a church and setting it on fire? Did we also do that in Russia? Have we built our reputation on the fiendish execution of innocents?"

Lieutenant Weber was now aware of Kurt's intentions, but he didn't retreat. "Major Heisler, are you questioning me as a friend or as an inquisitor?"

Kurt didn't respond, but continued to stare at Otto. The strained silence continued in the fading sunlight. Finally, Weber cracked first. "Orders are orders, Major. You know that. Absolute acceptance to any order, however difficult or distasteful, is the foundation that we stand on. I can't say I enjoyed what I did, but I didn't question the order from Major Diekmann, and my men didn't question my orders. The results of our actions speak for themselves."

"Otto, have we descended so deep into the abyss that we can't see out of it? Are we just creatures mindlessly following orders we cannot understand or justify? Is there no event, however horrible, that we can't reject? There must be a point where we recognize evil for what it is."

"Major Heisler, you've apparently developed a disease that must be cured if you're to remain a member of the Waffen SS: a conscience. It makes you sentimental and weak, with a desire to coddle and help lesser beings than yourself. The only concern we can have is for our own kind, the elite of the master race."

"Since when did you begin to read Nietzsche?"

"Since when did you begin to question the code of the Waffen SS or give a shit about civilians?"

"Lieutenant Weber, this is just an unofficial conversation between two old friends. What's been discussed here goes no further. Agreed?"

"Is that an order, Major?"

"I see no humor in that comment, but if you need it to be, yes, it is. Actually, Lieutenant, what you just said reinforces my point. Do all our actions need to be ordered? Have we become incapable of thinking for ourselves? Are we unable to make moral choices?"

A shrill whistle pierced the evening calmness.

"Another order, Major. It's time to resume our march to destiny. I hope to see you again when your head injury has healed sufficiently, and you've returned to normal. Remember, I was with you in Russia, and I saw you perform as a true soldier of the Fatherland. The 'code' was your life. You never questioned orders. You never sought morality. Morality doesn't exist, except to justify the survival of the fittest, and we must survive, whatever it takes."

"The question is, Lieutenant, what do you mean by 'we'? Humanity demands that 'we' retain some degree of compassion, even in a world gone mad. We can be loyal to the code without slaughtering innocent women and children."

"We have always been a law unto ourselves. Nothing has happened to change that. Goodbye, Major, and Heil Hitler!"

Kurt drove back to headquarters with Weber's last words ringing in his ears.

———

The next month's events challenged Kurt's search for sanity. Sent into the German defensive positions south of St. Lo, Das Reich immersed itself in a desperate attempt to halt the Allied breakout from the Normandy beachhead. Allied airpower, along with the terribly destructive force of naval bombardments, destroyed German men and equipment at an alarming rate. In an eerie atmosphere reminiscent of an earlier world war, the opposing sides dug in and slaughtered each other, day after day, with little advance by either side. The men of Das Reich, however, could tell they were no longer fighting on the Eastern Front. Unlike the Russian Front, at rare moments, a truce would be called, and stretcher-bearers from both sides would be allowed to retrieve their wounded. Although Kurt was not actively engaged in leading men into battle, his situation was still extremely dangerous; the Divisional Headquarters were located so close to the front that he could almost witness the fighting firsthand.

Kurt's face now permanently bore a strained, edgy look. As if the terror and tension of war weren't enough, Erika's due date was approaching, and he was nervously awaiting the expected message from Count Kresbach. His fretful state prevented him from getting much sleep, and he began to get confused about what he should be most concerned about, his life, Erika, the baby, Germany's future or Kresbach's assignment.

Rationalization is the religion of desperate men, and Kurt was desperate. He decided that whatever responsibilities the Count had in store for him, he felt more committed to Hitler's removal than ever. Kurt reasoned that the Allies must also see the Russians as a threat to their own civilizations, and Germany would be needed to help stop the Russian advance. If Hitler and his regime were replaced by a normal German government, the Western Allies would naturally see a truce as a way to save millions of lives in the Western Front, while at the same time allowing the Germans to stop the spread of the Red Menace. If the truce could be accomplished, Kurt believed all his other worries would be resolved. Still, whenever Kurt allowed himself to think the situation through, he could never quite escape a feeling of guilt regarding the fact that he was actively engaged in leading men who were devoted to Hitler while he was joining an attempt to eliminate him. Regardless, he was convinced that history would prove him right, and he hoped his fellow SS comrades would come to understand the logic and righteousness of his decision.

As for Oradour, Kurt's hopes for justice regarding the mass killings died on June 29. Major Diekmann left his bunker without his helmet and was killed by a shell fragment. In the ensuing days most of the battalion that Diekmann had led into Oradour would also die in Normandy. With the commanding officer and so many other participants dead and Germany's very existence at stake, the incident was swept away, and Kurt relegated it to the back of his mind.

By early July the British still had not taken Caen, but the German forces were being decimated, and replacements were unavailable. By now Kurt was living in a dream world, a fantasyland of hope and despair, of exhilaration and exhaustion, of determination and self-doubt. He gave orders, he followed orders, he watched men die, and he saw men survive, all in the torrent of destruction that seemed to have gone on forever. The Leibstandarte, Das Reich and the Twelfth SS Panzer Division (the Hitler Jugend) were especially paying a heavy price for containing the Normandy bridgehead. Das Reich was also fighting the Americans near St. Lo, but at this point Kurt was more concerned about a strange order he had been given: He was asked to attend a meeting of the German High Command in Paris in the middle of July.

In Paris a nervous Kurt Heisler reported to General Stuelpnagel, who turned out to be the leader of the local conspirators. Kurt and Stuelpnagel then had a secret meeting with Count Kresbach. For obvious reasons Kurt was given only as much information as he needed, and names and places were kept to a minimum. Any doubts he had about the commitment or capabilities of the conspirators quickly evaporated as he learned of the depth, breadth and number of people involved in the plot to take over the German government. The timeline called for Hitler to be assassinated soon, followed quickly by major cities being taken over simultaneously as a new government was being established in Berlin.

Kurt's role was to meet with the commanding officer of Das Reich and convince him to participate with the new government. Kurt told the group that he interacted with Lammerding almost daily and wasn't sure that he could be persuaded to support a group that had killed Hitler.

General Stuelpnagel responded, "Major, many high-ranking generals know of our plan, and they have said if Hitler is killed, they will become involved in the new government. Even the commander of the Leibstandarte, Sepp Dietrich, has voiced his displeasure with Hitler's unrealistic orders and has stated privately that Hitler must go. I have a hunch Field Marshals Rommel and von Kluge will join us, so General Lammerding might not be as hard to persuade as you think. As you can see, you're in very good company, but the less you know, the safer we all are, especially if we fail somehow. I need to return to my headquarters now, and I leave the rest of this briefing to Colonel Kresbach. Good luck, Major, and may God grant us success."

"I'll do my best, General."

The General gave Kurt a funny glance and laughed. "I forgot that you in the Waffen SS do not use the term 'sir.' Good day, gentlemen."

"Kurt, I'm surprised General Stuelpnagel gave you so much information. He must have really had you checked out before giving you all those names."

"I didn't know Hitler was going to be killed for sure, maybe just placed under arrest or put on trial."

"Assassination is the only way. In this case the end does justify the means."

Kurt said, "There's that term again, 'The end justifies the means,' only this time I believe it's true. Okay, I'm committed, but how will I know when Hitler has been killed and when to act?"

Colonel Kresbach got up and walked over to where Kurt was sitting and talked softly, as if someone were trying to listen in. "Starting on the nineteenth of this month you must be near a phone where you can be reached. We're lucky that you're at Headquarters and more available then a front line officer. We know how fluid the fighting is, but if you need to get sick or have a relapse from your injury, just be near your Headquarters to receive a message. It's now critical that your bravery be for our cause rather than for fighting the Allies."

"I'll do my best to be available, but the fighting is going to get even more unpredictable as the Allies get closer."

"I know. Let's hope we get lucky with the timing. Say, I just remembered, isn't Erika about to have a baby?"

"Yes, it could be any day now."

"Congratulations! You can use the impending birth as an excuse to stay by a phone. I'm sure you've considered this, but your actions can certainly help bring your child into a better world."

"I think about it all the time. What else can you tell me about the plot that the General didn't?"

"Only that when you get a phone call and hear the words 'Valkyrie successful,' it will mean Hitler is dead and the coup is in progress. We hope to get the British and Americans to agree to a ceasefire immediately so we can negotiate with them. It may take a little time for them to recognize our new government, and things may continue as they are for a short time. But they're smart, civilized people, and I see no reason for them to continue this bloodbath as long as we've removed the madman who started it."

"What if General Lammerding refuses my offer?"

"The plot will succeed with or without Das Reich. It will just be a lot easier if we can all unite behind the new government and not have internal fighting among ourselves. All the main Nazi leaders—Himmler, Goring, Goebbels—will be arrested and jailed pending trial, so we'll be Lammerding's only option. You do realize, Kurt, that you're putting your life in danger? Lammerding could have you shot for being a traitor without even really thinking about his choices."

"I know, Count. I guess it's up to me to make sure I do my job before it gets to that point. I know we can't fail, but what if we do? What if Hitler isn't killed?"

"Then we'll all be dead, and there will be no hope of saving Germany. God help us." Colonel Kresbach paused and then offered Kurt a slight degree of comfort. "Only three people in the conspiracy actually know your name: Stuelpnagel, me, and one other unnamed person. So if the plot fails, the odds are good you'll not be implicated. I know Stuelpnagel won't talk, and I promise you if I am captured, I'll never reveal your name. As for the other person, if the plot fails, he'll be dead. But we won't fail. We can't."

"Let's pray, then, that we're successful for Germany's sake. By the way, how are your wounds healing? You seem to be getting around pretty well."

"I've been given my permanent leave from the Third Panzer, and now I just sit around counting my money," laughed the Count. "But I must hurry back to Berlin before I arouse any suspicion. Someday you and your family will be proud to say you were a part of this, my young friend. Good luck, Major."

The two men embraced and parted.

Back at headquarters Kurt took every opportunity to be near General Lammerding, knowing he would soon have to confront him with the conspirator's offer. Kurt hoped that by talking with the General and showing him what a brave and loyal soldier he was, he would have additional influence when that moment arrived.

Kurt also knew he could be called into action any time. Despite his misgivings about Hitler, Kurt still felt a sense of pride every time Das Reich went into battle. He strongly believed that their sense of loyalty was to each other more than to anyone else, and if Hitler were gone, this sense of honor and duty could be channeled for the good of the new Germany. In the meantime Kurt waited and worried about when his call would come.

On July 18, 1944, two important events occurred that greatly altered the course of Kurt's life: The Allies conducted a massive air attack on the St. Lo area that pulverized the German units there, and Erika Heisler gave birth to a son, Jochen. The attack on St. Lo severely disrupted German communications, so Kurt would not learn of Jochen's birth for nearly a week. Kurt tried to stay near a phone at divisional headquarters in case the call for Operation Valkyrie came through, despite the dangers of being so close to the front lines during this attack,

At noon on July 20 an exhausted Kurt met with members of Das Reich staff to devise plans to stop the Allied offensive. He was functioning on pure adrenalin, fatigued from the constant strain of battle and the anticipation of the birth of his first child. But most of all, he was on edge waiting for the phone call announcing Hitler's death. Kurt was wolfing down a hasty lunch when a young officer told him he had a phone call. Electricity coursed through Kurt's body as he walked to the phone station.

"Major Heisler here."

"Valkyrie successful," said the unknown person on the other end of the phone. Kurt's world instantly entered a new dimension; his heart was beating so hard he felt it would explode. He had tried to prepare for this moment many times by rehearsing his speech to General Lammerding, but he was still unprepared for the surge of emotions that the message had created. A chance now existed to change the course of history, the history of the world, the history of Germany, and the history of Kurt Heisler and all the people he knew. Kurt took a deep breath and gathered himself to meet with General Lammerding.

"Major Heisler, General Lammerding wants to see you immediately!" The General's aide had appeared out of nowhere, but his timing could not have been better. Kurt literally ran to see the General, but his emotions were racing even faster. Arriving at the half-track that the General was using as a mobile command post, Kurt could see that the General and his subordinate were highly agitated. General Lammerding wasted no time explaining. "Major Heisler, the enemy is breaking through on our southern flank. I want you to gather every reserve we have and take anyone and anything that can move and plug the gap. Get started now and good luck."

"Yes, General," was all Kurt could say. Clearly, this was not the time to talk with the General about switching the allegiance of the Division. As Kurt rushed to mobilize a strike force to attack the enemy threat, he had a terrifying thought: What if he were killed before he could talk with Lammerding?

Kurt and the rest of his attack force tore into the flank of the Allied spearhead with the customary Waffen SS disdain for death and impossible odds. By sheer audacity and bravery, they were able to stall the Allied advance and bring momentary stability to the situation on the southern flank. After a day and night of unceasing combat, Kurt—covered with sweat, dirt, and a little of his own blood from a bullet that had grazed his shoulder—reported back to General Lammerding. Kurt had succeeded in his mission and proved again that he was a worthy member of the SS, so he felt this was the perfect time to explain the situation to General Lammerding. The General, however, was even more agitated than he had been the day before. "Congratulations, Major. You and your men did a fine job. Try to catch a few minutes' rest while I bring you up to date. I don't know all the details, but I was informed early this morning that an attempt was made on the Fuhrer's life at his headquarters at Wolf's Lair. Thank God he survived the bomb. Some traitor named Stauffenberg hoped to overthrow Hitler. He and some others have already been executed, and we can only hope the rest of the collaborators will be found and eliminated soon. We of the Waffen SS need to be even stronger than ever to our oath and prove to Hitler how fortunate he is to have men like us supporting him. See to your wound and rest up, Major. I'm sure you'll be back in action soon."

Kurt walked back to his quarters in a daze. He could not remember what his response to General Lammerding had been. He was totally numb, adrift in an immense black universe of despair and pure fear. Paralysis set in as he tried to eat. His hands shook so badly he could barely get food to his mouth. He needed time to sort out what had happened. What should he do? He needed to think, but there was no time to be alone and sort things out; the war was all-consuming.

The ensuing days challenged the very core of Kurt's sanity. Struggling to stay alive and still do his duty, he was debilitated by a steady diet of war and worry. He was in battle almost constantly, but even when he had a chance to rest, he was unable to sleep. He was in constant dread of being identified as a conspirator, especially after he heard that Stuelpnagel and Kresbach had been arrested. Horrifying thoughts ran through his over-worked mind. Would they implicate him while they were being tortured? If he were found out, would Erika also suffer the consequences? Kurt's fear and anxiety consumed him. Even his first quick surge of joy over Jochen's birth was quickly replaced by an even more intense sense of foreboding concerning the events of July 20. And the internal questions never ceased. Would he ever see his son? Even worse, would his son suffer because of the failed plot to kill Hitler? Would Jochen be taken from Erika and raised without knowing his real parents?

Meanwhile, the fighting grew even worse. On July 25 Das Reich suffered through thirteen Allied attacks and repulsed every one. The shelling had been so intense that the terrain surrounding Das Reich resembled the surface of the moon. Eventually, Das Reich became so decimated Kurt was forced to assemble a platoon of cooks, clerks and other non-combatants to fill gaps in the line. Between the constant combat and worrying about being identified as a conspirator, Kurt felt like a walking corpse. In early August the constant stress finally broke Kurt. The event that drove him over the edge was the news of the death of his brother. Jurgen— the perfect soldier, Kurt's role model, the best man at his wedding, his last surviving family member—was gone, killed in Normandy in late July. When Kurt got the news a few days later, his emotional foundation crumbled; he had a complete mental and physical breakdown and was sent home to Germany to recover.

A week later Kurt lay recuperating in a military hospital in Berlin, being treated for severe shell shock. He had virtually no feelings left, and his doctors had ordered complete bed rest with no visitors, fearful that any additional strain, good or bad, might send him into an irreversible void. Fortunately for him, no one knew the real cause of his mental stress, so his condition was blamed on combat stress and the head injury he had suffered in Russia the previous year. So, for a time, he was able to escape the daily tension of war, but not the fear of being discovered as a traitor to the Third Reich.

Heavily sedated, Kurt slept constantly. By week's end he appeared much better, at least outwardly, but internally he was still a mess. As a soldier who had seen so much death, Kurt accepted the reality of Jurgen's death rather quickly; Jurgen had chosen to be a soldier and knew the risks. So, while Kurt continued to grieve the loss of his only brother, at least the doctors knew about that condition and could treat it. What they didn't know was the all-consuming fear Kurt harbored inside, the fear of being exposed as a conspirator. He ached to tell Erika about his involvement in the plot and prayed that she would understand his motives, but every time he considered telling her, the image of Captain Anderson's mutilated body appeared before him. As much as Kurt longed for Erika's comfort and support, he knew he could not include her, so he continued to suffer in silence.

To help quiet all the voices in his head, Kurt finally formed a plan of action for dealing with his agony in true Waffen SS fashion: He would proceed with a full frontal attack. Kurt reasoned that if General Stuelpnagel or Count von Kresbach had named him as a conspirator, the Gestapo certainly wouldn't have shown him any pity just because he was recuperating; he would have been hauled out of the hospital, tortured and executed immediately. Still, even if he hadn't been named, it was well known that he had been the Count's roommate in the hospital and that he had visited the Count at his estate near Berlin. If the Gestapo didn't have this information already, they would find out eventually, and it would be routine to check Kurt out. So, to counter this action, Kurt decided to call the Gestapo just before he left the hospital and offer up what he knew about the Count. If the Gestapo did come to question him before he could make the call, Kurt decided that he would have to assume the Count had not revealed anything about his involvement; he would steadfastly deny any knowledge of the plot until the bitter end. Armed with this plan of action, Kurt tried to focus his remaining time on the joy of being reunited with Erika and seeing his son for the first time.

After two weeks of rest and therapy Kurt was ready to be discharged from the hospital. The day before he was released, he made two phone calls, one to Erika and one to the Gestapo Headquarters in Berlin.

———

The day of his release from the hospital Kurt sat quietly on the chair in his room, nauseated beyond anything he had ever felt before, even in combat. He was swimming in his own sweat, afraid he was going to pass out. Fear gripped him in a vise of indecision and vacillation. Should he run? Should he commit suicide? That would be a clear admission of guilt, and then what would happen to Erika and Jochen? After an hour of creating the worst possible scenarios, Kurt gradually began to calm down by convincing himself that meeting with the Gestapo would be a good thing: He could finally confront the demons of doubt that had plagued him since July. Drawing on that hope, Kurt got up, threw some cold water on his face, and changed his sweat-soaked clothing. He then gathered his few belongings and waited for the discharge nurse to escort him to the waiting staff car so he could depart to face his fears head-on.

———

Upon Kurt's arrival at the Gestapo administration building, he was taken to a small room and seated at a desk opposite a single Gestapo interrogator. "Good afternoon, Major Heisler. Thank you for contacting us and offering to come in. How's your recovery going?"

Kurt had rehearsed his performance many times, so he decided to force the issue immediately. "Splendid. I'm about ready to rejoin my division and help bring a successful conclusion to this damn war. I know you're busy, so let's not waste time. I'll tell you why I called you about Count von Kresbach. I saw his name on a list of the traitors that the People's Court had already executed as part of the assassination plot. Obviously, you need to question anyone he came in contact with, so I wanted to tell you about my encounters with Kresbach as soon as my doctors felt I was able." Kurt's outward performance was truly remarkable, because inwardly he was in a state of shock. He forced his body to remain calm enough to observe his interrogator's reaction for any sign that Kresbach had revealed his involvement in the attempted coup.

The agent was caught a bit off guard, but recovered quickly. "Well, yes, Major, we'd certainly be interested in such information. Please, tell me about your relationship with the Count."

"He was my roommate in the hospital during my recovery in the fall of 1943, and we got to know each other a bit during our daily conversations. When we were released, I went to Berlin and visited him a couple of times at his invitation. I found him to be a charming man and a gracious host. We mostly drank sherry and traded stories about the war in Russia and what needed to be done to defeat the Soviets. He never mentioned any plot against Hitler or even expressed any dissatisfaction with the war effort. I'm sure he never intended—nor would he be so stupid—to tell a member of the Waffen SS that he was involved in a plot to kill Hitler. If he had, I would have turned him in immediately."

"Did he mention any other names to you? Did he say anything you can think of that would help us in our continuing investigation?"

"I've been thinking of that since I saw his name on the list—and believe me, I had plenty of thinking time lying in a hospital bed—but I really can't recall anything he said that was unusual, either spoken or implied.

He was a delightful host, and we talked about our families a lot. In our last meeting he insisted that I bring my wife Erika on my next visit, but I was deployed again before we could accept that invitation."

"Tell me, Major, why would a man of the Count's social standing form a friendship with you? You certainly don't have any royal bloodlines, nor has your family accumulated any great wealth."

"You're absolutely right, but I never thought I was his ultimate target. I'm sure you're aware—as was the Count—that I married into the powerful von Klugemann family, which has many contacts within the Nazi Party. I assumed he was using me to get to them so he could social climb a bit. Perhaps he was even hoping to recruit some of the new aristocracy to his cause."

The interrogator eyed Kurt coldly for what seemed an eternity. "We're quite sure we've identified all those involved in the plot, but you never know. We've also known all about your meetings with Kresbach for quite some time, Major. We'd have talked to you much sooner, but our background check revealed that you have a brother, Jurgen, who is a steadfast defender of the Reich, and he has vouched for your unquestioning loyalty to der Fuhrer. Besides, had you been involved, Kresbach couldn't possibly have kept that information from us after what we put him through; no mortal could have."

"Kresbach sure had me fooled. He seemed like a good soldier and a fine gentleman, but I'm glad he got what he deserved."

The nameless form behind the desk rose. "Very well, Major, we're both busy men, and you're free to go."

Kurt got up, exchanged "Heil Hitlers" and left the agent to his pile of forms.

As soon as he was outside Kurt breathed a heavy sigh of relief, but he knew he was not completely free from concern. He was well aware how devious the Gestapo could be. They could be testing him, and he resolved to continue to be careful. As he left to join Erika and the von Klugemanns, he felt great pain thinking about the agony his friend Count Kresbach must have endured in order to keep their secret, a selfless, courageous act that had allowed Kurt to keep his life and family intact.

"Isn't he perfect?" beamed Erika.

The joy that filled Kurt as he held his young son for the first time was indescribable. He held Jochen for some time without speaking before finally finding his voice. "Well, with you for a mother and Maria for a grandmother, what else could Jochen be but perfect?"

It was impossible to tell who was more pleased with Kurt's comment, Erika or Maria.

"Yes, Jochen, you'll grow up to be a fine man, just like your father, and you'll perform great deeds of valor, just as he has done," proclaimed Maria.

"Let's hope he won't need to. This war can't go on forever, Mother. Germany has lost far too many young men doing heroic deeds of glory in war. Maybe we need people to do great things during peacetime."

"Germany will prevail. Our scientists are coming up with new weapons, and our armies are still strong, and your father says our factories are still producing at full capacity."

"Mother, face reality. We're losing the war. Our cities are being reduced to rubble, and our people are facing hardships unimaginable a short time ago. I refuse to let my son grow up in such an insane world."

"And what do you propose to do to solve our problems? I'm sure Hitler would like to hear your solutions."

"From what I've heard, Hitler doesn't listen to anybody but himself. Maybe that's our biggest problem."

"Erika, you don't know what you're saying! The Fuhrer will lead us through this, mark my words. Enough of this talk. I want to enjoy my grandson and savor this moment."

Kurt listened in silent amazement at the exchange between mother and daughter. Maria's loyalty to the Reich to the bitter end was predictable, but Erika's attitude had come as a surprise. Erika appeared quite disillusioned with Hitler and the war, and Kurt wondered what the source was for her newly-expressed cynicism. Just maybe, Kurt allowed himself to hope, she would understand his involvement with the conspirators. Still, he didn't dare tell her about it.

That night the von Klugemanns held a private family supper at their home. Frederick and Maria, Kurt and Erika, and Uncle Konrad and Aunt Hilda sat around the table, where the conversation centered on two obvious topics, Kurt and Jochen, and, of course, the war. The first part of the evening was very emotional as condolences and remembrances of Kurt's parents and Jurgen and Hans brought everyone to tears.

"Kurt, you and I are all that's left on our side of the family," lamented Konrad.

"Yes, I know, Uncle. That's why we must win this war to avenge their deaths. Don't worry. Somehow we'll get through all of this. I won't deny that we're in serious trouble, but there's still a chance for us to win if we can fight on just one front. We must somehow get the Allies to agree to a truce, get them to stop the bombing and let us stop Stalin before it's too late."

"Why would the Allies ever agree to a truce now? They've pushed us back all the way across France and are right on Germany's doorstep. Why would they want to stop?"

"We must convince them it's in their best interest to have a cease fire, that the world will be safer if they allow us to stop the spread of Bolshevism. Also, the Americans are more protective of their troops in battle; not having to invade Germany would save them a lot of casualties."

Uncle Konrad gave Kurt a look of bewilderment. "Sounds like a good idea, but I can't imagine how that would convince them when they know they have the upper hand. Just drive around any German city and see if you can find more than three streets in a row without damage. Sooner or later there won't be a building standing in Nuremberg. I'm not a defeatist, but something has to happen soon, or we'll all be living in holes in the ground."

"Don't worry, Uncle, the Waffen SS will come to the rescue. Remember our code: Nothing is impossible!"

Kurt could not believe he was acting so full of bravado, but he felt everyone needed a little dose of optimism—even if it was only a patriotic boast without solid support—before redirecting the conversation.

"Frederick, how much longer can the factory system continue to produce what the military needs?"

"Since you first asked me that question about a year ago, I've made some interesting calculations. First, we'll run short of qualified pilots and soldiers before we lose the ability to produce machines for them. Second, no matter what we can do, the Russians and the Western Allies can produce far more than we can. America herself doubles our output. America's economy is fueling the Allied success, most notably by enabling the Soviet Union to survive, even though, historically, the United States and the Soviet Union have always disliked each other. That's why I agree with you, Kurt. We must somehow drive a wedge between America and the Soviet Union. We must negotiate a peace with the Western Allies. It is our best option."

Maria von Klugemann summoned all her charismatic bearing, stood up and banged on the table with her fork. After getting everyone's attention, she made a toast. "To Hitler, to Germany, to the German people, to the SS, and to Jochen Heisler, the future hope of the Fatherland."

———

Later that night in the privacy of their bedroom, Erika and Kurt were finally able to share their hopes, fears, and feelings about the future.

"Jochen sleeps soundly. You've trained him well, Erika. You should be an officer with such leadership abilities."

"Why do you always have to put a military slant on everything, Kurt?"

"It's what I am, and I guess I've become too much of what I am."

"That's a ridiculous statement, and I'm not even sure what it means."

"I'm not sure I do either, Erika. I know I carry a lot of guilt about things I've done during the war, and I won't do them again. I'll never shoot another prisoner or another civilian. I look at Jochen, and I think about all the people dying in this war on both sides. I think about all the people I've killed, and I see them as small children. Why do we kill so easily and with no remorse during war? I ask myself, and then I remember that is what I've been trained to do and what I am."

Erika gently encircled Kurt with her arms and pulled him into her bosom. "Kurt, what we've done, or who we are is not as important as what we can become. I know I'm changing my beliefs about the world. I never really had any of my own before; I just copied mother and followed along. It all seemed so wonderful to be respected and to belong to an important family in a country that was dazzling the world. I'm afraid there's no hope for my mother and father. They'll die as true Nazis, but my son will never be one, and neither will I, at least not anymore."

"Are you just talking like that because we're losing? Would you feel the same if we were winning and still dazzling the world?"

"I hope so. I now know about what we're doing to the Jews in the concentration camps, and I'm horrified. Human beings don't do that to other human beings. Most German people know something about what's going on, but they pretend not to, or say it's none of their business. Well, whose business is it?"

Kurt reflected for minute, debating how much to reveal and decided it wasn't the time yet. "Speaking of business, do you spend much time working with your father?"

"Some. It gives me something to do, and it keeps me from having to do something worse. A number of my friends have been injured or killed in this stupid war. Women are driving buses, working in factories, serving in bomb clean-up squads and manning air defenses. It's ridiculous what Germany is being reduced to, and because of what? Our Aryan superiority?"

"Erika, all that is sobering, but what worries me most, regardless of what I said at dinner, is that time is now against us. Things should never have gotten to this point, but they have. What are our choices now? What can we do? In my case, I think the best thing I can do is fight with my division to see if we can reach a stalemate on our Western border. So I have to remain what I am, at least for the immediate future. I think you need to concentrate on taking care of Jochen—whatever happens—and making sure the two of you survive to help rebuild Germany in the future."

"You make it sound like you won't survive."

"I don't mean that. Have I ever failed you?"

"I hope you don't fail us, you, me and Jochen. Please hold me, Kurt."

———

In mid-September Erika paid a visit to her father at his factory. Frederick was not in his office, but was supposed to be returning shortly, so Erika waited for him. She had been her father's private secretary until the latter stages of her pregnancy, but had not been back in his office for more than six months. Browsing through his records, she discovered just how much work was being done by slave labor. As the minutes ticked by, she walked over to a large window and looked out over a sprawling expanse of industrial development, which now seemed to her to be a monument to man's capacity to improve his life at the expense of others. Erika's awareness of the true nature of the Nazi policy toward non-Aryans was growing, and she was becoming concerned about the morality of her father's business practices.

As Erika was looking at the pictures on her father's desk, Frederick entered the room and closed the door. Without saying a word, Erika went over and gave her father a hug.

"What a pleasant surprise to see you, Erika. Is this a social visit, or are you coming back to work? I think Jochen needs you more than I do."

"I'll be back, but not for a while. I suppose we could discuss this at home some time."

Frederick sat down at his large mahogany desk while Erika remained standing at his side. "Just before you came in I was looking at the picture of Hans on your desk. I know how much you wanted him to take over the business. What a waste his death was."

Frederick's face flashed with unaccustomed emotion. Recovering quickly, he said, "I guess you'll have to help run the business until Jochen is ready to take over, and don't ever say that Hans died a wasteful death."

Erika walked over to the front of the desk and sat down in a large leather chair. "I would rather focus on another issue than the death of my brother. Hans died doing what he thought was best for Germany; time will soon prove if he was right."

Frederick couldn't contain his composure any longer and pounded the table with his fists. "Hans was right, and we shall win this war and prove to the world that Germany is the greatest nation on earth."

Erika hesitated, wondering if this was the time and place to challenge her father. She stood up and began pacing in front of the desk. "Father, I hope I'm not about to offend you, but if we are such a great country, why do we need to use Russians and Jews as slave labor in our factories? Why do we need to work people to death to prove we are a master race? How can we abuse other human beings in such a manner?"

Frederick remained calm this time. "Apparently, I've given you too much credit. I always assumed—even though you're a woman—that you were able to understand such matters. I assumed you recognized the fact that a business can survive only if it makes a profit. I assumed you accepted the reality that whatever enables the Third Reich to survive is justified. I assumed you were a daughter who trusted and loved her father. I've treated you more like a son than a daughter, especially since Hans' death. Have I been wrong to do so?"

Erika pulled a chair next to Frederick and sat down. Leaning toward him, she said softly, "Father, I love you, and I hope I'm not being disrespectful, but I don't want you to lose your soul to money or to something that is evil."

"Erika, this conversation has gone on long enough. What you are saying borders on treason."

Erika knew that she would never be able to talk with her father like this again, but the image of Sophie Scholl waiting for her execution was uppermost in her mind, so she continued to pursue the issue. "What about Jochen? Do you want your grandson to inherit a legacy of greed, corruption and inhumanity? Do you want him to be heir to a kingdom built on the suffering of others? If we do win this war, what lesson will we have taught the world? That only power matters and justice does not exist except to give legitimacy to rule by dictator?"

In a harsh, sarcastic voice Frederick replied, "In the past you seemed quite happy with the advantages this 'evil wealth' provided. Only the strong and loyal will survive these times. I hope you are one of them. Your mother and I love Germany. We fully support Hitler and still see him as the savior of our country. I suggest that you return to the attitude you held when you were younger and appreciated the destiny of Aryan superiority. Ours is still a noble cause."

"I guess I'm finally growing up."

Frederick stood up and shook a finger at his daughter. "Erika, I will not allow you to speak like this again! You are not in a position to question your father or your leaders. Your place is to support your husband, have children, and help win the war. Don't trouble yourself with matters that are beyond your understanding. We won't speak of this again. Return to Kurt and Jochen. I have work to do." He gave her one last, stern glance before he walked out and slammed the door.

Erika returned home, satisfied that she had finally expressed her opinions to her father, but disillusioned with his response. For the immediate future Erika decided she would appear loyal and obedient, but beyond that she was unsure how her loyalty to home and country would unfold.

That night as she lay in bed with Kurt, Erika continued to think about her father. It had been a while since Kurt had turned his back to her and become silent. Erika nudged him. "Kurt, are you asleep?"

"Yes, can't you tell?"

"Good, then I can ask you a question. What do you think of my father?"

"I said I was asleep."

"And I asked you a question. Be serious now and answer me."

Turning around to face Erika, but keeping his eyes closed, Kurt said, "Erika, I suppose if I'm ever going to get some sleep, I'd better answer your question. Your father is a fine man. Good night."

"Do you know what my father said to me today when I visited him at work? I asked him about the slave labor he uses to keep his factory going, and he said he had no choice, that there were no other workers available. When I continued to question him, he told me to mind my own business. Me, his own daughter!"

Kurt's snoring ended Erika's story.

CHAPTER XVII

The End of Life

Shortly before he was to return to active duty Kurt received a phone call that caused him great joy and some concern. Jurgen called to inform everyone that he was alive and well. He and a few of his staff had been cut off behind enemy lines during the fighting in Normandy. They had hidden in the cellar of a farmhouse for five days and then made their escape back to the German lines. In all the confusion from the Allied attack, the information regarding his safe return had somehow never been sent to any family members. Jurgen was now stationed in Berlin on a special assignment for the Leibstandarte.

Kurt expressed his profound joy to Jurgen, but was puzzled by his brother's rather distant tone and mysterious goodbye. Jurgen ended the conversation by saying, "Major Heisler, I would like to see you about a very important matter as soon as possible. I'll come down for a visit as soon as you get settled again in Das Reich. I'm looking forward to our meeting. Heil Hitler!"

The doubt of being discovered is always the greatest fear of the guilty, and something in Jurgen's chilly voice created sharp pangs of fear that gnawed at Kurt's confidence. Even though he had convinced the Gestapo he hadn't been involved, he knew Jurgen was well connected throughout the Nazi hierarchy and had other sources of information. Did Jurgen know about his involvement in the plot? The question trickled like a river of acid through Kurt's mind, eroding all rational thinking about his brother's intent. No matter how hard he admonished himself for being such a worrier, Kurt could not escape the feeling that Jurgen knew.

As Kurt went about his life before the meeting with Jurgen, he surmised that if Jurgen did know about his involvement in the plot, he had kept the information to himself, or else Kurt would already be in the Gestapo's custody or dead. Kurt also considered the possibility that Jurgen and the Gestapo were setting an elaborate trap. He hoped that his fears were groundless and that he would celebrate a happy reunion with his brother, but he needed to prepare for the worst. Analyzing possible purposes for the meeting and planning his responses consumed much of Kurt's free time during the next few weeks. He wanted to warn Erika, but what if his fears were unfounded? Kurt calculated that if Jurgen knew about his involvement in the plot, Jurgen would deal with his younger brother personally. If Jurgen challenged him concerning the attempt on Hitler's life, he would stand up to him, explain his reasons for becoming involved, question Jurgen on his steadfast loyalty to a lost and evil cause and suffer the consequences.

Kurt doubted that he could sway Jurgen, but the time had come to stand up for his beliefs and admit that following Hitler had been a colossal mistake. As he thought about Jurgen, he toyed with the idea of confronting his brother about his change of loyalties, even if Jurgen didn't know anything. Maybe he could save his brother. The only thing Kurt was afraid of at this point was that his involvement might bring harm to Erika or Jochen. Kurt felt sure Jurgen wouldn't involve them as long as Erika didn't know about Kurt's involvement, but it was still a risk to assume that. Although the risk was slight, it was a good enough reason to keep Erika in the dark.

Despite Kurt's tenuous situation and the war's expanding impact on Germany, he was determined to make the most of his last days with his extended Nuremberg family before rejoining his unit. Between the constant air raids and the incessant speeches by Minister of Propaganda

Goebbels, the Heisler-Klugemann entourage tried not to let the war intrude on their private time together, which worked until they were forced to look outside and see the devastating effects of the Allied bombs. Still, refreshed by his time with Erika and his introduction to his son, Kurt reported back to active duty fortified by the knowledge that he was fighting not just to save Germany, but his family.

———

Jurgen arrived at Das Reich headquarters without warning a few days after Kurt was back at work. Everyone understood the natural desire of the two brothers to see each other after all they had been through, so nothing seemed unusual when Kurt invited Jurgen into the room that served as his office and dismissed his staff.

"Heil Hitler, Colonel Heisler. I'm very glad to see you. You look well after your ordeal," Kurt said.

"And I'm glad to have a chance to finally talk to you, brother. Are we alone, if you know what I mean?"

"Yes, Colonel, no one else can hear our conversation. Now, what's all this mystery and seriousness about?"

"Sit down at your desk, Major. I prefer to remain standing."

"Is that an order, Colonel?"

"Do as you wish."

Kurt sat down and looked intently at Jurgen, who paced back and forth as he started talking. "This is no time for small talk, so I'll get straight to the point. I'm going to ask you a question, but don't answer until I've explained my reasons for asking. That will give you a little time to consider your answer. Were you involved in the July 20 attempt on Hitler's life?"

After a dramatic pause while he stared at Kurt, Jurgen continued. "I know you've satisfied the Gestapo about not being involved, but now I need to hear it from you in person. Here's why I'm not satisfied, even though the experts believed you. Everyone did see a remarkable set of coincidences concerning your relationship with Kresbach. You were his roommate at the hospital, you visited him at his estate, and then you just happened to be called to make a report to the German High Command in Paris shortly before the July attempt on Hitler's life. Considering the fact that most members of the German High Command in Paris were involved in the plot, it all seemed rather convenient."

Jurgen stopped and looked at Kurt inquiringly, but Kurt said nothing, so Jurgen continued. "That was a clever trick calling the Gestapo and offering up information about your association with Kresbach before they brought you in for questioning. You didn't know I had already visited with the Gestapo before you met with them. I listened to tapes of both Stuelpnagel and Kresbach being interrogated about you, and let me just say, the creative juices of the Gestapo must have been flowing because the agony in the traitors' voices was enough to make my skin crawl. However, they never implicated you. That seemed to satisfy the Gestapo, especially with your record in the Waffen SS and the glowing account I gave them about your dedication to Hitler. But I need to be convinced, because I understand something about you that the Gestapo does not. You are your mother's son; you've always been the sensitive, caring, religious one in the family. I thought these strains of weakness had been erased, and maybe they have, but I need to be assured. Now please answer my question!"

With a forcefulness and sense of purpose that he had never before felt in the presence of his brother, Kurt stood up. "Please sit down, Colonel. It's now my turn to talk. Please allow me the same courtesy I gave you, and let me finish before you respond."

Anticipating what was coming, Jurgen gave Kurt an icy stare and rigidly took a seat.

"Yes, Jurgen, I was involved in the plot in a rather small way. I had no connection to the actual physical attempt by Stauffenberg, but that's immaterial. I knew about the plot, and I approved of it. I'm now firmly convinced that we've been following a fantasy, a fantasy that has turned into a nightmare of evil that has destroyed our souls, destroyed Germany, and slaughtered millions of innocent people. I'm afraid that after the failure of the attempt at Wolf's Lair, there is little hope to save Germany from total and utter destruction. I think even you can see that, and I hope you can also see that we've both chosen the wrong path and must do whatever we can to make up for our sins. I love you as a brother, but not what you stand for."

Jurgen could not contain himself any longer. "You weak, spineless traitor! I should've known better than to believe you could change; you were always too much like mother. Now you've brought shame to the Heisler name and to the Waffen SS. Mark my words, you'll forever regret the day you betrayed your oath to be loyal to Hitler until death. And what do you propose to do to make up for these 'sins,' as you call them? Kill Hitler by yourself? Is that how you intend to redeem yourself?"

"I think that depends on what you intend to do, brother. I'm surprised you haven't already attempted to shoot me."

"In due time, Major!" snapped Jurgen.

"Before I ask you to explain that comment, let me finish. I see no alternative except to keep fighting and try to get the Allies on the Western Front to seek peace. I know we're working on some plan to accomplish that goal, and if Das Reich is involved, I'll fight as fanatically as ever, but I'll behave as correctly as the war will allow me to. We need to be strong enough to stop Russia from entering Germany; there's no alternative to that issue. As for Hitler, sooner or later he and the Nazi Party have to go. There's no alternative to that issue, either."

"As despicable as you are, part of what you say is true. This is not the time or the place to solve my problem of how to remove your traitorous stain from my good name. So don't worry, I won't turn you in, although sometimes I think it would have been better for all of us if you had been exposed and executed along with all the rest of the treasonous bastards. The truth is, I'd never trust your fate to a court. I want to take care of you myself. So, for now, I trust you to do your duty, but as soon as the right opportunity presents itself, be assured I will kill you. By the way, do you even know what happened to your fellow conspirators?"

"Other than Stuelpnagel and Kresbach I don't even know who any of them were, nor do I know any details about the plot itself. I know Kresbach was tortured and killed by the Gestapo and Stuelpnagel was executed, but Hitler's been executing officers for all kinds of reasons late-ly, and there's no way for me to know which of them were involved. If you want me to stay alive long enough to kill me yourself, why don't you fill me in so I don't accidentally say something that would implicate me before you get your chance?"

"As you wish! Maybe you'll realize the futility of your actions when you see how quickly these vermin were discovered and exterminated. The leader of this stupidity, which was called Operation Valkyrie, was Colonel Claus von Stauffenberg, a wounded, decorated soldier of the Wehrmacht. On July 19 Stauffenberg was called to a meeting at Hitler's East Prussia Headquarters at Wolf's Lair, and the plan was for him to plant a bomb there. Fortunately for our beloved Fuhrer, the meeting was moved from an underground concrete bunker to a wooden building so the windows could be opened because of the unseasonable heat. On July 20 Stauffenberg planted the bomb under the conference table, excused himself, got in a car with his driver and witnessed the explosion. He didn't think Hitler could possibly have survived the blast, and he flew back to Berlin to join his fellow traitors. The trip took three hours, and the plane had no radio, so Stauffenberg was sure the coup was in motion.

"The open windows defused the blast, and the heavy oak table ab-sorbed much of the explosion, so the damage was minimal. A few officers were killed, but Hitler was only slightly injured. Stauffenberg's absence was quickly noted, and orders for his arrest were issued immediately. While Stauffenberg was flying to Berlin the other conspirators failed to put Operation Valkyrie into action, so they didn't seize control of the critical buildings and personnel as planned. This failure allowed Herr Goebbels to announce from the Berlin radio station that Hitler was indeed alive, and the rest of the plan fell apart quickly. Stauffenberg and a number of oth-ers were marched into a courtyard and executed by a firing squad. Field Marshal von Kluge, who was going to lead the coup in Paris, refused to take part in the coup when he learned Hitler had survived, and later commit-ted suicide, fearful that his knowledge of the plot would be discovered and he would be arrested. Field Marshal Rommel was also forced to commit suicide because of his involvement. Another traitor, General Stuelpnagel, tried to commit suicide, but was unsuccessful, and was later tortured and eventually hanged. Still another, General Beck, asked permission to take his own life, but was only able to wound himself in the head, and the final shot was happily delivered by an arresting officer. These were the type of fools you were aligned with, Major. They couldn't even kill themselves properly, much less kill the Fuhrer. What do you have to say for yourself now?"

"Your information changes nothing. Like me, they all knew the risks and believed Hitler had to be killed to save Germany. He's disgraced Germany forever. I want to raise Jochen in a world without Hitler and all that he stands for. If I survive this war, I'll work to rebuild Germany's image, if that's even possible. But don't worry, I'll do my best to stay alive, but for my family, not to fight you."

"Does Erika know of your disloyal behavior?"

"No, I haven't told her a thing."

"At least you've done one smart thing. I won't tell Erika, either, because your family doesn't deserve to suffer for your mistakes. Jochen deserves to grow up thinking his father was a man of honor, not a cowardly turncoat to his own comrades. Lucky for you the Gestapo doesn't know what I know. After Count von Kresbach was executed, his wife and daughter were thrown into prison, and his land and wealth were confiscated. Luckily, his son had been killed in the war, so at least he was spared the agony of knowing his father had committed treason."

"I'd thank you for your silence, but I know you're not doing it out of any kindness to me or my family. You're just protecting yourself. We both know the Gestapo won't go easy on you, either, if this gets out."

"Be that as it may, Major, as soon as the war permits, you and I will go to Ansbach and drive out to the woods where you first expressed a desire to follow in my footsteps. We'll have a duel, and my problem will be solved. Don't disappoint me and die in battle. I don't want to be robbed of the pleasure of erasing your disgrace myself."

Jurgen turned and stomped out, leaving Kurt to ponder the immensity of the confrontation.

During October and November Das Reich was again refitted and made battle-ready for Germany's last great offensive of World War II, but only a few high-ranking generals knew what Hitler's final gamble would be. The planning was meticulously carried out and kept extremely secret, and code words were changed constantly. No one at the divisional level knew what plans were being formulated by their superiors; even divisional commanders only found out their missions at the last moment. Given the duress that the German economy and transportation network were under and the losses suffered by the German military, a near miracle of logistics was achieved in setting up the formidable force assembled for the final attack on the Western Allies.

The daring German plan, Watch on the Rhine, called for the attacking force to begin in the mountainous region of the Ardennes on December 16, 1944, smash through Luxembourg and Belgium, and then push on to Antwerp. If successful, the German forces would drive a wedge between the Allies, destroy some thirty British and American divisions and force a stalemate on the Western Front. Most of the high-ranking generals who were consulted about the plan felt it was too ambitious. However, Hitler was not to be denied his chance to snatch final victory from the clutches of certain defeat. Besides the location of the initial attack point, the biggest surprise of the German attack was the magnitude of the army Hitler and his generals had been able to assemble. Across an eighty-five mile front, a quarter million troops, a thousand tanks and assault guns, and nineteen hundred pieces of artillery had been moved into position for the Ardennes surprise attack that the Americans later named The Battle of the Bulge.

During the preparations for the final attack, Kurt encountered Otto Weber. The two friends had not seen each other since their discussion of the Oradour incident back in Normandy. Kurt was inspecting some new equipment late one cold, crisp December afternoon when he heard a loud voice calling above the noise of the passing vehicles, "Major Heisler, Major Heisler."

An officer in a half-track gave a command, and a column of assorted military machines ground to a halt. The officer and his men wore white camouflage that matched their white vehicles. Kurt didn't recognize the officer until he had walked within twenty feet. "Captain Weber! Otto, I haven't seen you since Normandy. How the hell have you been?"

Otto wrapped Kurt in a joyful embrace. Otto sported a week-old beard, and, with his white whiskers and white uniform, could have passed for a polar bear. Kurt saluted and said, "Congratulations, Otto. I never thought you'd become a Captain."

Otto chuckled as a smile split the snowy mat covering his face. "I don't understand why I keep getting promoted, either. Times must be getting pretty desperate. I'm glad to see you, Major. We've just missed seeing each other a number of times. My transfer to another regiment didn't help matters any, either. How's your head?"

"Still attached, thankfully, but Erika thinks I'm crazy at times. You seem to have survived Normandy in one piece. How're you feeling?"

Otto leaned against Kurt, feigning old age, and said, "It's tough getting around at my age, especially carrying the added burden of being an officer. But I guess you know all about that. I picked up a few new nicks during Normandy, but nothing too serious. I was just thinking last night about all the shit we've been through since the summer of '41. I can't believe any of us are still around. By the way, congratulations on becoming a father. I hear mother and son are doing fine. See, I try to keep up on the status of my old friends—at least the few I still have."

Kurt smiled. "Thank you, Captain Weber. I'm ashamed to admit that I haven't kept track of you very well; my head injury kept me out of the game for quite a while. How's your love life? You should be ready to settle down soon, given your advanced age."

The roar of a passing Tiger tank interrupted their conversation, giving Kurt time to reflect on the fact that Otto was barely twenty-one. As the growling Tiger crawled away, Otto joked, "I suppose I could also be a father. Where and who I couldn't possibly guess. There would be a certain irony if I had a Russian son."

"I thought you always said Russians were just for killing."

"Well, I made a few exceptions, but I'd guess that by now those women are all dead. It's more likely I have a French or German son. I should check with the Lebensborn and see if my sense of duty produced any results."

Kurt shook his head. "Captain Weber, some day your excessive sense of duty will get you into some serious trouble."

Indignantly, Otto replied, "My sense of duty is still to kill Russians, not to fuck them. I enjoy the art of killing—British, French, Americans—but especially Russians."

"How much more killing do you think we'll have to do before this war is over?"

Otto peered into the winter haze and, without turning to look at Kurt, said, "I'm not sure I could live in a world without war. The exhilaration of the hunt, of killing or being killed, is a very powerful drug. Once you've tasted it and become addicted to its thrill, normal existence seems drab and mundane. Kurt, we're professional killers, and we're the best. Someday we'll be killed, too. We must expect violent death; it's our natural end. However, we can't ever lose sight of our purpose, to inflict more death than we absorb."

Kurt grabbed Otto by the shoulders and turned him so they were face-to-face. "Otto, I think we can save Germany without dying, and I think we can live in a world that is at peace."

A sneer crossed Otto's face, and he gently pushed Kurt away. "The only way we can live in peace is if we eliminate the Russian vermin. That's our purpose and it will be our legacy. Our sacrifice will only be justified with the defeat of Russia. A world free of Bolshevik filth will be our monument."

"I think you're being too cynical, Otto. Life is more than endless conflict terminated only by death."

"Being superior has a tendency to make a person cynical, Major, but superiority gives validity to our actions."

Kurt shuffled his feet in the shallow snow and then took a step forward to meet Otto's eyes. "Captain Weber, we must be careful not to become part of the filth, or we'll have to destroy ourselves."

"The only way we can become filth is if we become weak and sentimental. Remember, it's the birthright of the strong to dominate the weak." Otto clicked his heels together, saluted Kurt and exclaimed, "Heil Hitler!"

Kurt returned Otto's salute, and Captain Weber climbed back into his half-track. Captain Weber gave a command, and the column resumed its journey. As he disappeared around the bend, Otto yelled to Kurt, "Remember the code. Stay strong and we'll meet again."

Kurt watched in melancholy fascination as the SS column slowly vanished, and Otto's final words echoed deep in Kurt's conscience.

———•———

Before he left Nuremberg to rejoin his division for Watch on the Rhine, Kurt and Erika discussed her options for the future, depending on what happened to Kurt and to Germany in the coming months. The emotional, tearful talks ranged from near despair to an almost euphoric sense of hope. In the end a heavy dose of reality forced them to make a number of difficult decisions. They agreed that if things went bad, Erika would remain in Nuremberg or move west; she could not allow herself or Jochen to become prisoners of the Russians. They also agreed that if Kurt was killed, Erika would use her family's influence to somehow make an escape to safety. In reality, Kurt and Erika didn't know what safety really meant, especially if Germany lost and was occupied by the enemy. Their final plan—or dream, really—was that they would survive and find each other. Amid the anguish, frustration, and bewilderment that dominated their final goodbye, Erika had pulled Kurt to her with an intensity she had never displayed before and yelled in his face, "No matter what happens, we will find each other. No matter how long it takes, or how hard it is. Find me. I'll wait for you, and we will survive!"

———•———

The German High command counted on two factors for Watch on the Rhine to succeed: complete surprise and bad weather to ground Allied planes. On December 16 at five o'clock on a dark, foggy morning the German attack in the Ardennes began with a massive artillery barrage.

Kurt was in charge of a special Das Reich attack group of the Sixth Panzer Army under Waffen SS General Sepp Dietrich. The Sixth Panzer was the most powerful of the three army groups involved in the German attack and included all the participating Waffen SS Divisions. Dietrich's group was joined by Baron Hasso von Manteuffel and his Fifth Panzer Army in the middle section of the German attack force, while General Brandenberger commanded the Seventh Army in the southern sector. Dietrich and his force had been assigned the best troops and, unlike the offensive in Russia, were issued winter equipment; many of the German tanks had been painted white, and the troops' new white uniforms blended in with the snow-covered countryside. Given his group's superior strength, General Dietrich was given the campaign's most important objective: crash through Elsenborn Ridge, cross the Meuse River and seize Antwerp.

The German forces accomplished their first objective by completely surprising the Allies. The initial attack area had been designated a rest area by the Allies, who were convinced no German attack was imminent in the vicinity. But the northern sector of the battlefield assigned to General Dietrich and the Sixth Panzer Army was very hilly, and the defenders had a great geographic advantage. Roadblocks could be held by small, determined forces that were able to create bottlenecks and hold back vastly superior forces. Also, the narrow roads twisted and turned at sharp angles, making it extremely difficult for tanks to maneuver, especially in the dead of winter. Navigating these "goat trails" led to a slow, costly advance by the German Panzers, and General Dietrich's group failed to achieve its quick breakthrough.

Kurt and Das Reich were initially held in reserve, ready to sweep into the gap created by Dietrich's Sixth Panzers and race toward Antwerp. Unfortunately for Germany, that gap never materialized. Kurt and Das Reich waited in relief for a couple of days before an impatient Hitler, dissatisfied with General Dietrich's inability to break through the Elsenborn Ridge, diverted Das Reich south into the sector being attacked by Manteuffel's Fifth Panzer Army. There, Kurt's group was ordered to penetrate and rapidly expand the gaps created in this section. Kurt participated in the capture and destruction of St. Vith, and then his group wheeled north to capture the tiny village of Baraque de Fraiture, which sat at a key point on the main road leading from Bastogne to Liege.

Overall, things went well with Watch on the Rhine for the first few days; the Germans had caught the Allies completely off guard, and the weather kept the Allied air force grounded for about a week. During that time, though, the Americans had their own surprise for Hitler, the tenacity, flexibility, and bravery of small groups of GIs who disrupted the German timetable, allowing additional Allied forces to be rushed to shore up the Ardennes. When the weather broke and the Allied planes started flying again, Watch on the Rhine began to lose its momentum.

On December 23 Kurt Heisler was leading the advance element of his attack force when he ordered his driver to try a short cut down a twisted hillside path. Kurt's half-track turned a blind corner and was suddenly cut off and surrounded by American troops and forced to surrender. When Kurt was identified as an officer of the Second SS Panzer Division, the Allies used this intelligence to quickly adjust their troop deployment and send additional forces to stop this new threat.

Just like that—one quick turn on a hilly road—and Kurt was out of the war. For several days he was subjected to Allied interrogation to verify the existence of the powerful new German force, and then he was sent to the temporary oblivion of a POW camp. While he was relieved to be out of immediate danger and hopeful that he and Erika and Jochen would somehow survive and be reunited, Kurt was sick with worry about what might be happening on the home front. Rumors were running rampant about whole German cities being reduced to rubble. Kurt grilled new prisoners daily, trying to find out information about Nuremberg, but no one had any reliable updates. As bad as his situation was, though, Kurt realized it did offer some relief: He was safe from the Gestapo and from a confrontation with Jurgen.

As Kurt languished in the American POW camp, Erika was undergoing a time of shattering emotional upheaval and tragedy. Upon hearing that her husband had become a prisoner of the Americans, Erika quickly overcame her initial shock and gave thanks that he was safe and out of the war. At least she didn't have to worry about him being killed in battle any more, and she believed more than ever that Kurt would survive and they would be reunited. Erika then focused her energy on her own survival and that of her family and friends.

On January 2, 1945, Erika left Jochen with her parents and drove to Berlin to see Louisa and try to convince her to leave Berlin and stay with her in Nuremberg. By this time many Germans knew the end was coming, and Berlin was in danger of being taken by the Russians. Because travel was severely restricted and public transportation had largely been disabled, most civilians in Germany did not travel. Those who did were usually fleeing from the advance of the Red Army and moving toward the West and the safety of the Allies. Despite these obstacles and dangers, Erika felt she had to see Louisa. In addition to convincing Louisa to come and stay in Nuremberg, Erika needed some private time with her friend to deal with the trauma of Kurt's capture.

Shortly after Erika's arrival in Berlin, she and Louisa were sitting at a coffee table in the study of Louisa's apartment as a few snowflakes fluttered haphazardly in the grey afternoon sky. The table was next to a large window, where the staggered bomb craters and gutted buildings added a feeling of desperation as the two young women discussed their fates in a war that was going badly.

"When did you find out that Kurt was an American prisoner?" Louisa asked between sips of coffee.

"Yesterday." Erika paused to keep her emotions under control and then continued, "A friend of mother's called and told us. We've received no official notification yet, but the source is reliable. If it's true, at least he's not a prisoner of the Russians."

Erika paused again, looking to Louisa for support. Louisa sat silently, waiting for Erika to finish her story, so Erika continued. "I just had to get away from Nuremberg for a few days. I needed to be with someone besides my family. Someone who understands what it's like to have a husband whose life dangles on the whim of war."

"Unfortunately, Jurgen's not my husband, but I do understand what you're feeling. As women who are intimately connected to brothers in the Waffen SS, we do have a special bond."

"Have you heard from Jurgen lately?"

"Nothing for about a month. I know he's leading a regiment of the Leibstandarte, and I hope he's alive and well. You know how slow and unreliable battlefield information is."

"Yes, it's another one of the rewards of being stationed at the home front," Erika said sarcastically as she folded her hands and looked heavenward. "Have you and Jurgen made any plans for the future?"

"The last time we were together about six weeks ago, we were talking about getting married, but that conversation ended abruptly when I said something about how badly the war was going, and Jurgen got very angry with me. He was actually screaming at me that we would prevail and be victorious in the end."

Erika placed her cup carefully into the porcelain saucer. "I know Jurgen's intense, but it sounds like he's feeling the strain like the rest of us. But you're right to be concerned. That's one of the reasons I'm here. What if we do lose the war, Louisa? What'll you do? Do you plan to stay in Berlin? You can't allow yourself to be captured by those barbarians from the East. Why don't you come and stay with me in Nuremberg until we know what's going to happen? At least until things get better."

"Do you really think things will get better? It sounds like our western offensive failed, and I don't see signs of hope anywhere."

Erika reached across the table and squeezed Louisa's hands. "All the more reason to come to Nuremberg."

Louisa's face assumed a calm look of resignation as she stood up and gazed at a picture of Jurgen. "Erika, don't tell anyone, but I'm pregnant with Jurgen's child. He doesn't know, and I'm not sure if I'll tell him."

Erika jumped up excitedly and hugged Louisa. "This is wonderful! You must tell Jurgen as soon as possible and get married. Now you must come back with me to Nuremberg. This is so exciting, Louisa! Now Jochen will have a cousin, and Kurt will be an uncle."

Louisa forced a laugh. "And you'll be a doting aunt. Let's sit down and have another cup of coffee."

As soon as their cups were full, Louisa began answering Erika's rapid-fire questions about her immediate future. "I appreciate your offer to stay with you in Nuremberg, but I must say no. The same day Jurgen scolded me for being pessimistic about the war, he made some rather strange comments about the future. Shortly after screaming at me that we'd still be victorious, he became very somber. He said that no matter what happened, I must stay in Berlin. He mentioned some vague plan that if the worst happened, the SS would take care of their own. I assume by what he said that Jurgen would get me out of Berlin before it fell. I have no idea how he plans to get me out or where we'd go, but at least I have hope."

Erika took a deep breath, pushed her chair back and stood straight up. She grasped Louisa by both shoulders and said, "My God, Louisa, you can't risk your life and your child's future on such vague promises. I've no idea what plans the SS has for saving themselves, but, given Jurgen's obligations as a soldier, how can he be here to save you? He'll be lucky to save himself. How will he get to Berlin if he's still fighting somewhere else, especially if we're losing the war and defeat is inevitable? Soldiers can't control when they die or get captured, but you can take steps to make things better for yourself and your child. You'll both be much safer with me in Nuremberg."

Louisa smiled, but didn't answer Erika's questions. "What about you and Kurt? Had you discussed the possibility of his becoming a prisoner of war?"

"Not specifically, but we did discuss a number of possibilities. When Kurt said goodbye, we promised to find each other, no matter what happened to either of us. I've heard the Americans treat their prisoners well. If we win the war, Kurt will be rescued; if we lose, he'll eventually be released. My task is to make sure that Jochen and I will be there to greet him whenever he's freed."

"I hope it works out that easily for Kurt. He's a member of the Waffen SS, after all, and I've heard rumors that the Allies plan to deal harshly with all SS members."

Erika banged the table with her fist and said, "The Americans, the British, the French, they're all civilized people. They understand the nature of war and its necessary horrors, and they'll protect us from excessive punishment by the Russians."

"Will they understand the concentration camps?"

"Louisa, do we understand the concentration camps?"

Louisa shrugged her shoulders. "I don't think about such matters. I only know that Germany's enemies need to be eliminated, and we must do what our leaders tell us if we're to survive."

Erika laughed. "Yeah, that's sure worked for us so far, hasn't it? We've been following Hitler without question for years. Look out the window and see the results."

"Erika, you speak treason! If Jurgen or Kurt could hear you, they'd be shocked."

Afraid she might push Louisa too far, Erika shifted the conversation back to the reasons why Louisa should move to Nuremberg. Louisa listened carefully to all of Erika's arguments, including the hideous consequences of a woman being captured by the soldiers of Bolshevism, but remained unmoved. She told Erika not to worry, that somehow Berlin would survive, and if the city fell, she would be rescued by Jurgen or would "take matters into her own hands."

Erika realized further discussion was useless and dropped the subject for the remainder of her visit.

On the third day of Erika's stay with Louisa terrifying news reached them. On the night of January 2, 1945—the very day Erika had left for Berlin— British Lancaster bombers had pummeled Nuremberg into oblivion. According to initial reports, only the firebombing of Dresden had produced a more horrific one-day holocaust. Fear gripped Erika, and she became frantic worrying about Jochen and her parents; it took all of her resolve to gather herself mentally for the trip home. Furiously throwing her things into her suitcase, she said farewell to Louisa. As they tearfully embraced, Erika promised to keep in touch, fearing that she was probably seeing her friend for the last time.

Erika started for home in a state of frenzied anxiety, enveloped by a sense of foreboding for the fates of Jochen and her parents. Unfortunately, her return to Nuremberg took much longer than the trip to Berlin. Even though her father's car bore the symbol of the Allgemeine SS—the main SS arm in which Frederick had been bestowed honorary membership— Nazi officials stopped her at every checkpoint, demanding to see her papers. At every stop Erika pleaded for information about the situation in Nuremberg, and the news got worse with each request. She learned that the bombing had started over three thousand fires throughout the city and ruptured most of the gas lines, making travel within and around Nuremberg almost impossible. So Erika crept along for several days, dodging military vehicles and harried officials, all the while wiping away tears. At night she sought refuge in bomb shelters when all non-military traffic was at a standstill.

When Erika finally made it back to Nuremberg, she entered a scene of unspeakable destruction. The British bombers had pulverized the city, especially the von Klugemanns' neighborhood. The devastation was so complete Erika had to park many blocks away and agonizingly struggle toward her house through rubble-filled streets clogged with dazed and injured residents. She staggered onward in the direction of her home and family, but the mountain of debris had erased all familiar landmarks. Everything was encased in a mist of fine powder. The stench of burned flesh permeated the acres of twisted wreckage and human suffering, but Erika forced herself to continue toward her greatest fear. Her heart was pounding so rapidly she could scarcely think. She struggled on, compelled by a mother's protective instinct. Scrambling over and around obstacles that had once been the homes of friends and neighbors, Erika finally found what remained of her home. There was no evidence, living or dead, of any humans.

Erika began to tear at the pyramid of powder and stone, screaming over and over, "Jochen – Jochen – Jochen." Such anguish and wailing was a common scene in German cities during the last months of the war, but even amid those cries, Erika's heart-searing screams stood out. A group of men left their digging in the nearby rubble and came over to see if they could help her. They were all either very old or very young, bone-weary from having already spent days digging for survivors. A kindly white-haired man in tattered clothes gently grabbed Erika and forced her to stop her crazed attempt at excavation. Erika's hands were cut and bleeding, covered with gray powder. Her face was painted with an ashen gray film that had turned to paste by her stream of tears.

"I'm sorry, my dear, but we found no survivors in that building. We've searched for two days and haven't found so much as a shoe. Are you family?"

Erika couldn't speak, so the old man continued, "Give me your name, and I'll help you find some friends or relatives to stay with or a shelter to go where you can get some aid."

Her lips trembled as Erika tried to form some words, but all she could produce were anguished sobs. Eventually she managed to blurt out the name "von Klugemann" and the old man said with as much compassion as he could muster. "I'm so sorry, my dear, but I must tell you there is no hope. Some men from one of Herr von Klugemann's factories came over and searched the building as thoroughly as they could and found nothing. Apparently the von Klugemanns were at home when the bombs struck. Please, let me help you to a shelter where you can call someone."

Beyond shock and grief, Erika numbly followed the old man, wearing the look of the undead.

———

Most of the meaning of life ended for Erika upon her return to Nuremberg. It was as if hell had descended upon her, and her life became nearly unbearable. After a few days in a shelter, one of her father's business associates came and took her to his home, where she was given as much care as possible. Helpful friends kept her alive, but her mind and soul were gone, buried in the dust with her mother, father, and son. For the next few months she existed as one of the countless walking dead.

Time, the universal healer, eventually came to Erika's rescue. One of her greatest challenges was overcoming the sense of failure she felt; she had promised to keep Jochen safe so they could be reunited with Kurt again, no matter what. Once she convinced herself that half a promise was better than none—she was still alive—she slowly began to face reality and reclaim the identity of Erika Heisler, wife of SS Major Kurt Heisler and daughter of Frederick and Maria von Klugemann. Erika vowed to find Kurt and begin life anew. And, to give her life more meaning while she waited, she started working with the people at the shelters, trying to return the comfort the old man had given her on her day of terror. There were days when Erika occasionally disappeared into a melancholy state, but her work helped her maintain some sense of purpose. By April she felt strong enough to return to the tomb of rubble that encased her family; there she planted three white crosses and a pot of flowers before kneeling down in a prayer for her departed loved ones. When she was finished, Erika took one final look at the devastation, turned, and rejoined the living.

CHAPTER XVIII

Exiles in Another World

Kurt had been living the life of a normal prisoner of war for two months. After his capture on December 23 he had undergone a series of interrogations during his first two weeks of captivity, and then he was left with other captured officers of the German armed forces. Members of the Waffen SS still aroused mixed feelings among the regular Wehrmacht, and Kurt faced some hostility, but the fellowship of captured comrades proved greater than any political differences. At the end of February Kurt was placed in special quarters reserved only for captured soldiers of the Waffen SS. It seemed that they were a breed apart after all, even to the Americans.

Living in the limbo of a POW camp was the worst situation possible for soldiers with a country and a family to defend. They knew that Germany was losing, and they desperately sought information about their families, but except for random bits and pieces of news from newly-captured prisoners, they remained in the dark. Kurt had heard absolutely nothing of Erika and Jochen's status, and his concern became acute when he heard that Nuremberg had been heavily bombed. That information, coupled with a lot of time on his hands, fueled his anxieties with doubt, but eventually he realized that everything was beyond his control, and he just started marking time until the war was over.

Near the end of April Kurt was taken to a special building in the POW compound for a meeting with Colonel Johnson of the Office of Strategic Services, or the OSS. After some small talk Johnson handed Kurt a lengthy questionnaire and asked him to read it to see if he would be willing to answer the questions. Kurt took his time scanning the document. The questions, which were written in flawless German, were about the activities of the Waffen SS. Except for some questions about the extent of Kurt's involvement in various campaigns, the survey was rather innocuous, which puzzled Kurt; surely the Allies knew most this information already. Still, he reasoned, they must be looking for something, and it wouldn't hurt to play along for a while. He handed the document back to Colonel Johnson. "I'll help you out and answer these questions if you help me with my problem."

"What's that?"

"I haven't heard a thing about my wife and son since I've been here, but I know Nuremberg was heavily bombed in January, and that's where they were living. If you take the information in my file and find out what's happened to them, I'll answer these questions. Do we have a deal, Colonel?"

"I can't make any promises that we'll find out anything for sure, but we can start the process. So many people have been killed or displaced that it's difficult to trace someone. But I'll give you my word, one officer to another, that I'll do my best to see if I can find out about them. If you can live with that, we have a deal. I'm willing to do this as a gesture of good faith, Major, but you know you are in no position to bargain."

What Kurt did know was that finding out about Erika and Jochen was the most important thing in his life, and he couldn't even think about making plans for the future without knowing their fate. Then he remembered he did have a bargaining chip. "Since you have made a gesture of good faith, Colonel, I will do the same. I met an American agent under some unfortunate circumstances, and I think you might be interested in what happened to him."

"Really? That's an extraordinary coincidence. Who was it, and how did you meet?"

"An agent named Captain Anderson. I had the chance to interview him before he was turned over to the Gestapo and killed. Did you know him?"

A flash of recognition crossed Johnson's face. "Anderson's a pretty common name in America. Tell me a little more about your contact with him."

"It was just before the Normandy invasion when Das Reich was stationed in southern France. One of our patrols captured him while he was working with the French resistance, the Maquis. He seemed very bright and well-educated."

"Yes, I did know him. He was a fine man and very good at his job. We assumed he'd been killed in action, but this is the first confirmation we've received. Are you sure he was killed, not just taken away to another location?"

"Unfortunately, Colonel, there's no mistake about it. I interviewed him before he was taken by the Gestapo, and I later saw his body after they had finished with him. The Gestapo said he didn't give up a thing. I know it's only a small consolation to offer to someone who's lost a comrade, but I can tell you your Captain Anderson was a very bold character right up to the end. He fully understood his predicament, but that didn't stop him from throwing a glass of water in my face when he felt insulted by some of the questions I was asking him. I think he also called me a pompous ass and Nazi swine for good measure."

"I don't know what kind of questions you put to Captain Anderson to evoke such responses," Johnson said with a slight grin, "because he was usually composed and in complete control in just about any situation. At least now we know why we never made contact with him. I appreciate your sharing this information with me."

Colonel Johnson paused for a minute and shuffled the papers on his desk, looking like he was weighing alternatives about how to proceed. "Major, I'm going to be as blunt as I can with you to move this along. I need to get some answers to this questionnaire, and the faster I get them, the faster this war will be over for you. There's a reason I picked you to speak with, but I can't reveal that just yet. I promise I'll try to find out about your family as soon as I can, but this war isn't going to wait for anybody. If you don't answer these questions, I'm going to have to find someone who will, and that won't be hard given Germany's position right now. You're going to have to trust me, or the deal goes away. What do you say?"

Kurt felt like he had nothing to lose, so he agreed. It took him about an hour to complete the survey, whereupon he was returned to his quarters. Almost two weeks went by and he didn't hear anything about Erika and Jochen, despite his attempts through the guards to get back in touch with Colonel Johnson. Just about the time Kurt figured he had been duped and was about to give up hope, he was summoned to Johnson's office on May 6.

"Relax and sit down, Major Heisler. Can I get you a glass of water?"

"Yes, thank you, sir."

"You don't have to call me sir. Colonel will do."

Colonel Johnson returned with two glasses of water, handed one to Kurt and put the other on his desk. "I promised you I'd find out about your family, and I've fulfilled my end of the bargain." Johnson looked down at Kurt and waited a few painful seconds before talking. "I hate to be so abrupt about this, but there's no easy way to break this kind of news. Major, I'm afraid your son Jochen is dead, along with your wife's parents and your aunt and uncle. They all died in an Allied bombing raid on Nuremberg last January, but there is one piece of good news. Erika was out of town and survived." Johnson paused for a few seconds. "Like I said, there's no easy way to break this. I'm sorry for your loss, Major Heisler."

Kurt had been mentally preparing himself for some bad news, but the announcement about Jochen's death tore his heart out. He actually felt faint. Colonel Johnson handed him the glass of water, and Kurt took a drink. He tried valiantly to regain his equilibrium in the spinning room, but he was sure he was going to vomit. The Colonel's hand suddenly shook him gently by the shoulder and stopped his flight into nausea. As Kurt finished the glass of water, he composed himself, and for some unknown reason he simply said, "You speak perfect German, Colonel."

Colonel Johnson just let the remark sit for a while before eventually responding. "I know this is all coming at you very fast, Major, and you probably think I'm a heartless bastard for being so blunt and matter-of-fact, but we really need to move quickly. I have to discuss the questions you answered, and I can give you until tomorrow morning to process this news about your family, but then we have to move. I understand if you can't handle that, but if you can't, I'm prepared to make an offer to someone else. I'm sorry, Major, but I have no choice."

By now Kurt had regained his composure and was starting to think clearly again. "Does whatever you plan on offering me include Erika?"

"I'm not sure I can tell you exactly what the offer ... "

"Colonel, we're well past the point of being coy with each other. I answered your questions, and I'm sure you've had my answers and my background checked out or I wouldn't be here. Just tell me what this is all about, and we can finish this right now. I don't need twenty-four hours to think about anything. Erika is now the only future I have, and if this doesn't include her, there's no point in moving forward, and you can take your offer to someone else."

"Very well, Major, I'll get straight to the point. Yes, we have checked out your answers, but we still need more verification from you before we proceed. Let me get very specific, here. This war is going to end very soon, and America may soon have a new enemy. It should come as no surprise to you that we think the Soviet Union is just as big a threat to world democracy as Germany was. In fact, we're already preparing to defend ourselves against them, which is where you come in. We know about your combat record on the Eastern Front and your familiarity with Russian battle tactics, their soldiers, and their equipment. We also know you spent some time in German intelligence. We need people with your expertise to advise us on certain military aspects as we face future confrontations with the Soviet Union. Are you with me so far, Major?"

"Yes, many of us realized long ago the threat that the Soviet Union posed to the U.S., and we were hoping to form an alliance with you to stop them. Unfortunately, we couldn't talk sense into the right people soon enough. There were even attempts on Hitler's life, but he managed to escape every time. But tell me, Colonel, why all the secrecy about all of this if the war's ending soon? Won't I just be released like all the other prisoners so Erika and I can go home and get on with our lives? What do I get out of this? I still don't understand."

"This is where it starts to get a little complicated, Major, so I want you to bear with me for a few minutes. How about a cup of coffee while I walk you through the details?"

Kurt shrugged and nodded, and Johnson called for his aide to bring in a pot of coffee and two cups. Johnson picked up Kurt's file and started pulling out pages. "As soon as this war is over—and trust me, it's going to be over very soon—one of the first orders of business will be setting up trials for Germans who committed war crimes. According to our records, you behaved honorably on the Western Front, but your record on the Eastern Front doesn't look as clean. What you get out of this, Major, is that we can provide you immunity from prosecution for any of your war crimes if you agree to work with us. But before I can even officially make you that offer, I need a little more detail on some of those questions you answered."

Kurt was stunned. He knew he'd done some terrible things in the heat of battle, like so many soldiers on both sides, but it never occurred to him that he might have to face a trial for his actions. "Colonel, with all the atrocities committed by the leaders on both sides on the Eastern Front, are you telling me you'd waste time prosecuting a combat officer who was just trying to survive every day?"

"Major, you and I know the difference between killing soldiers in combat and wiping out entire villages of civilians. The Russians, the Poles, the French, the Jews have all suffered horribly at the hands of the Nazis, and the whole world will be watching to see how the monsters who committed these acts will be punished. We don't know exactly what you've been involved in, which is why I need more information, but do you want to risk being tried in court, especially when we can detain war criminals indefinitely?"

Kurt shook his head and sighed. "I know I did some questionable things while I was in the line of fire, but I always thought I was just a soldier doing his duty for his country. I just can't believe I'd wind up being tried for surviving a war."

"Look, Major, we both know war is a dirty business. The fact is, you don't have many options here. Let me get through the rest of my questions, and I think you'll see that I'm offering you a very attractive alternative. You said you joined the Waffen SS because you thought they were the most committed soldiers and best able to help Germany succeed, but that you were not actually a member of the Nazi Party, correct?"

"Yes."

"On the questionnaire you didn't mention any involvement in the destruction of the French village of Oradour, even though we know that your unit of Das Reich destroyed the village and slaughtered its inhabitants. Care to comment?"

Kurt bristled at the mere suggestion of Oradour. "Colonel, I wasn't involved in the field on that campaign. I was assigned a desk job doing intelligence work and never even set foot in the village. As a matter of fact, as soon as I heard about Das Reich's conduct at Oradour, I lodged a protest with my commanding officer."

Johnson paused and studied one of the pages. "Well, that matches our intelligence records, and we're satisfied concerning your explanation of Oradour, but I doubt our French allies will be. Let's hope you never fall into their hands. They're very passionate about seeking retribution for Oradour, and who could blame them?

"No one, Colonel. I was just as disgusted as you by Das Reich's behavior at Oradour. That's not what I stand for as a soldier."

"From what I can gather from the rest of your file, I believe that. Let's move on. Now that we've verified the sad news about Jochen and your other relatives, it appears that you have no other family left here other than your brother Jurgen. Is that correct?"

Kurt nodded in agreement. "Yes, Jurgen's a colonel in the Leibstandarte, but I have no idea if he has survived."

"We know a lot about Jurgen and his reputation in the Waffen SS. The OSS has been trying to locate him, but we've been unsuccessful so far. He seems to have vanished during the confusion of these final days. We hope to find him, and if we do, he has a lot to answer for, and there will be no deal for him. Is that clear?"

"That's probably for the best. My brother and I had a falling out right before I was captured, and if we ever meet again, it won't be under pleasant circumstances."

"Well, Major, from what we know about your brother Jurgen, that's to your credit." Colonel Johnson paused for a moment and refilled their coffee cups. "I know this is a lot to absorb at one time, so before I continue, do you have any questions?"

"Yes, one obvious one, Colonel. Why me? There must be many higher-ranking Waffen SS officers with a great deal more knowledge about Soviet military tactics."

"Yes, there are, but men like Dietrich, Hausser, Peiper, Mayer, and others are too high profile. If they disappear from Germany without a trial or explanation, people will ask questions. They'll have to stand trial for very visible war crimes, while you, on the other hand, have much of the same knowledge but aren't guilty of masterminding major atrocities and won't be as readily missed."

"What do you mean by missed?"

"That's the next part of our offer to you and Erika. Your identities will be changed, and you'll be sent to live in the United States and work for the OSS. All contact between you and any family members or friends will be forever severed, and you can never return to Germany, unless you're on an assignment for the OSS. You'll need to learn to speak and write English, learn about our history and culture in order to fit in, but we'll tutor you. While you're becoming Americanized, you'll live under wraps with the OSS and work with us at the same time. After you're comfortable with your new life, you'll be allowed to move out of our protective custody and begin a new life on your own, but you'll still work for us, and you can never tell people exactly what you do or who you really are. In return you'll be safe from any charges of war crimes and will be given the opportunity to perform a vital service for America."

The Colonel paused to take a breath and let everything sink in. "Excuse me, Major, I'm getting way ahead of myself. All of the details will be worked out later if your background checks out and we make you the offer, but we assume that Erika has to agree with this or you won't accept. Are you interested, and do you think Erika will be as well?"

Kurt thought about the offer for a moment and considered his options. His parents and most of his close friends were dead, and Jurgen might as well be. Germany was in ruins. If he stayed, word was bound to get out about his involvement in the assassination attempt on Hitler, making him a marked man among the surviving fanatics from the Third Reich. Jurgen might have already exposed him, and even if he hadn't and was still alive, Kurt faced a confrontation with him. Given some of Erika's critical comments about Hitler and the Reich in their last days together, Kurt was sure she would agree to take the deal. It offered their best chance to start a new life together.

"Yes, Colonel, I'm interested, and you're right about needing Erika's consent, but I think she'll agree. But I guarantee she'll have the same question I do. What exactly will we be doing?"

"That is still classified information, but between you and me, we don't even know yet. It'll depend upon how well you assimilate into our culture and the depth and breadth of your knowledge. I'm afraid that's all I can give you right now."

"What's our next step then, Colonel? You obviously know where Erika is, so when can I see her to discuss this?"

"You'll have to be a little patient. Given the secrecy of this assignment and Erika's parents' strong Nazi ties, we have to be very careful about how we set that up, but you'll see her soon. Until then, Major, sit tight while we verify the rest of your information. I'm speaking a little out of turn here, but at this point I'm confident the OSS will make you an offer."

Kurt sat in dazed silence, contemplating the adventure that lay ahead and mourning the loss of a son he hardly knew. Everything about the life he and Erika knew was about to change, but he was excited by the chance for a fresh start in a new environment. "Is there anything else I have to do, Colonel Johnson, or am I dismissed?"

"Yes, you're dismissed, but before you go, you might find this of interest. If you hadn't held out on the questionnaire by getting me to agree to check on your family, we wouldn't be sitting here now. I never would have followed up on your case file because we had a lot of SS officers to choose from, but when I found out you had almost no family left here and examined your experiences on the Eastern Front, you moved to the top of our list. You know, we've probably all seen some weird circumstances in this war, but yours ranks right up there."

"What do you mean, Colonel?"

"I was intrigued by your mention of Captain Anderson in Normandy. I couldn't tell you then that he was one of ours, an OSS agent, and part of our first experience with covert operations. General Donovan, the head of the OSS, likes to recruit Wall Street lawyers because they're known for maintaining a certain flair under pressure, and that's where he found Anderson. He was specially trained as part of the Jedburgh Program to work with the Maquis to disrupt German forces in Normandy after the invasion, and he was actually the first Jed to parachute into France on a special mission prior to D-Day. For the record, the Jedburgh Program was actually a British idea. I'm sure they really didn't want to work with us because they felt we were unprepared for real espionage work, but they were losing so many agents in France they were running out of manpower. Anyway, the Jeds were organized in three-man teams, usually an American, a Frenchman and a Brit. On D-Day and afterwards many Jed teams parachuted into France and organized, trained and led the various Maquis units. We supplied them with weapons and ammunition, trained them in hit-and-run tactics and supplied their targets. The Maquis were brave and ruthless, but they lacked leadership, so we provided it. General Eisenhower hesitated to send the Jeds into France before the invasion began because he was afraid one of them might be captured and reveal the date and location of D-Day, so Anderson was sent in not knowing. Ironically, we never made radio contact with him, so there was nothing for him to reveal. When you encountered Captain Anderson, I'm sure you couldn't in your wildest dreams imagine that you'd be working for the same organization within a year."

Kurt thought of Anderson's mutilated body strapped to a chair and shuddered. "I hope I have better luck than he had. I'm sorry he didn't make it. I respected him and hoped he'd be able to save himself."

"There wasn't much chance of that under any circumstances. All of the agents were issued L-Pills—potassium cyanide capsules—and were instructed to commit suicide to avoid the possibility that they might reveal vital information while being tortured. You can swallow an L-Pill and nothing will happen—it will just pass through you—but if you bite down, you die almost instantly. Obviously, Anderson didn't use his, and I guess we'll never know why. Perhaps one day you'll meet some of the survivors of the Jedburgh Program, and they can tell you some interesting stories about Captain Anderson."

Colonel Johnson looked at his watch, stood up and ushered Kurt to the door. "That's all for now, Major. We'll have plenty of time for more stories later. I'll send for you soon."

As Kurt returned to his barracks, he laughed inwardly about the absurd irony of one part of his situation. He had almost mentioned his involvement in the July 20 attempt on Hitler's life, but thought better of it at the last moment. He was sure it would increase his status with his new superiors, but without proof, it would probably have come off as desperate begging. But because he had been protected so well by the other conspirators, no one was left alive to corroborate his story, except for Jurgen.

Two days later on May 8, 1945, the war in Europe ended with Germany's unconditional surrender. Many German prisoners were scheduled for release within a few months, but discussions were already being held by the Allies on how to deal with Nazi war criminals, and anyone connected with a wartime atrocity was being held indefinitely. Kurt sweated it out until the end of May when Colonel Johnson told him that he had been accepted into the OSS program. However, they hadn't been able to make the arrangements with Erika yet, and Kurt was told to remain patient.

CHAPTER XIX

Reunion

The day after he got the news from Colonel Johnson that he was part of the program, Kurt was separated from the other prisoners to begin the process of disappearing. He was given quarters in solitary confinement, but he was treated more like a protected witness than a prisoner. And he was still without Erika. In July he was relocated to a tiny, dingy apartment within the OSS complex in Munich. The windowless flat was too cramped to even be described as cute. The kitchen—really just a counter with two stools, an icebox and an ancient stove—extended into an equally small living room, where a spindly, weather-beaten table and three mismatched chairs took up most of the floor space. The corner bathroom was a converted closet, its tiny mirror capable of reflecting only a part of Kurt's face. The bedroom was just that, a single bed in a room. Despite these glaring drawbacks, Kurt reveled in his new freedom and privacy.

One morning shortly after moving in, Kurt sat at the table studying an American history textbook, half listening to the one station that the ancient radio somehow managed to pull in. Stacked next to him, courtesy of the OSS, were several English instructional books. A knock on the door interrupted his reading.

"Kurt, you have a visitor," announced Colonel Johnson, smiling broadly as he entered, followed by Erika. "I'm sure you'll have no problem finding things to talk about, so I'll leave you two alone for a couple hours. If things go well, Erika can move in with you soon. Enjoy your time together."

Kurt and Erika hardly heard a word the Colonel said; they just stared at each other, mentally reconnecting to all the emotions they had been burying during their months apart. Erika's eyes welled up, while Kurt was unable to utter a sound. Finally, he began to softly wipe away her tears and whispered, "I've missed you, my love."

His words unleashed a liquid avalanche, and Erika threw her arms around his neck. "Oh, Kurt, I'm never going to let you leave me again. I can't describe the horrible feeling of loss I've been living with these last months. I've failed you. I know I promised you that Jochen and I would survive the war, but I failed. I can't tell you how much I miss him and my parents. Thank God you're all right. I couldn't go on if you had died. I ... "

"Enough, Erika, enough, we're together now. You didn't fail me or Jochen or your parents. As much as I mourn their deaths, I'm just thankful that you found the strength to carry on and survive so we could be together again. That's what we must build on. Now, just let me hold you."

In the silence of their dreary surroundings Kurt and Erika remained locked in an embrace of reunion, drawing strength from each other, slowly allowing their hopes to reawaken. Kurt spoke first. "Erika, I haven't even allowed myself to dream about this day, because I was so afraid it would never come. I want to hear about everything that happened. I have so much to tell you, too, but you'll have to be patient with me as I sort everything out. I'm so sorry that you had to go through this alone, that I wasn't there for you when you needed me."

Taking her hand and leading her to the bedroom, he said, "Come, let me show you the rest of our new home." After considerable effort, they found a comfortable position on the narrow bed, with Kurt flat on his back and Erika lying sideways, partially wrapped around him, her head on his chest.

"Erika, I've thought a lot about where to go from here, and I'm sure you have too. We can't forget the past, but we need to live in the present and build for the future. We have a responsibility to Jochen, our parents,

Konrad and Hilda and all the friends we've lost in the war to help build a better world, one free from the dangers of Communism."

Erika kissed Kurt's neck and then pressed her head against his chest. "Please, Kurt, why don't we forget the rest of the world and start getting to know each other again? My body aches just to lie here next to you and hear the sound of your voice and feel your touch on my skin. Let someone else save mankind today. Let's just save each other."

Kurt laughed softly and drew her closer. "You're right, my darling, we can make much better use of this time." He pulled himself on top of her and started unbuttoning her blouse as he teasingly left a trail of lingering kisses from her forehead to her eyelids to her lips to her neck and to her marvelous breasts. "Which parts should we start getting to know again first? I know I have some personal favorites that I need to be reintroduced to."

An hour later, still giggling like school kids, they hurriedly dressed while Colonel Johnson patiently pretended to listen to the radio in the living room.

———

Erika was allowed to return almost daily from then on, and her visits with Kurt became longer each day. By the end of the week the sense of urgency in their meetings began to subside, and they were starting to feel like a normal married couple again. The best news was that Colonel Johnson had told them that Erika could move in the next week, and that they would be moved to a larger apartment in a month.

Kurt had been waiting for the right time to tell Erika about his involvement in the Hitler assassination plot, and one afternoon while they were practicing their English over coffee, he thought the time was right. As he cleared his voice to speak, Erika gave him a smile, that enigmatic smile hinting of mystery, contradiction, and flirtation that used to drive him crazy, but now warmed him to his core. He hadn't seen it for a long time, but it convinced him that Erika was back, and that she had something up her sleeve.

"Kurt, I have a confession to make, so please hear me out, and don't be mad at me for not telling you this earlier. When you were off fighting the war, I didn't think you could save the world by yourself, so I decided to help. What do you know about the White Rose?"

Kurt smiled. "Quite a lot, actually. During my discussions with Count Kresbach we talked about the heroic struggle of the young students of the White Rose. Who would've thought that they'd be right about Hitler's effect on Germany? It's too bad they couldn't convince more Germans to help their cause earlier. Maybe we could've avoided total annihilation. Don't tell me the daughter of Maria and Frederick von Klugemann got involved with Sophie Scholl."

"Well, I was never directly involved with Sophie or the White Rose, but someone sent me a copy of their leaflets, and I became deeply influenced by them. I decided to try to do something to protest the war, but time ran out on me before I could do much. I wanted so badly to talk with you about my feelings, but I didn't know how a Das Reich officer fighting for Hitler on the Russian front would react to his wife believing in an anti-war group. You had enough things to deal with, and I didn't want to burden you with my problems."

Kurt gave Erika a wry smile. "Well, here's how this member of Das Reich would have reacted. How much do you know about the July 20 attempt to kill Hitler?"

"Actually, quite a bit. I was deeply disappointed that the plot failed. You're not saying you were ... "

"I won't go into the details, but I was part of that conspiracy. Kresbach was the one who got me involved with the conspirators. The bomb should've killed Hitler, but he got lucky. Somehow my role was never discovered. Kresbach wasn't so lucky, but he saved my life—and gave us a future—by not giving me up while he was being tortured."

"Kurt, I can't believe this. The irony here is ridiculous, sad really. All this time we were keeping secrets from each other. And not just little secrets, either, secrets of conscience. I think we have a lot to talk about."

"I wanted to tell you everything, but I couldn't endanger you and Jochen more than I already had. When I went into the hospital last fall, it wasn't shell shock; I was so worried about being discovered, I finally had a breakdown." Kurt took a slow sip of his coffee. "I've seen firsthand what the Gestapo will do to get information from someone."

Erika leaned over and gave Kurt a hug, "I understand, and thank you for thinking of me and Jochen. It's funny, but all the time that I was feeling sorry for myself that you weren't around to take care of us, you were taking care of us in the most honorable way. I'm sorry we couldn't be there to help each other. It must have been terrible living with such fears. That explains your strange behavior in the fall of 1944, too."

"Yes, if the consequences of being discovered weren't so severe, I'd say the irony is almost comical. I often thought you also seemed preoccupied, and now I know why. Erika, let's agree not to keep secrets anymore."

"Agreed," said Erika, coyly retreating behind her taunting blue eyes, "but first I have one more secret to reveal." She paused, smiled and took a sip of coffee to prolong the suspense. "I'm working for the OSS, too!"

"What?" Kurt sat straight up, a look of total bewilderment on his face. "For how long? In what capacity? And why did you wait this long to tell me?" Before she could even answer, Kurt started laughing out loud and shaking his head. "What's this all about? Are you telling me we're working together? Woman, you're really something! Every time I think I know you, you show me something different. I can hardly wait to hear this story, so out with it."

"How much has Colonel Johnson told you about me? I know he told you how Jochen and my family died, and that I was living with a friend of my father's. Did he also tell you I was working in a homeless shelter?"

"Yes, he told me all of that, and that you were well, but that was all. He said we could fill each other in when we were reunited. I sure as hell didn't know I'd be told my wife was a spy!"

"I couldn't tell you earlier because Colonel Johnson said our deal could be jeopardized if I told you without his permission. It could have been a test, but I didn't want to take the chance. Anyway, while you were resting comfortably in the safety of your POW camp, my life was in danger while I was being chased by Russian spies." Erika gave Kurt a mysterious look that hinted at murky dealings in dark alleys.

"Yes, my princess, you're really suited for physical danger. Now tell me the real story, and, remember, no secrets." Kurt tapped Erika lightly on the nose and repeated, "No more secrets."

"Yes, dear, now let me finish. How much do you know about the German atomic research program or the V-2 rocket program?"

"Virtually nothing. You know I was a little busy on the front lines."

Erika leaned over and gave Kurt a quick kiss. "Now get comfortable. Here comes the whole story. In May a race was already underway between the Russians and the Americans to acquire the scientists and equipment of the German space program. When the Soviets captured Berlin, they seized the German atomic research labs at the Kaiser Wilhelm Institute, and the Americans were afraid they'd also get all the V-2 scientists and rockets."

"Why are you saying 'German' instead of 'our'?"

"Because we're on the other side now, and don't interrupt me again. The V-2 rocket complex was located in central Germany in the Hartz Mountains, where a massive underground plant had been constructed at Nordhausen. The Soviets were about to gain control of the area, but the Americans got there first. They removed the V-2 missiles and recruited the scientists. You've certainly heard of Werner von Braun, haven't you?"

"Of course, everyone in Germany—and apparently Russia and America as well—has heard of him."

"So, can you guess where I fit in with all this?"

Kurt rolled his eyes and shook his head back and forth. "Well, I'm sure it has something to do with your superior intellect and probably one of your father's factories."

"Yes, my sarcastic and observant husband. You're proving to be as smart as I'd hoped way back when we first met. Now, for the rest of the story. Do you remember meeting a Dr. Heinz Manheim?"

"Was he one of the scientists I met at one of your parents' parties?"

"Yes, and his presence was no coincidence. He ran a secret program at one of father's underground factories directing a group of scientists who were secretly making the guidance systems for the V-2s being assembled at Nordhausen. It was Professor Manheim who offered to let me stay at his home after I lost my family. He disappeared in early May, probably because he was afraid of being arrested for using slave labor. I was contacted by Colonel Johnson to find the professor and convince him to work for the Americans. I reported to Johnson, but I actually worked for Major Robert Staver of the rocket research section of the Ordinance Office of the Army. Staver's job was to find and interrogate the German rocket scientists who built the V-2. I've helped locate and recruit over a hundred such specialists out of the Soviet zone into the safety of the American zone."

"One hundred? Now, I'm really impressed! Were you ever in danger?"

Erika coyly replied, "Not really, but it did get a little tense at times. Actually, I've pretty much done all I can, so by the time we leave for America, I'll be out of the OSS and ready to be a full time wife." Erika flashed her most alluring smile, stood up and tilted her head at Kurt. "Maybe you should consider the possibility that Colonel Johnson was more interested in me than you all along? After all, what have you been doing to save the world lately?"

"Erika, I always knew that being married to you would be a challenge, but, lucky for you, I'm just the man for the job. It's good to see you back to your old teasing self. It's no surprise that the Americans are doing everything they can to contain the Russians, and I'm glad that we're on the same team." He paused and took a deep breath. "Now, are there any more secrets, or can we declare a moratorium on conversation to take advantage of the time we have left before Colonel Johnson returns?"

They almost tripped over each other as they raced to the bedroom, shedding clothes along the way. A half hour later, Erika lifted her head off Kurt's chest and said, "I'd say we performed admirably, considering the circumstances."

Kurt smiled, but said nothing, so Erika read his mind. "Are you lost in the past or the future?"

"I'm just wondering what our new world will be like."

"What new world are you referring to?"

"Two worlds, actually. I hope we can be happy in our world and do something to make the real world a better place, too. After what Germany's done, we owe a debt that can never be paid, but I want to try. I hope the Americans have learned from Germany's mistakes. Government exists to serve all of the people, not just the people in the government ... Wow, listen to me preach. Anyway, we'll have lots of time during the next year to figure out what to do."

"We'll be working for the government of the most powerful country in the world, so we should be able to help make a better world for others," Erika offered. "But to start, I'm more concerned with making our world a better place. We deserve some happiness and a chance to make meaningful lives for ourselves, and America will provide us with a fresh start."

Erika looked at her watch. "Right now, though, we better get dressed. Colonel Johnson will be here in about five minutes, and for once I'd like to greet him with all of my clothes on. And Kurt, there's just one other thing; If we have a daughter, I want to name her Sophie."

TOM'S STORY

PART TWO

CHAPTER 21

THURSDAY, JANUARY 15, 1998
Grand Forks, North Dakota

So that's Kurt and Erika's story right up until the time they left for the United States in 1946. I wanted to continue with the rest of their story, covering their lives from their arrival in America up until the time they disappeared, but, unfortunately, the hodgepodge of material they gave me in the duffle bag didn't reveal anything new about those years, so all I could do was speculate about what was missing. Given their track record, they probably would have misled me anyway. For all I know, maybe their CIA contracts allowed them to give me details about their lives in Germany but prohibited them from disclosing their work during their years in America. Or maybe what they gave me was all fiction; I have no way of knowing, since I don't even know their real names.

When I finished writing the book in the summer of 1983, I didn't know if I would ever hear from Kurt or Erika again, so the pages sat gathering dust until Erika's phone call in 1998. During the fifteen years in between, Sophie and I resumed our mundane, middle-class lives, continuing our teaching careers and watching Sara and Bruce grow up and start college.

As for the "dangers" Kurt and Erika had frequently alluded to in our conversations, I didn't worry about them much except to wonder every once
in a while if someone might try to prevent me from publishing the book
if I ever decided to take that step. I almost tried once or twice, just to test
the system, but my curiosity and my rebellious nature both dimmed over
time, and I could never muster up enough enthusiasm to take the process
that far. So until Erika's phone call, the only printed copies of the book
were the one I typed originally and a second one that Sophie had printed
out after she typed it into our first home computer sometime in the early
Nineties; we had also saved it on floppy disks and then on a CD when that
format became available. A couple days before our meeting with Erika in
Fargo, I printed out a third copy—amazed by how technology had made
the home printing process so quick and easy—and mailed it to her in care
of the Holiday Inn with instructions to hold it for her arrival.

CHAPTER 22

SATURDAY, JANUARY 17, 1998
Grand Forks, North Dakota

On Saturday morning Sophie and I began the journey to Fargo filled with hope and fear, anticipation and anxiety. We left a little early because she had an errand to run before arriving at the Holiday Inn. A North Dakota winter is not to be trifled with, so the trunk was filled with winter survival gear: extra boots, coats, scarves, socks, hats, matches, candles, and some food items. My folks would have been proud of me.

It was a clear, sunny day, only about ten degrees above zero, but the morning sun was already working hard trying to burn the shallow snow off the plowed fields as we headed south on Interstate 29. The drive from Grand Forks to Fargo would never make the national registry of scenic routes, even though the highway is surrounded by some of the best farmland in the world. Unfortunately—at least from an aesthetic sense—good farmland is usually flat, so it doesn't provide much visual stimulation.

For a while we sat silently, each of us contemplating the same questions. How would the reunion with Erika go? Why had Erika finally broken two decades of silence? Why had she chosen to meet in Fargo, a city seventy miles south of Grand Forks? And where was Kurt?

We were fifteen minutes into the journey before Sophie spoke first. "Did you remember to bring our copy of the book?"

"Yes, dear, and I sent Erika one. I hope it was waiting for her at the Holiday Inn."

"I hope so, too. I can't believe how nervous I am. Here I am a middle-aged mother of two adult children, and I feel like a teenager going to my first rock concert."

"I don't want to get you mad, but you look a little tired. What time did you come to bed last night?"

"Three. I read your book again."

"Really, how many times is that?"

"That makes seventeen. I read it twice the first year and once every year since."

Sophie turned the radio down and poked me on my shoulder, as if she needed to get all of my attention. After making sure I was listening, she boasted, "I guess that makes me an expert on Nazi Germany and World War II, especially on the SS."

"How about being an expert on Kurt and Erika Heisler?"

Before she answered, Sophie turned and looked out the car window. She appeared to be counting the telephone poles as she pondered some unknown. "Yes, I guess you could say I know a lot about my parents, but not nearly as much as I should. Do you realize I don't even know their real names? How ridiculous is that?"

"After reading the book so many times, what gets you the most?"

"It's always the same—finding out who I'm named after and what she stands for. It makes me want to do something to make this a better world."

"Well, you've made my world better, but I know what you mean. Maybe someday we can get your parents' story published, and others will get the same feeling."

"That would be good. I'd like people to realize that not everyone who follows the wrong cause is evil. Do you think my dad can ever be forgiven for what he was a part of … I mean, really?"

"I don't know. We don't get to decide that."

Sophie retreated into her thoughts again, and we continued for several miles before she spoke again. "It seems like some people just never forgive or forget. I'm still bothered by that story you told me about President Reagan going to Europe a while back, and what happened when he was going to lay a wreath at that cemetery in Germany."

"You mean when he was at Bitberg to help celebrate the 40th anniversary of the end of World War II? That's when he had to cancel because so many people objected because there were some Waffen SS graves among those of the regular German soldiers."

"Yes, that shows me that people like my father will always be considered war criminals, that the stigma will never go away. I think my dad was a good man, and I hope he and my mother can forgive me. Let's not talk for a while. I just want to daydream and try to relax."

I allowed Sophie her request. Listening to the radio as I continued down I-29, I became so engrossed with my thoughts, I failed to realize we were almost to Fargo until I was approaching the first exit.

"Sophie, wake up. We're almost there."

"Don't worry, I'm not asleep. Do you think the CIA knows about your book?"

"What?"

"You heard me. Do you?"

"I really don't know. Who knows what the CIA knows? What brought that up?"

"I'm just wondering about a lot of things. I wonder what my mom will look like. I haven't even seen a picture of her in thirty years."

"They looked good back in 1979."

"You shithead! I can't believe you hid that visit from me for that long. Sometimes I think you'd have fit right in with the SS."

"Funny, but while you were resting, I was thinking about the book and how you reacted the first time you read it back in '83 . How mad you got at yourself for cutting them off, and how mad you got at me for keeping all that information to myself for so long." I sneaked a glance in Sophie's direction to gauge her level of irritation.

"Now is not the time to remind me about how pissed off I was at you. I can't believe it's been fifteen years since I first read my parents' story. I still can't understand why we've had no contact in all that time except for that one note from dad. If something happened to him, mom would surely know about it, so why has it taken so long for her to contact us?"

"I think we're about to find out. My guess is that it had something to do with the CIA, your Uncle Jurgen, or … "

"Or shut up! Don't you dare mention that creepy Brossard guy. I still get the chills when I think of him actually being in our house. Maybe mom can tell us something about him, because the CIA sure won't. Even when I threatened to tell the media about dad's past, they just shrugged it off and said they didn't know anything. I guess they're just not that smart. Hey, maybe you could work for the CIA?"

Ignoring her insult, I asked, "What's the address of the flower shop you want to stop at? I think our exit's coming up soon."

"I'll tell you where to go," Sophie laughed, adding, "and don't say, 'What's new?' Just take the next exit."

"Thanks. We have enough time to stop at the flower shop and then go over any final questions you might have before we go to meet your mother."

"I'll run in and you can wait in the car. I'm not sure about going over anything, though. I've thought and talked about my parents so much with you during the past fifteen years that I have nothing left to say, except to them. I hope mom can forgive me and she'll tell us dad's okay. I'll be right back."

———

The three numerals on the motel room door had Sophie paralyzed. Finally turning to me, she uttered, "Tom, this is Room 216. My mother is behind that door, but I'm too scared to knock."

"Sophie, you've waited a long time for this moment, so make the most of it. I'm sure she's more nervous than you are. Just knock."

Sophie knocked, the door opened and Erika was standing before us. A few wrinkles had dared to crease the perfect face, but the complexion was still pure, the hair blond, and the eyes the same blue, except they glistened from behind a river of tears. Sophie threw her arms around her mother, and they hugged and swayed, locked in a long emotional embrace. It was hard to distinguish who was saying "I love you" and "I'm so sorry" as they simultaneously exchanged similar greetings. Finally, Sophie broke their embrace, stepped back and opened her coat, and produced a single white rose.

"Mother, this is for you. Forgive me for my youthful ignorance that drove us apart."

Erika was visibly staggered. Her hand shook as she reached out to accept her daughter's token of love and reconciliation. "A white rose from my Sophie."

Then I saw something I never thought I'd experience: Erika losing her composure. She just sobbed, "Sophie, Sophie, Sophie," repeatedly as they clutched each other tightly.

I watched silently from the corner, transfixed by the mirror image of twins, separated by thirty years' time. After several minutes I interrupted the flood of emotions. "Maybe I should leave you two alone for a while to catch up on things."

Wiping her tears away with her hand, Erika answered, "I'm sorry, Tom, I'm not being a very good host, ignoring you like that, am I? I'm just so happy I can't let go of my Sophie. But don't be foolish and leave us. You're family, too. Besides, the less we go in and out, the better. Now, does either of you want something to drink?"

Just like that, the Erika I knew had reverted to form, taking control of the situation.

Before I could answer, Sophie blurted out, "Where's dad?" challenging Kurt's obvious absence.

Erika sighed in resignation. "I wanted to celebrate our reunion a little longer, but I do have some serious things to discuss, and Kurt's not being here is obviously first on the list. This is going to take a while, so let me take your coats so you can sit down and be comfortable. I'll get us all a drink. Unfortunately, the pop machine has a rather slim selection, so you can have a Diet Coke or a glass of water. How about Diet Coke all the way around?"

Sophie and I agreed and we sat on one of the double beds. Erika brought us our drinks and sat on the other bed facing us, only a few feet away.

Sophie asked again, this time with more urgency, "Where is dad?"

Erika gazed sadly at Sophie, drew a deep breath and said, "I honestly don't know, Liebchen. I'll do the best I can to explain, but I need to go back to 1982. Kurt was due to retire, and we were hoping things would somehow become normal, and we could reunite with our daughter and her family."

"I'm sorry to interrupt," I said, "but the last note we got from Kurt was a strange message saying his retirement had been delayed, and he was being sent overseas on a special assignment. I know you weren't supposed to have any contact with us, but Kurt did manage to send me a few notes. This one, though, seemed more ominous than any of the others, and I'm sure he wasn't supposed to tell anyone where he was going. I think this was back in 1985."

Erika smiled sadly at me. "You're right on two counts. He did go to Germany in 1985, and he shouldn't have told you. Actually, I'm surprised he even told me what I'm about to tell you. I think he had a premonition about going to Germany. Anyway, let me continue. In 1981, William Casey became head of the CIA. During World War II he'd been an OSS station chief in London in charge of secret intelligence, and during the Battle of the Bulge he was placed in charge of Operation Faust, a plan to recruit Germans to work as spies inside Germany for the OSS. Casey knew about Kurt being recruited and trained by Colonel Johnson. They were actually introduced by the Colonel. In 1982 the CIA became concerned because many of their agents in Europe—especially those in East Germany and the Soviet Union—were disappearing. Someone figured out that there was a mole in the organization who had been a member of the Waffen SS. Casey asked Kurt to delay his retirement to take on the project of finding the mole. Kurt stayed in D.C. for two years, coordinating a special task force and trying to run down leads. The CIA finally came up with a name: Otto Weber."

"Otto Weber!" I couldn't contain myself. "He was one of Kurt's SS comrades, but Claude Brossard told me he'd killed him. You mean he's not dead?"

"I thought he was dead, too, but in 1985 Casey said he was still alive. Kurt was the only person left who actually knew Weber during the war, and Casey thought they might be able to leverage that relationship in finding Weber. He sent Kurt to Germany to see if he could track him down."

I couldn't help but inwardly rejoice as I conjured up the image of the smug, arrogant Brossard sitting at my kitchen table hearing the news that he'd killed the wrong man. "So it appears our cocky Mr. Brossard wasn't as meticulous as he made out to be, after all. Man, I'd give anything to see that pencil-thin mustache start twitching as the flop sweat runs down that weasel's clammy forehead."

"I'm afraid you'll never get the satisfaction. Claude Brossard was run over and killed in 1988. The official report said it was a hit and run, but I'm sure it was an assassination. Any number of groups could have done it—Odessa, the CIA, Syria, or, most likely, the Runic Butterfly."

"Odessa? Runic Butterfly? What the hell are you two talking about? This is starting to sound like some video game," Sophie said, her voice rising. "Can we please get back to important things, like where's dad? Mom, do you have any idea where he is?"

Erika rested an elbow on each knee and looked sorrowfully at Sophie. "Sadly, no. I know Kurt was still in Berlin in 1986, but then he just disappeared. I haven't heard from him since, and the CIA says they don't know what happened to him. I've spent the last ten years trying to find out, but I have nothing to show for it. Remember, Sophie, how you said you didn't want any of your parents' dirty Nazi money? Well, you'll get your wish, because I've spent most of it trying to find your dad. I've bugged the CIA, the FBI, the West German Government, and the Soviet Union, and nobody knows anything, or will admit to knowing anything."

"So that's it? Dad's been missing for ten years, and I'm just finding out about it now? You're the spy with all the tricks. Couldn't you have found some way to tell me this before today?"

Erika got up, bent over Sophie and lightly stroked her cheek. "Liebchen, please don't be mad at me. You know I couldn't have told you, and there was nothing you could have done except put us in more danger by asking questions."

"Do you have any idea how frustrating this has been for me, Mother? It took years of Tom's nagging for me to finally give in and give you a second chance. Then, after I'd started hoping that maybe you and dad were actually the good people that he was telling me about, I reviewed all of Tom's research, several times, actually. After that I spent years researching on my own at the library and over the internet, hoping to find some little proof of your existence."

"It's true, Erika." I said. "Now she thinks she's the World War II expert. Can you imagine what it's been like for me living with that?"

Sophie was so upset she ignored me. "I even violated protocol with my old handlers, pestering them relentlessly to give me something—anything—about you and dad, but they wouldn't tell me a thing. I finally gave up and just waited for you to contact me, hoping I'd get the chance to tell you I'd forgiven you, that I'd like for us to be family again so you could get to know your grandkids and … " Sophie's voice trailed off as she choked back tears. After a few seconds she regained her composure and said sternly. "Mother, silence isn't always golden you know!"

Erika put her arm around Sophie and drew her close. "I'm sorry, but I've done the best I could, Sophie. I thought about contacting you several times, but it was impossible. Kurt and I had a falling out with the CIA, and for a while we were 'off the reservation' as they say, and no one knew where we were. But there's nothing we can do about that now, child, so let's just cherish this time we have as mother and daughter. I don't want our last hours to be spent with you mad at me. Please, Sophie?"

"Last hours? What do you mean, last hours? Mom, what's going on here?"

Erika sat back down on the bed, motioned to Sophie to join her and took both Sophie's hands. "I'm sorry to break this to you this way, but I'm going back to Germany late tonight to make one final attempt to find out what happened to Kurt. I still have a few contacts left there, and a CIA friend of Kurt's is helping me with arrangements, but this trip is totally unofficial. I have a ticket under an assumed name, so you can't say anything to anyone. I need some freedom for a while, and I don't want to be bothered by the CIA. By the way, I don't think we've ever told you any-thing that would put you in any real danger, but I'm sure the CIA has been checking on you. Even if they haven't, as soon as they find out about the book, at the very least they'll want to read it and check your sources, so be ready for that. Do you think they've been bugging you, no pun intended?"

I couldn't help but laugh at Erika's attempt at humor. "No, I don't think they've been sniffing around too much lately. Back when all this hit years ago they grilled us both pretty good, but they finally backed off when we could never give them any useful information. Every now and then, though, I get the feeling that someone's looking over my shoulder, even though I can't prove it. What's that saying, 'Just because you're para-noid doesn't mean they're not out to get you'? Sophie, have you noticed anything out of the ordinary for a while?"

"Not really, but I've been a lot less guarded these past few years. Mom, you're the one who should really be careful because one of dad's CIA friends is helping you. It seems those secrets never stay secret very long, so watch your back. And, assuming someone at the CIA will spill the beans, what should we say if they ask us if we saw you here?"

"If they ask, it means they already know, so don't deny you saw me. Just tell them I wanted to see my daughter and son-in-law for a few hours, and I didn't tell you where I'd been or where I was going. You can even tell them you put me on a plane to Minneapolis, because by the time they talk to you, I'll be lost in Germany where they won't be able to find me unless I let them."

Sophie gave Erika a concerned look. "Mother, do you really think there's a chance that dad's still alive?"

"I've never given up hope, but after all these years I'd say the odds are slim. He'd have found some way to contact me, unless he's being held in a prison somewhere, which is a possibility. But I still need some clo-sure, and I think the key lies in Germany. I went there once and snooped around a little, but the CIA got upset and sent me back home. They told me I couldn't return to Germany, that some people might cause me harm because of my work for the CIA."

Erika paused with a bemused look and almost started laughing before she continued. "Maybe it's all a moot point. Have you heard of the Nazi

War Crimes Disclosure Act? Not many people have, but President Clinton will sign it this fall. It'll release thousands of documents about Nazi war criminals used by the United States Government. Wouldn't that be something? Here I am trying to sneak out of America back to Germany, and America might be getting ready to deport me anyway. Some of this just seems too absurd to be believable."

I couldn't stay silent after that comment. "Erika, just sitting here now reflecting on the events of the last thirty years, I can't believe any of this happened, and I lived it. If I tried telling this story to anyone, I'd probably get hauled off to the loony bin. No one would believe me. But since we're sitting here face to face, I've got to ask you a question that's puzzled me all this time. Just what were you and Kurt doing in Bremen in 1966? I know the CIA didn't send you to spy on your own daughter."

Erika shook her head and chuckled. "Kurt really had to pull some strings to get that assignment. We had to agree to have absolutely no contact with Sophie under any circumstances. As I'm sure you remember, there was quite a bit of anti-war activity at the University of North Dakota during the late Sixties and early Seventies. With the U.S Air Force bases at Grand Forks and Minot and all of the underground ICBMs near Langdon, there were lots of targets for the protestors. President Johnson was convinced the long-haired radicals were getting money from the Soviet Union and China, so he ordered the CIA to confirm it. The CIA needed someone undercover to keep track of the protestors in North Dakota. That was our job, or at least it was until Tom accidentally broke our cover."

"So, you were spying on your own daughter?" Sophie shrieked. "I'll bet you had Tom find me so he could tell you about me. I think I have grounds for a divorce!"

"Careful, dear," I warned. "You know I always give you what you want."

Erika broke in, "Now, children, don't tease in front of an old lady. Sophie, we knew nothing about you and Tom until after you were married, because the CIA moved us before you two ever met. Before we left, we did see you at some of the protest events, and it took all of our will power not to reveal ourselves, but there was just too much at stake for us to take that kind of chance."

"Mother, I have a great idea. Why don't you come and stay with us? We'll keep you safe, and you'll get to know your grandchildren. Bruce and Sara both attend UND. Bruce is twenty-four and is in law school. Sara's twenty-two and is a senior in nursing. They don't live at home, but you could see them as much as you like. Also, I could make up for being such a snot."

Erika stroked her daughter's hair. "I'd love to spend time with all of you, but I can't. As for your being a snot, I guess you come by that naturally."

Sophie started to cry. Erika started to cry. I sat looking dumb, which by now wasn't a stretch for me. After a series of hugs, "sorrys," and "I love yous," Erika regained her composure.

I seized the opportunity to change the subject. "Erika, there's one other thing I want to ask you. You mentioned the Runic Butterfly earlier, and I don't remember that name coming up in any of our conversations. Claude Brossard mentioned the name to me during his visit, and later I asked a CIA agent about them; he said he'd never heard the name before. Do you know anything about the Butterfly?"

"A little. I was going to explain about the Runic Butterfly later, but this is as good a time as any. It's better if you don't know much about them, but I owe you a little information."

As if to emphasize the secrecy surrounding the organization, Erika looked around the room before continuing in a lowered voice. "They exist in a strange dimension. They're sort of an offshoot of Odessa, formed back in the early 1950s in the southern United States by escaped members of the Waffen SS, including Kurt's brother Jurgen. Their symbol was two runic characters signifying authority and rebirth that, joined together, looked like a butterfly. Today they no longer use the term Runic Butterfly and are known by a variety of names. Most of the old SS founders are long gone, so the Butterfly group is now run by second and third generation members. They're only after power, wealth, and control. They operate behind the scenes and draw no publicity to themselves. Their membership includes many respectable people, people that you don't want to cross. As you know, Jurgen was in Syria for a while, but he came back to the United States in 1980 to serve as an elder statesman for the Butterfly. I don't know if he's still alive, but I have a feeling he is."

"Mom, you don't think Jurgen had something to do with dad's disappearance?"

"I don't think so, but anything's possible. The whole situation is very confusing, and I'm getting frustrated trying to figure it out." Erika got up and paced around the room. "Excuse me, but I need to stretch a little; these old bones need to move around once in a while."

Sophie and I continued to sit with blank expressions, wondering what was coming next. Sophie put her arm around my neck and pulled my head closer and whispered, "Tom, we can't let her leave. We can't."

Before I could respond, Erika—who seemed to be gaining energy as she moved about the room—started up again. "You two stay sitting, but I'm going to keep moving," she said as she continued walking. "So now—considering our past, our clandestine CIA activities, Claude Brossard and Jurgen and his band of ex-Nazis chasing us, and this new threat from the Runic Butterfly—can you appreciate why Kurt and I were paranoid about getting you involved?"

"Yes!" Sophie and I answered in unison.

Erika walked between the beds and looked down at us. Crossing her arms, she asked, "Well, guess what? Everything I just told you about the Butterfly was wrong, totally wrong. The group was really a cover-up, a front for an ultra secret unit of CIA double agents who worked in the Middle East. How ironic is that? Kurt's been wondering what happened to Jurgen since 1945, and it turns out that they've both been working for the CIA since the 1960s. I only found this out a few years ago, and I'm not sure if I'm relieved or if I should be more concerned than ever."

"I'm a little confused here, so help me get some things straight. Did you and Kurt know about the Runic Butterfly?" I asked.

"No!" Erika almost spat the words out. "I never heard Kurt mention them, and I certainly knew nothing about them until two years ago. The CIA did tell us that there was an organization of ex-Nazis in the U.S. working against our government, and apparently that's why they were so careful with Kurt's identity. They were very secretive with us, but now I'm sure they were just being careful that Jurgen and Kurt never found out about each other."

"Do you think Jurgen ever had any idea Kurt was with the CIA?"

"Not according to what I was told."

Erika was getting very worked up, and I was starting to worry about her. "Erika, please sit down and relax a bit. Who in the hell told you all this?"

"I'm as relaxed as I can get, so don't worry about me. The CIA told me. I guess they felt there was no longer a reason to keep two old men apart. I asked them if Jurgen and Kurt were still alive—and get this—they said they didn't know."

"Maybe the CIA had a more devious reason to tell you. Maybe they want you to lead them somewhere," I said.

"Who cares?"

I was still confused. "And why would they use a one-armed man as a double agent? I think it would be hard to hide someone like that."

"The CIA always has their reasons, even if they don't make sense to any of the rest of us, but I don't care anymore. I'm really tired of all this spy crap. You know, people would be amazed if they knew all the stuff their government gets involved in. They just wouldn't believe it. I guess that's why governments get away with it. Sophie, don't you have anything to say? Are you just going to sit back and let Tom ask all the questions?"

Sophie reached across the narrow space between the beds and placed a hand on each of her mother's shoulders. "Yes, I do. Enough of this CIA crap, as you so eloquently put it. I want my dad back, and I want to celebrate a reunion with you." Sophie shook her mother and pleaded, "Mother, you can't go! We won't let you. I might never see you or dad again, and Bruce and Sara will never have a conversation with their German grandparents. How can you possibly leave me after a one-day reunion?"

Erika gently removed Sophie's hands from her shoulders and held them. "I'm sorry, but I have to go and try to find out what happened to the love of my life. Now, let's just make good use of the time we have left."

Erika's face had lost its glow, and she had become very melancholy. "I'm also speaking for Kurt when I say we're so sorry for our absence during the last thirty years, but we had to play the cards we dealt ourselves. There are many things we'd do differently if we had the chance, but we did the best we could. We're responsible for our actions, and nothing can ever totally erase our guilt, but we hope our lives in America have made up for some of our mistakes in Germany. It pained us beyond words to have to sacrifice our daughter for all these years, but it was necessary for your safety and for Kurt to do his job. It was both our mission and our punishment. I suppose I should have contacted you earlier about Kurt's disappearance, but I was always afraid and a little paranoid about what might happen if I did. Above all, I wanted to make sure nothing about us could harm you or your family. Lately I've felt safer, and I just had to see you one last time before going to Germany. I don't think the CIA wants to mess with an old lady any more, but you never know."

It was hard for me to tell who was more choked up, Sophie or her mother. No words were spoken throughout one long, tearful embrace. Erika ended the silence. "I love you Sophie, my Liebchen."

"I love you, Mom. If you get a chance, tell dad I love him, and that I'm sorry I was such a jerk. I would give anything to be able to tell him that myself."

"I will, but I'm sure he already knows. Now, let's talk about something more cheerful. Tom, your book is wonderful. It's even more than I had hoped for. I spent all morning reading it, and I felt things I hadn't felt in many years. Memories—good and bad—nearly overwhelmed me. For a few short hours, yesterday became today. Do you think we can ever be forgiven for some of the terrible things we've done?"

"Well, for what it's worth, I think you've made amends for your mistakes. But, as they say, history will be the judge. I'm glad the book meets with your approval, though. I tried to be as fair as possible."

Sophie jumped in. "Enough of this talk about the past. Let's celebrate this night together. We should get some champagne."

"Good idea. You've just read my mind," Erika said as she got up and walked into the bathroom. She returned with a bottle of champagne in an ice bucket and a tray of cheese and crackers. "I had these hidden in the shower. There's another bottle that I just put on ice in the sink. The room is paid for and after you've left me at the airport, I want you to come back here and spend the night. That is, unless you're too old for a little romantic getaway. Tom, why the smile?"

"Nothing, really. I was just thinking that you probably sounded just like your mother talking to you and Kurt way back when."

Erika laughed, "You're right. I must be more careful."

As we sat sipping champagne, Erika asked, "Has anyone else read your book? I know you weren't supposed to let anyone read it except Sophie until we gave our approval, but I know it's human nature to want to show your hard work to somebody."

"No, but if you count the number of times Sophie's read it, about twenty."

Sophie kicked me in the shin. "I just wanted to memorize the book in case the CIA confiscated it. You know, like in that book *Fahrenheit 451,* where people memorized books before the government came and burned them all?"

"I know you mean that as a joke, Sophie, but it's not too far-fetched. I'm sure the CIA will want to read it, so, Tom, don't add anything uncomplimentary about them, or you could be in trouble. I think you should try to get it published. There are a lot of people, especially in government, who would benefit from reading it, and, besides, it's a good story. Make sure Bruce and Sara read it, and your parents, too, Tom. We've been dead to them long enough."

Erika looked at her watch. "Okay, kids, I'm packed and ready. It's time for me to go to the airport."

———

Describing the emotions of Sophie and Erika saying goodbye at the airport is beyond my abilities as a writer. They knew as they hugged at the departure doorway that it was probably for the last time. Then, in a quiet North Dakota airport in the black gloom of a winter night, Erika kissed her daughter and climbed up the steps to the plane. Before entering the cabin, she turned and held the white rose over her heart and smiled wistfully at Sophie. We watched in silence as the plane vanished into the darkness.

———

Later in the hotel room as we were propped up on pillows in bed drinking Erika's champagne, I tried my best to distract Sophie from her melancholy by talking about everything under the sun, but she was lost in her thoughts. Realizing my efforts were fruitless, I got up to get the TV remote and an envelope fell out of the bed from under a pillow. The envelope was marked "Sophie," so I handed it to her. She looked at it numbly for a minute or so, turning it over and over gently in her hands. Finally, she said, "There's something in here other than a letter. I'm not sure if I dare open this, but I don't think I have a choice, do I?"

"I guess not."

She opened the envelope gingerly, took the letter out and started reading. After the day's events I didn't think Sophie had any more tears left, but they soon started dotting the paper, as she broke into a sob and handed me the letter. She then took something out of the bottom of the envelope while I started reading.

My darling Sophie,

I'm leaving my wedding ring for you because it has come to hold deep meaning for both of us and ties us together in more ways than you realize. Before you get upset worrying that I'm leaving you Nazi memorabilia, please read this entire note. This ring was the only symbol of my marriage to Kurt that survived the war. When I see it, I don't see a Nazi emblem, I see only a symbol of a love that endured a war and grew stronger with time. When we started working for the OSS, I was ordered to get rid of it, but I couldn't bring myself to do it. I hid it for quite some time—the CIA didn't even know I had it—but Kurt knew; he told me not to ever wear it in public, and I didn't. But I was wearing it around the house the day Tom discovered us in North Dakota. I took it off when I washed my hands and left it in the soap dish without a thought that some college kid would have a clue as to its meaning. When Tom discovered our secret, I told him that I felt there was a reason he had come into our lives, but even then I couldn't imagine that his discovery would reunite us with you. So you see, Liebchen, this ring has brought me closer to the two greatest loves of my life, and it will give me great pleasure knowing that you have this little part of me and Kurt with you forever.

All my love,
Mother

"Amazing," Sophie said, wiping away tears before trying the ring on her finger. "I didn't even know she still had this. I remember reading about it in the book, but it never occurred to me to ask her to see it. Is it like you remembered?"

"Yes, it's exactly like I remembered, but I've never thought about it again, either. I'm glad she left you with something better than a bottle of champagne."

"Yes, you have dad's Nordic statue, and now I have mom's ring. It's not much, but it's at least something, considering the circumstances." She was studying it carefully when a look of utter dismay suddenly crossed her face.

"What's the matter, Sophie? Is there something wrong?"

"Damn, I can't believe it. I forgot to ask mom the one thing that's been on my mind ever since we reconnected. I forgot to ask her my real name! Can you believe I forgot to do that? I still don't know who the hell I really am!"

———

We drove home early the next morning. About nine o'clock that night the telephone rang, and I picked it up in time to hear a voice I did not recognize say, "Just thought you'd like to know. Sophie's mother arrived safely in Germany." Then the line went dead.

CHAPTER 23

Our children, Bruce and Sara, read the book in February after we made them promise not to discuss it with anyone. At first they were both full of questions, interrogating Sophie and me unmercifully about their newly-discovered grandparents and wanting to know when they could meet them. But the novelty of the discovery wore off within a few months, and their attentions turned back to school, friends, and their own futures. Sophie and I shrugged off their indifference, but remained hopeful that their curiosity about their German grandparents would return someday when they could better comprehend the significance of their story.

I had intended to send the book to my parents in early March, but circumstances changed my plans. Sophie and I had always suspected that the CIA kept us under surveillance, and our suspicions were confirmed on the bitter cold evening of February 28 when the doorbell rang about eight o'clock. Two men dressed in dark suits stood on our doorstep; one was middle-aged, the other in his late twenties. The older man, who called himself John and appeared to have at least a trace of a personality, did most of the talking. The younger one introduced himself as Paul. After flashing their credentials, they joined us at the kitchen table and fumbled nervously over a cup of coffee before the actual interrogation began.

"You have a nice home. How long have you lived here?"

"I'm sure you already know the answer, so why ask us? Why don't you just cut to the chase and stop wasting our time?" Sophie was already primed for a fight.

John ignored the sarcasm. "I know your dad, Sophie. He's a fine man. I hope we can reach some kind of closure regarding his situation."

Sophie answered, "Closure? What the hell does that mean? Do you know anything about where my dad is? Is that what this is all about?"

John continued, "No, I'm afraid we don't have anything new to tell you about that. We know your mom is in Germany looking for him again. We've protected her and brought her back from Germany once already. Erika's a wonderful person, but she's a loose cannon at times. Right now she's really no threat to the agency, so we'll just let her roam for a while." John then looked directly at me. "Actually, Tom, we're more interested in your book and some of the research you've been doing. We'd like to take the book for a time and look it over, and Paul would like to take a peek at your computer."

"Do you have a search warrant? If you don't, I think that's an infringement of my personal liberties."

John gave me a long, knowing look. "Tom, we know a lot about you and your research. Your computer has a lot of hits in some sensitive areas, such as Monarch and Paperclip. They're public information, but because of your wife's heritage, we have a special interest in just why you're researching those particular projects. And as for a warrant, well, you know there's the law and then there's *the law*. Yes, we do have a search warrant, but ordinary search warrants might not cover all our needs, so we're exercising our power under the umbrella of protecting national security. That gives us all the authority we need. Please just cooperate and things will go smoothly."

I nodded at Paul. "Go ahead. The computer's down at the end of the hallway in the office on the right. If you guys are as sharp as you pretend to be, you should already know everything that's in there."

As Paul walked down the hallway, Sophie stood up, strode over to John, rested her hand on the table directly in front of him and said, "So if the CIA protects us from terrorists, who protects us from the CIA?"

John gave Sophie an ominous look. "You should have asked your father that question. Look, we're not here to debate political views. We're just here to do our job."

"Why do you need to take my book? It's the only copy I've got," I said.

"Well, Tom, you'll just have to print another copy off the CD I'm sure you've stashed somewhere. I assume you'll eventually try to get your book published, but that will be very hard if we find anything in it that we don't like. Don't forget, Kurt and Erika's confidentiality agreement is still in effect, and anything they told you is under our control. We've kept close tabs on you and Sophie. Things have gone well so far, so don't try to push your luck now."

Paul reappeared and announced, "I've got what I need. Do you have the book?"

I assumed Paul had copied the entire hard drive off my computer, and as I handed John the printed copy, I couldn't resist a parting shot. "Did you guys ever see the movie *Enemy of the State* with Will Smith? I'm beginning to know what he felt like."

They ignored my comment as they walked out the door.

About six months later the book showed up in my mailbox with a note attached. The book was cleared for publication, as long as I made no mention of Kurt's and Erika's activities after 1946. In late August I mailed a copy to my parents. I included a letter telling them that Sophie's parents had not been killed in a car accident as everyone had been told but were really Kurt and Erika Heisler, the subjects of the book. I told them to read it, not tell anyone about it, and not even mention it to us on the phone until we drove down to discuss it with them.

CHAPTER 24

SEPTEMBER 15, 1998

It was mid-afternoon when Sophie and I arrived in Wahpeton, North Dakota, for our first visit with my parents since I had sent them the book. They had moved there in 1992, a sensible move for them. My younger brother lived there, it had better medical facilities than New Rockford, and it was still small enough for them to feel comfortable getting around. The only downside for me was that it had eliminated my hunting quarters in New Rockford, and since their move I had been forced to mooch off friends for lodging during my hunting excursions.

I turned off Dakota Avenue onto Fourth Street, drove two blocks north and turned right at the large white building that housed the Wahpeton Police Department. We parked in the lot of my parents' nearby duplex and headed upstairs. On the second floor landing outside the entrance, dad's walking shoes rested neatly on the mat next to an antique oak table adorned with mom's artificial daisies and assorted knick-knacks with clever Norwegian sayings. I knocked twice on the door and dad quickly greeted us with, "What are you doing here, Tom? It's only the middle of September and hunting season doesn't start for another two weeks."

"I just came for some good food and free beer. How've you been?"

Before dad could answer, mom yelled from the kitchen, "Don't mind your grumpy old dad; he just wishes he could still go hunting. I hope you brought your lovely wife along."

"Yeah, dad's squeezing the life out of her with one of his hugs right now."

As we entered the living room, mom joined us from the kitchen, almost hidden behind her large blue and white checkered apron. Hugging both of us, she exclaimed, "I'm so happy you're here. We have so much to talk about. We aren't eating until five, so what can I get you for a snack?"

Dad charged straight to the point, quickly answering any questions we had regarding whether he had mellowed. "I think we need to discuss the book before we do anything else. Let's all get comfortable, and I'll get the ball rolling."

Sophie and I took seats on the flowery brown and blue love seat while mom and dad sat on the matching couch. There was no food or drink anywhere in sight, which signaled the importance of the pending conversation.

Dad started things off. "Tom, we think you've written a wonderful book. The battle scenes are realistic to this veteran, and I've checked on the historical accuracy of a number of things and they all seem to line up. Sophie, you certainly have some unique and fascinating parents. We don't understand the need for all the secrecy or what has happened between you and your parents, but I guess you'll tell us when the time is right. Tom, there are points in the book I'm going to ask you about, things that bother me a little, but I'll get back to them later. Sophie, you're my son's wife, the mother of my wonderful grandchildren, and I love you deeply, but it feels strange to think that I fought against your dad and that your grandparents were Nazi aristocrats. I think the book has broadened my horizons a little, but I apologize beforehand if I make some rash comments."

Dad finally paused for a breath, and mom jumped right in. "Not you, Frank. I can't possibly imagine you making a rash comment." She seemed proud of her little dig as she continued, "I'd love to meet your parents, Sophie. It would be so interesting to talk with them and compare notes about the times we've lived through."

"I'm sure my parents would love to meet you also."

Acting very proud of himself, my dad clapped his hands together loudly. "I have a revelation to announce. I think I've met your parents, but I didn't realize it until I read Tom's book. I'm not one hundred percent positive, but all the evidence supports my theory, so let me explain. Way back in the summer of 1968, two strangers came into my store. I remember the date because I'd just bought a new silver Pontiac, and I was filling out some insurance forms for Uncle Dick. I was in the store alone and in walked two people I'd never seen before, a man and a woman, both blond-haired and blue-eyed. The woman was so striking I even took special notice."

Mom raised her eyebrows and said, "Oh? Why didn't you ever tell me about her?"

Blushing slightly, dad replied, "Guess I didn't want you to get jealous. Anyway, the man and I made small talk, but the woman hardly spoke. I asked them where they were from, and they said they were from the eastern part of North Dakota but were moving to California. They'd just stopped in New Rockford to get gas and stretch a bit. The man had a slight German accent, but his English was perfect. Now comes the interesting part. It'd been a slow day, and I'd taken my company picture of the Rainbow Division from the war down to dust, and I'd left it on the counter near the cash register. The man noticed it and asked if I'd been in World War II. I told him yes, and he asked me where and when. When I mentioned the Battle of the Bulge, he seemed to get unsettled. I asked him if he had served, and he mumbled something about fighting all over Europe and losing most of his friends. Abruptly, he told me I had a nice store, thanked me for our visit, and left … with a limp. As they went out the door the woman turned, smiled and wished me and my family well. I thought it a little odd at the time, but I understood that a lot of veterans have a hard time talking about the war, and I kind of forgot about it until I read your book."

"Dad, how can you possibly remember all those details after so many years?" I asked.

"I don't know, but your descriptions of Kurt and Erika in the book perfectly match those two people who came into my store. And now, looking at the beauty sitting beside you confirms my suspicion; I just never realized the connection before."

I shrugged my shoulders and took a long chug of my beer. "Careful, Dad, about throwing out too many of those compliments. It might make her even harder to live with."

Sophie responded with an elbow to my ribs, but I kept talking. "Well, Kurt and Erika never mentioned the visit to me, but it sounds like it certainly could have been them. They probably wanted to see what kind of people could have produced such a perfect son."

After a round of laughter at my expense, I stood up and headed for the kitchen. "We need a break. Dad must be running out of breath. Who needs something to drink?"

After playing the host and supplying everyone with beverages, I sat down as dad produced another surprise, "I've got one more thing to add to this mystery. Do you remember your Aunt Mary in Fessenden?"

"Of course I do."

"Well, I forgot all about this, too, until I read your book. I remembered Mary coming into the store in—I'm not sure, probably around 1980—and telling me she'd seen you at a Fessenden gas station. You were sitting in a car in your hunting gear and you were with a man she didn't recognize. Before she could come over and say hi to you, a woman—a very attractive blond woman, she said—came out of the gas station, got into the car, and you all drove away. Were those strangers Kurt and Erika?"

I had to laugh at dad's observation. Once again, despite my caution that day, events proved that nothing goes unnoticed in small communities. "Yes, that was me. That's the only time I've seen Kurt and Erika since 1968. It was a secret visit to tell me what they'd been up to, stuff that I'm not going to tell you right now. You were in Minneapolis for business, so I didn't even have to try and hide it from you. I never noticed Aunt Mary. Any more surprises from either of you?"

They didn't have any, so Sophie and I spent the next half hour telling them about Sophie's estrangement from her parents, about how I had met Kurt and Erika and gained their confidence, and about Kurt and the CIA. We warned mom and dad that Kurt's CIA affiliation was classified information, and they were to tell no one. After finishing our background briefing, we mentioned we didn't know where Kurt and Erika were, and that subject was off limits. The four of us then took a break and adjourned to the kitchen for snacks and conversation about Bruce and Sara, but we were soon back in the living room engaged in dialogue about Sophie's parents.

This time it was my mother's turn to dominate the conversation. "Let me tell you something I found very interesting. Your book starts in 1937, the year when Kurt goes to Nuremberg and meets Erika. That's the same year your dad and I had our first date. We went to a movie starring Cary Grant and Irene Dunne; it was one of those screwball comedies so popular during the Thirties. Everyone liked happy movies back then because they wanted to laugh and forget the Depression for a couple of hours. Your dad and I were both working in Carrington. Dad worked at Gambles Hardware Store, and I worked at JC Penney's. We met at a dance at the Rainbow Gardens in Carrington. You know, the big band sound, real music. Boy, your dad could really dance."

"What do you mean could?" Dad got up and shuffled—very slowly—through a few dance moves across the living room and fell back onto the couch.

"That was wonderful, dear. Should I call an ambulance? Anyway, as I was saying, most Americans in 1937 were not much into politics, except for hoping FDR would get us out of the Depression. We were too worried about the basics to be concerned about world affairs. I contrast that with your parents, Sophie, all caught up with Hitler and the Nazis. I was just struck by how two couples about the same age at the same time in two different parts of the world were experiencing such conflicting sets of circumstances, Adolf Hitler versus Benny Goodman."

"Benny who?" I asked,

Mom took the bait. "You know, the famous band leader, the King of Swing. I remember you played dad's old records of the swing era and ... " Mom saw the smile on my face and knew she'd been had.

Dad came to her rescue. "Well, at least for a while you listened to real music. I do think Inga brings up a valid point about the contrast between life in Germany and America in the Thirties. It's funny how things develop, look at how Tom and Sophie wound up getting together."

"Mom, do you even remember the name of that movie you were talking about?" I asked.

"The Awful Truth."

The timer on the stove saved us from an analysis of the hidden meaning of the movie title, and as the women went into the kitchen, dad came over and sat next to me.

"Tom, I want to talk softly enough so your mother and Sophie can't hear us. I didn't want to say anything in front of Sophie. You know I love her, and I don't want to hurt her feelings, but her dad belonged to a real bad-ass organization."

"That doesn't necessarily mean Kurt was bad."

"Haven't you ever heard of guilt by association? I don't even like the fact that our government has worked with people like that. How the hell did Kurt even get into the CIA?"

I didn't answer, and dad got straight to the point, "Tom, I said I wanted to talk with you about a few points in your book. Well, here's my main question. Why do you seem so sympathetic to Kurt most of the time?"

"What do you mean?"

"The Waffen SS were really evil characters. They killed with no remorse, yet you make Kurt sound almost noble at times. To me, that doesn't seem to fit."

"Dad, do you remember taking me to the movie, *The Young Lions,* back in 1958? I think I was a freshman in high school."

"I think so. Isn't that the one with Marlon Brando playing a German soldier?"

"He was a young German officer, Christian, I think his name was. I vividly recall a couple scenes from that movie. In the first he becomes visibly upset when wounded British soldiers are machine-gunned to death in the desert; in the second he tries to surrender to some Americans who don't understand German, and a character played by Dean Martin kills him. The impression that remained with me is that sometimes good people wind up on the wrong side, and sometimes the reverse is true."

"Son, that happens in every war. I won't deny that, but that doesn't excuse the Waffen SS. Where are you going with this?"

"Do you remember our discussions about the draft back when I was getting ready to graduate?"

"Yes, that had to be the fall of '66 or so. Say, that's about when you met Kurt and Erika, wasn't it? Is that the connection? Are you saying you were taking advice from him about whether to serve your country?"

"No, Dad, at least not directly. What I'm trying to explain is that Kurt's situation just caused me to see things from another perspective. I still wonder about the decision I made. Was I wrong or right? Most of the time we judge our choices by how they turn out. History has shown that Vietnam was a mistake. Does that mean my choice was right? If the war had been successful, would my choice have been wrong? Was Kurt wrong because Germany lost, or because he fought for a cause that was evil? Remember, there was no Holocaust when Kurt joined the Waffen SS. The Final Solution to the Jewish question wasn't decided upon until 1942."

Dad leaned back in his chair, stretched his legs, and paused before answering. I could tell he was getting upset because he was humming as he tried to stay calm. Then he exploded, "You made a choice, a choice that was right for you. Live with it. As for Kurt, that's all bullshit. A person is judged by the company he keeps. The SS knew where Hitler was headed."

"I know, but I'm leading up to the whole point of my book. When do you follow your country's leaders without question? When do you start to question them? When do you protest? Was Kurt wrong to join the Waffen SS when he thought he was defending his country? Would a soldier be wrong for refusing to go to a war he thought was wrong? What if I hadn't got a teaching job and decided to go to Canada or become a Conscientious Objector? What is a patriot, really? I don't think you can ... "

"You never change, do you, son? Things aren't always black or white. You can't analyze every event in the hope there's a perfect answer. All we can do in these gray areas is follow our conscience and do our best until the correct solution becomes clear."

"But what if that answer never becomes clear, like the conflict between national security and individual rights? Was it right—or even legal—for Hoover to spy on Americans while he was heading the FBI? Was it right for Nixon to keep an 'enemies list' of 10,000 Americans that disagreed with him? I mean, how far should a country go under the vague cover of 'national security?' Do you think America was ever in danger of being attacked by John Lennon or a bunch of Hollywood movie stars?"

Dad tapped his fingers on his knee, smiled weakly, but didn't respond for a while. I pretty much knew what he was thinking. Dad was "old school" all the way—decorated veteran, self-made businessman, solid Republican, devout Catholic, and unapologetic patriot—and I loved and respected him for all of those things. Our political discussions were usually good-natured, full of exaggerated opinions and a few well-placed barbs, but he actually sounded mad when he started talking again.

"I thought this discussion was going to be about your book, not another of your predictably liberal political sermons. Tom, let me put it this way, sometimes you have to err on the side of the whole of society rather than on the side of an individual."

"But, Dad, society is made up of individuals, and that's what our Constitution is supposed to protect, the rights of the individual citizen, not the rights of the society."

"These are very difficult times. It's not like World War II. Today there are these damn international terrorists who float from country to country under no official flag. Look at what they did to the World Trade Center a few years ago. How do you stop bombings like that if you're not keeping an eye on people like this?" Dad paused and took a deep breath.

"But that's exactly what I'm talking about. Do you think I pose any kind of threat to America? That I should be treated the same way as potential terrorist bombers? The CIA has been watching me for thirty years, and all I ever did was accidentally meet some people who worked for them. Hell, they even confiscated my book and all my research and told me what I could and couldn't write, even though most of the stuff they censored is a matter of public record. Are you saying they had the right to do this to protect society? From what? Where does this madness stop, Dad?"

"Hell, knowing what I know now, I'd have been watching you, too. For God's sake, you're married to the daughter of an SS war criminal who escaped punishment because he cut a deal with the CIA. For all I know, I could be in trouble with the CIA, too." He reached over and picked up the phone. "Hello, CIA? Just in case you're listening, I'm not responsible for my son's terrorist tendencies, so leave me and my wife alone."

"Here, would you like their number?" I said, reaching for my wallet. "But the next time you ask me why I don't come around more often to talk, just think of this conversation."

"Okay, we disagree, but in the end we're just talking about apples and oranges. The debate will go on forever; it's all a matter of degree and who's in power to interpret and enforce that degree."

"Precisely! See if you can tell me who said this," I said, taking out a piece of paper from my shirt pocket and reading ... *"Of course the people don't want war. But after all, it's the leaders of the country who determine the policy, and it's always a simple matter to drag the people along whether it's a democracy, a fascist dictatorship, or a parliament, or a communist dictatorship. Voice or no voice the people can always be brought to the bidding of the leaders. That is easy. All you have to do is tell them they are being attacked, and denounce the pacifists for lack of patriotism, and exposing the country to greater danger."*

"You were obviously planning this, so I suppose this quote is from one of my heroes that you want to pick on, like Rush."

"No, not exactly. Herman Goring said it during the Nuremberg Trials."

Dad shook his head and gave me a bemused look. "Really, so what's your point? FDR got us into World War II under false pretenses? Lyndon Johnson used the Gulf of Tonkin incident to escalate the war in Vietnam?"

"Don't get your conservative feathers ruffled, Dad. I'm not just talking about the government getting us into unnecessary wars. I'm also talking about a government using some vague threat in order to get the public to accept harsh measures to control individual liberties."

"Enough! I've had all I can take of this conversation." Dad got up, stuck out his hand and said, "Shake. No hard feelings son, but this is going nowhere." After a quick handshake, he headed into the kitchen to see what was going on.

I stood up to stretch and walked out the door to the landing area at the top of the stairs. Staring at dad's walking shoes aligned neatly on the welcome mat, I realized how much I loved him, even though we lived on opposite ends of the political spectrum.

Mom yelled, "Tommy, get back in here. You can't read Norwegian anyway."

"So what. Norwegians can't either."

I walked back into the living room. Mom and Sophie were seated on the couch. Dad was out of sight, nibbling on something in the kitchen. Mom handed me an article and asked me to read it. The article was from the Wahpeton paper and concerned the speaker at the last Kiwanis meeting; I was surprised mom even gave me the article without dad in the room. She usually took his lead in political matters. She was slightly more liberal than dad; she only liked Rush Limbaugh a little bit. Before I could even start to read it, mom told me the whole story, with additional commentary.

"Can you believe that article? How can people do such horrible things? When I saw that woman standing up in front of us, telling us how she was raped sixty-seven times by the Russians over two days and nights, and she was only thirteen years old! I can't imagine the horror she experienced. I realize the Russians had just captured Berlin and they needed to celebrate, but not like that, not in the modern world. And the Russians were on our side, the good guys. Why does war make us such animals? How can we tolerate behavior like that?"

"That's good, Inga. I'm glad you remembered to bring this up," Dad said as he returned, coffee in hand. "Yeah, Tom, it was really uncomfortable listening to her. Nobody should have to go through something like that. It was amazing she even survived. When I was listening to her, I thought of something you'd told me about that time you heard Elie Weisel speak at UND. You said that you were using his book, *Night*, in your class, and that as you looked at this calm, soft-spoken man dressed in a suit, you couldn't imagine him as a starving teenager in Auschwitz. I had that same feeling as I listened to that German woman; it was eerie listening to her talk about surviving such a terrible experience. Auschwitz, Berlin, I ask the same question as Inga. How can people do that to each other?"

"Because war is a contradiction to the rule of law." I knew I was only adding fuel to the fire, but I couldn't resist. "Why does society tend to glamorize war and make it so heroic? I remember playing cowboys and Indians when I was a little boy, and I loved going to war movies. Unfortunately, violence fascinates us, and nothing is more violent than war; it provides governments with an excuse to commit atrocities. Our leaders tell us we need to go to war in order to defend our country, or to save the world from some evil force, but whatever the reason, people die. Rules don't count for much when you're told that your very existence is threatened and all that counts is that you win. After all, we shot prisoners during World War II, we firebombed German and Japanese cities, we dropped atomic bombs on Hiroshima and Nagasaki, we … "

"Dammit, Tom! Don't try getting philosophical on me and insinuating we were just as bad as the Germans and the Japanese. War is hell, but sometimes it's necessary. We can try to avoid it, but when that's impossible, the best we can do is follow a set of rules like the Geneva Convention or Nuremberg Laws and do our duty. Geeze, you get me so mad sometimes."

Dad's face was flushed and his hair was standing at attention. I responded calmly, "Dad, my point is, we certainly had good reasons for entering World War II; we were attacked, for God's sake! It was a just war on our part, and we needed to defeat Germany and Japan or be conquered. But, even a just war may have unjust consequences. It's the nature of the beast. War—any war—must be the last resort."

Sophie, sensing a prolonged argument between dad and me, intervened. "Maybe we should spend more time preventing wars and less time making up rules. I mean, who decides when a leader or a country is becoming dangerous enough to threaten the rest of the world? And I'm not just talking about which leaders, I also mean which countries decide? Who gets to decide who's good and who's bad?"

"The closest thing we've got right now to sort those things out is the UN," I said grudgingly, not wanting to let dad off the hook, "but they certainly have their limitations, given all the international politics involved."

"I agree," dad said, sounding relieved that the conversation had taken a different turn, "but in the end, sometimes you just have to act on your own to get things done. I don't agree with President Clinton very often, but after our embassies in Kenya and Tanzania were bombed last month, we did the right thing when we fired those cruise missiles and tried to take out bin Laden. We need to identify who our real enemies are and remove them, and we can't sit around while the UN debates the issues. I think everyone knows bin Laden and al Qaeda are public enemy number one, and we can't rest until we get them. Maybe we'll get a good Republican president in the next election, and he'll keep after bin Laden until we get the bastard. We just can't get side-tracked with some secondary target."

Sophie laughed and said, "Frank, I think you just used an oxymoron, 'good Republican President.'"

"Very funny, liberal bias person, but you know I'm right."

Mom stepped in, "Let's end this political discussion. All we've done is talk about serious stuff. Let's enjoy ourselves before Tom and Sophie have to leave."

Dad replied, "Just one more thing. I just hope ten years from now—I'm not sure I'll still be around in September, 2008, but hopefully we'll have a Republican administration—bin Laden will be gone, and the world will be a better, safer place."

"Dad, I'm sure you'll still be here in 2008, and I hope for all the same things, except for the Republican administration, of course."

Sophie got up and walked over to my parents. "I think I need to say something before we sit down for dinner. It's obvious that the two of you are uncomfortable with my parents' past, and I don't blame you. All I can say is that they regret their involvement with the Nazi movement, and they've tried to make amends ever since. Why else would they have named me Sophie? I love them and I forgive them, and I hope you can as well. Let's go eat and talk about the coming hunting season."

"I'd like to add something, too, Sophie," Inga said. "I can't imagine what this has been like for you all these years. I'm so sorry you and Tom had to face this alone and that we didn't know about this so we could have provided support for you. None of this is your fault, and there's nothing for you to feel guilty about. I hope that someday you can be reunited with your parents so this story can have a happy ending. Don't you agree, Frank?"

"Amen to that, dear," dad said.

We adjourned to the kitchen in a much lighter mood.

Driving back to Grand Forks that night I had to laugh to myself about the exchange with my parents. Toward the end of our visit mom had asked me what I knew about Kurt and Erika's CIA activities, and I just told her that was a story for another day. As for dad and me, I was glad things had ended on a cheerful note. I knew dad wouldn't stop watching Rush Limbaugh or Bill O'Reilly any time soon, but maybe, just maybe, he'd be a bit more skeptical about their rants. And even though we didn't agree on solutions to our country's problems, I felt as if I'd completed the journey I'd started forty years ago.

As I nudged the car into our garage, I wondered how the hardworking, patriotic folks around Bremen would have reacted if they had known that an SS Prince and a Nazi Princess had lived among them. I wondered why we humans fail to learn from the past. And I wondered how much of Kurt and Erika live within all of us.

EPILOGUE

A few days after our trip to Wahpeton, I came home and found Sophie standing next to the kitchen table sorting the mail. She was holding a photograph in her hand.

"How was your day, dear?"

Sophie made no response. She was transfixed by the photo she was holding. I waited a few moments and then asked, "Anything special?"

Sophie looked at me and shrugged, but said nothing. She put the photo back in the envelope, dropped it with the other mail on the table and left the room.

I noticed the envelope was postmarked "Zurich, Switzerland." I picked it up and took out a photo of Erika and a distinguished elderly gentleman; they looked like they were attending a picnic somewhere in the Alps. I stared at the picture for at least a minute, and then looked in the envelope to see if I had missed anything. I hadn't. I turned the picture over and discovered a short message scrawled in black ink. "We need to talk. I'll contact you soon. Love, Mom."

The man in the picture had only one arm.

AUTHORS' NOTES

In *Patriot Acts* we mention a number of programs and organizations, and we describe them in more detail in the following pages. However, these descriptions reveal elements of the plot, so we respectfully suggest that you consider finishing *Patriot Acts* before reading these notes.

Patriot Acts is a work of fiction constructed around historical events. Although much of the history of this period is common knowledge, in seeking historical correctness we consulted standard reference sources and the books listed in the bibliography at the end of this section. While we have attempted to make this book as accurate as possible regarding timelines, actual participants, settings, troop movements, government programs and the like, some details might have been altered in service of the plot; we also took obvious liberties with prominent historical figures by imagining conversations and interactions they had with our fictitious characters.

That being said, we feel some further explanation is necessary regarding our main characters:

Tom Johnson is fictitious, even though many of his incidents and those of other supporting fictional characters were taken from our own life experiences of growing up in New Rockford, North Dakota, attending college at the University of North Dakota in Grand Forks and teaching in the Grand Forks Public School System.

Tom's fictional family is based on Jim's real parents, James Lies, Sr., and Ruth Lies, but, again, we have embellished some details and created new ones where necessary. It is true, however, that during World War II James, Sr., enlisted in the U.S. Army in July of 1942 and served proudly with the 42nd Rainbow Division in Europe, earning a Bronze Star with two clusters before retiring as a Major in the Army Reserve in 1953.

Kurt, Erika and Sophie Heisler are fictional, as are their activities, although many Nazi military members were brought into the United States after the war through Operation Paperclip, which is described in one of the following sections.

The many other characters enhancing both Tom's story and Kurt and Erika's story are fictional composites based on reported events of their respective time periods, and any similarity to real people, living or dead, is coincidental and unintended.

U. S. Government Programs/Committees/Legislative Acts.

We profess to having absolutely no knowledge of the workings of the Central Intelligence Agency, so if any of the CIA meetings and activities described in the book strain credulity for our readers, we apologize and remind them that those sections are the fictional parts of the book; however, all of the U.S. Government and CIA-affiliated programs mentioned in *Patriot Acts* (except for the Runic Butterfly, which is a figment of our imaginations) are real. Even though the existence of these programs has been public knowledge for decades, most Americans have never heard of them. The following pages provide basic information about these government programs, and we encourage readers who are interested in learning more to consult the wealth of information readily available on the internet, as these programs characterize a most intriguing time period in America's history. A good starting point is www.archives.gov, the website for The National Archives and Records Administration (NARA), the official record keeper *"of all documents and materials created in the course of business conducted by the United States Federal Government."* We also found several books listed in the bibliography to be great resources regarding the formation of the CIA.

(Note: All direct quotations used in the following sections are taken from official U.S. documents located in the NARA files.)

The Jedburgh Program.

Our Captain Anderson is a fictional character, but the Jedburgh Program was the real thing, although it remained pretty much a secret until the CIA declassified many of its records in the 1980s. The program was a joint creation of the United States

Office of Strategic Services (OSS) and the British Special Operations Executive (SOE) to train the French resistance forces (FFI, for Force Forces of the Interior, also called the Maquis) to provide support for the Allied landings on D-Day and the battles afterward. The Jedburghs, after receiving comprehensive physical and mental training, were organized into independent, resourceful three-man teams. The first team parachuted into France early on the morning of D-Day, with other teams following shortly thereafter. With the Jedburghs' help, the Maquis' guerilla tactics against the Germans assisted the Allies in the invasion of France. After the war some American Jedburghs played prominent roles in major institutions, with Major William Colby becoming the CIA Director in 1973 and Colonel Aaron Bank commanding the first U.S. Special Forces group ever activated.

Office of Strategic Services (OSS). This precursor to the Central Intelligence Agency (CIA) was created by President Franklin Roosevelt on June 13, 1942, as a wartime intelligence agency authorized to conduct special operations not assigned to existing government agencies. Specifically, the OSS was designed to coordinate behind-enemy-lines espionage activities for the United States military, but its purview soon expanded well beyond that description to include recruiting, training, arming and supplying resistance movements as well as the use of various other tactics, such as propaganda management, psychological warfare, subversive acts and post-war planning. From 1943 to 1945 OSS agents performed such activities in China, Burma, French Indochina and all the Axis-controlled territories in Europe. After the war the OSS was dissolved by President Harry Truman in September of 1945, and over the next two years its responsibilities were divided among several existing and newly-formed government agencies. The National Security Act of 1947 created the first peacetime intelligence organization, the Central Intelligence Agency, which incorporated the wide-ranging functions of the old OSS under one banner.

Operation Paperclip. This program, which brought our fictional *Patriot Acts* characters Kurt and Erika Heisler into the United States, was controversial at its inception and remains so today. Given its history, this is not surprising.

Even though the United States and Russia, by necessity, were allies in defeating Hitler during World War II, both parties knew that their countries' political differences would force the end of the partnership at the war's end. Each country was wary of the other's motives, and many American military and political experts had already concluded that Russia would be the next threat to western democracy. Some, like General George Patton, even suggested that as long as America had a standing army in Europe, it might as well continue with the advancement all the way into Russia and finish the job, an idea that was, of course, rejected. Both Russia and the United States coveted the physical and human resources of the German V-2 rocket program, and as World War II drew to a close and the defeat of Germany was imminent, the two countries waged a capture and recruitment war in advance of what would eventually become the Cold War. There was an intense effort by each country to capture intact as many of these rocket resources as possible before Germany's surrender and the signing of the peace treaties; short of that, where necessary, the Americans destroyed rocket resources rather than letting them fall into Soviet hands.

To facilitate bringing scientists to the United States, the Joint Chiefs of Staff created the top secret Project Overcast to *"exploit...chosen rare minds whose continuing intellectual productivity we wish to use."* On July 6, 1945, 350 specialists, mostly Germans and Austrians, were chosen to be brought immediately to the United States. In 1946 the program was expanded by the Joint Intelligence Objectives Agency and renamed Operation Paperclip; its purpose was to recruit as many German scientists as possible for the United States while denying this intellectual expertise to the Russians. Of particular interest to America were scientists in the fields of rocketry, aerodynamics, radiation, chemical and biological weapons, and medicine. Although the program's guidelines prohibited the acceptance of scientists who had been "ardent Nazis" or were convicted of war crimes, these restrictions were routinely violated. From the end of the war until the early 1970s more than 1,600 German scientists, some of whom had also worked on brainwashing and torture techniques, were quietly brought into the United States with their families. Prominent among them were Werner von Braun and some of his associates, who became major contributors to America's space program, and General Reinhard Gehlen,

Hitler's Chief of Intelligence against Russia, who helped America set up a covert intelligence program that became the Central Intelligence Agency. Through the years the military also benefitted from Paperclip émigrés: The U.S. Air Force's School of Aviation Medicine (SAM) utilized German scientists during the Cold War to conduct human radiation experiments, and the Department of Defense worked with the CIA on many MKULTRA mind control experiments (discussed in the following section).

In 1979 (partly because of the public release of secret MKULTRA documents in the mid-1970s), the Justice Department's Office of Special Operations was created to deport Nazi war criminals from the United States, including some who were in America through Operation Paperclip. Among their findings was the discovery that the U.S. Army Counterintelligence Corps (CIC) had employed and protected Nazi Klaus Barbie, the infamous "Butcher of Lyon," and had even helped him escape to South America after the war. In 1999 the Justice Department undertook a secret investigation into the intelligence community's involvement in protecting Nazi war criminals in the United States. The final report was finished in 2006, but was kept secret until the Justice Department released a heavily redacted version in October, 2010, in compliance with a request under the Freedom of Information Act. On November 13, 2010, The *New York Times* released a copy of the entire 600-page report, which concluded that the CIA and even some Justice Department officials had collaborated with many Nazis and created a "safe haven" for war criminals, even after the Justice Department had initiated deportation proceedings for some Nazis subject to the 1979 OSI investigation. (The entire report is available in the *New York Times* archives: www.newyorktimesarchives.com.) The released files revealed that in the post-World War II run-up to the Cold War—even though many U.S. officials questioned the morality of using Nazi war criminals for research purposes—America was more concerned about the threat of Communism than in prosecuting Nazis or denying them entry to the United States. In the end, it appears that most of the questionable Germans were brought in by the intelligence groups while government enforcement officials looked the other way.

MKULTRA. Shortly after World War II ended, two secret U.S. government programs arose from Operation Paperclip to take advantage of specific expertise offered by German scientists. Project Chatter and Project Bluebird (later renamed Project Artichoke) experimented in mind control, behavior modification, and enhanced interrogation techniques, often involving the use of hypnosis and mind-altering drugs like LSD. These two projects were positioned as a response to Chinese, North Korean and Soviet mind control experiments allegedly used on American POWs in Korea and became the precursors to MKULTRA, a project created in 1953 by CIA Director Allen Dulles (whose brother, John Foster Dulles, had been Secretary of State under President Eisenhower). MKULTRA became the cover for more than 150 secret, illegal CIA human research experiments that ran well into the late 1960s. The CIA leadership clearly knew the programs were illegal, as revealed by this statement in the 1957 CIA Inspector General Report: *"Precautions must be taken not only to protect operations from exposure to enemy forces but also to conceal these activities from the American public in general. The knowledge that the agency is engaging in unethical and illicit activities would have serious repercussions in political and diplomatic circles."*

It wasn't until December of 1974, when The *New York Times* printed an article claiming the CIA had run illegal experiments on U.S. citizens in the 1960s, that the work of MKULTRA came to light. The government responded in 1975 by creating the Rockefeller Commission and then the Church Committee (see following sections) to investigate these and a variety of other CIA activities. Many questions remain about the true nature and scope of the program because in 1973 CIA Director Richard Helms, fearing that the project might be discovered, ordered the destruction of all MKULTRA documents. However, in 1977 a Freedom of Information Act request for information by journalist John Marks led to the discovery of 20,000 MKULTRA documents that had escaped destruction because they had been mistakenly stored in the wrong building. The discovery prompted a U.S. Senate hearing in 1977 and eventually most of the documents were declassified. Although the 20,000 documents represent only a fraction of the MKULTRA's total, they tell a very chilling story. The files reveal that, in addition to the CIA and the U.S. military branches, over thirty American colleges and universities and several major American drug companies participated in covert human behavioral experiments (although some didn't know the studies' originators because the CIA sponsorship was funneled through shadow organizations) on mostly unsuspecting citizens. Multiple methodologies—hypnosis, sensory deprivation, isolation, verbal and sexual abuse, electro-shock, radiation, and the administration of drugs, chemicals and lethal biological agents—were employed to influence subjects' mental states and alter brain functions, primarily for the purpose of developing dependable torture and interrogation methods. Experiments were designed for offensive purposes (techniques to elicit information from enemies) and defensive purposes (techniques to prevent enemies from getting information from American agents). There were also programs (Project Monarch) to develop unknowing "sleeper" assassins, as in a "Manchurian Candidate." Subjects included college students, government employees (including CIA agents), military personnel, medical staff, institutionalized mental patients, prostitutes, prisoners, and even children, most of the time without their knowledge; even those who volunteered were never told the nature of the experiments or the dangers involved, which was a clear violation of the Nuremberg Code which the United States had signed after World War II.

The fallout from these programs is ongoing. There have been several deaths resulting from the experiments (the U.S. government made a payment of $750,000 to one family in 1975) and allegations of many others. Additionally, a number of surviving subjects have filed lawsuits against the U.S. government for damages, and, although the government has aggressively denied legal liability, some subjects have been awarded damages. There have been several notable people who were subjects in MKULTRA experiments: Theodore Kaczynski, the famous Unabomber, started participating at the age of sixteen while a Harvard undergraduate student; Ken Kesey, author of *One Flew Over the Cuckoo's Nest,* volunteered to take LSD and other drugs at the Veterans Administration Hospital as a Stanford University student; James "Whitey" Bulger, a Boston mobster, volunteered while serving time in prison. While the CIA claimed to have stopped MKULTRA programs in the early 1970s, some former CIA agents contend that programs remained in place long after that. As for the value of the experiments themselves, it is believed that many of the interrogation and torture techniques developed in the MKULTRA experiments of the 1960s, such as waterboarding and sensory deprivation, were used on prisoners in Iraq and at Guantanamo Bay in Cuba after the 9/11 attacks.

The National Security Act of 1947. This Act not only established the CIA as our country's first peacetime intelligence agency, giving it the duty of collecting and evaluating intelligence, but it also created many familiar, long-standing American entities, such as the National Security Council (NSC), the Department of Defense (DOD), which included the Joint Chiefs of Staff (JCS), and the United States Air Force (USAF), which was separated from its affiliation with the U.S. Army. For the CIA, however, the Act's real impact rested in the ambiguously worded responsibility ... *"to perform such other functions and duties related to intelligence affecting the national security as the National Security Council may from time to time direct."* Shortly after the passage of this Act, the NSC created the Office of Special Projects to run a variety of covert human behavioral projects, including experiments in psychological and biological warfare and mind control, mostly on unsuspecting American and Canadian citizens; these and subsequent covert CIA activities were defined and defended under the "other functions and duties" clause of this Act. Eventually, most of the covert CIA experiments were brought under the umbrella of MKULTRA in 1953. Some of the key scientists involved in these projects were Nazi war criminals who had conducted human experiments in these areas and were brought into the United States via Operation Paperclip.

The Doolittle Report. In 1954 President Dwight Eisenhower commissioned Lieutenant General James Doolittle (USAF) to prepare a report on the covert activities of the CIA and to make recommendations for the organization's improvement; the report was presented to President Eisenhower privately in September, 1954, and wasn't declassified until 1976. While the report listed a thorough and wide-ranging list of recommendations for improvements in anticipated areas—staffing, budgets, agent training, better coordination among the various intelligence agencies, stronger oversight, etc.—it included this sobering statement: *"It is now clear that we are facing an implacable enemy whose avowed objective is world domination by whatever means and at whatever cost. There are no rules in such a game ... If the United States is to survive, long-standing American concepts of 'fair play' must be reconsidered. We must develop effective* *espionage and counterespionage services and must learn to subvert, sabotage and destroy our enemies by more clever, more sophisticated and more effective methods than those used against us. It may become necessary that the American people be made acquainted with, understand and support this fundamentally repugnant philosophy."*

The National Security Act of 1947 had far-reaching effects. On the domestic front it opened the door for the myriad of covert operations that were eventually folded into the MKULTRA program, and it also heavily influenced U.S. foreign policy. Although President Harry Truman had conducted independent covert operations in Greece and Indochina, President Eisenhower was the first President to incorporate covert action as an integral part of his overall foreign policy. At Eisenhower's direction the CIA conducted several clandestine operations to overthrow governments that were not supportive of the United States; the efforts were successful in Iran in 1953 and Guatemala in 1954, but failed in Indonesia in 1958. One of America's most embarrassing intelligence incidents occurred during Eisenhower's tenure on May 1, 1960, when Francis Gary Powers crashed his U-2 spy plane in the Soviet Union while flying a mission for the CIA. Eisenhower initially denied the spying charges, but was caught in a lie when Soviet Premier Nikita Khrushchev publicly produced the downed aircraft and its living pilot as proof. The episode had humiliating repercussions for the United States: For the first time many Americans started doubting its own government, and other nations started questioning America's "white hat" image concerning world affairs. The incident also forced a cancellation of the Paris Peace Summit that had been scheduled for the United States, the USSR, Great Britain and France, which, some historians believe, prolonged the Cold War.

Despite this very public embarrassment, presidents succeeding Eisenhower continued their own clandestine operations, with some suffering similar fates: In 1961 President Kennedy's attempt to overthrow Fidel Castro's government in Cuba using Cuban exiles as an invasion force failed miserably, as did several subsequent CIA-backed assassination attempts on Castro. In 1983-85 President Reagan's administration conducted two covert operations, selling weapons to Iran and then using the profits of the sales to help the Nicaraguan contras overthrow the Sandinista government, both of which violated existing law. The discovery of Reagan's operations in 1986 resulted in congressional hearings and the appointment of a special prosecutor, which led to charges of an administration cover-up and several criminal convictions.

The Rockefeller Commission, the Church Committee and the Pike Committee. (*Note: While each of these committees made comprehensive recommendations across a wide variety of issues, we have only mentioned here those recommendations that are related to the plot lines of Patriot Acts.*)

By 1975 the Vietnam War, the Watergate break-in, the discovery of CIA assassination plots, media reports of alleged CIA experiments on civilians, and rumors of other intelligence abuses spawned three separate government investigations, each of which held its own hearings and issued its own reports. The Rockefeller Commission (or the U.S. President's Commission on CIA activities within the United States) was an Executive Branch effort created by President Gerald Ford in 1975 and chaired by Vice President Nelson Rockefeller. Its task was to investigate whether the CIA had violated provisions of the National Security Act of 1947. It reviewed CIA abuses within the United States, such as illegal surveillance of American citizens, illegal mail opening, issues relating to the John F. Kennedy assassination and other domestic items. Also of note, it provided the first public verification of Project MKULTRA's secret and illegal mind control experiments on unsuspecting Americans and recommended that the programs be stopped.

The Church Committee (or Senate Select Committee to Study Governmental Operations with Respect to Intelligence Activities) was a U.S. Senate investigation headed by Senator Frank Church of Idaho. Its scope was much broader than that of the Rockefeller Commission, including not only the CIA, but all U.S. intelligence operations. While both committees made recommendations regarding organizational improvements, they focused primarily on illegalities and misconduct within the intelligence community and remedies for misconduct. The Church Committee also addressed the covert CIA experiments on American citizens and recommended that ... *"The CIA should not use in experimentation on human subjects, any drug, device or procedure which is designed or intended to harm, or is reasonably likely to harm, the physical or mental health of the human subject, except with the informed written consent, witnessed by a disinterested third party, of each human subject, and in accordance with the guidelines issued by the National Commission for the Protection of Human Subjects for Biomedical and Behavioral Research."* The Committee also recommended *"... establishing a legislative scheme which will afford effective redress to people who are injured by improper federal intelligence activity."*

The Pike Committee (House Select Committee on Intelligence), headed by Representative Otis G. Pike of New York, focused its attention on budgetary issues of the intelligence community, hoping that the budgets would reveal the inner workings of the CIA so the American public could assess whether they were getting their money's worth for CIA programs. Pike and CIA Director William Colby butted heads almost immediately; the relationship proved so adversarial and distracting that the U.S. House of Representatives, under pressure from White House and CIA threats that the committee's final report would endanger America's security, voted not to release it, even though large sections of a draft of the report had already been leaked and printed in The *New York Times*. Although the final report was never officially released, it was published in its entirety in *The Village Voice,* having been given to the paper by journalist Daniel Schorr. The House Committee on Standards of Official Conduct investigated the leak to Schorr, but failed to identify his government source.

The Nazi War Crimes Disclosure Act. President William Clinton created the Nazi War Criminal Records Interagency Working Group (IWG) with this Act in 1998 amid growing public concern about residual World War II issues, including the government's role in using and protecting war criminals for intelligence purposes. The IWG was tasked with locating, declassifying and releasing to the public all government records regarding people who committed war crimes or seized assets from victims associated with Nazi Germany and its allies from March 23, 1933, to May 8, 1945. The information was to be used to help deport Nazi war criminals and locate assets of victims looted by the Nazis. This

Act refocused attention on programs like Project Overcast and Project Paperclip that had brought hundreds of German scientists into the United States after the war. The IWG's mission became the largest congressionally mandated declassification effort in history, resulting in the release of 8.5 million pages of relevant files relating to World War II war crimes. However, the group's final report in 2007 underscored the difficulty of penetrating the shroud of secrecy surrounding this period of American history. Despite the IWG's exhaustive efforts, in December, 2010, the National Archives issued a new report on Nazi war crimes, *Hitler's Shadow: Nazi War Criminals, U.S. Intelligence and the Cold War,* which stated: *"Of particular importance to this volume are many declassified intelligence records from the Central Intelligence Agency and the Army Intelligence Command, which were not fully processed and available at the time that the IWG issued its Final Report in 2007. As a consequence, Congress [in HR 110-920] charged the National Archives in 2009 to prepare an additional historical volume as a companion piece to its 2005 volume U. S. Intelligence and the Nazis ... This volume of essays points to the significant impact that flowed from Congress and the Executive Branch agencies in adopting a broader and fuller release of previously security classified war crimes documentation."*

According to the National Archives press release, this new trove of information may total as many as two million pages, much of it which is yet to be reviewed at the time of this book's publishing.

SELECTED BIBLIOGRAPHY

Colin Beavan, *Operation Jedburgh: D-Day and America's First Shadow War,* New York: Penguin Books, 2007.

Chris Bishop & David Jordan, *The Rise and Fall of the Third Reich,* London: Amber Books Ltd, 2007.

Chris Bishop & Chris McNab, *Campaigns of World War II Day By Day,* London: Amber Books Ltd, 2007.

Paul Carell, *Hitler Moves East 1941-1943,* Boston: Little, Brown and Company, 1964.

Paul Carell, *Scorched Earth: The Russian-German War 1943-1944,* Boston: Little, Brown and Company, 1970.

I.C.B Dear, ed. *The Oxford Guide to World War II, Oxford:* Oxford University Press, 1995.

Joachim C. Fest, *Hitler,* New York: Harcourt Brace Jovanovich, 1974.

Heinz Hohne, *The Order of the Death's Head: The Story of Hitler's SS,* New York: Ballantine Books, 1971.

Geoffrey Jukes, *Kursk: the clash of armour,* New York: Ballantine Books, 1969.

John Keegan, *Barbarossa: invasion of Russia 1941,* New York: Ballantine Books, 1971.

John Keegan, *Waffen SS: the asphalt soldiers,* New York: Ballantine Books, 1970.

James Lucas, *Das Reich: The Military Role of the 2nd SS Division*, London: Cassell, 1999.

John Marks, *The Search for the "Manchurian Candidate"*: The CIA and Mind Control, New York: McGraw-Hill, 1980.

Timothy Snyder, *Bloodlands: Europe Between Hitler and Stalin,* New York: Basic Books, 2010.

Evan Thomas, *The Very Best Men: Four Who Dared: The Early Years of the CIA,* New York: Simon and Schuster, 1995.

John Toland, Battle: *The Story of the Bulge,* New York: Random House, 1959.

Douglas Waller, *Wild Bill Donovan: The Spymaster Who Created the OSS and Modern American Espionage,* New York: Free Press, 2011.

Website: http:// www.archives.gov. (The website for The National Archives and Records Administration [NARA], the official record keeper *"of all documents and materials created in the course of business conducted by the United States Federal Government."*)

Tim Weiner, *Legacy of Ashes: The History of the CIA,* New York: Doubleday, 2007.

Alan Wykes, *The Nuremberg Rallies,* New York: Ballantine Books, 1970.

Made in the USA
Charleston, SC
05 October 2014